GREAT EXPECTATIONS

Charles Dickens

GREAT EXPECTATIONS

Charles Dickens

Edited by
Graham Law
&
Adrian J. Pinnington

broadview literary texts

Canadian Cataloguing in Publication Data

Dickens, Charles, 1812–1870
    Great expectations
(Broadview literary texts)
Includes bibliographical references.
ISBN 1-55111-174-8

I. Law, Graham. II. Pinnington, Adrian J. (Adrian James), 1955-   .
III. Title. IV. Series.

PR4560.A2L38 1998   823'.8   C98-930545-7

broadview press
P.O. Box 1243
Peterborough, Ontario
K9J 7H5   Canada

broadview press
3576 California Road
Orchard Park, NY
14127   USA

**B.R.A.D. Book Representation
& Distribution Ltd.**
244a, London Road
Hadleigh, Essex
SS7 2DE   United Kingdom

Bruce Watson,
St. Clair Press
P.O. Box 287
Rozelle, NSW
2039 Australia

PRINTED IN CANADA

Contents

Introduction

Great Expectations is, in many ways, Dickens's masterpiece, yet it is also at the same time an unrepresentative work. It is true that in it he returns to the myth of the foundling which informs the plot of so many of his novels — the narrative in which the hero moves from an isolated and precarious existence at the margins of society to a secure and settled respectability. This time, however, he offers his readers a new and radical interrogation both of the myth and of the sources of its appeal. Like other great works of literature, *Great Expectations* has attracted, and continues to attract, a great variety of modern readings — Freudian, Marxist, Foucauldian and so on — yet it is also a novel which gains greatly in force and subtlety when placed in its original historical context. Indeed, looking at it in this way only helps us to grasp more firmly its continued relevance and importance. The aim of this new edition of the novel is above all to assist readers without the time or the facilities to consult the original documents, to study *Great Expectations* in the context of the social and cultural debates to which it belongs. In addition to the more familiar features of a chronology of the writer and explanatory notes, this volume contains extensive appendices of contemporary documents, including both those related to the production and reception of the novel, and typical contributions to the discussion of the key issues of Class and Language, and Crime and Punishment. In what follows, this introduction will attempt a brief overview of the relevance of those documents to the understanding of the novel.

Undoubtedly the motif of the orphaned boy who struggles to regain his rightful inheritance was one which held a profound autobiographical significance for Dickens himself. In fact, this is signalled in an odd way within the novel itself, when Joe and Wopsle tell Pip that they have been to see "the Blacking Ware'us" (p. 252). This reference is odd because the significance of it cannot have been understood by the novel's original readers, for it was only after Dickens's death that his friend and biographer, John Forster, published the autobiographical fragment in which Dickens revealed the — to him — deeply painful and shameful episode of being set to work in a "blacking warehouse" at the age of eleven or twelve (Appendix C 1).[1] As we read this autobiographical sketch, however, we cannot help being struck by the ambiguity of Dickens's response to this early experience of poverty and social insecurity. On the one hand, there is a profound sense of resentment that his family and others should have set such an obviously "special" child — "a child of singular abilities: quick, eager, delicate, and soon hurt" — to such degrading work; on the other, there is the painful recognition that "but for the mercy of God, I might easily have been ... a little robber or vagabond." Here, we can see that the figure of the orphaned child, who is a gentleman by birth, and yet needs to recover his own rightful status by work and struggle — the story essentially of *David Copperfield* — was one which allowed Dickens to express both his sense of personal humiliation and his awareness of the arbitrariness of the social hierarchy.

When we look at the letters Dickens wrote during the period when he conceived and composed *Great Expectations*,[2] it is clear that his thoughts at this time were continually returning to this question of his own childhood and the meaning of the personal success which he had secured. This success was symbolised for Dickens by his ownership of Gad's Hill Place, the country house located in that area of Kent which framed his happiest childhood memories, and which, significantly enough, he also used as the setting for the early scenes of the novel. Dickens had bought this house in 1856, describing it as "literally 'a dream of my childhood',"[3] and, following the breakdown of his marriage soon after, he had sold his London house and moved there in 1860. In an autobiographical piece, "Travelling Abroad," written just before *Great Expectations*, he uses the figure of a child, clearly based on himself, who gazes with longing at Gad's Hill Place and is reassured by his father that, if he works hard enough, he may come to

---

1. Citations in this form refer to the contemporary documents collected in the Appendices to this volume.
2. The latest volume in the Pilgrim Edition of *The Letters of Charles Dickens*, Vol. IX 1859–61, edited by Graham Storey, represents the most comprehensive collection of Dickens's letters from the period ever published. Extracts relevant to the composition of the novel are reproduced in Appendix A 2.
3. Cited in *Charles Dickens as Editor*, ed. R.C. Lehmann (London: Smith, Elder, 1912): 158.

live in the house himself one day (Appendix C 2). It is unsurprising to find that the germ of the story which became *Great Expectations* was itself conceived in this house (Appendix A 2/1), and that Dickens may have originally intended it for another story in the same semi-autobiographical series (Appendix A 2/3). The autobiographical resonance of the novel is also revealed in the way in which it is linked in Dickens's mind with the much more straightforwardly autobiographical *David Copperfield* — we even find him going back to read the earlier novel so as to avoid repetition (Appendix A 2/7).

At the same time, however, the novel's theme of the climb to respectability was one which had enormous resonance for the society in which Dickens lived. This is not to say that *Great Expectations* was a topical novel, in the sense of attacking some contemporary evil, in the way that many of Dickens's novels did. On the contrary, it is set very consciously in a period which is not only earlier than that of its composition, but which is also felt to be very different. While there are some difficulties with establishing a precise chronology for the novel,[1] it is clear that Dickens gave this careful thought and took great pains to make it historically authentic, as the maps and illustrations included in this edition help to verify. Roughly speaking, the life of Pip coincides with the century itself — making him ten years or so older than Dickens — and the main action takes place between 1807–10 and 1823–6. This chronology is carefully signalled, and the sense of historical depth maintained, by many details in the text: there are no railways, no photographs, no matches, no police; the soldiers act in the name of a king, not a queen; most houses are still built of wood; and so on.

More importantly the evils which the novel so powerfully depicts were ones which had largely disappeared, for the period of Pip's lifetime had also been a period of major penal reform (see Collins 1962, Emsley, & Gatrell). The first half of the nineteenth century saw the gradual relaxation of the "Bloody Code," under which more than two hundred offences, and as many as half of those committed for trial, were subject

---

1. See Jerome Meckier, "Dating the Action in *Great Expectations*," *Dickens Studies Annual* 21 (1992): 157–94.

to the death penalty, and which had been administered in ways as arbitrary and inefficient as it was savage and severe. Unsurprisingly in these circumstances, juries had been frequently reluctant to convict for minor offences, and capital sentences had been regularly though randomly commuted; nevertheless, in the popular imagination (see Appendix D 1) as well as in Pip's (p. 51), minor strayings from the path of virtue were seen to lead direct to the gallows. From the mid 1830s Prison Inspectors were appointed, and many of the old local criminal gaols like Newgate, which were notoriously corrupt and insanitary, were gradually superseded by new model penitentiaries under state control, like Coldbath Fields or Pentonville. Prisons like Newgate were widely seen to foster crime, whereas the new purpose-built institutions attempted systematically to rehabilitate their prisoners, according to various competing theories. The transportation of convicts to the Australian colony of New South Wales, originally initiated in 1786 as a substitute for the death penalty under the Bloody Code, had peaked in the 1820s, been severely criticised by a Parliamentary Select Committee in 1837 (see Appendix D 4), and was phased out by 1840; transportation to other Australian colonies continued in diminishing numbers until 1868 (see Hughes). The last of the hulks or prison ships, which had originally been introduced in 1776 for a temporary period of two years, when the transportation of convicts to America had been interrupted, had finally been closed in 1858, and the horrendous conditions on board such prisons widely recognised (see Appendix B 9).

These reforms in the criminal justice system, moreover, had taken place against a background of reforms of many other aspects of society, including schools (both elite and popular), government (both national and local), public health, and social welfare. Although these reforms were far, in both scope and spirit, from anything Western liberals might today find satisfactory, they represented to the Victorians themselves an enormous advance, a movement from a society which was in many ways still feudal in outlook, to one which was recognisably modern. It was this history, coinciding with a marked improvement in economic conditions, which gave the Victorians their powerful sense of progress and which they felt to be linked to a dramatic improvement in both morals and manners (see Briggs).

Great Expectations is thus not so much a protest against social evils as a sustained meditation upon this process of reform. It is this which gives such importance to the book's handling of the theme of the nature of a gentleman, a theme central both to the book and to Dickens's society (see Sadrin Pt. 2 and Gilmour). Stated in the broadest terms, British society in this period, transformed by industrialisation, had been moving from one in which the social hierarchy was justified chiefly in terms of birth and pedigree, towards one in which it was chiefly justified (as modern societies generally are) by reference to education and skills. This shift aroused intense debate and interest among the Victorians themselves. Many, following Tocqueville (Appendix C 3), saw Britain as having a uniquely "open" elite, in which successful men of any background could easily be absorbed and find a place. To such thinkers the progressive moralisation of the concept of a gentleman, and its detachment from mere questions of family or birth, was an inevitable accompaniment of progress (see Stephen's argument in Appendix C 4), and also a path to modernity which would avoid the dangers and upheavals of revolution. Yet this moralisation, especially in terms of sensitivity, sympathy, and civility, was a double-edged weapon, for it could easily become little more than a new and more powerful legitimation of class distinction and privilege, as, grotesquely, in the case of Sewell (Appendix C 5) or more subtly in the case of a thinker like Ruskin (Appendix C 6) or indeed Stephen himself. (The view that the lower orders were inherently less sensitive or civilised was one which Dickens himself attacked explicitly, notably in *David Copperfield*, Ch. 20.) Moreover, such a "moralisation" in terms of sensibility and manners was, as Newman pointed out, only superficially moral in the first place (Appendix C 7).

Such issues were widely aired in the period in which *Great Expectations* was written, perhaps most famously in Samuel Smiles's *Self-Help* (Appendix C 9). Here we see that, contrary to his later reputation, Smiles himself, influenced by Carlyle's "gospel of work" with its resounding condemnation of the idleness or dilettantism of the fashionable aristocracy (Appendix C 8), has a deeply moral notion of the "gentleman," one which apparently detaches it completely from questions of birth. Yet, in fact there is little in Smiles which actually challenges privilege, and indeed there is a sense that moral excellence will be rewarded with social success, and that the model of a gentleman will still naturally be provided by upper-class figures. The same ambiguity is also evident in Mrs. Craik's *John Halifax, Gentleman* (Appendix C 10), the most famous of the fictional treatments of the theme of the "self-made man." Although her hero suffers from social discrimination and prejudice, and, like Pip, loves a woman from a higher social class, he knows himself to be the son of a "gentleman" and so there is the sense that during the course of the novel he is winning back a status rightfully his, rather than defying or challenging class distinctions as such. This ambiguity, as we have suggested, was also present both in Dickens's personal life, where he was sensitive to insinuations in the literary world that he was not himself quite a gentleman and insisted upon his right to use a family crest, and in his novels, where considerable sympathy is extended to members of the underworld of crime and poverty, but the heroes are often the orphaned sons of gentlemen. *Oliver Twist* is in this sense his most characteristic work.

Great Expectations, however, is different, for here we are given a deeply ironic, pessimistic and disabused commentary on the whole Victorian discourse of the gentleman. Moreover, the more closely one reads the novel, the more unsettling its message appears to be. This radical edge to the work has a great deal to do with Dickens's daring and innovative use of the novel's autobiographical form. Indeed, from the beginning, the novel has been rightly admired for its tightly constructed and disciplined plot (Appendix B 1–4). From Dickens's letters, it seems evident that it was indeed the possibilities of the plot which first excited him, and that the germ of the novel lay in the fascination of an artistic experiment: to construct a first-person narration in which the narrator himself is ignorant of the true meaning of the events which he is recounting (Appendix A 2/7). But this artistic experimentation, admired by reviewers and giving the lie to the widespread view that his artistic powers were in decline (see Appendix B 3 & 7), also led Dickens to write a peculiarly modern novel, one exploring those issues of identity and self-knowledge which have proved so important to modernity itself.

The novel has in fact two plots — a false plot, which Pip for much of the novel believes himself to be living, in which Miss Havisham is training him to be a gentleman in preparation for marriage to Estella, and a true plot, the one designed and executed by Magwitch, which intersects with the first in a complex and subtle manner. Of these two plots, the first and false one essentially begins with Pip's summoning to Satis House and humiliation at the hands of Estella:

> "He calls the knaves, Jacks, this boy!" said Estella with disdain, before our first game was out. "And what coarse hands he has. And what thick boots!"
>
> I had never thought of being ashamed of my hands before; but I began to consider them a very indifferent pair. Her contempt was so strong, that it became infectious, and I caught it. (p. 95)

This humiliation is at once social, sexual, and linguistic.[1] Behind the sense of linguistic humiliation lies the complex process whereby the vocabulary, syntax, and pronunciation of a certain elite had come increasingly to be seen as not merely smart or desirable, but as "standard" or "received."[2] This was in turn linked to the reform of the "public schools," initiated by Thomas Arnold during his headmastership of Rugby and given a celebratory and idealised portrait in Thomas Hughes's *Tom Brown's Schooldays* (see Appendix C 11). The acceptance of a public school education as a qualification to enter "Society" and "the professions" had rapidly led to the growth of a unified and distinct "gentlemanly" form of speech. On the other hand, the idea that the language of the poor was not merely different, but in some way inferior or corrupt, was also evident in the reports on the state of popular education submitted to Parliament in 1861 and the widespread sense of a link between education, correct speech, and social and moral improvement (Appendix C 12/2-4). At the same time, however, this growing consciousness of "standard English"

---

1. It is a mark of the continuity of English society that this same contrast, between "knaves" and "jacks," could be used, apparently quite independently, to illustrate the difference between upper-class and non-upper-class English speech as late as the 1950s. See *Noblesse Oblige*, ed. Nancy Mitford (1956; Harmondsworth, Middlesex: Penguin Books, 1959): 26.
2. See Crowley; John Honey, *Does Accent Matter?* (London: Faber and Faber, 1989); and Patrick Joyce, "The People's English: Language and Class in England c.1840–1920," *Language, Self, and Society*, ed. Peter Burke and Roy Porter (Cambridge: Polity Press, 1991): 154–190.

also generated a corresponding interest in and concern for the disappearance of "dialect." The way in which such different responses could be combined in the same argument may be seen in Ruskin's contrast between "corrupt" cockney speech and the purity of genuine "dialects" (Appendix C 6).

The novel itself, however, offers a more subtle perspective on this issue than appears at first sight. It is certainly true that Pip, unlike, say, Joe, Magwitch, and Orlick, or even, though less markedly, Mrs. Joe and Pumblechook, predominantly uses standard speech from the very beginning of the novel; this has an artistic function, for it only adds to our sense of injustice at Pip's treatment at the hands of Estella. Just before her expression of contempt for him cited above, for example, Pip has described the house to Miss Havisham as "'so new here, and so strange, and so fine — and melancholy'" which seems hardly the speech of "a stupid, clumsy, labouring-boy" (pp. 94–6). Of course, Dickens is partly motivated by a desire for transparency and a wish to encourage identification with Pip's standpoint; indeed the problem of how to represent non-standard speech in an unpatronising way is one which has afflicted many novelists. Moreover, Dickens also uses Pip's standard speech in a psychological way to stress his isolation as a boy. It is interesting, for example, to note the way in which Pip begins to use non-standard forms at his second encounter with Magwitch, in a way which serves to suggest the growing intimacy between the two figures (Vol. I Ch. 3). We should also notice, however, the fact that the novel contains more powerful suggestions that as a child Pip actually spoke like Joe, as in the first "letter" he writes (Vol. I Ch. 7). If this composition, with its rudimentary and phonetic spelling, is taken as an accurate transcript of Pip's speech, then this suggests that what is presented as his speech elsewhere is in fact distorted by its being filtered through the mind of the older Pip, who has of course become a "gentleman" and learnt the literary language. Momentarily the language of the narrative and of its middle-class readers is thrown into doubt in an unsettling way. This hint of alienation between the child and the man gives poignancy to the detail where Pip, after he has received Wemmick's warning not to return home, finds as he dozes that the warning becomes "a vast shadowy verb which I had to conjugate. Imperative mood, present tense: Do not thou go home, let him not go home ..." (p. 391) It is almost as if at this point Pip's own speech has become to him a dead language which he has learnt from textbooks.

In other ways, too, the novel suggests a sense of how the "standard" literary language in which the novel itself is written could look from the other side. This is obvious in the caricatured representation of the aristocratic lout, Bentley Drummle, but also more strikingly in, for example, Trabb's boy's mocking imitation of Pip's speech and gestures: "he pulled up his shirt-collar, twined his side-hair ... drawling to his attendants, 'Don't know yah, don't know yah, pon my soul don't know yah!'" (p. 275). Here, too, we are suddenly given by the novel a quite different perspective upon Pip's transformation into a gentleman. This feature is in turn linked to the powerful awareness in the novel of the damage done by the identification of speech and class, vividly exemplified by Magwitch's account of Compeyson who had "'set up fur a gentleman ... been to a public boarding-school and had learning'" (p. 371). The figure of the swindler, a gentleman who had fallen on hard times and exploited his background to dupe people, was a familiar one in Dickens's time (see Appendix D 5 & 8/1); but Magwitch's description of the way in which, during their trial, Compeyson is able to exploit the difference in their class backgrounds to gain the sympathy of the court and a lighter sentence (Vol. III Ch. 3) is one which has many parallels even today. The same damage is conveyed in a different way in the portrayal of the verbal alienation between Pip and Joe after Pip's status changes, as Joe becomes increasingly tongue-tied and inarticulate in his struggle to produce a form of speech appropriate to the new relationship between them (Vol. II Ch. 8).

Pip's humiliation at the hands of Estella is, as already indicated, not only social but also sexual, and here a closer look at the novel also reveals a radically unsettling picture of the relations between gender, violence, and power. Again the novel begins by enlisting the reader's sympathy for Pip, this time through the vivid portrait of the deeply repressive Mrs. Joe, ruling over a sexless household with an iron hand: "She was tall and bony, and almost always wore a coarse apron, fastened over her figure behind with two loops, and having a square impregnable bib, that was stuck full of pins and needles" (p. 44). Not only has the orphan Pip been denied the breast, but so also, hints Dickens, has the adult Joe. Of course, Pip's sister's harshness is balanced by Joe's gentleness and kindness, but this gentleness itself has a darker side, for, as Joe himself explains in a moving passage, his father was a violent alcoholic who regularly beat up both wife and child (Vol. I Ch. 7). It is Joe's memory of his mother's suffering, so he tells Pip, which prevents him from resisting his own wife's tyranny. Joe is clearly a positive figure in the novel — "this gentle Christian man" as Pip learns to call him (p. 483) — yet we should not overlook the fact that he is also a wounded character, incapable of protecting Pip from his sister's cruelty, a fact which he himself twice apologises for (p. 85 and 489), or of acting as a true father to the orphaned boy. This surely undercuts the simple claim that Dickens is recommending him as a model of true gentlemanliness.

The idea of a deep-rooted enmity between the sexes also lies behind Miss Havisham's twisted upbringing of Estella and cruelty to Pip, as well as the marriage between Estella and Bentley Drummle. But perhaps the most disturbing aspect of the novel is the way in which Pip and Joe are only released from Mrs. Joe's tyranny by Orlick's violent attack upon her. This is underlined by the puzzling change in Mrs. Joe's behaviour towards Orlick himself: "She manifested the greatest anxiety to be on good terms with him … she showed every possible desire to conciliate him, and there was an air of humble propitiation in all she did, such as I have seen pervade the bearing of a child towards a hard master" (p. 157). The final simile is deeply unsettling; but the difficulty is compounded by the fact that Pip himself is haunted by a strange guilt about his sister's fate. When he first encounters her stricken body he has the odd feeling that he may have had a hand in the attack (p. 153); when she finally dies, he finds himself haunted by her figure (p. 305); when he first hears Magwitch's foot on the stair, he thinks that it may be the footstep of his dead sister (p. 341); finally, when Orlick confesses to the attack, he nevertheless puts the blame for it squarely on Pip (p. 447).

Of course, part of the subtlety of the novel lies in the way in which the reader too is likely to feel to some degree implicated in Pip's guilt, because the reader also wishes to see him released from Mrs. Joe's tyranny, and is likely to feel some relief when that moment comes. The first-person narrative ensures that the reader, every bit as much as Pip, is in a position of struggling to make sense of the events as they occur. Indeed, the theme of reading is one which is highlighted in different ways within the novel itself.[1] Pip is himself anxious to learn to read and write, though Joe warns him that Mrs. Joe would not approve as reading is connected in her mind with rebellion against her rule (p. 84), just as, until the mid nineteenth century, the taxes on printed matter reflected the fear among the ruling class that popular literacy was a step on the road to sedition (see Altick, especially Ch. 14). In this way, reading becomes intimately associated with Pip's desire to escape from his claustrophobic situation, yet there seems little chance of him succeeding in his aim as long as his education is confined to Mrs. Wopsle's school — an accurate depiction, it seems, of "Dame schools" even in the time when the novel was written (see Appendix C 12/1). Indeed, the novel is full of "bad" readers — Joe, the Aged P., Magwitch — who nevertheless not only enjoy reading, but who seem to be in an odd sense protected by their very disability. Pip, by contrast, is almost too artful a reader; from the first scene, when he conjures up a portrait of his parents from the inscriptions on their tombstones, he is able to read far more into the world than is actually there. It is this which leads him on, despite mounting evidence to the contrary, to suppose that Miss Havisham intends him to marry Estella. This ingenuity, however, is matched by an equal inability to read the significant silences which occur at different points in the novel, from Magwitch's look when he is captured (p. 74), to Biddy's silence when he promises not to forget Joe (p. 311), to Jaggers's refusal to answer Pip's questions as to when the identity of his patron would be revealed (p. 316). The reader, confined to Pip's viewpoint, is also subtly challenged by these silences, and begins to sense the unreliability of the narrator.

These different forms of misreading in the novel are connected both to the difficulty of self-knowledge — as when Pip is unable to see himself in Herbert's description (p. 277) — and to the instability of identity in the book. This is one major way in which Dickens goes beyond a mere critique of Victorian snobbishness or the myth of the self-made man. This can best be seen in what one might call the "Frankenstein" theme in the novel. As the notes indicate, Mary Shelley's novel is specifically referred

---

1. For a fuller discussion of reading and writing in the novel, see Murray Baumgarten, "Calligraphy and Code: Writing in *Great Expectations*," *Dickens Studies Annual* XI (1983): 61–72.

to more than once in the course of the text, the most significant allusion being when Pip compares himself and Magwitch to Frankenstein and the monster: "The imaginary student pursued by the misshapen creature he had impiously made, was not more wretched than I, pursued by the creature who had made me, and recoiling from him with a stronger repulsion, the more he admired me and the fonder he was of me." (p. 363). Pip is actually the "creature" (the one who has been created) and the tortuous complexity of the comparison seems to enact his own struggle to avoid recognition of this fact, leaving the reader giddy with the difficulty of sorting out which is the monster and which not. A similar sense of paradox is also present in the argument between Miss Havisham and Estella, where the latter simply places all responsibility for her character on the former; "'I am what you have made me. Take all the praise, all the blame; take all the success, take all the failure; in short, take me.'" (p. 331) Here, too, we are left wondering which is the greater monster.

The Frankenstein comparison is an entirely appropriate one because the novel is not only haunted by a sense of the ease with which identities are made and unmade, but also by a sense of the uncontrollability of narratives, of a slippage between intention and result. These themes come together in a small way in the character of Wopsle, who as an actor is continually attempting to take on other identities, and yet only succeeds in creating something misshapen and ridiculous — an unsettling echo of Pip's own attempts to act the part of a gentleman. In their different ways, both Miss Havisham and Magwitch also fail disastrously, creating monsters in the process, but it is the "monsters" themselves — Pip and Estella — who are left with a nightmarish sense of having been caught in other people's narratives, and so of having had their identities defined from the outside, regardless of their own wishes. This is repeated in a minor key with the deeply unpleasant Pumblechook, who also continually spins narratives about Pip, none of which have the slightest relation to reality and yet which Pip finds himself unable to refute or escape from.

This feeling that the world consists of competing but incommensurate narratives, which jostle together for priority, leads us to the third meaning of Pip's initial encounter with Estella: the loss not only of childhood but also of the secure and settled culture of his village upbringing:

It is a most miserable thing to feel ashamed of home ... I
had believed in the best parlour as a most elegant saloon; I
had believed in the front door, as a mysterious portal of
the Temple of State whose solemn opening was attended
with a sacrifice of roast fowls; I had believed in the kitchen
as a chaste though not magnificent apartment; I had believed in the forge as the glowing road to manhood and
independence. Within a single year, all this was changed.
(p. 140)

Dickens's sympathetic and detailed account of the ordinary life and culture of the village, as in the opening account of the Christmas celebra-
tions or the later description of Mrs. Joe's funeral, forms an easily
overlooked but essential background to Pip's experience of the loss of
childhood. It is in this way that the novel can be seen as self-consciously
concerned with modernity. For Pip's loss of childhood is mapped onto
the loss of rural culture and the transition to the alienated world of the
metropolis; yet, and here too the irony of the title is deepened, this is not
experienced as a liberation or a gain. Thus the account of Pip's dandified
existence as a student, a milieu which Dickens treats far more positively
in other novels, is experienced as a dreary and meaningless round of con-
sumption, merely an accumulation of debts (Vol. II Ch. 15).

The deeper meaning of London, however, seems to be symbolised by
the figure of Wemmick, with his schizophrenic combination of amoral
rationality at work in the City and rich fantasy life at home in his mock-
castle. When Pip first meets Wemmick, he asks him about London:

"Is it a very wicked place?" I asked, more for the sake of
saying something than for information.

"You may get cheated, robbed, and murdered, in London. But there are plenty of people anywhere, who'll do
that for you."

"If there is bad blood between you and them," said I,
to soften it off a little.

"Oh! I don't know about bad blood," returned Mr.
Wemmick; "there's not much bad blood about. They'll do
it, if there's anything to be got by it." (p. 202)

Here London is not only associated with crime, but also with a peculiarly modern acquisitive rationality, amoral and emotionless, which is summed up in the mechanism of the Law and in the dark figure of the supremely successful lawyer, Jaggers, who is free to manipulate the narratives of others, and yet seems to remain above and beyond all narratives himself.

The turning point of the novel, and the final collapse of the "false" narrative, comes with the return of Magwitch. In a memorable analogy, Pip compares this event to an eastern story in which a heavy slab of rock is suspended above a bed, ready to be dropped on any impostor who should usurp the rightful sultan. One day, after the sultan has been deposed, the awaited moment arrives, the rope is cut, and the slab falls (p. 338). The point of the analogy in the first place is the enormous and careful labour which has gone into the preparation of the trap, and in this sense it is an oddly self-conscious reflection on the tight construction of the novel itself, and on the narrative skills of the older Pip. But the analogy also contains the implication that Pip is in some sense an impostor, and that the return of Magwitch exposes his acquired gentility as a sham. Of course, this denouement has been carefully prepared for in the novel, especially in Pip's sense that he can never completely shake off a "taint of prison and crime" (p. 292). Again, this corresponds to a deep ambivalence within Dickens himself towards both crime and prisons — what John Forster called, in another context, his "attraction of repulsion."[1] This we can see clearly in his early descriptions of the Old Bailey and Newgate Prison (Appendix D 2 and 3), where he not only recalls his childhood fascination with the prison, but also seems himself torn between a humane sympathy towards the prisoners and their plight, entering imaginatively into their circumstances and appalled by the indifference of the judicial system, and an attitude of derision or even revulsion towards individual criminals.

Pip's horror and shame when he discovers the "tainted" source of his wealth and expectations is perhaps the point at which the novel is most

---

1.   The phrase was originally used with reference to the St. Giles area of London, known as a sink of poverty and crime. See Forster Bk. 1 Ch. 1.

remote in sensibility from contemporary readers. Yet it is striking how impressed the early reviewers were by this aspect of the work and the extent to which they shared Pip's attitude (Appendix B 1, 4, & 6). Even the highly unenthusiastic Mrs. Oliphant was sympathetic to Pip's "utter despair when he finds himself held fast in the clutches of this man's gratitude and bounty" and found his predicament "perhaps as strange and frightful as could be conceived" (Appendix B 8).

Yet the intensity of Pip's horror may also reflect Dickens's own increasingly reactionary and punitive attitude towards criminals in this period. In this, as in so many of his social attitudes, Dickens was undoubtedly influenced by Carlyle, who had launched a rabid attack on model prisons in 1850 (Appendix D 9). Although Dickens interested himself throughout his life in prison reform — as he did in many other kinds of social reform — whereas his attitudes as a younger man were on the whole progressive and enlightened, as he grew older he became increasingly disillusioned with the changes which had been carried out, and even to some extent began to regret them. We can see this attitude in some of his journalistic work while the novel was in progress (see Appendix D 10); while Dickens never doubted that the prisons of his youth were a scandal, he increasingly came to feel that the reforms had gone too far, and that society was growing too "soft" on crime. Sadly, although, among other writers, he had warmly supported the idea in the 1840s (see Collins 1962 Ch. 10), when the public execution of criminals was belatedly halted in 1868, Dickens made no comment on the decision, but instead issued one of his most illiberal contributions to the criminal debate (Appendix D 11). To a significant degree this also reflected a general shift in public attitudes, as people came to realise that the reforms, which, it had been naively hoped, would have a dramatic effect on crime and the rehabilitation of criminals, had not in fact solved the problem, and that crime persisted despite the general "progress" of society. (This is of course another issue which has an unpleasantly contemporary ring to it.) Dickens's later attitude is also evident within the novel itself, as in the older Pip's remarks on the condition of Newgate:

> At that time, jails were much neglected, and the period of
> exaggerated reaction consequent on all public wrong-doing

— and which is always its heaviest and longest punishment — was still far off. So, felons were not lodged and fed better than soldiers (to say nothing of paupers) and seldom set fire to their prisons with the excusable object of improving the flavour of their soup. (p. 288)

Here, again, the contrast between the past and present of the novel is stressed, but this passage is also a highly topical reference to the riots which took place in February 1861, at Chatham prison, in which prisoners protested a reduction in their diet. According to later evidence, the prisoners were in fact so hungry that they ate live frogs and worms when they could find them;[1] to Dickens, however, the riots were simply evidence of their pampered state.

At the same time, there is no doubt that the novel, while it uses such Victorian prejudices against the criminal to gain its effects, also offers an implicit critique of these attitudes. Just as Pip's love for Estella is seen as fatally linked to his desire for gentlemanly status, and thus renders him blind to her frigid and damaged character, so his horror of Magwitch is shown to be primarily linked to his own feelings of shame and longing for social respectability, which makes him blind to Magwitch's essential kindness and sense of justice. In an almost Brechtian way, Dickens balances Pip and Herbert's unthinking feelings of revulsion with Magwitch's at once brilliantly written and deeply sympathetic autobiographical narrative (Vol. III Ch.3), which can be compared with contemporary non-fictional equivalents (Appendix D 7 and 8/2). Here indeed Dickens seems able to feel empathy with the "little robber or vagabond" which he once feared that he might have become. In Pip's mind, however, Estella's charm had consisted precisely in her distance from the world of Newgate:

> I thought of the beautiful young Estella, proud and refined, coming towards me, and I thought with absolute abhorrence of the contrast between the jail and her.... I beat the prison dust off my feet as I sauntered to and fro, and I

---

1. Arthur Griffiths, *Fifty Years of Public Service* (London: Cassell & Co., 1904): 175–6.

shook it out of my dress, and I exhaled its air from my lungs. So contaminated did I feel, remembering who was coming, that the coach came quickly after all ... (p. 292)

The irony that Estella turns out to be the daughter of Magwitch and the murderess Molly, while not heavily emphasised in the novel, is a bleak one indeed. But the sense of contamination which Pip suffers from is also linked to his own ambiguous social position — it is notable that, whereas Magwitch seems to Pip to eat like a dog when he feeds him on the marshes (pp. 55–56), later it is Pip himself who feels that he is fed like a dog by Estella on his first visit to Satis House (p. 97).

Thus Pip's failure to understand the role of Magwitch in his life for much of the novel arises not so much from an inability to read the signs, as from a profound unwillingness to recognise their meaning. This desire to forget Magwitch is powerfully connected by Dickens with the theme of the transportation of convicts to Australia. Before he leaves the village, for example, Pip reflects:

> If I had often thought before, with something allied to shame, of my companionship with the fugitive whom I had once seen limping among those graves, what were my thoughts on this Sunday, when the place recalled the wretch, ragged and shivering, with his felon iron and badge! My comfort was, that it happened a long time ago, and that he had doubtless been transported a long way off, and that he was dead to me, and might be veritably dead into the bargain. (p. 179)

Britain's attitude to the transported convicts was much the same, as the utilitarian Jeremy Bentham, one of the first advocates of model penitentiaries, had pointed out as early as 1791, in a parody of the sentence of transportation:

> "I sentence you," says the Judge, "but to what I know not — perhaps to storm and shipwreck — perhaps to infectious disorders — perhaps to famine — perhaps to be massacred by savages — perhaps to be devoured by wild beasts. Away — take your chance — perish or prosper —

suffer or enjoy: I rid myself of the sight of you: the ship that bears you away saves me from witnessing your sufferings — I shall give myself no more trouble about you."[1]

The choice of Australia as the site of the penal colonies itself seems to have been influenced by the sense that this barren, remote land was especially suitable as a place of punishment. Yet Australia itself, by Dickens's time, could evoke two contrasting images (see Brantlinger Ch. 4). On the one hand, it had become synonymous with the horrors of transportation, both on the voyage and after arrival, well-known through first-hand accounts, novels (Appendix D 5–6), and official reports (Appendix D 4). At the same time, the chance — albeit remote — of convicts like Magwitch becoming wealthy in the new colony had become notorious, to the extent that some had even come to regard the possibility of being transported as an inducement to crime rather than a deterrence (Appendix D 4). This attitude is encapsulated in another famous parody of the transportation sentence, that of Sydney Smith in 1826:

> "Because you have committed this offence, the sentence of the Court is that you shall no longer be burdened with the support of your wife and family. You shall be immediately removed from a very bad climate and a country over burdened with people to one of the finest regions of the earth, where the demand for human labour is every hour increasing, and where it is highly probable you may ultimately gain your character and improve your future."[2]

Especially as transportation was wound down, Australia also came to be seen as a land of equality, a place where class distinctions ceased to apply, and commoner and gentleman could be united in honest industry.

---

1. Jeremy Bentham, *Principles of Penal Law* (1791) Bk. V Ch. 2. Bentham's attack on transportation to New South Wales here functions as a preface to the recommendation of his own model penitentiary, the Panopticon, which occurs in the following chapter.
2. Cited in *Sir Robert Peel: From His Private Papers*, 3 vols., ed. Charles Stuart Parker (London: John Murray, 1891) Vol. I: 400–1.

Emigration was widely seen as an answer to Britain's poverty and over-crowding, and Dickens himself became an enthusiastic advocate of voluntary emigration for the poor.

Yet, in *Great Expectations* itself, he seems once again to be making a rather subtler point about the role of Britain's overseas empire, which is seen as both off-stage — and something people would rather forget — and as providing the wealth to fuel the dreams of those who, like Pip, are caught within the cultural trammels of the British class system. In this sense, despite Pip's horror of Magwitch, we as readers recognise that at a deep level the two characters have much in common. For, in a sense, they both respond to the discrimination and contempt which they receive, not by challenging the status quo, but by becoming obsessed with it. Pip even repeats Magwitch's behaviour to the extent of himself secretly funding Herbert's business venture. Yet, Pip and Magwitch are also united by their blindness to the reality of the situation in which they find themselves; this is most poignantly evident when Magwitch is unable to grasp Pip's reaction to the revelation of the true source of his wealth (Vol. II Ch. 20).

Ironically, Pip himself does change sufficiently in his feelings towards the old man to keep from Magwitch his true sentiments and to allow him to go to his death believing himself to have accomplished his main goal. Critics have seen in this willingness to preserve Magwitch's illusions a profound change in Pip himself, so that he ends the novel a true rather than false gentleman. Yet, while Pip does alter to the extent that he comes to recognise Joe's true worth, and even to wish to marry Biddy and settle down (a wish in which he is frustrated, of course), this change seems to suggest a pervasive disillusionment with ambitions of any kind, rather than a moral transformation. In this sense it flows naturally from his first horrified reaction to Magwitch's revelations: "O, that he had never come! That he had left me at the forge — far from contented, yet, by comparison, happy!" (p. 347) In particular, the novel ends with a profound sense of disillusionment with romance. Indeed, we should not overlook the fact that, for Pip, Magwitch's appearance does not only reveal the tainted source of his own fortune, but it also exposes the falsity of the ingenious plot which he himself has woven around Estella and Miss Havisham, a plot which he is unwilling to relinquish until the bitter end.

This disillusionment with romance is especially evident with regard to the secret of Estella's birth and parentage; it is, significantly enough, the lawyer Jaggers who says to Pip:

> "For whose sake would you reveal the secret? For the father's? I think he would not be much the better for the mother. For the mother's? I think if she had done such a deed she would be safer where she was. For the daughter's? I think it could hardly serve her, to establish her parentage for the information of her husband, and to drag her back to disgrace, after an escape of twenty years, pretty secure to last for life." (p. 436)

This argument convinces Pip, as it does us, but only because we have already been shaken in our natural belief, as readers of novels, that it is better to know a secret than to remain ignorant. Even more strikingly, the revelation seems to make very little difference to how Pip — or we — perceive Estella. In the same way, unlike most Victorian novels working the foundling motif, this one ends with no revelation about the hero's parentage; he is simply an orphan, the child of parents whose poverty has driven them and his other siblings to an early grave. The calm acceptance of this fact, by the end of the novel, is perhaps Dickens's most telling refusal of the Victorian cult of the gentleman.

It is true that, in a sense, the novel ends happily, with Pip, the former blacksmith's apprentice, and Herbert, the son of gentlefolk, working in happy equality in the Eastern Branch of their firm. The tone, however, is one of mature disillusionment with greater ambitions: "I must not leave it to be supposed that we were ever a great House, or that we made mints of money. We were not in a grand way of business, but we had a good name, and worked for our profits, and did very well." (p. 499) It is against this background of disillusionment with romantic narratives that we must consider the question of the ending of the novel.[1] It was only in the final volume of his life of Dickens that Forster first revealed to readers the fact that the printed ending of the novel was not the one

---

1. For a fuller discussion of the ending, see Edgar Rosenburg, "Last Words on *Great Expectations*: A Textual Brief on the Six Endings," *Dickens Studies Annual* IX (1981): 87–115.

which Dickens had originally written (Appendix A 2/24). In his original ending, Pip had met Estella once again in London years later, finding her settled in a second and happier marriage (see Explanatory Note on p. 510). In many ways, this ending, in which Pip remains unambiguously single, does seem more plausible and in keeping with the rejection of romance in the novel, and the melancholy tone of the work as a whole. Critics have thus sometimes criticised Dickens for accepting Bulwer Lytton's advice, and changing the ending to the published one which allowed at least of the possibility of a reconciliation between the two. The newer ending, however, seems in many ways better written and more imaginative in its setting than the one which it replaced; it has the added advantage of linking Pip's renewed appeal to Estella with his final words to Magwitch. It is, moreover, by no means free of a note of ambiguity, as early reviewers recognised (Appendix B 1). Perhaps, in this most ambiguous and ironic of novels, such an uncertain conclusion to Pip's strivings for happiness is after all the most appropriate.

Acknowledgements

The editors and publishers are grateful to the Clarendon Press, Oxford, for permission to reproduce extracts from *The Letters of Charles Dickens: Volume IX 1859–1861* (1997), ed. Graham Storey.

We would like to thank the staff of the British Library Reading Room and Newspaper Library, the Wisbech and Fenland Museum Library, the Waseda University Central and Takata Libraries, and the Exeter University Library for assistance in locating and viewing materials. Professor George Hughes of Tokyo University and Dr. Chris Brooks of Exeter University were also generous in loaning materials.

Finally our special thanks are due to the staff of the Audio-Visual Department at Exeter University Library for their work on the illustrations.

A Note on the Text

The earliest undoubted references by Dickens to the new story which was to become *Great Expectations* are to be found in two letters of August 1860 (Appendix A 2/1–2). Dickens's original intention was to publish the novel in twenty monthly numbers, as he had done with most of his novels since *The Pickwick Papers*. However, before he began to write, he made a decision to reduce the length of the work by around half in order to publish it in weekly parts in his own family journal *All the Year Round*, as he had done recently with *A Tale of Two Cities*. The reason was economic. The serial then running in *All the Year Round*, Charles Lever's *A Day's Ride: A Life's Romance*, was rather discursive and had not "taken" with subscribers and the circulation was falling significantly. Since Lever's story was not scheduled to finish until the following March, Dickens acted to protect his own investment (Appendix A 2/4–6, 16). Despite this sudden change of plan, Dickens's working notes for the novel (transcribed in Appendix A 1) are noticeably less comprehensive than for any novel since he began the practice with *Dombey and Son* in 1846, and do not include number plans (see Butt and Stone). This suggests the completeness with which the story first took hold of his imagination.

He began writing at the end of September 1860 (Appendix A 2/3). Judging from the letters, he seems to have written most of the early parts at Gad's Hill Place, but to have worked on many of the later ones in London, at the house he rented near Regents Park during the first half of 1861. He considered the story concluded on 11 June 1861 (Appendix A 2/21-22). However, on the advice of Bulwer Lytton, whose own novel *A Strange Story* was due to commence in *All the Year Round* on the completion of *Great Expectations* (Appendix A 2/11 & 2/18), and who in turn had been reading Dickens's work in progress, Dickens altered the final pages of the novel (Appendix A 2/20 & 2/24–6; Explanatory Notes p. 510). The manuscript (including Dickens's working notes) was presented by Dickens to the dedicatee of the novel, the Reverend Chauncy Hare Townshend (Appendix A 2/27), who bequeathed the manuscript to the town of Wisbech, Cambridgeshire, on his death in 1868, where it remains in the Wisbech and Fenland Museum Library. According to Dickens's habitual practice in calculating the length of his novels, on the manuscript are marked nine monthly divisions (each corresponding to four weekly parts), although the novel was never published in monthly numbers. Surviving letters suggest that it was in fact generally written in weekly installments (Appendix A 2/8 & 2/14).

The story was first published in Britain in *All the Year Round* in thirty-six weekly parts commencing on 1 December 1860, as below. Serial publication in *Harper's Weekly* (New York) began and continued one week earlier, based on early sheets sent to America without the benefit of the author's final corrections (Appendix A 2/5).

		All the Year Round			Present Edition	
Part	Date	Issue No.	Page Nos.	Ch. Nos.	Ch. Nos.	Page Nos.
1	1 Dec 1860	IV 84	168–74	1–2	I 1–2	39–52
2	8 Dec	IV 85	193–8	3–4	I 3–4	53–66
3	15 Dec	IV 86	217–21	5	I 5	66–76
4	22 Dec	IV 87	241–5	6–7	I 6–7	76–88
5	29 Dec	IV 88	265–9	8	I 8	89–100
6	5 Jan 1861	IV 89	289–94	9–10	I 9–10	100–113
7	12 Jan	IV 90	313–8	11	I 11	114–126
8	19 Jan	IV 91	337–42	12–13	I 12–13	127–140
9	26 Jan	IV 92	361–6	14–15	I 14–15	140–152
10	2 Feb	IV 93	385–90	16–17	I 16–17	153–165
11	9 Feb	IV 94	409–14	18	I 18	165–178
12	16 Feb	IV 95	433–8	19	I 19	178–192
13	23 Feb	IV 96	457–62	20–21	II 1–2	193–206
14	2 Mar	IV 97	481–6	22	II 3	206–219
15	9 Mar	IV 98	505–10	23–24	II 4–5	219–233
16	16 Mar	IV 99	529–34	25–26	II 6–7	233–247
17	23 Mar	IV 100	553–8	27–28	II 8–9	247–261
18	30 Mar	V 101	1–6	29	II 10	261–273
19	6 Apr	V 102	25–30	30–31	II 11–12	273–287

All *the Year* Round					Present Edition	
Part	Date	Issue No.	Page Nos.	Ch. Nos.	Ch. Nos.	Page Nos.
20	13 Apr	V 103	49–54	32–33	II 13–14	287–299
21	20 Apr	V 104	72–8	34–35	II 15–16	299–313
22	27 Apr	V 105	97–102	36–37	II 17–18	313–326
23	4 May	V 106	121–6	38	II 19	326–339
24	11 May	V 107	145–9	39	II 20	339–350
25	18 May	V 108	169–74	40	III 1	351–364
26	25 May	V 109	193–8	41–42	III 2–3	364–377
27	1 Jun	V 110	217–21	43–44	III 4–5	377–389
28	8 Jun	V 111	241–6	45–46	III 6–7	389–404
29	15 Jun	V 112	265–70	47–48	III 8–9	404–417
30	22 Jun	V 113	289–94	49–50	III 10–11	417–430
31	29 Jun	V 114	313–8	51–52	III 12–13	430–442
32	6 Jul	V 115	337–42	53	III 14	443–454
33	13 Jul	V 116	361–6	54	III 15	455–468
34	20 Jul	V 117	385–90	55–56	III 16–17	468–481
35	27 Jul	V 118	409–13	57	III 18	481–492
36	3 Aug	V 119	433–7	58–59	III 19–20	493–503

Each issue of the journal had twenty-four pages of close double-column print without illustrations; the instalment from *Great Expectations* generally occupied around five to six columns. It led off the issue from the beginning, relegating *A Day's Ride* to the inside pages. The novel was first published as a book by Chapman and Hall in three volumes, unillustrated, on 6 July 1861. Apart from the addition of the dedication and the renumbering of the chapters to begin afresh in each volume, there were substantial revisions to the text as printed in *All the Year Round*.

This three-volume version went through five "editions" (in fact merely impressions) in 1861 (Appendix A 2/29–30 & 2/32–4). Two-volume editions of the novel were also published in English during 1861, by Harper's in New York (with illustrations by John McLenan) and by Tauchnitz in Leipzig (Appendix A 2/9, 2/12, & 2/29). Chapman and Hall brought out four further distinct editions of the novel during the author's lifetime: the one-volume edition of 1862, with illustrations by Marcus Stone, and three collected editions — the Cheap of 1863 (dated 1864), the Library of 1864, and the Charles Dickens of 1868. With the exception of a famous revision in the final sentence originating in the 1862 (see Explanatory Notes p. 511), there were few changes of substance in these later editions.

Like most recent editions, due in part to doubts about the thoroughness which the Charles Dickens edition was checked by the author, the present text is taken from the three-volume edition of 1861, with the exception of several readings restored from the manuscript, and a number of minor corrections in the interests of consistency. Following Margaret Cardwell in the Clarendon edition, three readings in the manuscript have been preferred over clear misprints in the 1861 and later volume editions: "correspondingly" for "corresponding" (p. 117), "disconcerted" for "discontented" (p. 119), and "narrowly" for "nervously" (p. 460). Most of the remaining variations from the 1861 text concern the representation of dialect or "uneducated" speech. Again following Cardwell, a number of non-standard forms found only in the manuscript have been restored. Typical examples are: Joe's "cander," "Howsumever," and "obserwation" (all p. 85), or "notsermuch" and "shouldser" (both p. 489); Pumblechook's "likeways" (p. 185); the Aged P.'s "arternoon" (p. 320); and Magwitch's "appinted" (p. 372) and "unnerstand" (p. 376). The forms "wot" and "wos," where found in the manuscript, have been preferred over the "what" and "was" often replacing them in the printed editions; this occurs especially in Magwitch's speech in Vol. III Chs. 1–3, and in Orlick's in Vol. III Ch. 14, although the usage remains far from consistent. The dominant forms "thankee" and "lookee," plus "ha'," "giv'," etc., have been used uniformly in place of the forms "thank'ee," "look'ee," or "ha," "giv," etc., which occasionally occur. Other obvious errors and inconsistencies have been corrected silently.

Number flags in the text mark brief editorial footnotes; asterisk flags refer to the more detailed Explanatory Notes at the end of the volume, which include discussion of significant textual problems. Those wishing to study in detail the complex variations between the manuscript, various surviving proofs, serial and volume editions, should consult the Clarendon edition of the novel.

Charles Dickens: A Brief Chronology

1812   Born Charles John Huffham Dickens at Portsmouth, second child and eldest son of John, a naval clerk, and Elizabeth Dickens.

1817   Family moves briefly to Sheerness and then to Chatham, both in Kent.

1822   Family moves to Camden Town in North London.

1824   Father imprisoned for three months for debt in the Marshalsea prison. Employed in a blacking warehouse. Enters Wellington House Academy.

1827   Enters solicitor's office as clerk.

1829   Studies shorthand and becomes a parliamentary and news reporter. Falls in love with Maria Beadell.

1833   Stories appear in the *Monthly Magazine*.

1834   Becomes reporter on the *Morning Chronicle*.

1835   "Sketches of London" appear in the *Evening Chronicle*.

1836   *Sketches by Boz* published in volume form in two series. Marries Catherine Hogarth, daughter of editor of the *Evening Chronicle*. Lives at Furnival's Inn, London. Meets John Forster.

1837   Becomes editor of *Bentley's Miscellany* for two years. *Pickwick Papers* appears in volume form, following publication in monthly parts. Son born, first of ten children by Catherine Hogarth. Family moves to Doughty Street, London. Death of wife's sister, Mary Hogarth.

1838   *Oliver Twist* appears in volume form following monthly serialization in *Bentley's Miscellany*. Visits schools in Yorkshire in preparing to write *Nicholas Nickleby*.

1839   *Nicholas Nickleby* appears in volume form following publication in monthly parts. Family moves to Devonshire Terrace, London.

1840   *Master Humphrey's Clock*, written entirely by Dickens, initially as a miscellany, appears weekly for around eighteen months.

1841   *The Old Curiosity Shop* and later *Barnaby Rudge* appear in volume form following serialization in *Master Humphrey's Clock*.

1842   Travels with his wife in USA and Canada for six months. *American Notes* published in volume form.

1843   *A Christmas Carol* appears as Christmas book.

1844   *Martin Chuzzlewit* appears in volume form following publication in monthly parts. Family move to Italy for around a year. *The Chimes* appears as Christmas book.

1845   *The Cricket on the Hearth* appears as Christmas book.

1846   Acts as founding editor of the *Daily News* for a brief period. *Pictures from Italy* appears in volume form following publication as a series of "Travelling Letters" in the *Daily News*. Family moves to Lausanne, Switzerland, and then Paris for a total period of over six months. *The Battle of Life* appears as Christmas book.

1847   Begins to assist Miss Burdett Coutts in the running of a home for reformed prostitutes (until 1858).

1848   *Dombey and Son* appears in volume form following publication in monthly parts. Begins to organize and act in private and charitable theatrical performances. *The Haunted Man* appears as Christmas book.

1850   Begins running *Household Words* as weekly journal, owned jointly with Bradbury & Evans. *David Copperfield* appears in volume form following publication in monthly parts.

1851   Father dies. Family moves to Tavistock House, Tavistock Square, London. Meets Wilkie Collins. *A Child's History of England* begins appearing in weekly parts in *Household Words*, continuing for three years.

1852   Last child born to Catherine Hogarth.

1853   *Bleak House* appears in volume form following publication in monthly parts. First public readings from his own works.

1854   Visits Preston, Lancashire, to observe strike by textile workers, in preparation for writing *Hard Times*. *Hard Times* appears in volume form following weekly serialization in *Household Words*.

1855   Moves to France with family for almost a year.

1856   Buys Gad's Hill Place, near Rochester, Kent.

1857   *Little Dorrit* appears in volume form following publication in monthly parts. Organizes and stars in charitable performances of *The Frozen Deep*, a melodrama by Wilkie Collins; falls in love with Ellen Ternan, a young actress in the company. *The Lazy Tour of Two Idle Apprentices* (in parts) and *The Perils of Certain English Prisoners* (Christmas number), written in collaboration with Wilkie Collins, appear in *Household Words*.

1858   *Reprinted Pieces* (articles from *Household Words*) published in volume form. Begins series of public readings for profit. Separates from his wife; issues personal statement defending his behavior in *Household Words*.

1859   Breaks off all links with Bradbury & Evans, buying out its share in *Household Words*, which was then replaced by *All the Year Round*, a similar weekly family journal. *A Tale of Two Cities* appears in volume form following publication as a weekly serial in *All the Year Round* and in monthly parts.

1860   Sells Tavistock House and lives permanently at Gad's Hill Place.

1861   *The Uncommercial Traveller*, series of papers reprinted from *All the Year Round*, published in volume form. *Great Expectations* appears in volume form following weekly serialization in *All the Year Round*. Begins second series of public readings (until 1863).

1863   Son Walter dies in India. Mother dies. "Mrs Lirriper's Lodgings" appears in Christmas number of *All the Year Round*.

1864   "Mrs Lirriper's Legacy" appears in Christmas number of *All the Year Round*.

1865   *Our Mutual Friend* appears in volume form following publication in monthly parts. Suffers serious train crash while traveling with Ellen Ternan. "Dr Marigold's Prescriptions" appears in Christmas number of *All the Year Round*.

1866   Begins third series of public readings (until 1867).

1867   Begins six-month public reading tour of USA. *No Thoroughfare*, in collaboration with Wilkie Collins, published in Christmas issue of *All the Year Round*.

1868   Begins fourth series of public readings (until 1869), leading to physical breakdown. Second expanded edition of *The Uncommercial Traveller*.

1870   Farewell season of public readings in London. First half of *The Mystery of Edwin Drood* issued in monthly parts and left incomplete. Collapses and dies at Gad's Hill Place. Buried in Westminster Abbey.

GREAT EXPECTATIONS

By
Charles Dickens

Affectionately inscribed
to
Chauncy Hare Townshend.*

---

* This and other asterisks throughout the text indicate that a detailed explanatory note appears at the end of the volume (pages 505-511).

VOLUME I

❧

CHAPTER I

MY FATHER'S family name being Pirrip, and my christian name Philip, my infant tongue could make of both names nothing longer or more explicit than Pip. So, I called myself Pip, and came to be called Pip.

I give Pirrip as my father's family name, on the authority of his tombstone and my sister — Mrs. Joe Gargery, who married the blacksmith. As I never saw my father or my mother, and never saw any likeness of either of them (for their days were long before the days of photographs),[1] my first fancies regarding what they were like, were unreasonably derived from their tombstones. The shape of the letters on my father's, gave me an odd idea that he was a square, stout, dark man, with curly black hair. From the character and turn of the inscription, "*Also Georgiana Wife of the Above*," I drew a childish conclusion that my mother was freckled and sickly. To five little stone lozenges,[2] each about a foot and a half long which were arranged in a neat row beside their grave, and were sacred to the memory of five little brothers of mine — who gave up trying to get a living, exceedingly early in that universal struggle* — I am indebted for a belief I religiously entertained that they had all been born on their backs with their hands in their trousers-pockets, and had never taken them out in this state of existence.

---

1. *long before the days of photographs:* i.e., well before 1839 when the photograph was invented almost simultaneously by Louis Daguerre in France and William Fox Talbot in England.
2. *lozenges:* tomb-stones in approximation of the recumbent human form, like an elongated diamond.

Ours was the marsh country, down by the river, within, as the river wound, twenty miles of the sea.* My first most vivid and broad impression of the identity of things, seems to me to have been gained on a memorable raw afternoon towards evening. At such a time I found out for certain, that this bleak place overgrown with nettles was the churchyard; and that Philip Pirrip, late of this parish, and also Georgiana wife of the above, were dead and buried; and that Alexander, Bartholomew, Abraham, Tobias, and Roger, infant children of the aforesaid, were also dead and buried; and that the dark flat wilderness beyond the churchyard, intersected with dykes and mounds and gates, with scattered cattle feeding on it, was the marshes; and that the low leaden line beyond, was the river; and that the distant savage lair from which the wind was rushing was the sea; and that the small bundle of shivers growing afraid of it all and beginning to cry, was Pip.

"Hold your noise!" cried a terrible voice, as a man started up from among the graves at the side of the church porch. "Keep still, you little devil, or I'll cut your throat!"*

A fearful man, all in coarse grey, with a great iron on his leg. A man with no hat, and with broken shoes, and with an old rag tied round his head. A man who had been soaked in water, and smothered in mud, and lamed by stones, and cut by flints, and stung by nettles, and torn by briars; who limped, and shivered, and glared and growled; and whose teeth chattered in his head as he seized me by the chin.

"O! Don't cut my throat, sir," I pleaded in terror. "Pray don't do it, sir."

"Tell us your name!" said the man. "Quick!"

"Pip, sir."

"Once more," said the man, staring at me. "Give it mouth!"

"Pip. Pip, sir."

"Show us where you live," said the man. "Pint out the place!"

I pointed to where our village lay, on the flat in-shore among the alder-trees and pollards,[1] a mile or more from the church.

The man, after looking at me for a moment, turned me upside-down, and emptied my pockets. There was nothing in them but a piece of bread. When the church came to itself — for he was so sudden and strong that

---

1. *pollards:* trees cut back (polled) to form a distinctive rounded head.

he made it go head over heels before me, and I saw the steeple under my feet — when the church came to itself, I say, I was seated on a high tombstone, trembling, while he ate the bread ravenously.

"You young dog," said the man, licking his lips, "what fat cheeks you ha' got."

I believe they were fat, though I was at that time undersized for my years, and not strong.

"Darn Me if I couldn't eat 'em," said the man, with a threatening shake of his head, "and if I han't half a mind to't!"

I earnestly expressed my hope that he wouldn't, and held tighter to the tombstone on which he had put me; partly, to keep myself upon it; partly, to keep myself from crying.

"Now then, lookee here!" said the man. "Where's your mother?"

"There, sir!" said I.

He started, made a short run, and stopped and looked over his shoulder.

"There, sir!" I timidly explained. "Also Georgiana. That's my mother."

"Oh!" said he, coming back. "And is that your father alonger your mother?"

"Yes, sir," said I; "him too; late of this parish."

"Ha!" he muttered then, considering. "Who d'ye live with — supposin' you're kindly let to live, which I han't made up my mind about?"

"My sister, sir — Mrs. Joe Gargery — wife of Joe Gargery, the blacksmith, sir."

"Blacksmith, eh?" said he. And looked down at his leg.

After darkly looking at his leg and me several times, he came closer to my tombstone, took me by both arms, and tilted me back as far as he could hold me; so that his eyes looked most powerfully down into mine, and mine looked most helplessly up into his.

"Now lookee here," he said, "the question being whether you're to be let to live. You know what a file is?"

"Yes, sir."

"And you know what wittles[1] is?"

---

1. *wittles:* food (dialect, variant of "victuals").

"Yes, sir."

After each question he tilted me over a little more, so as to give me a greater sense of helplessness and danger.

"You get me a file." He tilted me again. "And you get me wittles." He tilted me again. "You bring 'em both to me." He tilted me again. "Or I'll have your heart and liver out." He tilted me again.

I was dreadfully frightened, and so giddy that I clung to him with both hands, and said, "If you would kindly please to let me keep upright, sir, perhaps I shouldn't be sick, and perhaps I could attend more."

He gave me a most tremendous dip and roll, so that the church jumped over its own weather-cock. Then, he held me by the arms, in an upright position on the top of the stone, and went on in these fearful terms:

"You bring me, to-morrow morning early, that file and them wittles. You bring the lot to me, at that old Battery[1] over yonder. You do it, and you never dare to say a word or dare to make a sign concerning your having seen such a person as me, or any person sumever, and you shall be let to live. You fail, or you go from my words in any partickler, no matter how small it is, and your heart and your liver shall be tore out, roasted and ate. Now, I ain't alone, as you may think I am. There's a young man hid with me, in comparison with which young man I am a Angel. That young man hears the words I speak. That young man has a secret way pecooliar to himself, of getting at a boy, and at his heart, and at his liver. It is in wain for a boy to attempt to hide himself from that young man. A boy may lock his door, may be warm in bed, may tuck himself up, may draw the clothes over his head, may think himself comfortable and safe, but that young man will softly creep and creep his way to him and tear him open. I am a keeping that young man from harming of you at the present moment, with great difficulty. I find it wery hard to hold that young man off of your inside. Now, what do you say?"

I said that I would get him the file, and I would get him what broken bits of food I could, and I would come to him at the Battery early in the morning.

---

1. *Battery:* fortified platform where artillery used to be mounted, guarding the sea approach to London.

"Say Lord strike you dead if you don't!" said the man.

I said so, and he took me down.

"Now," he pursued, "you remember what you've undertook, and you remember that young man, and you get home!"

"Goo-good night, sir," I faltered.

"Much of that!" said he, glancing about him over the cold wet flat. "I wish I was a frog. Or a eel!"

At the same time, he hugged his shuddering body in both his arms — clasping himself, as if to hold himself together — and limped towards the low church wall. As I saw him go, picking his way among the nettles, and among the brambles that bound the green mounds, he looked in my young eyes as if he were eluding the hands of the dead people, stretching up cautiously out of their graves, to get a twist upon his ankle and pull him in.

When he came to the low church wall, he got over it, like a man whose legs were numbed and stiff, and then turned round to look for me. When I saw him turning, I set my face towards home, and made the best use of my legs. But presently I looked over my shoulder, and saw him going on again towards the river, still hugging himself in both arms, and picking his way with his sore feet among the great stones dropped into the marshes here and there for stepping-places when the rains were heavy, or the tide was in.

The marshes were just a long black horizontal line then, as I stopped to look after him; and the river was just another horizontal line, not nearly so broad nor yet so black; and the sky was just a row of long angry red lines and dense black lines intermixed. On the edge of the river I could faintly make out the only two black things in all the prospect that seemed to be standing upright; one of these was the beacon by which the sailors steered — like an unhooped cask upon a pole — an ugly thing when you were near it; the other a gibbet, with some chains hanging to it which had once held a pirate. The man was limping on towards this latter, as if he were the pirate come to life, and come down, and going back to hook himself up again. It gave me a terrible turn when I thought so; and as I saw the cattle lifting their heads to gaze after him, I wondered whether they thought so too. I looked all round for the horrible young man, and could see no signs of him. But, now I was frightened again, and ran home without stopping.

CHAPTER II

MY SISTER, Mrs. Joe Gargery, was more than twenty years older than I, and had established a great reputation with herself and the neighbours because she had brought me up "by hand".[1] Having at that time to find out for myself what the expression meant, and knowing her to have a hard and heavy hand, and to be much in the habit of laying it upon her husband as well as upon me, I supposed that Joe Gargery and I were both brought up by hand.

She was not a good-looking woman, my sister; and I had a general impression that she must have made Joe Gargery marry her by hand. Joe was a fair man, with curls of flaxen hair on each side of his smooth face, and with eyes of such a very undecided blue that they seemed to have somehow got mixed with their own whites. He was a mild, good-natured, sweet-tempered, easy-going, foolish, dear fellow — a sort of Hercules in strength, and also in weakness.

My sister, Mrs. Joe, with black hair and eyes, had such a prevailing redness of skin that I sometimes used to wonder whether it was possible she washed herself with a nutmeg-grater instead of soap. She was tall and bony, and almost always wore a coarse apron, fastened over her figure behind with two loops, and having a square impregnable bib in front, that was stuck full of pins and needles. She made it a powerful merit in herself, and a strong reproach against Joe, that she wore this apron so much. Though I really see no reason why she should have worn it at all: or why, if she did wear it at all, she should not have taken it off, every day of her life.

Joe's forge adjoined our house, which was a wooden house, as many of the dwellings in our country were — most of them, at that time. When I ran home from the churchyard, the forge was shut up, and Joe was sitting alone in the kitchen. Joe and I being fellow-sufferers, and having confidences as such, Joe imparted a confidence to me, the moment I raised the latch of the door and peeped in at him opposite to it, sitting in the chimney corner.

---

1. *brought me up "by hand"*: i.e., fed him as a baby from a spoon or a bottle rather than at the breast.

"Mrs. Joe has been out a dozen times, looking for you, Pip. And she's out now, making it a baker's dozen."

"Is she?"

"Yes, Pip," said Joe; "and what's worse, she's got Tickler with her."

At this dismal intelligence, I twisted the only button on my waistcoat round and round, and looked in great depression at the fire. Tickler was a wax-ended piece of cane, worn smooth by collision with my tickled frame.

"She sot down," said Joe, "and she got up, and she made a grab at Tickler, and she Ram-paged out. That's what she did," said Joe, slowly clearing the fire between the lower bars with the poker, and looking at it: "she Ram-paged out, Pip."

"Has she been gone long, Joe?" I always treated him as a larger species of child, and as no more than my equal.

"Well," said Joe, glancing up at the Dutch clock,[1] "she's been on the Ram-page, this last spell, about five minutes, Pip. She's a coming! Get behind the door, old chap, and have the jack-towel[2] betwixt you."

I took the advice. My sister, Mrs. Joe, throwing the door wide open, and finding an obstruction behind it, immediately divined the cause, and applied Tickler to its further investigation. She concluded by throwing me — I often served her as a connubial missile — at Joe, who, glad to get hold of me on any terms, passed me on into the chimney and quietly fenced me up there with his great leg.

"Where have you been, you young monkey?" said Mrs. Joe, stamping her foot. "Tell me directly what you've been doing to wear me away with fret and fright and worrit, or I'd have you out of that corner if you was fifty Pips, and he was five hundred Gargerys."

"I have only been to the churchyard," said I, from my stool, crying and rubbing myself.

"Churchyard!" repeated my sister. "If it warn't for me you'd have been to the churchyard long ago, and stayed there. Who brought you up by hand?"

"You did," said I.

---

1. *Dutch clock:* striking wooden wall clocks made in the Black Forest (Dutch = Deutsch, i.e., German), cheap and popular in Victorian England.
2. *jack-towel:* roller-towel.

"And why did I do it, I should like to know!" exclaimed my sister. I whimpered, "I don't know."

"*I* don't!" said my sister. "I'd never do it again! I know that. I may truly say I've never had this apron of mine off, since born you were. It's bad enough to be a blacksmith's wife (and him a Gargery) without being your mother."

My thoughts strayed from that question as I looked disconsolately at the fire. For, the fugitive out on the marshes with the ironed leg, the mysterious young man, the file, the food, and the dreadful pledge I was under to commit a larceny on those sheltering premises, rose before me in the avenging coals.

"Hah!" said Mrs. Joe, restoring Tickler to his station. "Churchyard, indeed! You may well say churchyard, you two." One of us, by-the-by, had not said it at all. "You'll drive *me* to the churchyard betwixt you, one of these days, and oh, a pr-r-recious pair you'd be without me!"

As she applied herself to set the tea-things, Joe peeped down at me over his leg, as if he were mentally casting me and himself up, and calculating what kind of pair we practically should make, under the grievous circumstances foreshadowed. After that, he sat feeling his right-side flaxen curls and whisker, and following Mrs. Joe about with his blue eyes, as his manner always was at squally times.

My sister had a trenchant way of cutting our bread-and-butter for us, that never varied. First, with her left hand she jammed the loaf hard and fast against her bib — where it sometimes got a pin into it, and sometimes a needle, which we afterwards got into our mouths. Then she took some butter (not too much) on a knife and spread it on the loaf, in an apothecary kind of way, as if she were making a plaister[1] — using both sides of the knife with a slapping dexterity, and trimming and moulding the butter off round the crust. Then, she gave the knife a final smart wipe on the edge of the plaister, and then sawed a very thick round off the loaf: which she finally, before separating from the loaf, hewed into two halves, of which Joe got one, and I the other.

---

1. *plaister:* patch of muslin spread with ointment, etc. and applied to the skin or a wound (plaster).

On the present occasion, though I was hungry, I dared not eat my slice. I felt that I must have something in reserve for my dreadful acquaintance, and his ally the still more dreadful young man. I knew Mrs. Joe's housekeeping to be of the strictest kind, and that my larcenous researches might find nothing available in the safe.[1] Therefore I resolved to put my hunk of bread-and-butter down the leg of my trousers.

The effort of resolution necessary to the achievement of this purpose, I found to be quite awful. It was as if I had to make up my mind to leap from the top of a high house, or plunge into a great depth of water. And it was made the more difficult by the unconscious Joe. In our already-mentioned freemasonry as fellow-sufferers, and in his good-natured companionship with me, it was our evening habit to compare the way we bit through our slices, by silently holding them up to each other's admiration now and then — which stimulated us to new exertions. To-night, Joe several times invited me, by the display of his fast-diminishing slice, to enter upon our usual friendly competition; but he found me, each time, with my yellow mug of tea on one knee, and my untouched bread-and-butter on the other. At last, I desperately considered that the thing I contemplated must be done, and that it had best be done in the least improbable manner consistent with the circumstances. I took advantage of a moment when Joe had just looked at me, and got my bread-and-butter down my leg.

Joe was evidently made uncomfortable by what he supposed to be my loss of appetite, and took a thoughtful bite out of his slice, which he didn't seem to enjoy. He turned it about in his mouth much longer than usual, pondering over it a good deal, and after all gulped it down like a pill. He was about to take another bite, and had just got his head on one side for a good purchase on it, when his eye fell on me, and he saw that my bread-and-butter was gone.

The wonder and consternation with which Joe stopped on the threshold of his bite and stared at me, were too evident to escape my sister's observation.

"What's the matter now?" said she, smartly, as she put down her cup.

---

1. *safe:* ventilated cupboard for storing food; larder.

"I say, you know!" muttered Joe, shaking his head at me in very serious remonstrance. "Pip, old chap! You'll do yourself a mischief. It'll stick somewhere. You can't have chawed it, Pip."

"What's the matter *now*?" repeated my sister, more sharply than before.

"If you can cough any trifle on it up, Pip, I'd recommend you to do it," said Joe, all aghast. "Manners is manners, but still your elth's your elth."

By this time, my sister was quite desperate, so she pounced on Joe, and, taking him by the two whiskers, knocked his head for a little while against the wall behind him: while I sat in the corner, looking guiltily on.

"Now, perhaps you'll mention what's the matter," said my sister, out of breath, "you staring great stuck pig."

Joe looked at her in a helpless way; then took a helpless bite, and looked at me again.

"You know, Pip," said Joe, solemnly, with his last bite in his cheek, and speaking in a confidential voice, as if we two were quite alone, "you and me is always friends, and I'd be the last to tell upon you, any time. But such a" — he moved his chair and looked about the floor between us, and then again at me — "such a most oncommon Bolt as that!"

"Been bolting his food, has he?" cried my sister.

"You know, old chap," said Joe, looking at me, and not at Mrs. Joe, with his bite still in his cheek, "I Bolted, myself, when I was your age — frequent — and as a boy I've been among a many Bolters; but I never see your Bolting equal yet, Pip, and it's a mercy you ain't Bolted dead."

My sister made a dive at me, and fished me up by the hair: saying nothing more than the awful words, "You come along and be dosed."

Some medical beast had revived Tar-water[1] in those days as a fine medicine, and Mrs. Joe always kept a supply of it in the cupboard; having a belief in its virtues correspondent to its nastiness. At the best of times, so much of this elixir was administered to me as a choice restorative, that I was conscious of going about, smelling like a new fence. On this particular evening the urgency of my case demanded a pint of this mixture, which was poured down my throat, for my greater comfort, while Mrs.

---

1. *Tar-water*: coal-tar infused in cold water, a popular remedy from the mid eighteenth century.

Joe held my head under her arm, as a boot would be held in a boot-jack. Joe got off with half a pint; but was made to swallow that (much to his disturbance, as he sat slowly munching and meditating before the fire), "because he had had a turn." Judging from myself, I should say he certainly had a turn afterwards, if he had had none before.

Conscience is a dreadful thing when it accuses man or boy; but when, in the case of a boy, that secret burden co-operates with another secret burden down the leg of his trousers, it is (as I can testify) a great punishment. The guilty knowledge that I was going to rob Mrs. Joe — I never thought I was going to rob Joe, for I never thought of any of the housekeeping property as his — united to the necessity of always keeping one hand on my bread-and-butter as I sat, or when I was ordered about the kitchen on any small errand, almost drove me out of my mind. Then, as the marsh winds made the fire glow and flare, I thought I heard the voice outside, of the man with the iron on his leg who had sworn me to secrecy, declaring that he couldn't and wouldn't starve until to-morrow, but must be fed now. At other times, I thought, What if the young man who was with so much difficulty restrained from imbruing his hands in me, should yield to a constitutional impatience, or should mistake the time, and should think himself accredited to my heart and liver to-night, instead of to-morrow! If ever anybody's hair stood on end with terror, mine must have done so then. But, perhaps, nobody's ever did?

It was Christmas Eve, and I had to stir the pudding for next day, with the copper-stick,[1] from seven to eight by the Dutch clock. I tried it with the load upon my leg (and that made me think afresh of the man with the load on *his* leg), and found the tendency of exercise to bring the bread-and-butter out at my ankle, quite unmanageable. Happily, I slipped away, and deposited that part of my conscience in my garret bedroom.

"Hark!" said I, when I had done my stirring, and was taking a final warm in the chimney corner before being sent up to bed; "was that great guns, Joe?"

"Ah!" said Joe. "There's another conwict off."

---

1. *copper-stick:* long wooden paddle used for stirring the large copper boiler used for both cooking and laundry.

"What does that mean, Joe?" said I.

Mrs. Joe, who always took explanations upon herself, said, snappishly, "Escaped. Escaped." Administering the definition like Tar-water.

While Mrs. Joe sat with her head bending over her needlework, I put my mouth into the forms of saying to Joe, "What's a convict?" Joe put *his* mouth into the forms of returning such a highly elaborate answer, that I could make out nothing of it but the single word "Pip."

"There was a conwict off last night," said Joe, aloud, "after sunset-gun. And they fired warning of him. And now, it appears they're firing warning of another."

"*Who's* firing?" said I.

"Drat that boy," interposed my sister, frowning at me over her work, "what a questioner he is. Ask no questions, and you'll be told no lies."

It was not very polite to herself, I thought, to imply that I should be told lies by her, even if I did ask questions. But she never was polite, unless there was company.

At this point, Joe greatly augmented my curiosity by taking the utmost pains to open his mouth very wide, and to put it into the form of a word that looked to me like "sulks." Therefore, I naturally pointed to Mrs. Joe, and put my mouth into the form of saying "her?" But Joe wouldn't hear of that, at all, and again opened his mouth very wide, and shook the form of a most emphatic word out of it. But I could make nothing of the word.

"Mrs. Joe," said I, as a last resource, "I should like to know — if you wouldn't much mind — where the firing comes from?"

"Lord bless the boy!" exclaimed my sister, as if she didn't quite mean that, but rather the contrary. "From the Hulks!"[1]

"Oh-h!" said I, looking at Joe. "Hulks!"

Joe gave a reproachful cough, as much as to say, "Well, I told you so."

"And please what's Hulks?" said I.

"That's the way with this boy!" exclaimed my sister, pointing me out with her needle and thread, and shaking her head at me. "Answer him one question, and he'll ask you a dozen directly. Hulks are prison-ships,

---

1. *Hulks:* large, superannuated sailing ships used at anchor as prisons from the late eighteenth century, later sometimes purpose-built.

right 'cross th' meshes." We always used that name for marshes, in our country.

"I wonder who's put into prison-ships, and why they're put there?" said I, in a general way, and with quiet desperation.

It was too much for Mrs. Joe, who immediately rose. "I tell you what, young fellow," said she, "I didn't bring you up by hand to badger people's lives out. It would be blame to me, and not praise, if I had. People are put in the Hulks because they murder, and because they rob, and forge, and do all sorts of bad; and they always begin by asking questions. Now, you get along to bed!"

I was never allowed a candle to light me to bed, and, as I went upstairs in the dark, with my head tingling — from Mrs. Joe's thimble having played the tambourine upon it, to accompany her last words — I felt fearfully sensible of the great convenience that the Hulks were handy for me. I was clearly on my way there. I had begun by asking questions, and I was going to rob Mrs. Joe.

Since that time, which is far enough away now, I have often thought that few people know what secrecy there is in the young, under terror. No matter how unreasonable the terror, so that it be terror. I was in mortal terror of the young man who wanted my heart and liver; I was in mortal terror of my interlocutor with the ironed leg; I was in mortal terror of myself, from whom an awful promise had been extracted; I had no hope of deliverance through my all-powerful sister, who repulsed me at every turn; I am afraid to think of what I might have done, on requirement, in the secrecy of my terror.

If I slept at all that night, it was only to imagine myself drifting down the river on a strong spring tide, to the Hulks; a ghostly pirate calling out to me through a speaking-trumpet, as I passed the gibbet-station, that I had better come ashore and be hanged there at once and not put it off. I was afraid to sleep, even if I had been inclined, for I knew that at the first faint dawn of morning I must rob the pantry. There was no doing it in the night, for there was no getting a light by easy friction then;[1] to have

---

1. *no getting a light by easy friction then:* i.e., before the invention of sulphur matches or Lucifers in 1829.

got one, I must have struck it out of flint and steel, and have made a noise like the very pirate himself rattling his chains.

As soon as the great black velvet pall outside my little window was shot with grey, I got up and went down-stairs; every board upon the way, and every crack in every board, calling after me, "Stop thief!" and "Get up, Mrs. Joe!" In the pantry, which was far more abundantly supplied than usual, owing to the season, I was very much alarmed, by a hare hanging up by the heels, whom I rather thought I caught, when my back was half turned, winking. I had no time for verification, no time for selection, no time for anything, for I had no time to spare. I stole some bread, some rind of cheese, about half a jar of mincemeat (which I tied up in my pocket-handkerchief with my last night's slice), some brandy from a stone bottle (which I decanted into a glass bottle I had secretly used for making that intoxicating fluid, Spanish-liquorice-water,[1] up in my room: diluting the stone bottle from a jug in the kitchen cupboard), a meat bone with very little on it, and a beautiful round compact pork pie. I was nearly going away without the pie, but I was tempted to mount upon a shelf, to look what it was that was put away so carefully in a covered earthenware dish in a corner, and I found it was the pie, and I took it, in the hope that it was not intended for early use, and would not be missed for some time.

There was a door in the kitchen, communicating with the forge; I unlocked and unbolted that door, and got a file from among Joe's tools. Then, I put the fastenings as I had found them, opened the door at which I had entered when I ran home last night, shut it, and ran for the misty marshes.

---

1. *Spanish-liquorice-water:* a concoction made from cold water and stick (or Spanish) liquorice, a medicament or sweetmeat made in long thin cylinders from the sweetened extract of root liquorice.

CHAPTER III

IT WAS a rimy[1] morning, and very damp. I had seen the damp lying on the outside of my little window, as if some goblin had been crying there all night, and using the window for a pocket-handkerchief. Now, I saw the damp lying on the bare hedges and spare grass, like a coarser sort of spiders' webs; hanging itself from twig to twig and blade to blade. On every rail and gate, wet lay clammy; and the marsh-mist was so thick, that the wooden finger on the post directing people to our village — a direction which they never accepted, for they never came there — was invisible to me until I was quite close under it. Then, as I looked up at it, while it dripped, it seemed to my oppressed conscience like a phantom devoting me to the Hulks.

The mist was heavier yet when I got out upon the marshes, so that instead of my running at everything, everything seemed to run at me. This was very disagreeable to a guilty mind. The gates and dykes and banks came bursting at me through the mist, as if they cried as plainly as could be, "A boy with Somebody-else's pork pie! Stop him!" The cattle came upon me with like suddenness, staring out of their eyes, and steaming out of their nostrils, "Holloa, young thief!" One black ox, with a white cravat on — who even had to my awakened conscience something of a clerical air — fixed me so obstinately with his eyes, and moved his blunt head round in such an accusatory manner as I moved round, that I blubbered out to him, "I couldn't help it, sir! It wasn't for myself I took it!" Upon which he put down his head, blew a cloud of smoke out of his nose, and vanished with a kick-up of his hind-legs and a flourish of his tail.

All this time, I was getting on towards the river; but however fast I went, I couldn't warm my feet, to which the damp cold seemed riveted, as the iron was riveted to the leg of the man I was running to meet. I knew my way to the Battery, pretty straight, for I had been down there on a Sunday with Joe, and Joe, sitting on an old gun, had told me that when I was 'prentice to him regularly bound, we would have such Larks there! However, in the confusion of the mist, I found myself at last too

---

1. *rimy:* frosty.

far to the right, and consequently had to try back along the river-side, on the bank of loose stones above the mud and the stakes that staked the tide out. Making my way along here with all despatch, I had just crossed a ditch which I knew to be very near the Battery, and had just scrambled up the mound beyond the ditch, when I saw the man sitting before me. His back was towards me, and he had his arms folded, and was nodding forward, heavy with sleep.

I thought he would be more glad if I came upon him with his breakfast, in that unexpected manner, so I went forward softly and touched him on the shoulder. He instantly jumped up, and it was not the same man, but another man!

And yet this man was dressed in coarse grey, too, and had a great iron on his leg, and was lame, and hoarse, and cold, and was everything that the other man was; except that he had not the same face, and had a flat broad-brimmed low-crowned felt hat on. All this, I saw in a moment, for I had only a moment to see it in: he swore an oath at me, made a hit at me — it was a round weak blow that missed me and almost knocked himself down, for it made him stumble — and then he ran into the mist, stumbling twice as he went, and I lost him.

"It's the young man!" I thought, feeling my heart shoot as I identified him. I dare say I should have felt a pain in my liver, too, if I had known where it was.

I was soon at the Battery, after that, and there was the right man — hugging himself and limping to and fro, as if he had never all night left off hugging and limping — waiting for me. He was awfully cold, to be sure. I half expected to see him drop down before my face and die of deadly cold. His eyes looked so awfully hungry, too, that when I handed him the file and he laid it down on the grass, it occurred to me he would have tried to eat it, if he had not seen my bundle. He did not turn me upside down, this time, to get at what I had, but left me right side upwards while I opened the bundle and emptied my pockets.

"What's in the bottle, boy?" said he.

"Brandy," said I.

He was already handing mincemeat down his throat in the most curious manner — more like a man who was putting it away somewhere in a violent hurry, than a man who was eating it — but he left off to take some of the liquor. He shivered all the while, so violently, that it was quite as much as he could do to keep the neck of the bottle between his teeth, without biting it off.

"I think you have got the ague," said I.

"I'm much of your opinion, boy," said he.

"It's bad about here," I told him. "You've been lying out on the meshes, and they're dreadful aguish. Rheumatic, too."

"I'll eat my breakfast afore they're the death of me," said he. "I'd do that, if I was going to be strung up to that there gallows as there is over there, directly arterwards. I'll beat the shivers so far, I'll bet you."

He was gobbling mincemeat, meat-bone, bread, cheese, and pork pie, all at once: staring distrustfully while he did so at the mist all round us, and often stopping — even stopping his jaws — to listen. Some real or fancied sound, some clink upon the river or breathing of beast upon the marsh, now gave him a start, and he said, suddenly:

"You're not a deceiving imp? You brought no one with you?"

"No, sir! No!"

"Nor giv' no one the office to follow you?"

"No!"

"Well," said he, "I believe you. You'd be but a fierce young hound indeed, if at your time of life you could help to hunt a wretched warmint,[1] hunted as near death and dunghill as this poor wretched warmint is!"

Something clicked in his throat, as if he had works in him like a clock, and was going to strike. And he smeared his ragged rough sleeve over his eyes.

Pitying his desolation, and watching him as he gradually settled down upon the pie, I made bold to say, "I am glad you enjoy it."

"Did you speak?"

"I said I was glad you enjoyed it."

"Thankee, my boy. I do."

I had often watched a large dog of ours eating his food; and I now noticed a decided similarity between the dog's way of eating and the man's.

---

1. *warmint:* noxious animal (dialect, variant of "varment"), and, by extension, objectionable person.

The man took strong sharp sudden bites, just like the dog. He swallowed, or rather snapped up, every mouthful, too soon and too fast; and he looked sideways here and there while he ate, as if he thought there was danger in every direction, of somebody's coming to take the pie away. He was altogether too unsettled in his mind over it, to appreciate it comfortably, I thought, or to have anybody to dine with him, without making a chop with his jaws at the visitor. In all of which particulars he was very like the dog.

"I am afraid you won't leave any of it for him," said I, timidly; after a silence during which I had hesitated as to the politeness of making the remark. "There's no more to be got where that came from." It was the certainty of this fact that impelled me to offer the hint.

"Leave any for him? Who's him?" said my friend, stopping in his crunching of pie-crust.

"The young man. That you spoke of. That was hid with you."

"Oh ah!" he returned, with something like a gruff laugh. "Him? Yes, yes! *He* don't want no wittles."

"I thought he looked as if he did," said I.

The man stopped eating, and regarded me with the keenest scrutiny and the greatest surprise.

"Looked? When?"

"Just now."

"Where?"

"Yonder," said I, pointing; "over there, where I found him nodding asleep, and thought it was you."

He held me by the collar and stared at me so, that I began to think his first idea about cutting my throat had revived.

"Dressed like you, you know, only with a hat," I explained, trembling; "and — and" — I was very anxious to put this delicately — "and with — the same reason for wanting to borrow a file. Didn't you hear the cannon last night?"*

"Then, there *was* firing!" he said to himself.

"I wonder you shouldn't have been sure of that," I returned, "for we heard it up at home, and that's further away, and we were shut in besides."

"Why, see now!" said he. "When a man's alone on these flats, with a

light head and a light stomach, perishing of cold and want, he hears nothin'
all night, but guns firing, and voices calling. Hears? He sees the soldiers,
with their red coats lighted up by the torches carried afore, closing in
round him. Hears his number called, hears himself challenged, hears the
rattle of the muskets, hears the orders 'Make ready! Present! Cover him
steady, men!' and is laid hands on — and there's nothin'! Why, if I see one
pursuing party last night — coming up in order, Damn 'em, with their
tramp, tramp — I see a hundred. And as to firing! Why, I see the mist
shake with the cannon, arter it was broad day. — But this man;" he had
said all the rest, as if he had forgotten my being there; "did you notice
anything in him?"

"He had a badly bruised face," said I, recalling what I hardly knew I
knew.

"Not here?" exclaimed the man, striking his left cheek mercilessly, with
the flat of his hand.

"Yes, there!"

"Where is he?" He crammed what little food was left, into the breast
of his grey jacket. "Show me the way he went. I'll pull him down, like a
bloodhound. Curse this iron on my sore leg! Give us hold of the file,
boy."

I indicated in what direction the mist had shrouded the other man,
and he looked up at it for an instant. But he was down on the rank wet
grass, filing at his iron like a madman, and not minding me or minding
his own leg, which had an old chafe upon it and was bloody, but which
he handled as roughly as if it had no more feeling in it than the file. I was
very much afraid of him again, now that he had worked himself into this
fierce hurry, and I was likewise very much afraid of keeping away from
home any longer. I told him I must go, but he took no notice, so I thought
the best thing I could do was to slip off. The last I saw of him, his head
was bent over his knee and he was working hard at his fetter, muttering
impatient imprecations at it and at his leg. The last I heard of him, I stopped
in the mist to listen, and the file was still going.

CHAPTER IV

I FULLY expected to find a Constable in the kitchen, waiting to take me up. But not only was there no Constable there, but no discovery had yet been made of the robbery. Mrs. Joe was prodigiously busy in getting the house ready for the festivities of the day, and Joe had been put upon the kitchen door-step to keep him out of the dustpan — an article into which his destiny always led him sooner or later, when my sister was vigorously reaping the floors of her establishment.

"And where the deuce ha' *you* been?" was Mrs. Joe's Christmas salutation, when I and my conscience showed ourselves.

I said I had been down to hear the Carols. "Ah! well!" observed Mrs. Joe. "You might ha' done worse." Not a doubt of that, I thought.

"Perhaps if I warn't a blacksmith's wife, and (what's the same thing) a slave with her apron never off, *I* should have been to hear the Carols," said Mrs. Joe. "I'm rather partial to Carols, myself, and that's the best of reasons for my never hearing any."

Joe, who had ventured into the kitchen after me as the dustpan had retired before us, drew the back of his hand across his nose with a conciliatory air when Mrs. Joe darted a look at him, and, when her eyes were withdrawn, secretly crossed his two forefingers, and exhibited them to me, as our token that Mrs. Joe was in a cross temper. This was so much her normal state, that Joe and I would often, for weeks together, be, as to our fingers, like monumental Crusaders as to their legs.[1]

We were to have a superb dinner, consisting of a leg of pickled pork and greens, and a pair of roast stuffed fowls. A handsome mince-pie had been made yesterday morning (which accounted for the mincemeat not being missed), and the pudding was already on the boil. These extensive arrangements occasioned us to be cut off unceremoniously in respect of breakfast; "for I an't," said Mrs. Joe, "I an't a going to have no formal cramming and busting and washing up now, with what I've got before me, I promise you!"

---

1. *like monumental Crusaders as to their legs:* referring to the (mistaken) assumption that effigies of knights with crossed legs in Mediaeval churches indicated that the original had been on a Crusade.

So, we had our slices served out, as if we were two thousand troops on a forced march instead of a man and boy at home; and we took gulps of milk and water, with apologetic countenances, from a jug on the dresser. In the mean time, Mrs. Joe put clean white curtains up, and tacked a new flowered-flounce across the wide chimney to replace the old one, and uncovered the little state parlour across the passage, which was never uncovered at any other time, but passed the rest of the year in a cool haze of silver paper, which even extended to the four little white crockery poodles on the mantelshelf, each with a black nose and a basket of flowers in his mouth, and each the counterpart of the other. Mrs. Joe was a very clean housekeeper, but had an exquisite art of making her cleanliness more uncomfortable and unacceptable than dirt itself. Cleanliness is next to Godliness,[1] and some people do the same by their religion.

My sister having so much to do, was going to church vicariously; that is to say, Joe and I were going. In his working clothes, Joe was a well-knit characteristic-looking blacksmith; in his holiday clothes, he was more like a scarecrow in good circumstances, than anything else. Nothing that he wore then, fitted him or seemed to belong to him; and everything that he wore then, grazed him. On the present festive occasion he emerged from his room, when the blithe bells were going, the picture of misery, in a full suit of Sunday penitentials. As to me, I think my sister must have had some general idea that I was a young offender whom an Accoucheur Policeman[2] had taken up (on my birthday) and delivered over to her, to be dealt with according to the outraged majesty of the law. I was always treated as if I had insisted on being born, in opposition to the dictates of reason, religion, and morality, and against the dissuading arguments of my best friends. Even when I was taken to have a new suit of clothes, the tailor had orders to make them like a kind of Reformatory, and on no account to let me have the free use of my limbs.

Joe and I going to church, therefore, must have been a moving spectacle for compassionate minds. Yet, what I suffered outside, was nothing

---

1. *Cleanliness is next to Godliness:* the maxim derives from the Anglican reformer Charles Wesley's sermon "On Dress" of 1791.
2. *Accoucheur Policeman:* as though the male mid-wife were also an officer of the law and had arrested Pip at birth.

to what I underwent within. The terrors that had assailed me whenever Mrs. Joe had gone near the pantry, or out of the room, were only to be equalled by the remorse with which my mind dwelt on what my hands had done. Under the weight of my wicked secret, I pondered whether the Church would be powerful enough to shield me from the vengeance of the terrible young man, if I divulged to that establishment. I conceived the idea that the time when the banns were read and when the clergyman said, "Ye are now to declare it!" would be the time for me to rise and propose a private conference in the vestry. I am far from being sure that I might not have astonished our small congregation by resorting to this extreme measure, but for its being Christmas Day and no Sunday.

Mr. Wopsle, the clerk at church, was to dine with us; and Mr. Hubble the wheelwright and Mrs. Hubble; and Uncle Pumblechook (Joe's uncle, but Mrs. Joe appropriated him), who was a well-to-do corn-chandler in the nearest town, and drove his own chaise-cart. The dinner hour was half-past one. When Joe and I got home, we found the table laid, and Mrs. Joe dressed, and the dinner dressing, and the front door unlocked (it never was, at any other time) for the company to enter by, and everything most splendid. And still, not a word of the robbery.

The time came, without bringing with it any relief to my feelings, and the company came. Mr. Wopsle, united to a Roman nose and a large shining bald forehead, had a deep voice which he was uncommonly proud of; indeed it was understood among his acquaintance that if you could only give him his head, he would read the clergyman into fits; he himself confessed that if the Church was "thrown open," meaning to competition, he would not despair of making his mark in it. The Church not being "thrown open," he was, as I have said, our clerk. But he punished the Amens tremendously; and when he gave out the psalm — always giving the whole verse — he looked all round the congregation first, as much as to say, "You have heard my friend overhead;[1] oblige me with your opinion of this style!"

---

1. *my friend overhead:* Anglican pulpits commonly had three levels, with the lower used for the leading of prayers by the parish clerk, and the middle and upper levels used by the clergyman, respectively for the reading of the lessons and the delivery of the sermon.

I opened the door to the company — making believe that it was a habit of ours to open that door — and I opened it first to Mr. Wopsle, next to Mr. and Mrs. Hubble, and last of all to Uncle Pumblechook. N.B. *I* was not allowed to call him uncle, under the severest penalties.

"Mrs. Joe," said Uncle Pumblechook: a large hard-breathing middle-aged slow man, with a mouth like a fish, dull staring eyes, and sandy hair standing upright on his head, so that he looked as if he had just been all but choked, and had that moment come to; "I have brought you, as the compliments of the season — I have brought you, Mum, a bottle of sherry wine — and I have brought you, Mum, a bottle of port wine."

Every Christmas Day he presented himself, as a profound novelty, with exactly the same words, and carrying the two bottles like dumb-bells. Every Christmas Day, Mrs. Joe replied, as she now replied, "Oh, Un—cle Pum—ble—chook! This is kind!" Every Christmas Day, he retorted, as he now retorted, "It's no more than your merits. And now are you all bobbish, and how's Sixpennorth of halfpence?"[1] meaning me.

We dined on these occasions in the kitchen, and adjourned, for the nuts and oranges and apples, to the parlour; which was a change very like Joe's change from his working clothes to his Sunday dress. My sister was uncommonly lively on the present occasion, and indeed was generally more gracious in the society of Mrs. Hubble than in any other company. I remember Mrs. Hubble as a little curly sharp-edged person in sky-blue, who held a conventionally juvenile position, because she had married Mr. Hubble — I don't know at what remote period — when she was much younger than he. I remember Mr. Hubble as a tough high-shouldered stooping old man, of a sawdusty fragrance, with his legs extraordinarily wide apart: so that in my short days I always saw some miles of open country between them when I met him coming up the lane.

Among this good company I should have felt myself, even if I hadn't robbed the pantry, in a false position. Not because I was squeezed in at an

---

1. *And now are you all bobbish, and how's Sixpennorth of halfpence?* Pumblechook's well-worn joke relies on a pun linking "bobbish" (in good health) with "bob" (slang for a shilling, a coin equivalent to twelve pence, hence the reference to the diminutive Pip as sixpence made up of twelve halfpenny pieces). "Sixpennorth" is an abbreviation of "sixpennyworth."

acute angle of the tablecloth, with the table in my chest, and the Pumblechookian elbow in my eye, nor because I was not allowed to speak (I didn't want to speak), nor because I was regaled with the scaly tips of the drumsticks of the fowls, and with those obscure corners of pork of which the pig, when living, had had the least reason to be vain. No; I should not have minded that, if they would only have left me alone. But they wouldn't leave me alone. They seemed to think the opportunity lost, if they failed to point the conversation at me, every now and then, and stick the point into me. I might have been an unfortunate little bull in a Spanish arena, I got so smartingly touched up by these moral goads.

It began the moment we sat down to dinner. Mr. Wopsle said grace with theatrical declamation — as it now appears to me, something like a religious cross of the Ghost in Hamlet with Richard the Third — and ended with the very proper aspiration that we might be truly grateful. Upon which my sister fixed me with her eye, and said, in a low reproachful voice, "Do you hear that? Be grateful."

"Especially," said Mr. Pumblechook, "be grateful, boy, to them which brought you up by hand."

Mrs. Hubble shook her head, and contemplating me with a mournful presentiment that I should come to no good, asked, "Why is it that the young are never grateful?" This moral mystery seemed too much for the company until Mr. Hubble tersely solved it by saying, "Naterally wicious." Everybody then murmured "True!" and looked at me in a particularly unpleasant and personal manner.

Joe's station and influence were something feebler (if possible) when there was company, than when there was none. But he always aided and comforted me when he could, in some way of his own, and he always did so at dinner-time by giving me gravy, if there were any. There being plenty of gravy to-day, Joe spooned into my plate, at this point, about half a pint.

A little later on in the dinner, Mr. Wopsle reviewed the sermon with some severity, and intimated — in the usual hypothetical case of the Church being "thrown open" — what kind of sermon *he* would have given them. After favouring them with some heads of that discourse, he remarked that he considered the subject of the day's homily, ill chosen; which was the less excusable, he added, when there were so many subjects "going about."

"True again," said Uncle Pumblechook. "You've hit it, sir! Plenty of subjects going about, for them that know how to put salt upon their tails. That's what's wanted. A man needn't go far to find a subject, if he's ready with his salt-box."[1] Mr. Pumblechook added, after a short interval of reflection, "Look at Pork alone. There's a subject! If you want a subject, look at Pork!"

"True, sir. Many a moral for the young," returned Mr. Wopsle; and I knew he was going to lug me in, before he said it; "might be deduced from that text."

("You listen to this," said my sister to me, in a severe parenthesis.)

Joe gave me some more gravy.

"Swine," pursued Mr. Wopsle, in his deepest voice, and pointing his fork at my blushes, as if he were mentioning my christian name; "Swine were the companions of the prodigal.[2] The gluttony of Swine is put before us, as an example to the young." (I thought this pretty well in him who had been praising up the pork for being so plump and juicy.) "What is detestable in a pig, is more detestable in a boy."

"Or girl," suggested Mr. Hubble.

"Of course, or girl, Mr. Hubble," assented Mr. Wopsle, rather irritably, "but there is no girl present."

"Besides," said Mr. Pumblechook, turning sharp on me, "think what you've got to be grateful for. If you'd been born a Squeaker—"

"He *was*, if ever a child was," said my sister, most emphatically.

Joe gave me some more gravy.

"Well, but I mean a four-footed Squeaker," said Mr. Pumblechook. "If you had been born such, would you have been here now? Not you—"

"Unless in that form," said Mr. Wopsle, nodding towards the dish.

---

1. *for them that know how to put salt upon their tails ... if he's ready with his salt-box:* referring to the traditional jocular advice to children to catch birds by throwing salt on their tails, most familiar from the nursery rhyme of "Simple Simon": "He went to catch a dickey bird, / And thought he could not fail, / Because he'd got a little salt, / To put upon its tail." Domestic table salt was often kept in a covered salt-box instead of a perforated salt cellar.

2. *Swine were the companions of the prodigal:* see Jesus's parable of the prodigal son in Luke 15:11-32, specifically verse 15.

"But I don't mean in that form, sir," returned Mr. Pumblechook, who had an objection to being interrupted; "I mean, enjoying himself with his elders and betters, and improving himself with their conversation, and rolling in the lap of luxury. Would he have been doing that? No, he wouldn't. And what would have been your destination?" turning on me again. "You would have been disposed of for so many shillings according to the market price of the article, and Dunstable the butcher would have come up to you as you lay in your straw, and he would have whipped you under his left arm, and with his right he would have tucked up his frock to get a penknife from out of his waistcoat-pocket, and he would have shed your blood and had your life. No bringing up by hand then. Not a bit of it!"

Joe offered me more gravy, which I was afraid to take.

"He was a world of trouble to you, ma'am," said Mrs. Hubble, commiserating my sister.

"Trouble?" echoed my sister; "trouble?" And then entered on a fearful catalogue of all the illnesses I had been guilty of, and all the acts of sleeplessness I had committed, and all the high places I had tumbled from, and all the low places I had tumbled into, and all the injuries I had done myself, and all the times she had wished me in my grave, and I had contumaciously refused to go there.

I think the Romans must have aggravated one another very much, with their noses. Perhaps, they became the restless people they were, in consequence. Anyhow, Mr. Wopsle's Roman nose so aggravated me, during the recital of my misdemeanours, that I should have liked to pull it until he howled. But, all I had endured up to this time, was nothing in comparison with the awful feelings that took possession of me when the pause was broken which ensued upon my sister's recital, and in which pause everybody had looked at me (as I felt painfully conscious) with indignation and abhorrence.

"Yet," said Mr. Pumblechook, leading the company gently back to the theme from which they had strayed, "Pork — regarded as biled — is rich, too; ain't it?"

"Have a little brandy, uncle," said my sister.

O Heavens, it had come at last! He would find it was weak, he would say it was weak, and I was lost! I held tight to the leg of the table under the cloth, with both hands, and awaited my fate.

My sister went for the stone bottle, came back with the stone bottle, and poured his brandy out: no one else taking any. The wretched man trifled with his glass — took it up, looked at it through the light, put it down — prolonged my misery. All this time, Mrs. Joe and Joe were briskly clearing the table for the pie and pudding.

I couldn't keep my eyes off him. Always holding tight by the leg of the table with my hands and feet, I saw the miserable creature finger his glass playfully, take it up, smile, throw his head back, and drink the brandy off. Instantly afterwards, the company were seized with unspeakable consternation, owing to his springing to his feet, turning round several times in an appalling spasmodic whooping-cough dance, and rushing out at the door; he then became visible through the window, violently plunging and expectorating, making the most hideous faces, and apparently out of his mind.

I held on tight, while Mrs. Joe and Joe ran to him. I didn't know how I had done it, but I had no doubt I had murdered him somehow. In my dreadful situation, it was a relief when he was brought back, and, surveying the company all round as if *they* had disagreed with him, sank down into his chair with the one significant gasp, "Tar!"

I had filled up the bottle from the tar-water jug. I knew he would be worse by-and-by. I moved the table, like a Medium of the present day,* by the vigour of my unseen hold upon it.

"Tar!" cried my sister, in amazement. "Why, how ever could Tar come there?"

But, Uncle Pumblechook, who was omnipotent in that kitchen, wouldn't hear the word, wouldn't hear of the subject, imperiously waved it all away with his hand, and asked for hot gin-and-water. My sister, who had begun to be alarmingly meditative, had to employ herself actively in getting the gin, the hot water, the sugar, and the lemon-peel, and mixing them. For the time at least, I was saved. I still held on the leg of the table, but clutched it now with the fervour of gratitude.

By degrees, I became calm enough to release my grasp and partake of pudding. Mr. Pumblechook partook of pudding. All partook of pudding. The course terminated, and Mr. Pumblechook had begun to beam under the genial influence of gin-and-water. I began to think I should get over the day, when my sister said to Joe, "Clean plates — cold."

I clutched the leg of the table again immediately, and pressed it to my bosom as if it had been the companion of my youth and friend of my soul. I foresaw what was coming, and I felt that this time I really was gone.

"You must taste," said my sister, addressing the guests with her best grace, "you must taste, to finish with, such a delightful and delicious present of Uncle Pumblechook's!"

Must they! Let them not hope to taste it!

"You must know," said my sister, rising, "it's a pie; a savoury pork pie."

The company murmured their compliments. Uncle Pumblechook, sensible of having deserved well of his fellow-creatures, said — quite vivaciously, all things considered — "Well, Mrs. Joe, we'll do our best endeavours; let us have a cut at this same pie."

My sister went out to get it. I heard her steps proceed to the pantry. I saw Mr. Pumblechook balance his knife. I saw reawakening appetite in the Roman nostrils of Mr. Wopsle. I heard Mr. Hubble remark that "a bit of savoury pork pie would lay atop of anything you could mention, and do no harm," and I heard Joe say, "You shall have some, Pip." I have never been absolutely certain whether I uttered a shrill yell of terror, merely in spirit, or in the bodily hearing of the company. I felt that I could bear no more, and that I must run away. I released the leg of the table, and ran for my life.

But, I ran no further than the house door, for there I ran head foremost into a party of soldiers with their muskets: one of whom held out a pair of handcuffs to me, saying, "Here you are, look sharp, come on!"

CHAPTER V

THE APPARITION of a file of soldiers ringing down the butt-ends of their loaded muskets on our door-step, caused the dinner-party to rise from table in confusion, and caused Mrs. Joe re-entering the kitchen empty-handed, to stop short and stare, in her wondering lament of "Gracious goodness gracious me, what's gone — with the — pie!"

The sergeant and I were in the kitchen when Mrs. Joe stood staring;

at which crisis I partially recovered the use of my senses. It was the sergeant who had spoken to me, and he was now looking round at the company, with his handcuffs invitingly extended towards them in his right hand, and his left on my shoulder.

"Excuse me, ladies and gentlemen," said the sergeant, "but as I have mentioned at the door to this smart young shaver" (which he hadn't), "I am on a chase in the name of the King, and I want the blacksmith."

"And pray what might you want with *him*?" retorted my sister, quick to resent his being wanted at all.

"Missis," returned the gallant sergeant, "speaking for myself, I should reply, the honour and pleasure of his fine wife's acquaintance; speaking for the King, I answer, a little job done."

This was received as rather neat in the sergeant; insomuch that Mr. Pumblechook cried audibly, "Good again!"

"You see, blacksmith," said the sergeant, who had by this time picked out Joe with his eye, "we have had an accident with these, and I find the lock of one of 'em goes wrong, and the coupling don't act pretty. As they are wanted for immediate service, will you throw your eye over them?"

Joe threw his eye over them, and pronounced that the job would necessitate the lighting of his forge fire, and would take nearer two hours than one. "Will it? Then will you set about it at once, blacksmith?" said the off-hand sergeant, "as it's on his Majesty's service. And if my men can bear a hand anywhere, they'll make themselves useful." With that, he called to his men, who came trooping into the kitchen one after another, and piled their arms in a corner. And then they stood about, as soldiers do; now, with their hands loosely clasped before them; now, resting a knee or a shoulder; now, easing a belt or a pouch; now, opening the door to spit stiffly over their high stocks,[1] out into the yard.

All these things I saw without then knowing that I saw them, for I was in an agony of apprehension. But, beginning to perceive that the handcuffs were not for me, and that the military had so far got the better of the pie as to put it in the background, I collected a little more of my scattered wits.

---

1. *stocks:* stiff military collars.

"Would you give me the Time?" said the sergeant, addressing himself to Mr. Pumblechook, as to a man whose appreciative powers justified the inference that he was equal to the time.

"It's just gone half-past two."

"That's not so bad," said the sergeant, reflecting; "even if I was forced to halt here nigh two hours, that'll do. How far might you call yourselves from the marshes, hereabouts? Not above a mile, I reckon?"

"Just a mile," said Mrs. Joe.

"That'll do. We begin to close in upon 'em about dusk. A little before dusk, my orders are. That'll do."

"Convicts, sergeant?" asked Mr. Wopsle, in a matter-of-course way.

"Ay!" returned the sergeant, "two. They're pretty well known to be out on the marshes still, and they won't try to get clear of 'em before dusk. Anybody here seen anything of any such game?"

Everybody, myself excepted, said no, with confidence. Nobody thought of me.

"Well!" said the sergeant, "they'll find themselves trapped in a circle, I expect, sooner than they count on. Now, blacksmith! If you're ready, His Majesty the King is."

Joe had got his coat and waistcoat and cravat off, and his leather apron on, and passed into the forge. One of the soldiers opened its wooden windows, another lighted the fire, another turned to at the bellows, the rest stood round the blaze, which was soon roaring. Then Joe began to hammer and clink, hammer and clink, and we all looked on.

The interest of the impending pursuit not only absorbed the general attention, but even made my sister liberal. She drew a pitcher of beer from the cask, for the soldiers, and invited the sergeant to take a glass of brandy. But Mr. Pumblechook said, sharply, "Give him wine, Mum. I'll engage there's no Tar in that:" so, the sergeant thanked him and said that as he preferred his drink without tar, he would take wine, if it was equally convenient. When it was given him, he drank his Majesty's health and Compliments of the Season, and took it all at a mouthful and smacked his lips.

"Good stuff, eh, sergeant?" said Mr. Pumblechook.

"I'll tell you something," returned the sergeant; "I suspect that stuff's of *your* providing."

Mr. Pumblechook, with a fat sort of laugh, said, "Ay, ay? Why?"

"Because," returned the sergeant, clapping him on the shoulder, "you're a man that knows what's what."

"D'ye think so?" said Mr. Pumblechook, with his former laugh. "Have another glass!"

"With you. Hob and nob,"[1] returned the sergeant. "The top of mine to the foot of yours — the foot of yours to the top of mine — Ring once, ring twice — the best tune on the Musical Glasses! Your health. May you live a thousand years, and never be a worse judge of the right sort than you are at the present moment of your life!"

The sergeant tossed off his glass again and seemed quite ready for another glass. I noticed that Mr. Pumblechook in his hospitality appeared to forget that he had made a present of the wine, but took the bottle from Mrs. Joe and had all the credit of handing it about in a gush of joviality. Even I got some. And he was so very free of the wine that he even called for the other bottle, and handed that about with the same liberality, when the first was gone.

As I watched them while they all stood clustering about the forge, enjoying themselves so much, I thought what terrible good sauce for a dinner my fugitive friend on the marshes was. They had not enjoyed themselves a quarter so much, before the entertainment was brightened with the excitement he furnished. And now, when they were all in lively anticipation of "the two villains" being taken, and when the bellows seemed to roar for the fugitives, the fire to flare for them, the smoke to hurry away in pursuit of them, Joe to hammer and clink for them, and all the murky shadows on the wall to shake at them in menace as the blaze rose and sank and the red-hot sparks dropped and died, the pale afternoon outside, almost seemed in my pitying young fancy to have turned pale on their account, poor wretches.

At last, Joe's job was done, and the ringing and roaring stopped. As Joe got on his coat, he mustered courage to propose that some of us should go down with the soldiers and see what came of the hunt. Mr. Pumblechook and Mr. Hubble declined, on the plea of a pipe and ladies' society; but Mr. Wopsle said he would go, if Joe would. Joe said he was

---

1. *Hob and nob:* a toast employed by a pair of drinkers.

agreeable, and would take me, if Mrs. Joe approved. We never should have got leave to go, I am sure, but for Mrs. Joe's curiosity to know all about it and how it ended. As it was, she merely stipulated, "If you bring the boy back with his head blown to bits by a musket, don't look to me to put it together again."

The sergeant took a polite leave of the ladies, and parted from Mr. Pumblechook as from a comrade; though I doubt if he were quite as fully sensible of that gentleman's merits under arid conditions, as when something moist was going. His men resumed their muskets and fell in. Mr. Wopsle, Joe, and I, received strict charge to keep in the rear, and to speak no word after we reached the marshes. When we were all out in the raw air and were steadily moving towards our business, I treasonably whispered to Joe, "I hope, Joe, we shan't find them." And Joe whispered to me, "I'd give a shilling if they had cut and run, Pip."

We were joined by no stragglers from the village, for the weather was cold and threatening, the way dreary, the footing bad, darkness coming on, and the people had good fires in-doors and were keeping the day. A few faces hurried to glowing windows and looked after us, but none came out. We passed the finger-post, and held straight on to the churchyard. There, we were stopped a few minutes by a signal from the sergeant's hand, while two or three of his men dispersed themselves among the graves, and also examined the porch. They came in again without finding anything, and then we struck out on the open marshes, through the gate at the side of the churchyard. A bitter sleet came rattling against us here on the east wind, and Joe took me on his back.

Now that we were out upon the dismal wilderness where they little thought I had been within eight or nine hours and had seen both men hiding, I considered for the first time, with great dread, if we should come upon them, would my particular convict suppose that it was I who had brought the soldiers there? He had asked me if I was a deceiving imp, and he had said I should be a fierce young hound if I joined the hunt against him. Would he believe that I was both imp and hound in treacherous earnest, and had betrayed him?

It was of no use asking myself this question now. There I was, on Joe's back, and there was Joe beneath me, charging at the ditches like a hunter, and stimulating Mr. Wopsle not to tumble on his Roman nose, and to keep up with us. The soldiers were in front of us, extended into a pretty wide line with an interval between man and man. We were taking the course I had begun with, and from which I had diverged in the mist. Either the mist was not out again yet, or the wind had dispelled it. Under the low red glare of sunset, the beacon, and the gibbet, and the mound of the Battery, and the opposite shore of the river, were plain, though all of a watery lead colour.

With my heart thumping like a blacksmith at Joe's broad shoulder, I looked all about for any sign of the convicts. I could see none, I could hear none. Mr. Wopsle had greatly alarmed me more than once, by his blowing and hard breathing; but I knew the sounds by this time, and could dissociate them from the object of pursuit. I got a dreadful start, when I thought I heard the file still going; but it was only a sheep bell. The sheep stopped in their eating and looked timidly at us; and the cattle, their heads turned from the wind and sleet, stared angrily as if they held us responsible for both annoyances; but, except these things, and the shudder of the dying day in every blade of grass, there was no break in the bleak stillness of the marshes.

The soldiers were moving on in the direction of the old Battery, and we were moving on a little way behind them, when, all of a sudden, we all stopped. For, there had reached us on the wings of the wind and rain, a long shout. It was repeated. It was at a distance towards the east, but it was long and loud. Nay, there seemed to be two or more shouts raised together — if one might judge from a confusion in the sound.

To this effect the sergeant and the nearest men were speaking under their breath, when Joe and I came up. After another moment's listening, Joe (who was a good judge) agreed, and Mr. Wopsle (who was a bad judge) agreed. The sergeant, a decisive man, ordered that the sound should not be answered, but that the course should be changed, and that his men should make towards it "at the double." So we slanted to the right (where the East was), and Joe pounded away so wonderfully, that I had to hold on tight to keep my seat.

It was a run indeed now, and what Joe called, in the only two words he spoke all the time, "a Winder." Down banks and up banks, and over gates, and splashing into dykes, and breaking among coarse rushes: no man cared where he went. As we came nearer to the shouting, it became more and more apparent that it was made by more than one voice. Sometimes, it seemed to stop altogether, and then the soldiers stopped. When it broke out again, the soldiers made for it at a greater rate than ever, and we after them. After a while, we had so run it down, that we could hear one voice calling "Murder!" and another voice, "Convicts! Runaways! Guard! This way for the runaway convicts!" Then both voices would seem to be stifled in a struggle, and then would break out again. And when it had come to this, the soldiers ran like deer, and Joe too.

The sergeant ran in first, when we had run the noise quite down, and two of his men ran in close upon him. Their pieces were cocked and levelled when we all ran in.

"Here are both men!" panted the sergeant, struggling at the bottom of a ditch. "Surrender, you two! and confound you for two wild beasts! Come asunder!"

Water was splashing, and mud was flying, and oaths were being sworn, and blows were being struck, when some more men went down into the ditch to help the sergeant, and dragged out, separately, my convict and the other one. Both were bleeding and panting and execrating and struggling; but of course I knew them both directly.

"Mind!" said my convict, wiping blood from his face with his ragged sleeves, and shaking torn hair from his fingers; "*I* took him! *I* give him up to you! Mind that!"

"It's not much to be particular about," said the sergeant; "it'll do you small good, my man, being in the same plight yourself. Handcuffs there!"

"I don't expect it to do me any good. I don't want it to do me more good than it does now," said my convict, with a greedy laugh. "I took him. He knows it. That's enough for me."

The other convict was livid to look at, and, in addition to the old bruised left side of his face, seemed to be bruised and torn all over. He could not so much as get his breath to speak, until they were both separately handcuffed, but leaned upon a soldier to keep himself from falling.

"Take notice, guard — he tried to murder me," were his first words.

"Tried to murder him?" said my convict, disdainfully. "Try, and not do it? I took him, and giv' him up; that's what I done. I not only prevented him getting off the marshes, but I dragged him here — dragged him this far on his way back. He's a gentleman, if you please, this villain. Now, the

Hulks has got its gentleman again, through me. Murder him? Worth my while, too, to murder him, when I could do worse and drag him back!"

The other one still gasped, "He tried — he tried — to — murder me. Bear — bear witness."

"Lookee here!" said my convict to the sergeant. "Single-handed I got clear of the prison-ship; I made a dash and I done it. I could ha' got clear of these death-cold flats likewise — look at my leg: you won't find much iron on it — if I hadn't made discovery that *he* was here. Let *him* go free? Let *him* profit by the means as I found out? Let *him* make a tool of me afresh and again? Once more? No, no, no. If I had died at the bottom there;" and he made an emphatic swing at the ditch with his manacled hands; "I'd have held to him with that grip, that you should have been safe to find him in my hold."

The other fugitive, who was evidently in extreme horror of his companion, repeated, "He tried to murder me. I should have been a dead man if you had not come up."

"He lies!" said my convict, with fierce energy. "He's a liar born, and he'll die a liar. Look at his face; ain't it written there? Let him turn those eyes of his on me. I defy him to do it."

The other, with an effort at a scornful smile — which could not, however, collect the nervous working of his mouth into any set expression — looked at the soldiers, and looked about at the marshes and at the sky, but certainly did not look at the speaker.

"Do you see him?" pursued my convict. "Do you see what a villain he is? Do you see those grovelling and wandering eyes? That's how he looked when we were tried together. He never looked at me."

The other, always working and working his dry lips and turning his eyes restlessly about him far and near, did at last turn them for a moment on the speaker, with the words, "You are not much to look at," and with a half-taunting glance at the bound hands. At that point, my convict became so frantically exasperated, that he would have rushed upon him but for the interposition of the soldiers. "Didn't I tell you," said the other convict then, "that he would murder me, if he could?" And any one could see that he shook with fear, and that there broke out upon his lips, curious white flakes, like thin snow.

"Enough of this parley," said the sergeant. "Light those torches."

As one of the soldiers, who carried a basket in lieu of a gun, went down on his knee to open it, my convict looked round him for the first time, and saw me. I had alighted from Joe's back on the brink of the ditch when we came up, and had not moved since. I looked at him eagerly when he looked at me, and slightly moved my hands and shook my head. I had been waiting for him to see me, that I might try to assure him of my innocence. It was not at all expressed to me that he even comprehended my intention, for he gave me a look that I did not understand, and it all passed in a moment. But if he had looked at me for an hour or for a day, I could not have remembered his face ever afterwards, as having been more attentive.

The soldier with the basket soon got a light, and lighted three or four torches, and took one himself and distributed the others. It had been almost dark before, but now it seemed quite dark, and soon afterwards very dark. Before we departed from that spot, four soldiers standing in a ring, fired twice into the air. Presently we saw other torches kindled at some distance behind us, and others on the marshes on the opposite bank of the river. "All right," said the sergeant. "March."

We had not gone far when three cannon were fired ahead of us with a sound that seemed to burst something inside my ear. "You are expected on board," said the sergeant to my convict; "they know you are coming. Don't straggle, my man. Close up here."

The two were kept apart, and each walked surrounded by a separate guard. I had hold of Joe's hand now, and Joe carried one of the torches. Mr. Wopsle had been for going back, but Joe was resolved to see it out, so we went on with the party. There was a reasonably good path now, mostly on the edge of the river, with a divergence here and there where a dyke came, with a miniature windmill on it and a muddy sluice-gate. When I looked round, I could see the other lights coming in after us. The torches we carried, dropped great blotches of fire upon the track, and I could see those, too, lying smoking and flaring. I could see nothing else but black darkness. Our lights warmed the air about us with their pitchy blaze, and the two prisoners seemed rather to like that, as they limped along in the midst of the muskets. We could not go fast, because of their lameness; and they were so spent, that two or three times we had to halt while they rested.

After an hour or so of this travelling, we came to a rough wooden hut and a landing-place. There was a guard in the hut, and they challenged, and the sergeant answered. Then, we went into the hut where there was a smell of tobacco and whitewash, and a bright fire, and a lamp, and a stand of muskets, and a drum, and a low wooden bedstead, like an overgrown mangle without the machinery,[1] capable of holding about a dozen soldiers all at once. Three or four soldiers who lay upon it in their great-coats, were not much interested in us, but just lifted their heads and took a sleepy stare, and then lay down again. The sergeant made some kind of report, and some entry in a book, and then the convict whom I call the other convict was drafted off with his guard, to go on board first.

My convict never looked at me, except that once. While we stood in the hut, he stood before the fire looking thoughtfully at it, or putting up his feet by turns upon the hob, and looking thoughtfully at them as if he pitied them for their recent adventures. Suddenly, he turned to the sergeant, and remarked:

"I wish to say something respecting this escape. It may prevent some persons laying under suspicion alonger me."

"You can say what you like," returned the sergeant, standing coolly looking at him with his arms folded, "but you have no call to say it here. You'll have opportunity enough to say about it, and hear about it, before it's done with, you know."

"I know, but this is another pint, a separate matter. A man can't starve; at least *I* can't. I took some wittles, up at the willage over yonder — where the church stands a'most out on the marshes."

"You mean stole," said the sergeant.

"And I'll tell you where from. From the blacksmith's."

"Halloa!" said the sergeant, staring at Joe.

"Halloa, Pip!" said Joe, staring at me.

"It was some broken wittles — that's what it was — and a dram of liquor, and a pie."

---

1. *like an overgrown mangle without the machinery:* an old-fashioned flat mangle for rolling and pressing laundry, consisting of a large polished table up to six feet in length on which the articles were placed. They were flattened by the action of a wooden box filled with stones pressing down on two horizontal rollers, and worked back and forth using a rack and pinion system.

"Have you happened to miss such an article as a pie, blacksmith?" asked the sergeant, confidentially.

"My wife did, at the very moment when you came in. Don't you know, Pip?"

"So," said my convict, turning his eyes on Joe in a moody manner, and without the least glance at me; "so you're the blacksmith, are you? Then I'm sorry to say, I've eat your pie."

"God knows you're welcome to it — so far as it was ever mine," returned Joe, with a saving remembrance of Mrs. Joe. "We don't know what you have done, but we wouldn't have you starved to death for it, poor miserable fellow-creatur. — Would us, Pip?"

The something that I had noticed before, clicked in the man's throat again, and he turned his back. The boat had returned, and his guard were ready, so we followed him to the landing-place made of rough stakes and stones, and saw him put into the boat, which was rowed by a crew of convicts like himself. No one seemed surprised to see him, or interested in seeing him, or glad to see him, or sorry to see him, or spoke a word, except that somebody in the boat growled as if to dogs, "Give way, you!" which was the signal for the dip of the oars. By the light of the torches, we saw the black Hulk lying out a little way from the mud of the shore, like a wicked Noah's ark. Cribbed and barred and moored by massive rusty chains, the prison-ship seemed in my young eyes to be ironed like the prisoners. We saw the boat go alongside, and we saw him taken up the side and disappear. Then, the ends of the torches were flung hissing into the water, and went out, as if it were all over with him.

CHAPTER VI

MY STATE of mind regarding the pilfering from which I had been so unexpectedly exonerated, did not impel me to frank disclosure; but I hope it had some dregs of good at the bottom of it.

I do not recal that I felt any tenderness of conscience in reference to Mrs. Joe, when the fear of being found out was lifted off me. But I loved Joe — perhaps for no better reason in those early days than because the dear fellow let me love him — and, as to him, my inner self was not so easily composed. It was much upon my mind (particularly when I first saw him looking about for his file) that I ought to tell Joe the whole truth. Yet I did not, and for the reason that I mistrusted that if I did, he would think me worse than I was. The fear of losing Joe's confidence, and of thenceforth sitting in the chimney corner at night staring drearily at my for ever lost companion and friend, tied up my tongue. I morbidly represented to myself that if Joe knew it, I never afterwards could see him at the fireside feeling his fair whisker, without thinking that he was meditating on it. That, if Joe knew it, I never afterwards could see him glance, however casually, at yesterday's meat or pudding when it came on to-day's table, without thinking that he was debating whether I had been in the pantry. That, if Joe knew it, and at any subsequent period of our joint domestic life remarked that his beer was flat or thick, the conviction that he suspected Tar in it, would bring a rush of blood to my face. In a word, I was too cowardly to do what I knew to be right, as I had been too cowardly to avoid doing what I knew to be wrong. I had had no intercourse with the world at that time, and I imitated none of its many inhabitants who act in this manner. Quite an untaught genius, I made the discovery of the line of action for myself.

As I was sleepy before we were far away from the prison-ship, Joe took me on his back again and carried me home. He must have had a tiresome journey of it, for Mr. Wopsle, being knocked up, was in such a very bad temper that if the Church had been thrown open, he would probably have excommunicated the whole expedition, beginning with Joe and myself. In his lay capacity, he persisted in sitting down in the damp to such an insane extent, that when his coat was taken off to be dried at the kitchen fire, the circumstantial evidence on his trousers would have hanged him if it had been a capital offence.

By that time, I was staggering on the kitchen floor like a little drunkard, through having been newly set upon my feet, and through having been fast asleep, and through waking in the heat and lights and noise of tongues. As I came to myself (with the aid of a heavy thump between the shoulders, and the restorative exclamation "Yah! Was there ever such a boy as this!" from my sister), I found Joe telling them about the convict's confession, and all the visitors suggesting different ways by which he had got into the pantry. Mr. Pumblechook made out, after carefully surveying the premises, that he had first got upon the roof of the forge, and had then got upon the roof of the house, and had then let himself down the kitchen chimney by a rope made of his bedding cut into strips; and as Mr. Pumblechook was very positive and drove his own chaise-cart — over everybody — it was agreed that it must be so. Mr. Wopsle, indeed, wildly cried out "No!" with the feeble malice of a tired man; but, as he had no theory, and no coat on, he was unanimously set at nought — not to mention his smoking hard behind, as he stood with his back to the kitchen fire to draw the damp out: which was not calculated to inspire confidence.

This was all I heard that night before my sister clutched me, as a slumberous offence to the company's eyesight, and assisted me up to bed with such a strong hand that I seemed to have fifty boots on, and to be dangling them all against the edges of the stairs. My state of mind, as I have described it, began before I was up in the morning, and lasted long after the subject had died out, and had ceased to be mentioned saving on exceptional occasions.

CHAPTER VII

AT THE time when I stood in the churchyard, reading the family tombstones, I had just enough learning to be able to spell them out. My construction even of their simple meaning was not very correct, for I read "wife of the Above" as a complimentary reference to my father's exaltation to a better world; and if any one of my deceased relations had been referred to as "Below," I have no doubt I should have formed the worst opinions of that member of the family. Neither, were my notions of the theological positions to which my Catechism bound me, at all accurate; for, I have a lively remembrance that I supposed my declaration that I was to "walk in the same all the days of my life,"[1] laid me under an obligation always to go

---

1. *the theological positions ... days of my life:* the Catechism is the document for the instruction of children in the fundamental beliefs of the Church of England, in the

through the village from our house in one particular direction, and never to vary it by turning down by the wheelwright's or up by the mill.

When I was old enough, I was to be apprenticed to Joe, and until I could assume that dignity I was not to be what Mrs. Joe called "Pompeyed," or (as I render it) pampered. Therefore, I was not only odd-boy about the forge, but if any neighbour happened to want an extra boy to frighten birds, or pick up stones, or do any such job, I was favoured with the employment. In order, however, that our superior position might not be compromised thereby, a money-box was kept on the kitchen mantelshelf, into which it was publicly made known that all my earnings were dropped. I have an impression that they were to be contributed eventually towards the liquidation of the National Debt,[2] but I know I had no hope of any personal participation in the treasure.

Mr. Wopsle's great-aunt kept an evening school in the village; that is to say, she was a ridiculous old woman of limited means and unlimited infirmity, who used to go to sleep from six to seven every evening, in the society of youth who paid twopence per week each, for the improving opportunity of seeing her do it.* She rented a small cottage, and Mr. Wopsle had the room up-stairs, where we students used to overhear him reading aloud in a most dignified and terrific manner, and occasionally bumping on the ceiling. There was a fiction that Mr. Wopsle "examined" the scholars, once a quarter. What he did on those occasions was to turn up his cuffs, stick up his hair, and give us Mark Antony's oration over the body of Caesar.[3] This was always followed by Collins's Ode on the Passions,[4]

---

form of question and response, contained in the rite of Confirmation from the Book of Common Prayer. The response Pip comically misinterprets runs: "I should keep God's holy will and commandments, and walk in the same all the days of my life."

2. *the National Debt:* central government borrowing, particularly high in the early years of the nineteenth century on account of the Napoleonic Wars. Saving banks, as they were then known, grew up in this period with the aims of rewarding working-class thrift and helping to finance the National Debt.

3. *Mark Antony's oration over the body of Caesar:* beginning famously, "Friends, Romans, countrymen, lend me your ears." See Shakespeare's *Julius Caesar* III ii 73-107.

4. *Collins's Ode on the Passions:* the poet William Collins (1721-59) whose work influenced the early Romantics. Dickens cites the sixth stanza of the "Ode to the Passions" (1747) almost verbatim.

wherein I particularly venerated Mr. Wopsle as Revenge, throwing his blood-stain'd sword in thunder down, and taking the War denouncing trumpet with a withering look. It was not with me then, as it was in later life, when I fell into the society of the Passions, and compared them with Collins and Wopsle, rather to the disadvantage of both gentlemen.

Mr. Wopsle's great-aunt, besides keeping this Educational Institution, kept — in the same room — a little general shop. She had no idea what stock she had, or what the price of anything in it was; but there was a little greasy memorandum-book kept in a drawer, which served as a Catalogue of Prices, and by this oracle Biddy arranged all the shop transactions. Biddy was Mr. Wopsle's great-aunt's granddaughter; I confess myself quite unequal to the working out of the problem, what relation she was to Mr. Wopsle. She was an orphan like myself; like me, too, had been brought up by hand. She was most noticeable, I thought, in respect of her extremities; for, her hair always wanted brushing, her hands always wanted washing, and her shoes always wanted mending and pulling up at heel. This description must be received with a week-day limitation. On Sundays, she went to church elaborated.

Much of my unassisted self, and more by the help of Biddy than of Mr. Wopsle's great-aunt, I struggled through the alphabet as if it had been a bramble-bush; getting considerably worried and scratched by every letter. After that, I fell among those thieves,[1] the nine figures, who seemed every evening to do something new to disguise themselves and baffle recognition. But, at last I began, in a purblind groping way, to read, write, and cipher, on the very smallest scale.

One night, I was sitting in the chimney corner with my slate, expending great efforts on the production of a letter to Joe. I think it must have been a full year after our hunt upon the marshes, for it was a long time after, and it was winter and a hard frost. With an alphabet on the hearth at my feet for reference, I contrived in an hour or two to print and smear this epistle:

---

1. *fell among those thieves:* echoing the words of Jesus in the parable of the Good Samaritan in Luke 10:30-35.

"MI DEER JO i OPE U R KRWITE WELL i OPE i SHAL SON B HABELL 4 2 TEEDGE U JO AN THEN WE SHORL B SO GLODD AN WEN i M PRENGTD 2 U JO WOT LARX AN BLEVE ME INF XN PIP."

There was no indispensable necessity for my communicating with Joe by letter, inasmuch as he sat beside me and we were alone. But, I delivered this written communication (slate and all) with my own hand, and Joe received it as a miracle of erudition.

"I say, Pip, old chap!" cried Joe, opening his blue eyes wide, "what a scholar you are! An't you?"

"I should like to be," said I, glancing at the slate as he held it: with a misgiving that the writing was rather hilly.

"Why, here's a J," said Joe, "and a O equal to anythink! Here's a J and a O, Pip, and a J-O, Joe."

I had never heard Joe read aloud to any greater extent than this monosyllable, and I had observed at church last Sunday when I accidentally held our Prayer-Book upside down, that it seemed to suit his convenience quite as well as if it had been all right. Wishing to embrace the present occasion of finding out whether in teaching Joe, I should have to begin quite at the beginning, I said, "Ah! But read the rest, Joe."

"The rest, eh, Pip?" said Joe, looking at it with a slowly searching eye, "One, two, three. Why, here's three Js, and three Os, and three J-O, Joes in it, Pip!"

I leaned over Joe, and, with the aid of my forefinger, read him the whole letter.

"Astonishing!" said Joe, when I had finished. "You ARE a scholar."

"How do you spell Gargery, Joe?" I asked him, with a modest patronage.

"I don't spell it at all," said Joe.

"But supposing you did?"

"It *can't* be supposed," said Joe. "Tho' I'm oncommon fond of reading, too."

"Are you, Joe?"

"On-common. Give me," said Joe, "a good book, or a good newspaper, and sit me down afore a good fire, and I ask no better. Lord!" he continued, after rubbing his knees a little, "when you *do* come to a J and a O, and says you, 'Here, at last, is a J-O, Joe,' how interesting reading is!"

I derived from this, that Joe's education, like Steam, was yet in its infancy. Pursuing the subject, I inquired:

"Didn't you ever go to school, Joe, when you were as little as me?"

"No, Pip."

"Why didn't you ever go to school, Joe, when you were as little as me?"

"Well, Pip," said Joe, taking up the poker, and settling himself to his usual occupation when he was thoughtful, of slowly raking the fire between the lower bars: "I'll tell you. My father, Pip, he were given to drink, and when he were overtook with drink, he hammered away at my mother, most onmerciful. It were a'most the only hammering he did, indeed, 'xcepting at myself. And he hammered at me with a wigour only to be equalled by the wigour with which he didn't hammer at his anwil. — You're a listening and understanding, Pip?"

"Yes, Joe."

"'Consequence, my mother and me we ran away from my father, several times; and then my mother she'd go out to work, and she'd say, 'Joe,' she'd say, 'now, please God, you shall have some schooling, child,' and she'd put me to school. But my father were that good in his hart that he couldn't abear to be without us. So, he'd come with a most tremenjous crowd and make such a row at the doors of the houses where we was, that they used to be obligated to have no more to do with us and to give us up to him. And then he took us home and hammered us. Which, you see, Pip," said Joe, pausing in his meditative raking of the fire, and looking at me, "were a drawback on my learning."

"Certainly, poor Joe!"

"Though mind you, Pip," said Joe, with a judicial touch or two of the poker on the top bar, "rendering unto all their doo, and maintaining equal justice betwixt man and man, my father were that good in his hart, don't you see?"

I didn't see; but I didn't say so.

"Well!" Joe pursued, "somebody must keep the pot a biling Pip, or the pot won't bile, don't you know?"

I saw that, and said so.

"'Consequence, my father didn't make objections to my going to work; so I went to work at my present calling, which were his too, if he would have followed it, and I worked tolerable hard, I assure *you*, Pip. In time I were able to keep him, and I kep him till he went off in a purple leptic fit. And it were my intentions to have had put upon his tombstone that Whatsume'er the failings on his part, Remember reader he were that good in his hart."

Joe recited this couplet with such manifest pride and careful perspicuity, that I asked him if he had made it himself?

"I made it," said Joe, "my own self. I made it in a moment. It was like striking out a horseshoe complete, in a single blow. I never was so much surprised in all my life — couldn't credit my own ed — to tell you the truth, hardly believed it *were* my own ed. As I was saying, Pip, it were my intentions to have had it cut over him; but poetry costs money, cut it how you will, small or large, and it were not done. Not to mention bearers, all the money that could be spared were wanted for my mother. She were in poor elth, and quite broke. She weren't long of following, poor soul, and her share of peace come round at last."

Joe's blue eyes turned a little watery; he rubbed, first one of them, and then the other, in a most uncongenial and uncomfortable manner, with the round knob on the top of the poker.

"It were but lonesome then," said Joe, "living here alone, and I got acquainted with your sister. Now, Pip;" Joe looked firmly at me, as if he knew I was not going to agree with him; "your sister is a fine figure of a woman."

I could not help looking at the fire, in an obvious state of doubt.

"Whatever family opinions, or whatever the world's opinions, on that subject may be, Pip, your sister is," Joe tapped the top bar with the poker after every word following, "a—fine—figure—of—a—woman!"

I could think of nothing better to say than "I am glad you think so, Joe."

"So am I," returned Joe, catching me up. "*I* am glad I think so, Pip. A little redness, or a little matter of Bone, here or there, what does it signify to Me?"

I sagaciously observed, if it didn't signify to him, to whom did it signify?

"Certainly!" assented Joe. "That's it. You're right, old chap! When I got acquainted with your sister, it were the talk how she was bringing you up by hand. Very kind of her too, all the folks said, and I said, along with all the folks. As to you," Joe pursued, with a countenance expressive of seeing something very nasty indeed: "if you could have been aware how small and flabby and mean you was, dear me, you'd have formed the most contemptible opinions of yourself!"

Not exactly relishing this, I said, "Never mind me, Joe."

"But I did mind you, Pip," he returned, with tender simplicity. "When I offered to your sister to keep company, and to be asked in church at such times as she was willing and ready to come to the forge, I said to her, 'And bring the poor little child. God bless the poor little child,' I said to your sister, 'there's room for *him* at the forge!'"

I broke out crying and begging pardon, and hugged Joe round the neck: who dropped the poker to hug me, and to say, "Ever the best of friends; an't us, Pip? Don't cry, old chap!"

When this little interruption was over, Joe resumed:

"Well, you see, Pip, and here we are! That's about where it lights; here we are! Now, when you take me in hand in my learning, Pip (and I tell you beforehand I am awful dull, most awful dull), Mrs. Joe mustn't see too much of what we're up to. It must be done, as I may say, on the sly. And why on the sly? I'll tell you why, Pip."

He had taken up the poker again; without which, I doubt if he could have proceeded in his demonstration.

"Your sister is given to government."

"Given to government Joe?" I was startled, for I had some shadowy idea (and I am afraid I must add, hope) that Joe had divorced her in favour of the Lords of the Admiralty, or Treasury.

"Given to government," said Joe. "Which I meantersay the government of you and myself."

"Oh!"

"And she an't over partial to having scholars on the premises," Joe continued, "and in partickler would not be over partial to my being a scholar, for fear as I might rise. Like a sort of rebel, don't you see?"

I was going to retort with an inquiry, and had got as far as "Why—" when Joe stopped me.

"Stay a bit. I know what you're a going to say, Pip; stay a bit! I don't deny that your sister comes the Mo-gul over us,[1] now and again. I don't

---

1. *comes the Mo-gul over us:* behaves like a tyrant; after the Grand Mogul, the common European designation for the emperors of Delhi whose line continued until 1857.

deny that she do throw us back-falls, and that she do drop down upon us heavy. At such times as when your sister is on the Ram-page, Pip," Joe sank his voice to a whisper and glanced at the door, "cander compels fur to admit that she is a Buster."

Joe pronounced this word, as if it began with at least twelve capital Bs.

"Why don't I rise? That were your obserwation when I broke it off, Pip?"

"Yes, Joe."

"Well," said Joe, passing the poker into his left hand, that he might feel his whisker; and I had no hope of him whenever he took to that placid occupation; "your sister's a master-mind. A master-mind."

"What's that?" I asked, in some hope of bringing him to a stand. But, Joe was readier with his definition than I had expected, and completely stopped me by arguing circularly, and answering with a fixed look, "Her."

"And I an't a master-mind," Joe resumed, when he had unfixed his look, and got back to his whisker. "And last of all, Pip — and this I want to say very serous to you, old chap — I see so much in my poor mother, of a woman drudging and slaving and breaking her honest hart and never getting no peace in her mortal days, that I'm dead afeerd of going wrong in the way of not doing what's right by a woman, and I'd fur rather of the two go wrong the t'other way, and be a little ill-conwenienced myself. I wish it was only me that got put out, Pip; I wish there warn't no Tickler for you, old chap; I wish I could take it all on myself; but this is the up-and-down-and-straight on it, Pip, and I hope you'll overlook shortcomings."

Young as I was, I believe that I dated a new admiration of Joe from that night. We were equals afterwards, as we had been before; but, afterwards at quiet times when I sat looking at Joe and thinking about him, I had a new sensation of feeling conscious that I was looking up to Joe in my heart.

"Howsumever," said Joe, rising to replenish the fire; "here's the Dutch-clock a working himself up to being equal to strike Eight of 'em, and she's not come home yet! I hope Uncle Pumblechook's mare mayn't have set a fore-foot on a piece o' ice, and gone down."

Mrs. Joe made occasional trips with Uncle Pumblechook on market-days, to assist him in buying such household stuffs and goods as required a woman's judgment; Uncle Pumblechook being a bachelor and reposing no confidences in his domestic servant. This was market-day, and Mrs. Joe was out on one of these expeditions.

Joe made the fire and swept the hearth, and then we went to the door to listen for the chaise-cart. It was a dry cold night, and the wind blew keenly, and the frost was white and hard. A man would die to-night of lying out on the marshes, I thought. And then I looked at the stars, and considered how awful it would be for a man to turn his face up to them as he froze to death, and see no help or pity in all the glittering multitude.

"Here comes the mare," said Joe, "ringing like a peal of bells!"

The sound of her iron shoes upon the hard road was quite musical, as she came along at a much brisker trot than usual. We got a chair out, ready for Mrs. Joe's alighting, and stirred up the fire that they might see a bright window, and took a final survey of the kitchen that nothing might be out of its place. When we had completed these preparations, they drove up, wrapped to the eyes. Mrs. Joe was soon landed, and Uncle Pumblechook was soon down too, covering the mare with a cloth, and we were soon all in the kitchen, carrying so much cold air in with us that it seemed to drive all the heat out of the fire.

"Now," said Mrs. Joe, unwrapping herself with haste and excitement, and throwing her bonnet back on her shoulders where it hung by the strings: "if this boy an't grateful this night, he never will be!"

I looked as grateful as any boy possibly could, who was wholly uninformed why he ought to assume that expression.

"It's only to be hoped," said my sister, "that he won't be Pompeyed. But I have my fears."

"She an't in that line, Mum," said Mr. Pumblechook. "She knows better."

She? I looked at Joe, making the motion with my lips and eyebrows, "She?" Joe looked at me, making the motion with *his* lips and eyebrows, "She?" My sister catching him in the act, he drew the back of his hand across his nose with his usual conciliatory air on such occasions, and looked at her.

"Well?" said my sister, in her snappish way. "What are you staring at? Is the house a-fire?"

"— Which some indiwidual," Joe politely hinted, "mentioned — she."
"And she is a she, I suppose?" said my sister. "Unless you call Miss
Havisham a he. And I doubt if even you'll go so far as that."
"Miss Havisham, up town?" said Joe.
"Is there any Miss Havisham down town?" returned my sister. "She
wants this boy to go and play there. And of course he's going. And he had
better play there," said my sister, shaking her head at me as an encourage-
ment to be extremely light and sportive, "or I'll work him."

I had heard of Miss Havisham up town — everybody for miles round,
had heard of Miss Havisham up town — as an immensely rich and grim
lady who lived in a large and dismal house barricaded against robbers,
and who led a life of seclusion.

"Well to be sure!" said Joe, astounded. "I wonder how she come to
know Pip!"

"Noodle!" cried my sister. "Who said she knew him?"

"— Which some indiwidual," Joe again politely hinted, "mentioned
that she wanted him to go and play there."

"And couldn't she ask Uncle Pumblechook if he knew of a boy to
go and play there? Isn't it just barely possible that Uncle Pumblechook
may be a tenant of hers, and that he may sometimes — we won't say
quarterly or half yearly, for that would be requiring too much of you —
but sometimes — go there to pay his rent? And couldn't she then ask
Uncle Pumblechook if he knew of a boy to go and play there? And
couldn't Uncle Pumblechook, being always considerate and thoughtful
for us — though you may not think it, Joseph," in a tone of the deepest
reproach, as if he were the most callous of nephews, "then mention this
boy, standing Prancing here" — which I solemnly declare I was not doing — "that I have for ever been a willing slave to?"

"Good again!" cried Uncle Pumblechook. "Well put! Prettily pointed!
Good indeed! Now Joseph, you know the case."

"No, Joseph," said my sister, still in a reproachful manner, while Joe
apologetically drew the back of his hand across and across his nose, "you
do not yet — though you may not think it — know the case. You may
consider that you do, but you do *not*, Joseph. For you do not know that
Uncle Pumblechook, being sensible that for anything we can tell, this boy's
fortune may be made by his going to Miss Havisham's, has offered to take

him into town to-night in his own chaise-cart, and to keep him to-night, and to take him with his own hands to Miss Havisham's to-morrow morning. And Lor-a-mussy me!" cried my sister, casting off her bonnet in sudden desperation, "here I stand talking to mere Mooncalfs,[1] with Uncle Pumblechook waiting, and the mare catching cold at the door, and the boy grimed with crock[2] and dirt from the hair of his head to the sole of his foot!"

With that, she pounced upon me, like an eagle on a lamb, and my face was squeezed into wooden bowls in sinks, and my head was put under taps of water-butts, and I was soaped, and kneaded, and towelled, and thumped, and harrowed, and rasped, until I really was quite beside myself. (I may here remark that I suppose myself to be better acquainted than any living authority, with the ridgy effect of a wedding-ring, passing unsympathetically over the human countenance.)

When my ablutions were completed, I was put into clean linen of the stiffest character, like a young penitent into sackcloth, and was trussed up in my tightest and fearfullest suit. I was then delivered over to Mr. Pumblechook, who formally received me as if he were the Sheriff, and who let off upon me the speech that I knew he had been dying to make all along: "Boy, be for ever grateful to all friends, but especially unto them which brought you up by hand!"

"Good-by, Joe!"

"God bless you, Pip, old chap!"

I had never parted from him before, and what with my feelings and what with soap-suds, I could at first see no stars from the chaise-cart. But they twinkled out one by one, without throwing any light on the questions why on earth I was going to play at Miss Havisham's, and what on earth I was expected to play at.

---

1. *Mooncalfs:* born fools (congenital idiocy being traditionally attributed to the influence of the moon).
2. *crock:* smut, soot (dialect).

CHAPTER VIII

MR. PUMBLECHOOK'S premises in the High-street of the market town, were of a peppercorny and farinaceous character, as the premises of a corn-chandler and seedsman should be. It appeared to me that he must be a very happy man indeed, to have so many little drawers in his shop; and I wondered when I peeped into one or two on the lower tiers, and saw the tied-up brown paper packets inside, whether the flower-seeds and bulbs ever wanted of a fine day to break out of those jails, and bloom.

It was in the early morning after my arrival that I entertained this speculation. On the previous night, I had been sent straight to bed in an attic with a sloping roof, which was so low in the corner where the bed-stead was, that I calculated the tiles as being within a foot of my eyebrows. In the same early morning, I discovered a singular affinity between seeds and corduroys. Mr. Pumblechook wore corduroys, and so did his shopman; and somehow, there was a general air and flavour about the corduroys, so much in the nature of seeds, and a general air and flavour about the seeds, so much in the nature of corduroys, that I hardly knew which was which. The same opportunity served me for noticing that Mr. Pumblechook appeared to conduct his business by looking across the street at the saddler, who appeared to transact *his* business by keeping his eye on the coachmaker, who appeared to get on in life by putting his hands in his pockets and contemplating the baker, who in his turn folded his arms and stared at the grocer, who stood at his door and yawned at the chemist. The watchmaker, always poring over a little desk with a magnifying glass at his eye, and always inspected by a group of smock-frocks poring over him through the glass of his shop-window, seemed to be about the only person in the High-street whose trade engaged his attention.

Mr. Pumblechook and I breakfasted at eight o'clock in the parlour behind the shop, while the shopman took his mug of tea and hunch of bread-and-butter on a sack of peas in the front premises. I considered Mr. Pumblechook wretched company. Besides being possessed by my sister's idea that a mortifying and penitential character ought to be imparted to my diet — besides giving me as much crumb as possible in combination with as little butter, and putting such a quantity of warm water into my milk that it would have been more candid to have left the milk out altogether — his conversation consisted of nothing but arithmetic. On my politely bidding him Good morning, he said, pompously, "Seven times nine, boy?" And how should *I* be able to answer, dodged in that way, in a strange place, on an empty stomach! I was hungry, but before I had swallowed a morsel, he began a running sum that lasted all through the breakfast. "Seven?" "And four?" "And eight?" "And six?" "And two?" "And ten?" And so on. And after each figure was disposed of, it was as much as I could do to get a bite or a sup, before the next came; while he sat at his ease guessing nothing, and eating bacon and hot roll, in (if I may be allowed the expression) a gorging and gormandising manner.

For such reasons I was very glad when ten o'clock came and we started for Miss Havisham's; though I was not at all at my ease regarding the manner in which I should acquit myself under that lady's roof. Within a quarter of an hour we came to Miss Havisham's house, which was of old brick, and dismal, and had a great many iron bars to it. Some of the windows had been walled up; of those that remained, all the lower were rustily barred. There was a court-yard in front, and that was barred; so, we had to wait, after ringing the bell, until some one should come to open it. While we waited at the gate, I peeped in (even then Mr. Pumblechook said, "And fourteen?" but I pretended not to hear him), and saw that at the side of the house there was a large brewery. No brewing was going on in it, and none seemed to have gone on for a long long time.

A window was raised, and a clear voice demanded "What name?" To which my conductor replied, "Pumblechook." The voice returned, "Quite right," and the window was shut again, and a young lady came across the court-yard, with keys in her hand.

"This," said Mr. Pumblechook, "is Pip."

"This is Pip, is it?" returned the young lady, who was very pretty and seemed very proud; "come in, Pip."

Mr. Pumblechook was coming in also, when she stopped him with the gate.

"Oh!" she said. "Did you wish to see Miss Havisham?"

"If Miss Havisham wished to see me," returned Mr. Pumblechook discomfited.

"Ah!" said the girl; "but you see she don't."

She said it so finally, and in such an undiscussible way, that Mr.

Pumblechook, though in a condition of ruffled dignity, could not protest. But he eyed me severely — as if *I* had done anything to him! — and departed with the words reproachfully delivered: "Boy! Let your behaviour here be a credit unto them which brought you up by hand!" I was not free from apprehension that he would come back to propound through the gate, "And sixteen?" But he didn't.

My young conductress locked the gate, and we went across the court-yard. It was paved and clean, but grass was growing in every crevice. The brewery buildings had a little lane of communication with it; and the wooden gates of that lane stood open, and all the brewery beyond, stood open, away to the high enclosing wall; and all was empty and disused. The cold wind seemed to blow colder there, than outside the gate; and it made a shrill noise in howling in and out at the open sides of the brew-ery, like the noise of wind in the rigging of a ship at sea.

She saw me looking at it, and she said, "You could drink without hurt all the strong beer that's brewed there now, boy."

"I should think I could, miss," said I, in a shy way.

"Better not try to brew beer there now, or it would turn out sour, boy; don't you think so?"

"It looks like it, miss."

"Not that anybody means to try," she added, "for that's all done with, and the place will stand as idle as it is, till it falls. As to strong beer, there's enough of it in the cellars already, to drown the Manor House."

"Is that the name of this house, miss?"

"One of its names, boy."

"It has more than one, then, miss?"

"One more. Its other name was Satis; which is Greek, or Latin, or Hebrew, or all three — or all one to me — for enough."[1]

"Enough House," said I; "that's a curious name, miss."

"Yes," she replied; "but it meant more than it said. It meant, when it was given, that whoever had this house, could want nothing else. They must have been easily satisfied in those days, I should think. But don't loiter, boy."

---

1. *Satis; which is Greek, or Latin, or Hebrew, or all three — or all one to me — for enough:* in fact Latin only.

Though she called me "boy" so often, and with a carelessness that was far from complimentary, she was of about my own age. She seemed much older than I, of course, being a girl, and beautiful and self-possessed; and she was as scornful of me as if she had been one-and-twenty, and a queen.

We went into the house by a side door — the great front entrance had two chains across it outside — and the first thing I noticed was, that the passages were all dark, and that she had left a candle burning there. She took it up, and we went through more passages and up a staircase, and still it was all dark, and only the candle lighted us.

At last we came to the door of a room, and she said, "Go in."

I answered, more in shyness than politeness, "After you, miss."

To this, she returned: "Don't be ridiculous, boy; I am not going in." And scornfully walked away, and — what was worse — took the candle with her.

This was very uncomfortable, and I was half afraid. However, the only thing to be done being to knock at the door, I knocked, and was told from within to enter. I entered, therefore, and found myself in a pretty large room, well lighted with wax candles. No glimpse of daylight was to be seen in it. It was a dressing-room, as I supposed from the furniture, though much of it was of forms and uses then quite unknown to me. But prominent in it was a draped table with a gilded looking-glass, and that I made out at first sight to be a fine lady's dressing-table.

Whether I should have made out this object so soon, if there had been no fine lady sitting at it, I cannot say. In an arm-chair, with an elbow resting on the table and her head leaning on that hand, sat the strangest lady I have ever seen, or shall ever see.

She was dressed in rich materials — satins, and lace, and silks — all of white. Her shoes were white. And she had a long white veil dependent from her hair, and she had bridal flowers in her hair, but her hair was white. Some bright jewels sparkled on her neck and on her hands, and some other jewels lay sparkling on the table. Dresses, less splendid than the dress she wore, and half-packed trunks, were scattered about. She had not quite finished dressing for she had but one shoe on — the other was on the table near her hand — her veil was but half arranged, her watch and chain were not put on, and some lace for her bosom lay with those trinkets, and with her handkerchief, and gloves, and some flowers, and a prayer-book, all confusedly heaped about the looking-glass.

It was not in the first moments that I saw all these things, though I saw more of them in the first moments than might be supposed. But, I saw that everything within my view which ought to be white, had been white long ago, and had lost its lustre, and was faded and yellow. I saw that the bride within the bridal dress had withered like the dress, and like the flowers, and had no brightness left but the brightness of her sunken eyes. I saw that the dress had been put upon the rounded figure of a young woman, and that the figure upon which it now hung loose, had shrunk to skin and bone. Once, I had been taken to see some ghastly wax-work at the Fair, representing I know not what impossible personage lying in state. Once, I had been taken to one of our old marsh churches to see a skeleton in the ashes of a rich dress, that had been dug out of a vault under the church pavement. Now, wax-work and skeleton seemed to have dark eyes that moved and looked at me. I should have cried out, if I could.

"Who is it?" said the lady at the table.

"Pip, ma'am."

"Pip?"

"Mr. Pumblechook's boy, ma'am. Come — to play."

"Come nearer; let me look at you. Come close."

It was when I stood before her, avoiding her eyes, that I took note of the surrounding objects in detail, and saw that her watch had stopped at twenty minutes to nine, and that a clock in the room had stopped at twenty minutes to nine.

"Look at me," said Miss Havisham. "You are not afraid of a woman who has never seen the sun since you were born?"

I regret to state that I was not afraid of telling the enormous lie comprehended in the answer "No."

"Do you know what I touch here?" she said, laying her hands, one upon the other, on her left side.

"Yes, ma'am." (It made me think of the young man.)

"What do I touch?"

"Your heart."

"Broken!"

She uttered the word with an eager look, and with strong emphasis, and with a weird smile that had a kind of boast in it. Afterwards, she kept her hands there for a little while, and slowly took them away as if they were heavy.

"I am tired," said Miss Havisham. "I want diversion, and I have done with men and women. Play."

I think it will be conceded by my most disputatious reader, that she could hardly have directed an unfortunate boy to do anything in the wide world more difficult to be done under the circumstances.

"I sometimes have sick fancies," she went on, "and I have a sick fancy that I want to see some play. There, there!" with an impatient movement of the fingers of her right hand; "play, play, play!"

For a moment, with the fear of my sister's working me before my eyes, I had a desperate idea of starting round the room in the assumed character of Mr. Pumblechook's chaise-cart. But, I felt myself so unequal to the performance that I gave it up, and stood looking at Miss Havisham in what I suppose she took for a dogged manner, inasmuch as she said, when we had taken a good look at each other:

"Are you sullen and obstinate?"

"No, ma'am, I am very sorry for you, and very sorry I can't play just now. If you complain of me I shall get into trouble with my sister, so I would do it if I could; but it's so new here, and so strange, and so fine — and melancholy —" I stopped, fearing I might say too much, or had already said it, and we took another look at each other.

Before she spoke again, she turned her eyes from me, and looked at the dress she wore, and at the dressing-table, and finally at herself in the looking-glass.

"So new to him," she muttered, "so old to me; so strange to him, so familiar to me; so melancholy to both of us! Call Estella."

As she was still looking at the reflection of herself, I thought she was still talking to herself, and kept quiet.

"Call Estella," she repeated, flashing a look at me. "You can do that. Call Estella. At the door."

To stand in the dark in a mysterious passage of an unknown house, bawling Estella to a scornful young lady neither visible nor responsive, and feeling it a dreadful liberty so to roar out her name, was almost as bad as playing to order. But, she answered at last, and her light came along the long dark passage like a star.

Miss Havisham beckoned her to come close, and took up a jewel from the table, and tried its effect upon her fair young bosom and against her pretty brown hair. "Your own, one day, my dear, and you will use it well. Let me see you play cards with this boy."

"With this boy! Why, he is a common labouring-boy!"

I thought I overheard Miss Havisham answer — only it seemed so unlikely — "Well? You can break his heart."

"What do you play, boy?" asked Estella of myself, with the greatest disdain.

"Nothing but beggar my neighbour, miss."

"Beggar him," said Miss Havisham to Estella. So we sat down to cards.

It was then I began to understand that everything in the room had stopped, like the watch and the clock, a long time ago. I noticed that Miss Havisham put down the jewel exactly on the spot from which she had taken it up. As Estella dealt the cards, I glanced at the dressing-table again, and saw that the shoe upon it, once white, now yellow, had never been worn. I glanced down at the foot from which the shoe was absent, and saw that the silk stocking on it, once white, now yellow, had been trodden ragged. Without this arrest of everything, this standing still of all the pale decayed objects, not even the withered bridal dress on the collapsed form could have looked so like grave-clothes, or the long veil so like a shroud.

So she sat, corpse-like, as we played at cards; the frillings and trimmings on her bridal dress, looking like earthy paper. I knew nothing then, of the discoveries that are occasionally made of bodies buried in ancient times, which fall to powder in the moment of being distinctly seen; but, I have often thought since, that she must have looked as if the admission of the natural light of day would have struck her to dust.

"He calls the knaves, Jacks, this boy!" said Estella with disdain, before our first game was out. "And what coarse hands he has! And what thick boots!"

I had never thought of being ashamed of my hands before; but I began to consider them a very indifferent pair. Her contempt was so strong, that it became infectious, and I caught it.

She won the game, and I dealt. I misdealt, as was only natural, when I knew she was lying in wait for me to do wrong; and she denounced me for a stupid, clumsy labouring-boy.

"You say nothing of her," remarked Miss Havisham to me, as she looked on. "She says many hard things of you, but you say nothing of her. What do you think of her?"

"I don't like to say," I stammered.

"Tell me in my ear," said Miss Havisham, bending down.

"I think she is very proud," I replied, in a whisper.

"Anything else?"

"I think she is very pretty."

"Anything else?"

"I think she is very insulting." (She was looking at me then with a look of supreme aversion.)

"Anything else?"

"I think I should like to go home."

"And never see her again, though she is so pretty?"

"I am not sure that I shouldn't like to see her again, but I should like to go home now."

"You shall go soon," said Miss Havisham, aloud. "Play the game out."

Saving for the one weird smile at first, I should have felt almost sure that Miss Havisham's face could not smile. It had dropped into a watchful and brooding expression — most likely when all the things about her had become transfixed — and it looked as if nothing could ever lift it up again. Her chest had dropped, so that she stooped; and her voice had dropped, so that she spoke low, and with a dead lull upon her; altogether, she had the appearance of having dropped, body and soul, within and without, under the weight of a crushing blow.

I played the game to an end with Estella, and she beggared me. She threw the cards down on the table when she had won them all, as if she despised them for having been won of me.

"When shall I have you here again?" said Miss Havisham. "Let me think."

I was beginning to remind her that to-day was Wednesday, when she checked me with her former impatient movement of the fingers of her right hand.

"There, there! I know nothing of days of the week; I know nothing of weeks of the year. Come again after six days. You hear?"

"Yes, ma'am."

"Estella, take him down. Let him have something to eat, and let him roam and look about him while he eats. Go, Pip."

I followed the candle down, as I had followed the candle up, and she stood it in the place where we had found it. Until she opened the side entrance, I had fancied, without thinking about it, that it must necessarily be night-time. The rush of the daylight quite confounded me, and made me feel as if I had been in the candlelight of the strange room many hours.

"You are to wait here, you boy," said Estella; and disappeared and closed the door.

I took the opportunity of being alone in the court-yard, to look at my coarse hands and my common boots. My opinion of those accessories was not favourable. They had never troubled me before, but they troubled me now, as vulgar appendages. I determined to ask Joe why he had ever taught me to call those picture-cards, Jacks, which ought to be called knaves. I wished Joe had been rather more genteelly brought up, and then I should have been so too.

She came back, with some bread and meat and a little mug of beer. She put the mug down on the stones of the yard, and gave me the bread and meat without looking at me, as insolently as if I were a dog in disgrace. I was so humiliated, hurt, spurned, offended, angry, sorry — I cannot hit upon the right name for the smart — God knows what its name was — that tears started to my eyes. The moment they sprang there, the girl looked at me with a quick delight in having been the cause of them. This gave me power to keep them back and to look at her: so, she gave a contemptuous toss — but with a sense, I thought, of having made too sure that I was so wounded — and left me.

But, when she was gone, I looked about me for a place to hide my face in, and got behind one of the gates in the brewery-lane, and leaned my sleeve against the wall there, and leaned my forehead on it and cried. As I cried, I kicked the wall, and took a hard twist at my hair; so bitter were my feelings, and so sharp was the smart without a name, that needed counteraction.

My sister's bringing up had made me sensitive. In the little world in which children have their existence whosoever brings them up, there is nothing so finely perceived and so finely felt, as injustice. It may be only small injustice that the child can be exposed to; but the child is small, and its world is small, and its rocking-horse stands as many hands high, according to scale, as a big-boned Irish hunter. Within myself, I had sustained, from my babyhood, a perpetual conflict with injustice. I had known, from the time when I could speak, that my sister, in her capricious and violent coercion, was unjust to me. I had cherished a profound conviction that her bringing me up by hand, gave her no right to bring me up by jerks. Through all my punishments, disgraces, fasts and vigils, and other penitential performances, I had nursed this assurance; and to my communing so much with it, in a solitary and unprotected way, I in great part refer the fact that I was morally timid and very sensitive.

I got rid of my injured feelings for the time, by kicking them into the brewery wall, and twisting them out of my hair, and then I smoothed my face with my sleeve, and came from behind the gate. The bread and meat were acceptable, and the beer was warming and tingling, and I was soon in spirits to look about me.

To be sure, it was a deserted place, down to the pigeon-house in the brewery-yard, which had been blown crooked on its pole by some high wind, and would have made the pigeons think themselves at sea, if there had been any pigeons there to be rocked by it. But, there were no pigeons in the dovecot, no horses in the stable, no pigs in the sty, no malt in the storehouse, no smells of grains and beer in the copper or the vat. All the uses and scents of the brewery might have evaporated with its last reek of smoke. In a by-yard, there was a wilderness of empty casks, which had a certain sour remembrance of better days lingering about them; but it was too sour to be accepted as a sample of the beer that was gone — and in this respect I remember those recluses as being like most others.

Behind the furthest end of the brewery, was a rank garden with an old wall: not so high but that I could struggle up and hold on long enough to look over it, and see that the rank garden was the garden of the house, and that it was overgrown with tangled weeds, but that there was a track upon the green and yellow paths, as if some one sometimes walked there, and that Estella was walking away from me even then. But she seemed to be everywhere. For, when I yielded to the temptation presented by the casks, and began to walk on them, I saw *her* walking on them at the end of the yard of casks. She had her back towards me, and held her pretty brown hair spread out in her two hands, and never looked round, and passed out of my view directly. So, in the brewery itself — by which I mean the large paved lofty place in which they used to make the beer, and where the brewing utensils still were. When I first went into it, and, rather oppressed by its gloom, stood near the door looking about me, I saw her pass among the extinguished fires, and ascend some light iron stairs, and go out by a gallery high overhead, as if she were going out into the sky.

It was in this place, and at this moment, that a strange thing happened to my fancy. I thought it a strange thing then, and I thought it a stranger thing long afterwards. I turned my eyes — a little dimmed by looking up at the frosty light — towards a great wooden beam in a low nook of the building near me on my right hand, and I saw a figure hanging there by the neck. A figure all in yellow white, with but one shoe to the feet; and it hung so, that I could see that the faded trimmings of the dress were like earthy paper, and that the face was Miss Havisham's, with a movement going over the whole countenance as if she were trying to call to me. In the terror of seeing the figure, and in the terror of being certain that it had not been there a moment before, I at first ran from it, and then ran towards it. And my terror was greatest of all, when I found no figure there.

Nothing less than the frosty light of the cheerful sky, the sight of people passing beyond the bars of the court-yard gate, and the reviving influence of the rest of the bread and meat and beer, would have brought me round. Even with those aids, I might not have come to myself as soon as I did, but that I saw Estella approaching with the keys, to let me out. She would have some fair reason for looking down upon me, I thought, if she saw me frightened; and she should have no fair reason.

She gave me a triumphant glance in passing me, as if she rejoiced that my hands were so coarse and my boots were so thick, and she opened the gate, and stood holding it. I was passing out without looking at her, when she touched me with a taunting hand.

"Why don't you cry?"

"Because I don't want to."

"You do," said she. "You have been crying till you are half blind, and you are near crying again now."

She laughed contemptuously, pushed me out, and locked the gate upon me. I went straight to Mr. Pumblechook's, and was immensely relieved to find him not at home. So, leaving word with the shopman on what day I was wanted at Miss Havisham's again, I set off on the four-mile walk to our forge; pondering, as I went along, on all I had seen, and deeply revolving that I was a common labouring-boy; that my hands were coarse; that my boots were thick; that I had fallen into a despicable habit of calling knaves Jacks; that I was much more ignorant than I had considered myself last night, and generally that I was in a low-lived bad way.

CHAPTER IX

WHEN I reached home, my sister was very curious to know all about Miss Havisham's, and asked a number of questions. And I soon found myself getting heavily bumped from behind in the nape of the neck and the small of the back, and having my face ignominiously shoved against the kitchen wall, because I did not answer those questions at sufficient length.

If a dread of not being understood be hidden in the breasts of other young people to anything like the extent to which it used to be hidden in mine — which I consider probable, as I have no particular reason to suspect myself of having been a monstrosity — it is the key to many reservations. I felt convinced that if I described Miss Havisham's as my eyes had seen it, I should not be understood. Not only that, but I felt convinced that Miss Havisham too would not be understood; and although she was perfectly incomprehensible to me, I entertained an impression that there would be something coarse and treacherous in my dragging her as she really was (to say nothing of Miss Estella) before the contemplation of Mrs. Joe. Consequently, I said as little as I could, and had my face shoved against the kitchen wall.

The worst of it was that that bullying old Pumblechook, preyed upon by a devouring curiosity to be informed of all I had seen and heard, came gaping over in his chaise-cart at tea-time, to have the details divulged to him. And the mere sight of the torment, with his fishy eyes and mouth open, his sandy hair inquisitively on end, and his waistcoat heaving with windy arithmetic, made me vicious in my reticence.

"Well, boy," Uncle Pumblechook began, as soon as he was seated in the chair of honour by the fire. "How did you get on up town?" I answered, "Pretty well, sir," and my sister shook her fist at me. "Pretty well?" Mr. Pumblechook repeated. "Pretty well is no answer. Tell us what you mean by pretty well, boy?"

Whitewash on the forehead hardens the brain into a state of obstinacy perhaps. Anyhow, with whitewash from the wall on my forehead, my obstinacy was adamantine. I reflected for some time, and then answered as if I had discovered a new idea, "I mean pretty well."

My sister with an exclamation of impatience was going to fly at me — I had no shadow of defence, for Joe was busy in the forge — when Mr. Pumblechook interposed with "No! Don't lose your temper. Leave this lad to me, ma'am; leave this lad to me." Mr. Pumblechook then turned me towards him, as if he were going to cut my hair, and said:

"First (to get our thoughts in order): Forty-three pence?"

I calculated the consequences of replying "Four Hundred Pound," and finding them against me, went as near the answer as I could — which was somewhere about eightpence off. Mr. Pumblechook then put me through my pence-table from "twelve pence make one shilling," up to "forty pence make three and fourpence," and then triumphantly demanded, as if he had done for me, "Now! How much is forty-three pence?" To which I replied, after a long interval of reflection, "I don't know." And I was so aggravated that I almost doubt if I did know.

Mr. Pumblechook worked his head like a screw to screw it out of me, and said, "Is forty-three pence seven and sixpence three fardens, for instance?"

"Yes!" said I. And although my sister instantly boxed my ears, it was highly gratifying to me to see that the answer spoilt his joke, and brought him to a dead stop.

"Boy! What like is Miss Havisham?" Mr. Pumblechook began again when he had recovered; folding his arms tight on his chest and applying the screw.

"Very tall and dark," I told him.

"Is she, uncle?" asked my sister.

Mr. Pumblechook winked assent; from which I at once inferred that he had never seen Miss Havisham, for she was nothing of the kind.

"Good!" said Mr. Pumblechook conceitedly. ("This is the way to have him! We are beginning to hold our own, I think, Mum?")

"I am sure, uncle," returned Mrs. Joe, "I wish you had him always: you know so well how to deal with him."

"Now, boy! What was she a doing of, when you went in to-day?" asked Mr. Pumblechook.

"She was sitting," I answered, "in a black velvet coach."

Mr. Pumblechook and Mrs. Joe stared at one another — as they well might — and both repeated, "In a black velvet coach?"

"Yes," said I. "And Miss Estella — that's her niece, I think — handed her in cake and wine at the coach-window, on a gold plate. And we all had cake and wine on gold plates. And I got up behind the coach to eat mine, because she told me to."

"Was anybody else there?" asked Mr. Pumblechook.

"Four dogs," said I.

"Large or small?"

"Immense," said I. "And they fought for veal cutlets out of a silver basket."

Mr. Pumblechook and Mrs. Joe stared at one another again, in utter amazement. I was perfectly frantic — a reckless witness under the torture — and would have told them anything.

"Where *was* this coach, in the name of gracious?" asked my sister.

"In Miss Havisham's room." They stared again. "But there weren't any horses to it." I added this saving clause, in the moment of rejecting four richly caparisoned coursers which I had had wild thoughts of harnessing.

"Can this be possible, uncle?" asked Mrs. Joe. "What can the boy mean?"

"I'll tell you, Mum," said Mr. Pumblechook. "My opinion is, it's a se-dan-chair. She's flighty,[1] you know — very flighty — quite flighty enough to pass her days in a sedan-chair."

---

1. *flighty:* whimsical, crazy.

"Did you ever see her in it, uncle?" asked Mrs. Joe.

"How could I," he returned, forced to the admission, "when I never see her in my life? Never clapped eyes upon her!"

"Goodness, uncle! And yet you have spoken to her?"

"Why, don't you know," said Mr. Pumblechook, testily, "that when I have been there, I have been took up to the outside of her door, and the door has stood ajar, and she has spoke to me that way. Don't say you don't know *that*, Mum. Howsever, the boy went there to play. What did you play at, boy?"

"We played with flags," I said. (I beg to observe that I think of myself with amazement, when I recal the lies I told on this occasion.)

"Flags!" echoed my sister.

"Yes," said I. "Estella waved a blue flag, and I waved a red one, and Miss Havisham waved one sprinkled all over with little gold stars, out at the coach-window. And then we all waved our swords and hurrahed."

"Swords!" repeated my sister. "Where did you get swords from?"

"Out of a cupboard," said I. "And I saw pistols in it — and jam — and pills. And there was no daylight in the room, but it was all lighted up with candles."

"That's true, Mum," said Mr. Pumblechook, with a grave nod. "That's the state of the case, for that much I've seen myself." And then they both stared at me, and I, with an obtrusive show of artlessness on my countenance, stared at them, and plaited the right leg of my trousers with my right hand.

If they had asked me any more questions I should undoubtedly have betrayed myself, for I was even then on the point of mentioning that there was a balloon in the yard, and should have hazarded the statement but for my invention being divided between that phenomenon and a bear in the brewery. They were so much occupied, however, in discussing the marvels I had already presented for their consideration, that I escaped. The subject still held them when Joe came in from his work to have a cup of tea. To whom my sister, more for the relief of her own mind than for the gratification of his, related my pretended experiences.

Now, when I saw Joe open his blue eyes and roll them all round the kitchen in helpless amazement, I was overtaken by penitence; but only as regarded him — not in the least as regarded the other two. Towards Joe, and Joe only, I considered myself a young monster, while they sat debating what results would ensue to me from Miss Havisham's acquaintance and favour. They had no doubt that Miss Havisham would "do something" for me; their doubts related to the form that something would take. My sister stood out for "property." Mr. Pumblechook was in favour of a handsome premium[1] for binding me apprentice to some genteel trade — say, the corn and seed trade, for instance. Joe fell into the deepest disgrace with both, for offering the bright suggestion that I might only be presented with one of the dogs who had fought for the veal-cutlets. "If a fool's head can't express better opinions than that," said my sister, "and you have got any work to do, you had better go and do it." So he went.

After Mr. Pumblechook had driven off, and when my sister was washing up, I stole into the forge to Joe, and remained by him until he had done for the night. Then I said, "Before the fire goes out, Joe, I should like to tell you something."

"Should you, Pip?" said Joe, drawing his shoeing-stool near the forge. "Then tell us. What is it, Pip?"

"Joe" said I, taking hold of his rolled-up shirt sleeve, and twisting it between my finger and thumb, "you remember all that about Miss Havisham's?"

"Remember?" said Joe. "I believe you! Wonderful!"

"It's a terrible thing, Joe; it ain't true."

"What are you telling of, Pip?" cried Joe, falling back in the greatest amazement. "You don't mean to say it's —"

"Yes I do; it's lies, Joe."

"But not all of it? Why sure you don't mean to say, Pip, that there was no black welwet co — eh?" For, I stood shaking my head. "But at least there was dogs, Pip? Come, Pip," said Joe, persuasively, "if there warn't no weal-cutlets, at least there was dogs?"

"No, Joe."

"*A* dog?" said Joe. "A puppy? Come?"

"No, Joe, there was nothing at all of the kind."

---

1. *premium:* a premium apprentice was one who had paid an initial fee to his master to receive instruction in his intended trade.

As I fixed my eyes hopelessly on Joe, Joe contemplated me in dismay. "Pip, old chap! This won't do, old fellow! I say! Where do you expect to go to?"

"It's terrible, Joe; an't it?"

"Terrible?" cried Joe. "Awful! What possessed you?"

"I don't know what possessed me, Joe," I replied, letting his shirt sleeve go, and sitting down in the ashes at his feet, hanging my head; "but I wish you hadn't taught me to call Knaves at cards, Jacks; and I wish my boots weren't so thick nor my hands so coarse."

And then I told Joe that I felt very miserable, and that I hadn't been able to explain myself to Mrs. Joe and Pumblechook who were so rude to me, and that there had been a beautiful young lady at Miss Havisham's who was dreadfully proud, and that she had said I was common, and that I knew I was common, and that I wished I was not common, and that the lies had come of it somehow, though I didn't know how.

This was a case of metaphysics, at least as difficult for Joe to deal with, as for me. But Joe took the case altogether out of the region of metaphysics, and by that means vanquished it.

"There's one thing you may be sure of, Pip," said Joe, after some rumination, "namely, that lies is lies. Howsever they come, they didn't ought to come, and they come from the father of lies, and work round to the same. Don't you tell no more of 'em, Pip. *That* ain't the way to get out of being common, old chap. And as to being common, I don't make it out at all clear. You are oncommon in some things. You're oncommon small. Likewise you're a oncommon scholar."

"No, I am ignorant and backward, Joe."

"Why, see what a letter you wrote last night! Wrote in print even! I've seen letters — Ah! and from gentlefolks! — that I'll swear weren't wrote in print," said Joe.

"I have learnt next to nothing, Joe. You think much of me. It's only that."

"Well, Pip," said Joe, "be it so or be it son't, you must be a common scholar afore you can be a oncommon one, I should hope! The king upon his throne, with his crown upon his ed, can't sit and write his acts of Parliament in print, without having begun, when he were a unpromoted Prince, with the alphabet — Ah!" added Joe, with a shake of the head that was full of meaning, "and begun at A too, and worked his way to Z. And *I* know what that is to do, though I can't say I've exactly done it."

There was some hope in this piece of wisdom, and it rather encouraged me.

"Whether common ones as to callings and earnings," pursued Joe, reflectively, "mightn't be the better of continuing fur to keep company with common ones, instead of going out to play with oncommon ones — which reminds me to hope that there were a flag, perhaps?"

"No, Joe."

"(I'm sorry there weren't a flag, Pip). Whether that might be, or mightn't be, is a thing as can't be looked into now, without putting your sister on the Rampage; and that's a thing not to be thought of, as being done intentional. Lookee here, Pip, at what is said to you by a true friend. Which this to you the true friend say. If you can't get to be oncommon through going straight, you'll never get to do it through going crooked. So don't tell no more on 'em, Pip, and live well and die happy."

"You are not angry with me, Joe?"

"No, old chap. But bearing in mind that them were which I meantersay of a stunning and outdacious sort — alluding to them which bordered on weal-cutlets and dog-fighting — a sincere well-wisher would adwise, Pip, their being dropped into your meditations, when you go up-stairs to bed. That's all, old chap, and don't never do it no more."

When I got up to my little room and said my prayers, I did not forget Joe's recommendation, and yet my young mind was in that disturbed and unthankful state, that I thought long after I laid me down, how common Estella would consider Joe, a mere blacksmith: how thick his boots, and how coarse his hands. I thought how Joe and my sister were then sitting in the kitchen, and how I had come up to bed from the kitchen, and how Miss Havisham and Estella never sat in a kitchen, but were far above the level of such common doings. I fell asleep recalling what I "used to do" when I was at Miss Havisham's; as though I had been there weeks or months, instead of hours; and as though it were quite an old subject of remembrance, instead of one that had arisen only that day.

That was a memorable day to me, for it made great changes in me. But, it is the same with any life. Imagine one selected day struck out of it, and think how different its course would have been. Pause you who read this, and think for a moment of the long chain of iron or gold, of thorns or flowers, that would never have bound you, but for the formation of the first link on one memorable day.

CHAPTER X

THE FELICITOUS idea occurred to me a morning or two later when I woke, that the best step I could take towards making myself uncommon was to get out of Biddy everything she knew. In pursuance of this luminous conception I mentioned to Biddy when I went to Mr. Wopsle's great-aunt's at night, that I had a particular reason for wishing to get on in life, and that I should feel very much obliged to her if she would impart all her learning to me. Biddy, who was the most obliging of girls, immediately said she would, and indeed began to carry out her promise within five minutes.

The Educational scheme or Course established by Mr. Wopsle's great-aunt may be resolved into the following synopsis. The pupils ate apples and put straws up one another's backs, until Mr. Wopsle's great-aunt collected her energies, and made an indiscriminate totter at them with a birch-rod. After receiving the charge with every mark of derision, the pupils formed in line and buzzingly passed a ragged book from hand to hand. The book had an alphabet in it, some figures and tables, and a little spelling — that is to say, it had had once. As soon as this volume began to circulate, Mr. Wopsle's great-aunt fell into a state of coma; arising either from sleep or a rheumatic paroxysm. The pupils then entered among themselves upon a competitive examination on the subject of Boots, with the view of ascertaining who could tread the hardest upon whose toes. This mental exercise lasted until Biddy made a rush at them and distributed three defaced[1] Bibles (shaped as if they had been unskilfully cut off the chump-end of something), more illegibly printed at the best than any curiosities of literature I have since met with, speckled all over with

---

1. *defaced:* probably here specifically meaning "with their covers removed."

ironmould, and having various specimens of the insect world smashed between their leaves. This part of the Course was usually lightened by several single combats between Biddy and refractory students. When the fights were over, Biddy gave out the number of a page, and then we all read aloud what we could — or what we couldn't — in a frightful chorus; Biddy leading with a high shrill monotonous voice, and none of us having the least notion of, or reverence for, what we were reading about. When this horrible din had lasted a certain time, it mechanically awoke Mr. Wopsle's great-aunt, who staggered at a boy fortuitously, and pulled his ears. This was understood to terminate the Course for the evening, and we emerged into the air with shrieks of intellectual victory. It is fair to remark that there was no prohibition against any pupil's entertaining himself with a slate or even with the ink (when there was any), but that it was not easy to pursue that branch of study in the winter season, on account of the little general shop in which the classes were holden — and which was also Mr. Wopsle's great-aunt's sitting-room and bed-chamber — being but faintly illuminated through the agency of one low-spirited dip-candle and no snuffers.[1]

It appeared to me that it would take time, to become uncommon under these circumstances: nevertheless, I resolved to try it, and that very evening Biddy entered on our special agreement, by imparting some information from her little catalogue of Prices, under the head of moist sugar, and lending me, to copy at home, a large old English D which she had imitated from the heading of some newspaper, and which I supposed, until she told me what it was, to be a design for a buckle.

Of course there was a public-house in the village, and of course Joe liked sometimes to smoke his pipe there. I had received strict orders from my sister to call for him at the Three Jolly Bargemen, that evening, on my way from school, and bring him home at my peril. To the Three Jolly Bargemen, therefore, I directed my steps.

There was a bar at the Jolly Bargemen, with some alarmingly long chalk scores in it on the wall at the side of the door, which seemed to me

---

1. *dip-candle and no snuffers:* the lowest-quality candle (made by dipping a wick repeatedly in melted tallow), and without the tool necessary for trimming the wick and thus increasing the light given off.

to be never paid off. They had been there ever since I could remember, and had grown more than I had. But there was a quantity of chalk about our country, and perhaps the people neglected no opportunity of turning it to account.[1]

It being Saturday night, I found the landlord looking rather grimly at these records, but as my business was with Joe and not with him, I merely wished him good evening, and passed into the common room at the end of the passage, where there was a bright large kitchen fire, and where Joe was smoking his pipe in company with Mr. Wopsle and a stranger. Joe greeted me as usual with "Halloa, Pip, old chap!" and the moment he said that, the stranger turned his head and looked at me.

He was a secret-looking man whom I had never seen before. His head was all on one side, and one of his eyes was half shut up, as if he were taking aim at something with an invisible gun. He had a pipe in his mouth, and he took it out, and, after slowly blowing all his smoke away and looking hard at me all the time, nodded. So, I nodded, and then he nodded again, and made room on the settle beside him that I might sit down there.

But, as I was used to sit beside Joe whenever I entered that place of resort, I said "No, thank you, sir," and fell into the space Joe made for me on the opposite settle. The strange man, after glancing at Joe, and seeing that his attention was otherwise engaged, nodded to me again when I had taken my seat, and then rubbed his leg — in a very odd way, as it struck me.

"You was saying," said the strange man, turning to Joe, "that you was a blacksmith."

"Yes. I said it, you know," said Joe.

"What'll you drink, Mr. —? You didn't mention your name, by-the-by."

Joe mentioned it now, and the strange man called him by it. "What'll you drink, Mr. Gargery? At my expense? To top up with?"

"Well," said Joe, "to tell you the truth, I ain't much in the habit of drinking at anybody's expense but my own."

"Habit? No," returned the stranger, "but once and away, and on a Saturday night too. Come! Put a name to it, Mr. Gargery."

---

1. *alarmingly long chalk scores … turning it to account:* referring to the custom at alehouses of writing up with chalk a "score" indicating items bought on "tick" (credit).

"I wouldn't wish to be stiff company," said Joe. "Rum."

"Rum," repeated the stranger. "And will the other gentleman originate a sentiment?"

"Rum," said Mr. Wopsle.

"Three Rums!" cried the stranger, calling to the landlord. "Glasses round!"

"This other gentleman," observed Joe, by way of introducing Mr. Wopsle, "is a gentleman that you would like to hear give it out. Our clerk at church."

"Aha!" said the stranger, quickly, and cocking his eye at me. "The lonely church, right out on the marshes, with the graves round it!"

"That's it," said Joe.

The stranger, with a comfortable kind of grunt over his pipe, put his legs up on the settle that he had to himself. He wore a flapping broad-brimmed traveller's hat, and under it a handkerchief tied over his head in the manner of a cap: so that he showed no hair. As he looked at the fire, I thought I saw a cunning expression, followed by a half laugh, come into his face.

"I am not acquainted with this country, gentlemen, but it seems a solitary country towards the river."

"Most meshes is solitary," said Joe.

"No doubt, no doubt. Do you find any gipsies, now, or tramps, or vagrants of any sort, out there?"

"No," said Joe; "none but a runaway convict now and then. And we don't find *them*, easy. Eh, Mr. Wopsle?"

Mr. Wopsle, with a majestic remembrance of old discomfiture, assented; but not warmly.

"Seems you have been out after such?" asked the stranger.

"Once," returned Joe. "Not that we wanted to take them you understand; we went out as lookers on; me, and Mr. Wopsle, and Pip. Didn't us, Pip?"

"Yes, Joe."

The stranger looked at me again — still cocking his eye, as if he were expressly taking aim at me with his invisible gun — and said, "He's a likely young parcel of bones that. What is it you call him?"

"Pip," said Joe.

"Christened Pip?"

"No, not christened Pip."

"Surname Pip?"

"No," said Joe, "it's a kind of a family name what he gave himself when a infant, and is called by."

"Son of yours?"

"Well," said Joe, meditatively — not, of course, that it could be in any wise necessary to consider about it, but because it was the way at the Jolly Bargemen to seem to consider deeply about everything that was discussed over pipes; "well — no. No, he ain't."

"Nevvy?" said the strange man.

"Well," said Joe, with the same appearance of profound cogitation, "he is not — no, not to deceive you, he is *not* — my nevvy."

"What the Blue Blazes is he?" asked the stranger. Which appeared to me to be an inquiry of unnecessary strength.

Mr. Wopsle struck in upon that; as one who knew all about relationships, having professional occasion to bear in mind what female relations a man might not marry;[1] and expounded the ties between me and Joe. Having his hand in, Mr. Wopsle finished off with a most terrifically snarling passage from Richard the Third,[2] and seemed to think he had done quite enough to account for it when he added, — "as the poet says."

And here I may remark that when Mr. Wopsle referred to me, he considered it a necessary part of such reference to rumple my hair and poke it into my eyes. I cannot conceive why everybody of his standing who visited at our house should always have put me through the same inflammatory process under similar circumstances. Yet I do not call to mind that I was ever in my earlier youth the subject of remark in our social family circle, but some large-handed person took some such ophthalmic steps to patronise me.

---

1. *having professional occasion to bear in mind what female relations a man might not marry:* as laid down by the Church of England in the "Table of Kindred and Affinity" found in the *Book of Common Prayer*, based on the injunctions in Leviticus 18.

2. *a most terrifically snarling passage from Richard the Third:* from Shakespeare's history play, presumably the speech beginning "I must be married to my brother's daughter" (IV ii 60-5).

All this while, the strange man looked at nobody but me, and looked at me as if he were determined to have a shot at me at last, and bring me down. But he said nothing after offering his Blue Blazes observation, until the glasses of rum-and-water were brought; and then he made his shot, and a most extraordinary shot it was.

It was not a verbal remark, but a proceeding in dumb-show, and was pointedly addressed to me. He stirred his rum-and-water pointedly at me, and he tasted his rum-and-water pointedly at me. And he stirred it and he tasted it: not with a spoon that was brought to him, but *with a file.*

He did this so that nobody but I saw the file; and when he had done it he wiped the file and put it in a breast-pocket. I knew it to be Joe's file, and I knew that he knew my convict, the moment I saw the instrument. I sat gazing at him, spell-bound. But he now reclined on his settle, taking very little notice of me, and talking principally about turnips.

There was a delicious sense of cleaning-up and making a quiet pause before going on in life afresh, in our village on Saturday nights, which stimulated Joe to dare to stay out half an hour longer on Saturdays than at other times. The half-hour and the rum-and-water running out together, Joe got up to go, and took me by the hand.

"Stop half a moment, Mr. Gargery," said the strange man. "I think I've got a bright new shilling somewhere in my pocket, and if I have, the boy shall have it."

He looked it out from a handful of small change, folded it in some crumpled paper, and gave it to me. "Yours!" said he. "Mind! Your own."

I thanked him, staring at him far beyond the bounds of good manners, and holding tight to Joe. He gave Joe good-night, and he gave Mr. Wopsle good-night (who went out with us), and he gave me only a look with his aiming eye — no, not a look, for he shut it up, but wonders may be done with an eye by hiding it.

On the way home, if I had been in a humour for talking, the talk must have been all on my side, for Mr. Wopsle parted from us at the door of the Jolly Bargemen, and Joe went all the way home with his mouth wide open, to rinse the rum out with as much air as possible. But I was in a manner stupefied by this turning up of my old misdeed and old acquaintance, and could think of nothing else.

My sister was not in a very bad temper when we presented ourselves in the kitchen, and Joe was encouraged by that unusual circumstance to tell her about the bright shilling. "A bad un, I'll be bound," said Mrs. Joe triumphantly, "or he wouldn't have given it to the boy! Let's look at it."

I took it out of the paper, and it proved to be a good one. "But what's this?" said Mrs. Joe, throwing down the shilling and catching up the paper. "Two One-Pound notes?"*

Nothing less than two fat sweltering one-pound notes that seemed to have been on terms of the warmest intimacy with all the cattle markets in the county. Joe caught up his hat again, and ran with them to the Jolly Bargemen to restore them to their owner. While he was gone, I sat down on my usual stool and looked vacantly at my sister, feeling pretty sure that the man would not be there.

Presently, Joe came back, saying that the man was gone, but that he, Joe, had left word at the Three Jolly Bargemen concerning the notes. Then my sister sealed them up in a piece of paper, and put them under some dried rose-leaves in an ornamental teapot on the top of a press[1] in the state parlour. There they remained, a nightmare to me, many and many a night and day.

I had sadly broken sleep when I got to bed, through thinking of the strange man taking aim at me with his invisible gun, and of the guiltily coarse and common thing it was, to be on secret terms of conspiracy with convicts — a feature in my low career that I had previously forgotten. I was haunted by the file too. A dread possessed me that when I least expected it, the file would reappear. I coaxed myself to sleep by thinking of Miss Havisham's, next Wednesday; and in my sleep I saw the file coming at me out of a door, without seeing who held it, and I screamed myself awake.

---

1. *press:* large cupboard, usually shelved and located in a recess.

CHAPTER XI

AT THE appointed time I returned to Miss Havisham's, and my hesitating ring at the gate brought out Estella. She locked it after admitting me, as she had done before, and again preceded me into the dark passage where her candle stood. She took no notice of me until she had the candle in her hand, when she looked over her shoulder, superciliously saying, "You are to come this way to-day," and took me to quite another part of the house.

The passage was a long one, and seemed to pervade the whole square basement of the Manor House. We traversed but one side of the square, however, and at the end of it she stopped, and put her candle down and opened a door. Here, the daylight reappeared, and I found myself in a small paved court-yard, the opposite side of which was formed by a detached dwelling-house, that looked as if it had once belonged to the manager or head clerk of the extinct brewery. There was a clock in the outer wall of this house. Like the clock in Miss Havisham's room, and like Miss Havisham's watch, it had stopped at twenty minutes to nine.

We went in at the door, which stood open, and into a gloomy room with a low ceiling, on the ground floor at the back. There was some company in the room, and Estella said to me as she joined it, "You are to go and stand there, boy, till you are wanted." "There," being the window, I crossed to it, and stood "there," in a very uncomfortable state of mind, looking out.

It opened to the ground, and looked into a most miserable corner of the neglected garden, upon a rank ruin of cabbage-stalks, and one box-tree that had been clipped round long ago, like a pudding, and had a new growth at the top of it, out of shape and of a different colour, as if that part of the pudding had stuck to the saucepan and got burnt. This was my homely thought, as I contemplated the box-tree. There had been some light snow, overnight, and it lay nowhere else to my knowledge; but, it had not quite melted from the cold shadow of this bit of garden, and the wind caught it up in little eddies and threw it at the window, as if it pelted me for coming there.

I divined that my coming had stopped conversation in the room, and that its other occupants were looking at me. I could see nothing of the room except the shining of the fire in the window-glass, but I stiffened in all my joints with the consciousness that I was under close inspection. There were three ladies in the room and one gentleman. Before I had been standing at the window five minutes, they somehow conveyed to me that they were all toadies and humbugs, but that each of them pretended not to know that the others were toadies and humbugs: because the admission that he or she did know it, would have made him or her out to be a toady and humbug.

They all had a listless and dreary air of waiting somebody's pleasure, and the most talkative of the ladies had to speak quite rigidly to repress a yawn. This lady, whose name was Camilla, very much reminded me of my sister, with the difference that she was older, and (as I found when I caught sight of her) of a blunter cast of features. Indeed, when I knew her better I began to think it was a Mercy she had any features at all, so very blank and high was the dead wall of her face.

"Poor dear soul!" said this lady, with an abruptness of manner quite my sister's. "Nobody's enemy but his own!"

"It would be much more commendable to be somebody else's enemy," said the gentleman; "far more natural."

"Cousin Raymond," observed another lady, "we are to love our neighbour."

"Sarah Pocket," returned Cousin Raymond, "if a man is not his own neighbour, who is?"

Miss Pocket laughed, and Camilla laughed and said (checking a yawn), "The idea!" But I thought they seemed to think it rather a good idea too. The other lady, who had not spoken yet, said gravely and emphatically, "*Very* true!"

"Poor soul!" Camilla presently went on (I knew they had all been looking at me in the mean time), "he is so very strange! Would anyone believe that when Tom's wife died, he actually could not be induced to see the importance of the children's having the deepest of trimmings to their mourning? 'Good Lord!' says he, 'Camilla, what can it signify so long as the poor bereaved little things are in black?' So like Matthew! The idea!"

"Good points in him, good points in him," said Cousin Raymond; "Heaven forbid I should deny good points in him; but he never had, and he never will have, any sense of the proprieties."

"You know I was obliged," said Camilla, "I was obliged to be firm. I said, 'It WILL NOT DO, for the credit of the family.' I told him that, without deep trimmings, the family was disgraced. I cried about it from breakfast till dinner. I injured my digestion. And at last he flung out in his violent way, and said, with a D, 'Then do as you like.' Thank Goodness it will always be a consolation to me to know that I instantly went out in a pouring rain and bought the things."

"*He* paid for them, did he not?" asked Estella.

"It's not the question, my dear child, who paid for them," returned Camilla, "*I* bought them. And I shall often think of that with peace, when I wake up in the night."

The ringing of a distant bell, combined with the echoing of some cry or call along the passage by which I had come, interrupted the conversation and caused Estella to say to me, "Now, boy!" On my turning round, they all looked at me with the utmost contempt, and, as I went out, I heard Sarah Pocket say, "Well I am sure! What next!" and Camilla add, with indignation, "Was there ever such a fancy! The i-de-a!"

As we were going with our candle along the dark passage, Estella stopped all of a sudden, and, facing round, said in her taunting manner with her face quite close to mine:

"Well?"

"Well, miss?" I answered, almost falling over her and checking myself. She stood looking at me, and, of course, I stood looking at her.

"Am I pretty?"

"Yes; I think you are very pretty."

"Am I insulting?"

"Not so much so as you were last time," said I.

"Not so much so?"

"No."

She fired when she asked the last question, and she slapped my face with such force as she had, when I answered it.

"Now?" said she. "You little coarse monster, what do you think of me now?"

"I shall not tell you."

"Because you are going to tell, up-stairs. Is that it?"

"No," said I, "that's not it."

"Why don't you cry again, you little wretch?"

"Because I'll never cry for you again," said I. Which was, I suppose, as false a declaration as ever was made; for I was inwardly crying for her then, and I know what I know of the pain she cost me afterwards.

We went on our way up-stairs after this episode; and, as we were going up, we met a gentleman groping his way down.

"Whom have we here?" asked the gentleman, stopping and looking at me.

"A boy," said Estella.

He was a burly man of an exceedingly dark complexion, with an exceedingly large head and a correspondingly large hand. He took my chin in his large hand and turned up my face to have a look at me by the light of the candle. He was prematurely bald on the top of his head, and had bushy black eyebrows that wouldn't lie down but stood up bristling. His eyes were set very deep in his head, and were disagreeably sharp and suspicious. He had a large watch-chain, and strong black dots where his beard and whiskers would have been if he had let them. He was nothing to me, and I could have had no foresight then, that he ever would be anything to me, but it happened that I had this opportunity of observing him well.

"Boy of the neighbourhood? Hey?" said he.

"Yes, sir," said I.

"How do *you* come here?"

"Miss Havisham sent for me, sir," I explained.

"Well! Behave yourself. I have a pretty large experience of boys, and you're a bad set of fellows. Now mind!" said he, biting the side of his great forefinger as he frowned at me, "you behave yourself!"

With those words, he released me — which I was glad of, for his hand smelt of scented soap — and went his way down-stairs. I wondered whether he could be a doctor; but no, I thought; he couldn't be a doctor, or he would have a quieter and more persuasive manner. There was not much time to consider the subject, for we were soon in Miss Havisham's room, where she and everything else were just as I had left them. Estella left me standing near the door, and I stood there until Miss Havisham cast her eyes upon me from the dressing-table.

"So!" she said, without being startled or surprised; "the days have worn away, have they?"

"Yes, ma'am. To-day is —"

"There, there, there!" with the impatient movement of her fingers. "I don't want to know. Are you ready to play?"

I was obliged to answer in some confusion, "I don't think I am, ma'am."

"Not at cards again?" she demanded, with a searching look.

"Yes, ma'am; I could do that, if I was wanted."

"Since this house strikes you old and grave, boy," said Miss Havisham, impatiently, "and you are unwilling to play, are you willing to work?"

I could answer this inquiry with a better heart than I had been able to find for the other question, and I said I was quite willing.

"Then go into that opposite room," said she, pointing at the door behind me with her withered hand, "and wait there till I come."

I crossed the staircase landing, and entered the room she indicated. From that room, too, the daylight was completely excluded, and it had an airless smell that was oppressive. A fire had been lately kindled in the damp old-fashioned grate, and it was more disposed to go out than to burn up, and the reluctant smoke which hung in the room seemed colder than the clearer air — like our own marsh mist. Certain wintry branches of candles on the high chimney-piece faintly lighted the chamber: or, it would be more expressive to say, faintly troubled its darkness. It was spacious, and I dare say had once been handsome, but every discernible thing in it was covered with dust and mould, and dropping to pieces. The most prominent object was a long table with a tablecloth spread on it, as if a feast had been in preparation when the house and the clocks all stopped together. An epergne or centre-piece of some kind was in the middle of this cloth; it was so heavily overhung with cobwebs that its form was quite undistinguishable; and, as I looked along the yellow expanse out of which I remember its seeming to grow, like a black fungus, I saw speckled-legged spiders with blotchy bodies running home to it, and running out from it, as if some circumstance of the greatest public importance had just transpired in the spider community.

I heard the mice too, rattling behind the panels, as if the same occurrence were important to their interests. But, the black-beetles took no notice of the agitation, and groped about the hearth in a ponderous elderly way, as if they were short-sighted and hard of hearing, and not on terms with one another.

These crawling things had fascinated my attention and I was watching them from a distance, when Miss Havisham laid a hand upon my shoulder. In her other hand she had a crutch-headed stick on which she leaned, and she looked like the Witch of the place.

"This," said she, pointing to the long table with her stick, "is where I will be laid when I am dead. They shall come and look at me here."

With some vague misgiving that she might get upon the table then and there and die at once, the complete realisation of the ghastly waxwork at the Fair, I shrank under her touch.

"What do you think that is?" she asked me, again pointing with her stick; "that, where those cobwebs are?"

"I can't guess what it is, ma'am."

"It's a great cake. A bride-cake. Mine!"

She looked all round the room in a glaring manner, and then said, leaning on me while her hand twitched my shoulder, "Come, come, come! Walk me, walk me!"

I made out from this, that the work I had to do, was to walk Miss Havisham round and round the room. Accordingly, I started at once, and she leaned upon my shoulder, and we went away at a pace that might have been an imitation (founded on my first impulse under that roof) of Mr. Pumblechook's chaise-cart.

She was not physically strong, and after a little time said, "Slower!" Still, we went at an impatient fitful speed, and as we went, she twitched the hand upon my shoulder, and worked her mouth, and led me to believe that we were going fast because her thoughts went fast. After a while she said, "Call Estella!" so I went out on the landing and roared that name as I had done on the previous occasion. When her light appeared, I returned to Miss Havisham, and we started away again round and round the room.

If only Estella had come to be a spectator of our proceedings, I should have felt sufficiently disconcerted; but, as she brought with her the three ladies and the gentleman whom I had seen below, I didn't know what to do. In my politeness, I would have stopped; but, Miss Havisham twitched my shoulder, and we posted on — with a shamefaced consciousness on my part that they would think it was all my doing.

"Dear Miss Havisham," said Miss Sarah Pocket. "How well you look!"

"I do not," returned Miss Havisham. "I am yellow skin and bone."

Camilla brightened when Miss Pocket met with this rebuff; and she murmured, as she plaintively contemplated Miss Havisham, "Poor dear soul! Certainly not to be expected to look well, poor thing. The idea!"

"And how are *you*?" said Miss Havisham to Camilla. As we were close to Camilla then, I would have stopped as a matter of course, only Miss Havisham wouldn't stop. We swept on, and I felt that I was highly obnoxious to Camilla.

"Thank you, Miss Havisham," she returned, "I am as well as can be expected."

"Why, what's the matter with you?" asked Miss Havisham, with exceeding sharpness.

"Nothing worth mentioning," replied Camilla. "I don't wish to make a display of my feelings, but I have habitually thought of you more in the night than I am quite equal to."

"Then don't think of me," retorted Miss Havisham.

"Very easily said!" remarked Camilla, amiably repressing a sob, while a hitch came into her upper lip, and her tears overflowed. "Raymond is a witness what ginger and sal volatile I am obliged to take in the night. Raymond is a witness what nervous jerkings I have in my legs. Chokings and nervous jerkings, however, are nothing new to me when I think with anxiety of those I love. If I could be less affectionate and sensitive, I should have a better digestion and an iron set of nerves. I am sure I wish it could be so. But as to not thinking you in the night — The idea!" Here, a burst of tears.

The Raymond referred to, I understood to be the gentleman present, and him I understood to be Mr. Camilla. He came to the rescue at this point, and said in a consolatory and complimentary voice, "Camilla, my dear, it is well known that your family feelings are gradually undermining you to the extent of making one of your legs shorter than the other."

"I am not aware," observed the grave lady whose voice I had heard but once, "that to think of any person is to make a great claim upon that person, my dear."

Miss Sarah Pocket, whom I now saw to be a little dry brown corrugated old woman, with a small face that might have been made of walnut shells, and a large mouth like a cat's without the whiskers, supported this position by saying, "No, indeed, my dear. Hem!"

"Thinking is easy enough," said the grave lady.

"What is easier, you know?" assented Miss Sarah Pocket.

"Oh, yes, yes!" cried Camilla, whose fermenting feelings appeared to rise from her legs to her bosom. "It's all very true! It's a weakness to be so affectionate, but I can't help it. No doubt my health would be much better if it was otherwise, still I wouldn't change my disposition if I could. It's the cause of much suffering, but it's a consolation to know I possess it, when I wake up in the night." Here another burst of feeling.

Miss Havisham and I had never stopped all this time, but kept going round and round the room: now, brushing against the skirts of the visitors: now, giving them the whole length of the dismal chamber.

"There's Matthew!" said Camilla. "Never mixing with any natural ties, never coming here to see how Miss Havisham is! I have taken to the sofa with my staylace cut, and have lain there hours, insensible, with my head over the side, and my hair all down, and my feet I don't know where —"

("Much higher than your head, my love," said Mr. Camilla.)

"I have gone off into that state, hours and hours, on account of Matthew's strange and inexplicable conduct, and nobody has thanked me."

"Really I must say I should think not!" interposed the grave lady.

"You see, my dear," added Miss Sarah Pocket (a blandly vicious personage), "the question to put to yourself is, who did you expect to thank you, my love?"

"Without expecting any thanks, or anything of the sort," resumed Camilla, "I have remained in that state, hours and hours, and Raymond is a witness of the extent to which I have choked, and what the total inefficacy of ginger has been, and I have been heard at the pianoforte-tuner's across the street, where the poor mistaken children have even supposed it to be pigeons cooing at a distance — and now to be told —" Here Camilla put her hand to her throat, and began to be quite chemical as to the formation of new combinations there.[1]

When this same Matthew was mentioned, Miss Havisham stopped me and herself, and stood looking at the speaker. This change had a great influence in bringing Camilla's chemistry to a sudden end.

---

1. *began to be quite chemical as to the formation of new combinations there:* i.e., Camilla, who is a hypochondriac, starts to cough and choke.

"Matthew will come and see me at last," said Miss Havisham, sternly, "when I am laid on that table. That will be his place — there," striking the table with her stick, "at my head! And yours will be there! And your husband's there! And Sarah Pocket's there! And Georgiana's there! Now you all know where to take your stations when you come to feast upon me. And now go!"

At the mention of each name, she had struck the table with her stick in a new place. She now said, "Walk me, walk me!" and we went on again.

"I suppose there's nothing to be done," exclaimed Camilla, "but comply and depart. It's something to have seen the object of one's love and duty, for even so short a time. I shall think of it with a melancholy satisfaction when I wake up in the night. I wish Matthew could have that comfort, but he sets it at defiance. I am determined not to make a display of my feelings, but it's very hard to be told one wants to feast on one's relations — as if one was a Giant[1] — and to be told to go. The bare idea!"

Mr. Camilla interposing, as Mrs. Camilla laid her hand upon her heaving bosom, that lady assumed an unnatural fortitude of manner which I supposed to be expressive of an intention to drop and choke when out of view, and kissing her hand to Miss Havisham, was escorted forth. Sarah Pocket and Georgiana contended who should remain last; but, Sarah was too knowing to be outdone, and ambled round Georgiana with that artful slipperiness, that the latter was obliged to take precedence. Sarah Pocket then made her separate effect of departing with "Bless you, Miss Havisham dear!" and with a smile of forgiving pity on her walnut-shell countenance for the weaknesses of the rest.

While Estella was away lighting them down, Miss Havisham still walked with her hand on my shoulder, but more and more slowly. At last she stopped before the fire, and said, after muttering and looking at it some seconds:

"This is my birthday, Pip."

I was going to wish her many happy returns, when she lifted her stick.

"I don't suffer it to be spoken of. I don't suffer those who were here

---

1. *as if one was a Giant:* Cronus, one of the giant Titan gods in Greek myth, ate his children as soon as they were born.

just now, or any one, to speak of it. They come here on the day, but they dare not refer to it."

Of course I made no further effort to refer to it.

"On this day of the year, long before you were born, this heap of decay," stabbing with her crutched stick at the pile of cobwebs on the table but not touching it, "was brought here. It and I have worn away together. The mice have gnawed at it, and sharper teeth than teeth of mice have gnawed at me."

She held the head of her stick against her heart as she stood looking at the table; she in her once white dress, all yellow and withered; the once white cloth all yellow and withered; everything around, in a state to crumble under a touch.

"When the ruin is complete," said she, with a ghastly look, "and when they lay me dead, in my bride's dress on the bride's table — which shall be done, and which will be the finished curse upon him — so much the better if it is done on this day!"

She stood looking at the table as if she stood looking at her own figure lying there. I remained quiet. Estella returned, and she too remained quiet. It seemed to me that we continued thus for a long time. In the heavy air of the room, and the heavy darkness that brooded in its remoter corners, I even had an alarming fancy that Estella and I might presently begin to decay.

At length, not coming out of her distraught state by degrees, but in an instant, Miss Havisham said, "Let me see you two play cards; why have you not begun?" With that, we returned to her room, and sat down as before; I was beggared, as before; and again, as before, Miss Havisham watched us all the time, directed my attention to Estella's beauty, and made me notice it the more by trying her jewels on Estella's breast and hair.

Estella, for her part, likewise treated me as before; except that she did not condescend to speak. When we had played some half-dozen games, a day was appointed for my return, and I was taken down into the yard to be fed in the former dog-like manner. There, too, I was again left to wander about as I liked.

It is not much to the purpose whether a gate in that garden wall which I had scrambled up to peep over on the last occasion was, on that last occasion, open or shut. Enough that I saw no gate then, and that I saw one now. As it stood open, and as I knew that Estella had let the visitors out — for, she had returned with the keys in her hand — I strolled into the garden and strolled all over it. It was quite a wilderness, and there were old melon-frames and cucumber-frames in it, which seemed in their decline to have produced a spontaneous growth of weak attempts at pieces of old hats and boots, with now and then a weedy offshoot into the likeness of a battered saucepan.

When I had exhausted the garden, and a greenhouse with nothing in it but a fallen-down grape-vine and some bottles, I found myself in the dismal corner upon which I had looked out of window. Never questioning for a moment that the house was now empty, I looked in at another window, and found myself, to my great surprise, exchanging a broad stare with a pale young gentleman with red eyelids and light hair.

This pale young gentleman quickly disappeared, and re-appeared beside me. He had been at his books when I had found myself staring at him, and I now saw that he was inky.

"Halloa!" said he, "young fellow!"

Halloa being a general observation which I have usually observed to be best answered by itself, I said, "Halloa!" politely omitting young fellow.

"Who let *you* in?" said he.

"Miss Estella."

"Who gave you leave to prowl about?"

"Miss Estella."

"Come and fight," said the pale young gentleman.

What could I do but follow him? I have often asked myself the question since: but, what else could I do? His manner was so final and I was so astonished, that I followed where he led, as if I had been under a spell.

"Stop a minute, though," he said, wheeling round before we had gone many paces. "I ought to give you a reason for fighting, too. There it is!" In a most irritating manner he instantly slapped his hands against one another, daintily flung one of his legs up behind him, pulled my hair, slapped his hands again, dipped his head, and butted it into my stomach.

The bull-like proceeding last mentioned, besides that it was unquestionably to be regarded in the light of a liberty, was particularly disagreeable just after bread and meat. I therefore hit out at him and was going to hit out again, when he said, "Aha! Would you?" and began dancing backwards and forwards in a manner quite unparalleled within my limited experience.

"Laws of the game!" said he. Here, he skipped from his left leg on to his right. "Regular rules!" Here, he skipped from his right leg on to his left. "Come to the ground, and go through the preliminaries!" Here, he dodged backwards and forwards, and did all sorts of things while I looked helplessly at him.

I was secretly afraid of him when I saw him so dexterous; but, I felt morally and physically convinced that his light head of hair could have had no business in the pit of my stomach, and that I had a right to consider it irrelevant when so obtruded on my attention. Therefore, I followed him without a word, to a retired nook of the garden, formed by the junction of two walls and screened by some rubbish. On his asking me if I was satisfied with the ground, and on my replying Yes, he begged my leave to absent himself for a moment, and quickly returned with a bottle of water and a sponge dipped in vinegar. "Available for both," he said, placing these against the wall. And then fell to pulling off, not only his jacket and waistcoat, but his shirt too, in a manner at once light-hearted, business-like, and bloodthirsty.

Although he did not look very healthy — having pimples on his face, and a breaking out at his mouth — these dreadful preparations quite appalled me. I judged him to be about my own age, but he was much taller, and he had a way of spinning himself about that was full of appearance. For the rest, he was a young gentleman in a grey suit (when not denuded for battle), with his elbows, knees, wrists, and heels, considerably in advance of the rest of him as to development.

My heart failed me when I saw him squaring at me with every demonstration of mechanical nicety, and eyeing my anatomy as if he were minutely choosing his bone. I never have been so surprised in my life, as I was when I let out the first blow, and saw him lying on his back, looking up at me with a bloody nose and his face exceedingly fore-shortened.

But, he was on his feet directly, and after sponging himself with a great show of dexterity began squaring again. The second greatest surprise I have ever had in my life was seeing him on his back again, looking up at me out of a black eye.

His spirit inspired me with great respect. He seemed to have no strength, and he never once hit me hard, and he was always knocked down; but, he would be up again in a moment, sponging himself or drinking out of the water-bottle, with the greatest satisfaction in seconding himself according to form, and then came at me with an air and a show that made me believe he really was going to do for me at last. He got heavily bruised, for I am sorry to record that the more I hit him, the harder I hit him; but, he came up again and again and again, until at last he got a bad fall with the back of his head against the wall. Even after that crisis in our affairs, he got up and turned round and round confusedly a few times, not knowing where I was; but finally went on his knees to his sponge and threw it up: at the same time panting out, "That means you have won."

He seemed so brave and innocent, that although I had not proposed the contest I felt but a gloomy satisfaction in my victory. Indeed, I go so far as to hope that I regarded myself while dressing, as a species of savage young wolf, or other wild beast. However, I got dressed, darkly wiping my sanguinary face at intervals, and I said, "Can I help you?" and he said "No thankee," and I said "Good afternoon," and *he* said "Same to you."

When I got into the court-yard, I found Estella waiting with the keys. But, she neither asked me where I had been, nor why I had kept her waiting; and there was a bright flush upon her face, as though something had happened to delight her. Instead of going straight to the gate, too, she stepped back into the passage, and beckoned me.

"Come here! You may kiss me, if you like."

I kissed her cheek as she turned it to me. I think I would have gone through a great deal to kiss her cheek. But, I felt that the kiss was given to the coarse common boy as a piece of money might have been, and that it was worth nothing.

What with the birthday visitors, and what with the cards, and what with the fight, my stay had lasted so long, that when I neared home the light on the spit of sand off the point on the marshes was gleaming against a black night-sky, and Joe's furnace was flinging a path of fire across the road.

CHAPTER XII

MY MIND grew very uneasy on the subject of the pale young gentleman. The more I thought of the fight, and recalled the pale young gentleman on his back in various stages of puffy and incrimsoned countenance, the more certain it appeared that something would be done to me. I felt that the pale young gentleman's blood was on my head, and that the Law would avenge it. Without having any definite idea of the penalties I had incurred, it was clear to me that village boys could not go stalking about the country, ravaging the houses of gentlefolks and pitching into the studious youth of England, without laying themselves open to severe punishment. For some days, I even kept close at home, and looked out at the kitchen door with the greatest caution and trepidation before going on an errand, lest the officers of the County Jail should pounce upon me. The pale young gentleman's nose had stained my trousers, and I tried to wash out that evidence of my guilt in the dead of night. I had cut my knuckles against the pale young gentleman's teeth, and I twisted my imagination into a thousand tangles, as I devised incredible ways of accounting for that damnatory circumstance when I should be haled before the Judges.

When the day came round for my return to the scene of the deed of violence, my terrors reached their height. Whether myrmidons of Justice,[1] specially sent down from London, would be lying in ambush behind the gate? Whether Miss Havisham, preferring to take personal vengeance for an outrage done to her house, might rise in those grave-clothes of hers, draw a pistol, and shoot me dead? Whether suborned boys — a numerous band of mercenaries — might be engaged to fall upon me in the brewery, and cuff me until I was no more? It was high testimony to my confidence in the spirit of the pale young gentleman, that I never imagined *him* accessory to these retaliations; they always came into my mind as the acts of injudicious relatives of his, goaded on by the state of his visage and an indignant sympathy with the family features.

---

1. *myrmidons of Justice:* stock phrase referring jocularly to the police; the Myrmidons were the remorseless followers of Achilles at the battle of Troy, according to Homer's *Iliad*.

However, go to Miss Havisham's I must, and go I did. And behold! nothing came of the late struggle. It was not alluded to in any way, and no pale young gentleman was to be discovered on the premises. I found the same gate open, and I explored the garden and even looked in at the windows of the detached house; but, my view was suddenly stopped by the closed shutters within, and all was lifeless. Only in the corner where the combat had taken place, could I detect any evidence of the young gentleman's existence. There were traces of his gore in that spot, and I covered them with garden-mould from the eye of man.

On the broad landing between Miss Havisham's own room and that other room in which the long table was laid out, I saw a garden-chair — a light chair on wheels, that you pushed from behind. It had been placed there since my last visit, and I entered, that same day, on a regular occupation of pushing Miss Havisham in this chair (when she was tired of walking with her hand upon my shoulder) round her own room, and across the landing, and round the other room. Over and over and over again, we would make these journeys, and sometimes they would last as long as three hours at a stretch. I insensibly fall into a general mention of these journeys as numerous, because it was at once settled that I should return every alternate day at noon for these purposes, and because I am now going to sum up a period of at least eight or ten months.

As we began to be more used to one another, Miss Havisham talked more to me, and asked me such questions as what had I learnt and what was I going to be? I told her I was going to be apprenticed to Joe, I believed; and I enlarged upon my knowing nothing and wanting to know everything, in the hope that she might offer some help towards that desirable end. But, she did not; on the contrary, she seemed to prefer my being ignorant. Neither did she ever give me any money — or anything but my daily dinner — nor ever stipulate that I should be paid for my services.

Estella was always about, and always let me in and out, but never told me I might kiss her again. Sometimes, she would coldly tolerate me; sometimes, she would condescend to me; sometimes, she would be quite familiar with me; sometimes, she would tell me energetically that she hated me. Miss Havisham would often ask me in a whisper, or when we were alone, "Does she grow prettier and prettier, Pip?" And when I said yes (for indeed she did), would seem to enjoy it greedily. Also, when we played at cards Miss Havisham would look on, with a miserly relish of Estella's moods, whatever they were. And sometimes, when her moods were so many and so contradictory of one another that I was puzzled what to say or do, Miss Havisham would embrace her with lavish fondness, murmuring something in her ear that sounded like "Break their hearts my pride and hope, break their hearts and have no mercy!"

There was a song Joe used to hum fragments of at the forge, of which the burden was Old Clem.[1] This was not a very ceremonious way of rendering homage to a patron saint; but, I believe Old Clem stood in that relation towards smiths. It was a song that imitated the measure of beating upon iron, and was a mere lyrical excuse for the introduction of Old Clem's respected name. Thus, you were to hammer boys round — Old Clem! With a thump and a sound — Old Clem! Beat it out, beat it out — Old Clem! With a clink for the stout — Old Clem! Blow the fire, blow the fire — Old Clem! Roaring dryer, soaring higher — Old Clem! One day soon after the appearance of the chair, Miss Havisham suddenly saying to me with the impatient movement of her fingers, "There, there, there! Sing!" I was surprised into crooning this ditty as I pushed her over the floor. It happened so to catch her fancy, that she took it up in a low brooding voice as if she were singing in her sleep. After that, it became customary with us to have it as we moved about, and Estella would often join in; though the whole strain was so subdued, even when there were three of us, that it made less noise in the grim old house than the lightest breath of wind.

What could I become with these surroundings? How could my character fail to be influenced by them? Is it to be wondered at if my thoughts were dazed, as my eyes were, when I came out into the natural light from the misty yellow rooms?

Perhaps, I might have told Joe about the pale young gentleman, if I had not previously been betrayed into those enormous inventions to which I had confessed. Under the circumstances, I felt that Joe could hardly fail

---

1. *Old Clem:* St. Clement, celebrated in this traditional song, was conventionally the guardian saint of the Mediaeval guilds of blacksmiths.

to discern in the pale young gentleman, an appropriate passenger to be put into the black velvet coach; therefore, I said nothing of him. Besides: that shrinking from having Miss Havisham and Estella discussed, which had come upon me in the beginning, grew much more potent as time went on. I reposed complete confidence in no one but Biddy; but, I told poor Biddy everything. Why it came natural to me to do so, and why Biddy had a deep concern in everything I told her, I did not know then, though I think I know now.

Meanwhile, councils went on in the kitchen at home, fraught with almost insupportable aggravation to my exasperated spirit. That ass, Pumblechook, used often to come over of a night for the purpose of discussing my prospects with my sister; and I really do believe (to this hour with less penitence than I ought to feel), that if these hands could have taken a linchpin out of his chaise-cart, they would have done it. The miserable man was a man of that confined stolidity of mind, that he could not discuss my prospects without having me before him — as it were, to operate upon — and he would drag me up from my stool (usually by the collar) where I was quiet in a corner, and, putting me before the fire as if I were going to be cooked, would begin by saying, "Now, Mum, here is this boy! Here is this boy which you brought up by hand. Hold up your head, boy, and be for ever grateful unto them which so did do. Now, Mum, with respections to this boy!" And then he would rumple my hair the wrong way — which from my earliest remembrance, as already hinted, I have in my soul denied the right of any fellow-creature to do — and would hold me before him by the sleeve: a spectacle of imbecility only to be equalled by himself.

Then, he and my sister would pair off in such nonsensical speculations about Miss Havisham, and about what she would do with me and for me, that I used to want — quite painfully — to burst into spiteful tears, fly at Pumblechook, and pummel him all over. In these dialogues, my sister spoke of me as if she were morally wrenching one of my teeth out at every reference; while Pumblechook himself, self-constituted my patron, would sit supervising me with a depreciatory eye, like the architect of my fortunes who thought himself engaged on a very unremunerative job.

In these discussions, Joe bore no part. But he was often talked at, while they were in progress, by reason of Mrs. Joe's perceiving that he was not favourable to my being taken from the forge. I was fully old enough now, to be apprenticed to Joe; and when Joe sat with the poker on his knees thoughtfully raking out the ashes between the lower bars, my sister would so distinctly construe that innocent action into opposition on his part, that she would dive at him, take the poker out of his hands, shake him, and put it away. There was a most irritating end to every one of these debates. All in a moment, with nothing to lead up to it, my sister would stop herself in a yawn, and catching sight of me as it were incidentally, would swoop upon me with, "Come! there's enough of *you! You* get along to bed; *you*'ve given trouble enough for one night, I hope!" As if I had besought them as a favour to bother my life out.

We went on in this way for a long time, and it seemed likely that we should continue to go on in this way for a long time, when, one day, Miss Havisham stopped short as she and I were walking, she leaning on my shoulder; and said with some displeasure:

"You are growing tall, Pip!"

I thought it best to hint, through the medium of a meditative look, that this might be occasioned by circumstances over which I had no control.

She said no more at the time; but, she presently stopped and looked at me again; and presently again; and after that, looked frowning and moody. On the next day of my attendance when our usual exercise was over, and I had landed her at her dressing-table, she stayed me with a movement of her impatient fingers:

"Tell me the name again of that blacksmith of yours."

"Joe Gargery, ma'am."

"Meaning the master you were to be apprenticed to?"

"Yes, Miss Havisham."

"You had better be apprenticed at once. Would Gargery come here with you, and bring your indentures,[1] do you think?"

I signified that I had no doubt he would take it as an honour to be asked.

---

1. *indentures:* the paired copies of the contract by which the apprentice was bound to his master, who in turn undertook to teach him his trade.

"Then let him come."

"At any particular time, Miss Havisham?"

"There, there! I know nothing about times. Let him come soon, and come alone with you."

When I got home at night, and delivered this message for Joe, my sister "went on the Rampage," in a more alarming degree than at any previous period. She asked me and Joe whether we supposed she was doormats under our feet, and how we dared to use her so, and what company we graciously thought she *was* fit for? When she had exhausted a torrent of such inquiries, she threw a candlestick at Joe, burst into a loud sobbing, got out the dustpan — which was always a very bad sign — put on her coarse apron, and began cleaning up to a terrible extent. Not satisfied with a dry cleaning, she took to a pail and scrubbing-brush, and cleaned us out of house and home, so that we stood shivering in the back yard. It was ten o'clock at night before we ventured to creep in again, and then she asked Joe why he hadn't married a Negress Slave at once? Joe offered no answer, poor fellow, but stood feeling his whisker and looking dejectedly at me, as if he thought it really might have been a better speculation.

CHAPTER XIII

IT WAS a trial to my feelings on the next day but one, to see Joe arraying himself in his Sunday clothes to accompany me to Miss Havisham's. However, as he thought his court-suit necessary to the occasion, it was not for me to tell him that he looked far better in his working dress; the rather, because I knew he made himself so dreadfully uncomfortable, entirely on my account, and that it was for me he pulled up his shirt-collar so very high behind, that it made the hair on the crown of his head stand up like a tuft of feathers.

At breakfast-time my sister declared her intention of going to town with us, and being left at Uncle Pumblechook's, and called for "when we had done with our fine ladies" — a way of putting the case, from which Joe appeared inclined to augur the worst. The forge was shut up for the day, and Joe inscribed in chalk upon the door (as it was his custom to do on the very rare occasions when he was not at work) the monosyllable HOUT, accompanied by a sketch of an arrow supposed to be flying in the direction he had taken.

We walked to town, my sister leading the way in a very large beaver bonnet, and carrying a basket like the Great Seal of England[1] in plaited straw, a pair of pattens,[2] a spare shawl, and an umbrella, though it was a fine bright day. I am not quite clear whether these articles were carried penitentially or ostentatiously; but, I rather think they were displayed as articles of property — much as Cleopatra or any other sovereign lady on the Rampage might exhibit her wealth in a pageant or procession.

When we came to Pumblechook's, my sister bounced in and left us. As it was almost noon, Joe and I held straight on to Miss Havisham's house. Estella opened the gate as usual, and, the moment she appeared, Joe took his hat off and stood weighing it by the brim in both his hands: as if he had some urgent reason in his mind for being particular to half a quarter of an ounce.

Estella took no notice of either of us, but led us the way that I knew so well. I followed next to her, and Joe came last. When I looked back at Joe in the long passage, he was still weighing his hat with the greatest care, and was coming after us in long strides on the tips of his toes.

Estella told me we were both to go in, so I took Joe by the coat-cuff and conducted him into Miss Havisham's presence. She was seated at her dressing-table, and looked round at us immediately.

"Oh!" said she to Joe. "You are the husband of the sister of this boy?"

I could hardly have imagined dear old Joe looking so unlike himself or so like some extraordinary bird; standing, as he did, speechless, with his tuft of feathers ruffled, and his mouth open, as if he wanted a worm.

"You are the husband," repeated Miss Havisham, "of the sister of this boy?"

It was very aggravating; but, throughout the interview Joe persisted in addressing Me instead of Miss Havisham.

---

1. *the Great Seal of England:* the large round metal stamp bearing the image of the sovereign, used by the Chancellor to authenticate important state documents.

2. *a pair of pattens:* overshoes used in wet or muddy areas, consisting of a wooden sole secured to the shoe with a leather strap and mounted on an oval iron ring.

"Which I meantersay, Pip," Joe now observed in a manner that was at once expressive of forcible argumentation, strict confidence, and great politeness, "as I hup and married your sister, and I were at the time what you might call (if you was anyways inclined) a single man."

"Well!" said Miss Havisham. "And you have reared the boy, with the intention of taking him for your apprentice; is that so, Mr. Gargery?"

"You know, Pip," replied Joe, "as you and me were ever friends, and it were look'd for'ard to betwixt us, as being calc'lated to lead to larks. Not but what, Pip, if you had ever made objections to the business — such as its being open to black and sut, or such-like — not but what they would have been attended to, don't you see?"

"Has the boy," said Miss Havisham, "ever made any objection? Does he like the trade?"

"Which it is well beknown to yourself, Pip," returned Joe, strengthening his former mixture of argumentation, confidence, and politeness, "that it were the wish of your own hart." (I saw the idea suddenly break upon him that he would adapt his epitaph to the occasion, before he went on to say) "And there weren't no objection on your part, and Pip it were the great wish of your hart!"

It was quite in vain for me to endeavour to make him sensible that he ought to speak to Miss Havisham. The more I made faces and gestures to him to do it, the more confidential, argumentative, and polite, he persisted in being to Me.

"Have you brought his indentures with you?" asked Miss Havisham.

"Well Pip, you know," replied Joe, as if that were a little unreasonable, "you yourself see me put 'em in my 'at, and therefore you know as they are here." With which he took them out, and gave them, not to Miss Havisham, but to me. I am afraid I was ashamed of the dear good fellow — I *know* I was ashamed of him — when I saw that Estella stood at the back of Miss Havisham's chair, and that her eyes laughed mischievously. I took the indentures out of his hand and gave them to Miss Havisham.

"You expected," said Miss Havisham, as she looked them over, "no premium with the boy?"

"Joe!" I remonstrated; for he made no reply at all. "Why don't you answer —"

"Pip," returned Joe, cutting me short as if he were hurt, "which I meantersay that were not a question requiring a answer betwixt yourself and me, and which you know the answer to be full well No. You know it to be No, Pip, and wherefore should I say it?"

Miss Havisham glanced at him as if she understood what he really was, better than I had thought possible, seeing what he was there; and took up a little bag from the table beside her.

"Pip has earned a premium here," she said, "and here it is. There are five-and-twenty guineas in this bag. Give it to your master, Pip."

As if he were absolutely out of his mind with the wonder awakened in him by her strange figure and the strange room, Joe, even at this pass, persisted in addressing me.

"This is wery liberal on your part, Pip," said Joe, "and it is as such received and grateful welcome, though never looked for, far nor near nor nowheres. And now, old chap," said Joe, conveying to me a sensation, first of burning and then of freezing, for I felt as if that familiar expression were applied to Miss Havisham; "and now, old chap, may we do our duty! May you and me do our duty, both on us by one and another, and by them which your liberal present — have — conweyed — to be — for the satisfaction of mind — of — them as never —" here Joe showed that he felt he had fallen into frightful difficulties, until he triumphantly rescued himself with the words, "and from myself far be it!" These words had such a round and convincing sound for him that he said them twice.

"Good-by, Pip!" said Miss Havisham. "Let them out, Estella."

"Am I to come again, Miss Havisham?" I asked.

"No. Gargery is your master now. Gargery! One word!"

Thus calling him back as I went out of the door, I heard her say to Joe, in a distinct emphatic voice, "The boy has been a good boy here, and that is his reward. Of course, as an honest man, you will expect no other and no more."

How Joe got out of the room, I have never been able to determine; but, I know that when he did get out he was steadily proceeding up-stairs instead of coming down, and was deaf to all remonstrances until I went after him and laid hold of him. In another minute we were outside the gate, and it was locked, and Estella was gone.

When we stood in the daylight alone again, Joe backed up against a wall, and said to me, "Astonishing!" And there he remained so long, saying "Astonishing" at intervals, so often, that I began to think his senses were never coming back. At length he prolonged his remark into "Pip, I do assure *you* this is as-TON-ishing!" and so, by degrees, became conversational and able to walk away.

I have reason to think that Joe's intellects were brightened by the encounter they had passed through, and that on our way to Pumblechook's he invented a subtle and deep design. My reason is to be found in what took place in Mr. Pumblechook's parlour: where, on our presenting ourselves, my sister sat in conference with that detested seedsman.

"Well?" cried my sister, addressing us both at once. "And what's happened to *you?* I wonder you condescend to come back to such poor society as this, I am sure I do!"

"Miss Havisham," said Joe, with a fixed look at me, like an effort of remembrance, "made it wery partick'ler that we should give her — were it compliments or respects, Pip?"

"Compliments," I said.

"Which that were my own belief," assented Joe — "her compliments to Mrs. J. Gargery —"

"Much good they'll do me!" observed my sister; but rather gratified too.

"And wishing," pursued Joe, with another fixed look at me, like another effort of remembrance, "that the state of Miss Havisham's elth were sitch as would have — allowed, were it, Pip?"

"Of her having the pleasure," I added.

"Of ladies' company," said Joe. And drew a long breath.

"Well!" cried my sister, with a mollified glance at Mr. Pumblechook. "She might have had the politeness to send that message at first, but it's better late than never. And what did she give young Rantipole[1] here?"

"She giv' him," said Joe, "nothing."

Mrs. Joe was going to break out, but Joe went on.

"What she giv'," said Joe, "she giv' to his friends. 'And by his friends,' were her explanation, 'I mean into the hands of his sister Mrs. J. Gargery.'

---

1. *Rantipole:* a wild or disorderly person.

Them were her words; 'Mrs. J. Gargery.' She mayn't have know'd," added Joe, with an appearance of reflection, "whether it were Joe, or Jorge."

My sister looked at Pumblechook: who smoothed the elbows of his wooden arm-chair, and nodded at her and at the fire, as if he had known all about it beforehand.

"And how much have you got?" asked my sister, laughing. Positively, laughing!

"What would present company say to ten pound?" demanded Joe.

"They'd say," returned my sister, curtly, "pretty well. Not too much, but pretty well."

"It's more than that, then," said Joe.

That fearful Impostor, Pumblechook, immediately nodded, and said, as he rubbed the arms of his chair: "It's more than that, Mum."

"Why, you don't mean to say —" began my sister.

"Yes I do, Mum," said Pumblechook; "but wait a bit. Go on, Joseph. Good in you! Go on!"

"What would present company say," proceeded Joe, "to twenty pound?"

"Handsome would be the word," returned my sister.

"Well, then," said Joe, "it's more than twenty pound."

That abject hypocrite, Pumblechook, nodded again, and said, with a patronising laugh, "It's more than that, Mum. Good again! Follow her up, Joseph!"

"Then to make an end of it," said Joe, delightedly handing the bag to my sister; "it's five-and-twenty pound."*

"It's five-and-twenty pound, Mum," echoed that basest of swindlers, Pumblechook, rising to shake hands with her; "and it's no more than your merits (as I said when my opinion was asked), and I wish you joy of the money!"

If the villain had stopped here, his case would have been sufficiently awful, but he blackened his guilt by proceeding to take me into custody, with a right of patronage that left all his former criminality far behind.

"Now you see, Joseph and wife," said Pumblechook, as he took me by the arm above the elbow, "I am one of them that always go right through with what they've begun. This boy must be bound, out of hand. That's *my* way. Bound out of hand."

"Goodness knows, Uncle Pumblechook," said my sister (grasping the money), "we're deeply beholden to you."

"Never mind me, Mum, returned that diabolical corn-chandler. "A pleasure's a pleasure, all the world over. But this boy, you know; we must have him bound. I said I'd see to it — to tell you the truth."

The Justices were sitting in the Town Hall near at hand, and we at once went over to have me bound apprentice to Joe in the Magisterial presence. I say, we went over, but I was pushed over by Pumblechook, exactly as if I had that moment picked a pocket or fired a rick; indeed, it was the general impression in Court that I had been taken red-handed, for, as Pumblechook shoved me before him through the crowd, I heard some people say, "What's he done?" and others, "He's a young 'un, too, but looks bad, don't he?" One person of mild and benevolent aspect even gave me a tract ornamented with a woodcut of a malevolent young man fitted up with a perfect sausage-shop of fetters, and entitled, TO BE READ IN MY CELL.

The Hall was a queer place, I thought, with higher pews in it than a church — and with people hanging over the pews looking on — and with mighty Justices (one with a powdered head) leaning back in chairs, with folded arms, or taking snuff, or going to sleep, or writing, or reading the newspapers — and with some shining black portraits on the walls, which my unartistic eye regarded as a composition of hardbake[1] and sticking-plaister.[2] Here, in a corner, my indentures were duly signed and attested, and I was "bound"; Mr. Pumblechook holding me all the while as if we had looked in on our way to the scaffold, to have those little preliminaries disposed of.

When we had come out again, and had got rid of the boys who had been put into great spirits by the expectation of seeing me publicly tortured, and who were much disappointed to find that my friends were merely rallying round me, we went back to Pumblechook's. And there my sister became so excited by the twenty-five guineas, that nothing would serve her but we must have a dinner out of that windfall, at the Blue

---

1. *hardbake:* a sweetmeat made of caramelised sugar or treacle with blanched almonds, known in Britain today as almond toffee.
2. *sticking-plaister:* any medicinal plaster with its own adhesive (see explanation in note on p. 46).

Boar, and that Pumblechook must go over in his chaise-cart, and bring the Hubbles and Mr. Wopsle.

It was agreed to be done; and a most melancholy day I passed. For, it inscrutably appeared to stand to reason, in the minds of the whole company, that I was an excrescence on the entertainment. And to make it worse, they all asked me from time to time — in short, whenever they had nothing else to do — why I didn't enjoy myself. And what could I possibly do then, but say I *was* enjoying myself — when I wasn't?

However, they were grown up and had their own way, and they made the most of it. That swindling Pumblechook, exalted into the beneficent contriver of the whole occasion, actually took the top of the table; and, when he addressed them on the subject of my being bound, and fiendishly congratulated them on my being liable to imprisonment if I played at cards, drank strong liquors, kept late hours or bad company, or indulged in other vagaries which the form of my indentures appeared to contemplate as next to inevitable, he placed me standing on a chair beside him, to illustrate his remarks.

My only other remembrances of the great festival are, That they wouldn't let me go to sleep, but whenever they saw me dropping off, woke me up and told me to enjoy myself. That, rather late in the evening Mr. Wopsle gave us Collins's ode,[1] and threw his blood-stain'd sword in thunder down, with such effect, that a waiter came in and said "The Commercials underneath sent up their compliments, and it wasn't the Tumblers' Arms." That, they were all in excellent spirits on the road home, and sang O Lady Fair![2] Mr. Wopsle taking the bass, and asserting with a tremendously strong voice (in reply to the inquisitive bore who leads that piece of music in a most impertinent manner, by wanting to know all about everybody's private affairs) that *he* was the man with his white locks flowing, and that he was upon the whole the weakest pilgrim going.

---

1. *Collins's ode:* see note on p. 79.
2. *O Lady Fair!* Popular ballad for three voices by Irish song-writer Thomas Moore (1779-1852). The lines in question run: "And who is the man, with his white locks flowing? / Oh, Lady Fair! where is he going? / A wandering Pilgrim weak, I falter, / To tell my beads at Agnes' altar."

Finally, I remember that when I got into my little bedroom I was truly wretched, and had a strong conviction on me that I should never like Joe's trade. I had liked it once, but once was not now.

CHAPTER XIV

IT IS a most miserable thing to feel ashamed of home. There may be black ingratitude in the thing, and the punishment may be retributive and well deserved; but, that it is a miserable thing, I can testify.

Home had never been a very pleasant place to me, because of my sister's temper. But, Joe had sanctified it, and I had believed in it. I had believed in the best parlour as a most elegant saloon; I had believed in the front door, as a mysterious portal of the Temple of State whose solemn opening was attended with a sacrifice of roast fowls; I had believed in the kitchen as a chaste though not magnificent apartment; I had believed in the forge as the glowing road to manhood and independence. Within a single year, all this was changed. Now, it was all coarse and common, and I would not have had Miss Havisham and Estella see it on any account.

How much of my ungracious condition of mind may have been my own fault, how much Miss Havisham's, how much my sister's, is now of no moment to me or to any one. The change was made in me; the thing was done. Well or ill done, excusably or inexcusably, it was done.

Once it had seemed to me that when I should at last roll up my shirt-sleeves and go into the forge, Joe's 'prentice, I should be distinguished and happy. Now the reality was in my hold, I only felt that I was dusty with the dust of small-coal, and that I had a weight upon my daily remembrance to which the anvil was a feather. There have been occasions in my later life (I suppose as in most lives) when I have felt for a time as if a thick curtain had fallen on all its interest and romance, to shut me out from anything save dull endurance any more. Never has that curtain dropped so heavy and blank, as when my way in life lay stretched out straight before me through the newly-entered road of apprenticeship to Joe.

I remember that at a later period of my "time," I used to stand about the churchyard on Sunday evenings when night was falling, comparing my own perspective with the windy marsh view, and making out some likeness between them by thinking how flat and low both were, and how on both there came an unknown way and a dark mist and then the sea. I was quite as dejected on the first working-day of my apprenticeship as in that after-time; but I am glad to know that I never breathed a murmur to Joe while my indentures lasted. It is about the only thing I *am* glad to know of myself in that connexion.

For, though it includes what I proceed to add, all the merit of what I proceed to add was Joe's. It was not because I was faithful, but because Joe was faithful, that I never ran away and went for a soldier or a sailor. It was not because I had a strong sense of the virtue of industry, but because Joe had a strong sense of the virtue of industry, that I worked with tolerable zeal against the grain. It is not possible to know how far the influence of any amiable honest-hearted duty-doing man flies out into the world; but it is very possible to know how it has touched one's self in going by, and I know right well, that any good that intermixed itself with my apprenticeship came of plain contented Joe, and not of restlessly aspiring discontented me.

What I wanted, who can say? How can *I* say, when I never knew? What I dreaded was, that in some unlucky hour I, being at my grimiest and commonest, should lift up my eyes and see Estella looking in at one of the wooden windows of the forge. I was haunted by the fear that she would, sooner or later, find me out, with a black face and hands, doing the coarsest part of my work, and would exult over me and despise me. Often after dark, when I was pulling the bellows for Joe, and we were singing Old Clem, and when the thought how we used to sing it at Miss Havisham's would seem to show me Estella's face in the fire, with her pretty hair fluttering in the wind and her eyes scorning me, — often at such a time I would look towards those panels of black night in the wall which the wooden windows then were, and would fancy that I saw her just drawing her face away, and would believe that she had come at last.

After that, when we went in to supper, the place and the meal would have a more homely look than ever, and I would feel more ashamed of home than ever, in my own ungracious breast.

CHAPTER XV

AS I was getting too big for Mr. Wopsle's great-aunt's room, my education under that preposterous female terminated. Not, however, until Biddy had imparted to me everything she knew, from the little catalogue of prices, to a comic song she had once bought for a halfpenny.[1] Although the only coherent part of the latter piece of literature were the opening lines,

> When I went to Lunnon town sirs,
>> Too rul loo rul
>> Too rul loo rul
> Wasn't I done very brown sirs,
>> Too rul loo rul
>> Too rul loo rul

— still, in my desire to be wiser, I got this composition by heart with the utmost gravity; nor do I recollect that I questioned its merit, except that I thought (as I still do) the amount of Too rul somewhat in excess of the poetry. In my hunger for information, I made proposals to Mr. Wopsle to bestow some intellectual crumbs upon me; with which he kindly complied. As it turned out, however, that he only wanted me for a dramatic lay-figure, to be contradicted and embraced and wept over and bullied and clutched and stabbed and knocked about in a variety of ways, I soon declined that course of instruction; though not until Mr. Wopsle in his poetic fury had severely mauled me.

Whatever I acquired, I tried to impart to Joe. This statement sounds so well, that I cannot in my conscience let it pass unexplained. I wanted to make Joe less ignorant and common, that he might be worthier of my society and less open to Estella's reproach.

The old Battery out on the marshes was our place of study, and a broken slate and a short piece of slate pencil were our educational imple-

---

1. *a comic song she had once bought for a halfpenny:* ballads and comic songs, printed on broadsheets and sold by tinkers, were popular from the early days of printing. The theme of the naive country-dweller fleeced by metropolitan rogues is also of long standing, though the song specifically referred to here has not been traced.

ments: to which Joe always added a pipe of tobacco. I never knew Joe to remember anything from one Sunday to another, or to acquire, under my tuition, any piece of information whatever. Yet he would smoke his pipe at the Battery with a far more sagacious air than anywhere else — even with a learned air — as if he considered himself to be advancing immensely. Dear fellow, I hope he did.

It was pleasant and quiet, out there with the sails on the river passing beyond the earthwork, and sometimes, when the tide was low, looking as if they belonged to sunken ships that were still sailing on at the bottom of the water. Whenever I watched the vessels standing out to sea with their white sails spread, I somehow thought of Miss Havisham and Estella; and whenever the light struck aslant, afar off, upon a cloud or sail or green hill-side or water-line, it was just the same. — Miss Havisham and Estella and the strange house and the strange life appeared to have something to do with everything that was picturesque.

One Sunday when Joe, greatly enjoying his pipe, had so plumed himself on being "most awful dull," that I had given him up for the day, I lay on the earthwork for some time with my chin on my hand, descrying traces of Miss Havisham and Estella all over the prospect, in the sky and in the water, until at last I resolved to mention a thought concerning them that had been much in my head.

"Joe," said I; "don't you think I ought to make Miss Havisham a visit?"

"Well, Pip," returned Joe, slowly considering. "What for?"

"What for, Joe? What is any visit made for?"

"There is some wisits, p'r'aps," said Joe, "as for ever remains open to the question, Pip. But in regard of wisiting Miss Havisham. She might think you wanted something — expected something of her."

"Don't you think I might say that I did not, Joe?"

"You might, old chap," said Joe. "And she might credit it. Similarly she mightn't."

Joe felt, as I did, that he had made a point there, and he pulled hard at his pipe to keep himself from weakening it by repetition.

"You see, Pip," Joe pursued, as soon as he was past that danger, "Miss Havisham done the handsome thing by you. When Miss Havisham done the handsome thing by you, she called me back to say to me as that were all."

"Yes, Joe. I heard her."

"ALL," Joe repeated, very emphatically.

"Yes, Joe. I tell you, I heard her."

"Which I meantersay, Pip, it might be that her meaning were — Make a end on it! — As you was! — Me to the North, and you to the South! — Keep in sunders!"

I had thought of that too, and it was very far from comforting to me to find that he had thought of it; for it seemed to render it more probable.

"But, Joe."

"Yes, old chap."

"Here am I, getting on in the first year of my time, and, since the day of my being bound, I have never thanked Miss Havisham, or asked after her, or shown that I remember her."

"That's true, Pip; and unless you was to turn her out a set of shoes all four round — and which I meantersay as even a set of shoes all four round might not act acceptable as a present, in a total wacancy of hoofs —"

"I don't mean that sort of remembrance, Joe; I don't mean a present."

But Joe had got the idea of a present in his head and must harp upon it. "Or even," said he, "if you was helped to knocking her up a new chain for the front door — or say a gross or two of shark-headed screws[1] for general use — or some light fancy article, such as a toasting-fork when she took her muffins — or a gridiron when she took a sprat or such like —"

"I don't mean any present at all, Joe," I interposed.

"Well," said Joe, still harping on it as though I had particularly pressed it, "if I was yourself, Pip, I wouldn't. No, I would *not*. For what's a door-chain when she's got one always up? And shark-headers is open to mis-representations. And if it was a toasting-fork, you'd go into brass and do yourself no credit. And the oncommonest workman can't show himself oncommon in a gridiron — for a gridiron IS a gridiron," said Joe, stead-fastly impressing it upon me, as if he were endeavouring to rouse me from a fixed delusion, "and you may haim at what you like, but a gridiron it will come out, either by your leave or again your leave, and you can't help yourself —"

---

1. *shark-headed screws:* i.e., screws with round rather than flat heads.

"My dear Joe," I cried, in desperation, taking hold of his coat, "don't go on in that way. I never thought of making Miss Havisham any present."

"No, Pip," Joe assented, as if he had been contending for that, all along; "and what I say to you is, you are right, Pip."

"Yes, Joe; but what I wanted to say, was, that as we are rather slack just now, if you would give me a half-holiday to-morrow, I think I would go up-town and make a call on Miss Est — Havisham."

"Which her name," said Joe, gravely, "ain't Estavisham, Pip, unless she have been rechris'ened."

"I know, Joe, I know. It was a slip of mine. What do you think of it, Joe?"

In brief, Joe thought that if I thought well of it, he thought well of it. But, he was particular in stipulating that if I were not received with cordiality, or if I were not encouraged to repeat my visit as a visit which had no ulterior object but was simply one of gratitude for a favour received, then this experimental trip should have no successor. By these conditions I promised to abide.

Now, Joe kept a journeyman at weekly wages whose name was Orlick. He pretended that his christian name was Dolge — a clear impossibility — but he was a fellow of that obstinate disposition that I believe him to have been the prey of no delusion in this particular, but wilfully to have imposed that name upon the village as an affront to its understanding. He was a broad-shouldered loose-limbed swarthy fellow of great strength, never in a hurry, and always slouching. He never even seemed to come to his work on purpose, but would slouch in as if by mere accident; and when he went to the Jolly Bargemen to eat his dinner, or went away at night, he would slouch out, like Cain or the Wandering Jew,[1] as if he had no idea where he was going and no intention of ever coming back. He lodged at a sluice-keeper's out on the marshes, and on working days would come slouching from his hermitage, with his hands in his pockets and his dinner loosely

---

1. *like Cain or the Wandering Jew:* both legendary outcasts in the Judaeo-Christian tradition; the story of Cain murdering his brother Abel and being condemned to be a fugitive is found in Genesis 4:1-16, while that of the Jew who insulted Christ on the road to Calvary, and was condemned to wander the earth until the Second Coming, has no Biblical source but is found in various versions from Mediaeval times.

tied in a bundle round his neck and dangling on his back. On Sundays he mostly lay all day on sluice-gates, or stood against ricks and barns. He always slouched, locomotively, with his eyes on the ground; and, when accosted or otherwise required to raise them, he looked up in a half resentful, half puzzled way, as though the only thought he ever had, was, that it was rather an odd and injurious fact that he should never be thinking.

This morose journeyman had no liking for me. When I was very small and timid, he gave me to understand that the Devil lived in a black corner of the forge, and that he knew the fiend very well: also that it was necessary to make up the fire, once in seven years, with a live boy, and that I might consider myself fuel. When I became Joe's 'prentice, Orlick was perhaps confirmed in some suspicion that I should displace him; howbeit, he liked me still less. Not that he ever said anything, or did anything, openly importing hostility; I only noticed that he always beat his sparks in my direction, and that whenever I sang Old Clem, he came in out of time.

Dolge Orlick was at work and present, next day, when I reminded Joe of my half-holiday. He said nothing at the moment, for he and Joe had just got a piece of hot iron between them, and I was at the bellows; but by-and-by he said, leaning on his hammer:

"Now, master! Sure you're not a going to favour only one of us. If Young Pip has a half-holiday, do as much for Old Orlick." I suppose he was about five-and-twenty, but he usually spoke of himself as an ancient person.

"Why, what'll you do with a half-holiday, if you get it?" said Joe.

"What'll *I* do with it! What'll *he* do with it? I'll do as much with it as *him*," said Orlick.

"As to Pip, he's going up-town," said Joe.

"Well then, as to Old Orlick, *he's* a going up-town," retorted that worthy. "Two can go up-town. Tan't only one wot can go up-town."

"Don't lose your temper," said Joe.

"Shall if I like," growled Orlick. "Some and their up-towning! Now, master! Come. No favouring in this shop. Be a man!"

The master refusing to entertain the subject until the journeyman was in a better temper, Orlick plunged at the furnace, drew out a red-hot bar, made at me with it as if he were going to run it through my body, whisked it round my head, laid it on the anvil, hammered it out — as if it were I, I thought, and the sparks were my spirting blood — and finally said, when he had hammered himself hot and the iron cold, and he again leaned on his hammer:

"Now, master!"

"Are you all right now?" demanded Joe.

"Ah! I am all right," said gruff Old Orlick.

"Then, as in general you stick to your work as well as most men," said Joe, "let it be a half-holiday for all."

My sister had been standing silent in the yard, within hearing — she was a most unscrupulous spy and listener — and she instantly looked in at one of the windows.

"Like you, you fool!" said she to Joe, "giving holidays to great idle hulkers like that. You are a rich man, upon my life, to waste wages in that way. I wish *I* was his master!"

"You'd be everybody's master, if you durst," retorted Orlick, with an ill-favoured grin.

("Let her alone," said Joe.)

"I'd be a match for all noodles and all rogues," returned my sister, beginning to work herself into a mighty rage. "And I couldn't be a match for the noodles, without being a match for your master, who's the dunderheaded king of the noodles. And I couldn't be a match for the rogues, without being a match for you, who are the blackest-looking and the worst rogue between this and France. Now!"

"You're a foul shrew, Mother Gargery," growled the journeyman. "If that makes a judge of rogues, you ought to be a good'un."

("Let her alone, will you?" said Joe.)

"What did you say?" cried my sister, beginning to scream. "What did you say? What did that fellow Orlick say to me, Pip? What did he call me, with my husband standing by? O! O! O!" Each of these exclamations was a shriek; and I must remark of my sister, what is equally true of all the violent women I have ever seen, that passion was no excuse for her, because it is undeniable that instead of lapsing into passion, she consciously and deliberately took extraordinary pains to force herself into it, and became blindly furious by regular stages; "what was the name he gave me before the base man who swore to defend me? O! Hold me! O!"

"Ah-h-h!" growled the journeyman, between his teeth, "I'd hold you, if you was my wife. I'd hold you under the pump, and choke it out of you."

("I tell you, let her alone," said Joe.)

"O! To hear him!" cried my sister, with a clap of her hands and a scream together — which was her next stage. "To hear the names he's giving me! That Orlick! In my own house! Me, a married woman! With my husband standing by! O! O!" Here my sister, after a fit of clappings and screamings, beat her hands upon her bosom and upon her knees, and threw her cap off, and pulled her hair down — which were the last stages on her road to frenzy. Being by this time a perfect Fury and a complete success, she made a dash at the door, which I had fortunately locked.

What could the wretched Joe do now, after his disregarded parenthetical interruptions, but stand up to his journeyman, and ask him what he meant by interfering betwixt himself and Mrs. Joe; and further whether he was man enough to come on? Old Orlick felt that the situation admitted of nothing less than coming on, and was on his defence straightway; so, without so much as pulling off their singed and burnt aprons, they went at one another, like two giants. But, if any man in that neighbourhood could stand up long against Joe, I never saw the man. Orlick, as if he had been of no more account than the pale young gentleman, was very soon among the coal-dust, and in no hurry to come out of it. Then, Joe unlocked the door and picked up my sister, who had dropped insensible at the window (but who had seen the fight first, I think), and who was carried into the house and laid down, and who was recommended to revive, and would do nothing but struggle and clench her hands in Joe's hair. Then, came that singular calm and silence which succeed all uproars; and then, with the vague sensation which I have always connected with such a lull — namely, that it was Sunday, and somebody was dead — I went up-stairs to dress myself.

When I came down again, I found Joe and Orlick sweeping up, without any other traces of discomposure than a slit in one of Orlick's nostrils, which was neither expressive nor ornamental. A pot of beer had appeared from the Jolly Bargemen, and they were sharing it by turns in a peaceable manner. The lull had a sedative and philosophical influence on Joe, who followed me out into the road to say, as a parting observation that might do me good, "On the Rampage, Pip, and off the Rampage, Pip — such is Life!"

With what absurd emotions (for, we think the feelings that are very serious in a man quite comical in a boy) I found myself again going to Miss Havisham's, matters little here. Nor, how I passed and repassed the gate many times before I could make up my mind to ring. Nor, how I debated whether I should go away without ringing; nor, how I should undoubtedly have gone, if my time had been my own, to come back.

Miss Sarah Pocket came to the gate. No Estella.

"How, then? You here again?" said Miss Pocket. "What do you want?"

When I said that I only came to see how Miss Havisham was, Sarah evidently deliberated whether or no she should send me about my business. But, unwilling to hazard the responsibility, she let me in, and presently brought the sharp message that I was to "come up."

Everything was unchanged, and Miss Havisham was alone. "Well?" said she, fixing her eyes upon me. "I hope you want nothing? You'll get nothing."

"No, indeed, Miss Havisham. I only wanted you to know that I am doing very well in my apprenticeship, and am always much obliged to you."

"There, there!" with the old restless fingers. "Come now and then; come on your birthday. — Ay!" she cried suddenly turning herself and her chair towards me, "You are looking round for Estella? Hey?"

I had been looking round — in fact, for Estella — and I stammered that I hoped she was well.

"Abroad," said Miss Havisham; "educating for a lady; far out of reach; prettier than ever; admired by all who see her. Do you feel that you have lost her?"

There was such a malignant enjoyment in her utterance of the last words, and she broke into such a disagreeable laugh, that I was at a loss what to say. She spared me the trouble of considering, by dismissing me. When the gate was closed upon me by Sarah of the walnut-shell countenance, I felt more than ever dissatisfied with my home and with my trade and with everything; and that was all I took by *that* motion.

As I was loitering along the High-street, looking in disconsolately at the shop-windows, and thinking what I would buy if I were a gentleman,

who should come out of the bookshop but Mr. Wopsle. Mr. Wopsle had
in his hand the affecting tragedy of George Barnwell,[1] in which he had
that moment invested sixpence, with the view of heaping every word of
it on the head of Pumblechook, with whom he was going to drink tea.
No sooner did he see me, than he appeared to consider that a special
Providence had put a 'prentice in his way to be read at; and he laid hold
of me, and insisted on my accompanying him to the Pumblechookian
parlour. As I knew it would be miserable at home, and as the nights were
dark and the way was dreary, and almost any companionship on the road
was better than none, I made no great resistance; consequently, we turned
into Pumblechook's just as the street and the shops were lighting up.

As I never assisted at any other representation of George Barnwell, I
don't know how long it may usually take; but I know very well that it
took until half-past nine o'clock that night, and that when Mr. Wopsle
got into Newgate, I thought he never would go to the scaffold, he became so much slower than at any former period of his disgraceful career.
I thought it a little too much that he should complain of being cut short
in his flower after all, as if he had not been running to seed, leaf after leaf,
ever since his course began. This, however, was a mere question of length
and wearisomeness. What stung me, was the identification of the whole
affair with my unoffending self. When Barnwell began to go wrong, I
declare that I felt positively apologetic, Pumblechook's indignant stare so
taxed me with it. Wopsle, too, took pains to present me in the worst light.
At once ferocious and maudlin, I was made to murder my uncle with no
extenuating circumstances whatever; Millwood put me down in argument,
on every occasion; it became sheer monomania in my master's daughter
to care a button for me; and all I can say for my gasping and procrastinat-
ing conduct on the fatal morning, is, that it was worthy of the general
feebleness of my character. Even after I was happily hanged and Wopsle
had closed the book, Pumblechook sat staring at me, and shaking his head,

---

1. *the affecting tragedy of George Barnwell:* the popular low-life tragedy, *The London Merchant, or the History of George Barnwell* by George Lillo (1693-1739), based on a ballad and first performed in 1731. Barnwell is a weak young apprentice who is seduced
by a loose woman, Sarah Millwood, and persuaded by her to rob his master. He
murders his uncle, is taken to Newgate Prison, and hanged.

and saying, "Take warning, boy, take warning!" as if it were a well-known fact that I contemplated murdering a near relation, provided I could only induce one to have the weakness to become my benefactor.

It was a very dark night when it was all over, and when I set out with Mr. Wopsle on the walk home. Beyond town, we found a heavy mist out, and it fell wet and thick. The turnpike lamp was a blur, quite out of the lamp's usual place apparently, and its rays looked solid substance on the fog. We were noticing this, and saying how that the mist rose with a change of wind from a certain quarter of our marshes, when we came upon a man, slouching under the lee of the turnpike house.

"Halloa!" we said, stopping. "Orlick, there?"

"Ah!" he answered, slouching out. "I was standing by, a minute, on the chance of company."

"You are late," I remarked.

Orlick not unnaturally answered, "Well? And *you*'re late."

"We have been," said Mr. Wopsle, exalted with his late performance, "we have been indulging, Mr. Orlick, in an intellectual evening."

Old Orlick growled, as if he had nothing to say about that, and we all went on together. I asked him presently whether he had been spending his half-holiday up and down town?

"Yes," said he, "all of it. I come in behind yourself. I didn't see you, but I must have been pretty close behind you. By-the-by, the guns is going again."

"At the Hulks?" said I.

"Ay! There's some of the birds flown from the cages. The guns have been going since dark, about. You'll hear one presently."

In effect, we had not walked many yards further, when the well-remembered boom came towards us, deadened by the mist, and heavily rolled away along the low grounds by the river, as if it were pursuing and threatening the fugitives.

"A good night for cutting off in," said Orlick. "We'd be puzzled how to bring down a jail-bird on the wing, to-night."

The subject was a suggestive one to me, and I thought about it in silence. Mr. Wopsle, as the ill-requited uncle of the evening's tragedy, fell to meditating aloud in his garden at Camberwell. Orlick, with his hands in his pockets, slouched heavily at my side. It was very dark, very wet, very muddy, and so we splashed along. Now and then, the sound of the signal cannon broke upon us again, and again rolled sulkily along the course of the river. I kept myself to myself and my thoughts. Mr. Wopsle died amiably at Camberwell, and exceedingly game on Bosworth Field, and in the greatest agonies at Glastonbury.[1] Orlick sometimes growled, "Beat it out, beat it out — Old Clem! With a clink for the stout — Old Clem!" I thought he had been drinking, but he was not drunk.

Thus, we came to the village. The way by which we approached it, took us past the Three Jolly Bargemen, which we were surprised to find — it being eleven o'clock — in a state of commotion, with the door wide open, and unwonted lights that had been hastily caught up and put down, scattered about. Mr. Wopsle dropped in to ask what was the matter (surmising that a convict had been taken), but came running out in a great hurry.

"There's something wrong," said he, without stopping, "up at your place, Pip. Run all!"

"What is it?" I asked, keeping up with him. So did Orlick, at my side.

"I can't quite understand. The house seems to have been violently entered when Joe Gargery was out. Supposed by convicts. Somebody has been attacked and hurt."

We were running too fast to admit of more being said, and we made no stop until we got into our kitchen. It was full of people; the whole village was there, or in the yard; and there was a surgeon, and there was Joe, and there were a group of women, all on the floor in the midst of the kitchen. The unemployed bystanders drew back when they saw me, and so I became aware of my sister — lying without sense or movement on the bare boards where she had been knocked down by a tremendous blow on the back of the head, dealt by some unknown hand when her face was turned towards the fire — destined never to be on the Rampage again, while she was wife of Joe.

---

1. *died amiably at Camberwell, exceedingly game on Bosworth Field, and in the greatest agonies at Glastonbury:* three stage deaths: that of George Barnwell's uncle in Lillo's play; that of Shakespeare's Richard III; in the absence of any well-known plays based on deaths at Glastonbury, it is assumed that the third reference is a slip by Dickens who probably intended to cite the death of Shakespeare's King John at Swinstead Abbey.

CHAPTER XVI

WITH MY head full of George Barnwell, I was at first disposed to believe that *I* must have had some hand in the attack upon my sister, or at
all events that as her near relation, popularly known to be under obliga-
tions to her, I was a more legitimate object of suspicion than any one
else. But when, in the clearer light of next morning, I began to recon-
sider the matter and to hear it discussed around me on all sides, I took
another view of the case, which was more reasonable.

Joe had been at the Three Jolly Bargemen, smoking his pipe, from a
quarter after eight o'clock to a quarter before ten. While he was there,
my sister had been seen standing at the kitchen door, and had exchanged
Good Night with a farm-labourer going home. The man could not be
more particular as to the time at which he saw her (he got into dense
confusion when he tried to be), than that it must have been before nine.
When Joe went home at five minutes before ten, he found her struck
down on the floor, and promptly called in assistance. The fire had not
then burnt unusually low, nor was the snuff of the candle very long; the
candle, however, had been blown out.

Nothing had been taken away from any part of the house. Neither,
beyond the blowing out of the candle — which stood on a table between the door and my sister, and was behind her when she stood facing
the fire and was struck — was there any disarrangement of the kitchen,
excepting such as she herself had made, in falling and bleeding. But, there
was one remarkable piece of evidence on the spot. She had been struck
with something blunt and heavy, on the head and spine; after the blows
were dealt, something heavy had been thrown down at her with considerable violence, as she lay on her face. And on the ground beside her,
when Joe picked her up, was a convict's leg-iron which had been filed
asunder.

Now, Joe, examining this iron with a smith's eye, declared it to have
been filed asunder some time ago. The hue and cry going off to the Hulks,
and people coming thence to examine the iron, Joe's opinion was cor-
roborated. They did not undertake to say when it had left the prison-
ships to which it undoubtedly had once belonged; but they claimed to
know for certain that that particular manacle had not been worn by either

of two convicts who had escaped last night. Further, one of those two was already retaken, and had not freed himself of his iron.

Knowing what I knew, I set up an inference of my own here. I believed the iron to be my convict's iron — the iron I had seen and heard him filing at, on the marshes — but my mind did not accuse him of having put it to its latest use. For, I believed one of two other persons to have become possessed of it, and to have turned it to this cruel account. Either Orlick, or the strange man who had shown me the file.

Now, as to Orlick; he had gone to town exactly as he told us when we picked him up at the turnpike, he had been seen about town all the evening, he had been in divers companies in several public-houses, and he had come back with myself and Mr. Wopsle. There was nothing against him, save the quarrel; and my sister had quarrelled with him, and with everybody else about her, ten thousand times. As to the strange man; if he had come back for his two bank-notes there could have been no dispute about them, because my sister was fully prepared to restore them. Besides, there had been no altercation; the assailant had come in so silently and suddenly, that she had been felled before she could look round.

It was horrible to think that I had provided the weapon, however undesignedly, but I could hardly think otherwise. I suffered unspeakable trouble while I considered and reconsidered whether I should at last dissolve that spell of my childhood, and tell Joe all the story. For months afterwards, I every day settled the question finally in the negative, and reopened and reargued it next morning. The contention came, after all, to this; — the secret was such an old one now, had so grown into me and become a part of myself, that I could not tear it away. In addition to the dread that, having led up to so much mischief, it would be now more likely than ever to alienate Joe from me if he believed it, I had the further restraining dread that he would not believe it, but would assort it with the fabulous dogs and veal-cutlets as a monstrous invention. However, I temporised with myself, of course — for, was I not wavering between right and wrong, when the thing is always done? — and resolved to make a full disclosure if I should see any such new occasion as a new chance of helping in the discovery of the assailant.

The Constables, and the Bow-street men from London — for, this happened in the days of the extinct red-waistcoated police* — were about the house for a week or two, and did pretty much what I have heard and read of like authorities doing in other such cases. They took up several obviously wrong people, and they ran their heads very hard against wrong ideas, and persisted in trying to fit the circumstances to the ideas, instead of trying to extract ideas from the circumstances. Also, they stood about the door of the Jolly Bargemen, with knowing and reserved looks that filled the whole neighbourhood with admiration; and they had a mysterious manner of taking their drink, that was almost as good as taking the culprit. But not quite, for they never did it.

Long after these constitutional powers had dispersed, my sister lay very ill in bed. Her sight was disturbed, so that she saw objects multiplied, and grasped at visionary teacups and wine-glasses instead of the realities; her hearing was greatly impaired; her memory also; and her speech was unintelligible. When, at last, she came round so far as to be helped downstairs, it was still necessary to keep my slate always by her, that she might indicate in writing what she could not indicate in speech. As she was (very bad handwriting apart) a more than indifferent speller, and as Joe was a more than indifferent reader, extraordinary complications arose between them, which I was always called in to solve. The administration of mutton instead of medicine, the substitution of Tea for Joe, and the baker for bacon, were among the mildest of my own mistakes.

However, her temper was greatly improved, and she was patient. A tremulous uncertainty of the action of all her limbs soon became a part of her regular state, and afterwards, at intervals of two or three months, she would often put her hands to her head, and would then remain for about a week at a time in some gloomy aberration of mind. We were at a loss to find a suitable attendant for her, until a circumstance happened conveniently to relieve us. Mr. Wopsle's great-aunt conquered a confirmed habit of living into which she had fallen,[1] and Biddy became a part of our establishment.

It may have been about a month after my sister's reappearance in the kitchen, when Biddy came to us with a small speckled box containing

---

1. *conquered a confirmed habit of living into which she had fallen:* echoing the tract *Hydriotaphia, or Urn Burial* (1658) by Sir Thomas Browne (1605-82): "The long habit of living indisposeth us for dying" (Ch. V).

the whole of her worldly effects, and became a blessing to the household. Above all, she was a blessing to Joe, for the dear old fellow was sadly cut up by the constant contemplation of the wreck of his wife, and had been accustomed, while attending on her of an evening, to turn to me every now and then and say, with his blue eyes moistened, "Such a fine figure of a woman as she once were, Pip!" Biddy instantly taking the cleverest charge of her as though she had studied her from infancy, Joe became able in some sort to appreciate the greater quiet of his life, and to get down to the Jolly Bargemen now and then for a change that did him good. It was characteristic of the police people that they had all more or less suspected poor Joe (though he never knew it), and that they had to a man concurred in regarding him as one of the deepest spirits they had ever encountered.

Biddy's first triumph in her new office, was to solve a difficulty that had completely vanquished me. I had tried hard at it, but had made nothing of it. Thus it was:

Again and again and again, my sister had traced upon the slate, a character that looked like a curious T, and then with the utmost eagerness had called our attention to it as something she particularly wanted. I had in vain tried everything producible that began with a T, from tar to toast and tub. At length it had come into my head that the sign looked like a hammer, and on my lustily calling that word in my sister's ear, she had begun to hammer on the table and had expressed a qualified assent. Thereupon, I had brought in all our hammers, one after another, but without avail. Then I bethought me of a crutch, the shape being much the same and I borrowed one in the village, and displayed it to my sister with considerable confidence. But she shook her head to that extent when she was shown it, that we were terrified lest in her weak and shattered state she should dislocate her neck.

When my sister found that Biddy was very quick to understand her, this mysterious sign reappeared on the slate. Biddy looked thoughtfully at it, heard my explanation, looked thoughtfully at my sister, looked thoughtfully at Joe (who was always represented on the slate by his initial letter), and ran into the forge, followed by Joe and me.

"Why, of course!" cried Biddy, with an exultant face. "Don't you see? It's *him*!"

Orlick, without a doubt! She had lost his name, and could only signify him by his hammer. We told him why we wanted him to come into the kitchen, and he slowly laid down his hammer, wiped his brow with his arm, took another wipe at it with his apron, and came slouching out, with a curious loose vagabond bend in the knees that strongly distinguished him.

I confess that I expected to see my sister denounce him, and that I was disappointed by the different result. She manifested the greatest anxiety to be on good terms with him, was evidently much pleased by his being at length produced, and motioned that she would have him given something to drink. She watched his countenance as if she were particularly wishful to be assured that he took kindly to his reception, she showed every possible desire to conciliate him, and there was an air of humble propitiation in all she did, such as I have seen pervade the bearing of a child towards a hard master. After that day, a day rarely passed without her drawing the hammer on her slate, and without Orlick's slouching in and standing doggedly before her, as if he knew no more than I did what to make of it.

CHAPTER XVII

I NOW fell into a regular routine of apprenticeship-life, which was varied beyond the limits of the village and the marshes, by no more remarkable circumstance than the arrival of my birthday and my paying another visit to Miss Havisham. I found Miss Sarah Pocket still on duty at the gate, I found Miss Havisham just as I had left her, and she spoke of Estella in the very same way, if not in the very same words. The interview lasted but a few minutes, and she gave me a guinea when I was going, and told me to come again on my next birthday. I may mention at once that this became an annual custom. I tried to decline taking the guinea on the first occasion, but with no better effect than causing her to ask me very angrily, if I expected more? Then, and after that, I took it.

So unchanging was the dull old house, the yellow light in the darkened room, the faded spectre in the chair by the dressing-table glass, that

I felt as if the stopping of the clocks had stopped Time in that mysterious place, and, while I and everything else outside it grew older, it stood still. Daylight never entered the house as to my thoughts and remembrances of it, any more than as to the actual fact. It bewildered me, and under its influence I continued at heart to hate my trade and to be ashamed of home.

Imperceptibly I became conscious of a change in Biddy, however. Her shoes came up at the heel, her hair grew bright and neat, her hands were always clean. She was not beautiful — she was common, and could not be like Estella — but she was pleasant and wholesome and sweet-tempered. She had not been with us more than a year (I remember her being newly out of mourning at the time it struck me), when I observed to myself one evening that she had curiously thoughtful and attentive eyes; eyes that were very pretty and very good.

It came of my lifting up my own eyes from a task I was poring at — writing some passages from a book, to improve myself in two ways at once by a sort of stratagem — and seeing Biddy observant of what I was about. I laid down my pen, and Biddy stopped in her needlework without laying it down.

"Biddy," said I, "how do you manage it? Either I am very stupid, or you are very clever."

"What is it that I manage? I don't know," returned Biddy, smiling.

She managed our whole domestic life, and wonderfully too; but I did not mean that, though that made what I did mean, more surprising.

"How do you manage, Biddy," said I, "to learn everything that I learn, and always to keep up with me?" I was beginning to be rather vain of my knowledge, for I spent my birthday guineas on it, and set aside the greater part of my pocket-money for similar investment; though I have no doubt, now, that the little I knew was extremely dear at the price.

"I might as well ask you," said Biddy, "how *you* manage?"

"No; because when I come in from the forge of a night, any one can see me turning to at it. But you never turn to at it, Biddy."

"I suppose I must catch it — like a cough," said Biddy, quietly; and went on with her sewing.

Pursuing my idea as I leaned back in my wooden chair and looked at Biddy sewing away with her head on one side, I began to think her rather an extraordinary girl. For, I called to mind now, that she was equally accomplished in the terms of our trade, and the names of our different sorts of work, and our various tools. In short, whatever I knew, Biddy knew. Theoretically, she was already as good a blacksmith as I, or better.

"You are one of those, Biddy," said I, "who make the most of every chance. You never had a chance before you came here, and see how improved you are!"

Biddy looked at me for an instant, and went on with her sewing. "I was your first teacher though; wasn't I?" said she, as she sewed.

"Biddy!" I exclaimed, in amazement. "Why, you are crying!"

"No I am not," said Biddy, looking up and laughing. "What put that in your head?"

What could have put it in my head, but the glistening of a tear as it dropped on her work? I sat silent, recalling what a drudge she had been until Mr. Wopsle's great-aunt successfully overcame that bad habit of living, so highly desirable to be got rid of by some people. I recalled the hopeless circumstances by which she had been surrounded in the miserable little shop and the miserable little noisy evening school, with that miserable old bundle of incompetence always to be dragged and shouldered. I reflected that even in those untoward times there must have been latent in Biddy what was now developing, for, in my first uneasiness and discontent I had turned to her for help, as a matter of course. Biddy sat quietly sewing, shedding no more tears, and while I looked at her and thought about it all, it occurred to me that perhaps I had not been sufficiently grateful to Biddy. I might have been too reserved, and should have patronised her more (though I did not use that precise word in my meditations), with my confidence.

"Yes, Biddy," I observed, when I had done turning it over, "you were my first teacher, and that at a time when we little thought of ever being together like this, in this kitchen."

"Ah, poor thing!" replied Biddy. It was like her self-forgetfulness, to transfer the remark to my sister, and to get up and be busy about her, making her more comfortable; "that's sadly true!"

"Well!" said I, "we must talk together a little more, as we used to do. And I must consult you a little more, as I used to do. Let us have a quiet walk on the marshes next Sunday, Biddy, and a long chat."

My sister was never left alone now; but Joe more than readily under-took the care of her on that Sunday afternoon, and Biddy and I went out together. It was summer-time, and lovely weather. When we had passed the village and the church and the churchyard, and were out on the marshes and began to see the sails of the ships as they sailed on, I began to combine Miss Havisham and Estella with the prospect, in my usual way. When we came to the river-side and sat down on the bank, with the water rippling at our feet, making it all more quiet than it would have been without that sound, I resolved that it was a good time and place for the admission of Biddy into my inner confidence.

"Biddy," said I, after binding her to secrecy, "I want to be a gentleman."

"Oh, I wouldn't, if I was you!" she returned. "I don't think it would answer."

"Biddy," said I, with some severity, "I have particular reasons for wanting to be a gentleman."

"You know best, Pip; but don't you think you are happier as you are?"

"Biddy," I exclaimed, impatiently, "I am not at all happy as I am. I am disgusted with my calling and with my life. I have never taken to either, since I was bound. Don't be absurd."

"Was I absurd?" said Biddy, quietly raising her eyebrows; "I am sorry for that; I didn't mean to be. I only want you to do well, and to be comfortable."

"Well then, understand once for all that I never shall or can be comfortable — or anything but miserable — there, Biddy! — unless I can lead a very different sort of life from the life I lead now."

"That's a pity!" said Biddy, shaking her head with a sorrowful air.

Now, I too had so often thought it a pity, that, in the singular kind of quarrel with myself which I was always carrying on, I was half inclined to shed tears of vexation and distress when Biddy gave utterance to her sentiment and my own. I told her she was right, and I knew it was much to be regretted, but still it was not to be helped.

"If I could have settled down," I said to Biddy, plucking up the short grass within reach, much as I had once upon a time pulled my feelings out of my hair and kicked them into the brewery wall: "if I could have settled down and been but half as fond of the forge as I was when I was little, I know it would have been much better for me. You and I and Joe would have wanted nothing then, and Joe and I would perhaps have gone partners when I was out of my time, and I might even have grown up to keep company with you and we might have sat on this very bank on a fine Sunday, quite different people. I should have been good enough for *you*; shouldn't I, Biddy?"

Biddy sighed as she looked at the ships sailing on, and returned for answer, "Yes; I am not over-particular." It scarcely sounded flattering, but I knew she meant well.

"Instead of that," said I, plucking up more grass and chewing a blade or two, "see how I am going on. Dissatisfied, and uncomfortable, and — what would it signify to me, being coarse and common, if nobody had told me so!"

Biddy turned her face suddenly towards mine, and looked far more attentively at me than she had looked at the sailing ships.

"It was neither a very true nor a very polite thing to say," she remarked, directing her eyes to the ships again. "Who said it?"

I was disconcerted, for I had broken away without quite seeing where I was going. It was not to be shuffled off now, however, and I answered, "The beautiful young lady at Miss Havisham's, and she's more beautiful than anybody ever was, and I admire her dreadfully, and I want to be a gentleman on her account." Having made this lunatic confession, I began to throw my torn-up grass into the river, as if I had some thoughts of following it.

"Do you want to be a gentleman, to spite her or to gain her over?" Biddy quietly asked me, after a pause.

"I don't know," I moodily answered.

"Because, if it is to spite her," Biddy pursued, "I should think — but you know best — that might be better and more independently done by caring nothing for her words. And if it is to gain her over, I should think — but you know best — she was not worth gaining over."

Exactly what I myself had thought, many times. Exactly what was perfectly manifest to me at the moment. But how could I, a poor dazed village lad, avoid that wonderful inconsistency into which the best and wisest of men fall every day?

"It may be all quite true," said I to Biddy, "but I admire her dreadfully."

In short, I turned over on my face when I came to that, and got a good grasp on the hair on each side of my head, and wrenched it well. All the while knowing the madness of my heart to be so very mad and misplaced, that I was quite conscious it would have served my face right, if I had lifted it up by my hair, and knocked it against the pebbles as a punishment for belonging to such an idiot.

Biddy was the wisest of girls, and she tried to reason no more with me. She put her hand, which was a comfortable hand though roughened by work, upon my hands, one after another, and gently took them out of my hair. Then she softly patted my shoulder in a soothing way, while with my face upon my sleeve I cried a little — exactly as I had done in the brewery yard — and felt vaguely convinced that I was very much ill used by somebody, or by everybody; I can't say which.

"I am glad of one thing," said Biddy, "and that is, that you have felt you could give me your confidence, Pip. And I am glad of another thing, and that is, that of course you know you may depend upon my keeping it and always so far deserving it. If your first teacher (dear! such a poor one, and so much in need of being taught herself!) had been your teacher at the present time, she thinks she knows what lesson she would set. But it would be a hard one to learn, and you have got beyond her, and it's of no use now." So, with a quiet sigh for me, Biddy rose from the bank, and said, with a fresh and pleasant change of voice, "Shall we walk a little further, or go home?"

"Biddy," I cried, getting up, putting my arm round her neck, and giving her a kiss, "I shall always tell you everything."

"Till you're a gentleman," said Biddy.

"You know I never shall be, so that's always. Not that I have any occasion to tell you anything, for you know everything I know — as I told you at home the other night."

"Ah!" said Biddy, quite in a whisper, as she looked away at the ships. And then repeated, with her former pleasant change; "shall we walk a little further, or go home?"

I said to Biddy we would walk a little further, and we did so, and the summer afternoon toned down into the summer evening, and it was very beautiful. I began to consider whether I was not more naturally and wholesomely situated, after all, in these circumstances, than playing beggar my neighbour by candlelight in the room with the stopped clocks, and being despised by Estella. I thought it would be very good for me if I could get her out of my head, with all the rest of those remembrances and fancies, and could go to work determined to relish what I had to do, and stick to it, and make the best of it. I asked myself the question whether I did not surely know that if Estella were beside me at that moment instead of Biddy, she would make me miserable? I was obliged to admit that I did know it for a certainty, and I said to myself, "Pip, what a fool you are!"

We talked a good deal as we walked, and all that Biddy said seemed right. Biddy was never insulting, or capricious, or Biddy to-day and somebody else to-morrow; she would have derived only pain, and no pleasure, from giving me pain; she would far rather have wounded her own breast than mine. How could it be, then, that I did not like her much the better of the two?

"Biddy," said I, when we were walking homeward, "I wish you could put me right."

"I wish I could!" said Biddy.

"If I could only get myself to fall in love with you — you don't mind my speaking so openly to such an old acquaintance?"

"Oh dear, not at all!" said Biddy. "Don't mind me."

"If I could only get myself to do it, *that* would be the thing for me."

"But you never will, you see," said Biddy.

It did not appear quite so unlikely to me that evening, as it would have done if we had discussed it a few hours before. I therefore observed I was not quite sure of that. But Biddy said she *was*, and she said it decisively. In my heart I believed her to be right; and yet I took it rather ill, too, that she should be so positive on the point.

When we came near the churchyard, we had to cross an embankment, and get over a stile near a sluice-gate. There started up, from the gate, or from the rushes, or from the ooze (which was quite in his stagnant way), old Orlick.

"Halloa!" he growled, "where are you two going?"

Where should we be going, but home? "Well then," said he, "I'm jiggered if I don't see you home!"

This penalty of being jiggered was a favourite supposititious case of his. He attached no definite meaning to the word that I am aware of, but used it, like his own pretended christian name, to affront mankind, and convey an idea of something savagely damaging. When I was younger, I had had a general belief that if he had jiggered me personally, he would have done it with a sharp and twisted hook.

Biddy was much against his going with us, and said to me in a whisper, "Don't let him come; I don't like him." As I did not like him either, I took the liberty of saying that we thanked him, but we didn't want seeing home. He received that piece of information with a yell of laughter, and dropped back, but came slouching after us at a little distance.

Curious to know whether Biddy suspected him of having had a hand in that murderous attack of which my sister had never been able to give any account, I asked her why she did not like him?

"Oh!" she replied, glancing over her shoulder as he slouched after us, "because I — I am afraid he likes me."

"Did he ever tell you he liked you?" I asked, indignantly.

"No," said Biddy, glancing over her shoulder again, "he never told me so; but he dances at me, whenever he can catch my eye."

However novel and peculiar this testimony of attachment, I did not doubt the accuracy of the interpretation. I was very hot indeed upon Old Orlick's daring to admire her; as hot as if it were an outrage on myself.

"But it makes no difference to you, you know," said Biddy, calmly.

"No, Biddy, it makes no difference to me; only I don't like it; I don't approve of it."

"Nor I neither," said Biddy. "Though *that* makes no difference to you."

"Exactly," said I; "but I must tell you I should have no opinion of you Biddy, if he danced at you with your own consent."

I kept an eye on Orlick after that night, and, whenever circumstances were favourable to his dancing at Biddy, got before him, to obscure that demonstration. He had struck root in Joe's establishment, by reason of my sister's sudden fancy for him, or I should have tried to get him dismissed. He quite understood and reciprocated my good intentions, as I had reason to know thereafter.

And now, because my mind was not confused enough before, I complicated its confusion fifty thousand-fold, by having states and seasons when I was clear that Biddy was immeasurably better than Estella, and that the plain honest working life to which I was born, had nothing in it to be ashamed of, but offered me sufficient means of self-respect and happiness. At those times, I would decide conclusively that my disaffection to dear old Joe and the forge, was gone, and that I was growing up in a fair way to be partners with Joe and to keep company with Biddy — when all in a moment some confounding remembrance of the Havisham days would fall upon me, like a destructive missile, and scatter my wits again. Scattered wits take a long time picking up; and often, before I had got them well together, they would be dispersed in all directions by one stray thought, that perhaps after all Miss Havisham was going to make my fortune when my time was out.

If my time had run out, it would have left me still at the height of my perplexities, I dare say. It never did run out, however, but was brought to a premature end, as I proceed to relate.

CHAPTER XVIII

IT WAS in the fourth year of my apprenticeship to Joe, and it was a Saturday night. There was a group assembled round the fire at the Three Jolly Bargemen, attentive to Mr. Wopsle as he read the newspaper aloud. Of that group I was one.

A highly popular murder had been committed, and Mr. Wopsle was imbrued in blood to the eyebrows. He gloated over every abhorrent adjective in the description, and identified himself with every witness at the Inquest. He faintly moaned, "I am done for," as the victim, and he barbarously bellowed, "I'll serve you out," as the murderer. He gave the medical testimony, in pointed imitation of our local practitioner; and he piped and shook, as the aged turnpike-keeper who had heard blows, to an extent so very paralytic as to suggest a doubt regarding the mental competency of that witness. The coroner, in Mr. Wopsle's hands, became Timon of Athens; the beadle, Coriolanus.[1] He enjoyed himself thoroughly, and

---

1. *The coroner, in Mr. Wopsle's hands, became Timon of Athens; the beadle, Coriolanus:* both heroes of the Shakespeare plays bearing their names; the former is a type of misanthropy and the latter of arrogance.

we all enjoyed ourselves, and were delightfully comfortable. In this cozy state of mind we came to the verdict Wilful Murder.

Then, and not sooner, I became aware of a strange gentleman leaning over the back of the settle opposite me, looking on. There was an expression of contempt on his face, and he bit the side of a great forefinger as he watched the group of faces. "Well!" said the stranger to Mr. Wopsle, when the reading was done, "you have settled it all to your own satisfaction, I have no doubt?"

Everybody started and looked up, as if it were the murderer. He looked at everybody coldly and sarcastically.

"Guilty, of course?" said he. "Out with it. Come!"

"Sir," returned Mr. Wopsle, "without having the honour of your acquaintance, I do say Guilty." Upon this, we all took courage to unite in a confirmatory murmur.

"I know you do," said the stranger; "I knew you would. I told you so. But now I'll ask you a question. Do you know, or do you not know, that the law of England supposes every man to be innocent, until he is proved — proved — to be guilty?"

"Sir," Mr. Wopsle began to reply, "as an Englishman myself, I —"

"Come!" said the stranger, biting his forefinger at him. "Don't evade the question. Either you know it, or you don't know it. Which is it to be?"

He stood with his head on one side and himself on one side, in a bullying interrogative manner, and he threw his forefinger at Mr. Wopsle — as it were to mark him out — before biting it again.

"Now!" said he. "Do you know it, or don't you know it?"

"Certainly I know it," replied Mr. Wopsle.

"Certainly you know it. Then why didn't you say so at first? Now, I'll ask you another question;" taking possession of Mr. Wopsle, as if he had a right to him. "*Do* you know that none of these witnesses have yet been cross-examined?"

Mr. Wopsle was beginning, "I can only say —" when the stranger stopped him.

"What? You won't answer the question, yes or no? Now, I'll try you again." Throwing his finger at him again. "Attend to me. Are you aware, or are you not aware, that none of these witnesses have yet been cross-examined? Come, I only want one word from you. Yes, or no?"

Mr. Wopsle hesitated, and we all began to conceive rather a poor opinion of him.

"Come!" said the stranger, "I'll help you. You don't deserve help, but I'll help you. Look at that paper you hold in your hand. What is it?"

"What is it?" repeated Mr. Wopsle, eyeing it, much at a loss.

"Is it," pursued the stranger in his most sarcastic and suspicious manner, "the printed paper you have just been reading from?"

"Undoubtedly."

"Undoubtedly. Now, turn to that paper, and tell me whether it distinctly states that the prisoner expressly said that his legal advisers instructed him altogether to reserve his defence?"

"I read that just now," Mr. Wopsle pleaded.

"Never mind what you read just now, sir; I don't ask you what you read just now. You may read the Lord's Prayer backwards, if you like — and, perhaps, have done it before to-day. Turn to the paper. No, no, no, my friend; not to the top of the column; you know better than that; to the bottom, to the bottom." (We all began to think Mr. Wopsle full of subterfuge.) "Well? Have you found it?"

"Here it is," said Mr. Wopsle.

"Now, follow that passage with your eye, and tell me whether it distinctly states that the prisoner expressly said that he was instructed by his legal advisers wholly to reserve his defence? Come! Do you make that of it?"

Mr. Wopsle answered, "Those are not the exact words."

"Not the exact words!" repeated the gentleman, bitterly. "Is that the exact substance?"

"Yes," said Mr. Wopsle.

"Yes," repeated the stranger, looking round at the rest of the company with his right hand extended towards the witness, Wopsle. "And now I ask you what you say to the conscience of that man who, with that passage before his eyes, can lay his head upon his pillow after having pronounced a fellow-creature guilty, unheard?"

We all began to suspect that Mr. Wopsle was not the man we had thought him, and that he was beginning to be found out.

"And that same man, remember," pursued the gentleman, throwing his finger at Mr. Wopsle heavily; "that same man might be summoned as a juryman upon this very trial, and, having thus deeply committed himself, might return to the bosom of his family and lay his head upon his pillow, after deliberately swearing that he would well and truly try the issue joined between Our Sovereign Lord the King and the prisoner at the bar, and would a true verdict give according to the evidence, so help him God!"

We were all deeply persuaded that the unfortunate Wopsle had gone too far, and had better stop in his reckless career while there was yet time.

The strange gentleman, with an air of authority not to be disputed, and with a manner expressive of knowing something secret about every one of us that would effectually do for each individual if he chose to disclose it, left the back of the settle, and came into the space between the two settles, in front of the fire, where he remained standing: his left hand in his pocket, and he biting the forefinger of his right.

"From information I have received," said he, looking round at us as we all quailed before him, "I have reason to believe there is a blacksmith among you, by name Joseph — or Joe — Gargery. Which is the man?"

"Here is the man," said Joe.

The strange gentleman beckoned him out of his place, and Joe went.

"You have an apprentice," pursued the stranger, "commonly known as Pip? Is he here?"

"I am here!" I cried.

The stranger did not recognise me, but I recognised him as the gentleman I had met on the stairs, on the occasion of my second visit to Miss Havisham. I had known him the moment I saw him looking over the settle, and now that I stood confronting him with his hand upon my shoulder, I checked off again in detail, his large head, his dark complexion, his deep-set eyes, his bushy black eyebrows, his large watch-chain, his strong black dots of beard and whisker, and even the smell of scented soap on his great hand.

"I wish to have a private conference with you two," said he, when he had surveyed me at his leisure. "It will take a little time. Perhaps we had better go to your place of residence. I prefer not to anticipate my communication here; you will impart as much or as little of it as you please to your friends afterwards; I have nothing to do with that."

Amidst a wondering silence, we three walked out of the Jolly Bargemen, and in a wondering silence walked home. While going along, the strange gentleman occasionally looked at me, and occasionally bit the side of his finger. As we neared home, Joe vaguely acknowledging the occasion as an impressive and ceremonious one, went on ahead to open the front door. Our conference was held in the state parlour, which was feebly lighted by one candle.

It began with the strange gentleman's sitting down at the table, drawing the candle to him, and looking over some entries in his pocket-book. He then put up the pocket-book and set the candle a little aside: after peering round it into the darkness at Joe and me, to ascertain which was which.

"My name," he said, "is Jaggers, and I am a lawyer in London. I am pretty well known. I have unusual business to transact with you, and I commence by explaining that it is not of my originating. If my advice had been asked, I should not have been here. It was not asked, and you see me here. What I have to do as the confidential agent of another, I do. No less, no more."

Finding that he could not see us very well from where he sat, he got up, and threw one leg over the back of a chair and leaned upon it; thus having one foot on the seat of the chair, and one foot on the ground.

"Now, Joseph Gargery, I am the bearer of an offer to relieve you of this young fellow your apprentice. You would not object to cancel his indentures, at his request and for his good? You would not want anything for so doing?"

"Lord forbid that I should want anything for not standing in Pip's way," said Joe, staring.

"Lord forbidding is pious, but not to the purpose," returned Mr. Jaggers. "The question is, Would you want anything? Do you want anything?"

"The answer is," returned Joe, sternly, "No."

I thought Mr. Jaggers glanced at Joe, as if he considered him a fool for his disinterestedness. But I was too much bewildered between breathless curiosity and surprise, to be sure of it.

"Very well," said Mr. Jaggers. "Recollect the admission you have made, and don't try to go from it presently."

"Who's a going to try?" retorted Joe.

"I don't say anybody is. Do you keep a dog?"

"Yes, I do keep a dog."

"Bear in mind then, that Brag is a good dog, but Holdfast is a better.[1] Bear that in mind, will you?" repeated Mr. Jaggers, shutting his eyes and nodding his head at Joe, as if he were forgiving him something. "Now, I return to this young fellow. And the communication I have got to make is, that he has great expectations."

Joe and I gasped, and looked at one another.

"I am instructed to communicate to him," said Mr. Jaggers, throwing his finger at me sideways, "that he will come into a handsome property. Further, that it is the desire of the present possessor of that property, that he be immediately removed from his present sphere of life and from this place, and be brought up as a gentleman — in a word, as a young fellow of great expectations."

My dream was out; my wild fancy was surpassed by sober reality; Miss Havisham was going to make my fortune on a grand scale.

"Now, Mr. Pip," pursued the lawyer, "I address the rest of what I have to say, to you. You are to understand, first, that it is the request of the person from whom I take my instructions, that you always bear the name of Pip. You will have no objection, I dare say, to your great expectations being encumbered with that easy condition. But if you have any objection, this is the time to mention it."

My heart was beating so fast, and there was such a singing in my ears, that I could scarcely stammer I had no objection.

"I should think not! Now you are to understand, secondly, Mr. Pip, that the name of the person who is your liberal benefactor remains a profound secret, until the person chooses to reveal it. I am empowered to mention that it is the intention of the person to reveal it at first hand by word of mouth to yourself. When or where that intention may be carried out, I cannot say; no one can say. It may be years hence. Now, you are distinctly to understand that you are most positively prohibited from making any inquiry on this head, or any allusion or reference, however distant, to any individual whomsoever as *the* individual, in all the communications you may have with me. If you have a suspicion in your own

---

1. *Brag is a good dog, but Holdfast is a better:* a proverbial phrase, meaning that discretion is preferable to boastfulness.

breast, keep that suspicion in your own breast. It is not the least to the purpose what the reasons of this prohibition are; they may be the strongest and gravest reasons, or they may be mere whim. That is not for you to inquire into. The condition is laid down. Your acceptance of it, and your observance of it as binding, is the only remaining condition that I am charged with, by the person from whom I take my instructions, and for whom I am not otherwise responsible. That person is the person from whom you derive your expectations, and the secret is solely held by that person and by me. Again, not a very difficult condition with which to encumber such a rise in fortune; but if you have any objection to it, this is the time to mention it. Speak out."

Once more, I stammered with difficulty that I had no objection.

"I should think not! Now, Mr. Pip, I have done with stipulations." Though he called me Mr. Pip, and began rather to make up to me, he still could not get rid of a certain air of bullying suspicion; and even now he occasionally shut his eyes and threw his finger at me while he spoke, as much as to express that he knew all kinds of things to my disparagement, if he only chose to mention them. "We come next, to mere details of arrangement. You must know that, although I have used the term 'expectations' more than once, you are not endowed with expectations only. There is already lodged in my hands, a sum of money amply sufficient for your suitable education and maintenance. You will please consider me your guardian. Oh!" for I was going to thank him, "I tell you at once, I am paid for my services, or I shouldn't render them. It is considered that you must be better educated, in accordance with your altered position, and that you will be alive to the importance and necessity of at once entering on that advantage."

I said I had always longed for it.

"Never mind what you have always longed for, Mr. Pip," he retorted; "keep to the record. If you long for it now, that's enough. Am I answered that you are ready to be placed at once, under some proper tutor? Is that it?"

I stammered yes, that was it.

"Good. Now, your inclinations are to be consulted. I don't think that wise, mind, but it's my trust. Have you ever heard of any tutor whom you would prefer to another?"

I had never heard of any tutor but Biddy and Mr. Wopsle's great-aunt; so, I replied in the negative.

"There is a certain tutor, of whom I have some knowledge, who I think might suit the purpose," said Mr. Jaggers. "I don't recommend him, observe; because I never recommend anybody. The gentleman I speak of, is one Mr. Matthew Pocket."

Ah! I caught at the name directly. Miss Havisham's relation. The Matthew whom Mr. and Mrs. Camilla had spoken of. The Matthew whose place was to be at Miss Havisham's head, when she lay dead, in her bride's dress on the bride's table.

"You know the name?" said Mr. Jaggers, looking shrewdly at me, and then shutting up his eyes while he waited for my answer.

My answer was, that I had heard of the name.

"Oh!" said he. "You have heard of the name. But the question is, what do you say of it?"

I said, or tried to say, that I was much obliged to him for his recommendation —

"No, my young friend!" he interrupted, shaking his great head very slowly. "Recollect yourself!"

Not recollecting myself, I began again that I was much obliged to him for his recommendation —

"No, my young friend," he interrupted, shaking his head and frowning and smiling both at once; "no, no, no; it's very well done, but it won't do; you are too young to fix me with it. Recommendation is not the word, Mr. Pip. Try another."

Correcting myself, I said that I was much obliged to him for his mention of Mr. Matthew Pocket —

"*That's* more like it!" cried Mr. Jaggers.

— And (I added), I would gladly try that gentleman.

"Good. You had better try him in his own house. The way shall be prepared for you, and you can see his son first, who is in London. When will you come to London?"

I said (glancing at Joe, who stood looking on, motionless), that I supposed I could come directly.

"First," said Mr. Jaggers, "you should have some new clothes to come in, and they should not be working clothes. Say this day week. You'll want some money. Shall I leave you twenty guineas?"

He produced a long purse, with the greatest coolness, and counted them out on the table and pushed them over to me. This was the first time he had taken his leg from the chair. He sat astride of the chair when he had pushed the money over, and sat swinging his purse and eyeing Joe.

"Well, Joseph Gargery? You look dumbfoundered?"

"I *am*!" said Joe, in a very decided manner.

"It was understood that you wanted nothing for yourself, remember?"

"It were understood," said Joe. "And it are understood. And it ever will be similar according."

"But what," said Mr. Jaggers, swinging his purse, "what if it was in my instructions to make you a present, as compensation?"

"As compensation what for?" Joe demanded.

"For the loss of his services."

Joe laid his hand upon my shoulder with the touch of a woman. I have often thought him since, like the steam-hammer, that can crush a man or pat an eggshell, in his combination of strength with gentleness. "Pip is that harty welcome," said Joe, "to go free with his services, to honour and fortun', as no words can tell him. But if you think as Money — can make compensation to me — for the loss of the little child — what come to the forge — and ever the best of friends! —"

O dear good Joe, whom I was so ready to leave and so unthankful to, I see you again, with your muscular blacksmith's arm before your eyes, and your broad chest heaving, and your voice dying away. O dear good faithful tender Joe, I feel the loving tremble of your hand upon my arm, as solemnly this day as if it had been the rustle of an angel's wing!

But I encouraged Joe at the time. I was lost in the mazes of my future fortunes, and could not retrace the by-paths we had trodden together. I begged Joe to be comforted, for (as he said) we had ever been the best of friends, and (as I said) we ever would be so. Joe scooped his eyes with his disengaged wrist, as if he were bent on gouging himself, but said not another word.

Mr. Jaggers had looked on at this, as one who recognised in Joe the village idiot, and in me his keeper. When it was over, he said, weighing in his hand the purse he had ceased to swing:

"Now, Joseph Gargery, I warn you this is your last chance. No half measures with me. If you mean to take a present that I have it in charge to make you, speak out, and you shall have it. If on the contrary you mean to say —" Here, to his great amazement, he was stopped by Joe's suddenly working round him with every demonstration of a fell pugilistic purpose.

"Which I meantersay," cried Joe, "that if you come into my place bull-baiting and badgering me, come out! Which I meantersay as sech if you're a man, come on! Which I meantersay that what I say, I meantersay and stand or fall by!"

I drew Joe away, and he immediately became placable; merely stating to me, in an obliging manner and as a polite expostulatory notice to any one whom it might happen to concern, that he were not a going to be bull-baited and badgered in his own place. Mr. Jaggers had risen when Joe demonstrated, and had backed near the door. Without evincing any inclination to come in again, he there delivered his valedictory remarks. They were these.

"Well, Mr. Pip, I think the sooner you leave here — as you are to be a gentleman — the better. Let it stand for this day week, and you shall receive my printed address in the meantime. You can take a hackney-coach at the stage-coach office in London, and come straight to me. Understand, that I express no opinion, one way or other, on the trust I undertake. I am paid for undertaking it, and I do so. Now, understand that, finally. Understand that!"

He was throwing his finger at both of us, and I think would have gone on, but for his seeming to think Joe dangerous, and going off.

Something came into my head which induced me to run after him, as he was going down to the Jolly Bargemen where he had left a hired carriage.

"I beg your pardon, Mr. Jaggers."

"Halloa!" said he, facing round, "what's the matter?"

"I wish to be quite right, Mr. Jaggers, and to keep to your directions; so I thought I had better ask. Would there be any objection to my taking leave of any one I know, about here, before I go away?"

"No," said he, looking as if he hardly understood me.

"I don't mean in the village only, but up town?"

"No," said he. "No objection."

I thanked him and ran home again, and there I found that Joe had already locked the front door and vacated the state parlour, and was seated by the kitchen fire with a hand on each knee, gazing intently at the burning coals. I too sat down before the fire and gazed at the coals, and nothing was said for a long time.

My sister was in her cushioned chair in her corner, and Biddy sat at her needlework before the fire, and Joe sat next Biddy, and I sat next Joe in the corner opposite my sister. The more I looked into the glowing coals, the more incapable I became of looking at Joe; the longer the silence lasted, the more unable I felt to speak.

At length I got out, "Joe, have you told Biddy?"

"No, Pip," returned Joe, still looking at the fire, and holding his knees tight, as if he had private information that they intended to make off somewhere, "which I left it to yourself, Pip."

"I would rather you told, Joe."

"Pip's a gentleman of fortun' then," said Joe, "and God bless him in it!"

Biddy dropped her work, and looked at me. Joe held his knees and looked at me. I looked at both of them. After a pause, they both heartily congratulated me; but there was a certain touch of sadness in their congratulations, that I rather resented.

I took it upon myself to impress Biddy (and through Biddy, Joe) with the grave obligation I considered my friends under, to know nothing and say nothing about the maker of my fortune. It would all come out in good time, I observed, and in the meanwhile nothing was to be said, save that I had come into great expectations from a mysterious patron. Biddy nodded her head thoughtfully at the fire as she took up her work again, and said she would be very particular; and Joe, still detaining his knees, said, "Ay, ay, I'll be ekervally[1] partickler, Pip;" and then they congratulated me again, and went on to express so much wonder at the notion of my being a gentleman, that I didn't half like it.

Infinite pains were then taken by Biddy to convey to my sister some idea of what had happened. To the best of my belief, those efforts entirely

---

1. *ekervally:* Joe's idiosyncratic version of "equally."

failed. She laughed and nodded her head a great many times, and even repeated after Biddy, the words "Pip" and "Property." But I doubt if they had more meaning in them than an election cry,[1] and I cannot suggest a darker picture of her state of mind.

I never could have believed it without experience, but as Joe and Biddy became more at their cheerful ease again, I became quite gloomy. Dissatisfied with my fortune, of course I could not be; but it is possible that I may have been, without quite knowing it, dissatisfied with myself.

Anyhow, I sat with my elbow on my knee and my face upon my hand, looking into the fire, as those two talked about my going away, and about what they should do without me, and all that. And whenever I caught one of them looking at me, though never so pleasantly (and they often looked at me — particularly Biddy), I felt offended: as if they were expressing some mistrust of me. Though Heaven knows they never did by word or sign.

At those times I would get up and look out at the door; for, our kitchen door opened at once upon the night, and stood open on summer evenings to air the room. The very stars to which I then raised my eyes, I am afraid I took to be but poor and humble stars for glittering on the rustic objects among which I had passed my life.

"Saturday night," said I, when we sat at our supper of bread-and-cheese and beer. "Five more days, and then the day before *the* day! They'll soon go."

"Yes, Pip," observed Joe, whose voice sounded hollow in his beer mug. "They'll soon go."

"Soon, soon go," said Biddy.

"I have been thinking, Joe, that when I go down on Monday, and order my new clothes, I shall tell the tailor that I'll come and put them on there, or that I'll have them sent to Mr. Pumblechook's. It would be very disagreeable to be stared at by all the people here."

"Mr. and Mrs. Hubble might like to see you in your new gen-teel figure too, Pip," said Joe, industriously cutting his bread, with his cheese on it, in the palm of his left hand, and glancing at my untasted supper as

---

1. *an election cry:* a political slogan used at election time.

if he thought of the time when we used to compare slices. "So might Wopsle. And the Jolly Bargemen might take it as a compliment."

"That's just what I don't want, Joe. They would make such a business of it — such a coarse and common business — that I couldn't bear myself."

"Ah, that indeed, Pip!" said Joe. "If you couldn't abear yourself —"

Biddy asked me here, as she sat holding my sister's plate, "Have you thought about when you'll show yourself to Mr. Gargery, and your sister, and me? You will show yourself to us; won't you?"

"Biddy," I returned with some resentment, "you are so exceedingly quick that it's difficult to keep up with you."

("She always were quick," observed Joe.)

"If you had waited another moment, Biddy, you would have heard me say that I shall bring my clothes here in a bundle one evening — most likely on the evening before I go away."

Biddy said no more. Handsomely forgiving her, I soon exchanged an affectionate good night with her and Joe, and went up to bed. When I got into my little room, I sat down and took a long look at it, as a mean little room that I should soon be parted from and raised above, for ever. It was furnished with fresh young remembrances too, and even at the same moment I fell into much the same confused division of mind between it and the better rooms to which I was going, as I had been in so often between the forge and Miss Havisham's, and Biddy and Estella.

The sun had been shining brightly all day on the roof of my attic, and the room was warm. As I put the window open and stood looking out, I saw Joe come slowly forth at the dark door below, and take a turn or two in the air; and then I saw Biddy come, and bring him a pipe and light it for him. He never smoked so late, and it seemed to hint to me that he wanted comforting, for some reason or other.

He presently stood at the door immediately beneath me, smoking his pipe, and Biddy stood there too, quietly talking to him, and I knew that they talked of me, for I heard my name mentioned in an endearing tone by both of them more than once. I would not have listened for more, if I could have heard more: so, I drew away from the window, and sat down in my one chair by the bedside, feeling it very sorrowful and strange that this first night of my bright fortunes should be the loneliest I had ever known.

Looking towards the open window, I saw light wreaths from Joe's pipe floating there, and I fancied it was like a blessing from Joe — not obtruded on me or paraded before me, but pervading the air we shared together. I put my light out, and crept into bed; and it was an uneasy bed now, and I never slept the old sound sleep in it any more.

CHAPTER XIX

MORNING made a considerable difference in my general prospect of Life, and brightened it so much that it scarcely seemed the same. What lay heaviest on my mind, was, the consideration that six days intervened between me and the day of departure; for, I could not divest myself of a misgiving that something might happen to London in the meanwhile, and that, when I got there, it would be either greatly deteriorated or clean gone.

Joe and Biddy were very sympathetic and pleasant when I spoke of our approaching separation; but they only referred to it when I did. After breakfast, Joe brought out my indentures from the press in the best parlour, and we put them in the fire, and I felt that I was free. With all the novelty of my emancipation on me, I went to church with Joe, and thought, perhaps the clergyman wouldn't have read that about the rich man and the kingdom of Heaven,[1] if he had known all.

After our early dinner I strolled out alone, purposing to finish off the marshes at once, and get them done with. As I passed the church, I felt (as I had felt during service in the morning) a sublime compassion for the poor creatures who were destined to go there, Sunday after Sunday, all their lives through, and to lie obscurely at last among the low green mounds. I promised myself that I would do something for them one of these days, and formed a plan in outline for bestowing a dinner of roast beef and plum-pudding, a pint of ale, and a gallon of condescension, upon everybody in the village.

---

1. *that about the rich man and the kingdom of Heaven:* see Matthew 19:16-24.

If I had often thought before, with something allied to shame, of my companionship with the fugitive whom I had once seen limping among those graves, what were my thoughts on this Sunday, when the place recalled the wretch, ragged and shivering, with his felon iron and badge! My comfort was, that it happened a long time ago, and that he had doubtless been transported a long way off, and that he was dead to me, and might be veritably dead into the bargain.

No more low wet grounds, no more dykes and sluices, no more of these grazing cattle — though they seemed, in their dull manner, to wear a more respectful air now, and to face round, in order that they might stare as long as possible at the possessor of such great expectations — farewell, monotonous acquaintances of my childhood, henceforth I was for London and greatness: not for smith's work in general and for you! I made my exultant way to the old Battery, and, lying down there to consider the question whether Miss Havisham intended me for Estella, fell asleep.

When I awoke, I was much surprised to find Joe sitting beside me, smoking his pipe. He greeted me with a cheerful smile on my opening my eyes, and said:

"As being the last time, Pip, I thought I'd foller."

"And Joe, I am very glad you did so."

"Thankee, Pip."

"You may be sure, dear Joe," I went on, after we had shaken hands, "that I shall never forget you."

"No, no, Pip!" said Joe, in a comfortable tone, "I'm sure of that. Ay, ay, old chap! Bless you, it were only necessary to get it well round in a man's mind, to be certain on it. But it took a bit of time to get it well round, the change come so oncommon plump; didn't it?"

Somehow, I was not best pleased with Joe's being so mightily secure of me. I should have liked him to have betrayed emotion, or to have said, "It does you credit, Pip," or something of that sort. Therefore, I made no remark on Joe's first head: merely saying as to his second, that the tidings had indeed come suddenly, but that I had always wanted to be a gentleman, and had often and often speculated on what I would do, if I were one.

"Have you though?" said Joe. "Astonishing!"

"It's a pity now, Joe," said I, "that you did not get on a little more, when we had our lessons here; isn't it?"

"Well, I don't know," returned Joe. "I'm so awful dull. I'm only master of my own trade. It were always a pity as I was so awful dull; but it's no more of a pity now, than it was — this day twelvemonth — don't you see?"

What I had meant was, that when I came into my property and was able to do something for Joe, it would have been much more agreeable if he had been better qualified for a rise in station. He was so perfectly innocent of my meaning, however, that I thought I would mention it to Biddy in preference.

So, when we had walked home and had had tea, I took Biddy into our little garden by the side of the lane, and, after throwing out in a general way for the elevation of her spirits, that I should never forget her, said I had a favour to ask of her.

"And it is, Biddy," said I, "that you will not omit any opportunity of helping Joe on, a little."

"How helping him on?" asked Biddy, with a steady sort of glance.

"Well! Joe is a dear good fellow — in fact, I think he is the dearest fellow that ever lived — but he is rather backward in some things. For instance, Biddy, in his learning and his manners."

Although I was looking at Biddy as I spoke, and although she opened her eyes very wide when I had spoken, she did not look at me.

"Oh, his manners! Won't his manners do, then?" asked Biddy, plucking a black currant leaf.

"My dear Biddy, they do very well here —"

"Oh! they *do* very well here?" interposed Biddy, looking closely at the leaf in her hand.

"Hear me out — but if I were to remove Joe into a higher sphere, as I shall hope to remove him when I fully come into my property, they would hardly do him justice."

"And don't you think he knows that?" asked Biddy.

It was such a very provoking question (for it had never in the most distant manner occurred to me), that I said, snappishly, "Biddy, what do you mean?"

Biddy having rubbed the leaf to pieces between her hands — and the smell of a black currant bush has ever since recalled to me that evening in the little garden by the side of the lane — said, "Have you never considered that he may be proud?"

"Proud?" I repeated, with disdainful emphasis.

"Oh! there are many kinds of pride," said Biddy, looking full at me and shaking her head; "pride is not all of one kind —"

"Well? What are you stopping for?" said I.

"Not all of one kind," resumed Biddy. "He may be too proud to let any one take him out of a place that he is competent to fill, and fills well and with respect. To tell you the truth, I think he is: though it sounds bold in me to say so, for you must know him far better than I do."

"Now, Biddy," said I, "I am very sorry to see this in you. I did not expect to see this in you. You are envious, Biddy, and grudging. You are dissatisfied on account of my rise in fortune, and you can't help showing it."

"If you have the heart to think so," returned Biddy, "say so. Say so over and over again, if you have the heart to think so."

"If you have the heart to be so, you mean, Biddy," said I, in a virtuous and superior tone; "don't put it off upon me. I am very sorry to see it, and it's a — it's a bad side of human nature. I did intend to ask you to use any little opportunities you might have after I was gone, of improving dear Joe. But after this, I ask you nothing. I am extremely sorry to see this in you, Biddy," I repeated. "It's a — it's a bad side of human nature."

"Whether you scold me or approve of me," returned poor Biddy, "you may equally depend upon my trying to do all that lies in my power, here, at all times. And whatever opinion you take away of me, shall make no difference in my remembrance of you. Yet a gentleman should not be unjust neither," said Biddy, turning away her head.

I again warmly repeated that it was a bad side of human nature (in which sentiment, waiving its application, I have since seen reason to think I was right), and I walked down the little path away from Biddy, and Biddy went into the house, and I went out at the garden gate and took a dejected stroll until supper-time; again feeling it very sorrowful and strange that this, the second night of my bright fortunes, should be as lonely and unsatisfactory as the first.

But, morning once more brightened my view, and I extended my clemency to Biddy, and we dropped the subject. Putting on the best clothes I had, I went into town as early as I could hope to find the shops open, and presented myself before Mr. Trabb, the tailor: who was having his breakfast in the parlour behind his shop, and who did not think it worth his while to come out to me, but called me in to him.

"Well!" said Mr. Trabb, in a hail-fellow-well-met kind of way. "How are you, and what can I do for you?"

Mr. Trabb had sliced his hot roll into three feather beds, and was slipping butter in between the blankets, and covering it up. He was a prosperous old bachelor, and his open window looked into a prosperous little garden and orchard, and there was a prosperous iron safe let into the wall at the side of his fireplace, and I did not doubt that heaps of his prosperity were put away in it in bags.

"Mr. Trabb," said I, "it's an unpleasant thing to have to mention, because it looks like boasting; but I have come into a handsome property."

A change passed over Mr. Trabb. He forgot the butter in bed, got up from the bedside, and wiped his fingers on the tablecloth, exclaiming, "Lord bless my soul!"

"I am going up to my guardian in London," said I, casually drawing some guineas out of my pocket and looking at them; "and I want a fashionable suit of clothes to go in. I wish to pay for them," I added — otherwise I thought he might only pretend to make them — "with ready money."

"My dear sir," said Mr. Trabb, as he respectfully bent his body, opened his arms, and took the liberty of touching me on the outside of each elbow, "don't hurt me by mentioning that. May I venture to congratulate you? Would you do me the favour of stepping into the shop?"

Mr. Trabb's boy was the most audacious boy in all that countryside. When I had entered he was sweeping the shop, and he had sweetened his labours by sweeping over me. He was still sweeping when I came out into the shop with Mr. Trabb, and he knocked the broom against all possible corners and obstacles, to express (as I understood it) equality with any blacksmith, alive or dead.

"Hold that noise," said Mr. Trabb, with the greatest sternness, "or I'll knock your head off! Do me the favour to be seated, sir. Now, this," said Mr. Trabb, taking down a roll of cloth, and tiding it out in a flowing manner over the counter, preparatory to getting his hand under it to show the gloss, "is a very sweet article. I can recommend it for your purpose, sir, because it really is extra super. But you shall see some others. Give me

Number Four, you!" (To the boy, and with a dreadfully severe stare: fore-seeing the danger of that miscreant's brushing me with it, or making some other sign of familiarity.)

Mr. Trabb never removed his stern eye from the boy until he had deposited number four on the counter and was at a safe distance again. Then, he commanded him to bring number five, and number eight. "And let me have none of your tricks here," said Mr. Trabb, "or you shall repent it, you young scoundrel, the longest day you have to live."

Mr. Trabb then bent over number four, and in a sort of deferential confidence recommended it to me as a light article for summer wear, an article much in vogue among the nobility and gentry, an article that it would ever be an honour to him to reflect upon a distinguished fellow-townsman's (if he might claim me for a fellow-townsman) having worn. "Are you bringing numbers five and eight, you vagabond," said Mr. Trabb to the boy after that, "or shall I kick you out of the shop and bring them myself?"

I selected the materials for a suit, with the assistance of Mr. Trabb's judgment, and re-entered the parlour to be measured. For, although Mr. Trabb had my measure already, and had previously been quite contented with it, he said apologetically that it "wouldn't do under existing circumstances, sir — wouldn't do at all." So, Mr. Trabb measured and calculated me, in the parlour, as if I were an estate and he the finest species of surveyor, and gave himself such a world of trouble that I felt that no suit of clothes could possibly remunerate him for his pains. When he had at last done and had appointed to send the articles to Mr. Pumblechook's on the Thursday evening, he said, with his hand upon the parlour lock, "I know, sir, that London gentlemen cannot be expected to patronise local work, as a rule; but if you would give me a turn now and then in the quality of a townsman, I should greatly esteem it. Good morning, sir, much obliged. — Door!"

The last word was flung at the boy, who had not the least notion what it meant. But I saw him collapse as his master rubbed me out with his hands, and my first decided experience of the stupendous power of money, was, that it had morally laid upon his back, Trabb's boy.

After this memorable event, I went to the hatter's, and the bootmaker's, and the hosier's, and felt rather like Mother Hubbard's dog whose outfit required the services of so many trades.[1] I also went to the coach-office and took my place for seven o'clock on Saturday morning. It was not necessary to explain everywhere that I had come into a handsome property; but whenever I said anything to that effect, it followed that the officiating tradesman ceased to have his attention diverted through the window by the Highstreet, and concentrated his mind upon me. When I had ordered everything I wanted, I directed my steps towards Pumblechook's, and, as I approached that gentleman's place of business, I saw him standing at his door.

He was waiting for me with great impatience. He had been out early with the chaise-cart, and had called at the forge and heard the news. He had prepared a collation for me in the Barnwell parlour, and he too ordered his shopman to "come out of the gangway" as my sacred person passed.

"My dear friend," said Mr. Pumblechook, taking me by both hands, when he and I and the collation were alone, "I give you joy of your good fortune. Well deserved, well deserved!"

This was coming to the point, and I thought it a sensible way of expressing himself.

"To think," said Mr. Pumblechook, after snorting admiration at me for some moments, "that I should have been the humble instrument of leading up to this, is a proud reward."

I begged Mr. Pumblechook to remember that nothing was to be ever said or hinted, on that point.

"My dear young friend," said Mr. Pumblechook, "if you will allow me to call you so —"

I murmured "Certainly," and Mr. Pumblechook took me by both hands again, and communicated a movement to his waistcoat, which had an emotional appearance, though it was rather low down, "My dear young friend, rely upon my doing my little all in your absence, by keeping the fact before the mind of Joseph. — Joseph!" said Mr. Pumblechook, in the way of a compassionate adjuration. "Joseph!! Joseph!!!" Thereupon he shook his head and tapped it, expressing his sense of deficiency in Joseph.

---

1. *Mother Hubbard's dog whose outfit required the services of so many trades:* in the nursery rhyme published at the beginning of the nineteenth century, Old Mother Hubbard goes in turn to the tailor's, hatter's, barber's, cobbler's, seamstress's, and hosier's to fit out her dog.

"But my dear young friend," said Mr. Pumblechook, "you must be hungry, you must be exhausted. Be seated. Here is a chicken had round from the Boar, here is a tongue had round from the Boar, here's one or two little things had round from the Boar, that I hope you may not despise. But do I," said Mr. Pumblechook, getting up again the moment after he had sat down, "see afore me, him as I ever sported with in his times of happy infancy? And may I — *may* I —?"

This May I, meant might he shake hands? I consented, and he was fervent, and then sat down again.

"Here is wine," said Mr. Pumblechook. "Let us drink, Thanks to Fortune, and may she ever pick out her favourites with equal judgment! And yet I cannot," said Mr. Pumblechook, getting up again, "see afore me One — and likeways drink to One — without again expressing — May I — *may* I?"

I said he might, and he shook hands with me again, and emptied his glass and turned it upside down. I did the same; and if I had turned myself upside down before drinking, the wine could not have gone more direct to my head.

Mr. Pumblechook helped me to the liver wing,[1] and to the best slice of tongue (none of those out-of-the-way No Thoroughfares of Pork now),[2] and took, comparatively speaking, no care of himself at all. "Ah! poultry, poultry! You little thought," said Mr. Pumblechook, apostrophising the fowl in the dish, "when you was a young fledgling, what was in store for you. You little thought you was to be refreshment beneath this humble roof for One as — Call it a weakness, if you will," said Mr. Pumblechook, getting up again, "but may I? *may* I —?"

It began to be unnecessary to repeat the form of saying he might, so he did it at once. How he ever did it so often without wounding himself with my knife, I don't know.

---

1. *liver wing:* when dressed for cooking, a chicken, etc. traditionally has the liver tucked under its right wing.
2. *none of those out-of-the-way No Thoroughfares of Pork now:* referring back to "those obscure corners of pork" with which Pip was regaled at Christmas in his childhood, as described on p. 62.

"And your sister," he resumed, after a little steady eating, "which had the honour of bringing you up by hand! It's a sad picter, to reflect that she's no longer equal to fully understanding the honour. May —"

I saw he was about to come at me again, and I stopped him.

"We'll drink her health," said I.

"Ah!" cried Mr. Pumblechook, leaning back in his chair, quite flaccid with admiration, "that's the way you know 'em, sir!" (I don't know who Sir was, but he certainly was not I, and there was no third person present); "that's the way you know the noble minded, sir! Ever forgiving and ever affable. It might," said the servile Pumblechook, putting down his untasted glass in a hurry and getting up again, "to a common person, have the appearance of repeating — but may I —?"

When he had done it, he resumed his seat and drank to my sister. "Let us never be blind," said Mr. Pumblechook, "to her faults of temper, but it is to be hoped she meant well."

At about this time, I began to observe that he was getting flushed in the face; as to myself, I felt all face, steeped in wine and smarting.

I mentioned to Mr. Pumblechook that I wished to have my new clothes sent to his house, and he was ecstatic on my so distinguishing him. I mentioned my reason for desiring to avoid observation in the village, and he lauded it to the skies. There was nobody but himself, he intimated, worthy of my confidence, and — in short, might he? Then he asked me tenderly if I remembered our boyish games at sums, and how we had gone together to have me bound apprentice, and, in effect, how he had ever been my favourite fancy and my chosen friend? If I had taken ten times as many glasses of wine as I had, I should have known that he never had stood in that relation towards me, and should in my heart of hearts have repudiated the idea. Yet for all that, I remember feeling convinced that I had been much mistaken in him, and that he was a sensible practical good-hearted prime fellow.

By degrees he fell to reposing such great confidence in me, as to ask my advice in reference to his own affairs. He mentioned that there was an opportunity for a great amalgamation and monopoly of the corn and seed trade on those premises, if enlarged, such as had never occurred before in that, or any other neighbourhood. What alone was wanting to the realisation of a vast fortune, he considered to be More Capital. Those were the two little words, more capital. Now it appeared to him (Pumblechook) that if that capital were got into the business, through a sleeping partner, sir — which sleeping partner would have nothing to do but walk in, by self or deputy, whenever he pleased, and examine the books — and walk in twice a year and take his profits away in his pocket, to the tune of fifty per cent — it appeared to him that that might be an opening for a young gentleman of spirit combined with property, which would be worthy of his attention. But what did I think? He had great confidence in my opinion, and what did I think? I gave it as my opinion. "Wait a bit!" The united vastness and distinctness of this view so struck him, that he no longer asked if he might shake hands with me, but said he really must — and did.

We drank all the wine, and Mr. Pumblechook pledged himself over and over again to keep Joseph up to the mark (I don't know what mark), and to render me efficient and constant service (I don't know what service). He also made known to me for the first time in my life, and certainly after having kept his secret wonderfully well, that he had always said of me, "That boy is no common boy, and mark me, his fortun' will be no common fortun'." He said with a tearful smile that it was a singular thing to think of now, and I said so too. Finally I went out into the air, with a dim perception that there was something unwonted in the conduct of the sunshine, and found that I had slumberously got to the turnpike without having taken any account of the road.

There, I was roused by Mr. Pumblechook's hailing me. He was a long way down the sunny street, and was making expressive gestures for me to stop. I stopped, and he came up breathless.

"No, my dear friend," said he, when he had recovered wind for speech. "Not if I can help it. This occasion shall not entirely pass without that affability on your part. — May I, as an old friend and well-wisher? *May* I?"

We shook hands for the hundredth time at least, and he ordered a young carter out of my way with the greatest indignation. Then, he blessed me and stood waving his hand to me until I had passed the crook in the road; and then I turned into a field and had a long nap under a hedge before I pursued my way home.

I had scant luggage to take with me to London, for little of the little I possessed was adapted to my new station. But, I began packing that same afternoon, and wildly packed up things that I knew I should want next morning, in a fiction that there was not a moment to be lost.

So, Tuesday, Wednesday, and Thursday, passed; and on Friday morning I went to Mr. Pumblechook's, to put on my new clothes and pay my visit to Miss Havisham. Mr. Pumblechook's own room was given up to me to dress in, and was decorated with clean towels expressly for the event. My clothes were rather a disappointment, of course. Probably every new and eagerly expected garment ever put on since clothes came in, fell a trifle short of the wearer's expectation. But after I had had my new suit on, some half an hour, and had gone through an immensity of posturing with Mr. Pumblechook's very limited dressing-glass, in the futile endeavour to see my legs, it seemed to fit me better. It being market morning at a neighbouring town some ten miles off, Mr. Pumblechook was not at home. I had not told him exactly when I meant to leave, and was not likely to shake hands with him again before departing. This was all as it should be, and I went out in my new array: fearfully ashamed of having to pass the shopman, and suspicious after all that I was at a personal disadvantage, something like Joe's in his Sunday suit.

I went circuitously to Miss Havisham's by all the back ways, and rang at the bell constrainedly, on account of the stiff long fingers of my gloves. Sarah Pocket came to the gate, and positively reeled back when she saw me so changed; her walnut-shell countenance likewise, turned from brown to green and yellow.

"You?" said she. "You, good gracious! What do you want?"

"I am going to London, Miss Pocket," said I, "and want to say good-by to Miss Havisham."

I was not expected, for she left me locked in the yard, while she went to ask if I were to be admitted. After a very short delay, she returned and took me up, staring at me all the way.

Miss Havisham was taking exercise in the room with the long spread table, leaning on her crutch stick. The room was lighted as of yore, and at the sound of our entrance, she stopped and turned. She was then just abreast of the rotted bride-cake.

"Don't go, Sarah," she said. "Well, Pip?"

"I start for London, Miss Havisham, to-morrow," I was exceedingly careful what I said, "and I thought you would kindly not mind my taking leave of you."

"This is a gay figure, Pip," said she, making her crutch stick play round me, as if she, the fairy godmother who had changed me, were bestowing the finishing gift.

"I have come into such good fortune since I saw you last, Miss Havisham," I murmured. "And I am so grateful for it, Miss Havisham!"

"Ay, ay!" said she, looking at the discomfited and envious Sarah, with delight. "I have seen Mr. Jaggers. I have heard about it, Pip. So you go tomorrow?"

"Yes, Miss Havisham."

"And you are adopted by a rich person?"

"Yes, Miss Havisham."

"Not named?"

"No, Miss Havisham."

"And Mr. Jaggers is made your guardian?"

"Yes, Miss Havisham."

She quite gloated on these questions and answers, so keen was her enjoyment of Sarah Pocket's jealous dismay. "Well!" she went on; "you have a promising career before you. Be good — deserve it — and abide by Mr. Jaggers's instructions." She looked at me, and looked at Sarah, and Sarah's countenance wrung out of her watchful face a cruel smile. "Good-by, Pip! — you will always keep the name of Pip, you know."

"Yes, Miss Havisham."

"Good-by, Pip!"

She stretched out her hand, and I went down on my knee and put it to my lips. I had not considered how I should take leave of her; it came naturally to me at the moment, to do this. She looked at Sarah Pocket with triumph in her weird eyes, and so I left my fairy godmother, with both her hands on her crutch stick, standing in the midst of the dimly lighted room beside the rotten bride-cake that was hidden in cobwebs.

Sarah Pocket conducted me down, as if I were a ghost who must be seen out. She could not get over my appearance, and was in the last degree confounded. I said "Good-by, Miss Pocket;" but she merely stared, and did not seem collected enough to know that I had spoken. Clear of the house, I made the best of my way back to Pumblechook's, took off my new clothes, made them into a bundle, and went back home in my older dress, carrying it — to speak the truth — much more at my ease too, though I had the bundle to carry.

And now, those six days which were to have run out so slowly, had run out fast and were gone, and to-morrow looked me in the face more steadily than I could look at it. As the six evenings had dwindled away, to five, to four, to three, to two, I had become more and more appreciative of the society of Joe and Biddy. On this last evening, I dressed myself out in my new clothes, for their delight, and sat in my splendour until bed-time. We had a hot supper on the occasion, graced by the inevitable roast fowl, and we had some flip[1] to finish with. We were all very low, and none the higher for pretending to be in spirits.

I was to leave our village at five in the morning, carrying my little hand-portmanteau, and I had told Joe that I wished to walk away all alone. I am afraid — sore afraid — that this purpose originated in my sense of the contrast there would be between me and Joe, if we went to the coach together. I had pretended with myself that there was nothing of this taint in the arrangement; but when I went up to my little room on this last night, I felt compelled to admit that it might be so, and had an impulse upon me to go down again and entreat Joe to walk with me in the morning. I did not.

All night there were coaches in my broken sleep, going to wrong places instead of to London, and having in the traces, now dogs, now cats, now pigs, now men — never horses. Fantastic failures of journeys occupied me until the day dawned and the birds were singing. Then, I got up and partly dressed, and sat at the window to take a last look out, and in taking it fell asleep.

Biddy was astir so early to get my breakfast, that, although I did not sleep at the window an hour, I smelt the smoke of the kitchen fire when I started up with a terrible idea that it must be late in the afternoon. But long after that, and long after I had heard the clinking of the teacups and was quite ready, I wanted the resolution to go down-stairs. After all, I remained up there, repeatedly unlocking and unstrapping my small port-

---

1. *flip:* a mixture of beer and spirits sweetened with sugar and heated with a hot poker.

manteau and locking and strapping it up again, until Biddy called to me that I was late.

It was a hurried breakfast with no taste in it. I got up from the meal, saying with a sort of briskness, as if it had only just occurred to me, "Well! I suppose I must be off!" and then I kissed my sister who was laughing and nodding and shaking in her usual chair, and kissed Biddy, and threw my arms around Joe's neck. Then I took up my little portmanteau and walked out. The last I saw of them was, when I presently heard a scuffle behind me, and looking back, saw Joe throwing an old shoe after me and Biddy throwing another old shoe.[1] I stopped then, to wave my hat, and dear old Joe waved his strong right arm above his head, crying huskily "Hooroar!" and Biddy put her apron to her face.

I walked away at a good pace, thinking it was easier to go than I had supposed it would be, and reflecting that it would never have done to have had an old shoe thrown after the coach, in sight of all the High-street. I whistled and made nothing of going. But the village was very peaceful and quiet, and the light mists were solemnly rising, as if to show me the world, and I had been so innocent and little there, and all beyond was so unknown and great, that in a moment with a strong heave and sob I broke into tears. It was by the finger-post at the end of the village, and I laid my hand upon it, and said, "Good-by O my dear, dear friend!"

Heaven knows we need never be ashamed of our tears, for they are rain upon the blinding dust of earth, overlaying our hard hearts. I was better after I had cried, than before — more sorry, more aware of my own ingratitude, more gentle. If I had cried before, I should have had Joe with me then.

So subdued I was by those tears, and by their breaking out again in the course of the quiet walk, that when I was on the coach, and it was clear of the town, I deliberated with an aching heart whether I would not get down when we changed horses and walk back, and have another evening at home, and a better parting. We changed, and I had not made up my mind, and still reflected for my comfort that it would be quite

---

1. *Joe throwing an old shoe after me and Biddy throwing another old shoe:* casting an old shoe after someone, at a wedding for example, was a traditional means of invoking good fortune.

practicable to get down and walk back, when we changed again. And while I was occupied with these deliberations, I would fancy an exact resemblance to Joe in some man coming along the road towards us, and my heart would beat high. — As if he could possibly be there!

We changed again, and yet again, and it was now too late and too far to go back, and I went on. And the mists had all solemnly risen now, and the world lay spread before me.

THIS IS THE END OF THE FIRST STAGE OF
PIP'S EXPECTATIONS

VOLUME II

⟨decorative ornament⟩

CHAPTER I

THE JOURNEY from our town to the metropolis, was a journey of about five hours. It was a little past mid-day when the four-horse stage-coach by which I was a passenger, got into the ravel of traffic frayed out about the Cross-Keys, Wood-street, Cheapside, London.*

We Britons had at that time particularly settled that it was treasonable to doubt our having and our being the best of everything:[1] otherwise, while I was scared by the immensity of London, I think I might have had some faint doubts whether it was not rather ugly, crooked, narrow, and dirty.

Mr. Jaggers had duly sent me his address; it was, Little Britain, and he had written after it on his card, "just out of Smithfield, and close by the coach-office."[2] Nevertheless, a hackney-coachman, who seemed to have as many capes to his greasy great-coat as he was years old, packed me up in his coach and hemmed me in with a folding and jingling barrier of steps, as if he were going to take me fifty miles. His getting on his box, which I remember to have been decorated with an old weather-stained pea-green hammercloth[3] motheaten into rags, was quite a work of time.

---

1. *We Britons had at that time particularly settled that it was treasonable to doubt our having and our being the best of everything:* presumably referring to the period of patriotic fervour following the victory over Napoleon at Waterloo in 1815.
2. *his address; it was, Little Britain, and he had written after it on his card, "just out of Smithfield, and close by the coach-office."* Smithfield was the square where the open cattle market was held until the mid century. See Map B and Illustration A.
3. *hammercloth:* cloth covering the driver's box (seat) in a coach.

It was a wonderful equipage, with six great coronets outside, and ragged things behind for I don't know how many footmen to hold on by, and a harrow[1] below them, to prevent amateur footmen from yielding to the temptation.

I had scarcely had time to enjoy the coach and to think how like a straw-yard it was, and yet how like a rag-shop, and to wonder why the horses' nose-bags were kept inside, when I observed the coachman beginning to get down, as if we were going to stop presently. And stop we presently did, in a gloomy street, at certain offices with an open door, whereon was painted MR. JAGGERS.

"How much?" I asked the coachman.

The coachman answered, "A shilling — unless you wish to make it more."

I naturally said I had no wish to make it more.

"Then it must be a shilling," observed the coachman. "I don't want to get into trouble. *I* know *him!*' He darkly closed an eye at Mr. Jaggers's name, and shook his head.

When he had got his shilling, and had in course of time completed the ascent to his box, and had got away (which appeared to relieve his mind), I went into the front office with my little portmanteau in my hand and asked, Was Mr. Jaggers at home?

"He is not," returned the clerk. "He is in Court at present. Am I addressing Mr. Pip?"

I signified that he was addressing Mr. Pip.

"Mr. Jaggers left word would you wait in his room. He couldn't say how long he might be, having a case on. But it stands to reason his time being valuable, that he won't be longer than he can help."

With those words, the clerk opened a door, and ushered me into an inner chamber at the back. Here, we found a gentleman with one eye, in a velveteen suit and knee-breeches, who wiped his nose with his sleeve on being interrupted in the perusal of the newspaper.

"Go and wait outside, Mike," said the clerk.

---

1. *harrow:* literally, an agricultural implement, comprising a heavy frame set with iron teeth, which is dragged over ploughed land to break up clods of earth etc.

I began to say that I hoped I was not interrupting — when the clerk shoved this gentleman out with as little ceremony as I ever saw used, and tossing his fur cap out after him, left me alone.

Mr. Jaggers's room was lighted by a skylight only, and was a most dismal place; the skylight, eccentrically patched like a broken head, and the distorted adjoining houses looking as if they had twisted themselves to peep down at me through it. There were not so many papers about, as I should have expected to see; and there were some odd objects about, that I should not have expected to see — such as an old rusty pistol, a sword in a scabbard, several strange-looking boxes and packages, and two dreadful casts on a shelf, of faces peculiarly swollen, and twitchy about the nose. Mr. Jaggers's own high-backed chair was of deadly black horse-hair, with rows of brass nails round it, like a coffin; and I fancied I could see how he leaned back in it, and bit his forefinger at the clients. The room was but small, and the clients seemed to have had a habit of backing up against the wall: the wall, especially opposite to Mr. Jaggers's chair, being greasy with shoulders. I recalled, too, that the one-eyed gentleman had shuffled forth against the wall when I was the innocent cause of his being turned out.

I sat down in the cliental chair placed over against Mr. Jaggers's chair, and became fascinated by the dismal atmosphere of the place. I called to mind that the clerk had the same air of knowing something to every-body else's disadvantage, as his master had. I wondered how many other clerks there were up-stairs, and whether they all claimed to have the same detrimental mastery of their fellow-creatures. I wondered what was the history of all the odd litter about the room, and how it came there. I wondered whether the two swollen faces were of Mr. Jaggers's family, and, if he were so unfortunate as to have had a pair of such ill-looking rela-tions, why he stuck them on that dusty perch for the blacks[1] and flies to settle on, instead of giving them a place at home. Of course I had no experience of a London summer day, and my spirits may have been op-pressed by the hot exhausted air, and by the dust and grit that lay thick on everything. But I sat wondering and waiting in Mr. Jaggers's close room,

---

1. *blacks:* particles of coal soot.

until I really could not bear the two casts on the shelf above Mr. Jaggers's chair, and got up and went out.

When I told the clerk that I would take a turn in the air while I waited, he advised me to go round the corner and I should come into Smithfield. So, I came into Smithfield; and the shameful place, being all asmear with filth and fat and blood and foam, seemed to stick to me. So, I rubbed it off with all possible speed by turning into a street where I saw the great black dome of Saint Paul's bulging at me from behind a grim stone building which a bystander said was Newgate Prison.[1] Following the wall of the jail, I found the roadway covered with straw to deaden the noise of passing vehicles; and from this, and from the quantity of people standing about, smelling strongly of spirits and beer, I inferred that the trials were on.

While I looked about me here, an exceedingly dirty and partially drunk minister of justice asked me if I would like to step in and hear a trial or so: informing me that he could give me a front place for half-a-crown, whence I should command a full view of the Lord Chief Justice in his wig and robes — mentioning that awful personage like waxwork, and presently offering him at the reduced price of eighteenpence. As I declined the proposal on the plea of an appointment, he was so good as to take me into a yard and show me where the gallows was kept, and also where people were publicly whipped, and then he showed me the Debtors' Door, out of which culprits came to be hanged: heightening the interest of that dreadful portal by giving me to understand that "four on 'em" would come out at that door the day after to-morrow at eight in the morning, to be killed in a row. This was horrible, and gave me a sickening idea of London: the more so as the Lord Chief Justice's proprietor wore (from his hat down to his boots and up again to his pocket-handkerchief inclusive) mildewed clothes, which had evidently not belonged

---

1. *the great black dome of Saint Paul's bulging at me from behind a grim stone building which a bystander said was Newgate Prison:* see Map B. St. Paul's Cathedral was rebuilt with its famous baroque dome by Sir Christopher Wren in 1675-1710 after the Great Fire of London, while Newgate Prison was rebuilt after the original building was destroyed by fire during the Gordon Riots of 1780.

to him originally, and which, I took it into my head, he had bought cheap of the executioner. Under these circumstances I thought myself well rid of him for a shilling.

I dropped into the office to ask if Mr. Jaggers had come in yet, and I found he had not, and I strolled out again. This time, I made the tour of Little Britain, and turned into Bartholomew Close; and now I became aware that other people were waiting about for Mr. Jaggers, as well as I. There were two men of secret appearance lounging in Bartholomew Close, and thoughtfully fitting their feet into the cracks of the pavement as they talked together, one of whom said to the other when they first passed me, that "Jaggers would do it if it was to be done." There was a knot of three men and two women standing at a corner, and one of the women was crying on her dirty shawl, and the other comforted her by saying as she pulled her own shawl over her shoulders, "Jaggers is for him, 'Melia, and what more *could* you have?" There was a red-eyed little Jew who came into the Close while I was loitering there, in company with a second little Jew whom he sent upon an errand; and while the messenger was gone, I remarked this Jew, who was of a highly excitable temperament, performing a jig of anxiety under a lamp-post, and accompanying himself, in a kind of frenzy, with the words, "Oh Jaggerth, Jaggerth, Jaggerth! all otherth ith Cag-Maggerth,[1] give me Jaggerth!" These testimonies to the popularity of my guardian made a deep impression on me, and I admired and wondered more than ever.

At length, as I was looking out at the iron gate of Bartholomew Close into Little Britain, I saw Mr. Jaggers coming across the road towards me. All the others who were waiting, saw him at the same time, and there was quite a rush at him. Mr. Jaggers, putting a hand on my shoulder and walking me on at his side without saying anything to me, addressed himself to his followers.

First, he took the two secret men.

"Now, I have nothing to say to *you*," said Mr. Jaggers, throwing his finger at them. "I want to know no more than I know. As to the result, it's

---

1. *Cag-Maggerth:* from "cagmag," dialect or slang for rotten meat, or by extension, anything worthless. Dickens often employs the lisp as a marker of Jewish speech.

a toss-up. I told you from the first it was a toss-up. Have you paid Wemmick?"

"We made the money up this morning, sir," said one of the men, submissively, while the other perused Mr. Jaggers's face.

"I don't ask you when you made it up, or where, or whether you made it up at all. Has Wemmick got it?"

"Yes, sir," said both the men together.

"Very well; then you may go. Now, I won't have it!" said Mr. Jaggers, waving his hand at them to put them behind him. "If you say a word to me, I'll throw up the case."

"We thought, Mr. Jaggers —" one of the men began, pulling off his hat.

"That's what I told you not to do," said Mr. Jaggers. "*You* thought! I think for you; that's enough for you. If I want you, I know where to find you; I don't want you to find me. Now I won't have it. I won't hear a word."

The two men looked at one another as Mr. Jaggers waved them behind again, and humbly fell back and were heard no more.

"And now *you!*' said Mr. Jaggers, suddenly stopping, and turning on the two women with the shawls, from whom the three men had meekly separated. — "Oh! Amelia, is it?"

"Yes, Mr. Jaggers."

"And do you remember," retorted Mr. Jaggers, "that but for me you wouldn't be here and couldn't be here?"

"Oh yes, sir!" exclaimed both women together. "Lord bless you, sir, well we knows that!"

"Then why," said Mr. Jaggers, "do you come here?"

"My Bill, sir!" the crying woman pleaded.

"Now, I tell you what!" said Mr. Jaggers. "Once for all. If you don't know that your Bill's in good hands, I know it. And if you come here, bothering about your Bill, I'll make an example of both your Bill and you, and let him slip through my fingers. Have you paid Wemmick?"

"Oh yes, sir! Every farden."

"Very well. Then you have done all you have got to do. Say another word — one single word — and Wemmick shall give you your money back."

This terrible threat caused the two women to fall off immediately. No one remained now but the excitable Jew, who had already raised the skirts of Mr. Jaggers's coat to his lips several times. "I don't know this man!" said Mr. Jaggers, in the same devastating strain. "What does this fellow want?"

"Ma thear Mithter Jaggerth. Hown brother to Habraham Latharuth!"

"Who's he?" said Mr. Jaggers. "Let go of my coat."

The suitor, kissing the hem of the garment again before relinquishing it, replied, "Habraham Latharuth, on thuthpithion of plate."

"You're too late," said Mr. Jaggers. "I am over the way."

"Holy father, Mithter Jaggerth!" cried my excitable acquaintance, turning white, "don't thay you're again Habraham Latharuth!"

"I am," said Mr. Jaggers, "and there's an end of it. Get out of the way."

"Mithter Jaggerth! Half a moment! My hown cuthen'th gone to Mithter Wemmick at thith prethent minute, to hoffer him hany termth. Mithter Jaggerth! Half a quarter of a moment! If you'd have the condethenthun to be bought off from the t'other thide — at hany thuperior prithe! — money no object! — Mithter Jaggerth — Mithter —!"

My guardian threw his supplicant off with supreme indifference, and left him dancing on the pavement as if it were red-hot. Without further interruption, we reached the front office, where we found the clerk and the man in velveteen with the fur cap.

"Here's Mike," said the clerk, getting down from his stool, and approaching Mr. Jaggers confidentially.

"Oh!" said Mr. Jaggers, turning to the man, who was pulling a lock of hair in the middle of his forehead, like the Bull in Cock Robin pulling at the bell-rope;[1] "your man comes on this afternoon. Well?"

"Well, Mas'r Jaggers," returned Mike, in the voice of a sufferer from a constitutional cold; "arter a deal o' trouble, I've found one, sir, as might do."

"What is he prepared to swear?"

---

1. *the Bull in Cock Robin pulling at the bell-rope:* in the nursery rhyme "The Death and Burial of Cock Robin," the bull (bullfinch?) offers to toll the bell.

"Well, Mas'r Jaggers," said Mike, wiping his nose on his fur cap this time; "in a general way, anythink."

Mr. Jaggers suddenly became most irate. "Now, I warned you before," said he, throwing his forefinger at the terrified client, "that if you ever presumed to talk in that way here, I'd make an example of you. You infernal scoundrel, how dare you tell ME that?"

The client looked scared, but bewildered too, as if he were unconscious what he had done.

"Spooney!"[1] said the clerk, in a low voice, giving him a stir with his elbow. "Soft Head! Need you say it face to face?"

"Now, I ask you, you blundering booby," said my guardian, very sternly, "once more and for the last time, what the man you have brought here is prepared to swear?"

Mike looked hard at my guardian, as if he were trying to learn a lesson from his face, and slowly replied, "Ayther to character, or to having been in his company and never left him all the night in question."

"Now, be careful. In what station of life is this man?"

Mike looked at his cap, and looked at the floor, and looked at the ceiling, and looked at the clerk, and even looked at me, before beginning to reply in a nervous manner, "We've dressed him up like —" when my guardian blustered out:

"What? You WILL, will you?"

("Spooney!" added the clerk again, with another stir.)

After some helpless casting about, Mike brightened and began again: "He is dressed like a 'spectable pieman. A sort of a pastrycook."

"Is he here?" asked my guardian.

"I left him," said Mike, "a settin on some door-steps round the corner."

"Take him past that window, and let me see him."

The window indicated, was the office window. We all three went to it, behind the wire blind, and presently saw the client go by in an accidental manner, with a murderous-looking tall individual, in a short suit of white linen and a paper cap. This guileless confectioner was not by any means sober, and had a black eye in the green stage of recovery, which was painted over.

---

1. *Spooney:* foolish.

"Tell him to take his witness away directly," said my guardian to the clerk, in extreme disgust, "and ask him what he means by bringing such a fellow as that."

My guardian then took me into his own room, and while he lunched, standing, from a sandwich-box and a pocket-flask of sherry (he seemed to bully his very sandwich as he ate it), informed me what arrangements he had made for me. I was to go to "Barnard's Inn,"[1] to young Mr. Pocket's rooms, where a bed had been sent in for my accommodation; I was to remain with young Mr. Pocket until Monday; on Monday I was to go with him to his father's house on a visit, that I might try how I liked it. Also, I was told what my allowance was to be — it was a very liberal one — and had handed to me from one of my guardian's drawers, the cards of certain tradesmen with whom I was to deal for all kinds of clothes, and such other things as I could in reason want. "You will find your credit good, Mr. Pip," said my guardian, whose flask of sherry smelt like a whole cask-full, as he hastily refreshed himself, "but I shall by this means be able to check your bills, and to pull you up if I find you outrunning the constable.[2] Of course you'll go wrong somehow, but that's no fault of mine."

After I had pondered a little over this encouraging sentiment, I asked Mr. Jaggers if I could send for a coach? He said it was not worth while, I was so near my destination; Wemmick should walk round with me, if I pleased.

I then found that Wemmick was the clerk in the next room. Another clerk was rung down from up-stairs to take his place while he was out, and I accompanied him into the street, after shaking hands with my guardian. We found a new set of people lingering outside, but Wemmick made a way among them by saying coolly yet decisively, "I tell you it's no use; he won't have a word to say to one of you;" and we soon got clear of them, and went on side by side.

---

1. *"Barnard's Inn"*: formerly one of the "Inns of Chancery," i.e., lawyer's chambers or residences for students of the law, but already used for private lodgings by the early nineteenth century. See Map B and Illustration B.
2. *outrunning the constable*: falling into debt (idiomatic).

CHAPTER II

CASTING MY eyes on Mr. Wemmick as we went along, to see what he was like in the light of day, I found him to be a dry man, rather short in stature, with a square wooden face, whose expression seemed to have been imperfectly chipped out with a dull-edged chisel. There were some marks in it that might have been dimples, if the material had been softer and the instrument finer, but which, as it was, were only dints. The chisel had made three or four of these attempts at embellishment over his nose, but had given them up without an effort to smooth them off. I judged him to be a bachelor from the frayed condition of his linen, and he appeared to have sustained a good many bereavements; for, he wore at least four mourning rings, besides a brooch representing a lady and a weeping willow at a tomb with an urn on it. I noticed, too, that several rings and seals hung at his watch chain, as if he were quite laden with remembrances of departed friends. He had glittering eyes — small, keen, and black — and thin wide mottled lips. He had had them, to the best of my belief, from forty to fifty years.

"So you were never in London before?" said Mr. Wemmick to me.

"No," said I.

"*I* was new here once," said Mr. Wemmick. "Rum to think of now!"

"You are well acquainted with it now?"

"Why, yes," said Mr. Wemmick. "I know the moves of it."

"Is it a very wicked place?" I asked, more for the sake of saying something than for information.

"You may get cheated, robbed, and murdered, in London. But there are plenty of people anywhere, who'll do that for you."

"If there is bad blood between you and them," said I, to soften it off a little.

"Oh! I don't know about bad blood," returned Mr. Wemmick; "there's not much bad blood about. They'll do it, if there's anything to be got by it."

"That makes it worse."

"You think so?" returned Mr. Wemmick. "Much about the same, I should say."

He wore his hat on the back of his head, and looked straight before him: walking in a self-contained way as if there were nothing in the streets to claim his attention. His mouth was such a post-office of a mouth that he had a mechanical appearance of smiling. We had got to the top of Holborn Hill before I knew that it was merely a mechanical appearance, and that he was not smiling at all.

"Do you know where Mr. Matthew Pocket lives?" I asked Mr. Wemmick.

"Yes," said he, nodding in the direction. "At Hammersmith, west of London."[1]

"Is that far?"

"Well! Say five miles."

"Do you know him?"

"Why, you're a regular cross-examiner!" said Mr. Wemmick, looking at me with an approving air. "Yes, I know him. *I* know him!"

There was an air of toleration or depreciation about his utterance of these words, that rather depressed me; and I was still looking sideways at his block of a face in search of any encouraging note to the text, when he said here we were at Barnard's Inn. My depression was not alleviated by the announcement, for, I had supposed that establishment to be an hotel kept by Mr. Barnard, to which the Blue Boar in our town was a mere public-house. Whereas I now found Barnard to be a disembodied spirit, or a fiction, and his inn the dingiest collection of shabby buildings ever squeezed together in a rank corner as a club for Tom-cats.

We entered this haven through a wicket-gate, and were disgorged by an introductory passage into a melancholy little square that looked to me like a flat burying-ground. I thought it had the most dismal trees in it, and the most dismal sparrows, and the most dismal cats, and the most dismal houses (in number half a dozen or so), that I had ever seen. I thought the windows of the sets of chambers into which these houses were divided, were in every stage of dilapidated blind and curtain, crippled flower-pot, cracked glass, dusty decay, and miserable makeshift; while To Let To Let To Let, glared at me from empty rooms, as if no new wretches ever came there, and the vengeance of the soul of Barnard were being slowly appeased by the gradual suicide of the present occupants and their unholy

---

1. *At Hammersmith, west of London:* then a riverside village. See Map C and Illustration C.

interment under the gravel. A frouzy mourning of soot and smoke attired this forlorn creation of Barnard, and it had strewn ashes on its head, and was undergoing penance and humiliation as a mere dust-hole. Thus far my sense of sight; while dry rot and wet rot and all the silent rots that rot in neglected roof and cellar — rot of rat and mouse and bug and coaching-stables near at hand besides — addressed themselves faintly to my sense of smell, and moaned, "Try Barnard's Mixture."[1]

So imperfect was this realisation of the first of my great expectations, that I looked in dismay at Mr. Wemmick. "Ah!" said he, mistaking me; "the retirement reminds you of the country. So it does me."

He led me into a corner and conducted me up a flight of stairs — which appeared to me to be slowly collapsing into sawdust, so that one of those days the upper lodgers would look out at their doors and find themselves without the means of coming down — to a set of chambers on the top floor. MR. POCKET, JUN., was painted on the door, and there was a label on the letter-box, "Return shortly."

"He hardly thought you'd come so soon," Mr. Wemmick explained. "You don't want me any more?"

"No, thank you," said I.

"As I keep the cash," Mr. Wemmick observed, "we shall most likely meet pretty often. Good day."

"Good day."

I put out my hand, and Mr. Wemmick at first looked at it as if he thought I wanted something. Then he looked at me, and said, correcting himself,

"To be sure! Yes. You're in the habit of shaking hands?"

I was rather confused, thinking it must be out of the London fashion, but said yes.

"I have got so out of it!" said Mr. Wemmick — "except at last. Very glad, I'm sure, to make your acquaintance. Good day!"

When we had shaken hands and he was gone, I opened the staircase

---

1. *"Try Barnard's Mixture"*: like an advertisement for a noxious patent medicine. Compare Dickens's description of Gray's Inn in "Living in Chambers" in *All the Year Round* 18 August 1860, reprinted in *The Uncommercial Traveller*.

window and had nearly beheaded myself, for, the lines had rotted away, and it came down like the guillotine. Happily it was so quick that I had not put my head out. After this escape, I was content to take a foggy view of the Inn through the window's encrusting dirt, and to stand dolefully looking out, saying to myself that London was decidedly overrated.

Mr. Pocket, Junior's, idea of Shortly was not mine, for I had nearly maddened myself with looking out for half an hour, and had written my name with my finger several times in the dirt of every pane in the window, before I heard footsteps on the stairs. Gradually there arose before me the hat, head, neckcloth, waistcoat, trousers, boots, of a member of society of about my own standing. He had a paper-bag under each arm and a pottle[1] of strawberries in one hand, and was out of breath.

"Mr. Pip?" said he.

"Mr. Pocket?" said I.

"Dear me!" he exclaimed. "I am extremely sorry; but I knew there was a coach from your part of the country at mid-day, and I thought you would come by that one. The fact is, I have been out on your account — not that that is any excuse — for I thought, coming from the country, you might like a little fruit after dinner, and I went to Covent Garden Market[2] to get it good."

For a reason that I had, I felt as if my eyes would start out of my head. I acknowledged his attention incoherently, and began to think this was a dream.

"Dear me!" said Mr. Pocket, Junior. "This door sticks so!"

As he was fast making jam of his fruit by wrestling with the door while the paper-bags were under his arms, I begged him to allow me to hold them. He relinquished them with an agreeable smile, and combated with the door as if it were a wild beast. It yielded so suddenly at last, that he staggered back upon me, and I staggered back upon the opposite door, and we both laughed. But still I felt as if my eyes must start out of my head, and as if this must be a dream.

---

1. *pottle:* a small cone-shaped basket.
2. *Covent Garden Market:* large fruit, vegetable and flower market west of the City. See Map C and Illustration D.

"Pray come in," said Mr. Pocket, Junior. "Allow me to lead the way. I am rather bare here, but I hope you'll be able to make out tolerably well till Monday. My father thought you would get on more agreeably through to-morrow with me than with him, and might like to take a walk about London. I am sure I shall be very happy to show London to you. As to our table, you won't find that bad, I hope, for it will be supplied from our coffee-house here, and (it is only right I should add) at your expense, such being Mr. Jaggers's directions. As to our lodging, it's not by any means splendid, because I have my own bread to earn, and my father hasn't anything to give me, and I shouldn't be willing to take it, if he had. This is our sitting-room — just such chairs and tables and carpet and so forth, you see, as they could spare from home. You mustn't give me credit for the table-cloth and spoons and castors, because they come for you from the coffee-house. This is my little bedroom; rather musty, but Barnard's *is* musty. This is your bedroom; the furniture's hired for the occasion, but I trust it will answer the purpose; if you should want anything, I'll go and fetch it. The chambers are retired, and we shall be alone together, but we shan't fight, I dare say. But, dear me, I beg your pardon, you're holding the fruit all this time. Pray let me take these bags from you. I am quite ashamed."

As I stood opposite to Mr. Pocket, Junior, delivering him the bags, One, Two, I saw the starting appearance come into his own eyes that I knew to be in mine, and he said, falling back:

"Lord bless me, you're the prowling boy!"

"And you," said I, "are the pale young gentleman!"

CHAPTER III

THE PALE young gentleman and I stood contemplating one another in Barnard's Inn, until we both burst out laughing. "The idea of its being you!" said he. "The idea of its being *you!*" said I. And then we contemplated one another afresh, and laughed again. "Well!" said the pale young gentleman, reaching out his hand good humouredly, "it's all over now, I hope, and it will be magnanimous in you if you'll forgive me for having knocked you about so."

I derived from this speech that Mr. Herbert Pocket (for Herbert was the pale young gentleman's name) still rather confounded his intention with his execution. But I made a modest reply, and we shook hands warmly.

"You hadn't come into your good fortune at that time?" said Herbert Pocket.

"No," said I.

"No," he acquiesced: "I heard it had happened very lately. I was rather on the look-out for good fortune then."

"Indeed?"

"Yes. Miss Havisham had sent for me, to see if she could take a fancy to me. But she couldn't — at all events, she didn't."

I thought it polite to remark that I was surprised to hear that.

"Bad taste," said Herbert, laughing, "but a fact. Yes, she had sent for me on a trial visit, and if I had come out of it successfully, I suppose I should have been provided for; perhaps I should have been what-you-may-called it to Estella."

"What's that?" I asked, with sudden gravity.

He was arranging his fruit in plates while we talked, which divided his attention, and was the cause of his having made this lapse of a word. "Affianced," he explained, still busy with the fruit. "Betrothed. Engaged. What's-his-named. Any word of that sort."

"How did you bear your disappointment?" I asked.

"Pooh!" said he, "I didn't care much for it. *She's* a Tartar."

"Miss Havisham?" I suggested.

"I don't say no to that, but I meant Estella. That girl's hard and haughty and capricious to the last degree, and has been brought up by Miss Havisham to wreak revenge on all the male sex."

"What relation is she to Miss Havisham?"

"None," said he. "Only adopted."

"Why should she wreak revenge on all the male sex? What revenge?"

"Lord, Mr. Pip!" said he. "Don't you know?"

"No," said I.

"Dear me! It's quite a story, and shall be saved till dinner-time. And now let me take the liberty of asking you a question. How did you come there, that day?"

I told him, and he was attentive until I had finished, and then burst out laughing again, and asked me if I was sore afterwards? I didn't ask him if *he* was, for my conviction on that point was perfectly established.

"Mr. Jaggers is your guardian, I understand?" he went on.

"Yes."

"You know he is Miss Havisham's man of business and solicitor, and has her confidence when nobody else has?"

This was bringing me (I felt) towards dangerous ground. I answered with a constraint I made no attempt to disguise, that I had seen Mr. Jaggers in Miss Havisham's house on the very day of our combat, but never at any other time, and that I believed he had no recollection of having ever seen me there.

"He was so obliging as to suggest my father for your tutor, and he called on my father to propose it. Of course he knew about my father from his connexion with Miss Havisham. My father is Miss Havisham's cousin; not that that implies familiar intercourse between them, for he is a bad courtier and will not propitiate her."

Herbert Pocket had a frank and easy way with him that was very taking. I had never seen any one then, and I have never seen any one since, who more strongly expressed to me, in every look and tone, a natural incapacity to do anything secret and mean. There was something wonderfully hopeful about his general air, and something that at the same time whispered to me he would never be very successful or rich. I don't know how this was. I became imbued with the notion on that first occasion before we sat down to dinner, but I cannot define by what means.

He was still a pale young gentleman, and had a certain conquered languor about him in the midst of his spirits and briskness, that did not seem indicative of natural strength. He had not a handsome face, but it was better than handsome: being extremely amiable and cheerful. His figure was a little ungainly, as in the days when my knuckles had taken such liberties with it, but it looked as if it would always be light and young. Whether Mr. Trabb's local work would have sat more gracefully on him than on me, may be a question; but I am conscious that he carried off his rather old clothes, much better than I carried off my new suit.

As he was so communicative, I felt that reserve on my part would be a bad return unsuited to our years. I therefore told him my small story, and laid stress on my being forbidden to inquire who my benefactor was.

I further mentioned that as I had been brought up a blacksmith in a country place, and knew very little of the ways of politeness, I would take it as a great kindness in him if he would give me a hint whenever he saw me at a loss or going wrong.

"With pleasure," said he, "though I venture to prophesy that you'll want very few hints. I dare say we shall be often together, and I should like to banish any needless restraint between us. Will you do me the favour to begin at once to call me by my christian name, Herbert?"

I thanked him, and said I would. I informed him in exchange that my christian name was Philip.

"I don't take to Philip," said he, smiling, "for it sounds like a moral boy out of the spelling-book,[1] who was so lazy that he fell into a pond, or so fat that he couldn't see out of his eyes, or so avaricious that he locked up his cake till the mice ate it, or so determined to go a birds'-nesting that he got himself eaten by bears who lived handy in the neighbourhood. I tell you what I should like. We are so harmonious, and you have been a blacksmith — would you mind it?"

"I shouldn't mind anything that you propose," I answered, "but I don't understand you."

"Would you mind Handel for a familiar name? There's a charming piece of music by Handel, called the Harmonious Blacksmith."

"I should like it very much."

"Then, my dear Handel," said he, turning round as the door opened, "here is the dinner, and I must beg of you to take the top of the table, because the dinner is of your providing."

This I would not hear of, so he took the top, and I faced him. It was a nice little dinner — seemed to me then, a very Lord Mayor's Feast — and it acquired additional relish from being eaten under those independent circumstances, with no old people by, and with London all around us. This again was heightened by a certain gipsy character that set the banquet

---

1. *a moral boy out of the spelling-book:* contemporary spelling primers, such as the *English Spelling-Book* by William Mavor (1750–1837) or the *Charity School Spelling Book* by Mrs. Sarah Trimmer (1741–1810), both published towards the end of the eighteenth century, typically progessed from lists of words to short narratives of an exemplary nature. See Appendix D 1.

off; for, while the table was, as Mr. Pumblechook might have said, the lap of luxury — being entirely furnished forth from the coffee-house — the circumjacent region of sitting-room was of a comparatively pastureless and shifty character: imposing on the waiter the wandering habits of putting the covers on the floor (where he fell over them), the melted butter in the armchair, the bread on the bookshelves, the cheese in the coal-scuttle, and the boiled fowl into my bed in the next room — where I found much of its parsley and butter in a state of congelation when I retired for the night. All this made the feast delightful, and when the waiter was not there to watch me, my pleasure was without alloy.

We had made some progress in the dinner, when I reminded Herbert of his promise to tell me about Miss Havisham.

"True," he replied. "I'll redeem it at once. Let me introduce the topic, Handel, by mentioning that in London it is not the custom to put the knife in the mouth — for fear of accidents — and that while the fork is reserved for that use, it is not put further in than is necessary. It is scarcely worth mentioning, only it's as well to do as other people do. Also, the spoon is not generally used over-hand, but under. This has two advantages. You get at your mouth better (which after all is the object), and you save a good deal of the attitude of opening oysters, on the part of the right elbow."

He offered these friendly suggestions in such a lively way, that we both laughed and I scarcely blushed.

"Now," he pursued, "concerning Miss Havisham. Miss Havisham, you must know, was a spoilt child. Her mother died when she was a baby, and her father denied her nothing. Her father was a country gentleman down in your part of the world, and was a brewer. I don't know why it should be a crack thing to be a brewer; but it is indisputable that while you cannot possibly be genteel and bake, you may be as genteel as never was and brew.* You see it every day."

"Yet a gentleman may not keep a public-house; may he?" said I.

"Not on any account," returned Herbert; "but a public-house may keep a gentleman. Well! Mr. Havisham was very rich and very proud. So was his daughter."

"Miss Havisham was an only child?" I hazarded.

"Stop a moment, I am coming to that. No, she was not an only child;

she had a half-brother. Her father privately married again — his cook, I rather think."

"I thought he was proud," said I.

"My good Handel, so he was. He married his second wife privately, because he was proud, and in course of time *she* died. When she was dead, I apprehend he first told his daughter what he had done, and then the son became a part of the family, residing in the house you are acquainted with. As the son grew a young man, he turned out riotous, extravagant, undutiful — altogether bad. At last his father disinherited him; but he softened when he was dying, and left him well off, though not nearly so well off as Miss Havisham. Take another glass of wine, and excuse my mentioning that society as a body does not expect one to be so strictly conscientious in emptying one's glass, as to turn it bottom upwards with the rim on one's nose."

I had been doing this, in an excess of attention to his recital. I thanked him, and apologised. He said, "Not at all," and resumed.

"Miss Havisham was now an heiress, and you may suppose was looked after as a great match. Her half-brother had now ample means again, but what with debts and what with new madness wasted them most fearfully again. There were stronger differences between him and her, than there had been between him and his father, and it is suspected that he cherished a deep and mortal grudge against her, as having influenced the father's anger. Now, I come to the cruel part of the story — merely breaking off, my dear Handel, to remark that a dinner-napkin will not go into a tumbler."

Why I was trying to pack mine into my tumbler, I am wholly unable to say. I only know that I found myself, with a perseverance worthy of a much better cause, making the most strenuous exertions to compress it within those limits. Again I thanked him and apologised, and again he said in the cheerfullest manner, "Not at all, I am sure!" and resumed.

"There appeared upon the scene — say at the races, or the public balls, or anywhere else you like — a certain man, who made love to Miss Havisham. I never saw him, for this happened five-and-twenty years ago (before you and I were, Handel), but I have heard my father mention that he was a showy-man, and the kind of man for the purpose. But that he was not to be, without ignorance or prejudice, mistaken for a gentleman, my father most strongly asseverates; because it is a principle of his that no man who was not a true gentleman at heart, ever was, since the world began, a true gentleman in manner. He says, no varnish can hide the grain of the wood; and that the more varnish you put on, the more the grain will express itself. Well! This man pursued Miss Havisham closely, and professed to be devoted to her. I believe she had not shown much susceptibility up to that time; but all she possessed, certainly came out then, and she passionately loved him. There is no doubt that she perfectly idolised him. He practised on her affection in that systematic way, that he got great sums of money from her, and he induced her to buy her brother out of a share in the brewery (which had been weakly left him by his father) at an immense price, on the plea that when he was her husband he must hold and manage it all. Your guardian was not at that time in Miss Havisham's councils, and she was too haughty and too much in love, to be advised by any one. Her relations were poor and scheming, with the exception of my father; he was poor enough, but not time-serving or jealous. The only independent one among them, he warned her that she was doing too much for this man, and was placing herself too unreservedly in his power. She took the first opportunity of angrily ordering my father out of the house, in his presence, and my father has never seen her since."

I thought of her having said, "Matthew will come and see me at last when I am laid dead upon that table;" and I asked Herbert whether his father was so inveterate against her?

"It's not that," said he, "but she charged him, in the presence of her intended husband, with being disappointed in the hope of fawning upon her for his own advancement, and, if he were to go to her now, it would look true — even to him — and even to her. To return to the man and make an end of him. The marriage day was fixed, the wedding dresses were bought, the wedding tour was planned out, the wedding guests were invited. The day came, but not the bridegroom. He wrote her a letter —"

"Which she received," I struck in, "when she was dressing for her marriage? At twenty minutes to nine?"

"At the hour and minute," said Herbert, nodding, "at which she afterwards stopped all the clocks. What was in it, further than that it most heartlessly broke the marriage off, I can't tell you, because I don't know. When she recovered from a bad illness that she had, she laid the whole place waste, as you have seen it, and she has never since looked upon the light of day."

"Is that all the story?" I asked, after considering it.

"All I know of it; and indeed I only know so much, through piecing it out for myself; for my father always avoids it, and, even when Miss Havisham invited me to go there, told me no more of it than it was absolutely requisite I should understand. But I have forgotten one thing. It has been supposed that the man to whom she gave her misplaced confidence, acted throughout in concert with her half-brother; that it was a conspiracy between them; and that they shared the profits."

"I wonder he didn't marry her and get all the property," said I.

"He may have been married already, and her cruel mortification may have been a part of her half-brother's scheme," said Herbert. "Mind! I don't know that."

"What became of the two men?" I asked, after again considering the subject.

"They fell into deeper shame and degradation — if there can be deeper — and ruin."

"Are they alive now?"

"I don't know."

"You said just now, that Estella was not related to Miss Havisham, but adopted. When adopted?"

Herbert shrugged his shoulders. "There has always been an Estella, since I have heard of a Miss Havisham. I know no more. And now, Handel," said he, finally throwing off the story as it were, "there is a perfectly open understanding between us. All that I know about Miss Havisham, you know."

"And all that I know," I retorted, "you know."

"I fully believe it. So there can be no competition or perplexity between you and me. And as to the condition on which you hold your advancement in life — namely, that you are not to inquire or discuss to whom you owe it — you may be very sure that it will never be encroached upon, or even approached, by me, or by any one belonging to me."

In truth, he said this with so much delicacy, that I felt the subject done with, even though I should be under his father's roof for years and years to come. Yet he said it with so much meaning, too, that I felt he as perfectly understood Miss Havisham to be my benefactress, as I understood the fact myself.

It had not occurred to me before, that he had led up to the theme for the purpose of clearing it out of our way; but we were so much the lighter and easier for having broached it, that I now perceived this to be the case. We were very gay and sociable, and I asked him, in the course of conversation, what he was? He replied, "A capitalist — an Insurer of Ships."* I suppose he saw me glancing about the room in search of some tokens of Shipping, or capital, for he added, "In the City."

I had grand ideas of the wealth and importance of Insurers of Ships in the City, and I began to think with awe, of having laid a young Insurer on his back, blackened his enterprising eye, and cut his responsible head open. But, again, there came upon me, for my relief that odd impression that Herbert Pocket would never be very successful or rich.

"I shall not rest satisfied with merely employing my capital in insuring ships. I shall buy up some good Life Assurance shares, and cut into the Direction. I shall also do a little in the mining way. None of these things will interfere with my chartering a few thousand tons on my own account. I think I shall trade," said he, leaning back in his chair, "to the East Indies, for silks, shawls, spices, dyes, drugs, and precious woods. It's an interesting trade."

"And the profits are large?" said I.

"Tremendous!" said he.

I wavered again, and began to think here were greater expectations than my own.

"I think I shall trade, also," said he, putting his thumbs in his waistcoat pockets, "to the West Indies, for sugar, tobacco, and rum. Also to Ceylon, specially for elephants' tusks."

"You will want a good many ships," said I.

"A perfect fleet," said he.

Quite overpowered by the magnificence of these transactions, I asked him where the ships he insured mostly traded to at present?

"I haven't begun insuring yet," he replied. "I am looking about me."

Somehow, that pursuit seemed more in keeping with Barnard's Inn. I said (in a tone of conviction), "Ah-h!"

"Yes. I am in a counting-house, and looking about me."

"Is a counting-house profitable?" I asked.

"To—do you mean to the young fellow who's in it?" he asked, in reply.

"Yes; to you."

"Why, n-no: not to me." He said this with the air of one carefully reckoning up and striking a balance. "Not directly profitable. That is, it doesn't pay me anything, and I have to — keep myself."

This certainly had not a profitable appearance, and I shook my head as if I would imply that it would be difficult to lay by much accumulative capital from such a source of income.

"But the thing is," said Herbert Pocket, "that you look about you. *That's* the grand thing. You are in a counting-house, you know, and you look about you."

It struck me as a singular implication that you couldn't be out of a counting-house, you know, and look about you; but I silently deferred to his experience.

"Then the time comes," said Herbert, "when you see your opening. And you go in, and you swoop upon it and you make your capital, and then there you are! When you have once made your capital, you have nothing to do but employ it."

This was very like his way of conducting that encounter in the garden; very like. His manner of bearing his poverty, too, exactly corresponded to his manner of bearing that defeat. It seemed to me that he took all blows and buffets now, with just the same air as he had taken mine then. It was evident that he had nothing around him but the simplest necessaries, for everything that I remarked upon turned out to have been sent in on my account from the coffee-house or somewhere else.

Yet, having already made his fortune in his own mind, he was so unassuming with it that I felt quite grateful to him for not being puffed up. It was a pleasant addition to his naturally pleasant ways, and we got on famously. In the evening we went out for a walk in the streets, and went half-price to the Theatre;[1] and next day we went to church at Westminster Abbey, and in the afternoon we walked in the Parks;[2] and I wondered who shod all the horses there, and wished Joe did.

---

1. *went half-price to the Theatre:* i.e., for the second half of the presentation only.
2. *and next day we went to church at Westminster Abbey, and in the afternoon we walked in the Parks:* popular resorts for visitors to London then as now; "the Parks" refers to the Royal Parks in the West End of London, Hyde Park, St. James Park and Green Park. See Map C.

On a moderate computation, it was many months, that Sunday, since I had left Joe and Biddy. The space interposed between myself and them, partook of that expansion, and our marshes were any distance off. That I could have been at our old church in my old church-going clothes, on the very last Sunday that ever was, seemed a combination of impossibilities, geographical and social, solar and lunar. Yet in the London streets, so crowded with people and so brilliantly lighted in the dusk of evening, there were depressing hints of reproaches for that I had put the poor old kitchen at home so far away; and in the dead of night, the footsteps of some incapable impostor of a porter mooning about Barnard's Inn, under pretence of watching it, fell hollow on my heart.

On the Monday morning at a quarter before nine, Herbert went to the counting-house to report himself — to look about him, too, I suppose — and I bore him company. He was to come away in an hour or two to attend me to Hammersmith, and I was to wait about for him. It appeared to me that the eggs from which young Insurers were hatched, were incubated in dust and heat, like the eggs of ostriches, judging from the places to which those incipient giants repaired on a Monday morning. Nor did the counting-house where Herbert assisted, show in my eyes as at all a good Observatory; being a back second floor up a yard, of a grimy presence in all particulars, and with a look into another back second floor, rather than a look out.

I waited about until it was noon, and I went upon 'Change,[1] and I saw fluey[2] men sitting there under the bills about shipping, whom I took to be great merchants, though I couldn't understand why they should all be out of spirits. When Herbert came, we went and had lunch at a celebrated house which I then quite venerated, but now believe to have been the most abject superstition in Europe, and where I could not help noticing, even then, that there was much more gravy on the tablecloths and knives and waiters' clothes, than in the steaks. This collation dis-

---

1. *went upon 'Change:* i.e., visited the Royal Exchange in Cornhill, in the City east of Cheapside (see Map C and Illustration E), where the shipping insurance giants Lloyd's operated throughout the nineteenth century. The old Exchange referred to here was burnt down in 1838.
2. *fluey:* covered in fluff (flue) from wool or cotton.

posed of at a moderate price (considering the grease: which was not charged for), we went back to Barnard's Inn and got my little portmanteau, and then took coach for Hammersmith. We arrived there at two or three o'clock in the afternoon, and had very little way to walk to Mr. Pocket's house. Lifting the latch of a gate, we passed direct into a little garden overlooking the river, where Mr. Pocket's children were playing about. And unless I deceive myself on a point where my interests or prepossessions are certainly not concerned, I saw that Mr. and Mrs. Pocket's children were not growing up or being brought up, but were tumbling up.

Mrs. Pocket was sitting on a garden chair under a tree, reading, with her legs upon another garden chair; and Mrs. Pocket's two nursemaids were looking about them while the children played. "Mamma," said Herbert, "this is young Mr. Pip." Upon which Mrs. Pocket received me with an appearance of amiable dignity.*

"Master Alick and Miss Jane," cried one of the nurses to two of the children "if you go a bouncing up against them bushes you'll fall over into the river and be drownded, and what'll your pa say then!"

At the same time this nurse picked up Mrs. Pocket's handkerchief, and said, "If that don't make six times you've dropped it, Mum!" Upon which Mrs. Pocket laughed and said, "Thank you, Flopson," and settling herself in one chair only, resumed her book. Her countenance immediately assumed a knitted and intent expression as if she had been reading for a week, but before she could have read half a dozen lines, she fixed her eyes upon me, and said, "I hope your mamma is quite well?" This unexpected inquiry put me into such a difficulty that I began saying in the absurdest way that if there had been any such person I had no doubt she would have been quite well and would have been very much obliged and would have sent her compliments, when the nurse came to my rescue.

"Well!" she cried, picking up the pocket handkerchief, "if that don't make seven times! What ARE you a doing of this afternoon, Mum!" Mrs. Pocket received her property, at first with a look of unutterable surprise as if she had never seen it before, and then with a laugh of recognition, and said, "Thank you, Flopson," and forgot me, and went on reading.

I found, now I had leisure to count them, that there were no fewer than six little Pockets present, in various stages of tumbling up. I had scarcely arrived at the total when a seventh was heard, as in the region of air, wailing dolefully.

"If there ain't Baby!" said Flopson, appearing to think it most surprising. "Make haste up, Millers."

Millers, who was the other nurse, retired into the house, and by degrees the child's wailing was hushed and stopped, as if it were a young ventriloquist with something in its mouth. Mrs. Pocket read all the time, and I was curious to know what the book could be.

We were waiting, I supposed, for Mr. Pocket to come out to us; at any rate we waited there, and so I had an opportunity of observing the remarkable family phenomenon that whenever any of the children strayed near Mrs. Pocket in their play, they always tripped themselves up and tumbled over her — always very much to her momentary astonishment, and their own more enduring lamentation. I was at a loss to account for this surprising circumstance, and could not help giving my mind to speculations about it, until by-and-by Millers came down with the baby, which baby was handed to Flopson, which Flopson was handing it to Mrs. Pocket, when she too went fairly head foremost over Mrs. Pocket, baby and all, and was caught by Herbert and myself.

"Gracious me, Flopson!" said Mrs. Pocket, looking off her book for a moment, "everybody's tumbling!"

"Gracious you, indeed, Mum!" returned Flopson, very red in the face; "what have you got there?"

"*I* got here, Flopson?" asked Mrs. Pocket.

"Why, if it ain't your footstool!" cried Flopson. "And if you keep it under your skirts like that, who's to help tumbling? Here! Take the baby, Mum, and give me your book."

Mrs. Pocket acted on the advice, and inexpertly danced the infant a little in her lap, while the other children played about it. This had lasted but a very short time, when Mrs. Pocket issued summary orders that they were all to be taken into the house for a nap. Thus I made the second discovery on that first occasion, that the nurture of the little Pockets consisted of alternately tumbling up and lying down.

Under these circumstances, when Flopson and Millers had got the children into the house, like a little flock of sheep, and Mr. Pocket came out of it to make my acquaintance, I was not much surprised to find that

Mr. Pocket was a gentleman with a rather perplexed expression of face, and with his very grey hair disordered on his head, as if he didn't quite see his way to putting anything straight.

CHAPTER IV

MR. POCKET said he was glad to see me, and he hoped I was not sorry to see him. "For, I really am not," he added, with his son's smile, "an alarming personage." He was a young-looking man, in spite of his perplexities and his very grey hair, and his manner seemed quite natural. I use the word natural, in the sense of its being unaffected; there was something comic in his distraught way, as though it would have been downright ludicrous but for his own perception that it was very near being so. When he had talked with me a little, he said to Mrs. Pocket, with a rather anxious contraction of his eyebrows, which were black and handsome, "Belinda, I hope you have welcomed Mr. Pip?" And she looked up from her book, and said, "Yes." She then smiled upon me in an absent state of mind, and asked me if I liked the taste of orange-flower water? As the question had no bearing, near or remote, on any foregone or subsequent transaction, I consider it to have been thrown out, like her previous approaches, in general conversational condescension.

I found out within a few hours, and may mention at once, that Mrs. Pocket was the only daughter of a certain quite accidental deceased Knight, who had invented for himself a conviction that his deceased father would have been made a Baronet but for somebody's determined opposition arising out of entirely personal motives — I forget whose, if I ever knew — the Sovereign's, the Prime Minister's, the Lord Chancellor's, the Archbishop of Canterbury's, anybody's — and had tacked himself on to the nobles of the earth in right of this quite supposititious fact. I believe he had been knighted himself for storming the English grammar at the point of the pen, in a desperate address engrossed on vellum, on the occasion of the laying of the first stone of some building or other, and for handing some Royal Personage either the trowel or the mortar. Be that as it may, he had directed Mrs. Pocket to be brought up from her cradle as one who in the nature of things must marry a title, and who was to be guarded from the acquisition of plebeian domestic knowledge. So successful a watch and ward had been established over the young lady by this judicious parent, that she had grown up highly ornamental, but perfectly helpless and useless. With her character thus happily formed, in the first bloom of her youth she had encountered Mr. Pocket: who was also in the first bloom of youth, and not quite decided whether to mount to the Woolsack, or to roof himself in with a mitre.[1] As his doing the one or the other was a mere question of time, he and Mrs. Pocket had taken Time by the forelock (when, to judge from its length, it would seem to have wanted cutting), and had married without the knowledge of the judicious parent. The judicious parent, having nothing to bestow or withhold but his blessing, had handsomely settled that dower upon them after a short struggle, and had informed Mr. Pocket that his wife was "a treasure for a Prince." Mr. Pocket had invested the Prince's treasure in the ways of the world ever since, and it was supposed to have brought him in but indifferent interest. Still, Mrs. Pocket was in general the object of a queer sort of respectful pity, because she had not married a title; while Mr. Pocket was the object of a queer sort of forgiving reproach, because he had never got one.

Mr. Pocket took me into the house and showed me my room: which was a pleasant one, and so furnished as that I could use it with comfort for my own private sitting-room. He then knocked at the doors of two other similar rooms, and introduced me to their occupants, by name Drummle and Startop.* Drummle, an old-looking young man of a heavy order of architecture, was whistling. Startop, younger in years and appearance, was reading and holding his head, as if he thought himself in danger of exploding it with too strong a charge of knowledge.

Both Mr. and Mrs. Pocket had such a noticeable air of being in somebody else's hands, that I wondered who really was in possession of the house and let them live there, until I found this unknown power to be the servants. It was a smooth way of going on, perhaps, in respect of sav-

---

1. *to mount to the Woolsack, or to roof himself in with a mitre:* symbols of the highest office in the Law (Lord Chancellor), or the Church (Archbishop).

ing trouble; but it had the appearance of being expensive, for the servants felt it a duty they owed to themselves to be nice in their eating and drinking, and to keep a deal of company down-stairs. They allowed a very liberal table to Mr. and Mrs. Pocket, yet it always appeared to me that by far the best part of the house to have boarded in, would have been the kitchen — always supposing the boarder capable of self-defence, for, before I had been there a week, a neighbouring lady with whom the family were personally unacquainted, wrote in to say that she had seen Millers slapping the baby. This greatly distressed Mrs. Pocket, who burst into tears on receiving the note, and said it was an extraordinary thing that the neighbours couldn't mind their own business.

By degrees I learnt, and chiefly from Herbert, that Mr. Pocket had been educated at Harrow and at Cambridge, where he had distinguished himself; but that when he had had the happiness of marrying Mrs. Pocket very early in life, he had impaired his prospects and taken up the calling of a Grinder.[1] After grinding a number of dull blades — of whom it was remarkable that their fathers, when influential, were always going to help him to preferment, but always forgot to do it when the blades had left the Grindstone — he had wearied of that poor work and had come to London. Here, after gradually failing in loftier hopes, he had "read" with divers who had lacked opportunities or neglected them, and had refurbished divers others for special occasions, and had turned his acquirements to the account of literary compilation and correction, and on such means, added to some very moderate private resources, still maintained the house I saw.

Mr. and Mrs. Pocket had a toady neighbour; a widow lady of that highly sympathetic nature that she agreed with everybody, blessed everybody, and shed smiles and tears on everybody, according to circumstances. This lady's name was Mrs. Coiler,* and I had the honour of taking her down to dinner on the day of my installation. She gave me to understand on the stairs, that it was a blow to dear Mrs. Pocket that dear Mr. Pocket should be under the necessity of receiving gentlemen to read with him. That did not extend to me, she told me in a gush of love and confidence

---

1. *the calling of a Grinder:* someone who prepares students for examinations; a crammer.

(at that time, I had known her something less than five minutes); if they were all like Me, it would be quite another thing.

"But dear Mrs. Pocket," said Mrs. Coiler, "after her early disappointment (not that dear Mr. Pocket was to blame in that), requires so much luxury and elegance —"

"Yes, ma'am," I said, to stop her, for I was afraid she was going to cry.

"And she is of so aristocratic a disposition —"

"Yes, ma'am," I said again, with the same object as before.

"— that it *is* hard," said Mrs. Coiler, "to have dear Mr. Pocket's time and attention diverted from dear Mrs. Pocket."

I could not help thinking that it might be harder if the butcher's time and attention were diverted from dear Mrs. Pocket; but I said nothing, and indeed had enough to do in keeping a bashful watch upon my company-manners.

It came to my knowledge, through what passed between Mrs. Pocket and Drummle while I was attentive to my knife and fork, spoon, glasses, and other instruments of self-destruction, that Drummle, whose christian name was Bentley, was actually the next heir but one to a baronetcy. It further appeared that the book I had seen Mrs. Pocket reading in the garden, was all about titles, and that she knew the exact date at which her grandpapa would have come into the book, if he ever had come at all. Drummle didn't say much, but in his limited way (he struck me as a sulky kind of fellow) he spoke as one of the elect, and recognised Mrs. Pocket as a woman and a sister.[1] No one but themselves and Mrs. Coiler the toady neighbour showed any interest in this part of the conversation, and it appeared to me that it was painful to Herbert; but it promised to last a long time, when the page came in with the announcement of a domestic affliction. It was, in effect, that the cook had mislaid the beef. To my unutterable amazement, I now, for the first time, saw Mr. Pocket relieve his mind by going through a performance that struck me as very extraordinary, but which made no impression on anybody else, and with which I soon became as familiar as the rest. He laid down the

---

1. *a woman and a sister:* an ironic reference to the famous anti-slavery picture showing a Negro slave chained and kneeling, with the legend "Am I not a man and a brother?"

carving-knife and fork — being engaged in carving, at the moment — put his two hands into his disturbed hair, and appeared to make an extraordinary effort to lift himself up by it. When he had done this, and had not lifted himself up at all, he quietly went on with what he was about.

Mrs. Coiler then changed the subject, and began to flatter me. I liked it for a few moments, but she flattered me so very grossly that the pleasure was soon over. She had a serpentine way of coming close at me when she pretended to be vitally interested in the friends and localities I had left, which was altogether snaky and fork-tongued; and when she made an occasional bounce upon Startop (who said very little to her), or upon Drummle (who said less), I rather envied them for being on the opposite side of the table.

After dinner the children were introduced, and Mrs. Coiler made admiring comments on their eyes, noses, and legs — a sagacious way of improving their minds. There were four little girls, and two little boys, besides the baby who might have been either, and the baby's next successor who was as yet neither. They were brought in by Flopson and Millers, much as though those two non-commissioned officers had been recruiting somewhere for children and had enlisted these: while Mrs. Pocket looked at the young Nobles that ought to have been, as if she rather thought she had had the pleasure of inspecting them before, but didn't quite know what to make of them.

"Here! Give me your fork, Mum, and take the baby," said Flopson. "Don't take it that way, or you'll get its head under the table."

Thus advised, Mrs. Pocket took it the other way, and got its head upon the table; which was announced to all present by a prodigious concussion.

"Dear, dear! Give it me back, Mum," said Flopson; "and Miss Jane, come and dance to baby, do!"

One of the little girls, a mere mite who seemed to have prematurely taken upon herself some charge of the others, stepped out of her place by me, and danced to and from the baby until it left off crying, and laughed. Then, all the children laughed, and Mr. Pocket (who in the meantime had twice endeavoured to lift himself up by the hair) laughed, and we all laughed and were glad.

Flopson, by dint of doubling the baby at the joints like a Dutch doll,[1] then got it safely into Mrs. Pocket's lap, and gave it the nutcrackers to play with: at the same time recommending Mrs. Pocket to take notice that the handles of that instrument were not likely to agree with its eyes, and sharply charging Miss Jane to look after the same. Then, the two nurses left the room, and had a lively scuffle on the staircase with a dissipated page who had waited at dinner, and who had clearly lost half his buttons at the gaming-table.

I was made very uneasy in my mind by Mrs. Pocket's falling into a discussion with Drummle respecting two baronetcies, while she ate a sliced orange steeped in sugar and wine, and forgetting all about the baby on her lap: who did most appalling things with the nutcrackers. At length, little Jane perceiving its young brains to be imperilled, softly left her place, and with many small artifices coaxed the dangerous weapon away. Mrs. Pocket finishing her orange at about the same time, and not approving of this, said to Jane:

"You naughty child, how dare you? Go and sit down this instant!"

"Mamma dear," lisped the little girl, "baby ood have put hith eyeth out."

"How dare you tell me so?" retorted Mrs. Pocket. "Go and sit down in your chair this moment!"

Mrs. Pocket's dignity was so crushing, that I felt quite abashed: as if I myself had done something to rouse it.

"Belinda," remonstrated Mr. Pocket, from the other end of the table, "how can you be so unreasonable? Jane only interfered for the protection of baby."

"I will not allow anybody to interfere," said Mrs. Pocket. "I am surprised, Matthew, that you should expose me to the affront of interference."

"Good God!" cried Mr. Pocket, in an outbreak of desolate desperation. "Are infants to be nutcrackered into their tombs, and is nobody to save them?"

"I will not be interfered with by Jane," said Mrs. Pocket, with a majestic glance at that innocent little offender. "I hope I know my poor grandpapa's position. Jane, indeed!"

---

1. *a Dutch doll:* a jointed wooden doll.

Mr. Pocket got his hands in his hair again, and this time really did lift himself some inches out of his chair. "Hear this!" he helplessly exclaimed to the elements. "Babies are to be nutcrackered dead, for people's poor grandpapa's positions!" Then he let himself down again, and became silent. We all looked awkwardly at the tablecloth while this was going on. A pause succeeded, during which the honest and irrepressible baby made a series of leaps and crows at little Jane, who appeared to me to be the only member of the family (irrespective of servants) with whom it had any decided acquaintance.

"Mr. Drummle," said Mrs. Pocket, "will you ring for Flopson? Jane, you undutiful little thing, go and lie down. Now, baby darling, come with ma!"

The baby was the soul of honour, and protested with all its might. It doubled itself up the wrong way over Mrs. Pocket's arm, exhibited a pair of knitted shoes and dimpled ankles to the company in lieu of its soft face, and was carried out in the highest state of mutiny. And it gained its point after all, for I saw it through the window within a few minutes, being nursed by little Jane.

It happened that the other five children were left behind at the dinner-table, through Flopson's having some private engagement, and their not being anybody else's business. I thus became aware of the mutual relations between them and Mr. Pocket, which were exemplified in the following manner. Mr. Pocket, with the normal perplexity of his face heightened and his hair rumpled, looked at them for some minutes, as if he couldn't make out how they came to be boarding and lodging in that establishment, and why they hadn't been billeted by Nature on somebody else. Then, in a distant, Missionary way he asked them certain questions — as why little Joe had that hole in his frill: who said, Pa, Flopson was going to mend it when she had time — and how little Fanny came by that whitlow:[1] who said, Pa, Millers was going to poultice it when she didn't forget. Then, he melted into parental tenderness, and gave them a shilling apiece and told them to go and play; and then as they went out, with one very strong effort to lift himself up by the hair he dismissed the hopeless subject.

---

1. *a whitlow:* a running sore on the finger.

In the evening there was rowing on the river. As Drummle and Startop had each a boat, I resolved to set up mine, and to cut them both out. I was pretty good at most exercises in which country-boys are adepts, but, as I was conscious of wanting elegance of style for the Thames — not to say for other waters — I at once engaged to place myself under the tuition of the winner of a prize-wherry who plied at our stairs,[1] and to whom I was introduced by my new allies. This practical authority confused me very much, by saying I had the arm of a blacksmith. If he could have known how nearly the compliment lost him his pupil, I doubt if he would have paid it.

There was a supper-tray after we got home at night, and I think we should all have enjoyed ourselves, but for a rather disagreeable domestic occurrence. Mr. Pocket was in good spirits, when a housemaid came in, and said, "If you please, sir, I should wish to speak to you."

"Speak to your master?" said Mrs. Pocket, whose dignity was roused again. "How can you think of such a thing? Go and speak to Flopson. Or speak to me — at some other time."

"Begging your pardon, ma'am?" returned the housemaid, "I should wish to speak at once, and to speak to master."

Hereupon, Mr. Pocket went out of the room, and we made the best of ourselves until he came back.

"This is a pretty thing, Belinda!" said Mr. Pocket, returning with a countenance expressive of grief and despair. "Here's the cook lying insensibly drunk on the kitchen floor, with a large bundle of fresh butter made up in the cupboard ready to sell for grease!"

Mrs. Pocket instantly showed much amiable emotion, and said, "This is that odious Sophia's doing!"

"What do you mean, Belinda?" demanded Mr. Pocket.

"Sophia has told you," said Mrs. Pocket. "Did I not see her with my own eyes and hear her with my own ears, come into the room just now and ask to speak to you?"

---

1. *the winner of a prize-wherry who plied at our stairs:* a champion oarsman at the light rowing-boat hired out to carry passengers and goods on the river; "stairs" refers to landing stages on the Thames, which typically include a flight of stone steps.

"But has she not taken me down-stairs, Belinda," returned Mr. Pocket, "and shown me the woman, and the bundle too?"

"And do you defend her, Matthew," said Mrs. Pocket, "for making mischief?"

Mr. Pocket uttered a dismal groan.

"Am I, grandpapa's granddaughter, to be nothing in the house?" said Mrs. Pocket. "Besides, the cook has always been a very nice respectful woman, and said in the most natural manner when she came to look after the situation, that she felt I was born to be a Duchess."

There was a sofa where Mr. Pocket stood, and he dropped upon it in the attitude of the Dying Gladiator.[1] Still in that attitude he said, with a hollow voice, "Good night, Mr. Pip," when I deemed it advisable to go to bed and leave him.

CHAPTER V

AFTER TWO or three days, when I had established myself in my room and had gone backwards and forwards to London several times, and had ordered all I wanted of my tradesmen, Mr. Pocket and I had a long talk together. He knew more of my intended career than I knew myself, for he referred to his having been told by Mr. Jaggers that I was not designed for any profession, and that I should be well enough educated for my destiny if I could "hold my own" with the average of young men in prosperous circumstances. I acquiesced, of course, knowing nothing to the contrary.

He advised my attending certain places in London, for the acquisition of such mere rudiments as I wanted, and my investing him with the functions of explainer and director of all my studies. He hoped that with intelligent assistance I should meet with little to discourage me, and should

---

1. *the Dying Gladiator:* classical statue of a figure lying propped on one arm and with bowed head, found in Rome in the Capitoline museum, and made famous by Byron's moving description in Canto IV of *Childe Harold's Pilgrimage.*

soon be able to dispense with any aid but his. Through his way of saying this, and much more to similar purpose, he placed himself on confidential terms with me in an admirable manner; and I may state at once that he was always so zealous and honourable in fulfilling his compact with me, that he made me zealous and honourable in fulfilling mine with him. If he had shown indifference as a master, I have no doubt I should have returned the compliment as a pupil; he gave me no such excuse, and each of us did the other justice. Nor, did I ever regard him as having anything ludicrous about him — or anything but what was serious, honest, and good — in his tutor communication with me.

When these points were settled, and so far carried out as that I had begun to work in earnest, it occurred to me that if I could retain my bedroom in Barnard's Inn, my life would be agreeably varied, while my manners would be none the worse for Herbert's society. Mr. Pocket did not object to this arrangement, but urged that before any step could possibly be taken in it, it must be submitted to my guardian. I felt that his delicacy arose out of the consideration that the plan would save Herbert some expense, so I went off to Little Britain and imparted my wish to Mr. Jaggers.

"If I could buy the furniture now hired for me," said I, "and one or two other little things, I should be quite at home there."

"Go it!" said Mr. Jaggers, with a short laugh. "I told you you'd get on. Well! How much do you want?"

I said I didn't know how much.

"Come!" retorted Mr. Jaggers. "How much? Fifty pounds?"

"Oh, not nearly so much."

"Five pounds?" said Mr. Jaggers.

This was such a great fall, that I said in discomfiture, "Oh! more than that."

"More than that, eh!" retorted Mr. Jaggers, lying in wait for me, with his hands in his pockets, his head on one side, and his eyes on the wall behind me; "how much more?"

"It is so difficult to fix a sum," said I, hesitating.

"Come!" said Mr. Jaggers. "Let's get at it. Twice five; will that do? Three times five; will that do? Four times five; will that do?"

I said I thought that would do handsomely.

"Four times five will do handsomely, will it?" said Mr. Jaggers, knitting his brows. "Now, what do you make of four times five?"

"What do I make of it?"

"Ah!" said Mr. Jaggers; "how much?"

"I suppose you make it twenty pounds," said I, smiling.

"Never mind what *I* make it, my friend," observed Mr. Jaggers, with a knowing and contradictory toss of his head. "I want to know what *you* make it."

"Twenty pounds, of course."

"Wemmick!" said Mr. Jaggers, opening his office door. "Take Mr. Pip's written order, and pay him twenty pounds."

This strongly marked way of doing business made a strongly marked impression on me, and that not of an agreeable kind. Mr. Jaggers never laughed; but he wore great bright creaking boots, and, in poising himself on these boots, with his large head bent down and his eyebrows joined together, awaiting an answer, he sometimes caused the boots to creak, as if *they* laughed in a dry and suspicious way. As he happened to go out now, and as Wemmick was brisk and talkative, I said to Wemmick that I hardly knew what to make of Mr. Jaggers's manner.

"Tell him that, and he'll take it as a compliment," answered Wemmick; "he don't mean that you *should* know what to make of it. — Oh!" for I looked surprised, "it's not personal; it's professional: only professional."

Wemmick was at his desk, lunching — and crunching — on a dry hard biscuit; pieces of which he threw from time to time into his slit of a mouth, as if he were posting them.

"Always seems to me," said Wemmick, "as if he had set a man-trap and was watching it. Suddenly — click — you're caught!"

Without remarking that man-traps were not among the amenities of life, I said I supposed he was very skilful?

"Deep," said Wemmick, "as Australia." Pointing with his pen at the office floor, to express that Australia was understood, for the purposes of the figure, to be symmetrically on the opposite spot of the globe. "If there was anything deeper," added Wemmick, bringing his pen to paper, "he'd be it."

Then, I said I supposed he had a fine business, and Wemmick said, "Ca-pi-tal!" Then I asked if there were many clerks? to which he replied:

"We don't run much into clerks, because there's only one Jaggers, and people won't have him at second hand. There are only four of us. Would you like to see 'em? You are one of us, as I may say."

I accepted the offer. When Mr. Wemmick had put all the biscuit into the post, and had paid me my money from a cash-box in a safe, the key of which safe he kept somewhere down his back and produced from his coat-collar like an iron pigtail, we went up-stairs. The house was dark and shabby, and the greasy shoulders that had left their mark in Mr. Jaggers's room, seemed to have been shuffling up and down the staircase for years. In the front first floor, a clerk who looked something between a publican and a rat-catcher — a large pale puffed swollen man — was attentively engaged with three or four people of shabby appearance, whom he treated as unceremoniously as everybody seemed to be treated who contributed to Mr. Jaggers's coffers. "Getting evidence together," said Mr. Wemmick, as we came out, "for the Bailey." In the room over that, a little flabby terrier of a clerk with dangling hair (his cropping seemed to have been forgotten when he was a puppy) was similarly engaged with a man with weak eyes, whom Mr. Wemmick presented to me as a smelter[1] who kept his pot always boiling, and who would melt me anything I pleased — and who was in an excessive white-perspiration, as if he had been trying his art on himself. In a back room, a high-shouldered man with a face-ache tied up in dirty flannel, who was dressed in old black clothes that bore the appearance of having been waxed, was stooping over his work of making fair copies of the notes of the other two gentlemen, for Mr. Jaggers's own use.

This was all the establishment. When we went down-stairs again, Wemmick led me into my guardian's room, and said, "This you've seen already."

"Pray," said I, as the two odious casts with the twitchy leer upon them caught my sight again, "whose likenesses are those?"

"These?" said Wemmick, getting upon a chair, and blowing the dust off the horrible heads before bringing them down. "These are two

---

1. *smelter:* literally, a workman engaged in heating ore to extract metal, seen as analogous to the process of extracting evidence from documents.

celebrated ones. Famous clients of ours that got us a world of credit. This chap (why you must have come down in the night and been peeping into the inkstand, to get this blot upon your eyebrow, you old rascal!) murdered his master, and, considering that he wasn't brought up to evidence, didn't plan it badly."

"Is it like him?" I asked, recoiling from the brute, as Wemmick spat upon his eyebrow and gave it a rub with his sleeve.

"Like him? It's himself, you know. The cast was made in Newgate, directly after he was taken down. You had a particular fancy for me, hadn't you, Old Artful?" said Wemmick. He then explained this affectionate apostrophe, by touching his brooch representing the lady and the weeping willow at the tomb with the urn upon it, and saying, "Had it made for me, express!"

"Is the lady anybody?" said I.

"No," returned Wemmick. "Only his game. (You liked your bit of game, didn't you?) No; deuce a bit of a lady in the case, Mr. Pip, except one — and she wasn't of this slender ladylike sort, and you wouldn't have caught *her* looking after this urn — unless there was something to drink in it." Wemmick's attention being thus directed to his brooch, he put down the cast, and polished the brooch with his pocket-handkerchief.

"Did that other creature come to the same end?" I asked. "He has the same look."

"You're right," said Wemmick; "it's the genuine look. Much as if one nostril was caught up with a horsehair and a little fish-hook. Yes, he came to the same end; quite the natural end here, I assure you. He forged wills, this blade did, if he didn't also put the supposed testators to sleep too. You were a gentlemanly Cove, though" (Mr. Wemmick was again apostrophising), "and you said you could write Greek. Yah, Bounceable![1] What a liar you were! I never met such a liar as you!" Before putting his late friend on his shelf again, Wemmick touched the largest of his mourning rings, and said, "Sent out to buy it for me, only the day before."

While he was putting up the other cast and coming down from the chair the thought crossed my mind that all his personal jewellery was

---

1. *Bounceable:* swaggering.

derived from like sources. As he had shown no diffidence on the subject, I ventured on the liberty of asking him the question, when he stood before me, dusting his hands.

"Oh yes," he returned, "these are all gifts of that kind. One brings another, you see; that's the way of it. I always take 'em. They're curiosities. And they're property. They may not be worth much, but, after all, they're property and portable. It don't signify to you with your brilliant lookout, but as to myself, my guiding-star always is, Get hold of portable property."

When I had rendered homage to this light, he went on to say, in a friendly manner:

"If at any odd time when you have nothing better to do, you wouldn't mind coming over to see me at Walworth,[1] I could offer you a bed, and I should consider it an honour. I have not much to show you; but such two or three curiosities as I have got, you might like to look over; and I am fond of a bit of garden and a summer-house."

I said I should be delighted to accept his hospitality.

"Thankee," said he; "then we'll consider that it's to come off, when convenient to you. Have you dined with Mr. Jaggers yet?"

"Not yet."

"Well," said Wemmick, "he'll give you wine, and good wine. I'll give you punch, and not bad punch. And now I'll tell you something. When you go to dine with Mr. Jaggers, look at his housekeeper."

"Shall I see something very uncommon?"

"Well," said Wemmick, "you'll see a wild beast tamed. Not so very uncommon, you'll tell me. I reply, that depends on the original wildness of the beast, and the amount of taming. It won't lower your opinion of Mr. Jaggers's powers. Keep your eye on it."

I told him I would do so, with all the interest and curiosity that his preparation awakened. As I was taking my departure, he asked me if I would like to devote five minutes to seeing Mr. Jaggers "at it?"

For several reasons, and not least because I didn't clearly know what Mr. Jaggers would be found to be "at," I replied in the affirmative. We

---

1. *Walworth:* then still largely rural suburb south of the Thames. See Map C.

dived into the City, and came up in a crowded police-court,* where a blood-relation (in the murderous sense) of the deceased with the fanciful taste in brooches, was standing at the bar, uncomfortably chewing something; while my guardian had a woman under examination or cross-examination — I don't know which — and was striking her, and the bench, and everybody present, with awe. If anybody, of whatsoever degree, said a word that he didn't approve of, he instantly required to have it "taken down." If anybody wouldn't make an admission, he said, "I'll have it out of you!" and if anybody made an admission, he said, "Now I have got you!" The magistrates shivered under a single bite of his finger. Thieves and thief-takers hung in dread rapture on his words, and shrank when a hair of his eyebrows turned in their direction. Which side he was on, I couldn't make out, for he seemed to me to be grinding the whole place in a mill; I only know that when I stole out on tiptoe, he was not on the side of the bench; for, he was making the legs of the old gentleman who presided, quite convulsive under the table, by his denunciations of his conduct as the representative of British law and justice in that chair that day.

CHAPTER VI

BENTLEY DRUMMLE, who was so sulky a fellow that he even took up a book as if its writer had done him an injury, did not take up an acquaintance in a more agreeable spirit. Heavy in figure, movement, and comprehension — in the sluggish complexion of his face, and in the large awkward tongue that seemed to loll about in his mouth as he himself lolled about in a room — he was idle, proud, niggardly, reserved, and suspicious. He came of rich people down in Somersetshire, who had nursed this combination of qualities until they made the discovery that it was just of age and a blockhead. Thus, Bentley Drummle had come to Mr. Pocket when he was a head taller than that gentleman, and half a dozen heads thicker than most gentlemen.

Startop had been spoilt by a weak mother and kept at home when he ought to have been at school, but he was devotedly attached to her, and admired her beyond measure. He had a woman's delicacy of feature, and was — "as you may see, though you never saw her," said Herbert to me — exactly like his mother. It was but natural that I should take to him much more kindly than to Drummle, and that, even in the earliest evenings of our boating, he and I should pull homeward abreast of one another, conversing from boat to boat, while Bentley Drummle came up in our wake alone, under the overhanging banks and among the rushes. He would always creep in-shore like some uncomfortable amphibious creature, even when the tide would have sent him fast upon his way; and I always think of him as coming after us in the dark or by the back-water, when our own two boats were breaking the sunset or the moonlight in mid-stream.

Herbert was my intimate companion and friend. I presented him with a half-share in my boat, which was the occasion of his often coming down to Hammersmith; and my possession of a half-share in his chambers often took me up to London. We used to walk between the two places at all hours. I have an affection for the road yet (though it is not so pleasant a road as it was then), formed in the impressibility of untried youth and hope.

When I had been in Mr. Pocket's family a month or two, Mr. and Mrs. Camilla turned up. Camilla was Mr. Pocket's sister. Georgiana, whom I had seen at Miss Havisham's on the same occasion, also turned up. She was a cousin — an indigestive single woman, who called her rigidity religion, and her liver love. These people hated me with the hatred of cupidity and disappointment. As a matter of course, they fawned upon me in my prosperity with the basest meanness. Towards Mr. Pocket, as a grownup infant with no notion of his own interests, they showed the complacent forbearance I had heard them express. Mrs. Pocket they held in contempt; but they allowed the poor soul to have been heavily disappointed in life, because that shed a feeble reflected light upon themselves.

These were the surroundings among which I settled down, and applied myself to my education. I soon contracted expensive habits, and began to spend an amount of money that within a few short months I should have thought almost fabulous; but through good and evil I stuck to my books. There was no other merit in this, than my having sense enough to feel my deficiencies. Between Mr. Pocket and Herbert I got on fast; and, with one or the other always at my elbow to give me the start I wanted, and clear obstructions out of my road, I must have been as great a dolt as Drummle if I had done less.

I had not seen Mr. Wemmick for some weeks, when I thought I would write him a note and propose to go home with him on a certain evening. He replied that it would give him much pleasure, and that he would expect me at the office at six o'clock. Thither I went, and there I found him, putting the key of his safe down his back as the clock struck.

"Did you think of walking down to Walworth?" said he.

"Certainly," said I, "if you approve."

"Very much," was Wemmick's reply, "for I have had my legs under the desk all day, and shall be glad to stretch them. Now I'll tell you what I have got for supper, Mr. Pip. I have got a stewed steak — which is of home preparation — and a cold roast fowl — which is from the cook's-shop. I think it's tender, because the master of the shop was a Juryman in some cases of ours the other day, and we let him down easy. I reminded him of it when I bought the fowl, and I said, 'Pick us out a good one, old Briton, because if we had chosen to keep you in the box another day or two, we could easily have done it.' He said to that, 'Let me make you a present of the best fowl in the shop.' I let him, of course. As far as it goes, it's property and portable. You don't object to an aged parent, I hope?"

I really thought he was still speaking of the fowl, until he added, "Because I have got an aged parent at my place." I then said what politeness required.

"So, you haven't dined with Mr. Jaggers yet?" he pursued, as we walked along.

"Not yet."

"He told me so this afternoon when he heard you were coming. I expect you'll have an invitation to-morrow. He's going to ask your pals, too. Three of 'em; ain't there?"

Although I was not in the habit of counting Drummle as one of my intimate associates, I answered, "Yes."

"Well, he's going to ask the whole gang;" I hardly felt complimented by the word; "and whatever he gives you, he'll give you good. Don't look forward to variety, but you'll have excellence. And there's another rum thing in his house," proceeded Wemmick, after a moment's pause, as if the remark followed on the housekeeper understood; "he never lets a door or window be fastened at night."

"Is he never robbed?"

"That's it!" returned Wemmick. "He says, and gives it out publicly, 'I want to see the man who'll rob *me*.' Lord bless you, I have heard him, a hundred times if I have heard him once, say to regular cracksmen in our front office, 'You know where I live; now, no bolt is ever drawn there; why don't you do a stroke of business with me? Come; can't I tempt you?' Not a man of them, sir, would be bold enough to try it on, for love or money."

"They dread him so much?" said I.

"Dread him," said Wemmick. "I believe you they dread him. Not but what he's artful, even in his defiance of them. No silver, sir. Britannia metal,[1] every spoon."

"So they wouldn't have much," I observed, "even if they —"

"Ah! But *he* would have much," said Wemmick, cutting me short, "and they know it. He'd have their lives, and the lives of scores of 'em. He'd have all he could get. And it's impossible to say what he couldn't get, if he gave his mind to it."

I was falling into meditation on my guardian's greatness, when Wemmick remarked:

"As to the absence of plate, that's only his natural depth, you know. A river's its natural depth, and he's his natural depth. Look at his watch-chain. That's real enough."

"It's very massive," said I.

"Massive?" repeated Wemmick. "I think so. And his watch is a gold repeater,[2] and worth a hundred pound if it's worth a penny. Mr. Pip, there are about seven hundred thieves in this town who know all about that watch; there's not a man, a woman, or a child, among them, who wouldn't identify the smallest link in that chain, and drop it as if it was red-hot, if inveigled into touching it."

At first with such discourse, and afterwards with conversation of a more general nature, did Mr. Wemmick and I beguile the time and the road, until he gave me to understand that we had arrived in the district of Walworth.

---

1. *Britannia metal:* tin alloy similar in appearance to silver.
2. *repeater:* expensive pocket-watch, first invented in the seventeenth century, which chimed the hour on demand.

It appeared to be a collection of back lanes, ditches, and little gardens, and to present the aspect of a rather dull retirement. Wemmick's house was a little wooden cottage in the midst of plots of garden, and the top of it was cut out and painted like a battery mounted with guns.

"My own doing," said Wemmick. "Looks pretty; don't it?"

I highly commended it. I think it was the smallest house I ever saw; with the queerest gothic windows (by far the greater part of them sham), and a gothic door, almost too small to get in at.

"That's a real flagstaff, you see," said Wemmick, "and on Sundays I run up a real flag. Then look here. After I have crossed this bridge, I hoist it up — so — and cut off the communication."

The bridge was a plank, and it crossed a chasm about four feet wide and two deep. But it was very pleasant to see the pride with which he hoisted it up and made it fast; smiling as he did so, with a relish and not merely mechanically.

"At nine o'clock every night, Greenwich time," said Wemmick, "the gun fires. There he is, you see! And when you hear him go, I think you'll say he's a Stinger."

The piece of ordnance referred to, was mounted in a separate fortress, constructed of lattice-work. It was protected from the weather by an ingenious little tarpaulin contrivance in the nature of an umbrella.

"Then, at the back," said Wemmick, "out of sight, so as not to impede the idea of fortifications — for it's a principle with me, if you have an idea, carry it out and keep it up — I don't know whether that's your opinion —"

I said, decidedly.

"At the back, there's a pig, and there are fowls and rabbits; then, I knock together my own little frame, you see, and grow cucumbers; and you'll judge at supper what sort of a salad I can raise. So, sir," said Wemmick, smiling again, but seriously too, as he shook his head, "if you can suppose the little place besieged, it would hold out a devil of a time in point of provisions."

Then, he conducted me to a bower about a dozen yards off, but which was approached by such ingenious twists of path that it took quite a long time to get at; and in this retreat our glasses were already set forth. Our punch was cooling in an ornamental lake on whose margin the bower was raised. This piece of water (with an island in the middle which might have been the salad for supper) was of a circular form, and he had constructed a fountain in it, which, when you set a little mill going and took a cork out of a pipe, played to that powerful extent that it made the back of your hand quite wet.

"I am my own engineer, and my own carpenter, and my own plumber, and my own gardener, and my own Jack of all Trades," said Wemmick, in acknowledging my compliments. "Well; it's a good thing, you know. It brushes the Newgate cobwebs away, and pleases the Aged. You wouldn't mind being at once introduced to the Aged, would you? It wouldn't put you out?"

I expressed the readiness I felt, and we went into the Castle. There, we found, sitting by a fire, a very old man in a flannel coat: clean, cheerful, comfortable, and well cared for, but intensely deaf.

"Well aged parent," said Wemmick, shaking hands with him in a cordial and jocose way, "how am you?"

"All right, John; all right!" replied the old man.

"Here's Mr. Pip, aged parent," said Wemmick, "and I wish you could hear his name. Nod away at him, Mr. Pip; that's what he likes. Nod away at him, if you please, like winking!"

"This is a fine place of my son's, sir," cried the old man, while I nodded as hard as I possibly could. "This is a pretty pleasure-ground, sir. This spot and these beautiful works upon it ought to be kept together by the Nation, after my son's time, for the people's enjoyment."

"You're as proud of it as Punch; ain't you, Aged?" said Wemmick, contemplating the old man, with his hard face really softened; "there's a nod for you;" giving him a tremendous one; "there's another for you;" giving him a still more tremendous one; "you like that, don't you? If you're not tired, Mr. Pip — though I know it's tiring to strangers — will you tip him one more? You can't think how it pleases him."

I tipped him several more, and he was in great spirits. We left him bestirring himself to feed the fowls, and we sat down to our punch in the arbour; where Wemmick told me as he smoked a pipe that it had taken him a good many years to bring the property up to its present pitch of perfection.

"Is it your own, Mr. Wemmick?"

"Oh yes," said Wemmick, "I have got hold of it, a bit at a time. It's a freehold, by George!"

"Is it, indeed? I hope Mr. Jaggers admires it?"

"Never seen it," said Wemmick. "Never heard of it. Never seen the Aged. Never heard of him. No; the office is one thing, and private life is another. When I go into the office, I leave the Castle behind me, and when I come into the Castle, I leave the office behind me. If it's not in any way disagreeable to you, you'll oblige me by doing the same. I don't wish it professionally spoken about."

Of course I felt my good faith involved in the observance of his request. The punch being very nice, we sat there drinking it and talking, until it was almost nine o'clock. "Getting near gun-fire," said Wemmick then, as he laid down his pipe; "it's the Aged's treat."

Proceeding into the Castle again, we found the Aged heating the poker, with expectant eyes, as a preliminary to the performance of this great nightly ceremony. Wemmick stood with his watch in his hand, until the moment was come for him to take the red-hot poker from the Aged, and repair to the battery. He took it, and went out, and presently the Stinger went off with a Bang that shook the crazy little box of a cottage as if it must fall to pieces, and made every glass and teacup in it ring. Upon this, the Aged — who I believe would have been blown out of his arm-chair but for holding on by the elbows — cried out exultingly, "He's fired! I heerd him!" and I nodded at the old gentleman until it is no figure of speech to declare that I absolutely could not see him.

The interval between that time and supper, Wemmick devoted to showing me his collection of curiosities. They were mostly of a felonious character; comprising the pen with which a celebrated forgery had been committed, a distinguished razor or two, some locks of hair, and several manuscript confessions written under condemnation — upon which Mr. Wemmick set particular value as being, to use his own words, "every one of 'em Lies, sir." These were agreeably dispersed among small specimens of china and glass various neat trifles made by the proprietor of the museum, and some tobacco-stoppers carved by the Aged. They were all displayed in that chamber of the Castle into which I had been first inducted, and which served, not only as the general sitting-room but as the kitchen too, if I might judge from a saucepan on the hob, and a brazen bijou[1] over the fireplace designed for the suspension of a roasting-jack.

There was a neat little girl in attendance, who looked after the Aged in the day. When she had laid the supper-cloth, the bridge was lowered to give her means of egress, and she withdrew for the night. The supper was excellent; and though the Castle was rather subject to dry-rot insomuch that it tasted like a bad nut, and though the pig might have been farther off, I was heartily pleased with my whole entertainment. Nor was there any drawback on my little turret bedroom, beyond there being such a very thin ceiling between me and the flagstaff, that when I lay down on my back in bed, it seemed as if I had to balance that pole on my forehead all night.

Wemmick was up early in the morning, and I am afraid I heard him cleaning my boots. After that, he fell to gardening, and I saw him from my gothic window pretending to employ the Aged, and nodding at him in a most devoted manner. Our breakfast was as good as the supper, and at half-past eight precisely we started for Little Britain. By degrees, Wemmick got dryer and harder as we went along, and his mouth tightened into a post-office again. At last, when we got to his place of business and he pulled out his key from his coat-collar, he looked as unconscious of his Walworth property as if the Castle and the drawbridge and the arbour and the lake and the fountain and the Aged, had all been blown into space together by the last discharge of the Stinger.

CHAPTER VII

IT FELL out as Wemmick had told me it would, that I had an early opportunity of comparing my guardian's establishment with that of his cashier and clerk. My guardian was in his room, washing his hands with his scented soap, when I went into the office from Walworth; and he called me to him, and gave me the invitation for myself and friends which Wemmick had prepared me to receive. "No ceremony," he stipulated, "and no din-

---

1. *brazen bijou:* brass ring.

ner dress, and say to-morrow." I asked him where we should come to (for I had no idea where he lived), and I believe it was in his general objection to make anything like an admission, that he replied, "Come here, and I'll take you home with me." I embrace this opportunity of remarking that he washed his clients off, as if he were a surgeon or a dentist. He had a closet in his room, fitted up for the purpose, which smelt of the scented soap like a perfumer's shop. It had an unusually large jack-towel on a roller inside the door, and he would wash his hands, and wipe them and dry them all over this towel, whenever he came in from a police-court or dismissed a client from his room. When I and my friends repaired to him at six o'clock next day, he seemed to have been engaged on a case of a darker complexion than usual, for, we found him with his head butted into this closet, not only washing his hands, but laving his face and gargling his throat. And even when he had done all that, and had gone all round the jack-towel, he took out his penknife and scraped the case¹ out of his nails before he put his coat on.

There were some people slinking about as usual when we passed out into the street, who were evidently anxious to speak with him; but there was something so conclusive in the halo of scented soap which encircled his presence, that they gave it up for that day. As we walked along westward, he was recognised ever and again by some face in the crowd of the streets, and whenever that happened he talked louder to me; but he never otherwise recognised anybody, or took notice that anybody recognised him.

He conducted us to Gerrard-street, Soho,² to a house on the south side of that street. Rather a stately house of its kind, but dolefully in want of painting, and with dirty windows. He took out his key and opened the door, and we all went into a stone hall, bare, gloomy, and little used. So, up a dark brown staircase into a series of three dark brown rooms on the first floor. There were carved garlands on the panelled walls, and as he stood among them giving us welcome, I know what kind of loops I thought they looked like.³

---

1. *case:* i.e., the law case.
2. *Gerrard-street, Soho:* at the time Soho was an area of rapidly fading splendour to the west of the City (see Map C). Gerard Street was laid out in the 1670s.
3. *what kind of loops I thought they looked like:* i.e., hangman's nooses.

Dinner was laid in the best of these rooms; the second was his dressing-room; the third, his bedroom. He told us that he held the whole house, but rarely used more of it than we saw. The table was comfortably laid — no silver in the service, of course — and at the side of his chair was a capacious dumb-waiter,[1] with a variety of bottles and decanters on it, and four dishes of fruit for dessert. I noticed throughout, that he kept everything under his own hand, and distributed everything himself.

There was a bookcase in the room; I saw, from the backs of the books, that they were about evidence, criminal law, criminal biography, trials, acts of parliament, and such things. The furniture was all very solid and good, like his watch-chain. It had an official look, however, and there was nothing merely ornamental to be seen. In a corner, was a little table of papers with a shaded lamp: so that he seemed to bring the office home with him in that respect too, and to wheel it out of an evening and fall to work.

As he had scarcely seen my three companions until now — for, he and I had walked together — he stood on the hearth-rug, after ringing the bell, and took a searching look at them. To my surprise, he seemed at once to be principally if not solely interested in Drummle.

"Pip," said he, putting his large hand on my shoulder and moving me to the window, "I don't know one from the other. Who's the Spider?"

"The spider?" said I.

"The blotchy, sprawly, sulky fellow."

"That's Bentley Drummle," I replied; "the one with the delicate face is Startop."

Not making the least account of "the one with the delicate face," he returned, "Bentley Drummle is his name, is it? I like the look of that fellow."

He immediately began to talk to Drummle: not at all deterred by his replying in his heavy reticent way, but apparently led on by it to screw discourse out of him. I was looking at the two, when there came between me and them, the housekeeper, with the first dish for the table.

---

1. *dumb-waiter:* a piece of dining-room furniture, usually consisting of revolving trays attached to a stand, and obviating the need for a servant to wait at table.

She was a woman of about forty, I supposed — but I may have thought her younger than she was. Rather tall, of a lithe nimble figure, extremely pale, with large faded eyes, and a quantity of streaming hair. I cannot say whether any diseased affection of the heart caused her lips to be parted as if she were panting, and her face to bear a curious expression of suddenness and flutter; but I know that I had been to see Macbeth at the theatre, a night or two before, and that her face looked to me as if it were all disturbed by fiery air, like the faces I had seen rise out of the Witches' caldron.

She set the dish on, touched my guardian quietly on the arm with a finger to notify that dinner was ready, and vanished. We took our seats at the round table, and my guardian kept Drummle on one side of him, while Startop sat on the other. It was a noble dish of fish that the housekeeper had put on table, and we had a joint of equally choice mutton afterwards, and then an equally choice bird. Sauces, wines, all the accessories we wanted, and all of the best, were given out by our host from his dumbwaiter; and when they had made the circuit of the table, he always put them back again. Similarly, he dealt us clean plates and knives and forks, for each course, and dropped those just disused into two baskets on the ground by his chair. No other attendant than the housekeeper appeared. She set on every dish; and I always saw in her face, a face rising out of the caldron. Years afterwards, I made a dreadful likeness of that woman, by causing a face that had no other natural resemblance to it than it derived from flowing hair, to pass behind a bowl of flaming spirits in a dark room.

Induced to take particular notice of the housekeeper, both by her own striking appearance and by Wemmick's preparation, I observed that whenever she was in the room, she kept her eyes attentively on my guardian, and that she would remove her hands from any dish she put before him, hesitatingly, as if she dreaded his calling her back, and wanted him to speak when she was nigh, if he had anything to say. I fancied that I could detect in his manner a consciousness of this, and a purpose of always holding her in suspense.

Dinner went off gaily, and, although my guardian seemed to follow rather than originate subjects, I knew that he wrenched the weakest part of our dispositions out of us. For myself, I found that I was expressing my tendency to lavish expenditure, and to patronise Herbert, and to boast of my great prospects, before I quite knew that I had opened my lips. It was so with all of us, but with no one more than Drummle: the development of whose inclination to gird in a grudging and suspicious way at the rest, was screwed out of him before the fish was taken off.

It was not then, but when we had got to the cheese, that our conversation turned upon our rowing feats, and that Drummle was rallied for coming up behind of a night in that slow amphibious way of his. Drummle upon this, informed our host that he much preferred our room to our company, and that as to skill he was more than our master, and that as to strength he could scatter us like chaff. By some invisible agency, my guardian wound him up to a pitch little short of ferocity about this trifle; and he fell to baring and spanning his arm to show how muscular it was, and we all fell to baring and spanning our arms in a ridiculous manner.

Now, the housekeeper was at that time clearing the table; my guardian, taking no heed of her, but with the side of his face turned from her, was leaning back in his chair biting the side of his forefinger and showing an interest in Drummle, that, to me, was quite inexplicable. Suddenly, he clapped his large hand on the housekeeper's, like a trap, as she stretched it across the table. So suddenly and smartly did he do this, that we all stopped in our foolish contention.

"If you talk of strength," said Mr. Jaggers, "I'll show you a wrist. Molly, let them see your wrist."

Her entrapped hand was on the table, but she had already put her other hand behind her waist. "Master," she said, in a low voice, with her eyes attentively and entreatingly fixed upon him. "Don't."

"I'll show you a wrist," repeated Mr. Jaggers, with an immovable determination to show it. "Molly, let them see your wrist."

"Master," she again murmured. "Please!"

"Molly," said Mr. Jaggers, not looking at her, but obstinately looking at the opposite side of the room, "let them see *both* your wrists. Show them. Come!"

He took his hand from hers, and turned that wrist up on the table. She brought her other hand from behind her, and held the two out side by side. The last wrist was much disfigured — deeply seamed and scarred across and across. When she held her hands out, she took her eyes from Mr. Jaggers, and turned them watchfully on every one of the rest of us in succession.

"There's power here," said Mr. Jaggers, coolly tracing out the sinews with his forefinger. "Very few men have the power of wrist that this woman has. It's remarkable what mere force of grip there is in these hands. I have had occasion to notice many hands; but I never saw stronger in that respect, man's or woman's, than these."

While he said these words in a leisurely critical style, she continued to look at every one of us in regular succession as we sat. The moment he ceased, she looked at him again. "That'll do, Molly," said Mr. Jaggers, giving her a slight nod; "you have been admired, and can go." She withdrew her hands and went out of the room, and Mr. Jaggers, putting the decanters on from his dumb-waiter, filled his glass and passed round the wine.

"At half-past nine, gentlemen," said he, "we must break up. Pray make the best use of your time. I am glad to see you all. Mr. Drummle, I drink to you."

If his object in singling out Drummle were to bring him out still more, it perfectly succeeded. In a sulky triumph, Drummle showed his morose depreciation of the rest of us, in a more and more offensive degree until he became downright intolerable. Through all his stages, Mr. Jaggers followed him with the same strange interest. He actually seemed to serve as a zest to Mr. Jaggers's wine.

In our boyish want of discretion I dare say we took too much to drink, and I know we talked too much. We became particularly hot upon some boorish sneer of Drummle's, to the effect that we were too free with our money. It led to my remarking, with more zeal than discretion, that it came with a bad grace from him, to whom Startop had lent money in my presence but a week or so before.

"Well" retorted Drummle; "he'll be paid."

"I don't mean to imply that he won't," said I, "but it might make you hold your tongue about us and our money, I should think."

"*You* should think!" retorted Drummle. "Oh Lord!"

"I dare say," I went on, meaning to be very severe, "that you wouldn't lend money to any of us, if we wanted it."

"You are right," said Drummle. "I wouldn't lend one of you a sixpence. I wouldn't lend anybody a sixpence."

"Rather mean to borrow under those circumstances, I should say."

"*You* should say," repeated Drummle. "Oh Lord!"

This was so very aggravating — the more especially as I found myself making no way against his surly obtuseness — that I said, disregarding Herbert's efforts to check me:

"Come, Mr. Drummle, since we are on the subject, I'll tell you what passed between Herbert here and me, when you borrowed that money."

"*I* don't want to know what passed between Herbert there and you," growled Drummle. And I think he added in a lower growl, that we might both go to the devil and shake ourselves.

"I'll tell you, however," said I, "whether you want to know or not. We said that as you put it in your pocket very glad to get it, you seemed to be immensely amused at his being so weak as to lend it."

Drummle laughed outright, and sat laughing in our faces, with his hands in his pockets and his round shoulders raised: plainly signifying that it was quite true, and that he despised us, as asses all.

Hereupon Startop took him in hand, though with a much better grace than I had shown, and exhorted him to be a little more agreeable. Startop, being a lively bright young fellow, and Drummle being the exact opposite, the latter was always disposed to resent him as a direct personal affront. He now retorted in a coarse lumpish way, and Startop tried to turn the discussion aside with some small pleasantry that made us all laugh. Resenting this little success more than anything, Drummle, without any threat or warning, pulled his hands out of his pockets, dropped his round shoulders, swore, took up a large glass, and would have flung it at his adversary's head, but for our entertainer's dexterously seizing it at the instant when it was raised for that purpose.

"Gentlemen," said Mr. Jaggers, deliberately putting down the glass, and hauling out his gold repeater by its massive chain, "I am exceedingly sorry to announce that it's half-past nine."

On this hint we all rose to depart. Before we got to the street door, Startop was cheerily calling Drummle "old boy," as if nothing had happened. But the old boy was so far from responding, that he would not even walk to Hammersmith on the same side of the way; so, Herbert and I, who remained in town, saw them going down the street on opposite sides; Startop leading, and Drummle lagging behind in the shadow of the houses, much as he was wont to follow in his boat.

As the door was not yet shut, I thought I would leave Herbert there for a moment, and run up-stairs again to say a word to my guardian. I found him in his dressing-room surrounded by his stock of boots, already hard at it, washing his hands of us.

I told him I had come up again, to say how sorry I was that anything disagreeable should have occurred, and that I hoped he would not blame me much.

"Pooh!" said he, sluicing his face, and speaking through the water-drops; "it's nothing, Pip. I like that Spider though."

He had turned towards me now, and was shaking his head, and blowing, and towelling himself.

"I am glad you like him, sir," said I — "but I don't."

"No, no," my guardian assented; "don't have too much to do with him. Keep as clear of him as you can. But I like the fellow, Pip; he is one of the true sort. Why, if I was a fortune-teller —"

Looking out of the towel, he caught my eye.

"But I am not a fortune-teller," he said, letting his head drop into a festoon of towel, and towelling away at his two ears. "You know what I am, don't you? Good night, Pip."

"Good night, sir."

In about a month after that, the Spider's time with Mr. Pocket was up for good, and, to the great relief of all the house but Mrs. Pocket, he went home to the family hole.

CHAPTER VIII

"MY DEAR MR. PIP,

"I write this by request of Mr. Gargery, for to let you know that he is going to London in company of Mr. Wopsle and would be glad if agreeable to be allowed to see you. He would call at Barnard's Hotel Tuesday morning 9 o'clock, when if not agreeable please leave word. Your poor sister is much the same as when you left. We talk of you in the kitchen every night, and wonder what you are saying and doing. If now considered in the light of a liberty, excuse it for the love of poor old days. No more, dear Mr. Pip, from

"Your ever obliged, and affectionate

"Servant,

"BIDDY.*

"P.S. He wishes me most particular to write *what larks*. He says you will understand. I hope and do not doubt it will be agreeable to see him even though a gentleman, for you had ever a good heart, and he is a worthy worthy man. I have read him all excepting only the last little sentence, and he wishes me most particular to write again *what larks*."

I received this letter by the post on Monday morning, and therefore its appointment was for next day. Let me confess exactly, with what feelings I looked forward to Joe's coming.

Not with pleasure, though I was bound to him by so many ties; no; with considerable disturbance, some mortification, and a keen sense of incongruity. If I could have kept him away by paying money, I certainly would have paid money. My greatest reassurance was, that he was coming to Barnard's Inn, not to Hammersmith, and consequently would not fall in Bentley Drummle's way. I had little objection to his being seen by Herbert or his father, for both of whom I had a respect; but I had the sharpest sensitiveness as to his being seen by Drummle, whom I held in contempt. So, throughout life, our worst weaknesses and meannesses are usually committed for the sake of the people whom we most despise.

I had begun to be always decorating the chambers in some quite unnecessary and inappropriate way or other, and very expensive those wrestles with Barnard proved to be. By this time, the rooms were vastly different from what I had found them, and I enjoyed the honour of occupying a few prominent pages in the books of a neighbouring upholsterer. I had got on so fast of late, that I had even started a boy in boots — top boots — in bondage and slavery to whom I might have been said to pass my days. For, after I had made the monster[1] (out of the refuse of my washerwoman's family) and had clothed him with a blue coat, canary waistcoat, white cravat, creamy breeches, and the boots already mentioned, I had to find him a little to do and a great deal to eat; and with both of those horrible requirements he haunted my existence.

This avenging phantom was ordered to be on duty at eight on Tuesday

---

1. *after I had made the monster:* first of a series of references ironically comparing Pip's servant to the monster created by Dr. Frankenstein, in Mary Shelley's Gothic tale *Frankenstein, or the Modern Prometheus* (1818).

morning in the hall (it was two feet square, as charged for floorcloth), and Herbert suggested certain things for breakfast that he thought Joe would like. While I felt sincerely obliged to him for being so interested and considerate, I had an odd half-provoked sense of suspicion upon me, that if Joe had been coming to see *him*, he wouldn't have been quite so brisk about it.

However, I came into town on the Monday night to be ready for Joe, and I got up early in the morning, and caused the sitting-room and breakfast-table to assume their most splendid appearance. Unfortunately the morning was drizzly, and an angel could not have concealed the fact that Barnard was shedding sooty tears outside the window, like some weak giant of a Sweep.[1]

As the time approached I should have liked to run away, but the Avenger pursuant to orders was in the hall, and presently I heard Joe on the staircase. I knew it was Joe, by his clumsy manner of coming up-stairs — his state boots being always too big for him — and by the time it took him to read the names on the other floors in the course of his ascent. When at last he stopped outside our door, I could hear his finger tracing over the painted letters of my name, and I afterwards distinctly heard him breathing in at the keyhole. Finally he gave a faint single rap, and Pepper — such was the compromising name of the avenging boy — announced "Mr. Gargery!" I thought he never would have done wiping his feet, and that I must have gone out to lift him off the mat, but at last he came in.

"Joe, how are you, Joe?"

"Pip, how AIR you, Pip?"

With his good honest face all glowing and shining, and his hat put down on the floor between us, he caught both my hands and worked them straight up and down, as if I had been the last-patented Pump.

"I am glad to see you, Joe. Give me your hat."

But Joe, taking it up carefully with both hands, like a bird's-nest with eggs in it, wouldn't hear of parting with that piece of property, and persisted in standing talking over it in a most uncomfortable way.

---

1. *like some weak giant of a Sweep:* i.e., a chimney sweep.

"Which you have that growed," said Joe, "and that swelled, and that gentlefolked;" Joe considered a little before he discovered this word; "as to be sure you are a honour to your king and country."

"And you, Joe, look wonderfully well."

"Thank God," said Joe, "I'm ekerval to most. And your sister, she's no worse than she were. And Biddy, she's ever right and ready. And all friends is no backerder, if not no forarder. 'Ceptin' Wopsle; he's had a drop."

All this time (still with both hands taking great care of the bird's-nest), Joe was rolling his eyes round and round the room, and round and round the flowered pattern of my dressing-gown.

"Had a drop, Joe?"

"Why yes," said Joe, lowering his voice, "he's left the Church, and went into the playacting. Which the playacting have likeways brought him to London along with me. And his wish were," said Joe, getting the bird's-nest under his left arm for the moment and groping in it for an egg with his right; "if no offence, as I would 'and you that."

I took what Joe gave me, and found it to be the crumpled playbill of a small metropolitan theatre, announcing the first appearance, in that very week, of "the celebrated Provincial Amateur of Roscian renown,[1] whose unique performance in the highest tragic walk of our National Bard has lately occasioned so great a sensation in local dramatic circles."

"Were you at his performance, Joe?" I inquired.

"I *were*," said Joe, with emphasis and solemnity.

"Was there a great sensation?"

"Why," said Joe, "yes, there certainly were a peck of orange-peel. Partickler, when he see the ghost. Though I put it to yourself, sir, whether it were calc'lated to keep a man up to his work with a good hart, to be continiwally cutting in betwixt him and the Ghost with 'Amen!' A man may have had a misfortun' and been in the Church," said Joe, lowering his voice to an argumentative and feeling tone, "but that is no reason why you should put him out at such a time. Which I meantersay, if the ghost of a man's own father cannot be allowed to claim his attention, what can,

---

1. *of Roscian renown:* after the famous ancient Roman actor Roscius. Wopsle's perform-ance referred to here is as the hero in Shakespeare's *Hamlet.*

Sir? Still more, when his mourning 'at is unfortunately made so small as that the weight of the black feathers brings it off, try to keep it on how you may."

A ghost-seeing effect in Joe's own countenance informed me that Herbert had entered the room. So, I presented Joe to Herbert, who held out his hand; but Joe backed from it, and held on by the bird's-nest.

"Your servant, Sir," said Joe, "which I hope as you and Pip" — here his eye fell on the Avenger, who was putting some toast on table, and so plainly denoted an intention to make that young gentleman one of the family, that I frowned it down and confused him more — "I meantersay, you two gentlemen — which I hope as you get your elths in this close spot? For the present may be a wery good inn, according to London opinions," said Joe, confidentially, "and I believe its character do stand i; but I wouldn't keep a pig in it myself — not in the case that I wished him to fatten wholesome and to eat with a meller flavour on him."

Having borne this flattering testimony to the merits of our dwelling-place, and having incidentally shown this tendency to call me "sir," Joe, being invited to sit down to table, looked all round the room for a suitable spot on which to deposit his hat — as if it were only on some very few rare substances in nature that it could find a resting place — and ultimately stood it on an extreme corner of the chimney-piece, from which it ever afterwards fell off at intervals.

"Do you take tea, or coffee, Mr. Gargery?" asked Herbert, who always presided of a morning.

"Thankee, Sir," said Joe, stiff from head to foot, "I'll take whichever is most agreeable to yourself."

"What do you say to coffee?"

"Thankee, Sir," returned Joe, evidently dispirited by the proposal, "since you *are* so kind as make chice of coffee, I will not run contrairy to your own opinions. But don't you never find it a little 'eating?"

"Say tea then," said Herbert, pouring it out.

Here Joe's hat tumbled off the mantelpiece, and he started out of his chair and picked it up, and fitted it to the same exact spot. As if it were an absolute point of good breeding that it should tumble off again soon.

"When did you come to town, Mr. Gargery?"

"Were it yesterday afternoon?" said Joe, after coughing behind his hand, as if he had had time to catch the whooping-cough since he came. "No it were not. Yes it were. Yes. It were yesterday afternoon" (with an appearance of mingled wisdom, relief, and strict impartiality).

"Have you seen anything of London, yet?"

"Why, yes, Sir," said Joe, "me and Wopsle went off straight to look at the Blacking Ware'us.* But we didn't find that it come up to its likeness in the red bills at the shop doors; which I meantersay," added Joe, in an explanatory manner, "as it is there drawd too architectooralooral."

I really believe Joe would have prolonged this word (mightily expressive to my mind of some architecture that I know) into a perfect Chorus, but for his attention being providentially attracted by his hat, which was toppling. Indeed, it demanded from him a constant attention, and a quickness of eye and hand, very like that exacted by wicket-keeping.[1] He made extraordinary play with it, and showed the greatest skill; now, rushing at it and catching it neatly as it dropped; now, merely stopping it midway, beating it up, and humouring it in various parts of the room and against a good deal of the pattern of the paper on the wall, before he felt it safe to close with it; finally, splashing it into the slop-basin, where I took the liberty of laying hands upon it.

As to his shirt-collar, and his coat-collar, they were perplexing to reflect upon — insoluble mysteries both. Why should a man scrape himself to that extent, before he could consider himself full dressed? Why should he suppose it necessary to be purified by suffering for his holiday clothes? Then he fell into such unaccountable fits of meditation, with his fork midway between his plate and his mouth; had his eyes attracted in such strange directions; was afflicted with such remarkable coughs; sat so far from the table, and dropped so much more than he ate, and pretended that he hadn't dropped it; that I was heartily glad when Herbert left us for the City.

I had neither the good sense nor the good feeling to know that this was all my fault, and that if I had been easier with Joe, Joe would have been easier with me. I felt impatient of him and out of temper with him; in which condition he heaped coals of fire on my head.

---

1. *wicket-keeping:* in the game of cricket, equivalent to the work of the catcher at baseball.

"Us two being now alone, Sir," — began Joe.

"Joe," I interrupted, pettishly, "how can you call me, Sir?"

Joe looked at me for a single instant with something faintly like reproach. Utterly preposterous as his cravat was, and as his collars were, I was conscious of a sort of dignity in the look.

"Us two being now alone," resumed Joe, "and me having the intentions and abilities to stay not many minutes more, I will now conclude — leastways begin — to mention what have led to my having had the present honour. For was it not," said Joe, with his old air of lucid exposition, "that my only wish were to be useful to you, I should not have had the honour of breaking wittles in the company and abode of gentlemen."

I was so unwilling to see the look again, that I made no remonstrance against this tone.

"Well, Sir," pursued Joe, "this is how it were. I were at the Bargemen t'other night, Pip;" whenever he subsided into affection, he called me Pip, and whenever he relapsed into politeness he called me Sir; "when there come up in his shay-cart, Pumblechook. Which that same identical," said Joe, going down a new track, "do comb my 'air the wrong way sometimes, awful, by giving out up and down town as it were him which ever had your infant companionation and were looked upon as a playfeller by yourself."

"Nonsense. It was you, Joe."

"Which I fully believed it were, Pip," said Joe, slightly tossing his head, "though it signify little now, Sir. Well, Pip; this same identical, which his manners is given to blusterous, come to me at the Bargemen (wot a pipe and a pint of beer do give refreshment to the working-man, Sir, and do not over stimulate), and his word were, 'Joseph, Miss Havisham she wish to speak to you.'"

"Miss Havisham, Joe?"

"'She wish,' were Pumblechook's word, 'to speak to you.'" Joe sat and rolled his eyes at the ceiling.

"Yes, Joe? Go on, please."

"Next day, Sir," said Joe, looking at me as if I were a long way off, "having cleaned myself, I go and I see Miss A."

"Miss A., Joe? Miss Havisham?"

"Which I say, Sir," replied Joe, with an air of legal formality, as if he were making his will, "Miss A., or otherways Havisham. Her expression air then as follering: 'Mr. Gargery. You air in correspondence with Mr. Pip?' Having had a letter from you, I were able to say 'I am.' (When I married your sister, Sir, I said 'I will;' and when I answered your friend, Pip, I said 'I am.') 'Would you tell him, then,' said she, 'that which Estella has come home and would be glad to see him.'"

I felt my face fire up as I looked at Joe. I hope one remote cause of its firing, may have been my consciousness that if I had known his errand, I should have given him more encouragement.

"Biddy," pursued Joe, "when I got home and asked her fur to write the message to you, a little hung back. Biddy says, 'I know he will be very glad to have it by word of mouth, it is holiday-time, you want to see him, go!' I have now concluded, Sir," said Joe, rising from his chair, "and, Pip, I wish you ever well and ever prospering to a greater and a greater heighth."

"But you are not going now, Joe?"

"Yes I am," said Joe.

"But you are coming back to dinner, Joe?"

"No I am not," said Joe.

Our eyes met, and all the "Sir" melted out of that manly heart as he gave me his hand.

"Pip, dear old chap, life is made of ever so many partings welded together, as I may say, and one man's a blacksmith, and one's a whitesmith, and one's a goldsmith, and one's a coppersmith. Diwisions among such must come, and must be met as they come. If there's been any fault at all to-day, it's mine. You and me is not two figures to be together in London; nor yet anywheres else but what is private, and beknown, and understood among friends. It ain't that I am proud, but that I want to be right, as you shall never see me no more in these clothes. I'm wrong in these clothes. I'm wrong out of the forge, the kitchen, or off th' meshes. You won't find half so much fault in me if you think of me in my forge dress, with my hammer in my hand, or even my pipe. You won't find half so much fault in me if, supposing as you should ever wish to see me, you come and put your head in at the forge winder and see Joe the blacksmith, there, at the old anvil, in the old burnt apron, sticking to the old work. I'm awful dull, but I hope I've beat out something nigh the rights of this at last. And so GOD bless you, dear old Pip, old chap, GOD bless you!"

I had not been mistaken in my fancy that there was a simple dignity in him. The fashion of his dress could no more come in its way when he spoke these words, than it could come in its way in Heaven. He touched me gently on the forehead, and went out. As soon as I could recover myself sufficiently, I hurried out after him and looked for him in the neighbouring streets; but he was gone.

CHAPTER IX

IT WAS clear that I must repair to our town next day, and in the first flow of my repentance it was equally clear that I must stay at Joe's. But, when I had secured my box-place by to-morrow's coach and had been down to Mr. Pocket's and back, I was not by any means convinced on the last point, and began to invent reasons and make excuses for putting up at the Blue Boar. I should be an inconvenience at Joe's; I was not expected, and my bed would not be ready; I should be too far from Miss Havisham's, and she was exacting and mightn't like it. All other swindlers upon earth are nothing to the self-swindlers, and with such pretences did I cheat myself. Surely a curious thing. That I should innocently take a bad half-crown of somebody else's manufacture, is reasonable enough; but that I should knowingly reckon the spurious coin of my own make, as good money! An obliging stranger, under pretence of compactly folding up my bank-notes for security's sake, abstracts the notes and gives me nutshells; but what is his sleight of hand to mine, when I fold up my own nutshells and pass them on myself as notes!

Having settled that I must go to the Blue Boar, my mind was much disturbed by indecision whether or no to take the Avenger. It was tempting to think of that expensive Mercenary publicly airing his boots in the archway of the Blue Boar's posting-yard; it was almost solemn to imagine him casually produced in the tailor's shop and confounding the disrespectful senses of Trabb's boy. On the other hand, Trabb's boy might worm himself into his intimacy and tell him things; or, reckless and desperate wretch as I knew he could be, might hoot him in the High-street. My patroness, too, might hear of him, and not approve. On the whole, I resolved to leave the Avenger behind.

It was the afternoon coach by which I had taken my place, and, as winter had now come round, I should not arrive at my destination until two or three hours after dark. Our time of starting from the Cross Keys was two o'clock. I arrived on the ground with a quarter of an hour to spare, attended by the Avenger — if I may connect that expression with one who never attended on me if he could possibly help it.

At that time it was customary to carry Convicts down to the dockyards by stage-coach. As I had often heard of them in the capacity of outside passengers, and had more than once seen them on the high road dangling their ironed legs over the coach roof, I had no cause to be surprised when Herbert, meeting me in the yard, came up and told me there were two convicts going down with me. But I had a reason that was an old reason now, for constitutionally faltering whenever I heard the word convict.

"You don't mind them, Handel?" said Herbert.

"Oh no!"

"I thought you seemed as if you didn't like them?"

"I can't pretend that I do like them, and I suppose you don't particularly. But I don't mind them."

"See! There they are," said Herbert, "coming out of the Tap. What a degraded and vile sight it is!"

They had been treating their guard, I suppose, for they had a gaoler with them, and all three came out wiping their mouths on their hands. The two convicts were handcuffed together, and had irons on their legs — irons of a pattern that I knew well. They wore the dress that I likewise knew well. Their keeper had a brace of pistols, and carried a thick-knobbed bludgeon under his arm; but he was on terms of good understanding with them, and stood, with them beside him, looking on at the putting-to of the horses, rather with an air as if the convicts were an interesting Exhibition not formally open at the moment, and he the Curator. One was a taller and stouter man than the other, and appeared as a matter of course, according to the mysterious ways of the world both convict and free, to have had allotted to him the smaller suit of clothes. His arms and legs were like great pincushions of those shapes, and his attire disguised him absurdly; but I knew his half-closed eye at one glance. There stood the man whom I had seen on the settle at the Three Jolly Bargemen on a Saturday night, and who had brought me down with his invisible gun!

It was easy to make sure that as yet he knew me no more than if he had never seen me in his life. He looked across at me, and his eye appraised my watch-chain, and then he incidentally spat and said something to the other convict, and they laughed and slued themselves round with a clink of their coupling manacle, and looked at something else. The great numbers on their backs, as if they were street doors; their coarse mangy ungainly outer surface, as if they were lower animals; their ironed legs, apologetically garlanded with pocket-handkerchiefs; and the way in which all present looked at them and kept from them; made them (as Herbert had said) a most disagreeable and degraded spectacle.

But this was not the worst of it. It came out that the whole of the back of the coach had been taken by a family removing from London, and that there were no places for the two prisoners but on the seat in front, behind the coachman. Hereupon, a choleric gentleman, who had taken the fourth place on that seat, flew into a most violent passion, and said that it was a breach of contract to mix him up with such villainous company, and that it was poisonous and pernicious and infamous and shameful, and I don't know what else. At this time the coach was ready and the coachman impatient, and we were all preparing to get up, and the prisoners had come over with their keeper — bringing with them that curious flavour of bread-poultice, baize, rope-yarn, and hearthstone, which attends the convict presence.*

"Don't take it so much amiss, sir," pleaded the keeper to the angry passenger; "I'll sit next you myself. I'll put 'em on the outside of the row. They won't interfere with you, sir. You needn't know they're there."

"And don't blame *me*," growled the convict I had recognised. "*I* don't want to go. *I* am quite ready to stay behind. As fur as I am concerned any one's welcome to *my* place."

"Or mine," said the other, gruffly. "*I* wouldn't have incommoded none of you, if I'd a had *my* way." Then, they both laughed, and began cracking nuts, and spitting the shells about. — As I really think I should have liked to do myself, if I had been in their place and so despised.

At length, it was voted that there was no help for the angry gentleman, and that he must either go in his chance company or remain behind. So, he got into his place, still making complaints, and the keeper got into the place next him, and the convicts hauled themselves up as well as they could, and the convict I had recognised sat behind me with his breath on the hair of my head.

"Good-by, Handel!" Herbert called out as we started. I thought what a blessed fortune it was, that he had found another name for me than Pip.

It is impossible to express with what acuteness I felt the convict's breathing, not only on the back of my head, but all along my spine. The sensation was like being touched in the marrow with some pungent and searching acid, and it set my very teeth on edge. He seemed to have more breathing business to do than another man, and to make more noise in doing it; and I was conscious of growing high-shouldered on one side, in my shrinking endeavours to fend him off.

The weather was miserably raw, and the two cursed the cold. It made us all lethargic before we had gone far, and when we had left the Half-way House[1] behind, we habitually dozed and shivered and were silent. I dozed off, myself, in considering the question whether I ought to restore a couple of pounds sterling to this creature before losing sight of him, and how it could best be done. In the act of dipping forward as if I were going to bathe among the horses, I woke in a fright and took the question up again.

But I must have lost it longer than I had thought, since, although I could recognise nothing in the darkness and the fitful lights and shadows of our lamps, I traced marsh country in the cold damp wind that blew at us. Cowering forward for warmth and to make me a screen against the wind, the convicts were closer to me than before. The very first words I heard them interchange as I became conscious were the words of my own thought, "Two One Pound notes."

"How did he get 'em?" said the convict I had never seen.

"How should I know?" returned the other. "He had 'em stowed away somehow. Giv' him by friends, I expect."

"I wish," said the other, with a bitter curse upon the cold, "that I had 'em here."

"Two one pound notes, or friends?"

---

1. *Half-way House:* the coaching inn on the road from London to Rochester marking the mid-point in the journey.

"Two one pound notes. I'd sell all the friends I ever had, for one, and think it a blessed good bargain. Well? So he says —?"

"So he says," resumed the convict I had recognised — "it was all said and done in half a minute, behind a pile of timber in the Dockyard — 'You're a going to be discharged?' Yes, I was. Would I find out that boy that had fed him and kep his secret, and give him them two one pound notes? Yes, I would. And I did."

"More fool you," growled the other. "I'd have spent 'em on a Man, in wittles and drink. He must have been a green one. Mean to say he knowed nothing of you?"

"Not a ha'porth. Different gangs and different ships. He was tried again for prison breaking, and got made a Lifer."

"And was that — Honour! — the only time you worked out, in this part of the country?"

"The only time."

"What might have been your opinion of the place?"

"A most beastly place. Mudbank, mist, swamp, and work; work, swamp, mist, and mudbank."

They both execrated the place in very strong language, and gradually growled themselves out, and had nothing left to say.

After overhearing this dialogue, I should assuredly have got down and been left in the solitude and darkness of the highway, but for feeling certain that the man had no suspicion of my identity. Indeed, I was not only so changed in the course of nature, but so differently dressed and so differently circumstanced, that it was not at all likely he could have known me without accidental help. Still, the coincidence of our being together on the coach, was sufficiently strange to fill me with a dread that some other coincidence might at any moment connect me, in his hearing, with my name. For this reason, I resolved to alight as soon as we touched the town, and put myself out of his hearing. This device I executed successfully. My little portmanteau was in the boot[1] under my feet; I had but to turn a hinge to get it out; I threw it down before me, got down after it, and was left at the first lamp on the first stones of the town pavement. As

---

1. *boot:* luggage compartment under the driver's seat of a coach.

to the convicts, they went their way with the coach, and I knew at what point they would be spirited off to the river. In my fancy, I saw the boat with its convict crew waiting for them at the slime-washed stairs, — again heard the gruff "Give way, you!" like an order to dogs — again saw the wicked Noah's Ark lying out on the black water.

I could not have said what I was afraid of, for my fear was altogether undefined and vague, but there was great fear upon me. As I walked on to the hotel, I felt that a dread, much exceeding the mere apprehension of a painful or disagreeable recognition, made me tremble. I am confident that it took no distinctness of shape, and that it was the revival for a few minutes of the terror of childhood.

The coffee-room at the Blue Boar was empty, and I had not only ordered my dinner there, but had sat down to it, before the waiter knew me. As soon as he had apologised for the remissness of his memory, he asked me if he should send Boots for Mr. Pumblechook?

"No," said I, "certainly not."

The waiter (it was he who had brought up the Great Remonstrance from the Commercials,[1] on the day when I was bound) appeared surprised, and took the earliest opportunity of putting a dirty old copy of a local newspaper so directly in my way, that I took it up and read this paragraph:

"Our readers will learn, not altogether without interest, in reference to the recent romantic rise in fortune of a young artificer in iron of this neighbourhood (what a theme, by the way, for the magic pen of our as yet not universally acknowledged townsman TOOBY, the poet of our columns!) that the youth's earliest patron, companion, and friend, was a highly-respected individual not entirely unconnected with the corn and seed trade, and whose eminently convenient and commodious business premises are situate within a hundred miles of the High-street. It is not wholly irrespective of our personal feelings that we record HIM as the Mentor of our young Telemachus,[2] for it is good to know that our town produced

---

1. *the Great Remonstrance from the Commercials:* by analogy with that presented in Parliament in 1641, listing the complaints of the Commons against King Charles I. Dickens's friend John Forster published a book on the subject in 1860.
2. *Mentor of our young Telemachus:* Mentor is the guardian of Telemachus, the young son of the absent Odysseus, in Homer's *Odyssey.*

the founder of the latter's fortunes. Does the thought-contracted brow of the local Sage or the lustrous eye of local Beauty inquire whose fortunes? We believe that Quintin Matsys[1] was the BLACKSMITH of Antwerp. VERB. SAP."[2]

I entertain a conviction, based upon large experience, that if in the days of my prosperity I had gone to the North Pole, I should have met somebody there, wandering Esquimaux or civilised man, who would have told me that Pumblechook was my earliest patron and the founder of my fortunes.

CHAPTER X

BETIMES IN the morning I was up and out. It was too early yet to go to Miss Havisham's, so I loitered into the country on Miss Havisham's side of town — which was not Joe's side; I could go there to-morrow — thinking about my patroness, and painting brilliant pictures of her plans for me.

She had adopted Estella, she had as good as adopted me, and it could not fail to be her intention to bring us together. She reserved it for me to restore the desolate house, admit the sunshine into the dark rooms, set the clocks a going and the cold hearths a blazing, tear down the cobwebs, destroy the vermin — in short, do all the shining deeds of the young Knight of romance, and marry the Princess. I had stopped to look at the house as I passed; and its seared red brick walls, blocked windows, and strong green ivy clasping even the stacks of chimneys with its twigs and tendons, as if with sinewy old arms, had made up a rich attractive mystery, of which I was the hero. Estella was the inspiration of it, and the heart of it, of course. But, though she had taken such strong possession of

---

1. *Quintin Matsys:* sixteenth-century painter of the Flemish school, traditionally understood to have started life as a blacksmith.
2. *VERB. SAP.:* "To wise people, a single word is sufficient for understanding" (Latin saw, *verbum sapienti sat est*).

me, though my fancy and my hope were so set upon her, though her influence on my boyish life and character had been all-powerful, I did not, even that romantic morning, invest her with any attributes save those she possessed. I mention this in this place, of a fixed purpose, because it is the clue by which I am to be followed into my poor labyrinth. According to my experience, the conventional notion of a lover cannot be always true. The unqualified truth is, that when I loved Estella with the love of a man, I loved her simply because I found her irresistible. Once for all; I knew to my sorrow, often and often, if not always, that I loved her against reason, against promise, against peace, against hope, against happiness, against all discouragement that could be. Once for all; I loved her none the less because I knew it, and it had no more influence in restraining me, than if I had devoutly believed her to be human perfection.

I so shaped out my walk as to arrive at the gate at my old time. When I had rung at the bell with an unsteady hand, I turned my back upon the gate, while I tried to get my breath and keep the beating of my heart moderately quiet. I heard the side door open, and steps come across the court-yard; but I pretended not to hear, even when the gate swung on its rusty hinges.

Being at last touched on the shoulder, I started and turned. I started much more naturally then, to find myself confronted by a man in a sober grey dress. The last man I should have expected to see in that place of porter at Miss Havisham's door.

"Orlick!"

"Ah, young master, there's more changes than yours. But come in, come in. It's opposed to my orders to hold the gate open."

I entered and he swung it, and locked it, and took the key out. "Yes!" said he, facing round, after doggedly preceding me a few steps towards the house. "Here I am!"

"How did you come here?"

"I come here," he retorted, "on my legs. I had my box brought alongside me in a barrow."

"Are you here for good?"

"I ain't here for harm, young master, I suppose?"

I was not so sure of that. I had leisure to entertain the retort in my mind, while he slowly lifted his heavy glance from the pavement, up my legs and arms, to my face.

"Then you have left the forge?" I said.

"Do this look like a forge?" replied Orlick, sending his glance all round him with an air of injury. "Now, do it look like it?"

I asked him how long he had left Gargery's forge?

"One day is so like another here," he replied, "that I don't know without casting it up. However, I come here some time since you left."

"I could have told you that, Orlick."

"Ah!" said he, drily. "But then you've got to be a scholar."

By this time we had come to the house, where I found his room to be one just within the side door, with a little window in it looking on the court-yard. In its small proportions, it was not unlike the kind of place usually assigned to a gate-porter in Paris. Certain keys were hanging on the wall, to which he now added the gate key; and his patchwork-covered bed was in a little inner division or recess. The whole had a slovenly confined and sleepy look, like a cage for a human dormouse: while he, looming dark and heavy in the shadow of a corner by the window, looked like the human dormouse for whom it was fitted up — as indeed he was.

"I never saw this room before," I remarked; "but there used to be no Porter here."

"No," said he; "not till it got about that there was no protection on the premises, and it come to be considered dangerous, with convicts and Tag and Rag and Bobtail going up and down. And then I was recommended to the place as a man who could give another man as good as he brought, and I took it. It's easier than bellowsing and hammering. — That's loaded, that is."

My eye had been caught by a gun with a brass-bound stock over the chimney-piece, and his eye had followed mine.

"Well," said I, not desirous of more conversation, "shall I go up to Miss Havisham?"

"Burn me, if I know!" he retorted, first stretching himself and then shaking himself; "my orders ends here, young master. I give this here bell a rap with this here hammer, and you go on along the passage till you meet somebody."

"I am expected, I believe?"

"Burn me twice over, if I can say!" said he.

Upon that, I turned down the long passage which I had first trodden in my thick boots, and he made his bell sound. At the end of the passage, while the bell was still reverberating, I found Sarah Pocket: who appeared to have now become constitutionally green and yellow by reason of me.

"Oh!" said she. "You, is it, Mr. Pip?"

"It is, Miss Pocket. I am glad to tell you that Mr. Pocket and family are all well."

"Are they any wiser?" said Sarah, with a dismal shake of the head; "they had better be wiser, than well. Ah, Matthew, Matthew! You know your way, sir?"

Tolerably, for I had gone up the staircase in the dark, many a time. I ascended it now, in lighter boots than of yore, and tapped in my old way at the door of Miss Havisham's room. "Pip's rap," I heard her say, immediately; "come in, Pip."

She was in her chair near the old table, in the old dress, with her two hands crossed on her stick, her chin resting on them, and her eyes on the fire. Sitting near her, with the white shoe that had never been worn, in her hand, and her head bent as she looked at it, was an elegant lady whom I had never seen.

"Come in, Pip," Miss Havisham continued to mutter, without looking round or up; "come in, Pip, how do you do, Pip? so you kiss my hand as if I were a queen, eh? — Well?"

She looked up at me suddenly, only moving her eyes, and repeated in a grimly playful manner,

"Well?"

"I heard, Miss Havisham," said I, rather at a loss, "that you were so kind as to wish me to come and see you, and I came directly."

"Well?"

The lady whom I had never seen before, lifted up her eyes and looked archly at me, and then I saw that the eyes were Estella's eyes. But she was so much changed, was so much more beautiful, so much more womanly, in all things winning admiration had made such wonderful advance, that I seemed to have made none. I fancied, as I looked at her, that I slipped hopelessly back into the coarse and common boy again. O the sense of distance and disparity that came upon me, and the inaccessibility that came about her!

She gave me her hand. I stammered something about the pleasure I felt in seeing her again, and about my having looked forward to it for a long, long time.

"Do you find her much changed, Pip?" asked Miss Havisham, with her greedy look, and striking her stick upon a chair that stood between them, as a sign to me to sit down there.

"When I came in, Miss Havisham, I thought there was nothing of Estella in the face or figure; but now it all settles down so curiously into the old —"

"What? You are not going to say into the old Estella?" Miss Havisham interrupted. "She was proud and insulting, and you wanted to go away from her. Don't you remember?"

I said confusedly that that was long ago, and that I knew no better then, and the like. Estella smiled with perfect composure, and said she had no doubt of my having been quite right, and of her having been very disagreeable.

"Is *he* changed?" Miss Havisham asked her.

"Very much," said Estella, looking at me.

"Less coarse and common?" said Miss Havisham, playing with Estella's hair.

Estella laughed, and looked at the shoe in her hand, and laughed again, and looked at me, and put the shoe down. She treated me as a boy still, but she lured me on.

We sat in the dreamy room among the old strange influences which had so wrought upon me, and I learnt that she had but just come home from France, and that she was going to London. Proud and wilful as of old, she had brought those qualities into such subjection to her beauty that it was impossible and out of nature — or I thought so — to separate them from her beauty. Truly it was impossible to dissociate her presence from all those wretched hankerings after money and gentility that had disturbed my boyhood — from all those ill-regulated aspirations that had first made me ashamed of home and Joe — from all those visions that had raised her face in the glowing fire, struck it out of the iron on the anvil, extracted it from the darkness of night to look in at the wooden window of the forge and flit away. In a word, it was impossible for me to separate her, in the past or in the present, from the innermost life of my life.

It was settled that I should stay there all the rest of the day, and return to the hotel at night, and to London to-morrow. When we had conversed for a while, Miss Havisham sent us two out to walk in the neglected garden: on our coming in by-and-by, she said, I should wheel her about a little as in times of yore.

So, Estella and I went out into the garden by the gate through which I had strayed to my encounter with the pale young gentleman, now Herbert; I, trembling in spirit and worshipping the very hem of her dress; she, quite composed and most decidedly not worshipping the hem of mine. As we drew near to the place of encounter, she stopped and said:

"I must have been a singular little creature to hide and see that fight that day: but I did, and I enjoyed it very much."

"You rewarded me very much."

"Did I?" she replied, in an incidental and forgetful way. "I remember I entertained a great objection to your adversary, because I took it ill that he should be brought here to pester me with his company."

"He and I are great friends now," said I.

"Are you? I think I recollect though, that you read with his father?"

"Yes."

I made the admission with reluctance, for it seemed to have a boyish look, and she already treated me more than enough like a boy.

"Since your change of fortune and prospects, you have changed your companions," said Estella.

"Naturally," said I.

"And necessarily," she added, in a haughty tone; "what was fit company for you once, would be quite unfit company for you now."

In my conscience, I doubt very much whether I had any lingering intention left, of going to see Joe; but if I had, this observation put it to flight.

"You had no idea of your impending good fortune, in those times?" said Estella, with a slight wave of her hand, signifying in the fighting times.

"Not the least."

The air of completeness and superiority with which she walked at my side, and the air of youthfulness and submission with which I walked at hers, made a contrast that I strongly felt. It would have rankled in me more than it did, if I had not regarded myself as eliciting it by being so set apart for her and assigned to her.

The garden was too overgrown and rank for walking in with ease, and after we had made the round of it twice or thrice, we came out again into the brewery yard. I showed her to a nicety where I had seen her walking on the casks, that first old day, and she said, with a cold and careless look in that direction, "Did I?" I reminded her where she had come out of the house and given me my meat and drink, and she said, "I don't remember." "Not remember that you made me cry?" said I. "No," said she, and shook her head and looked about her. I verily believe that her not remembering and not minding in the least, made me cry again, inwardly — and that is the sharpest crying of all.

"You must know," said Estella, condescending to me as a brilliant and beautiful woman might, "that I have no heart — if that has anything to do with my memory."

I got through some jargon to the effect that I took the liberty of doubting that. That I knew better. That there could be no such beauty without it.

"Oh! I have a heart to be stabbed in or shot in, I have no doubt," said Estella, "and, of course, if it ceased to beat I should cease to be. But you know what I mean. I have no softness there, no — sympathy — sentiment — nonsense."

What *was* it that was borne in upon my mind when she stood still and looked attentively at me? Anything that I had seen in Miss Havisham? No. In some of her looks and gestures there was that tinge of resemblance to Miss Havisham which may often be noticed to have been acquired by children, from grown persons with whom they have been much associated and secluded, and which, when childhood is past, will produce a remarkable occasional likeness of expression between faces that are otherwise quite different. And yet I could not trace this to Miss Havisham. I looked again, and though she was still looking at me, the suggestion was gone.

What *was* it?

"I am serious," said Estella, not so much with a frown (for her brow was smooth) as with a darkening of her face; "if we are to be thrown much together, you had better believe it at once. No!" imperiously stopping me as I opened my lips. "I have not bestowed my tenderness anywhere. I have never had any such thing."

In another moment we were in the brewery so long disused, and she pointed to the high gallery where I had seen her going out on that same first day, and told me she remembered to have been up there, and to have seen me standing scared below. As my eyes followed her white hand, again the same dim suggestion that I could not possibly grasp, crossed me. My involuntary start occasioned her to lay her hand upon my arm. Instantly the ghost passed once more, and was gone.

What *was* it?

"What is the matter?" asked Estella. "Are you scared again?"

"I should be, if I believed what you said just now," I replied, to turn it off.

"Then you don't? Very well. It is said, at any rate. Miss Havisham will soon be expecting you at your old post, though I think that might be laid aside now, with other old belongings. Let us make one more round of the garden, and then go in. Come! You shall not shed tears for my cruelty to-day; you shall be my Page, and give me your shoulder."

Her handsome dress had trailed upon the ground. She held it in one hand now, and with the other lightly touched my shoulder as we walked. We walked round the ruined garden twice or thrice more, and it was all in bloom for me. If the green and yellow growth of weed in the chinks of the old wall had been the most precious flowers that ever blew, it could not have been more cherished in my remembrance.

There was no discrepancy of years between us, to remove her far from me; we were of nearly the same age, though of course the age told for more in her case than in mine; but the air of inaccessibility which her beauty and her manner gave her, tormented me in the midst of my delight, and at the height of the assurance I felt that our patroness had chosen us for one another. Wretched boy!

At last we went back into the house, and there I heard, with surprise, that my guardian had come down to see Miss Havisham on business, and would come back to dinner. The old wintry branches of chandeliers in the room where the mouldering table was spread, had been lighted while we were out, and Miss Havisham was in her chair and waiting for me.

It was like pushing the chair itself back into the past, when we began the old slow circuit round about the ashes of the bridal feast. But, in the funereal room, with that figure of the grave fallen back in the chair fixing its eyes upon her, Estella looked more bright and beautiful than before, and I was under stronger enchantment.

The time so melted away, that our early dinner-hour drew close at hand, and Estella left us to prepare herself. We had stopped near the centre of the long table, and Miss Havisham, with one of her withered arms stretched out of the chair, rested that clenched hand upon the yellow cloth. As Estella looked back over her shoulder before going out at the door, Miss Havisham kissed that hand to her, with a ravenous intensity that was of its kind quite dreadful.

Then, Estella being gone and we two left alone, she turned to me, and said in a whisper:

"Is she beautiful, graceful, well-grown? Do you admire her?"

"Everybody must who sees her, Miss Havisham."

She drew an arm round my neck, and drew my head close down to hers as she sat in the chair. "Love her, love her, love her! How does she use you?"

Before I could answer (if I could have answered so difficult a question at all), she repeated, "Love her, love her, love her! If she favours you, love her. If she wounds you, love her. If she tears your heart to pieces — and as it gets older and stronger, it will tear deeper — love her, love her, love her!"

Never had I seen such passionate eagerness as was joined to her utterance of these words. I could feel the muscles of the thin arm round my neck, swell with the vehemence that possessed her.

"Hear me, Pip! I adopted her to be loved. I bred her and educated her, to be loved. I developed her into what she is, that she might be loved. Love her!"

She said the word often enough, and there could be no doubt that she meant to say it; but if the often repeated word had been hate instead of love — despair — revenge — dire death — it could not have sounded from her lips more like a curse.

"I'll tell you," said she, in the same hurried passionate whisper, "what real love is. It is blind devotion, unquestioning self-humiliation, utter submission, trust and belief against yourself and against the whole world, giving up your whole heart and soul to the smiter — as I did!"

When she came to that, and to a wild cry that followed that, I caught her round the waist. For she rose up in the chair, in her shroud of a dress, and struck at the air as if she would as soon have struck herself against the wall and fallen dead.

All this passed in a few seconds. As I drew her down into her chair, I was conscious of a scent that I knew, and turning, saw my guardian in the room.

He always carried (I have not yet mentioned it, I think) a pocket-handkerchief of rich silk and of imposing proportions, which was of great value to him in his profession. I have seen him so terrify a client or a witness by ceremoniously unfolding this pocket-handkerchief as if he were immediately going to blow his nose, and then pausing, as if he knew he should not have time to do it before such client or witness committed himself, that the self-committal has followed directly, quite as a matter of course. When I saw him in the room, he had this expressive pocket-hand-kerchief in both hands, and was looking at us. On meeting my eye, he said plainly, by a momentary and silent pause in that attitude, "Indeed? Singular!" and then put the handkerchief to its right use with wonderful effect.

Miss Havisham had seen him as soon as I, and was (like everybody else) afraid of him. She made a strong attempt to compose herself, and stammered that he was as punctual as ever.

"As punctual as ever," he repeated, coming up to us. "(How do you do, Pip? Shall I give you a ride, Miss Havisham? Once round?) And so you are here, Pip?"

I told him when I had arrived, and how Miss Havisham had wished me to come and see Estella. To which he replied, "Ah! Very fine young lady!" Then he pushed Miss Havisham in her chair before him, with one of his large hands, and put the other in his trousers-pocket as if the pocket were full of secrets.

"Well, Pip! How often have you seen Miss Estella before?" said he, when he came to a stop.

"How often?"

"Ah! How many times? Ten thousand times?"

"Oh! Certainly not so many."

"Twice?"

"Jaggers," interposed Miss Havisham, much to my relief; "leave my Pip alone, and go with him to your dinner."

He complied, and we groped our way down the dark stairs together. While we were still on our way to those detached apartments across the paved yard at the back, he asked me how often I had seen Miss Havisham eat and drink; offering me a breadth of choice, as usual, between a hundred times and once.

I considered, and said, "Never."

"And never will, Pip," he retorted, with a frowning smile. "She has never allowed herself to be seen doing either, since she lived this present life of hers. She wanders about in the night, and then lays hands on such food as she takes."

"Pray, sir," said I, "may I ask you a question?"

"You may," said he, "and I may decline to answer it. Put your question."

"Estella's name. Is it Havisham or —?" I had nothing to add.

"Or what?" said he.

"Is it Havisham?"

"It is Havisham."

This brought us to the dinner-table, where she and Sarah Pocket awaited us. Mr. Jaggers presided, Estella sat opposite to him, I faced my green and yellow friend. We dined very well, and were waited on by a maid servant whom I had never seen in all my comings and goings, but who, for anything I know, had been in that mysterious house the whole time. After dinner, a bottle of choice old port was placed before my guardian (he was evidently well acquainted with the vintage), and the two ladies left us.

Anything to equal the determined reticence of Mr. Jaggers under that roof, I never saw elsewhere, even in him. He kept his very looks to himself, and scarcely directed his eyes to Estella's face once during dinner. When she spoke to him, he listened, and in due course answered, but never looked at her, that I could see. On the other hand, she often looked at him, with interest and curiosity, if not distrust, but his face never showed the least consciousness. Throughout dinner he took a dry delight in making Sarah Pocket greener and yellower, by often referring in conversation with me to my expectations; but here, again, he showed no consciousness, and even made it appear that he extorted — and even did extort, though I don't know how — those references out of my innocent self.

And when he and I were left alone together, he sat with an air upon him of general lying by in consequence of information he possessed, that really was too much for me. He cross-examined his very wine when he had nothing else in hand. He held it between himself and the candle, tasted the port, rolled it in his mouth, swallowed it, looked at his glass again, smelt the port, tried it, drank it, filled again, and cross-examined the glass again, until I was as nervous as if I had known the wine to be telling him something to my disadvantage. Three or four times I feebly thought I would start conversation; but whenever he saw me going to ask him anything, he looked at me with his glass in his hand, and rolling his wine about in his mouth, as if requesting me to take notice that it was of no use, for he couldn't answer.

I think Miss Pocket was conscious that the sight of me involved her in the danger of being goaded to madness, and perhaps tearing off her cap — which was a very hideous one, in the nature of a muslin mop — and strewing the ground with her hair — which assuredly had never grown on *her* head. She did not appear when we afterwards went up to Miss Havisham's room, and we four played at whist. In the interval, Miss Havisham, in a fantastic way, had put some of the most beautiful jewels from her dressing-table into Estella's hair, and about her bosom and arms; and I saw even my guardian look at her from under his thick eyebrows, and raise them a little, when her loveliness was before him, with those rich flushes of glitter and colour in it.

Of the manner and extent to which he took our trumps into custody, and came out with mean little cards at the ends of hands, before which the glory of our Kings and Queens was utterly abased, I say nothing; nor, of the feeling that I had, respecting his looking upon us personally in the light of three very obvious and poor riddles that he had found out long ago. What I suffered from, was the incompatibility between his cold presence and my feelings towards Estella. It was not that I knew I could never bear to speak to him about her, that I knew I could never bear to hear him creak his boots at her, that I knew I could never bear to see him wash his hands of her; it was, that my admiration should be within a foot or two of him — it was, that my feelings should be in the same place with him — *that*, was the agonising circumstance.

We played until nine o'clock, and then it was arranged that when Estella came to London I should be forewarned of her coming and should meet her at the coach; and then I took leave of her, and touched her and left her.

My guardian lay at the Boar in the next room to mine. Far into the night, Miss Havisham's words, "Love her, love her, love her!" sounded in my ears. I adapted them for my own repetition, and said to my pillow, "I love her, I love her, I love her!" hundreds of times. Then, a burst of gratitude came upon me, that she should be destined for me, once the blacksmith's boy. Then, I thought if she were, as I feared, by no means rapturously grateful for that destiny yet, when would she begin to be interested in me? When should I awaken the heart within her, that was mute and sleeping now?

Ah me! I thought those were high and great emotions. But I never thought there was anything low and small in my keeping away from Joe, because I knew she would be contemptuous of him. It was but a day gone, and Joe had brought the tears into my eyes; they had soon dried, God forgive me! soon dried.

CHAPTER XI

AFTER WELL considering the matter while I was dressing at the Blue Boar in the morning, I resolved to tell my guardian that I doubted Orlick's being the right sort of man to fill a post of trust at Miss Havisham's. "Why, of course he is not the right sort of man, Pip," said my guardian, comfortably satisfied beforehand on the general head, "because the man who fills the post of trust never is the right sort of man." It seemed quite to put him into spirits, to find that this particular post was not exceptionally held by the right sort of man, and he listened in a satisfied manner while I told him what knowledge I had of Orlick. "Very good, Pip," he observed, when I had concluded, "I'll go round presently, and pay our friend off." Rather alarmed by this summary action, I was for a little delay, and even hinted that our friend himself might be difficult to deal with. "Oh no he won't," said my guardian, making his pocket-handkerchief-point, with perfect confidence; "I should like to see him argue the question with *me*."

As we were going back together to London by the mid-day coach, and as I breakfasted under such terrors of Pumblechook that I could scarcely hold my cup, this gave me an opportunity of saying that I wanted a walk, and that I would go on along the London-road while Mr. Jaggers was occupied, if he would let the coachman know that I would get into my place when overtaken. I was thus enabled to fly from the Blue Boar immediately after breakfast. By then making a loop of about a couple of miles into the open country at the back of Pumblechook's premises, I got round into the High-street again, a little beyond that pitfall, and felt myself in comparative security.

It was interesting to be in the quiet old town once more, and it was not disagreeable to be here and there suddenly recognised and stared after. One or two of the tradespeople even darted out of their shops and went a little way down the street before me, that they might turn, as if they had forgotten something, and pass me face to face — on which occasions I don't know whether they or I made the worse pretence; they of not doing it, or I of not seeing it. Still my position was a distinguished one, and I was not at all dissatisfied with it, until Fate threw me in the way of that unlimited miscreant, Trabb's boy.

Casting my eyes along the street at a certain point of my progress, I beheld Trabb's boy approaching, lashing himself with an empty blue bag. Deeming that a serene and unconscious contemplation of him would best beseem me, and would be most likely to quell his evil mind, I advanced with that expression of countenance, and was rather congratulating myself on my success, when suddenly the knees of Trabb's boy smote together, his hair uprose, his cap fell off, he trembled violently in every limb, staggered out into the road, and crying to the populace, "Hold me! I'm so frightened!" feigned to be in a paroxysm of terror and contrition, occasioned by the dignity of my appearance. As I passed him, his teeth loudly chattered in his head, and with every mark of extreme humiliation, he prostrated himself in the dust.

This was a hard thing to bear, but this was nothing. I had not advanced another two hundred yards, when, to my inexpressible terror, amazement, and indignation, I again beheld Trabb's boy approaching. He was coming round a narrow corner. His blue bag was slung over his shoulder, honest industry beamed in his eyes, a determination to proceed to Trabb's with cheerful briskness was indicated in his gait. With a shock he became aware of me, and was severely visited as before; but this time his motion was rotatory, and he staggered round and round me with knees more afflicted, and with uplifted hands as if beseeching for mercy. His sufferings were hailed with the greatest joy by a knot of spectators, and I felt utterly confounded.

I had not got as much further down the street as the post-office, when I again beheld Trabb's boy shooting round by a back way. This time, he was entirely changed. He wore the blue bag in the manner of my great-coat, and was strutting along the pavement towards me on the opposite side of the street, attended by a company of delighted young friends to whom he from time to time exclaimed, with a wave of his hand, "Don't know yah!" Words cannot state the amount of aggravation and injury wreaked upon me by Trabb's boy, when, passing abreast of me, he pulled up his shirt-collar, twined his side-hair, stuck an arm akimbo, and smirked extravagantly by, wriggling his elbows and body, and drawling to his at-tendants, "Don't know yah, don't know yah, pon my soul don't know yah!" The disgrace attendant on his immediately afterwards taking to crow-ing and pursuing me across the bridge with crows, as from an exceed-ingly dejected fowl who had known me when I was a blacksmith, culminated the disgrace with which I left the town, and was, so to speak, ejected by it into the open country.

But unless I had taken the life of Trabb's boy on that occasion, I really do not even now see what I could have done save endure. To have strug-gled with him in the street, or to have exacted any lower recompense from him than his heart's best blood, would have been futile and degrad-ing. Moreover, he was a boy whom no man could hurt; an invulnerable and dodging serpent who, when chased into a corner, flew out again be-tween his captor's legs, scornfully yelping. I wrote, however, to Mr. Trabb by next day's post, to say that Mr. Pip must decline to deal further with one who could so far forget what he owed to the best interests of society, as to employ a boy who excited Loathing in every respectable mind.

The coach, with Mr. Jaggers inside, came up in due time, and I took my box-seat again, and arrived in London safe — but not sound, for my heart was gone. As soon as I arrived, I sent a penitential codfish and bar-rel of oysters to Joe (as reparation for not having gone myself), and then went on to Barnard's Inn.

I found Herbert dining on cold meat, and delighted to welcome me back. Having despatched The Avenger to the coffee-house for an addition to the dinner, I felt that I must open my breast that very evening to my friend and chum.[1] As confidence was out of the question with The Avenger in the hall, which could merely be regarded in the light of an ante-chamber to the keyhole, I sent him to the Play. A better proof of the severity of my bondage to that taskmaster could scarcely be afforded, than the degrading shifts to which I was constantly driven to find him employment. So mean is extremity, that I sometimes sent him to Hyde Park-corner[2] to see what o'clock it was.

Dinner done and we sitting with our feet upon the fender, I said to Herbert, "My dear Herbert, I have something very particular to tell you."

"My dear Handel," he returned, "I shall esteem and respect your confidence."

"It concerns myself, Herbert," said I, "and one other person."

Herbert crossed his feet, looked at the fire with his head on one side, and having looked at it in vain for some time, looked at me because I didn't go on.

"Herbert," said I, laying my hand upon his knee, "I love — I adore — Estella."

Instead of being transfixed, Herbert replied in an easy matter-of-course way, "Exactly. Well?"

"Well, Herbert? Is that all you say? Well?"

"What next, I mean?" said Herbert. "Of course I know that."

"How do you know it?" said I.

"How do I know it, Handel? Why, from you."

"I never told you."

"Told me! You have never told me when you have got your hair cut, but I have had senses to perceive it. You have always adored her, ever since I have known you. You brought your adoration and your portmanteau here, together. Told me! Why, you have always told me all day long. When you told me your own story, you told me plainly that you began adoring her the first time you saw her, when you were very young indeed."

"Very well, then," said I, to whom this was a new and not unwel-

---

1. *chum:* person with whom an apartment is shared.
2. *Hyde Park-corner:* nearly three miles from Pip's residence. See Map C.

come light, "I have never left off adoring her. And she has come back, a most beautiful and most elegant creature. And I saw her yesterday. And if I adored her before, I now doubly adore her."

"Lucky for you then, Handel," said Herbert, "that you are picked out for her and allotted to her. Without encroaching on forbidden ground, we may venture to say that there can be no doubt between ourselves of that fact. Have you any idea yet, of Estella's views on the adoration question?"

I shook my head gloomily. "Oh! She is thousands of miles away, from me," said I.

"Patience, my dear Handel: time enough, time enough. But you have something more to say?"

"I am ashamed to say it," I returned, "and yet it's no worse to say it than to think it. You call me a lucky fellow. Of course, I am. I was a blacksmith's boy but yesterday; I am — what shall I say I am — to-day?"

"Say, a good fellow, if you want a phrase," returned Herbert, smiling, and clapping his hand on the back of mine, "a good fellow, with impetuosity and hesitation, boldness and diffidence, action and dreaming, curiously mixed in him."

I stopped for a moment to consider whether there really was this mixture in my character. On the whole, I by no means recognised the analysis, but thought it not worth disputing.

"When I ask what I am to call myself to-day, Herbert," I went on, "I suggest what I have in my thoughts. You say I am lucky. I know I have done nothing to raise myself in life, and that Fortune alone has raised me; that is being very lucky. And yet, when I think of Estella —"

("And when don't you, you know?" Herbert threw in, with his eyes on the fire; which I thought kind and sympathetic of him.)

"— Then, my dear Herbert, I cannot tell you how dependent and uncertain I feel, and how exposed to hundreds of chances. Avoiding forbidden ground, as you did just now, I may still say that on the constancy of one person (naming no person) all my expectations depend. And at the best, how indefinite and unsatisfactory, only to know so vaguely what they are!" In saying this, I relieved my mind of what had always been there, more or less, though no doubt most since yesterday.

"Now, Handel," Herbert replied, in his gay hopeful way, "it seems to me that in the despondency of the tender passion, we are looking into our gift-horse's mouth with a magnifying glass. Likewise, it seems to me that, concentrating our attention on the examination, we altogether overlook one of the best points of the animal. Didn't you tell me that your guardian, Mr. Jaggers, told you in the beginning, that you were not endowed with expectations only? And even if he had not told you so — though that is a very large If, I grant — could you believe that of all men in London, Mr. Jaggers is the man to hold his present relations towards you unless he were sure of his ground?"

I said I could not deny that this was a strong point. I said it (people often do so, in such cases) like a rather reluctant concession to truth and justice; — as if I wanted to deny it!

"I should think it *was* a strong point," said Herbert, "and I should think you would be puzzled to imagine a stronger; as to the rest, you must bide your guardian's time, and he must bide his client's time. You'll be one-and-twenty before you know where you are, and then perhaps you'll get some further enlightenment. At all events, you'll be nearer getting it, for it must come at last."

"What a hopeful disposition you have!" said I, gratefully admiring his cheery ways.

"I ought to have," said Herbert, "for I have not much else. I must acknowledge, by-the-by, that the good sense of what I have just said is not my own, but my father's. The only remark I ever heard him make on your story, was the final one: 'The thing is settled and done, or Mr. Jaggers would not be in it.' And now before I say anything more about my father, or my father's son, and repay confidence with confidence, I want to make myself seriously disagreeable to you for a moment — positively repulsive."

"You won't succeed," said I.

"Oh yes I shall!" said he. "One, two, three, and now I am in for it. Handel, my good fellow;" though he spoke in this light tone, he was very much in earnest: "I have been thinking since we have been talking with our feet on this fender, that Estella surely cannot be a condition of your inheritance, if she was never referred to by your guardian. Am I right in so understanding what you have told me, as that he never referred to her, directly or indirectly, in any way? Never even hinted, for instance, that your patron might have views as to your marriage ultimately?"

"Never."

"Now, Handel, I am quite free from the flavour of sour grapes, upon my soul and honour! Not being bound to her, can you not detach yourself from her? — I told you I should be disagreeable."

I turned my head aside, for, with a rush and a sweep, like the old marsh winds coming up from the sea, a feeling like that which had subdued me on the morning when I left the forge, when the mists were solemnly rising, and when I laid my hand upon the village finger-post, smote upon my heart again. There was silence between us for a little while.

"Yes; but my dear Handel," Herbert went on, as if we had been talking instead of silent, "its having been so strongly rooted in the breast of a boy whom nature and circumstances made so romantic, renders it very serious. Think of her bringing-up, and think of Miss Havisham. Think of what she is herself (now I am repulsive and you abominate me). This may lead to miserable things."

"I know it, Herbert," said I, with my head still turned away, "but I can't help it."

"You can't detach yourself?"

"No. Impossible!"

"You can't try, Handel?"

"No. Impossible!"

"Well!" said Herbert, getting up with a lively shake as if he had been asleep, and stirring the fire; "now I'll endeavour to make myself agreeable again!"

So he went round the room and shook the curtains out, put the chairs in their places, tidied the books and so forth that were lying about, looked into the hall, peeped into the letter-box, shut the door, and came back to his chair by the fire: where he sat down, nursing his left leg in both arms.

"I was going to say a word or two, Handel, concerning my father and my father's son. I am afraid it is scarcely necessary for my father's son to remark that my father's establishment is not particularly brilliant in its housekeeping."

"There is always plenty, Herbert," said I: to say something encouraging.

"Oh yes! and so the dustman says, I believe, with the strongest approval, and so does the marine store-shop in the back street. Gravely, Handel, for the subject is grave enough, you know how it is, as well as I do. I suppose there was a time once when my father had not given matters up; but if ever there was, the time is gone. May I ask you if you have ever had an opportunity of remarking, down in your part of the country, that the children of not exactly suitable marriages, are always most particularly anxious to be married?"

This was such a singular question, that I asked him in return, "Is it so?"

"I don't know," said Herbert, "that's what I want to know. Because it is decidedly the case with us. My poor sister Charlotte who was next me and died before she was fourteen, was a striking example. Little Jane is the same. In her desire to be matrimonially established, you might suppose her to have passed her short existence in the perpetual contemplation of domestic bliss. Little Alick in a frock has already made arrangements for his union with a suitable young person at Kew. And indeed, I think we are all engaged, except the baby."

"Then you are?" said I.

"I am," said Herbert; "but it's a secret."

I assured him of my keeping the secret, and begged to be favoured with further particulars. He had spoken so sensibly and feelingly of my weakness that I wanted to know something about his strength.

"May I ask the name?" I said.

"Name of Clara," said Herbert.

"Live in London?"

"Yes. Perhaps I ought to mention," said Herbert, who had become curiously crestfallen and meek, since we entered on the interesting theme, "that she is rather below my mother's nonsensical family notions. Her father had to do with the victualling of passenger-ships. I think he was a species of purser."

"What is he now?" said I.

"He's an invalid now," replied Herbert.

"Living on —?"

"On the first floor," said Herbert. Which was not at all what I meant, for I had intended my question to apply to his means. "I have never seen him, for he has always kept his room overhead, since I have known Clara. But I have heard him constantly. He makes tremendous rows — roars, and pegs at the floor with some frightful instrument." In looking at me and then laughing heartily, Herbert for the time recovered his usual lively manner.

"Don't you expect to see him?" said I.

"Oh yes, I constantly expect to see him," returned Herbert, "because I never hear him, without expecting him to come tumbling through the ceiling. But I don't know how long the rafters may hold."

When he had once more laughed heartily, he became meek again, and told me that the moment he began to realise Capital, it was his intention to marry this young lady. He added as a self-evident proposition, engendering low spirits, "But you *can't* marry, you know, while you're looking about you."

As we contemplated the fire, and as I thought what a difficult vision to realise this same Capital sometimes was, I put my hands in my pockets. A folded piece of paper in one of them attracting my attention, I opened it and found it to be the playbill I had received from Joe, relative to the celebrated provincial amateur of Roscian renown. "And bless my heart," I involuntarily added aloud, "it's to-night!"

This changed the subject in an instant, and made us hurriedly resolve to go to the play. So, when I had pledged myself to comfort and abet Herbert in the affair of his heart by all practicable and impracticable means, and when Herbert had told me that his affianced already knew me by reputation and that I should be presented to her, and when we had warmly shaken hands upon our mutual confidence, we blew out our candles, made up our fire, locked our door, and issued forth in quest of Mr. Wopsle and Denmark.[1]

CHAPTER XII

ON OUR arrival in Denmark, we found the king and queen of that country elevated in two arm-chairs on a kitchen-table, holding a Court. The whole of the Danish nobility were in attendance; consisting of a noble boy in the wash-leather boots of a gigantic ancestor, a venerable Peer with a dirty face who seemed to have risen from the people late in life,

---

1. *Denmark:* setting of Shakespeare's *Hamlet.* See note on p. 250.

and the Danish chivalry with a comb in its hair and a pair of white silk legs, and presenting on the whole a feminine appearance. My gifted townsman stood gloomily apart, with folded arms, and I could have wished that his curls and forehead had been more probable.

Several curious little circumstances transpired as the action proceeded. The late king of the country not only appeared to have been troubled with a cough at the time of his decease, but to have taken it with him to the tomb, and to have brought it back. The royal phantom also carried a ghostly manuscript round its truncheon, to which it had the appearance of occasionally referring and that, too, with an air of anxiety and a tendency to lose the place of reference which were suggestive of a state of mortality. It was this, I conceive, which led to the Shade's being advised by the gallery to "turn over!" — a recommendation which it took extremely ill. It was likewise to be noted of this majestic spirit that whereas it always appeared with an air of having been out a long time and walked an immense distance, it perceptibly came from a closely contiguous wall. This occasioned its terrors to be received derisively. The Queen of Denmark, a very buxom lady, though no doubt historically brazen, was considered by the public to have too much brass about her; her chin being attached to her diadem by a broad band of that metal (as if she had a gorgeous toothache), her waist being encircled by another, and each of her arms by another, so that she was openly mentioned as "the kettle-drum." The noble boy in the ancestral boots, was inconsistent; representing himself, as it were in one breath, as an able seaman, a strolling actor, a gravedigger, a clergyman, and a person of the utmost importance at a Court fencing-match, on the authority of whose practised eye and nice discrimination the finest strokes were judged. This gradually led to a want of toleration for him, and even — on his being detected in holy orders, and declining to perform the funeral service — to the general indignation taking the form of nuts. Lastly, Ophelia was a prey to such slow musical madness, that when, in course of time, she had taken off her white muslin scarf, folded it up, and buried it, a sulky man who had been long cooling his impatient nose against an iron bar in the front row of the gallery, growled, "Now the baby's put to bed let's have supper!" Which, to say the least of it, was out of keeping.

Upon my unfortunate townsman all these incidents accumulated with playful effect. Whenever that undecided Prince had to ask a question or state a doubt, the public helped him out with it. As for example; on the question whether 'twas nobler in the mind to suffer some roared yes, and some no, and some inclining to both opinions said "toss up for it;" and quite a Debating Society arose. When he asked what should such fellows as he do crawling between earth and heaven, he was encouraged with loud cries of "Hear, hear!" When he appeared with his stocking disordered (its disorder expressed, according to usage, by one very neat fold in the top, which I suppose to be always got up with a flat iron), a conversation took place in the gallery respecting the paleness of his leg, and whether it was occasioned by the turn the ghost had given him. On his taking the recorders — very like a little black flute that had just been played in the orchestra and handed out at the door — he was called upon unanimously for Rule Britannia. When he recommended the player not to saw the air thus, the sulky man said, "And don't *you* do it, neither; you're a deal worse than *him*!" And I grieve to add that peals of laughter greeted Mr. Wopsle on every one of these occasions.

But his greatest trials were in the churchyard: which had the appearance of a primeval forest, with a kind of small ecclesiastical wash-house on one side, and a turnpike-gate on the other. Mr. Wopsle in a comprehensive black cloak, being descried entering at the turnpike, the gravedigger was admonished in a friendly way, "Look out! Here's the undertaker a coming, to see how you're a getting on with your work!" I believe it is well known in a constitutional[1] country that Mr. Wopsle could not possibly have returned the skull, after moralising over it, without dusting his fingers on a white napkin taken from his breast; but even that innocent and indispensable action did not pass without the comment "Wai-ter!" The arrival of the body for interment (in an empty black box with the lid tumbling open), was the signal for a general joy which was much enhanced by the discovery, among the bearers, of an individual obnoxious to identification. The joy attended Mr. Wopsle through his struggle with Laertes on the brink of the orchestra and the grave, and slackened no more until he had tumbled the king off the kitchen-table, and had died by inches from the ankles upward.

---

1. *constitutional:* here implying "civilized."

We had made some pale efforts in the beginning to applaud Mr. Wopsle; but they were too hopeless to be persisted in. Therefore we had sat, feeling keenly for him, but laughing, nevertheless, from ear to ear. I laughed in spite of myself all the time, the whole thing was so droll; and yet I had a latent impression that there was something decidedly fine in Mr. Wopsle's elocution — not for old associations' sake, I am afraid, but because it was very slow, very dreary, very up-hill and down-hill, and very unlike any way in which any man in any natural circumstances of life or death ever expressed himself about anything. When the tragedy was over, and he had been called for and hooted, I said to Herbert, "Let us go at once, or perhaps we shall meet him."

We made all the haste we could down-stairs, but we were not quick enough either. Standing at the door was a Jewish man with an unnaturally heavy smear of eyebrow, who caught my eye as we advanced, and said, when we came up with him:

"Mr. Pip and friend?"

Identity of Mr. Pip and friend confessed.

"Mr. Waldengarver," said the man, "would be glad to have the honour."

"Waldengarver?" I repeated — when Herbert murmured in my ear, "Probably Wopsle."

"Oh!" said I. "Yes. Shall we follow you?"

"A few steps, please." When we were in a side alley, he turned and asked, "How did you think he looked? — I dressed him."

I don't know what he had looked like, except a funeral; with the addition of a large Danish sun or star hanging round his neck by a blue ribbon, that had given him the appearance of being insured in some extraordinary Fire Office.[1] But I said he had looked very nice.

"When he come to the grave," said our conductor, "he showed his cloak beautiful. But, judging from the wing, it looked to me that when he see the ghost in the queen's apartment, he might have made more of his stockings."

---

1. *a large Danish sun or star hanging round his neck by a blue ribbon, that had given him the appearance of being insured in some extraordinary Fire Office:* referring to the distinguishing signs employed in London by the private fire brigades maintained by property insurance companies before the foundation of a public force in 1865.

I modestly assented, and we all fell through a little dirty swing door, into a sort of hot packing-case immediately behind it. Here Mr. Wopsle was divesting himself of his Danish garments, and here there was just room for us to look at him over one another's shoulders, by keeping the packing-case door, or lid, wide open.

"Gentlemen," said Mr. Wopsle, "I am proud to see you. I hope, Mr. Pip, you will excuse my sending round. I had the happiness to know you in former times, and the Drama has ever had a claim which has ever been acknowledged, on the noble and the affluent."

Meanwhile, Mr. Waldengarver, in a frightful perspiration, was trying to get himself out of his princely sables.

"Skin the stockings off, Mr. Waldengarver," said the owner of that property, "or you'll bust 'em. Bust 'em, and you'll bust five-and-thirty shillings. Shakspeare never was complimented with a finer pair. Keep quiet in your chair now, and leave 'em to me."

With that, he went upon his knees, and began to flay his victim; who, on the first stocking coming off, would certainly have fallen over backward with his chair, but for there being no room to fall anyhow.

I had been afraid until then to say a word about the play. But then, Mr. Waldengarver looked up at us complacently, and said:

"Gentlemen, how did it seem to you, to go, in front?"

Herbert said from behind (at the same time poking me), "capitally." So I said "capitally."

"How did you like my reading of the character, gentlemen?" said Mr. Waldengarver, almost, if not quite, with patronage.

Herbert said from behind (again poking me), "massive and concrete." So I said boldly, as if I had originated it, and must beg to insist upon it, "massive and concrete."

"I am glad to have your approbation, gentlemen," said Mr. Waldengarver, with an air of dignity, in spite of his being ground against the wall at the time, and holding on by the seat of the chair.

"But I'll tell you one thing, Mr. Waldengarver," said the man who was on his knees, "in which you're out in your reading. Now mind! I don't care who says contrairy; I tell you so. You're out in your reading of Hamlet when you get your legs in profile. The last Hamlet as I dressed, made the same mistakes in his reading at rehearsal, till I got him to put a large red wafer on each of his shins, and then at that rehearsal (which was the last) I went in front, sir, to the back of the pit, and whenever his reading brought him into profile, I called out 'I don't see no wafers!' And at night his reading was lovely."

Mr. Waldengarver smiled at me, as much as to say "a faithful dependent — I overlook his folly;" and then said aloud, "My view is a little classic and thoughtful for them here; but they will improve, they will improve."

Herbert and I said together, Oh, no doubt they would improve.

"Did you observe, gentlemen," said Mr. Waldengarver, "that there was a man in the gallery who endeavoured to cast derision on the service — I mean, the representation?"

We basely replied that we rather thought we had noticed such a man. I added, "He was drunk, no doubt."

"Oh dear no, sir," said Mr. Wopsle, "not drunk. His employer would see to that, sir. His employer would not allow him to be drunk."

"You know his employer?" said I.

Mr. Wopsle shut his eyes, and opened them again; performing both ceremonies very slowly. "You must have observed, gentlemen," said he, "an ignorant and a blatant ass, with a rasping throat and a countenance expressive of low malignity, who went through — I will not say sustained — the rôle (if I may use a French expression) of Claudius King of Denmark. That is his employer, gentlemen. Such is the profession!"

Without distinctly knowing whether I should have been more sorry for Mr. Wopsle if he had been in despair, I was so sorry for him as it was, that I took the opportunity of his turning round to have his braces put on — which jostled us out at the doorway — to ask Herbert what he thought of having him home to supper? Herbert said he thought it would be kind to do so; therefore I invited him, and he went to Barnard's with us, wrapped up to the eyes, and we did our best for him, and he sat until two o'clock in the morning, reviewing his success and developing his plans. I forget in detail what they were, but I have a general recollection that he was to begin with reviving the Drama, and to end with crushing it; inasmuch as his decease would leave it utterly bereft and without a chance or hope.

Miserably I went to bed after all, and miserably thought of Estella, and miserably dreamed that my expectations were all cancelled, and that I had to give my hand in marriage to Herbert's Clara, or play Hamlet to

Miss Havisham's Ghost, before twenty thousand people, without knowing twenty words of it.

CHAPTER XIII

ONE DAY when I was busy with my books and Mr. Pocket, I received a note by the post, the mere outside of which threw me into a great flutter; for, though I had never seen the handwriting in which it was addressed, I divined whose hand it was. It had no set beginning, as Dear Mr. Pip, or Dear Pip, or Dear Sir, or Dear Anything, but ran thus:

"I am to come to London the day after to-morrow by the mid-day coach. I believe it was settled you should meet me? At all events Miss Havisham has that impression, and I write in obedience to it. She sends you her regard.

"Yours, ESTELLA."

If there had been time, I should probably have ordered several suits of clothes for this occasion; but as there was not, I was fain to be content with those I had. My appetite vanished instantly, and I knew no peace or rest until the day arrived. Not that its arrival brought me either; for, then I was worse than ever, and began haunting the coach-office in Wood-street, Cheapside, before the coach had left the Blue Boar in our town. For all that I knew this perfectly well, I still felt as if it were not safe to let the coach-office be out of my sight longer than five minutes at a time; and in this condition of unreason I had performed the first half-hour of a watch of four or five hours, when Wemmick ran against me.

"Halloa, Mr. Pip," said he; "how do you do? I should hardly have thought this was *your* beat."

I explained that I was waiting to meet somebody who was coming up by coach, and I inquired after the Castle and the Aged.

"Both flourishing, thankye," said Wemmick, "and particularly the Aged. He's in wonderful feather. He'll be eighty-two next birthday. I have a notion of firing eighty-two times, if the neighbourhood shouldn't complain, and that cannon of mine should prove equal to the pressure. However, this is not London talk. Where do you think I am going to?"

"To the office?" said I, for he was tending in that direction.

"Next thing to it," returned Wemmick, "I am going to Newgate. We are in a banker's-parcel case[1] just at present, and I have been down the road taking a squint at the scene of action, and thereupon must have a word or two with our client."

"Did your client commit the robbery?" I asked.

"Bless your soul and body, no," answered Wemmick, very drily. "But he is accused of it. So might you or I be. Either of us might be accused of it, you know."

"Only neither of us is," I remarked.

"Yah!" said Wemmick, touching me on the breast with his forefinger; "you're a deep one, Mr. Pip! Would you like to have a look at Newgate? Have you time to spare?"

I had so much time to spare, that the proposal came as a relief, notwithstanding its irreconcilability with my latent desire to keep my eye on the coach-office. Muttering that I would make the inquiry whether I had time to walk with him, I went into the office, and ascertained from the clerk with the nicest precision and much to the trying of his temper, the earliest moment at which the coach could be expected — which I knew beforehand, quite as well as he. I then rejoined Mr. Wemmick, and affecting to consult my watch and to be surprised by the information I had received, accepted his offer.

We were at Newgate in a few minutes, and we passed through the lodge where some fetters were hanging up on the bare walls among the prison rules, into the interior of the jail. At that time, jails were much neglected, and the period of exaggerated reaction consequent on all public wrong-doing — and which is always its heaviest and longest punishment — was still far off. So, felons were not lodged and fed better than soldiers (to say nothing of paupers), and seldom set fire to their prisons with the excusable object of improving the flavour of their soup.* It was visiting time when Wemmick took me in; and a potman was going his rounds with beer; and the prisoners, behind bars in yards, were buying beer, and

---

1. *banker's-parcel case:* fraud involving the substitution of a fake parcel for the real one.

talking to friends; and a frouzy, ugly, disorderly, depressing scene it was.

It struck me that Wemmick walked among the prisoners, much as a gardener might walk among his plants. This was first put into my head by his seeing a shoot that had come up in the night, and saying, "What, Captain Tom? Are *you* there? Ah, indeed!" and also "Is that Black Bill behind the cistern? Why I didn't look for you these two months; how do you find yourself?" Equally in his stopping at the bars and attending to anxious whisperers — always singly — Wemmick with his post-office in an immovable state, looked at them while in conference, as if he were taking particular notice of the advance they had made, since last observed, towards coming out in full blow at their trial.

He was highly popular, and I found that he took the familiar department of Mr. Jaggers's business: though something of the state of Mr. Jaggers hung about him too, forbidding approach beyond certain limits. His personal recognition of each successive client was comprised in a nod, and in his settling his hat a little easier on his head with both hands, and then tightening the post-office, and putting his hands in his pockets. In one or two instances, there was a difficulty respecting the raising of fees, and then Mr. Wemmick, backing as far as possible from the insufficient money produced, said, "It's no use, my boy. I'm only a subordinate. I can't take it. Don't go on in that way with a subordinate. If you are unable to make up your quantum, my boy, you had better address yourself to a principal; there are plenty of principals in the profession, you know, and what is not worth the while of one, may be worth the while of another; that's my recommendation to you, speaking as a subordinate. Don't try on useless measures. Why should you? Now, who's next?"

Thus, we walked through Wemmick's greenhouse, until he turned to me and said, "Notice the man I shall shake hands with." I should have done so, without the preparation, as he had shaken hands with no one yet.

Almost as soon as he had spoken, a portly upright man (whom I can see now, as I write) in a well-worn olive-coloured frock-coat, with a peculiar pallor overspreading the red in his complexion, and eyes that went wandering about when he tried to fix them, came up to a corner of the bars, and put his hand to his hat — which had a greasy spotty surface like cold broth — with a half-serious and half-jocose military salute.

"Colonel, to you!" said Wemmick; "how are you, Colonel?"

"All right, Mr. Wemmick."

"Everything was done that could be done, but the evidence was too strong for us, Colonel."

"Yes it was too strong, sir — but *I* don't care."

"No, no," said Wemmick, coolly, "*you* don't care." Then, turning to me, "Served His Majesty this man. Was a soldier in the line and bought his discharge."

I said, "Indeed?" and the man's eyes looked at me, and then looked over my head, and then looked all round me, and then he drew his hand across his lips and laughed.

"I think I shall be out of this on Monday, sir," he said to Wemmick.

"Perhaps," returned my friend, "but there's no knowing."

"I am glad to have the chance of bidding you good-by, Mr. Wemmick," said the man, stretching out his hand between two bars.

"Thankye," said Wemmick, shaking hands with him. "Same to you, Colonel."

"If what I had upon me when taken, had been real, Mr. Wemmick," said the man, unwilling to let his hand go, "I should have asked the favour of your wearing another ring — in acknowledgment of your attentions."

"I'll accept the will for the deed," said Wemmick. "By-the-by; you were quite a pigeon-fancier." The man looked up at the sky. "I am told you had a remarkable breed of tumblers. *Could* you commission any friend of yours to bring me a pair, if you've no further use for 'em?"

"It shall be done, sir."

"All right," said Wemmick, "they shall be taken care of. Good afternoon, Colonel. Good-by!" They shook hands again, and as we walked away Wemmick said to me, "A Coiner,[1] a very good workman. The Recorder's report is made to-day, and he is sure to be executed on Monday.[2] Still you see, as far as it goes, a pair of pigeons are portable property, all

---

1. *Coiner:* maker of counterfeit coins.
2. *The Recorder's report is made to-day, and he is sure to be executed on Monday:* The Recorder of the City of London, then appointed by the Lord Mayor and aldermen to be the "mouth of the City," acted as a justice of the peace and judge at the quarter sessions, delivered all sentences and judgements of the court, and reported them to the Secretary of State.

the same." With that, he looked back, and nodded at this dead plant, and then cast his eyes about him in walking out of the yard, as if he were considering what other pot would go best in its place.

As we came out of the prison through the lodge, I found that the great importance of my guardian was appreciated by the turnkeys, no less than by those whom they held in charge. "Well, Mr. Wemmick," said the turnkey, who kept us between the two studded and spiked lodge gates, and who carefully locked one before he unlocked the other, "what's Mr. Jaggers going to do with that waterside murder? Is he going to make it manslaughter, or what's he going to make of it?"

"Why don't you ask him?" returned Wemmick.

"Oh yes, I dare say!" said the turnkey.

"Now, that's the way with them here, Mr. Pip," remarked Wemmick, turning to me with his post-office elongated. "They don't mind what they ask of me, the subordinate; but you'll never catch 'em asking any questions of my principal."

"Is this young gentleman one of the 'prentices or articled ones of your office?" asked the turnkey, with a grin at Mr. Wemmick's humour.

"There he goes again, you see!" cried Wemmick, "I told you so! Asks another question of the subordinate before his first is dry! Well, supposing Mr. Pip is one of them?"

"Why then," said the turnkey, grinning again, "he knows what Mr. Jaggers is."

"Yah!" cried Wemmick, suddenly hitting out at the turnkey in a facetious way, "you're as dumb as one of your own keys when you have to do with my principal, you know you are. Let us out, you old fox, or I'll get him to bring an action against you for false imprisonment."

The turnkey laughed, and gave us good day, and stood laughing at us over the spikes of the wicket when we descended the steps into the street.

"Mind you, Mr. Pip," said Wemmick, gravely in my ear, as he took my arm to be more confidential; "I don't know that Mr. Jaggers does a better thing than the way in which he keeps himself so high. He's always so high. His constant height is of a piece with his immense abilities. That Colonel durst no more take leave of *him*, than that turnkey durst ask him his intentions respecting a case. Then, between his height and them, he slips in his subordinate — don't you see? — and so he has 'em, soul and body."

I was very much impressed, and not for the first time, by my guardian's subtlety. To confess the truth, I very heartily wished, and not for the first time, that I had had some other guardian of minor abilities.

Mr. Wemmick and I parted at the office in Little Britain, where suppliants for Mr. Jaggers's notice were lingering about as usual, and I returned to my watch in the street of the coach-office, with some three hours on hand. I consumed the whole time in thinking how strange it was that I should be encompassed by all this taint of prison and crime; that, in my childhood out on our lonely marshes on a winter evening I should have first encountered it; that, it should have reappeared on two occasions, starting out like a stain that was faded but not gone; that, it should in this new way pervade my fortune and advancement. While my mind was thus engaged, I thought of the beautiful young Estella, proud and refined, coming towards me, and I thought with absolute abhorrence of the contrast between the jail and her. I wished that Wemmick had not met me, or that I had not yielded to him and gone with him, so that, of all days in the year on this day, I might not have had Newgate in my breath and on my clothes. I beat the prison dust off my feet as I sauntered to and fro, and I shook it out of my dress, and I exhaled its air from my lungs. So contaminated did I feel, remembering who was coming, that the coach came quickly after all, and I was not yet free from the soiling consciousness of Mr. Wemmick's conservatory, when I saw her face at the coach window and her hand waving to me.

What *was* the nameless shadow which again in that one instant had passed?

CHAPTER XIV

IN HER furred travelling-dress, Estella seemed more delicately beautiful than she had ever seemed yet, even in my eyes. Her manner was more winning than she had cared to let it be to me before, and I thought I saw Miss Havisham's influence in the change.

We stood in the Inn Yard while she pointed out her luggage to me, and when it was all collected I remembered — having forgotten everything but herself in the meanwhile — that I knew nothing of her destination.

"I am going to Richmond," she told me. "Our lesson is, that there are two Richmonds, one in Surrey and one in Yorkshire, and that mine is the Surrey Richmond.[1] The distance is ten miles. I am to have a carriage, and you are to take me. This is my purse, and you are to pay my charges out of it. Oh, you must take the purse! We have no choice, you and I, but to obey our instructions. We are not free to follow our own devices, you and I."

As she looked at me in giving me the purse, I hoped there was an inner meaning in her words. She said them slightingly, but not with displeasure.

"A carriage will have to be sent for, Estella. Will you rest here a little?"

"Yes, I am to rest here a little, and I am to drink some tea, and you are to take care of me the while."

She drew her arm through mine, as if it must be done, and I requested a waiter who had been staring at the coach like a man who had never seen such a thing in his life, to show us a private sitting-room. Upon that, he pulled out a napkin, as if it were a magic clue without which he couldn't find the way up-stairs, and led us to the black hole of the establishment: fitted up with a diminishing mirror (quite a superfluous article considering the hole's proportions), an anchovy sauce-cruet, and somebody's pattens. On my objecting to this retreat, he took us into another room with a dinner-table for thirty, and in the grate a scorched leaf of a copy-book under a bushel of coal-dust. Having looked at this extinct conflagration and shaken his head, he took my order: which, proving to be merely "Some tea for the lady," sent him out of the room in a very low state of mind.

I was, and I am, sensible that the air of this chamber, in its strong combination of stable with soup-stock, might have led one to infer that the coaching department was not doing well, and that the enterprising proprietor was boiling down the horses for the refreshment department. Yet

---

1. *the Surrey Richmond:* fashionable riverside town to the south-west of London. See Map C.

the room was all in all to me, Estella being in it. I thought that with her I could have been happy there for life. (I was not at all happy there at the time, observe, and I knew it well.)

"Where are you going to, at Richmond?" I asked Estella.

"I am going to live," said she, "at a great expense, with a lady there, who has the power — or says she has — of taking me about, and introducing me, and showing people to me and showing me to people."

"I suppose you will be glad of variety and admiration?"

"Yes, I suppose so."

She answered so carelessly, that I said, "You speak of yourself as if you were some one else."

"Where did you learn how I speak of others? Come, come," said Estella, smiling delightfully, "you must not expect me to go to school to *you*; I must talk in my own way. How do you thrive with Mr. Pocket?"

"I live quite pleasantly there; at least —" It appeared to me that I was losing a chance.

"At least?" repeated Estella.

"As pleasantly as I could anywhere, away from you."

"You silly boy," said Estella, quite composedly, "how can you talk such nonsense? Your friend Mr. Matthew, I believe, is superior to the rest of his family?"

"Very superior indeed. He is nobody's enemy —"

"Don't add but his own," interposed Estella, "for I hate that class of man. But he really is disinterested, and above small jealousy and spite, I have heard?"

"I am sure I have every reason to say so."

"You have not every reason to say so of the rest of his people," said Estella, nodding at me with an expression of face that was at once grave and rallying, "for they beset Miss Havisham with reports and insinuations to your disadvantage. They watch you, misrepresent you, write letters about you (anonymous sometimes), and you are the torment and the occupation of their lives. You can scarcely realise to yourself the hatred those people feel for you."

"They do me no harm, I hope?" said I.

Instead of answering, Estella burst out laughing. This was very singular to me, and I looked at her in considerable perplexity. When she left off — and she had not laughed languidly, but with real enjoyment — I said, in my diffident way with her:

"I hope I may suppose that you would not be amused if they did me any harm."

"No, no, you may be sure of that," said Estella. "You may be certain that I laugh because they fail. Oh, those people with Miss Havisham, and the tortures they undergo!" She laughed again, and even now when she had told me why, her laughter was very singular to me, for I could not doubt its being genuine, and yet it seemed too much for the occasion. I thought there must really be something more here than I knew; she saw the thought in my mind, and answered it.

"It is not easy for even you," said Estella, "to know what satisfaction it gives me to see those people thwarted, or what an enjoyable sense of the ridiculous I have when they are made ridiculous. For you were not brought up in that strange house from a mere baby. — I was. You had not your little wits sharpened by their intriguing against you, suppressed and defenceless, under the mask of sympathy and pity and what not that is soft and soothing. — I had. You did not gradually open your round childish eyes wider and wider to the discovery of that impostor of a woman who calculates her stores of peace of mind for when she wakes up in the night. — I did."

It was no laughing matter with Estella now, nor was she summoning these remembrances from any shallow place. I would not have been the cause of that look of hers, for all my expectations in a heap.

"Two things I can tell you," said Estella. "First, notwithstanding the proverb that constant dropping will wear away a stone, you may set your mind at rest that these people never will — never would, in a hundred years — impair your ground with Miss Havisham, in any particular, great or small. Second, I am beholden to you as the cause of their being so busy and so mean in vain, and there is my hand upon it."

As she gave it me playfully — for her darker mood had been but momentary — I held it and put it to my lips. "You ridiculous boy," said Estella, "will you never take warning? Or do you kiss my hand in the spirit in which I once let you kiss my cheek?"

"What was it?" said I.

"I must think a moment. A spirit of contempt for the fawners and plotters."

"If I say yes, may I kiss the cheek again?"

"You should have asked before you touched the hand. But, yes, if you like."

I leaned down, and her calm face was like a statue's. "Now," said Estella, gliding away the instant I touched her cheek, "you are to take care that I have some tea, and you are to take me to Richmond."

Her reverting to this tone as if our association were forced upon us and we were mere puppets, gave me pain; but everything in our intercourse did give me pain. Whatever her tone with me happened to be, I could put no trust in it, and build no hope on it; and yet I went on against trust and against hope. Why repeat it a thousand times? So it always was.

I rang for the tea, and the waiter, reappearing with his magic clue, brought in by degrees some fifty adjuncts to that refreshment but of tea not a glimpse. A teaboard, cups and saucers, plates, knives and forks (including carvers), spoons (various), salt-cellars, a meek little muffin confined with the utmost precaution under a strong iron cover, Moses in the bullrushes[1] typified by a soft bit of butter in a quantity of parsley, a pale loaf with a powdered head, two proof impressions of the bars of the kitchen fireplace on triangular bits of bread, and ultimately a fat family urn: which the waiter staggered in with, expressing in his countenance burden and suffering. After a prolonged absence at this stage of the entertainment, he at length came back with a casket of precious appearance containing twigs. These I steeped in hot water, and so from the whole of these appliances extracted one cup of I don't know what, for Estella.

The bill paid, and the waiter remembered, and the ostler not forgotten, and the chambermaid taken into consideration — in a word, the whole house bribed into a state of contempt and animosity, and Estella's purse much lightened — we got into our post-coach and drove away. Turning into Cheapside and rattling up Newgate-street, we were soon under the walls of which I was so ashamed.

"What place is that?" Estella asked me.

I made a foolish pretence of not at first recognising it, and then told her. As she looked at it, and drew in her head again, murmuring "Wretches!"

---

1. *Moses in the bullrushes:* see Exodus 2:1–10.

I would not have confessed to my visit for any consideration.

"Mr. Jaggers," said I, by way of putting it neatly on somebody else, "has the reputation of being more in the secrets of that dismal place than any man in London."

"He is more in the secrets of every place, I think," said Estella, in a low voice.

"You have been accustomed to see him often, I suppose?"

"I have been accustomed to see him at uncertain intervals, ever since I can remember. But I know him no better now, than I did before I could speak plainly. What is your own experience of him? Do you advance with him?"

"Once habituated to his distrustful manner," said I, "I have done very well."

"Are you intimate?"

"I have dined with him at his private house."

"I fancy," said Estella, shrinking, "that must be a curious place."

"It is a curious place."

I should have been chary of discussing my guardian too freely even with her; but I should have gone on with the subject so far as to describe the dinner in Gerrard-street, if we had not then come into a sudden glare of gas. It seemed, while it lasted, to be all alight and alive with that inexplicable feeling I had had before; and when we were out of it, I was as much dazed for a few moments as if I had been in Lightning.

So, we fell into other talk, and it was principally about the way by which we were travelling, and about what parts of London lay on this side of it, and what on that. The great city was almost new to her, she told me, for she had never left Miss Havisham's neighbourhood until she had gone to France, and she had merely passed through London then in going and returning. I asked her if my guardian had any charge of her while she remained here? To that she emphatically said "God forbid!" and no more.

It was impossible for me to avoid seeing that she cared to attract me; that she made herself winning; and would have won me even if the task had needed pains. Yet this made me none the happier, for, even if she had not taken that tone of our being disposed of by others, I should have felt that she held my heart in her hand because she wilfully chose to do it, and not because it would have wrung any tenderness in her, to crush it and throw it away.

When we passed through Hammersmith, I showed her where Mr. Matthew Pocket lived, and said it was no great way from Richmond, and that I hoped I should see her sometimes.

"Oh yes, you are to see me; you are to come when you think proper; you are to be mentioned to the family; indeed you are already mentioned."

I inquired was it a large household she was going to be a member of?

"No; there are only two; mother and daughter. The mother is a lady of some station, I believe, though not averse to increasing her income."

"I wonder Miss Havisham could part with you again so soon."

"It is a part of Miss Havisham's plans for me, Pip," said Estella, with a sigh, as if she were tired; "I am to write to her constantly and see her regularly, and report how I go on — I and the jewels — for they are nearly all mine now."

It was the first time she had ever called me by my name. Of course she did so, purposely, and knew that I should treasure it up.

We came to Richmond all too soon, and our destination there, was a house by the Green; a staid old house, where hoops and powder and patches, embroidered coats rolled stockings ruffles and swords, had had their court days many a time. Some ancient trees before the house were still cut into fashions as formal and unnatural as the hoops and wigs and stiff skirts; but their own allotted places in the great procession of the dead were not far off, and they would soon drop into them and go the silent way of the rest.

A bell with an old voice — which I dare say in its time had often said to the house, Here is the green farthingale, Here is the diamond-hilted sword, Here are the shoes with red heels and the blue solitaire,[1] — sounded gravely in the moonlight, and two cherry-coloured maids came fluttering out to receive Estella. The doorway soon absorbed her boxes, and she gave me her hand and a smile, and said good night, and was

---

1. *Here is the green farthingale, Here is the diamond-hilted sword, Here are the shoes with red heels and the blue solitaire:* memories of fashionable visitors of the past; a "farthingale" is a framework of hoops for extending a lady's skirts, while a "solitaire" is a loose black silk neck-tie worn by men.

absorbed likewise. And still I stood looking at the house, thinking how happy I should be if I lived there with her, and knowing that I never was happy with her, but always miserable.

I got into the carriage to be taken back to Hammersmith, and I got in with a bad heart-ache, and I got out with a worse heart-ache. At our own door, I found little Jane Pocket coming home from a little party escorted by her little lover; and I envied her little lover, in spite of his being subject to Flopson.

Mr. Pocket was out lecturing; for, he was a most delightful lecturer on domestic economy, and his treatises on the management of children and servants were considered the very best text-books on those themes. But, Mrs. Pocket was at home, and was in a little difficulty, on account of the baby's having been accommodated with a needle-case to keep him quiet during the unaccountable absence (with a relative in the Foot Guards)[1] of Millers. And more needles were missing, than it could be regarded as quite wholesome for a patient of such tender years either to apply externally or to take as a tonic.

Mr. Pocket being justly celebrated for giving most excellent practical advice, and for having a clear and sound perception of things and a highly judicious mind, I had some notion in my heart-ache of begging him to accept my confidence. But, happening to look up at Mrs. Pocket as she sat reading her book of dignities after prescribing Bed as a sovereign remedy for baby, I thought — Well — No, I wouldn't.

CHAPTER XV

AS I HAD grown accustomed to my expectations, I had insensibly begun to notice their effect upon myself and those around me. Their influence on my own character, I disguised from my recognition as much as possible, but I knew very well that it was not all good. I lived in a state of

---

1. *(with a relative in the Foot Guards):* i.e., the servant has a romantic assignation with a soldier.

chronic uneasiness respecting my behaviour to Joe. My conscience was not by any means comfortable about Biddy. When I woke up in the night — like Camilla — I used to think, with a weariness on my spirits, that I should have been happier and better if I had never seen Miss Havisham's face, and had risen to manhood content to be partners with Joe in the honest old forge. Many a time of an evening, when I sat alone looking at the fire, I thought, after all, there was no fire like the forge fire and the kitchen fire at home.

Yet Estella was so inseparable from all my restlessness and disquiet of mind, that I really fell into confusion as to the limits of my own part in its production. That is to say, supposing I had had no expectations, and yet had had Estella to think of, I could not make out to my satisfaction that I should have done much better. Now, concerning the influence of my position on others, I was in no such difficulty, and so I perceived — though dimly enough perhaps — that it was not beneficial to anybody, and, above all, that it was not beneficial to Herbert. My lavish habits led his easy nature into expenses that he could not afford, corrupted the simplicity of his life, and disturbed his peace with anxieties and regrets. I was not at all remorseful for having unwittingly set those other branches of the Pocket family to the poor arts they practised: because such littlenesses were their natural bent, and would have been evoked by anybody else, if I had left them slumbering. But Herbert's was a very different case, and it often caused me a twinge to think that I had done him evil service in crowding his sparely-furnished chambers with incongruous upholstery work, and placing the canary-breasted Avenger at his disposal.

So now, as an infallible way of making little ease great ease, I began to contract a quantity of debt. I could hardly begin but Herbert must begin too, so he soon followed. At Startop's suggestion, we put ourselves down for election into a club called The Finches of the Grove:[1] the object of which institution I have never divined, if it were not that the members should dine expensively once a fortnight, to quarrel among themselves as much as possible after dinner, and to cause six waiters to get drunk on

---

1. *The Finches of the Grove:* the phrase derives from Tilburnia's mad speech in the play-within-the-play in Sheridan's comedy *The Critic* (1781), II ii.

the stairs. I know that these gratifying social ends were so invariably accomplished, that Herbert and I understood nothing else to be referred to
in the first standing toast of the society: which ran "Gentlemen, may the
present promotion of good feeling ever reign predominant among the
Finches of the Grove."

The Finches spent their money foolishly (the Hotel we dined at was
in Covent-garden),[1] and the first Finch I saw, when I had the honour of
joining the Grove, was Bentley Drummle: at that time floundering about
town in a cab of his own, and doing a great deal of damage to the posts
at the street corners. Occasionally, he shot himself out of his equipage
head-foremost over the apron; and I saw him on one occasion deliver
himself at the door of the Grove in this unintentional way — like coals.
But here I anticipate a little, for I was not a Finch, and could not be,
according to the sacred laws of the society, until I came of age.

In my confidence in my own resources, I would willingly have taken
Herbert's expenses on myself; but Herbert was proud, and I could make
no such proposal to him. So, he got into difficulties in every direction,
and continued to look about him. When we gradually fell into keeping
late hours and late company, I noticed that he looked about him with a
desponding eye at breakfast-time; that he began to look about him more
hopefully about mid-day; that he drooped when he came into dinner;
that he seemed to descry Capital in the distance rather clearly, after dinner; that he all but realised Capital towards midnight; and that at about
two o'clock in the morning, he became so deeply despondent again as to
talk of buying a rifle and going to America, with a general purpose of
compelling buffaloes to make his fortune.

I was usually at Hammersmith about half the week, and when I was
at Hammersmith I haunted Richmond: whereof separately by-and-by.
Herbert would often come to Hammersmith when I was there, and I
think at those seasons his father would occasionally have some passing
perception that the opening he was looking for, had not appeared yet.
But in the general tumbling up of the family, his tumbling out in life

---

1. *the Hotel we dined at was in Covent-garden:* the area around Covent Garden market
   then had a reputation for dissipation and immorality.

somewhere, was a thing to transact itself somehow. In the meantime Mr. Pocket grew greyer, and tried oftener to lift himself out of his perplexities by the hair. While Mrs. Pocket tripped up the family with her footstool, read her book of dignities, lost her pocket-handkerchief, told us about her grandpapa, and taught the young idea how to shoot, by shooting it into bed[1] whenever it attracted her notice.

As I am now generalising a period of my life with the object of clearing my way before me, I can scarcely do so better than by at once completing the description of our usual manners and customs at Barnard's Inn.

We spent as much money as we could, and got as little for it as people could make up their minds to give us. We were always more or less miserable, and most of our acquaintance were in the same condition. There was a gay fiction among us that we were constantly enjoying ourselves, and a skeleton truth that we never did. To the best of my belief, our case was in the last aspect a rather common one.

Every morning, with an air ever new, Herbert went into the City to look about him. I often paid him a visit in the dark back-room in which he consorted with an ink-jar, a hat-peg, a coal-box, a string-box, an almanack, a desk and stool, and a ruler; and I do not remember that I ever saw him do anything else but look about him. If we all did what we undertake to do, as faithfully as Herbert did, we might live in a Republic of the Virtues. He had nothing else to do, poor fellow, except at a certain hour of every afternoon to "go to Lloyd's" — in observance of a ceremony of seeing his principal, I think. He never did anything else in connexion with Lloyd's that I could find out, except come back again. When he felt his case unusually serious, and that he positively must find an opening, he would go on 'Change at a busy time, and walk in and out, in a kind of gloomy country dance figure, among the assembled magnates. "For," says Herbert to me, coming home to dinner on one of those

---

1. *taught the young idea how to shoot, by shooting it into bed:* referring ironically to a passage in James Thomson's poem "Spring," from *The Seasons* (1726–30), describing the joys of rearing young children: "Then infant Reason grows apace, and calls / For the kind Hand of an assiduous Care. / Delightful Task! to rear the tender Thought, / To teach the young Idea how to shoot" (ll. 1150-3).

special occasions, "I find the truth to be, Handel, that an opening won't come to one, but one must go to it — so I have been."

If we had been less attached to one another, I think we must have hated one another regularly every morning. I detested the chambers beyond expression at that period of repentance, and could not endure the sight of the Avenger's livery: which had a more expensive and a less remunerative appearance then, than at any other time in the four-and-twenty hours. As we got more and more into debt, breakfast became a hollower and hollower form, and, being on one occasion at breakfast-time threatened (by letter) with legal proceedings, "not unwholly unconnected," as my local paper might put it, "with jewellery," I went so far as to seize the Avenger by his blue collar and shake him off his feet — so that he was actually in the air, like a booted Cupid — for presuming to suppose that we wanted a roll.

At certain times — meaning at uncertain times, for they depended on our humour — I would say to Herbert, as if it were a remarkable discovery:

"My dear Herbert, we are getting on badly."

"My dear Handel," Herbert would say to me, in all sincerity, "if you will believe me, those very words were on my lips, by a strange coincidence."

"Then, Herbert," I would respond, "let us look into our affairs."

We always derived profound satisfaction from making an appointment for this purpose. I always thought this was business, this was the way to confront the thing, this was the way to take the foe by the throat. And I know Herbert thought so too.

We ordered something rather special for dinner, with a bottle of something similarly out of the common way, in order that our minds might be fortified for the occasion, and we might come well up to the mark. Dinner over, we produced a bundle of pens, a copious supply of ink, and a goodly show of writing and blotting paper. For, there was something very comfortable in having plenty of stationery.

I would then take a sheet of paper, and write across the top of it, in a neat hand, the heading, "Memorandum of Pip's debts;" with Barnard's Inn and the date very carefully added. Herbert would also take a sheet of paper, and write across it with similar formalities, "Memorandum of Herbert's debts."

Each of us would then refer to a confused heap of papers at his side, which had been thrown into drawers, worn into holes in pockets, half-burnt in lighting candles, stuck for weeks into the looking-glass, and otherwise damaged. The sound of our pens going, refreshed us exceedingly, insomuch that I sometimes found it difficult to distinguish between this edifying business proceeding and actually paying the money. In point of meritorious character, the two things seemed about equal.

When we had written a little while, I would ask Herbert how he got on? Herbert probably would have been scratching his head in a most rueful manner at the sight of his accumulating figures.

"They are mounting up, Handel," Herbert would say; "upon my life, they are mounting up."

"Be firm, Herbert," I would retort, plying my own pen with great assiduity. "Look the thing in the face. Look into your affairs. Stare them out of countenance."

"So I would, Handel, only they are staring *me* out of countenance."

However, my determined manner would have its effect, and Herbert would fall to work again. After a time he would give up once more, on the plea that he had not got Cobbs's bill, or Lobbs's, or Nobbs's, as the case might be.

"Then, Herbert estimate; estimate it in round numbers, and put it down."

"What a fellow of resource you are!" my friend would reply, with admiration. "Really your business powers are very remarkable."

I thought so too. I established with myself on these occasions, the reputation of a first-rate man of business — prompt, decisive, energetic, clear, cool-headed. When I had got all my responsibilities down upon my list, I compared each with the bill, and ticked it off. My self-approval when I ticked an entry was quite a luxurious sensation. When I had no more ticks to make, I folded all my bills up uniformly, docketed each on the back, and tied the whole into a symmetrical bundle. Then I did the same for Herbert (who modestly said he had not my administrative genius), and felt that I had brought his affairs into a focus for him.

My business habits had one other bright feature, which I called "leaving a Margin." For example; supposing Herbert's debts to be one hundred and sixty-four pounds four-and-twopence, I would say, "Leave a margin, and put them down at two hundred." Or, supposing my own to be four times as much, I would leave a margin, and put them down at seven hundred. I had the highest opinion of the wisdom of this same Margin, but I am bound to acknowledge that on looking back, I deem it to have been an expensive device. For, we always ran into new debt immediately, to the full extent of the margin, and sometimes, in the sense of freedom and solvency it imparted, got pretty far on into another margin.

But there was a calm, a rest, a virtuous hush, consequent on these examinations of our affairs that gave me, for the time, an admirable opinion of myself. Soothed by my exertions, my method, and Herbert's compliments, I would sit with his symmetrical bundle and my own on the table before me among the stationery, and feel like a bank of some sort, rather than a private individual.

We shut our outer door on these solemn occasions, in order that we might not be interrupted. I had fallen into my serene state one evening, when we heard a letter dropped through the slit in the said door, and fall on the ground. "It's for you, Handel," said Herbert, going out and coming back with it, "and I hope there is nothing the matter." This was in allusion to its heavy black seal and border.

The letter was signed TRABB & Co., and its contents were simply, that I was an honoured sir, and that they begged to inform me that Mrs. J. Gargery had departed this life on Monday last, at twenty minutes past six in the evening, and that my attendance was requested at the interment on Monday next at three o'clock in the afternoon.

CHAPTER XVI

IT WAS the first time that a grave had opened in my road of life, and the gap it made in the smooth ground was wonderful. The figure of my sister in her chair by the kitchen fire, haunted me night and day. That the place could possibly be, without her, was something my mind seemed unable to compass; and whereas she had seldom or never been in my thoughts of late, I had now the strangest ideas that she was coming towards me in the street, or that she would presently knock at the door. In my rooms too, with which she had never been at all associated, there was at once the blankness of death and a perpetual suggestion of the sound of her voice or the turn of her face or figure, as if she were still alive and had been often there.

Whatever my fortunes might have been, I could scarcely have recalled my sister with much tenderness. But I suppose there is a shock of regret which may exist without much tenderness. Under its influence (and perhaps to make up for the want of the softer feeling) I was seized with a violent indignation against the assailant from whom she had suffered so much; and I felt that on sufficient proof I could have revengefully pursued Orlick, or any one else, to the last extremity.

Having written to Joe, to offer consolation, and to assure him that I should come to the funeral, I passed the intermediate days in the curious state of mind I have glanced at. I went down early in the morning, and alighted at the Blue Boar in good time to walk over to the forge.

It was fine summer weather again, and, as I walked along, the times when I was a little helpless creature, and my sister did not spare me, vividly returned. But they returned with a gentle tone upon them that softened even the edge of Tickler. For now, the very breath of the beans and clover whispered to my heart that the day must come when it would be well for my memory that others walking in the sunshine should be softened as they thought of me.

At last I came within sight of the house, and saw that Trabb and Co. had put in a funereal execution and taken possession.[1] Two dismally absurd persons, each ostentatiously exhibiting a crutch done up in a black bandage — as if that instrument could possibly communicate any comfort to anybody — were posted at the front door; and in one of them I recognised a postboy discharged from the Boar for turning a young couple into a sawpit on their bridal morning, in consequence of intoxication rendering it necessary for him to ride his horse clasped round the neck with both arms. All the children of the village, and most of the women,

---

1. *put in a funereal execution and taken possession:* that is, the undertakers occupied the house in the manner of the Sheriff's officers taking possession of the property of a debtor.

were admiring these sable warders and the closed windows of the house and forge; and as I came up, one of the two warders (the postboy) knocked at the door — implying that I was far too much exhausted by grief, to have strength remaining to knock for myself.

Another sable warder (a carpenter, who had once eaten two geese for a wager) opened the door, and showed me into the best parlour. Here, Mr. Trabb had taken unto himself the best table, and had got all the leaves up, and was holding a kind of black Bazaar, with the aid of a quantity of black pins. At the moment of my arrival, he had just finished putting some-body's hat into black long-clothes, like an African baby; so he held out his hand for mine. But I, misled by the action, and confused by the occa-sion, shook hands with him with every testimony of warm affection.

Poor dear Joe, entangled in a little black cloak tied in a large bow under his chin, was seated apart at the upper end of the room; where, as chief mourner, he had evidently been stationed by Trabb. When I bent down and said to him, "Dear Joe, how are you?" he said, "Pip, old chap, you knowed her when she were a fine figure of a —" and clasped my hand and said no more.

Biddy, looking very neat and modest in her black dress, went quietly here and there, and was very helpful. When I had spoken to Biddy, as I thought it not a time for talking I went and sat down near Joe, and there began to wonder in what part of the house it — she — my sister — was. The air of the parlour being faint with the smell of sweet cake, I looked about for the table of refreshments; it was scarcely visible until one had got accustomed to the gloom, but there was a cut-up plum-cake upon it, and there were cut-up oranges, and sandwiches, and biscuits, and two de-canters that I knew very well as ornaments, but had never seen used in all my life; one full of port, and one of sherry. Standing at this table, I be-came conscious of the servile Pumblechook in a black cloak and several yards of hatband, who was alternately stuffing himself, and making obse-quious movements to catch my attention. The moment he succeeded, he came over to me (breathing sherry and crumbs), and said in a subdued voice, "May I, dear sir?" and did. I then descried Mr. and Mrs. Hubble; the last-named in a decent speechless paroxysm in a corner. We were all going to "follow," and were all in course of being tied up separately (by Trabb) into ridiculous bundles.

"Which I meantersay, Pip," Joe whispered me, as we were being what Mr. Trabb called "formed" in the parlour, two and two — and it was dreadfully like a preparation for some grim kind of dance; "which I meantersay, sir, as I would in preference have carried her to the church myself, along with three or four friendly ones wot come to it with willing harts and arms, but it were considered wot the neighbours would look down on such and would be of opinions as it were wanting in respect."

"Pocket-handkerchiefs out, all!" cried Mr. Trabb at this point, in a depressed business-like voice. "Pocket-handkerchiefs out! We are ready!"

So, we all put our pocket-handkerchiefs to our faces, as if our noses were bleeding, and filed out two and two; Joe and I; Biddy and Pumblechook; Mr. and Mrs. Hubble. The remains of my poor sister had been brought round by the kitchen door, and, it being a point of Undertaking ceremony that the six bearers must be stifled and blinded under a horrible black velvet housing with a white border, the whole looked like a blind monster with twelve human legs, shuffling and blundering along, under the guidance of two keepers — the postboy and his comrade.

The neighbourhood, however, highly approved of these arrangements, and we were much admired as we went through the village; the more youthful and vigorous part of the community making dashes now and then to cut us off, and lying in wait to intercept us at points of vantage. At such times the more exuberant among them called out in an excited manner on our emergence round some corner of expectancy, "Here they come!" "Here they are!" and we were all but cheered. In this progress I was much annoyed by the abject Pumblechook, who, being behind me, persisted all the way as a delicate attention in arranging my streaming hatband, and smoothing my cloak. My thoughts were further distracted by the excessive pride of Mr. and Mrs. Hubble, who were surpassingly conceited and vainglorious in being members of so distinguished a procession.

And now, the range of marshes lay clear before us, with the sails of the ships on the river growing out of it; and we went into the churchyard, close to the graves of my unknown parents, Philip Pirrip, late of this parish, and Also Georgiana, Wife of the Above. And there, my sister was laid quietly in the earth while the larks sang high above it, and the light wind strewed it with beautiful shadows of clouds and trees.

Of the conduct of the worldly-minded Pumblechook while this was doing, I desire to say no more than that it was all addressed to me; and that even when those noble passages were read which remind humanity how it brought nothing into the world and can take nothing out, and how it fleeth like a shadow and never continueth long in one stay,[1] I heard him cough a reservation of the case of a young gentleman who came unexpectedly into large property. When we got back, he had the hardihood to tell me that he wished my sister could have known I had done her so much honour, and to hint that she would have considered it reasonably purchased at the price of her death. After that, he drank all the rest of the sherry, and Mr. Hubble drank the port, and the two talked (which I have since observed to be customary in such cases) as if they were of quite another race from the deceased, and were notoriously immortal. Finally, he went away with Mr. and Mrs. Hubble — to make an evening of it, I felt sure, and to tell the Jolly Bargemen that he was the founder of my fortunes and my earliest benefactor.

When they were all gone, and when Trabb and his men — but not his boy: I looked for him — had crammed their mummery into bags, and were gone too, the house felt wholesomer. Soon afterwards, Biddy, Joe, and I, had a cold dinner together; but we dined in the best parlour, not in the old kitchen, and Joe was so exceedingly particular what he did with his knife and fork and the salt-cellar and what not, that there was great restraint upon us. But after dinner, when I made him take his pipe, and when I had loitered with him about the forge, and when we sat down together on the great block of stone outside it, we got on better. I noticed that after the funeral Joe changed his clothes so far, as to make a compromise between his Sunday dress and working dress: in which the dear fellow looked natural, and like the Man he was.

He was very much pleased by my asking if I might sleep in my own little room, and I was pleased too; for, I felt that I had done rather a great thing in making the request. When the shadows of evening were closing

---

1. *those noble passages were read which remind humanity ... never continueth long in one stay:*
From the "Order of the Burial of the Dead," the funeral service of the Anglican Church, found in the *Book of Common Prayer*, and echoing the words of the Bible in I Timothy 6:7, Psalm 102:11, and Job 14:2.

in, I took an opportunity of getting into the garden with Biddy for a little talk.

"Biddy," said I, "I think you might have written to me about these sad matters."

"Do you, Mr. Pip?" said Biddy. "I should have written if I had thought that."

"Don't suppose that I mean to be unkind, Biddy, when I say I consider that you ought to have thought that."

"Do you, Mr. Pip?"

She was so quiet, and had such an orderly, good, and pretty way with her, that I did not like the thought of making her cry again. After looking a little at her downcast eyes as she walked beside me, I gave up that point.

"I suppose it will be difficult for you to remain here now, Biddy dear?"

"Oh! I can't do so, Mr. Pip," said Biddy, in a tone of regret, but still of quiet conviction. "I have been speaking to Mrs. Hubble, and I am going to her to-morrow. I hope we shall be able to take some care of Mr. Gargery, together, until he settles down."

"How are you going to live, Biddy? If you want any mo —"

"How am I going to live?" repeated Biddy, striking in, with a momentary flush upon her face. "I'll tell you, Mr. Pip. I am going to try to get the place of mistress in the new school nearly finished here.* I can be well recommended by all the neighbours, and I hope I can be industrious and patient, and teach myself while I teach others. You know, Mr. Pip," pursued Biddy, with a smile, as she raised her eyes to my face, "the new schools are not like the old, but I learnt a good deal from you after that time, and have had time since then to improve."

"I think you would always improve, Biddy, under any circumstances."

"Ah! Except in my bad side of human nature," murmured Biddy.

It was not so much a reproach, as an irresistible thinking aloud. Well! I thought I would give up that point too. So, I walked a little further with Biddy, looking silently at her downcast eyes.

"I have not heard the particulars of my sister's death, Biddy."

"They are very slight, poor thing. She had been in one of her bad states — though they had got better of late, rather than worse — for four days, when she came out of it in the evening, just at tea-time, and said quite plainly, 'Joe.' As she had never said any word for a long while, I ran and fetched in Mr. Gargery from the forge. She made signs to me that she wanted him to sit down close to her, and wanted me to put her arms round his neck. So I put them round his neck, and she laid her head down on his shoulder quite content and satisfied. And so she presently said 'Joe' again, and once 'Pardon,' and once 'Pip.' And so she never lifted her head up any more, and it was just an hour later when we laid it down on her own bed, because we found she was gone."

Biddy cried; the darkening garden, and the lane, and the stars that were coming out, were blurred in my own sight.

"Nothing was ever discovered, Biddy?"

"Nothing."

"Do you know what is become of Orlick?"

"I should think from the colour of his clothes that he is working in the quarries."

"Of course you have seen him then? — Why are you looking at that dark tree in the lane?"

"I saw him there, on the night she died."

"That was not the last time either, Biddy?"

"No; I have seen him there, since we have been walking here. — It is of no use," said Biddy, laying her hand upon my arm, as I was for running out, "you know I would not deceive you; he was not there a minute, and he is gone."

It revived my utmost indignation to find that she was still pursued by this fellow, and I felt inveterate against him. I told her so, and told her that I would spend any money or take any pains to drive him out of that country. By degrees she led me into more temperate talk, and she told me how Joe loved me, and how Joe never complained of anything — she didn't say, of me; she had no need; I knew what she meant — but ever did his duty in his way of life, with a strong hand, a quiet tongue, and a gentle heart.

"Indeed, it would be hard to say too much for him," said I; "and Biddy, we must often speak of these things, for of course I shall be often down here now. I am not going to leave poor Joe alone."

Biddy said never a single word.

"Biddy, don't you hear me?"

"Yes, Mr. Pip."

"Not to mention your calling me Mr. Pip — which appears to me to be in bad taste, Biddy — what do you mean?"

"What do I mean?" asked Biddy, timidly.

"Biddy," said I, in a virtuously self-asserting manner, "I must request to know what you mean by this?"

"By this?" said Biddy.

"Now, don't echo," I retorted. "You used not to echo, Biddy."

"Used not!" said Biddy. "O Mr. Pip! Used!"

Well! I rather thought I would give up that point too. After another silent turn in the garden, I fell back on the main position.

"Biddy," said I, "I made a remark respecting my coming down here often, to see Joe, which you received with a marked silence. Have the goodness, Biddy, to tell me why."

"Are you quite sure, then, that you WILL come to see him often?" asked Biddy, stopping in the narrow garden walk, and looking at me under the stars with a clear and honest eye.

"Oh dear me!" said I, as if I found myself compelled to give up Biddy in despair. "This really is a very bad side of human nature! Don't say any more, if you please, Biddy. This shocks me very much."

For which cogent reason I kept Biddy at a distance during supper, and, when I went up to my own old little room, took as stately a leave of her as I could, in my murmuring soul, deem reconcilable with the church-yard and the event of the day. As often as I was restless in the night, and that was every quarter of an hour, I reflected what an unkindness, what an injury, what an injustice, Biddy had done me.

Early in the morning, I was to go. Early in the morning, I was out, and looking in, unseen, at one of the wooden windows of the forge. There I stood, for minutes, looking at Joe, already at work with a glow of health and strength upon his face that made it show as if the bright sun of the life in store for him were shining on it.

"Good-by, dear Joe! — No, don't wipe it off — for God's sake, give me your blackened hand! — I shall be down soon, and often."

"Never too soon, sir," said Joe, "and never too often, Pip!"

Biddy was waiting for me at the kitchen door, with a mug of new milk and a crust of bread. "Biddy," said I, when I gave her my hand at parting, "I am not angry, but I am hurt."

"No, don't be hurt," she pleaded quite pathetically; "let only me be hurt, if I have been ungenerous."

Once more, the mists were rising[1] as I walked away. If they disclosed to me, as I suspect they did, that I should not come back, and that Biddy was quite right, all I can say is — they were quite right too.

CHAPTER XVII

HERBERT and I went on from bad to worse, in the way of increasing our debts, looking into our affairs, leaving Margins, and the like exemplary transactions; and Time went on, whether or no, as he has a way of doing; and I came of age — in fulfilment of Herbert's prediction, that I should do so before I knew where I was.

Herbert himself had come of age, eight months before me. As he had nothing else than his majority to come into, the event did not make a profound sensation in Barnard's Inn. But we had looked forward to my one-and-twentieth birthday, with a crowd of speculations and anticipations, for we had both considered that my guardian could hardly help saying something definite on that occasion.

I had taken care to have it well understood in Little Britain, when my birthday was. On the day before it, I received an official note from Wemmick, informing me that Mr. Jaggers would be glad if I would call upon him at five in the afternoon of the auspicious day. This convinced us that something great was to happen, and threw me into an unusual flutter when I repaired to my guardian's office, a model of punctuality.

In the outer office Wemmick offered me his congratulations, and incidentally rubbed the side of his nose with a folded piece of tissue-paper that I liked the look of. But he said nothing respecting it, and motioned me with a nod into my guardian's room. It was November, and my guardian was standing before his fire leaning his back against the chimney-piece, with his hands under his coat-tails.

---

1. *Once more, the mists were rising:* referring back to Pip's first departure described at the closing of Vol. I on p. 192.

"Well, Pip," said he, "I must call you Mr. Pip to-day. Congratulations, Mr. Pip."

We shook hands — he was always a remarkably short shaker — and I thanked him.

"Take a chair, Mr. Pip," said my guardian.

As I sat down, and he preserved his attitude and bent his brows at his boots, I felt at a disadvantage, which reminded me of that old time when I had been put upon a tombstone. The two ghastly casts on the shelf were not far from him, and their expression was as if they were making a stupid apoplectic attempt to attend to the conversation.

"Now my young friend," my guardian began, as if I were a witness in the box, "I am going to have a word or two with you."

"If you please, sir."

"What do you suppose," said Mr. Jaggers, bending forward to look at the ground, and then throwing his head back to look at the ceiling, "what do you suppose you are living at the rate of?"

"At the rate of, sir?"

"At" repeated Mr. Jaggers, still looking at the ceiling, "the — rate — of?" And then looked all round the room, and paused with his pocket-handkerchief in his hand, half way to his nose.

I had looked into my affairs so often, that I had thoroughly destroyed any slight notion I might ever have had of their bearings. Reluctantly, I confessed myself quite unable to answer the question. This reply seemed agreeable to Mr. Jaggers, who said, "I thought so!" and blew his nose with an air of satisfaction.

"Now, I have asked *you* a question, my friend," said Mr. Jaggers. "Have you anything to ask *me?*"

"Of course it would be a great relief to me to ask you several questions, sir; but I remember your prohibition."

"Ask one," said Mr. Jaggers.

"Is my benefactor to be made known to me to-day?"

"No. Ask another."

"Is that confidence to be imparted to me soon?"

"Waive that, a moment," said Mr. Jaggers, "and ask another."

I looked about me, but there appeared to be now no possible escape from the inquiry, "Have — I — anything to receive, sir?" On that, Mr.

Jaggers said, triumphantly, "I thought we should come to it!" and called to Wemmick to give him that piece of paper. Wemmick appeared, handed it in, and disappeared.

"Now, Mr. Pip," said Mr. Jaggers, "attend, if you please. You have been drawing pretty freely here; your name occurs pretty often in Wemmick's cash-book; but you are in debt, of course?"

"I am afraid I must say yes, sir."

"You know you must say yes; don't you?" said Mr. Jaggers.

"Yes, sir."

"I don't ask you what you owe, because you don't know; and if you did know, you wouldn't tell me; you would say less. Yes, yes, my friend," cried Mr. Jaggers, waving his forefinger to stop me, as I made a show of protesting: "it's likely enough that you think you wouldn't, but you would. You'll excuse me, but I know better than you. Now, take this piece of paper in your hand. You have got it? Very good. Now, unfold it and tell me what it is."

"This is a bank-note," said I, "for five hundred pounds."

"That is a bank-note," repeated Mr. Jaggers, "for five hundred pounds. And a very handsome sum of money too, I think. You consider it so?"

"How could I do otherwise!"

"Ah! But answer the question," said Mr. Jaggers.

"Undoubtedly."

"You consider it, undoubtedly, a handsome sum of money. Now, that handsome sum of money, Pip, is your own. It is a present to you on this day, in earnest of your expectations. And at the rate of that handsome sum of money per annum, and at no higher rate, you are to live until the donor of the whole appears. That is to say, you will now take your money affairs entirely into your own hands, and you will draw from Wemmick one hundred and twenty-five pounds per quarter, until you are in communication with the fountain-head, and no longer with the mere agent. As I have told you before, I am the mere agent. I execute my instructions, and I am paid for doing so. I think them injudicious, but I am not paid for giving any opinion on their merits."

I was beginning to express my gratitude to my benefactor for the great liberality with which I was treated, when Mr. Jaggers stopped me. "I am not paid; Pip," said he, coolly, "to carry your words to any one;" and then gathered up his coat-tails, as he had gathered up the subject, and stood frowning at his boots as if he suspected them of designs against him.

After a pause, I hinted:

"There was a question just now, Mr. Jaggers, which you desired me to waive for a moment. I hope I am doing nothing wrong in asking it again?"

"What is it?" said he.

I might have known that he would never help me out; but it took me aback to have to shape the question afresh, as if it were quite new. "Is it likely," I said, after hesitating, "that my patron, the fountain-head you have spoken of, Mr. Jaggers, will soon —" there I delicately stopped.

"Will soon what?" asked Mr. Jaggers. "That's no question as it stands, you know."

"Will soon come to London," said I, after casting about for a precise form of words, "or summon me anywhere else?"

"Now here," replied Mr. Jaggers, fixing me for the first time with his dark deep-set eyes, "we must revert to the evening when we first encountered one another in your village. What did I tell you then, Pip?"

"You told me, Mr. Jaggers, that it might be years hence when that person appeared."

"Just so," said Mr. Jaggers; "that's my answer."

As we looked full at one another, I felt my breath come quicker in my strong desire to get something out of him. And as I felt that it came quicker, and as I felt that he saw that it came quicker, I felt that I had less chance than ever of getting anything out of him.

"Do you suppose it will still be years hence, Mr. Jaggers?"

Mr. Jaggers shook his head — not in negativing the question, but in altogether negativing the notion that he could anyhow be got to answer it — and the two horrible casts of the twitched faces looked, when my eyes strayed up to them, as if they had come to a crisis in their suspended attention, and were going to sneeze.

"Come!" said Mr. Jaggers, warming the backs of his legs with the backs of his warmed hands, "I'll be plain with you, my friend Pip. That's a question I must not be asked. You'll understand that, better, when I tell you it's a question that might compromise *me*. Come! I'll go a little further with you; I'll say something more."

He bent down so low to frown at his boots, that he was able to rub the calves of his legs in the pause he made.

"When that person discloses," said Mr. Jaggers, straightening himself, "you and that person will settle your own affairs. When that person discloses, my part in this business will cease and determine. When that person discloses, it will not be necessary for me to know anything about it. And that's all I have got to say."

We looked at one another until I withdrew my eyes, and looked thoughtfully at the floor. From this last speech I derived the notion that Miss Havisham, for some reason or no reason, had not taken him into her confidence as to her designing me for Estella; that he resented this, and felt a jealousy about it; or that he really did object to that scheme, and would have nothing to do with it. When I raised my eyes again, I found that he had been shrewdly looking at me all the time, and was doing so still.

"If that is all you have to say, sir," I remarked, "there can be nothing left for me to say."

He nodded assent, and pulled out his thief-dreaded watch, and asked me where I was going to dine? I replied at my own chambers, with Herbert. As a necessary sequence, I asked him if he would favour us with his company, and he promptly accepted the invitation. But he insisted on walking home with me, in order that I might make no extra preparation for him, and first he had a letter or two to write, and (of course) had his hands to wash. So, I said I would go into the outer office and talk to Wemmick.

The fact was, that when the five hundred pounds had come into my pocket, a thought had come into my head which had been often there before; and it appeared to me that Wemmick was a good person to advise with, concerning such thought.

He had already locked up his safe, and made preparations for going home. He had left his desk, brought out his two greasy office candlesticks and stood them in line with the snuffers on a slab near the door, ready to be extinguished; he had raked his fire low, put his hat and great-coat ready, and was beating himself all over the chest with his safe-key, as an athletic exercise after business.

"Mr. Wemmick," said I, "I want to ask your opinion. I am very desirous to serve a friend."

Wemmick tightened his post-office and shook his head, as if his opinion were dead against any fatal weakness of that sort.

"This friend," I pursued, "is trying to get on in commercial life, but has no money, and finds it difficult and disheartening to make a beginning. Now, I want somehow to help him to a beginning."

"With money down?" said Wemmick, in a tone drier than any sawdust.

"With *some* money down," I replied, for an uneasy remembrance shot across me of that symmetrical bundle of papers at home; "with *some* money down, and perhaps some anticipation of my expectations."

"Mr. Pip," said Wemmick, "I should like just to run over with you on my fingers, if you please, the names of the various bridges up as high as Chelsea Reach. Let's see; there's London, one; Southwark, two; Blackfriars, three; Waterloo, four; Westminster, five; Vauxhall, six."* He had checked off each bridge in its turn, with the handle of his safe-key on the palm of his hand. "There's as many as six, you see, to choose from."

"I don't understand you," said I.

"Choose your bridge, Mr. Pip," returned Wemmick, "and take a walk upon your bridge, and pitch your money into the Thames over the centre arch of your bridge, and you know the end of it. Serve a friend with it, and you may know the end of it too — but it's a less pleasant and profitable end."

I could have posted a newspaper in his mouth, he made it so wide after saying this.

"This is very discouraging," said I.

"Meant to be so," said Wemmick.

"Then is it your opinion," I inquired, with some little indignation, "that a man should never —"

"— Invest portable property in a friend?" said Wemmick. "Certainly he should not. Unless he wants to get rid of the friend — and then it becomes a question how much portable property it may be worth to get rid of him."

"And that," said I, "is your deliberate opinion, Mr. Wemmick?"

"That," he returned, "is my deliberate opinion in this office."

"Ah!" said I, pressing him, for I thought I saw him near a loophole here; "but would that be your opinion at Walworth?"

"Mr. Pip," he replied, with gravity, "Walworth is one place, and this office is another. Much as the Aged is one person, and Mr. Jaggers is another. They must not be confounded together. My Walworth sentiments must be taken at Walworth; none but my official sentiments can be taken in this office."

"Very well," said I, much relieved, "then I shall look you up at Walworth, you may depend upon it."

"Mr. Pip," he returned, "you will be welcome there, in a private and personal capacity."

We had held this conversation in a low voice, well knowing my guardian's ears to be the sharpest of the sharp. As he now appeared in his doorway, towelling his hands, Wemmick got on his great-coat and stood by to snuff out the candles. We all three went into the street together, and from the door-step Wemmick turned his way, and Mr. Jaggers and I turned ours.

I could not help wishing more than once that evening, that Mr. Jaggers had had an Aged in Gerrard-street, or a Stinger, or a Something, or a Somebody, to unbend his brows a little. It was an uncomfortable consideration on a twenty-first birthday, that coming of age at all seemed hardly worth while in such a guarded and suspicious world as he made of it. He was a thousand times better informed and cleverer than Wemmick, and yet I would a thousand times rather have had Wemmick to dinner. And Mr. Jaggers made not me alone intensely melancholy, because, after he was gone, Herbert said of himself, with his eyes fixed on the fire, that he thought he must have committed a felony and forgotten the details of it, he felt so dejected and guilty.

CHAPTER XVIII

DEEMING Sunday the best day for taking Mr. Wemmick's Walworth sentiments, I devoted the next ensuing Sunday afternoon to a pilgrimage to the Castle. On arriving before the battlements, I found the Union Jack flying and the drawbridge up; but undeterred by this show of defiance and resistance, I rang at the gate, and was admitted in a most pacific manner by the Aged.

"My son, sir," said the old man, after securing the drawbridge, "rather had it in his mind that you might happen to drop in, and he left word that he would soon be home from his arternoon walk. He is very regular in his walks, is my son. Very regular in everything, is my son."

I nodded at the old gentleman as Wemmick himself might have nodded, and we went in and sat down by the fireside.

"You made acquaintance with my son, sir," said the old man, in his chirping way, while he warmed his hands at the blaze, "at his office, I expect?" I nodded. "Hah! I have heerd that my son is a wonderful hand at his business, sir?" I nodded hard. "Yes; so they tell me. His business is the Law?" I nodded harder. "Which makes it more surprising in my son," said the old man, "for he was not brought up to the Law, but to the Wine-Coopering."

Curious to know how the old gentleman stood informed concerning the reputation of Mr. Jaggers, I roared that name at him. He threw me into the greatest confusion by laughing heartily and replying in a very sprightly manner, "No, to be sure; you're right." And to this hour I have not the faintest notion what he meant, or what joke he thought I had made.

As I could not sit there nodding at him perpetually, without making some other attempt to interest him, I shouted an inquiry whether his own calling in life had been "the Wine-Coopering." By dint of straining that term out of myself several times and tapping the old gentleman on the chest to associate it with him, I at last succeeded in making my meaning understood.

"No," said the old gentleman; "the warehousing, the warehousing. First, over yonder;" he appeared to mean up the chimney, but I believe he intended to refer me to Liverpool; "and then in the City of London here. However, having an infirmity — for I am hard of hearing, sir —"

I expressed in pantomime the greatest astonishment.

"— Yes, hard of hearing; having that infirmity coming upon me, my son he went into the Law, and he took charge of me, and he by little and little made out this elegant and beautiful property. But returning to what you said, you know," pursued the old man, again laughing heartily, "what I say is, No to be sure; you're right."

I was modestly wondering whether my utmost ingenuity would have enabled me to say anything that would have amused him half as much as this imaginary pleasantry, when I was startled by a sudden click in the wall on one side of the chimney, and the ghostly tumbling open of a little wooden flap with "JOHN" upon it. The old man, following my eyes, cried with great triumph, "My son's come home!" and we both went out to the drawbridge.

It was worth any money to see Wemmick waving a salute to me from the other side of the moat, when we might have shaken hands across it with the greatest ease. The Aged was so delighted to work the drawbridge, that I made no offer to assist him, but stood quiet until Wemmick had come across, and had presented me to Miss Skiffins: a lady by whom he was accompanied.

Miss Skiffins was of a wooden appearance, and was, like her escort, in the post-office branch of the service. She might have been some two or three years younger than Wemmick, and I judged her to stand possessed of portable property. The cut of her dress from the waist upward, both before and behind, made her figure very like a boy's kite; and I might have pronounced her gown a little too decidedly orange, and her gloves a little too intensely green. But she seemed to be a good sort of fellow, and showed a high regard for the Aged. I was not long in discovering that she was a frequent visitor at the Castle; for, on our going in, and my complimenting Wemmick on his ingenious contrivance for announcing himself to the Aged, he begged me to give my attention for a moment to the other side of the chimney, and disappeared. Presently another click came, and another little door tumbled open with "Miss Skiffins" on it; then Miss Skiffins shut up and John tumbled open; then Miss Skiffins and John both tumbled open together, and finally shut up together. On Wemmick's return from working these mechanical appliances, I expressed the great admiration with which I regarded them, and he said, "Well, you know, they're both pleasant and useful to the Aged. And by George, sir, it's a thing worth mentioning, that of all the people who come to this gate, the secret of those pulls is only known to the Aged, Miss Skiffins, and me!"

"And Mr. Wemmick made them," added Miss Skiffins, "with his own hands out of his own head."

While Miss Skiffins was taking off her bonnet (she retained her green gloves during the evening as an outward and visible sign that there was company),[1] Wemmick invited me to take a walk with him round the property, and see how the island looked in winter-time. Thinking that he did this to give me an opportunity of taking his Walworth sentiments, I seized the opportunity as soon as we were out of the Castle.

Having thought of the matter with care, I approached my subject as if I had never hinted at it before. I informed Wemmick that I was anxious in behalf of Herbert Pocket, and I told him how we had first met, and how we had fought. I glanced at Herbert's home, and at his character, and at his having no means but such as he was dependent on his father for: those, uncertain and unpunctual. I alluded to the advantages I had derived in my first rawness and ignorance from his society, and I confessed that I feared I had but ill repaid them, and that he might have done better without me and my expectations. Keeping Miss Havisham in the background at a great distance, I still hinted at the possibility of my having competed with him in his prospects, and at the certainty of his possessing a generous soul, and being far above any mean distrusts, retaliations, or designs. For all these reasons (I told Wemmick), and because he was my young companion and friend, and I had a great affection for him, I wished my own good fortune to reflect some rays upon him, and therefore I sought advice from Wemmick's experience and knowledge of men and affairs, how I could best try with my resources to help Herbert to some present income — say of a hundred a year, to keep him in good hope and heart — and gradually to buy him on to some small partnership. I begged Wemmick, in conclusion, to understand that my help must always be rendered without Herbert's knowledge or suspicion, and that there was no one else in the world with whom I could advise. I wound up by laying my hand upon his shoulder, and saying, "I can't help confiding in you, though I know it must be troublesome to you; but that is your fault, in having ever brought me here."

---

1. *an outward and visible sign that there was company:* a further ironic reference to the Catechism (see note on pp. 78–79). Compare:

   Q. What meanest thou by this word *sacrament?*

   A. I mean an outward and visible sign of an inward and spiritual grace, given unto us, ordained by Christ himself, as a means whereby we receive the same, and a pledge to assure us thereof.

Wemmick was silent for a little while, and then said with a kind of start, "Well you know, Mr. Pip, I must tell you one thing. This is devilish good of you."

"Say you'll help me to be good then," said I.

"Ecod," replied Wemmick, shaking his head, "that's not my trade."

"Nor is this your trading-place," said I.

"You are right," he returned. "You hit the nail on the head. Mr. Pip, I'll put on my considering-cap, and I think all you want to do, may be done by degrees. Skiffins (that's her brother) is an accountant and agent. I'll look him up and go to work for you."

"I thank you ten thousand times."

"On the contrary," said he, "I thank you, for though we are strictly in our private and personal capacity, still it may be mentioned that there *are* Newgate cobwebs about, and it brushes them away."

After a little further conversation to the same effect, we returned into the Castle where we found Miss Skiffins preparing tea. The responsible duty of making the toast was delegated to the Aged, and that excellent old gentleman was so intent upon it that he seemed to me in some danger of melting his eyes. It was no nominal meal that we were going to make, but a vigorous reality. The Aged prepared such a haystack of buttered toast, that I could scarcely see him over it as it simmered on an iron stand hooked on to the top-bar; while Miss Skiffins brewed such a jorum of tea, that the pig in the back premises became strongly excited, and repeatedly expressed his desire to participate in the entertainment.

The flag had been struck, and the gun had been fired, at the right moment of time, and I felt as snugly cut off from the rest of Walworth as if the moat were thirty feet wide by as many deep. Nothing disturbed the tranquillity of the Castle, but the occasional tumbling open of John and Miss Skiffins: which little doors were a prey to some spasmodic infirmity that made me sympathetically uncomfortable until I got used to it. I inferred from the methodical nature of Miss Skiffins's arrangements that she made tea there every Sunday night; and I rather suspected that a classic brooch she wore, representing the profile of an undesirable female with a very straight nose and a very new moon, was a piece of portable property that had been given her by Wemmick.

We ate the whole of the toast, and drank tea in proportion, and it was delightful to see how warm and greasy we all got after it. The Aged especially, might have passed for some clean old chief of a savage tribe, just oiled. After a short pause of repose, Miss Skiffins — in the absence of the little servant who, it seemed, retired to the bosom of her family on Sunday afternoons — washed up the tea-things, in a trifling lady-like amateur manner that compromised none of us. Then, she put on her gloves again, and we drew round the fire, and Wemmick said, "Now Aged Parent, tip us the paper."

Wemmick explained to me while the Aged got his spectacles out, that this was according to custom, and that it gave the old gentleman infinite satisfaction to read the news aloud. "I won't offer an apology," said Wemmick, "for he isn't capable of many pleasures — am you, Aged P.?"

"All right, John, all right," returned the old man seeing himself spoken to.

"Only tip him a nod every now and then when he looks off his paper," said Wemmick, "and he'll be as happy as a king. We are all attention, Aged One."

"All right, John, all right!" returned the cheerful old man: so busy and so pleased, that it really was quite charming.

The Aged's reading reminded me of the classes at Mr. Wopsle's great-aunt's, with the pleasanter peculiarity that it seemed to come through a keyhole. As he wanted the candles close to him, and as he was always on the verge of putting either his head or the newspaper into them, he required as much watching as a powder-mill. But Wemmick was equally untiring and gentle in his vigilance, and the Aged read on, quite unconscious of his many rescues. Whenever he looked at us, we all expressed the greatest interest and amazement, and nodded until he resumed again.

As Wemmick and Miss Skiffins sat side by side, and as I sat in a shadowy corner, I observed a slow and gradual elongation of Mr. Wemmick's mouth, powerfully suggestive of his slowly and gradually stealing his arm round Miss Skiffins's waist. In course of time I saw his hand appear on the other side of Miss Skiffins; but at that moment Miss Skiffins neatly stopped him with the green glove, unwound his arm again as if it were an article of dress, and with the greatest deliberation laid it on the table before her. Miss Skiffins's composure while she did this was one of the most remarkable sights I have ever seen, and if I could have thought the act consistent with abstraction of mind, I should have deemed that Miss Skiffins performed it mechanically.

By-and-by, I noticed Wemmick's arm beginning to disappear again, and gradually fading out of view. Shortly afterwards, his mouth began to widen again. After an interval of suspense on my part that was quite enthralling and almost painful, I saw his hand appear on the other side of Miss Skiffins. Instantly, Miss Skiffins stopped it with the neatness of a placid boxer, took off that girdle or cestus[1] as before, and laid it on the table. Taking the table to represent the path of virtue, I am justified in stating that during the whole time of the Aged's reading, Wemmick's arm was straying from the path of virtue and being recalled to it by Miss Skiffins.

At last, the Aged read himself into a light slumber. This was the time for Wemmick to produce a little kettle, a tray of glasses, and a black bottle with a porcelain-topped cork, representing some clerical dignitary of a rubicund and social aspect.[2] With the aid of these appliances we all had something warm to drink: including the Aged, who was soon awake again. Miss Skiffins mixed, and I observed that she and Wemmick drank out of one glass. Of course I knew better than to offer to see Miss Skiffins home, and under the circumstances I thought I had best go first: which I did, taking a cordial leave of the Aged, and having passed a pleasant evening.

Before a week was out, I received a note from Wemmick, dated Walworth, stating that he hoped he had made some advance in that matter appertaining to our private and personal capacities, and that he would be glad if I could come and see him again upon it. So, I went out to Walworth again, and yet again, and yet again, and I saw him by appointment in the City several times, but never held any communication with him on the subject in or near Little Britain. The upshot was, that we found a worthy young merchant or shipping-broker, not long established in business, who wanted intelligent help, and who wanted capital, and who in due course of time and receipt would want a partner. Between him and

---

1. *cestus:* literally, the symbolic belt worn by a betrothed woman in ancient Greece and Rome, and removed on her wedding night.
2. *a black bottle with a porcelain-topped cork, representing some clerical dignitary of a rubicund and social aspect:* by analogy with the stiff round white collar worn above a black cassock by Anglican or other clergy.

me, secret articles were signed of which Herbert was the subject, and I paid him half of my five hundred pounds down, and engaged for sundry other payments: some, to fall due at certain dates out of my income: some, contingent on my coming into my property. Miss Skiffins's brother conducted the negotiation. Wemmick pervaded it throughout, but never appeared in it.

The whole business was so cleverly managed, that Herbert had not the least suspicion of my hand being in it. I never shall forget the radiant face with which he came home one afternoon, and told me, as a mighty piece of news, of his having fallen in with one Clarriker (the young merchant's name), and of Clarriker's having shown an extraordinary inclination towards him, and of his belief that the opening had come at last. Day by day as his hopes grew stronger and his face brighter, he must have thought me a more and more affectionate friend, for I had the greatest difficulty in restraining my tears of triumph when I saw him so happy. At length, the thing being done, and he having that day entered Clarriker's House, and he having talked to me for a whole evening in a flush of pleasure and success, I did really cry in good earnest when I went to bed, to think that my expectations had done some good to somebody.

A great event in my life, the turning point of my life, now opens on my view. But, before I proceed to narrate it, and before I pass on to all the changes it involved, I must give one chapter to Estella. It is not much to give to the theme that so long filled my heart.

CHAPTER XIX

IF THAT staid old house near the Green at Richmond should ever come to be haunted when I am dead, it will be haunted, surely, by my ghost. O the many, many nights and days through which the unquiet spirit within me haunted that house when Estella lived there! Let my body be where it would, my spirit was always wandering, wandering, wandering, about that house.

The lady with whom Estella was placed, Mrs. Brandley by name, was a widow, with one daughter several years older than Estella. The mother looked young, and the daughter looked old; the mother's complexion was pink, and the daughter's was yellow; the mother set up for frivolity, and the daughter for theology. They were in what is called a good position, and visited, and were visited by, numbers of people. Little, if any, community of feeling subsisted between them and Estella, but the understanding was established that they were necessary to her, and that she was necessary to them. Mrs. Brandley had been a friend of Miss Havisham's before the time of her seclusion.

In Mrs. Brandley's house and out of Mrs. Brandley's house, I suffered every kind and degree of torture that Estella could cause me. The nature of my relations with her, which placed me on terms of familiarity without placing me on terms of favour, conduced to my distraction. She made use of me to tease other admirers, and she turned the very familiarity between herself and me, to the account of putting a constant slight on my devotion to her. If I had been her secretary, steward, half-brother, poor relation — if I had been a younger brother of her appointed husband — I could not have seemed to myself, further from my hopes when I was nearest to her. The privilege of calling her by her name and hearing her call me by mine, became under the circumstances an aggravation of my trials; and while I think it likely that it almost maddened her other lovers, I know too certainly that it almost maddened me.

She had admirers without end. No doubt my jealousy made an admirer of every one who went near her; but there were more than enough of them without that.

I saw her often at Richmond, I heard of her often in town, and I used often to take her and the Brandleys on the water; there were picnics, fête days, plays, operas, concerts, parties, all sorts of pleasures, through which I pursued her — and they were all miseries to me. I never had one hour's happiness in her society, and yet my mind all round the four-and-twenty hours was harping on the happiness of having her with me unto death.

Throughout this part of our intercourse — and it lasted, as will presently be seen, for what I then thought a long time — she habitually reverted to that tone which expressed that our association was forced upon us. There were other times when she would come to a sudden check in this tone and in all her many tones, and would seem to pity me.

"Pip, Pip," she said one evening, coming to such a check, when we sat apart at a darkening window of the house in Richmond; "will you never take warning?"

"Of what?"

"Of me."

"Warning not to be attracted by you, do you mean, Estella?"

"Do I mean! If you don't know what I mean, you are blind."

I should have replied that Love was commonly reputed blind, but for the reason that I always was restrained — and this was not the least of my miseries — by a feeling that it was ungenerous to press myself upon her, when she knew that she could not choose but obey Miss Havisham. My dread always was, that this knowledge on her part laid me under a heavy disadvantage with her pride, and made me the subject of a rebellious struggle in her bosom.

"At any rate" said I, "I have no warning given me just now, for you wrote to me to come to you, this time."

"That's true" said Estella, with a cold careless smile that always chilled me.

After looking at the twilight without, for a little while, she went on to say:

"The time has come round when Miss Havisham wishes to have me for a day at Satis. You are to take me there, and bring me back, if you will. She would rather I did not travel alone, and objects to receiving my maid, for she has a sensitive horror of being talked of by such people. Can you take me?"

"Can I take you, Estella!"

"You can then? The day after to-morrow, if you please. You are to pay all charges out of my purse. You hear the condition of your going?"

"And must obey," said I.

This was all the preparation I received for that visit, or for others like it: Miss Havisham never wrote to me, nor had I ever so much as seen her handwriting. We went down on the next day but one, and we found her in the room where I had first beheld her, and it is needless to add that there was no change in Satis House.

She was even more dreadfully fond of Estella than she had been when I last saw them together; I repeat the word advisedly, for there was something positively dreadful in the energy of her looks and embraces. She hung upon Estella's beauty, hung upon her words, hung upon her gestures, and sat mumbling her own trembling fingers while she looked at her, as though she were devouring the beautiful creature she had reared. From Estella she looked at me, with a searching glance that seemed to pry into my heart and probe its wounds. "How does she use you, Pip; how does she use you?" she asked me again, with her witch-like eagerness, even in Estella's hearing. But, when we sat by her flickering fire at night, she was most weird; for then, keeping Estella's hand drawn through her arm and clutched in her own hand, she extorted from her, by dint of referring back to what Estella had told her in her regular letters, the names and conditions of the men whom she had fascinated; and as Miss Havisham dwelt upon this roll, with the intensity of a mind mortally hurt and diseased, she sat with her other hand on her crutch stick, and her chin on that, and her wan bright eyes glaring at me, a very spectre.

I saw in this, wretched though it made me, and bitter the sense of dependence and even of degradation that it awakened — I saw in this, that Estella was set to wreak Miss Havisham's revenge on men, and that she was not to be given to me until she had gratified it for a term. I saw in this, a reason for her being beforehand assigned to me. Sending her out to attract and torment and do mischief, Miss Havisham sent her with the malicious assurance that she was beyond the reach of all admirers, and that all who staked upon that cast were secured to lose. I saw in this, that I, too, was tormented by a perversion of ingenuity, even while the prize was reserved for me. I saw in this, the reason for my being staved off so long, and the reason for my late guardian's declining to commit himself to the formal knowledge of such a scheme. In a word, I saw in this, Miss Havisham as I had her then and there before my eyes, and always had had her before my eyes; and I saw in this, the distinct shadow of the darkened and unhealthy house in which her life was hidden from the sun.

The candles that lighted that room of hers were placed in sconces on the wall. They were high from the ground, and they burnt with the steady dulness of artificial light in air that is seldom renewed. As I looked round at them, and at the pale gloom they made, and at the stopped clock, and at the withered articles of bridal dress upon the table and the ground, and at her own awful figure with its ghostly reflection thrown large by the fire upon the ceiling and the wall, I saw in everything the construction that my mind had come to, repeated and thrown back to me. My thoughts passed into the great room across the landing where the table was spread, and I saw it written, as it were, in the falls of the cobwebs from the centre-piece, in the crawlings of the spiders on the cloth, in the tracks of the mice as they betook their little quickened hearts behind the panels, and in the gropings and pausings of the beetles on the floor.

It happened on the occasion of this visit that some sharp words arose between Estella and Miss Havisham. It was the first time I had ever seen them opposed.

We were seated by the fire, as just now described, and Miss Havisham still had Estella's arm drawn through her own, and still clutched Estella's hand in hers, when Estella gradually began to detach herself. She had shown a proud impatience more than once before, and had rather endured that fierce affection than accepted or returned it.

"What!" said Miss Havisham, flashing her eyes upon her, "are you tired of me?"

"Only a little tired of myself," replied Estella, disengaging her arm, and moving to the great chimney-piece, where she stood looking down at the fire.

"Speak the truth, you ingrate!" cried Miss Havisham, passionately striking her stick upon the floor; "you are tired of me."

Estella looked at her with perfect composure, and again looked down at the fire. Her graceful figure and her beautiful face expressed a self-possessed indifference to the wild heat of the other, that was almost cruel.

"You stock and stone!"[1] exclaimed Miss Havisham. "You cold, cold heart!"

"What?" said Estella, preserving her attitude of indifference as she leaned against the great chimney-piece and only moving her eyes; "do you reproach me for being cold? You?"

"Are you not?" was the fierce retort.

---

1. *You stock and stone!* A stock is literally a block of wood; Dickens here uses the two epithets merely as types of heartlessness, although in combination the two more commonly refer to idols carved from wood or rock (see the entry for "stock *n*.1" in the *Oxford English Dictionary* 2nd edition).

"You should know," said Estella. "I am what you have made me. Take all the praise, take all the blame; take all the success, take all the failure; in short, take me."

"O, look at her, look at her!" cried Miss Havisham, bitterly; "Look at her, so hard and thankless, on the hearth where she was reared! Where I took her into this wretched breast when it was first bleeding from its stabs, and where I have lavished years of tenderness upon her!"

"At least I was no party to the compact," said Estella, "for if I could walk and speak, when it was made, it was as much as I could do. But what would you have? You have been very good to me, and I owe everything to you. What would you have?"

"Love," replied the other.

"You have it."

"I have not," said Miss Havisham.

"Mother by adoption," retorted Estella, never departing from the easy grace of her attitude, never raising her voice as the other did, never yielding either to anger or tenderness, "Mother by adoption, I have said that I owe everything to you. All I possess is freely yours. All that you have given me, is at your command to have again. Beyond that, I have nothing. And if you ask me to give you what you never gave me, my gratitude and duty cannot do impossibilities."

"Did I never give her love!" cried Miss Havisham, turning wildly to me. "Did I never give her a burning love, inseparable from jealousy at all times, and from sharp pain, while she speaks thus to me! Let her call me mad, let her call me mad!"

"Why should I call you mad," returned Estella, "I, of all people? Does any one live, who knows what set purposes you have, half as well as I do? Does any one live, who knows what a steady memory you have, half as well as I do? I who have sat on this same hearth on the little stool that is even now beside you there, learning your lessons and looking up into your face, when your face was strange and frightened me!"

"Soon forgotten!" moaned Miss Havisham. "Times soon forgotten!"

"No, not forgotten," retorted Estella. "Not forgotten, but treasured up in my memory. When have you found me false to your teaching? When have you found me unmindful of your lessons? When have you found me giving admission here," she touched her bosom with her hand, "to anything that you excluded? Be just to me."

"So proud, so proud!" moaned Miss Havisham, pushing away her grey hair with both her hands.

"Who taught me to be proud?" returned Estella. "Who praised me when I learnt my lesson?"

"So hard, so hard!" moaned Miss Havisham, with her former action.

"Who taught me to be hard?" returned Estella. "Who praised me when I learnt my lesson?"

"But to be proud and hard to *me*!" Miss Havisham quite shrieked, as she stretched out her arms. "Estella, Estella, Estella, to be proud and hard to *me*!"

Estella looked at her for a moment with a kind of calm wonder, but was not otherwise disturbed; when the moment was past, she looked down at the fire again.

"I cannot think," said Estella, raising her eyes after a silence, "why you should be so unreasonable when I come to see you after a separation. I have never forgotten your wrongs and their causes. I have never been unfaithful to you or your schooling. I have never shown any weakness that I can charge myself with."

"Would it be weakness to return my love?" exclaimed Miss Havisham. "But yes, yes, she would call it so!"

"I begin to think," said Estella, in a musing way, after another moment of calm wonder, "that I almost understand how this comes about. If you had brought up your adopted daughter wholly in the dark confinement of these rooms, and had never let her know that there was such a thing as the daylight by which she has never once seen your face — if you had done that, and then, for a purpose had wanted her to understand the daylight and know all about it, you would have been disappointed and angry?"

Miss Havisham, with her head in her hands, sat making a low moaning, and swaying herself on her chair, but gave no answer.

"Or," said Estella, "— which is a nearer case — if you had taught her, from the dawn of her intelligence, with your utmost energy and might, that there was such a thing as daylight, but that it was made to be her enemy and destroyer, and she must always turn against it, for it had blighted you and would else blight her; — if you had done this, and then, for a purpose, had wanted her to take naturally to the daylight and she could not do it, you would have been disappointed and angry?"

Miss Havisham sat listening (or it seemed so, for I could not see her face), but still made no answer.

"So," said Estella, "I must be taken as I have been made. The success is not mine, the failure is not mine, but the two together make me."

Miss Havisham had settled down, I hardly knew how, upon the floor, among the faded bridal relics with which it was strewn. I took advantage of the moment — I had sought one from the first — to leave the room, after beseeching Estella's attention to her, with a movement of my hand. When I left, Estella was yet standing by the great chimney-piece, just as she had stood throughout. Miss Havisham's grey hair was all adrift upon the ground, among the other bridal wrecks, and was a miserable sight to see.

It was with a depressed heart that I walked in the starlight for an hour and more, about the court-yard, and about the brewery, and about the ruined garden. When I at last took courage to return to the room, I found Estella sitting at Miss Havisham's knee, taking up some stitches in one of those old articles of dress that were dropping to pieces, and of which I have often been reminded since by the faded tatters of old banners that I have seen hanging up in cathedrals. Afterwards, Estella and I played cards, as of yore — only we were skilful now, and played French games — and so the evening wore away, and I went to bed.

I lay in that separate building across the court-yard. It was the first time I had ever lain down to rest in Satis House, and sleep refused to come near me. A thousand Miss Havishams haunted me. She was on this side of my pillow, on that, at the head of the bed, at the foot, behind the half-opened door of the dressing-room, in the dressing-room, in the room overhead, in the room beneath — everywhere. At last, when the night was slow to creep on towards two o'clock, I felt that I absolutely could no longer bear the place as a place to lie down in, and that I must get up. I therefore got up and put on my clothes, and went out across the yard into the long stone passage, designing to gain the outer court-yard and walk there for the relief of my mind. But, I was no sooner in the passage than I extinguished my candle; for, I saw Miss Havisham going along it in a ghostly manner, making a low cry. I followed her at a distance, and saw her go up the staircase. She carried a bare candle in her hand, which she had probably taken from one of the sconces in her own room, and was a most unearthly object by its light. Standing at the bottom of the staircase, I felt the mildewed air of the feast-chamber, without seeing her open the door, and I heard her walking there, and so across into her own room, and so across again into that, never ceasing the low cry. After a time, I tried in the dark both to get out, and to go back, but I could do neither until some streaks of day strayed in and showed me where to lay my hands. During the whole interval, whenever I went to the bottom of the staircase, I heard her footstep, saw her light pass above, and heard her ceaseless low cry.

Before we left next day, there was no revival of the difference between her and Estella, nor was it ever revived on any similar occasion; and there were four similar occasions, to the best of my remembrance. Nor, did Miss Havisham's manner towards Estella in anywise change, except that I believed it to have something like fear infused among its former characteristics.

It is impossible to turn this leaf of my life, without putting Bentley Drummle's name upon it; or I would, very gladly.

On a certain occasion when the Finches were assembled in force, and when good feeling was being promoted in the usual manner by nobody's agreeing with anybody else, the presiding Finch called the Grove to order, forasmuch as Mr. Drummle had not yet toasted a lady; which, according to the solemn constitution of the society it was the brute's turn to do that day. I thought I saw him leer in an ugly way at me while the decanters were going round, but as there was no love lost between us, that might easily be. What was my indignant surprise when he called upon the company to pledge him to "Estella!"

"Estella who?" said I.

"Never you mind," retorted Drummle.

"Estella of where?" said I. "You are bound to say of where." Which he was, as a Finch.

"Of Richmond, gentlemen," said Drummle, putting me out of the question, "and a peerless beauty."

Much he knew about peerless beauties, a mean miserable idiot! I whispered Herbert.

"I know that lady," said Herbert, across the table, when the toast had been honoured.

"*Do* you?" said Drummle.

"And so do I," I added, with a scarlet face.

"*Do* you?" said Drummle. "*Oh,* Lord!"

This was the only retort — except glass or crockery — that the heavy creature was capable of making; but, I became as highly incensed by it as if it had been barbed with wit, and I immediately rose in my place and said that I could not but regard it as being like the honourable Finch's impudence to come down to that Grove — we always talked about coming down to that Grove, as a neat Parliamentary turn of expression — down to that Grove, proposing a lady of whom he knew nothing. Mr. Drummle upon this, starting up, demanded what I meant by that? Whereupon, I made him the extreme reply that I believed he knew where I was to be found.[1]

Whether it was possible in a Christian country to get on without blood, after this, was a question on which the Finches were divided. The debate upon it grew so lively, indeed, that at least six more honourable members told six more, during the discussion, that they believed *they* knew where *they* were to be found. However, it was decided at last (the Grove being a Court of Honour) that if Mr Drummle would bring never so slight a certificate from the lady, importing that he had the honour of her acquaintance, Mr. Pip must express his regret, as a gentleman and a Finch, for "having been betrayed into a warmth which." Next day was appointed for the production (lest our honour should take cold from delay), and next day Drummle appeared with a polite little avowal in Estella's hand, that she had had the honour of dancing with him several times. This left me no course but to regret that I had been "betrayed into a warmth which," and on the whole to repudiate, as untenable, the idea that I was to be found anywhere. Drummle and I then sat snorting at one another for an hour, while the Grove engaged in indiscriminate contradiction, and finally the promotion of good feeling was declared to have gone ahead at an amazing rate.

I tell this lightly, but it was no light thing to me. For, I cannot adequately express what pain it gave me to think that Estella should show any favour to a contemptible, clumsy, sulky booby, so very far below the

---

1. *I believed he knew where I was to be found:* i.e., Pip challenged him to fight a duel for the vindication of honour.

average. To the present moment, I believe it to have been referable to some pure fire of generosity and disinterestedness in my love for her, that I could not endure the thought of her stooping to that hound. No doubt I should have been miserable whomsoever she had favoured; but a worthier object would have caused me a different kind and degree of distress.

It was easy for me to find out, and I did soon find out, that Drummle had begun to follow her closely, and that she allowed him to do it. A little while, and he was always in pursuit of her, and he and I crossed one another every day. He held on, in a dull persistent way, and Estella held him on; now with encouragement, now with discouragement, now almost flattering him, now openly despising him, now knowing him very well, now scarcely remembering who he was.

The Spider, as Mr. Jaggers had called him, was used to lying in wait, however, and had the patience of his tribe. Added to that, he had a blockhead confidence in his money and in his family greatness, which sometimes did him good service — almost taking the place of concentration and determined purpose. So, the Spider, doggedly watching Estella, outwatched many brighter insects, and would often uncoil himself and drop at the right nick of time.

At a certain Assembly Ball[1] at Richmond (there used to be Assembly Balls at most places then), where Estella had outshone all other beauties, this blundering Drummle so hung about her, and with so much toleration on her part, that I resolved to speak to her concerning him. I took the next opportunity: which was when she was waiting for Mrs. Brandley to take her home, and was sitting apart among some flowers, ready to go. I was with her, for I almost always accompanied them to and from such places.

"Are you tired, Estella?"

"Rather, Pip."

"You should be."

"Say rather, I should not be; for I have my letter to Satis House to write, before I go to sleep."

---

1. *Assembly Ball:* here "Assembly" probably refers back to the "public assembly," a general meeting of the members of polite society for conversation and dalliance, which formed a regular part of fashionable life in the eighteenth century.

"Recounting to-night's triumph?" said I. "Surely a very poor one, Estella."

"What do you mean? I didn't know there had been any."

"Estella," said I, "do look at that fellow in the corner yonder, who is looking over here at us."

"Why should I look at him?" returned Estella, with her eyes on me instead. "What is there in that fellow in the corner yonder — to use your words — that I need look at?"

"Indeed, that is the very question I want to ask you," said I. "For he has been hovering about you all night."

"Moths, and all sorts of ugly creatures," replied Estella, with a glance towards him, "hover about a lighted candle. Can the candle help it?"

"No" I returned; "but cannot the Estella help it?"

"Well!" said she, laughing, after a moment, "perhaps. Yes. Anything you like."

"But, Estella, do hear me speak. It makes me wretched that you should encourage a man so generally despised as Drummle. You know he is despised."

"Well?" said she.

"You know he is as ungainly within, as without. A deficient, ill-tempered, lowering, stupid fellow."

"Well?" said she.

"You know he has nothing to recommend him but money, and a ridiculous roll of addle-headed predecessors; now, don't you?"

"Well?" said she again; and each time she said it, she opened her lovely eyes the wider.

To overcome the difficulty of getting past that monosyllable, I took it from her, and said, repeating it with emphasis, "Well! Then, that is why it makes me wretched."

Now, if I could have believed that she favoured Drummle with any idea of making me — me — wretched, I should have been in better heart about it; but in that habitual way of hers, she put me so entirely out of the question, that I could believe nothing of the kind.

"Pip," said Estella, casting her glance over the room, "don't be foolish about its effect on you. It may have its effect on others, and may be meant to have. It's not worth discussing."

"Yes it is," said I, "because I cannot bear that people should say, 'she throws away her graces and attractions on a mere boor, the lowest in the crowd.'"

"I can bear it," said Estella.

"Oh! don't be so proud, Estella, and so inflexible."

"Calls me proud and inflexible in this breath!" said Estella, opening her hands. "And in his last breath reproached me for stooping to a boor!"

"There is no doubt you do," said I, something hurriedly, "for I have seen you give him looks and smiles this very night, such as you never give to — me."

"Do you want me then," said Estella, turning suddenly with a fixed and serious, if not angry, look, "to deceive and entrap you?"

"Do you deceive and entrap him, Estella?"

"Yes, and many others — all of them but you. Here is Mrs. Brandley. I'll say no more."

And now that I have given the one chapter to the theme that so filled my heart, and so often made it ache and ache again, I pass on, unhindered, to the event that had impended over me longer yet; the event that had begun to be prepared for, before I knew that the world held Estella, and in the days when her baby intelligence was receiving its first distortions from Miss Havisham's wasting hands.

In the Eastern story, the heavy slab that was to fall on the bed of state in the flush of conquest was slowly wrought out of the quarry, the tunnel for the rope to hold it in its place was slowly carried through the leagues of rock, the slab was slowly raised and fitted in the roof, the rope was rove to it and slowly taken through the miles of hollow to the great iron ring. All being made ready with much labour, and the hour come, the sultan was aroused in the dead of the night, and the sharpened axe that was to sever the rope from the great iron ring was put into his hand, and he struck with it, and the rope parted and rushed away, and the ceiling fell.[1] So, in my case; all the work, near and afar, that tended to the end,

1. *In the Eastern story, the heavy slab that was to fall on the bed of state ... and the rope parted and rushed away, and the ceiling fell.* The story referred to is "The Enchanters, or, Misnar

had been accomplished; and in an instant the blow was struck, and the roof of my stronghold dropped upon me.

CHAPTER XX

I WAS three-and-twenty years of age. Not another word had I heard to enlighten me on the subject of my expectations, and my twenty-third birthday was a week gone. We had left Barnard's Inn more than a year, and lived in the Temple.[2] Our chambers were in Garden-court, down by the river.

Mr. Pocket and I had for some time parted company as to our original relations, though we continued on the best terms. Notwithstanding my inability to settle to anything — which I hope arose out of the restless and incomplete tenure on which I held my means — I had a taste for reading, and read regularly so many hours a day. That matter of Herbert's was still progressing, and everything with me was as I have brought it down to the close of the last chapter.

Business had taken Herbert on a journey to Marseilles. I was alone, and had a dull sense of being alone. Dispirited and anxious, long hoping that to-morrow or next week would clear my way, and long disappointed, I sadly missed the cheerful face and ready response of my friend.

---

the Sultan of India" from *Tales of the Genii* (1764), a series of interconnected tales in the style of the *Arabian Nights*. A preface claimed that *Tales of the Genii* was translated from the Persian by one Sir Charles Morell, but the book was in fact written by James Ridley (1736–65). As a child Dickens was not only familiar with the story referred to here, but even composed a play on the subject. See the discussion of this simile in the Introduction, p. 20.

2. *the Temple:* see Map B and Illustration F. The site, on the north bank of the Thames below the Strand, was originally owned in the thirteenth century by the Knights Templar; it later became occupied by two of the four London legal societies, the Inner Temple and Middle Temple. As with many of the London "inns of court," by the early nineteenth century many of the chambers were rented out as general residences. Garden Court was in the Middle Temple, on the western side of the site, just above the Temple Gardens which reached down to the river.

It was wretched weather; stormy and wet, stormy and wet; and mud, mud, mud, deep in all the streets. Day after day, a vast heavy veil had been driving over London from the East, and it drove still, as if in the East there were an Eternity of cloud and wind. So furious had been the gusts, that high buildings in town had had the lead stripped off their roofs; and in the country, trees had been torn up, and sails of windmills carried away; and gloomy accounts had come in from the coast, of shipwreck and death. Violent blasts of rain had accompanied these rages of wind, and the day just closed as I sat down to read had been the worst of all.

Alterations have been made in that part of the Temple since that time, and it has not now so lonely a character as it had then, nor is it so exposed to the river. We lived at the top of the last house, and the wind rushing up the river shook the house that night, like discharges of cannon, or breakings of a sea. When the rain came with it and dashed against the windows, I thought, raising my eyes to them as they rocked, that I might have fancied myself in a storm-beaten lighthouse. Occasionally, the smoke came rolling down the chimney as though it could not bear to go out into such a night; and when I set the doors open and looked down the staircase, the staircase lamps were blown out; and when I shaded my face with my hands and looked through the black windows (opening them ever so little, was out of the question in the teeth of such wind and rain) I saw that the lamps in the court were blown out, and that the lamps on the bridges and the shore were shuddering, and that the coal fires in barges on the river were being carried away before the wind like red-hot splashes in the rain.

I read with my watch upon the table, purposing to close my book at eleven o'clock. As I shut it, Saint Paul's, and all the many church-clocks in the City — some leading, some accompanying, some following — struck that hour. The sound was curiously flawed[1] by the wind; and I was listening, and thinking how the wind assailed and tore it, when I heard a footstep on the stair.

---

1. *flawed:* an unusual transitive use of the verb, which usually implies the ruffling of a water surface by the wind. Perhaps the separate meaning, the cracking of a brittle object such as a bell, also comes into play here.

What nervous folly made me start, and awfully connect it with the footstep of my dead sister, matters not. It was past in a moment, and I listened again, and heard the footstep stumble in coming on. Remembering then, that the staircase-lights were blown out, I took up my reading-lamp and went out to the stair-head. Whoever was below had stopped on seeing my lamp, for all was quiet.

"There is some one down there, is there not?" I called out, looking down.

"Yes," said a voice from the darkness beneath.

"What floor do you want?"

"The top. Mr. Pip."

"That is my name. — There is nothing the matter?"

"Nothing the matter," returned the voice. And the man came on.

I stood with my lamp held out over the stair-rail, and he came slowly within its light. It was a shaded lamp, to shine upon a book, and its circle of light was very contracted; so that he was in it for a mere instant, and then out of it. In the instant, I had seen a face that was strange to me, looking up with an incomprehensible air of being touched and pleased by the sight of me.

Moving the lamp as the man moved, I made out that he was substantially dressed, but roughly; like a voyager by sea. That he had long iron grey hair. That his age was about sixty. That he was a muscular man, strong on his legs, and that he was browned and hardened by exposure to weather. As he ascended the last stair or two, and the light of my lamp included us both, I saw, with a stupid kind of amazement, that he was holding out both his hands to me.

"Pray what is your business?" I asked him.

"My business?" he repeated, pausing. "Ah! Yes. I will explain my business, by your leave."

"Do you wish to come in?"

"Yes," he replied; "I wish to come in, Master."

I had asked him the question inhospitably enough, for I resented the sort of bright and gratified recognition that still shone in his face. I resented it, because it seemed to imply that he expected me to respond to it. But, I took him into the room I had just left, and, having set the lamp on the table, asked him as civilly as I could, to explain himself.

He looked about him with the strangest air — an air of wondering pleasure as if he had some part in the things he admired — and he pulled off a rough outer coat, and his hat. Then, I saw that his head was furrowed and bald, and that the long iron grey hair grew only on its sides. But, I saw nothing that in the least explained him. On the contrary, I saw him next moment, once more holding out both his hands to me.

"What do you mean?" said I, half suspecting him to be mad.

He stopped in his looking at me, and slowly rubbed his right hand over his head. "It's disapinting to a man," he said, in a coarse broken voice, "arter having looked for'ard so distant, and come so fur; but you're not to blame for that — neither on us is to blame for that. I'll speak in half a minute. Give me half a minute, please."

He sat down on a chair that stood before the fire, and covered his forehead with his large brown veinous hands. I looked at him attentively then, and recoiled a little from him; but I did not know him.

"There's no one nigh," said he, looking over his shoulder; "is there?"

"Why do you, a stranger coming into my rooms at this time of the night, ask that question?" said I.

"You're a game one," he returned, shaking his head at me with a deliberate affection, at once most unintelligible and most exasperating; "I'm glad you've grow'd up, a game one! But don't catch hold of me. You'd be sorry arterwards to have done it."

I relinquished the intention he had detected, for I knew him! Even yet, I could not recal a single feature, but I knew him! If the wind and the rain had driven away the intervening years, had scattered all the intervening objects, had swept us to the churchyard where we first stood face to face on such different levels, I could not have known my convict more distinctly than I knew him now, as he sat in the chair before the fire. No need to take a file from his pocket and show it to me; no need to take the handkerchief from his neck and twist it round his head; no need to hug himself with both his arms, and take a shivering turn across the room, looking back at me for recognition. I knew him before he gave me one of those aids, though, a moment before, I had not been conscious of remotely suspecting his identity.

He came back to where I stood, and again held out both his hands. Not knowing what to do — for, in my astonishment I had lost my self-possession — I reluctantly gave him my hands. He grasped them heartily, raised them to his lips, kissed them, and still held them.

"You acted noble, my boy," said he. "Noble, Pip! And I have never forgot it!"

At a change in his manner as if he were even going to embrace me, I laid a hand upon his breast and put him away.

"Stay!" said I. "Keep off! If you are grateful to me for what I did when I was a little child, I hope you have shown your gratitude by mending your way of life. If you have come here to thank me, it was not necessary. Still, however you have found me out, there must be something good in the feeling that has brought you here, and I will not repulse you; but surely you must understand that — I —"

My attention was so attracted by the singularity of his fixed look at me, that the words died away on my tongue.

"You was a saying," he observed, when we had confronted one another in silence, "that surely I must understand. What, surely must I understand?"

"That I cannot wish to renew that chance intercourse with you of long ago, under these different circumstances. I am glad to believe you have repented and recovered yourself. I am glad to tell you so. I am glad that, thinking I deserve to be thanked, you have come to thank me. But our ways are different ways, none the less. You are wet, and you look weary. Will you drink something before you go?"

He had replaced his neckerchief loosely, and had stood, keenly observant of me, biting a long end of it. "I think," he answered, still with the end at his mouth and still observant of me, "that I *will* drink (I thank you) afore I go."

There was a tray ready on a side-table. I brought it to the table near the fire, and asked him what he would have? He touched one of the bottles without looking at it or speaking, and I made him some hot rum-and-water. I tried to keep my hand steady while I did so, but his look at me as he leaned back in his chair with the long draggled end of his neckerchief between his teeth — evidently forgotten — made my hand very difficult to master. When at last I put the glass to him, I saw with amazement that his eyes were full of tears.

Up to this time I had remained standing, not to disguise that I wished him gone. But I was softened by the softened aspect of the man, and felt a touch of reproach. "I hope," said I, hurriedly putting something into a glass for myself, and drawing a chair to the table, "that you will not think I spoke harshly to you just now. I had no intention of doing it, and I am sorry for it if I did. I wish you well, and happy!"

As I put my glass to my lips, he glanced with surprise at the end of his neckerchief, dropping from his mouth when he opened it, and stretched out his hand. I gave him mine, and then he drank, and drew his sleeve across his eyes and forehead.

"How are you living?" I asked him.

"I've been a sheep-farmer, stock-breeder, other trades besides, away in the new world," said he: "many a thousand mile of stormy water off from this."

"I hope you have done well?"

"I've done wonderful well. There's others went out alonger me as has done well too, but no man has done nigh as well as me. I'm famous for it."

"I am glad to hear it."

"I hope to hear you say so, my dear boy."

Without stopping to try to understand those words or the tone in which they were spoken, I turned off to a point that had just come into my mind.

"Have you ever seen a messenger you once sent to me," I inquired, "since he undertook that trust?"

"Never set eyes upon him. I warn't likely to it."

"He came faithfully, and he brought me the two one-pound notes. I was a poor boy then, as you know, and to a poor boy they were a little fortune. But, like you, I have done well since, and you must let me pay them back. You can put them to some other poor boy's use." I took out my purse.

He watched me as I laid my purse upon the table and opened it, and he watched me as I separated two one-pound notes from its contents. They were clean and new, and I spread them out and handed them over to him. Still watching me, he laid them one upon the other, folded them long-wise, gave them a twist, set fire to them at the lamp, and dropped the ashes into the tray.

"May I make so bold," he said then, with a smile that was like a frown, and with a frown that was like a smile, "as ask you *how* you have done well, since you and me was out on them lone shivering marshes?"

"How?"

"Ah!"

He emptied his glass, got up, and stood at the side of the fire, with his heavy brown hand on the mantelshelf. He put a foot up to the bars, to dry and warm it, and the wet boot began to steam; but, he neither looked at it, nor at the fire, but steadily looked at me. It was only now that I began to tremble.

When my lips had parted, and had shaped some words that were without sound, I forced myself to tell him (though I could not do it distinctly), that I had been chosen to succeed to some property.

"Might a mere warmint ask what property?" said he.

I faltered, "I don't know."

"Might a mere warmint ask whose property?" said he.

I faltered again, "I don't know."

"Could I make a guess, I wonder," said the Convict, "at your income since you come of age! As to the first figure now. Five?"

With my heart beating like a heavy hammer of disordered action, I rose out of my chair, and stood with my hand upon the back of it, looking wildly at him.

"Concerning a guardian," he went on. "There ought to have been some guardian, or such-like, whiles you was a minor. Some lawyer, maybe. As to the first letter of that lawyer's name now. Would it be J?"

All the truth of my position came flashing on me; and its disappointments, dangers, disgraces, consequences of all kinds, rushed in in such a multitude that I was borne down by them and had to struggle for every breath I drew.

"Put it," he resumed, "as the employer of that lawyer whose name begun with a J, and might be Jaggers — put it as he had come over sea to Portsmouth, and had landed there, and had wanted to come on to you. 'However you have found me out,' you says just now. Well! However did I find you out? Why, I wrote from Portsmouth to a person in London, for particulars of your address. That person's name? Why, Wemmick."

I could not have spoken one word, though it had been to save my life. I stood, with a hand on the chair-back and a hand on my breast, where I seemed to be suffocating — I stood so, looking wildly at him, until I grasped at the chair, when the room began to surge and turn. He caught me, drew me to the sofa, put me up against the cushions, and bent on one knee before me: bringing the face that I now well remembered, and that I shuddered at, very near to mine.

"Yes, Pip, dear boy, I've made a gentleman on you! It's me wot has done it! I swore that time, sure as ever I earned a guinea, that guinea should go to you. I swore afterwards, sure as ever I spec'lated and got rich, you should get rich. I lived rough, that you should live smooth; I worked hard, that you should be above work. What odds, dear boy? Do I tell it, fur you to feel a obligation? Not a bit. I tell it, fur you to know as that there hunted dunghill dog wot you kep life in, got his head so high that he could make a gentleman — and, Pip, you're him!"

The abhorrence in which I held the man, the dread I had of him, the repugnance with which I shrank from him, could not have been exceeded if he had been some terrible beast.

"Lookee here, Pip. I'm your second father. You're my son — more to me nor any son. I've put away money, only for you to spend. When I was a hired-out shepherd in a solitary hut, not seeing no faces but faces of sheep till I half forgot wot men's and women's faces wos like, I see yourn. I drops my knife many a time in that hut when I was a eating my dinner or my supper, and I says, 'Here's the boy again, a looking at me whiles I eats and drinks!' I see you there a many times, as plain as ever I see you on them misty marshes. 'Lord strike me dead!' I says each time — and I goes out in the air to say it under the open heavens — 'but wot, if I gets liberty and money, I'll make that boy a gentleman!' And I done it. Why, look at you, dear boy! Look at these here lodgings o' yourn, fit for a lord! A lord? Ah! You shall show money with lords for wagers, and beat 'em!"

In his heat and triumph, and in his knowledge that I had been nearly fainting, he did not remark on my reception of all this. It was the one grain of relief I had.

"Lookee here!" he went on, taking my watch out of my pocket, and turning towards him a ring on my finger, while I recoiled from his touch as if he had been a snake, "a gold 'un and a beauty: *that's* a gentleman's, I hope! A diamond all set round with rubies; *that's* a gentleman's, I hope!

Look at your linen; fine and beautiful! Look at your clothes; better ain't to be got! And your books too," turning his eyes round the room, "mounting up, on their shelves, by hundreds! And you read 'em; don't you? I see you'd been a reading of 'em when I come in. Ha, ha, ha! You shall read 'em to me, dear boy! And if they're in foreign languages wot I don't understand, I shall be just as proud as if I did."

Again he took both my hands and put them to his lips, while my blood ran cold within me.

"Don't you mind talking, Pip," said he, after again drawing his sleeve over his eyes and forehead, as the click came in his throat which I well remembered — and he was all the more horrible to me that he was so much in earnest; "you can't do better nor keep quiet, dear boy. You ain't looked slowly forward to this as I have; you wosn't prepared for this, as I wos. But didn't you never think it might be me?"

"O no, no, no," I returned. "Never, never!"

"Well, you see it wos me, and single-handed. Never a soul in it but my own self and Mr. Jaggers."

"Was there no one else?" I asked.

"No," said he, with a glance of surprise: "who else should there be? And, dear boy, how good looking you have growed! There's bright eyes somewheres — eh? Isn't there bright eyes somewheres, wot you love the thoughts on?"

O Estella, Estella!

"They shall be yourn, dear boy, if money can buy 'em. Not that a gentleman like you, so well set up as you, can't win 'em off of his own game; but money shall back you! Let me finish wot I was a telling you, dear boy. From that there hut and that there hiring-out, I got money left me by my master (which died, and had been the same as me), and got my liberty and went for myself. In every single thing I went for, I went for you. 'Lord strike a blight upon it,' I says, wotever it was I went for, 'if it ain't for him!' It all prospered wonderful. As I giv' you to understand just now, I'm famous for it. It was the money left me, and the gains of the first few year wot I sent home to Mr. Jaggers — all for you — when he first come arter you, agreeable to my letter."

O, that he had never come! That he had left me at the forge — far from contented, yet, by comparison, happy!

"And then, dear boy, it was a recompense to me, lookee here, to know in secret that I was making a gentleman. The blood horses[1] of them colonists might fling up the dust over me as I was walking; what do I say? I says to myself, 'I'm making a better gentleman nor ever *you*'ll be!' When one of 'em says to another, 'He was a convict, a few year ago, and is a ignorant common fellow now, for all he's lucky,' what do I say? I says to myself, 'If I ain't a gentleman, nor yet ain't got no learning, I'm the owner of such. All on you owns stock and land; which on you owns a brought-up London gentleman?' This way I kep myself a going. And this way I held steady afore my mind that I would for certain come one day and see my boy, and make myself known to him, on his own ground."

He laid his hand on my shoulder. I shuddered at the thought that for anything I knew, his hand might be stained with blood.

"It warn't easy, Pip, for me to leave them parts, nor yet it warn't safe. But I held to it, and the harder it was, the stronger I held, for I was determined, and my mind firm made up. At last I done it. Dear boy, I done it!"

I tried to collect my thoughts, but I was stunned. Throughout, I had seemed to myself to attend more to the wind and the rain than to him; even now, I could not separate his voice from those voices, though those were loud and his was silent.

"Where will you put me?" he asked, presently. "I must be put somewheres, dear boy."

"To sleep?" said I.

"Yes. And to sleep long and sound," he answered; "for I've been sea-tossed and sea-washed, months and months."

"My friend and companion," said I, rising from the sofa, "is absent; you must have his room."

"He won't come back to-morrow; will he?"

"No," said I, answering almost mechanically, in spite of my utmost efforts; "not to-morrow."

"Because, lookee here, dear boy," he said, dropping his voice, and laying a long finger on my breast in an impressive manner, "caution is necessary."

---

1. *blood horses:* i.e., thoroughbreds.

"How do you mean? Caution?"

"By G—, it's Death!"

"What's death?"

"I was sent for life. It's death to come back. There's been overmuch coming back of late years, and I should of a certainty be hanged if took."*

Nothing was needed but this; the wretched man, after loading wretched me with his gold and silver chains for years, had risked his life to come to me, and I held it there in my keeping! If I had loved him instead of abhorring him; if I had been attracted to him by the strongest admiration and affection, instead of shrinking from him with the strongest repugnance; it could have been no worse. On the contrary, it would have been better, for his preservation would then have naturally and tenderly addressed my heart.

My first care was to close the shutters, so that no light might be seen from without, and then to close and make fast the doors. While I did so, he stood at the table drinking rum and eating biscuit; and when I saw him thus engaged, I saw my convict on the marshes at his meal again. It almost seemed to me as if he must stoop down presently, to file at his leg.

When I had gone into Herbert's room, and had shut off any other communication between it and the staircase than through the room in which our conversation had been held, I asked him if he would go to bed? He said yes, but asked me for some of my "gentleman's linen" to put on in the morning. I brought it out, and laid it ready for him, and my blood again ran cold when he again took me by both hands to give me good night.

I got away from him, without knowing how I did it, and mended the fire in the room where we had been together, and sat down by it, afraid to go to bed. For an hour or more, I remained too stunned to think; and it was not until I began to think, that I began fully to know how wrecked I was, and how the ship in which I had sailed was gone to pieces.

Miss Havisham's intentions towards me, all a mere dream; Estella not designed for me; I only suffered in Satis House as a convenience, a sting for the greedy relations, a model with a mechanical heart to practise on when no other practice was at hand; those were the first smarts I had. But, sharpest and deepest pain of all — it was for the convict, guilty of I knew not what crimes, and liable to be taken out of those rooms where I sat thinking, and hanged at the Old Bailey door, that I had deserted Joe.

I would not have gone back to Joe now, I would not have gone back to Biddy now, for any consideration: simply, I suppose, because my sense of my own worthless conduct to them was greater than every consideration. No wisdom on earth could have given me the comfort that I should have derived from their simplicity and fidelity; but I could never, never, never, undo what I had done.

In every rage of wind and rush of rain, I heard pursuers. Twice, I could have sworn there was a knocking and whispering at the outer door. With these fears upon me, I began either to imagine or recal that I had had mysterious warnings of this man's approach. That, for weeks gone by, I had passed faces in the streets which I had thought like his. That, these likenesses had grown more numerous, as he, coming over the sea, had drawn nearer. That, his wicked spirit had somehow sent these messengers to mine, and that now on this stormy night he was as good as his word, and with me.

Crowding up with these reflections came the reflection that I had seen him with my childish eyes to be a desperately violent man; that I had heard that other convict reiterate that he had tried to murder him; that I had seen him down in the ditch tearing and fighting like a wild beast. Out of such remembrances I brought into the light of the fire, a half-formed terror that it might not be safe to be shut up there with him in the dead of the wild solitary night. This dilated until it filled the room, and impelled me to take a candle and go in and look at my dreadful burden.

He had rolled a handkerchief round his head, and his face was set and lowering in his sleep. But he was asleep, and quietly too, though he had a pistol lying on the pillow. Assured of this, I softly removed the key to the outside of his door, and turned it on him before I again sat down by the fire. Gradually I slipped from the chair and lay on the floor. When I awoke, without having parted in my sleep with the perception of my wretchedness, the clocks of the Eastward churches were striking five, the candles were wasted out, the fire was dead, and the wind and rain intensified the thick black darkness.

THIS IS THE END OF THE SECOND STAGE OF
PIP'S EXPECTATIONS.

VOLUME III

CHAPTER I

IT WAS fortunate for me that I had to take precautions to ensure (so far as I could) the safety of my dreaded visitor; for, this thought pressing on me when I awoke, held other thoughts in a confused concourse at a distance.

The impossibility of keeping him concealed in the chambers was self-evident. It could not be done, and the attempt to do it would inevitably engender suspicion. True, I had no Avenger in my service now, but I was looked after by an inflammatory old female, assisted by an animated rag-bag whom she called her niece, and to keep a room secret from them would be to invite curiosity and exaggeration. They both had weak eyes, which I had long attributed to their chronically looking in at keyholes, and they were always at hand when not wanted; indeed that was their only reliable quality besides larceny. Not to get up a mystery with these people, I resolved to announce in the morning that my uncle had unexpectedly come from the country.

This course I decided on while I was yet groping about in the darkness for the means of getting a light. Not stumbling on the means after all, I was fain to go out to the adjacent Lodge and get the watchman there to come with his lantern. Now, in groping my way down the black staircase I fell over something, and that something was a man crouching in a corner.

As the man made no answer when I asked him what he did there, but eluded my touch in silence, I ran to the Lodge and urged the watchman to come quickly: telling him of the incident on the way back. The wind being as fierce as ever, we did not care to endanger the light in the lantern by rekindling the extinguished lamps on the staircase, but we examined the staircase from the bottom to the top and found no one there. It then occurred to me as possible that the man might have slipped into my rooms; so, lighting my candle at the watchman's, and leaving him standing at the door, I examined them carefully, including the room in which my dreaded guest lay asleep. All was quiet, and assuredly no other man was in those chambers.

It troubled me that there should have been a lurker on the stairs, on that night of all nights in the year, and I asked the watchman, on the chance of eliciting some hopeful explanation as I handed him a dram at the door, whether he had admitted at his gate any gentleman who had perceptibly been dining out? Yes, he said; at different times of the night, three. One lived in Fountain Court, and the other two lived in the Lane,[1] and he had seen them all go home. Again, the only other man who dwelt in the house of which my chambers formed a part, had been in the country for some weeks; and he certainly had not returned in the night, because we had seen his door with his seal on it as we came up-stairs.

"The night being so bad, sir," said the watchman, as he gave me back my glass, "uncommon few have come in at my gate.[2] Besides them three gentlemen that I have named, I don't call to mind another since about eleven o'clock, when a stranger asked for you."

"My uncle," I muttered. "Yes."

"You saw him, sir?"

"Yes. Oh yes."

"Likewise the person with him?"

"Person with him!" I repeated.

"I judged the person to be with him," returned the watchman. "The person stopped, when he stopped to make inquiry of me, and the person took this way when he took this way."

"What sort of person?"

The watchman had not particularly noticed; he should say a working

---

1. *Fountain Court ... the Lane:* Fountain Court is also in the grounds of the Middle Temple; "the Lane" is Temple Lane. See Map B.
2. *my gate:* i.e., the gate at the end of Temple Lane.

person; to the best of his belief, he had a dust-coloured kind of clothes on, under a dark coat. The watchman made more light of the matter than I did, and naturally; not having my reason for attaching weight to it. When I had got rid of him, which I thought it well to do without prolonging explanations, my mind was much troubled by these two circumstances taken together. Whereas they were easy of innocent solution apart — as, for instance, some diner-out or diner-at-home, who had not gone near this watchman's gate, might have strayed to my staircase and dropped asleep there — and my nameless visitor might have brought some one with him to show him the way — still, joined, they had an ugly look to one as prone to distrust and fear as the changes of a few hours had made me.

I lighted my fire, which burnt with a raw pale flare at that time of the morning, and fell into a doze before it. I seemed to have been dozing a whole night when the clocks struck six. As there was full an hour and a half between me and daylight, I dozed again; now, waking up uneasily, with prolix conversations about nothing, in my ears; now, making thunder of the wind in the chimney; at length, falling off into a profound sleep from which the daylight woke me with a start.

All this time I had never been able to consider my own situation, nor could I do so yet. I had not the power to attend to it. I was greatly dejected and distressed, but in an incoherent wholesale sort of way. As to forming any plan for the future, I could as soon have formed an elephant. When I opened the shutters and looked out at the wet wild morning, all of a leaden hue; when I walked from room to room; when I sat down again shivering, before the fire, waiting for my laundress to appear; I thought how miserable I was, but hardly knew why, or how long I had been so, or on what day of the week I made the reflection, or even who I was that made it.

At last, the old woman and the niece came in — the latter with a head not easily distinguishable from her dusty broom — and testified surprise at sight of me and the fire. To whom I imparted how my uncle had come in the night and was then asleep, and how the breakfast preparations were to be modified accordingly. Then, I washed and dressed while they knocked the furniture about and made a dust; and so, in a sort of dream or sleep-waking, I found myself sitting by the fire again, waiting for — Him — to come to breakfast.

By-and-by, his door opened and he came out. I could not bring myself to bear the sight of him, and I thought he had a worse look by daylight.

"I do not even know," said I, speaking low as he took his seat at the
table, "by what name to call you. I have given out that you are my uncle."

"That's it, dear boy! Call me uncle."

"You assumed some name, I suppose, on board ship?"

"Yes, dear boy. I took the name of Provis."

"Do you mean to keep that name?"

"Why, yes, dear boy, it's as good as another — unless you'd like another."

"What is your real name?" I asked him in a whisper.

"Magwitch," he answered, in the same tone; "chrisen'd Abel."

"What were you brought up to be?"

"A warmint, dear boy."

He answered quite seriously, and used the word as if it denoted some
profession.

"When you came into the Temple last night —" said I, pausing to
wonder whether that could really have been last night, which seemed so
long ago.

"Yes, dear boy?"

"When you came in at the gate and asked the watchman the way
here, had you any one with you?"

"With me? No, dear boy."

"But there was some one there?"

"I didn't take particular notice," he said, dubiously, "not knowing the
ways of the place. But I think there *wos* a person, too, come in alonger me."

"Are you known in London?"

"I hope not!" said he, giving his neck a jerk with his forefinger that
made me turn hot and sick.

"Were you known in London, once?"

"Not over and above, dear boy. I *wos* in the provinces mostly."

"Were you — tried — in London?"

"Which time?" said he, with a sharp look.

"The last time."

He nodded. "First knowed Mr. Jaggers that way. Jaggers was for me."

It was on my lips to ask him what he was tried for, but he took up a knife, gave it a flourish, and with the words, "And wotever I done is worked out and paid for!" fell to at his breakfast.

He ate in a ravenous way that was very disagreeable, and all his actions were uncouth, noisy, and greedy. Some of his teeth had failed him since I saw him eat on the marshes, and as he turned his food in his mouth, and turned his head sideways to bring his strongest fangs to bear upon it, he looked terribly like a hungry old dog. If I had begun with any appetite, he would have taken it away, and I should have sat much as I did — repelled from him by an insurmountable aversion, and gloomily looking at the cloth.

"I'm a heavy grubber, dear boy," he said, as a polite kind of apology when he had made an end of his meal, "but I always wos. If it had been in my constitution to be a lighter grubber, I might ha' got into lighter trouble. Sim'larly, I must have my smoke. When I was first hired out as shepherd t'other side the world, it's my belief I should ha' turned into a molloncolly-mad sheep myself, if I hadn't a had my smoke."

As he said so, he got up from table, and putting his hand into the breast of the pea-coat[1] he wore, brought out a short black pipe, and a handful of loose tobacco of the kind that is called Negro-head.[2] Having filled his pipe, he put the surplus tobacco back again, as if his pocket were a drawer. Then, he took a live coal from the fire with the tongs, and lighted his pipe at it, and then turned round on the hearth-rug with his back to the fire, and went through his favourite action of holding out both his hands for mine.

"And this," said he, dandling my hands up and down in his, as he puffed at his pipe; "and this is the gentleman wot I made! The real genuine One! It does me good fur to look at you, Pip. All I stip'late, is, to stand by and look at you, dear boy!"

I released my hands as soon as I could, and found that I was beginning slowly to settle down to the contemplation of my condition. What I was chained to, and how heavily, became intelligible to me, as I heard his

---

1. *pea-coat:* a stout short woollen overcoat, worn by sailors.
2. *tobacco of the kind that is called Negro-head:* a strong coarse plug tobacco, black in colour.

hoarse voice, and sat looking up at his furrowed bald head with its iron grey hair at the sides.

"I mustn't see my gentleman a footing it in the mire of the streets; there mustn't be no mud on *his* boots. My gentleman must have horses, Pip! Horses to ride, and horses to drive, and horses for his servant to ride and drive as well. Shall colonists have their horses (and blood 'uns, if you please, good Lord!) and not my London gentleman? No, no. We'll show 'em another pair of shoes than that, Pip; won't us?"

He took out of his pocket a great thick pocket-book, bursting with papers, and tossed it on the table.

"There's something worth spending in that there book, dear boy. It's yourn. All I've got ain't mine; it's yourn. Don't you be afeerd on it. There's more where that come from. I've come to the old country fur to see my gentleman spend his money *like* a gentleman. That'll be *my* pleasure. My pleasure 'ull be fur to see him do it. And blast you all!" he wound up, looking round the room and snapping his fingers once with a loud snap, "blast you every one, from the judge in his wig, to the colonist a stirring up the dust, I'll show a better gentleman than the whole kit on you put together!"

"Stop!" said I, almost in a frenzy of fear and dislike, "I want to speak to you. I want to know what is to be done. I want to know how you are to be kept out of danger, how long you are going to stay, what projects you have."

"Lookee here, Pip," said he, laying his hand on my arm in a suddenly altered and subdued manner; "first of all, lookee here. I forgot myself half a minute ago. What I said was low; that's wot it was; low. Lookee here, Pip. Look over it. I ain't a going to be low."

"First," I resumed, half groaning, "what precautions can be taken against your being recognised and seized?"

"No, dear boy," he said, in the same tone as before, "that don't go first. Lowness goes first. I ain't took so many year to make a gentleman, not without knowing wot's due to him. Lookee here, Pip. I was low; that's wot I wos; low. Look over it, dear boy."

Some sense of the grimly-ludicrous moved me to a fretful laugh, as I replied, "I *have* looked over it. In Heaven's name, don't harp upon it!"

"Yes, but lookee here," he persisted. "Dear boy, I ain't come so fur to be low. Now, go on, dear boy. You was a saying —"

"How are you to be guarded from the danger you have incurred?"

"Well, dear boy, the danger ain't so great. Without I was informed agen, the danger ain't so much to signify. There's Jaggers, and there's Wemmick, and there's you. Who else is there to inform?"

"Is there no chance person who might identify you in the street?" said I.

"Well," he returned, "there ain't many. Nor yet I don't intend to advertise myself in the newspapers by the name of A. M. come back from Botany Bay;[1] and years has rolled away, and who's to gain by it? Still, lookee here, Pip. If the danger had been fifty times as great, I should ha' come to see you, mind you, just the same."

"And how long do you remain?"

"How long?" said he, taking his black pipe from his mouth, and dropping his jaw as he stared at me. "I'm not a going back. I've come for good."

"Where are you to live?" said I. "What is to be done with you? Where will you be safe?"

"Dear boy," he returned, "there's disguising wigs can be bought for money, and there's hair powder, and spectacles, and black clothes — shorts[2] and wot not. Others has done it safe afore, and wot others has done afore, others can do agen. As to the where and how of living, dear boy, give me your own opinions on it."

"You take it smoothly now," said I, "but you were very serious last night, when you swore it was Death."

"And so I swear it is Death," said he, putting his pipe back in his mouth, "and Death by the rope, in the open street not fur from this,[3] and it's serious that you should fully understand it to be so. Wot then, when that's once done? Here I am. To go back now, 'ud be as bad as to stand ground — worse. Besides, Pip, I'm here, because I've meant it by you, years and years. As to what I dare, I'm a old bird now, as has dared all manner of

---

1. *Botany Bay:* the principal British convict settlement from 1787 to 1840, in New South Wales, Australia.
2. *shorts:* knee-breeches, by then old-fashioned.
3. *Death by the rope, in the open street not fur from this:* i.e., at Newgate.

traps since first he was fledged, and I'm not afeerd to perch upon a scarecrow. If there's Death hid inside of it, there is, and let him come out, and I'll face him, and then I'll believe in him and not afore. And now let me have a look at my gentleman agen."

Once more, he took me by both hands and surveyed me with an air of admiring proprietorship: smoking with great complacency all the while.

It appeared to me that I could do no better than secure him some quiet lodging hard by, of which he might take possession when Herbert returned: whom I expected in two or three days. That the secret must be confided to Herbert as a matter of unavoidable necessity, even if I could have put the immense relief I should derive from sharing it with him out of the question, was plain to me. But it was by no means so plain to Mr. Provis (I resolved to call him by that name), who reserved his consent to Herbert's participation until he should have seen him and formed a favourable judgment of his physiognomy. "And even then, dear boy," said he, pulling a greasy little clasped black Testament out of his pocket, "we'll have him on his oath."

To state that my terrible patron carried this little black book about the world solely to swear people on in cases of emergency, would be to state what I never quite established — but this I can say, that I never knew him put it to any other use. The book itself had the appearance of having been stolen from some court of justice, and perhaps his knowledge of its antecedents, combined with his own experience in that wise, gave him a reliance on its powers as a sort of legal spell or charm. On this first occasion of his producing it, I recalled how he had made me swear fidelity in the churchyard long ago, and how he had described himself last night as always swearing to his resolutions in his solitude.

As he was at present dressed in a seafaring slop suit,[1] in which he looked as if he had some parrots and cigars to dispose of, I next discussed with him what dress he should wear. He cherished an extraordinary belief in the virtues of "shorts" as a disguise, and had in his own mind sketched a dress for himself that would have made him something between a dean and a dentist. It was with considerable difficulty that I won him over to

---

1. *a seafaring slop suit:* cheap ready-made and loose-fitting clothes for sailors, supplied from the ship's stores.

the assumption of a dress more like a prosperous farmer's; and we arranged that he should cut his hair close, and wear a little powder. Lastly, as he had not yet been seen by the laundress or her niece, he was to keep himself out of their view until his change of dress was made.

It would seem a simple matter to decide on these precautions; but in my dazed, not to say distracted, state, it took so long, that I did not get out to further them, until two or three in the afternoon. He was to remain shut up in the chambers while I was gone, and was on no account to open the door.

There being to my knowledge a respectable lodging-house in Essex-street, the back of which looked into the Temple, and was almost within hail of my windows, I first of all repaired to that house, and was so fortunate as to secure the second floor for my uncle, Mr. Provis. I then went from shop to shop, making such purchases as were necessary to the change in his appearance. This business transacted, I turned my face, on my own account, to Little Britain. Mr. Jaggers was at his desk, but, seeing me enter, got up immediately and stood before his fire.

"Now, Pip," said he, "be careful."

"I will, sir," I returned. For, I had thought well of what I was going to say coming along.

"Don't commit yourself," said Mr. Jaggers, "and don't commit any one. You understand — any one. Don't tell me anything: I don't want to know anything; I am not curious."

Of course I saw that he knew the man was come.

"I merely want, Mr. Jaggers," said I, "to assure myself that what I have been told, is true. I have no hope of its being untrue, but at least I may verify it."

Mr. Jaggers nodded. "But did you say 'told' or 'informed'?" he asked me, with his head on one side, and not looking at me, but looking in a listening way at the floor. "Told would seem to imply verbal communication. You can't have verbal communication with a man in New South Wales, you know."

"I will say, informed, Mr. Jaggers."

"Good."

"I have been informed by a person named Abel Magwitch, that he is the benefactor so long unknown to me."

"That is the man," said Mr. Jaggers, "— in New South Wales."

"And only he?" said I.

"And only he," said Mr. Jaggers.

"I am not so unreasonable, sir, as to think you at all responsible for my mistakes and wrong conclusions; but I always supposed it was Miss Havisham."

"As you say, Pip," returned Mr. Jaggers, turning his eyes upon me coolly, and taking a bite at his forefinger, "I am not at all responsible for that."

"And yet it looked so like it, sir," I pleaded with a downcast heart.

"Not a particle of evidence, Pip," said Mr. Jaggers, shaking his head and gathering up his skirts. "Take nothing on its looks; take everything on evidence. There's no better rule."

"I have no more to say," said I, with a sigh, after standing silent for a little while. "I have verified my information, and there an end."

"And Magwitch — in New South Wales — having at last disclosed himself," said Mr. Jaggers, "you will comprehend, Pip, how rigidly throughout my communication with you, I have always adhered to the strict line of fact. There has never been the least departure from the strict line of fact. You are quite aware of that?"

"Quite, sir."

"I communicated to Magwitch — in New South Wales — when he first wrote to me — from New South Wales — the caution that he must not expect me ever to deviate from the strict line of fact. I also communicated to him another caution. He appeared to me to have obscurely hinted in his letter at some distant idea he had of seeing you in England here. I cautioned him that I must hear no more of that; that he was not at all likely to obtain a pardon; that he was expatriated for the term of his natural life; and that his presenting himself in this country would be an act of felony, rendering him liable to the extreme penalty of the law. I gave Magwitch that caution," said Mr. Jaggers, looking hard at me; "I wrote it to New South Wales. He guided himself by it, no doubt."

"No doubt," said I.

"I have been informed by Wemmick," pursued Mr. Jaggers, still looking hard at me, "that he has received a letter, under date Portsmouth, from a colonist of the name of Purvis, or —"

"Or Provis," I suggested.

"Or Provis — thank you, Pip. Perhaps it *is* Provis? Perhaps you know it's Provis?"

"Yes," said I.

"You know it's Provis. A letter, under date Portsmouth, from a colonist of the name of Provis, asking for the particulars of your address, on behalf of Magwitch. Wemmick sent him the particulars, I understand, by return of post. Probably it is through Provis that you have received the explanation of Magwitch — in New South Wales?"

"It came through Provis," I replied.

"Good day, Pip," said Mr. Jaggers, offering his hand; "glad to have seen you. In writing by post to Magwitch — in New South Wales — or in communicating with him through Provis, have the goodness to mention that the particulars and vouchers of our long account shall be sent to you, together with the balance; for there is still a balance remaining. Good day, Pip!"

We shook hands, and he looked hard at me as long as he could see me. I turned at the door, and he was still looking hard at me, while the two vile casts on the shelf seemed to be trying to get their eyelids open, and to force out of their swollen throats, "O, what a man he is!"

Wemmick was out, and though he had been at his desk he could have done nothing for me. I went straight back to the Temple, where I found the terrible Provis drinking rum-and-water and smoking negro-head, in safety.

Next day the clothes I had ordered, all came home, and he put them on. Whatever he put on, became him less (it dismally seemed to me) than what he had worn before. To my thinking, there was something in him that made it hopeless to attempt to disguise him. The more I dressed him and the better I dressed him, the more he looked like the slouching fugitive on the marshes. This effect on my anxious fancy was partly referable, no doubt, to his old face and manner growing more familiar to me; but I believe too that he dragged one of his legs as if there were still a weight of iron on it, and that from head to foot there was Convict in the very grain of the man.

The influences of his solitary hut-life were upon him besides, and gave him a savage air that no dress could tame; added to these, were the influences of his subsequent branded life among men, and, crowning all, his consciousness that he was dodging and hiding now. In all his ways of sitting and standing, and eating and drinking — of brooding about, in a high-shouldered reluctant style — of taking out his great horn-handled jack-knife[1] and wiping it on his legs and cutting his food — of lifting light glasses and cups to his lips, as if they were clumsy pannikins — of chopping a wedge off his bread, and soaking up with it the last fragments of gravy round and round his plate, as if to make the most of an allowance, and then drying his finger-ends on it, and then swallowing it — in these ways and a thousand other small nameless instances arising every minute in the day, there was Prisoner, Felon, Bondsman, plain as plain could be.

It had been his own idea to wear that touch of powder, and I had conceded the powder after overcoming the shorts. But I can compare the effect of it, when on, to nothing but the probable effect of rouge upon the dead; so awful was the manner in which everything in him that it was most desirable to repress, started through that thin layer of pretence, and seemed to come blazing out at the crown of his head. It was abandoned as soon as tried, and he wore his grizzled hair cut short.

Words cannot tell what a sense I had, at the same time, of the dreadful mystery that he was to me. When he fell asleep of an evening, with his knotted hands clenching the sides of the easy-chair, and his bald head tattooed with deep wrinkles falling forward on his breast, I would sit and look at him, wondering what he had done, and loading him with all the crimes in the Calendar,[2] until the impulse was powerful on me to start up and fly from him. Every hour so increased my abhorrence of him, that I even think I might have yielded to this impulse in the first agonies of being so haunted, notwithstanding all he had done for me, and the risk he ran, but for the knowledge that Herbert must soon come back. Once, I actually did start out of bed in the night, and begin to dress myself in my worst clothes, hurriedly intending to leave him there with everything else I possessed, and enlist for India as a private soldier.

---

1. *jack-knife:* folding clasp-knife.
2. *all the crimes in the Calendar:* the *Newgate Calendar,* journal recounting the stories of notorious criminals, published irregularly between 1773 and 1845.

I doubt if a ghost could have been more terrible to me, up in those lonely rooms in the long evenings and long nights, with the wind and the rain always rushing by. A ghost could not have been taken and hanged on my account, and the consideration that he could be, and the dread that he would be, were no small addition to my horrors. When he was not asleep, or playing a complicated kind of Patience with a ragged pack of cards of his own — a game that I never saw before or since, and in which he recorded his winnings by sticking his jack-knife into the table — when he was not engaged in either of these pursuits, he would ask me to read to him — "Foreign language, dear boy!" While I complied, he, not comprehending a single word, would stand before the fire surveying me with the air of an Exhibitor, and I would see him, between the fingers of the hand with which I shaded my face, appealing in dumb show to the furniture to take notice of my proficiency. The imaginary student pursued by the misshapen creature he had impiously made,[1] was not more wretched than I, pursued by the creature who had made me, and recoiling from him with a stronger repulsion, the more he admired me and the fonder he was of me.

This is written of, I am sensible, as if it had lasted a year. It lasted about five days. Expecting Herbert all the time, I dared not go out, except when I took Provis for an airing after dark. At length, one evening when dinner was over and I had dropped into a slumber quite worn out — for my nights had been agitated and my rest broken by fearful dreams — I was roused by the welcome footstep on the staircase. Provis, who had been asleep too, staggered up at the noise I made, and in an instant I saw his jack-knife shining in his hand.

"Quiet! It's Herbert!" I said; and Herbert came bursting in, with the airy freshness of six hundred miles of France upon him.

"Handel, my dear fellow, how are you, and again how are you, and again how are you? I seem to have been gone a twelvemonth! Why, so I must have been, for you have grown quite thin and pale! Handel, my — Halloa! I beg your pardon."

---

1. *The imaginary student pursued by the misshapen creature he had impiously made:* a further reference to Mary Shelley's *Frankenstein* (see note on p. 248). See also Introduction pp. 17–18.

He was stopped in his running on and in his shaking hands with me, by seeing Provis. Provis, regarding him with a fixed attention, was slowly putting up his jack-knife, and groping in another pocket for something else.

"Herbert, my dear friend," said I, shutting the double doors, while Herbert stood staring and wondering, "something very strange has happened. This is — a visitor of mine."

"It's all right, dear boy!" said Provis coming forward, with his little clasped black book, and then addressing himself to Herbert. "Take it in your right hand. Lord strike you dead on the spot, if ever you split in any way sumever! Kiss it!"

"Do so, as he wishes it," I said to Herbert. So, Herbert, looking at me with a friendly uneasiness and amazement, complied, and Provis immediately shaking hands with him, said, "Now you're on your oath, you know. And never believe me on mine, if Pip shan't make a gentleman on you!"

CHAPTER II

IN VAIN should I attempt to describe the astonishment and disquiet of Herbert, when he and I and Provis sat down before the fire, and I recounted the whole of the secret. Enough, that I saw my own feelings reflected in Herbert's face, and, not least among them, my repugnance towards the man who had done so much for me.

What would alone have set a division between that man and us, if there had been no other dividing circumstance, was his triumph in my story. Saving his troublesome sense of having been "low" on one occasion since his return — on which point he began to hold forth to Herbert, the moment my revelation was finished — he had no perception of the possibility of my finding any fault with my good fortune. His boast that he had made me a gentleman, and that he had come to see me support the character on his ample resources, was made for me quite as much as for himself; and that it was a highly agreeable boast to both of us, and that we must both be very proud of it, was a conclusion quite established in his own mind.

"Though, lookee here, Pip's comrade," he said to Herbert, after having discoursed for some time, "I know very well that once since I come back — for half a minute — I've been low. I said to Pip, I knowed as I had been low. But don't you fret yourself on that score. I ain't made Pip a gentleman, and Pip ain't a going to make you a gentleman, not fur me not to know wot's due to ye both. Dear boy, and Pip's comrade, you two may count upon me always having a gen-teel muzzle on. Muzzled I have been since that half a minute when I was betrayed into lowness, muzzled I am at the present time, muzzled I ever will be."

Herbert said, "Certainly," but looked as if there were no specific consolation in this, and remained perplexed and dismayed. We were anxious for the time when he would go to his lodging, and leave us together, but he was evidently jealous of leaving us together, and sat late. It was midnight before I took him round to Essex-street, and saw him safely in at his own dark door. When it closed upon him, I experienced the first moment of relief I had known since the night of his arrival.

Never quite free from an uneasy remembrance of the man on the stairs, I had always looked about me in taking my guest out after dark, and in bringing him back; and I looked about me now. Difficult as it is in a large city to avoid the suspicion of being watched, when the mind is conscious of danger in that regard, I could not persuade myself that any of the people within sight cared about my movements. The few who were passing, passed on their several ways, and the street was empty when I turned back into the Temple. Nobody had come out at the gate with us, nobody went in at the gate with me. As I crossed by the fountain, I saw his lighted back windows looking bright and quiet, and, when I stood for a few moments in the doorway of the building where I lived, before going up the stairs, Garden-court was as still and lifeless as the staircase was when I ascended it.

Herbert received me with open arms, and I had never felt before, so blessedly, what it is to have a friend. When he had spoken some sound words of sympathy and encouragement, we sat down to consider the question, What was to be done?

The chair that Provis had occupied still remaining where it had stood — for he had a barrack way with him of hanging about one spot, in one unsettled manner, and going through one round of observances with his pipe and his negro-head and his jack-knife and his pack of cards, and what not, as if it were all put down for him on a slate — I say, his chair remaining where it had stood, Herbert unconsciously took it, but next moment started out of it, pushed it away, and took another. He had no occasion to say, after that, that he had conceived an aversion for my patron, neither had I occasion to confess my own. We interchanged that confidence without shaping a syllable.

"What," said I to Herbert, when he was safe in another chair, "what is to be done?"

"My poor dear Handel," he replied, holding his head, "I am too stunned to think."

"So was I, Herbert, when the blow first fell. Still, something must be done. He is intent upon various new expenses — horses, and carriages, and lavish appearance of all kinds. He must be stopped somehow."

"You mean that you can't accept —"

"How can I?" I interposed, as Herbert paused. "Think of him! Look at him!"

An involuntary shudder passed over both of us.

"Yet I am afraid the dreadful truth is, Herbert, that he is attached to me, strongly attached to me. Was there ever such a fate!"

"My poor dear Handel," Herbert repeated.

"Then," said I, "after all, stopping short here, never taking another penny from him, think what I owe him already! Then again: I am heavily in debt — very heavily for me, who have now no expectations — and I have been bred to no calling, and I am fit for nothing."

"Well, well, well!" Herbert remonstrated. "Don't say fit for nothing."

"What am I fit for? I know only one thing that I am fit for, and that is, to go for a soldier. And I might have gone, my dear Herbert, but for the prospect of taking counsel with your friendship and affection."

Of course I broke down there: and of course Herbert, beyond seizing a warm grip of my hand, pretended not to know it.

"Anyhow, my dear Handel," said he presently, "soldiering won't do. If you were to renounce this patronage and these favours, I suppose you would do so with some faint hope of one day repaying what you have already had. Not very strong, that hope, if you went soldiering! Besides, it's absurd. You would be infinitely better in Clarriker's house, small as it is. I am working up towards a partnership, you know."

Poor fellow! He little suspected with whose money.

"But there is another question," said Herbert. "This is an ignorant determined man, who has long had one fixed idea. More than that, he seems to me (I may misjudge him) to be a man of a desperate and fierce character."

"I know he is," I returned. "Let me tell you what evidence I have seen of it." And I told him what I had not mentioned in my narrative; of that encounter with the other convict.

"See, then," said Herbert; "think of this! He comes here at the peril of his life, for the realisation of his fixed idea. In the moment of realisation, after all his toil and waiting, you cut the ground from under his feet, destroy his idea, and make his gains worthless to him. Do you see nothing that he might do, under the disappointment?"

"I have seen it, Herbert, and dreamed of it, ever since the fatal night of his arrival. Nothing has been in my thoughts so distinctly, as his putting himself in the way of being taken."

"Then you may rely upon it," said Herbert, "that there would be great danger of his doing it. That is his power over you as long as he remains in England, and that would be his reckless course if you forsook him."

I was so struck by the horror of this idea, which had weighed upon me from the first, and the working out of which would make me regard myself, in some sort, as his murderer, that I could not rest in my chair but began pacing to and fro. I said to Herbert, meanwhile, that even if Provis were recognised and taken, in spite of himself, I should be wretched as the cause, however innocently. Yes; even though I was so wretched in having him at large and near me, and even though I would far far rather have worked at the forge all the days of my life than I would ever have come to this!

But there was no raving off* the question, What was to be done?

"The first and the main thing to be done," said Herbert, "is to get him out of England. You will have to go with him, and then he may be induced to go."

"But get him where I will, could I prevent his coming back?"

"My good Handel, is it not obvious that with Newgate in the next street, there must be far greater hazard in your breaking your mind to him and making him reckless, here, than elsewhere. If a pretext to get him away could be made out of that other convict, or out of anything else in his life, now."

"There, again!" said I, stopping before Herbert, with my open hands held out as if they contained the desperation of the case. "I know nothing of his life. It has almost made me mad to sit here of a night and see him before me, so bound up with my fortunes and misfortunes, and yet so unknown to me, except as the miserable wretch who terrified me two days in my childhood!"

Herbert got up, and linked his arm in mine, and we slowly walked to and fro together, studying the carpet.

"Handel," said Herbert, stopping, "you feel convinced that you can take no further benefits from him; do you?"

"Fully. Surely you would, too, if you were in my place?"

"And you feel convinced that you must break with him?"

"Herbert, can you ask me?"

"And you have, and are bound to have, that tenderness for the life he has risked on your account, that you must save him, if possible, from throwing it away. Then you must get him out of England before you stir a finger to extricate yourself. That done, extricate yourself, in Heaven's name, and we'll see it out together, dear old boy."

It was a comfort to shake hands upon it, and walk up and down again, with only that done.

"Now, Herbert," said I, "with reference to gaining some knowledge of his history. There is but one way that I know of. I must ask him pointblank."

"Yes. Ask him," said Herbert, "when we sit at breakfast in the morning." For, he had said, on taking leave of Herbert, that he would come to breakfast with us.

With this project formed, we went to bed. I had the wildest dreams concerning him, and woke unrefreshed; I woke, too, to recover the fear which I had lost in the night, of his being found out as a returned transport. Waking, I never lost that fear.

He came round at the appointed time, took out his jack-knife, and sat down to his meal. He was full of plans "for his gentleman's coming out strong, and like a gentleman," and urged me to begin speedily upon the pocket-book, which he had left in my possession. He considered the chambers and his own lodging as temporary residences, and advised me to look out at once for a "fashionable crib"[1] near Hyde Park, in which he could have "a shake-down."[2] When he had made an end of his breakfast, and was wiping his knife on his leg, I said to him, without a word of preface:

"After you were gone last night, I told my friend of the struggle that the soldiers found you engaged in on the marshes, when we came up. You remember?"

"Remember!" said he. "I think so!"

"We want to know something about that man — and about you. It is strange to know no more about either, and particularly you, than I was able to tell last night. Is not this as good a time as another for our knowing more?"

"Well!" he said, after consideration. "You're on your oath you know, Pip's comrade?"

"Assuredly," replied Herbert.

"As to anything I say, you know," he insisted. "The oath applies to all."

"I understand it to do so."

"And lookee here! Wotever I done, is worked out and paid for," he insisted again.

"So be it."

He took out his black pipe and was going to fill it with negro-head, when, looking at the tangle of tobacco in his hand, he seemed to think it might perplex the thread of his narrative. He put it back again, stuck his pipe in a button-hole of his coat, spread a hand on each knee, and, after turning an angry eye on the fire for a few silent moments, looked round at us and said what follows.

---

1. "*fashionable crib*": elegant dwelling (thieves' slang).
2. "*a shake-down*": temporary bed (colloquial).

CHAPTER III

"DEAR BOY and Pip's comrade. I am not a going fur to tell you my life, like a song or a story-book. But to give it you short and handy, I'll put it at once into a mouthful of English. In jail and out of jail, in jail and out of jail, in jail and out of jail. There, you've got it. That's *my* life pretty much, down to such times as I got shipped off, arter Pip stood my friend.

"I've been done everything to, pretty well — except hanged. I've been locked up, as much as a silver tea-kettle. I've been carted[1] here and carted there, and put out of this town and put out of that town, and stuck in the stocks, and whipped and worried and drove. I've no more notion where I was born, than you have — if so much. I first become aware of myself, down in Essex, a thieving turnips for my living. Summun had run away from me — a man — a tinker — and he'd took the fire with him, and left me wery cold.

"I know'd my name to be Magwitch, chrisen'd Abel. How did I know it? Much as I know'd the birds' names in the hedges to be chaffinch, sparrer, thrush. I might have thought it wos all lies together, only as the birds' names come out true, I supposed mine did.

"So fur as I could find, there warn't a soul that see young Abel Magwitch, with as little on him as in him, but wot caught fright at him, and either drove him off, or took him up. I wos took up, took up, took up, to that extent that I reg'larly grow'd up took up.

"This is the way it wos, that when I wos a ragged little creetur as much to be pitied as ever I see (not that I looked in the glass, for there warn't many insides of furnished houses known to me), I got the name of being hardened. 'This is a terrible hardened one,' they says to prison wisitors, picking out me. 'May be said to live in jails, this boy.' Then they looked at me, and I looked at them, and they measured my head,[2] some on 'em — they had better a measured my stomach — and others on 'em

---

1. *carted:* removed (carted off).
2. *measured my head:* based on the theory of phrenology originated by Gall and Spurzheim, where the physical configuration of the skull is thought to reflect mental and moral characteristics.

giv' me tracts what I couldn't read, and made me speeches wot I couldn't unnerstand. They always went on agen me about the Devil. But what the Devil wos I to do? I must put something into my stomach, mustn't I? — Howsomever, I'm a getting low, and I know wot's due. Dear boy and Pip's comrade, don't you be afeerd of me being low.

"Tramping, begging, thieving, working sometimes when I could — though that warn't as often as you may think, till you put the question whether you would ha' been over ready to give me work yourselves — a bit of a poacher, a bit of a labourer, a bit of a waggoner, a bit of a hay-maker, a bit of a hawker, a bit of most things that don't pay and lead to trouble, I got to be a man. A deserting soldier in a Travellers' Rest,[1] wot lay hid up to the chin under a lot of taturs,[2] learnt me to read; and a travelling Giant[3] wot signed his name at a penny a time learnt me to write. I warn't locked up as often now as formerly, but I wore out my good share of key-metal still.

"At Epsom races,[4] a matter of over twenty years ago, I got acquainted wi' a man whose skull I'd crack wi' this poker, like the claw of a lobster, if I'd got it on this hob. His right name was Compeyson; and that's the man, dear boy, wot you see me a pounding in the ditch, according to wot you truly told your comrade arter I was gone last night.

"He set up fur a gentleman, this Compeyson, and he'd been to a public boarding-school[5] and had learning. He was a smooth one to talk, and wos a dab at the ways of gentlefolks. He was good-looking too. It was the night afore the great race, when I found him on the heath, in a booth wot I know'd on. Him and some more was a sitting among the tables when I went in, and the landlord (which had a knowledge of me, and was a sporting one) called him out, and said, 'I think this is a man that might suit you' — meaning I was.

"Compeyson, he looks at me very noticing, and I look at him. He

---

1. *Travellers' Rest:* doss house.
2. *taturs:* potatoes (slang).
3. *a travelling Giant:* perhaps as part of a circus or freak show.
4. *Epsom races:* course for horseracing on the Surrey Downs, south-west of London.
5. *public boarding-school:* i.e., an English Public School for the sons of gentlemen.

has a watch and a chain and a ring and a breast-pin and a handsome suit of clothes.

"'To judge from appearances, you're out of luck,' says Compeyson to me.

"'Yes, master, and I've never been in it much.' (I had come out of Kingston Jail[1] last on a vagrancy committal. Not but wot it might have been for something else; but it warn't.)

"'Luck changes,' says Compeyson; 'perhaps yours is going to change.'

"I says, 'I hope it may be so. There's room.'

"'What can you do?' says Compeyson.

"'Eat and drink,' I says; 'if you'll find the materials.'

"Compeyson laughed, looked at me again very noticing, giv' me five shillings, and appinted me for next night. Same place.

"I went to Compeyson next night, same place, and Compeyson took me on to be his man and pardner. And wot was Compeyson's business in which we was to go pardners? Compeyson's business was the swindling, handwriting forging, stolen bank-note passing, and such-like. All sorts of traps as Compeyson could set with his head, and keep his own legs out of and get the profits from and let another man in for, was Compeyson's business. He'd no more heart than a iron file, he was as cold as death, and he had the head of the Devil afore mentioned.

"There was another in with Compeyson, as was called Arthur — not as being so chrisen'd, but as a surname. He was in a Decline, and wos a shadow to look at. Him and Compeyson had been in a bad thing with a rich lady some years afore, and they'd made a pot of money by it; but Compeyson betted and gamed, and he'd have run through the king's taxes. So, Arthur was a dying, and a dying poor and with the horrors on him, and Compeyson's wife (which Compeyson kicked mostly) was a having pity on him when she could, and Compeyson was a having pity on nothing and nobody.

"I might a took warning by Arthur, but I didn't; and I won't pretend I wos partick'ler — for where 'ud be the good on it, dear boy and comrade? So I begun wi' Compeyson, and a poor tool I was in his hands. Arthur lived at the top of Compeyson's house (over nigh Brentford[2] it

---

1. *Kingston Jail:* in the town on the Thames, south of Richmond.
2. *Brentford:* town on the Thames, north of Richmond.

was), and Compeyson kept a careful account agen him for board and lodging, in case he should ever get better to work it out. But Arthur soon settled the account. The second or third time as ever I see him, he come a tearing down into Compeyson's parlour late at night, in only a flannel gown, with his hair all in a sweat, and he says to Compeyson's wife, 'Sally, she really is up-stairs alonger me, now, and I can't get rid of her. She's all in white,' he says, 'wi' white flowers in her hair, and she's awful mad, and she's got a shroud hanging over her arm, and she says she'll put it on me at five in the morning.'

"Says Compeyson: 'Why, you fool, don't you know she's got a living body? And how should she be up there, without coming through the door, or in at the window, and up the stairs?'

"'I don't know how she's there,' says Arthur, shivering dreadful with the horrors, 'but she's standing in the corner at the foot of the bed, awful mad. And over where her heart's broke — *you* broke it! — there's drops of blood.'

"Compeyson spoke hardy, but he was always a coward. 'Go up alonger this drivelling sick man,' he says to his wife, 'and Magwitch, lend her a hand, will you?' But he never come nigh himself.

"Compeyson's wife and me took him up to bed agen, and he raved most dreadful. 'Why look at her!' he cries out. 'She's a shaking the shroud at me! Don't you see her? Look at her eyes! Ain't it awful to see her so mad?' Next, he cries, 'She'll put it on me, and then I'm done for! Take it away from her, take it away!' And then he catched hold of us, and kep on a talking to her, and answering of her, till I half believed I see her myself.

"Compeyson's wife, being used to him, giv' him some liquor to get the horrors off, and by-and-by he quieted. 'Oh, she's gone! Has her keeper been for her?' he says. 'Yes,' says Compeyson's wife. 'Did you tell him to lock her and bar her in?' 'Yes.' 'And to take that ugly thing away from her?' 'Yes, yes, all right.' 'You're a good creetur,' he says, 'don't leave me, wotever you do, and thank you!'

"He rested pretty quiet till it might want a few minutes of five, and then he starts up with a scream, and screams out, 'Here she is! She's got the shroud again. She's unfolding it. She's coming out of the corner. She's coming to the bed. Hold me, both on you — one of each side — don't let her touch me with it. Hah! she missed me that time. Don't let her throw it over my shoulders. Don't let her lift me up to get it round me. She's lifting me up. Keep me down!' Then he lifted himself up hard, and was dead.

"Compeyson took it easy as a good riddance for both sides. Him and me was soon busy, and first he swore me (being ever artful) on my own book — this here little black book, dear boy, wot I swore your comrade on.

"Not to go into the things that Compeyson planned, and I done — which 'ud take a week — I'll simply say to you, dear boy, and Pip's comrade, that that man got me into such nets as made me his black slave. I was always in debt to him, always under his thumb, always a working, always a getting into danger. He was younger than me, but he'd got craft, and he'd got learning, and he overmatched me five hundred times told and no mercy. My Missis[1] as I had the hard time wi' — Stop though! I ain't brought *her* in —"

He looked about him in a confused way, as if he had lost his place in the book of his remembrance; and he turned his face to the fire, and spread his hands broader on his knees, and lifted them off and put them on again.

"There ain't no need to go into it," he said, looking round once more. "The time wi' Compeyson was a'most as hard a time as ever I had; that said, all's said. Did I tell you as I was tried, alone, for misdemeanour, while with Compeyson?"

I answered, No.

"Well!" he said, "I *was*, and got convicted. As to took up on suspicion, that was twice or three times in the four or five year that it lasted; but evidence was wanting. At last, me and Compeyson was both committed for felony — on a charge of putting stolen notes in circulation — and there was other charges behind. Compeyson says to me, 'Separate defences, no communication,' and that was all. And I was so miserable poor, that I sold all the clothes I had, except wot hung on my back, afore I could get Jaggers.

"When we was put in the dock, I noticed first of all wot a gentleman Compeyson looked, wi' his curly hair and his black clothes and his white pocket-handkercher, and wot a common sort of wretch I looked. When the prosecution opened and the evidence was put short, aforehand, I no-

---

1. *Missis:* wife (slang).

ticed how heavy it all bore on me, and how light on him. When the evidence was giv' in the box, I noticed how it was always me that had come for'ard, and could be swore to, how it was always me that the money had been paid to, how it was always me that had seemed to work the thing and get the profit. But, when the defence come on, then I see the plan plainer; for, says the counsellor for Compeyson, 'My lord and gentlemen, here you has afore you, side by side, two persons as your eyes can separate wide; one, the younger, well brought up, who will be spoke to as such; one, the elder, ill brought up, who will be spoke to as such; one, the younger, seldom if ever seen in these here transactions, and only suspected; t'other, the elder, always seen in 'em and always wi' his guilt brought home. Can you doubt, if there is but one in it, which is the one, and, if there is two in it, which is much the worst one?' And such-like. And when it come to character, warn't it Compeyson as had been to the school, and warn't it his schoolfellows as was in this position and in that, and warn't it him as had been know'd by witnesses in such clubs and societies, and nowt to his disadvantage? And warn't it me as had been tried afore, and as had been know'd up hill and down dale in Bridewells and Lock-Ups?[1] And when it come to speech-making, warn't it Compeyson as could speak to 'em wi' his face dropping every now and then into his white pocket-handkercher — ah! and wi' verses in his speech, too — and warn't it me as could only say, 'Gentlemen, this man at my side is a most precious rascal'? And when the verdict come, warn't it Compeyson as was recommended to mercy on account of good character and bad company, and giving up all the information he could agen me, and warn't it me as got never a word but Guilty? And when I says to Compeyson, 'Once out of this court, I'll smash that face o' yourn!' ain't it Compeyson as prays the Judge to be protected, and gets two turnkeys stood betwixt us? And when we're sentenced, ain't it him as gets seven year, and me fourteen,[2] and ain't it him as the Judge is sorry for, because he might a done so well, and ain't it me

---

1. *Bridewells and Lock-Ups:* prisons (the original Bridewell Prison, in London just to the west of the Temple, survived until 1863).

2. *And when we're sentenced, ain't it him as gets seven year, and me fourteen:* the terms of sentences to transportation were then seven years, fourteen years, or life.

as the Judge perceives to be a old offender of wiolent passion, likely to come to worse?"

He had worked himself into a state of great excitement, but he checked it, took two or three short breaths, swallowed as often, and stretching out his hand towards me said, in a reassuring manner, "I ain't a going to be low, dear boy!"

He had so heated himself that he took out his handkerchief and wiped his face and head and neck and hands, before he could go on.

"I had said to Compeyson that I'd smash that face of his, and I swore Lord smash mine! to do it. We was in the same prison-ship, but I couldn't get at him for long, though I tried. At last I come behind him and hit him on the cheek to turn him round and get a smashing one at him, when I was seen and seized. The black-hole of that ship warn't a strong one, to a judge of black-holes that could swim and dive. I escaped to the shore, and I was a hiding among the graves there, envying them as was in 'em and all over, when I first see my boy!"

He regarded me with a look of affection that made him almost abhorrent to me again, though I had felt great pity for him.

"By my boy, I was giv' to unnerstand as Compeyson was out on them marshes too. Upon my soul, I half believe he escaped in his terror, to get quit of me, not knowing it was me as had got ashore. I hunted him down. I smashed his face. 'And now,' says I, 'as the worst thing I can do, caring nothing for myself, I'll drag you back.' And I'd have swum off, towing him by the hair, if it had come to that, and I'd a got him aboard without the soldiers.

"Of course he'd much the best of it to the last — his character was so good. He had escaped when he was made half wild by me and my murderous intentions; and his punishment was light. I was put in irons, brought to trial again, and sent for life. I didn't stop for life, dear boy and Pip's comrade, being here."

He wiped himself again, as he had done before, and then slowly took his tangle of tobacco from his pocket, and plucked his pipe from his button-hole, and slowly filled it, and began to smoke.

"Is he dead?" I asked, after a silence.

"Is who dead, dear boy?"

"Compeyson."

"He hopes *I* am, if he's alive, you may be sure," with a fierce look. "I never heerd no more of him."

Herbert had been writing with his pencil in the cover of a book. He soft'ı pushed the book over to me, as Provis stood smoking with his eyes on the fire, and I read in it:

"Young Havisham's name was Arthur. Compeyson is the man who professed to be Miss Havisham's lover."

I shut the book and nodded slightly to Herbert, and put the book by; but we neither of us said anything, and both looked at Provis as he stood smoking by the fire.

CHAPTER IV

WHY SHOULD I pause to ask how much of my shrinking from Provis might be traced to Estella? Why should I loiter on my road, to compare the state of mind in which I had tried to rid myself of the stain of the prison before meeting her at the coach-office, with the state of mind in which I now reflected on the abyss between Estella in her pride and beauty, and the returned transport whom I harboured? The road would be none the smoother for it, the end would be none the better for it, he would not be helped, nor I extenuated.

A new fear had been engendered in my mind by his narrative; or rather, his narrative had given form and purpose to the fear that was already there. If Compeyson were alive and should discover his return, I could hardly doubt the consequence. That, Compeyson stood in mortal fear of him, neither of the two could know much better than I; and that, any such man as that man had been described to be, would hesitate to release himself for good from a dreaded enemy by the safe means of becoming an informer, was scarcely to be imagined.

Never had I breathed, and never would I breathe — or so I resolved — a word of Estella to Provis. But, I said to Herbert that before I could go abroad, I must see both Estella and Miss Havisham. This was when we were left alone on the night of the day when Provis told us his story. I resolved to go out to Richmond next day, and I went.

On my presenting myself at Mrs. Brandley's, Estella's maid was called to tell me that Estella had gone into the country. Where? To Satis House, as usual. Not as usual, I said, for she had never yet gone there without me; when was she coming back? There was an air of reservation in the answer which increased my perplexity, and the answer was, that her maid believed she was only coming back at all for a little while. I could make nothing of this, except that it was meant that I should make nothing of it, and I went home again in complete discomfiture.

Another night-consultation with Herbert after Provis was gone home (I always took him home, and always looked well about me), led us to the conclusion that nothing should be said about going abroad until I came back from Miss Havisham's. In the meantime, Herbert and I were to consider separately what it would be best to say; whether we should devise any pretence of being afraid that he was under suspicious observation; or whether I, who had never yet been abroad, should propose an expedition. We both knew that I had but to propose anything, and he would consent. We agreed that his remaining many days in his present hazard was not to be thought of.

Next day, I had the meanness to feign that I was under a binding promise to go down to Joe; but I was capable of almost any meanness towards Joe or his name. Provis was to be strictly careful while I was gone, and Herbert was to take the charge of him that I had taken. I was to be absent only one night, and, on my return, the gratification of his impatience for my starting as a gentleman on a greater scale, was to be begun. It occurred to me then, and as I afterwards found to Herbert also, that he might be best got away across the water, on that pretence — as, to make purchases, or the like.

Having thus cleared the way for my expedition to Miss Havisham's, I set off by the early morning coach before it was yet light, and was out on the open country-road when the day came creeping on, halting and whimpering and shivering, and wrapped in patches of clouds and rags of mist, like a beggar. When we drove up to the Blue Boar after a drizzly ride, whom should I see come out under the gateway, toothpick in hand, to look at the coach, but Bentley Drummle!

As he pretended not to see me, I pretended not to see him. It was a very lame pretence on both sides; the lamer, because we both went into the coffee-room, where he had just finished his breakfast, and where I ordered mine. It was poisonous to me to see him in the town, for I very well knew why he had come there.

Pretending to read a smeary newspaper long out of date, which had nothing half so legible in its local news, as the foreign matter of coffee, pickles, fish sauces, gravy, melted butter, and wine, with which it was sprinkled all over, as if it had taken the measles in a highly irregular form, I sat at my table while he stood before the fire. By degrees it became an enormous injury to me that he stood before the fire, and I got up, determined to have my share of it. I had to put my hands behind his legs for the poker when I went up to the fireplace to stir the fire, but still pretended not to know him.

"Is this a cut?" said Mr. Drummle.

"Oh!" said I, poker in hand; "it's you, is it? How do you do? I was wondering who it was, who kept the fire off."

With that, I poked tremendously, and having done so, planted myself side by side with Mr. Drummle, my shoulders squared and my back to the fire.

"You have just come down?" said Mr. Drummle, edging me a little away with his shoulder.

"Yes," said I, edging *him* a little away with *my* shoulder.

"Beastly place," said Drummle. — "Your part of the country, I think?"

"Yes," I assented. "I am told it's very like your Shropshire."*

"Not in the least like it," said Drummle.

Here Mr. Drummle looked at his boots, and I looked at mine, and then Mr. Drummle looked at my boots, and I looked at his.

"Have you been here long?" I asked, determined not to yield an inch of the fire.

"Long enough to be tired of it," returned Drummle, pretending to yawn, but equally determined.

"Do you stay here long?"

"Can't say," answered Mr. Drummle. "Do you?"

"Can't say," said I.

I felt here, through a tingling in my blood, that if Mr. Drummle's shoulder had claimed another hair's breadth of room, I should have jerked him into the window; equally, that if my own shoulder had urged a similar claim, Mr. Drummle would have jerked me into the nearest box. He whistled a little. So did I.

"Large tract of marshes about here, I believe?" said Drummle.

"Yes. What of that?" said I.

Mr. Drummle looked at me, and then at my boots, and then said, "Oh!" and laughed.

"Are you amused, Mr. Drummle?"

"No," said he, "not particularly. I am going out for a ride in the saddle. I mean to explore those marshes for amusement. Out-of-the-way villages there, they tell me. Curious little public-houses — and smithies — and that. Waiter!"

"Yes, sir."

"Is that horse of mine ready?"

"Brought round to the door, sir."

"I say. Look here, you sir. The lady won't ride to-day; the weather won't do."

"Very good, sir."

"And I don't dine, because I'm going to dine at the lady's."

"Very good, sir."

Then, Drummle glanced at me, with an insolent triumph on his greatjowled face that cut me to the heart, dull as he was, and so exasperated me, that I felt inclined to take him in my arms (as the robber in the storybook is said to have taken the old lady),[1] and seat him on the fire.

One thing was manifest to both of us, and that was, that until relief came, neither of us could relinquish the fire. There we stood, well squared up before it, shoulder to shoulder and foot to foot, with our hands behind us, not budging an inch. The horse was visible outside in the drizzle at the door, my breakfast was put on table, Drummle's was cleared away, the waiter invited me to begin, I nodded, we both stood our ground.

"Have you been to the Grove since?" said Drummle.

"No," said I, "I had quite enough of the Finches the last time I was there."

---

1. *as the robber in the story-book is said to have taken the old lady:* told in the *Newgate Calendar* of the highwayman and folk-hero Dick Turpin, hung in 1739.

"Was that when we had a difference of opinion?"

"Yes," I replied, very shortly.

"Come, come! They let you off easily enough," sneered Drummle. "You shouldn't have lost your temper."

"Mr. Drummle," said I, "you are not competent to give advice on that subject. When I lose my temper (not that I admit having done so on that occasion), I don't throw glasses."

"I do," said Drummle.

After glancing at him once or twice, in an increased state of smouldering ferocity, I said:

"Mr. Drummle, I did not seek this conversation, and I don't think it an agreeable one."

"I am sure it's not," said he, superciliously over his shoulder; "I don't think anything about it."

"And therefore," I went on, "with your leave, I will suggest that we hold no kind of communication in future."

"Quite my opinion," said Drummle, "and what I should have suggested myself, or done — more likely — without suggesting. But don't lose your temper. Haven't you lost enough without that?"

"What do you mean, sir?"

"Wai-ter!" said Drummle, by way of answering me.

The waiter reappeared.

"Look here, you sir. You quite understand that the young lady don't ride to-day, and that I dine at the young lady's?"

"Quite so, sir!"

When the waiter had felt my fast-cooling tea-pot with the palm of his hand, and had looked imploringly at me, and had gone out, Drummle, careful not to move the shoulder next me, took a cigar from his pocket and bit the end off, but showed no sign of stirring. Choking and boiling as I was, I felt that we could not go a word further, without introducing Estella's name, which I could not endure to hear him utter; and therefore I looked stonily at the opposite wall, as if there were no one present, and forced myself to silence. How long we might have remained in this ridiculous position it is impossible to say, but for the incursion of three thriving farmers — laid on by the waiter, I think — who came into the coffee-room unbuttoning their great-coats and rubbing their hands, and before whom, as they charged at the fire, we were obliged to give way.

I saw him through the window, seizing his horse's mane, and mounting in his blundering brutal manner, and sidling and backing away. I thought he was gone, when he came back, calling for a light for the cigar in his mouth, which he had forgotten. A man in a dust-coloured dress appeared with what was wanted — I could not have said from where: whether from the inn yard, or the street, or where not — and as Drummle leaned down from the saddle and lighted his cigar and laughed, with a jerk of his head towards the coffee-room windows, the slouching shoulders and ragged hair of this man, whose back was towards me, reminded me of Orlick.

Too heavily out of sorts to care much at the time whether it were he or no, or after all to touch the breakfast, I washed the weather and the journey from my face and hands, and went out to the memorable old house that it would have been so much the better for me never to have entered, never to have seen.

CHAPTER V

IN THE room where the dressing-table stood, and where the wax candles burnt on the wall, I found Miss Havisham and Estella; Miss Havisham seated on a settee near the fire, and Estella on a cushion at her feet. Estella was knitting, and Miss Havisham was looking on. They both raised their eyes as I went in, and both saw an alteration in me. I derived that, from the look they interchanged.

"And what wind," said Miss Havisham, "blows you here, Pip?"

Though she looked steadily at me, I saw that she was rather confused. Estella, pausing for a moment in her knitting with her eyes upon me, and then going on, I fancied that I read in the action of her fingers, as plainly as if she had told me in the dumb alphabet, that she perceived I had discovered my real benefactor.

"Miss Havisham," said I, "I went to Richmond yesterday, to speak to Estella; and finding that some wind had blown *her* here, I followed."

Miss Havisham motioning to me for the third or fourth time to sit down, I took the chair by the dressing-table, which I had often seen her occupy. With all that ruin at my feet and about me, it seemed a natural place for me, that day.

"What I had to say to Estella, Miss Havisham, I will say before you, presently — in a few moments. It will not surprise you, it will not displease you. I am as unhappy as you can ever have meant me to be."

Miss Havisham continued to look steadily at me. I could see in the action of Estella's fingers as they worked, that she attended to what I said: but she did not look up.

"I have found out who my patron is. It is not a fortunate discovery, and is not likely ever to enrich me in reputation, station, fortune, anything. There are reasons why I must say no more of that. It is not my secret, but another's."

As I was silent for a while, looking at Estella and considering how to go on, Miss Havisham repeated, "It is not your secret, but another's. Well?"

"When you first caused me to be brought here, Miss Havisham; when I belonged to the village over yonder, that I wish I had never left; I suppose I did really come here, as any other chance boy might have come — as a kind of servant, to gratify a want or a whim, and to be paid for it?"

"Ay, Pip," replied Miss Havisham, steadily nodding her head; "you did."

"And that Mr. Jaggers —"

"Mr. Jaggers," said Miss Havisham, taking me up in a firm tone, "had nothing to do with it, and knew nothing of it. His being my lawyer, and his being the lawyer of your patron, is a coincidence. He holds the same relation towards numbers of people, and it might easily arise. Be that as it may, it did arise, and was not brought about by any one."

Any one might have seen in her haggard face that there was no suppression or evasion so far.

"But when I fell into the mistake I have so long remained in, at least you led me on?" said I.

"Yes," she returned, again nodding steadily, "I let you go on."

"Was that kind?"

"Who am I," cried Miss Havisham, striking her stick upon the floor and flashing into wrath so suddenly that Estella glanced up at her in surprise, "who am I, for God's sake, that I should be kind!"

It was a weak complaint to have made, and I had not meant to make it. I told her so, as she sat brooding after this outburst.

"Well, well, well!" she said. "What else?"

"I was liberally paid for my old attendance here," I said, to soothe her, "in being apprenticed, and I have asked these questions only for my own information. What follows has another (and I hope more disinterested) purpose. In humouring my mistake, Miss Havisham, you punished — practised on — perhaps you will supply whatever term expresses your intention, without offence — your self-seeking relations?"

"I did. Why, they would have it so! So would you. What has been my history, that I should be at the pains of entreating either them, or you, not to have it so! You made your own snares. *I* never made them."

Waiting until she was quiet again — for this, too, flashed out of her in a wild and sudden way — I went on.

"I have been thrown among one family of your relations, Miss Havisham, and have been constantly among them since I went to London. I know them to have been as honestly under my delusion as I myself. And I should be false and base if I did not tell you, whether it is acceptable to you or no, and whether you are inclined to give credence to it or no, that you deeply wrong both Mr. Matthew Pocket and his son Herbert, if you suppose them to be otherwise than generous, upright, open, and incapable of anything designing or mean."

"They are your friends," said Miss Havisham.

"They made themselves my friends," said I, "when they supposed me to have superseded them; and when Sarah Pocket, Miss Georgiana, and Mistress Camilla, were not my friends, I think."

This contrasting of them with the rest seemed, I was glad to see, to do them good with her. She looked at me keenly for a little while, and then said quietly:

"What do you want for them?"

"Only," said I, "that you would not confound them with the others. They may be of the same blood, but, believe me, they are not of the same nature."

Still looking at me keenly, Miss Havisham repeated:

"What do you want for them?"

"I am not so cunning, you see," I said, in answer, conscious that I reddened a little, "as that I could hide from you, even if I desired, that I do want something. Miss Havisham, if you would spare the money to do my friend Herbert a lasting service in life, but which from the nature of the case must be done without his knowledge, I could show you how."

"Why must it be done without his knowledge?" she asked, settling her hands upon her stick, that she might regard me the more attentively.

"Because," said I, "I began the service myself, more than two years ago, without his knowledge, and I don't want to be betrayed. Why I fail in my ability to finish it, I cannot explain. It is a part of the secret which is another person's and not mine."

She gradually withdrew her eyes from me, and turned them on the fire. After watching it for what appeared in the silence and by the light of the slowly wasting candles to be a long time, she was roused by the collapse of some of the red coals, and looked towards me again — at first, vacantly — then, with a gradually concentrating attention. All this time, Estella knitted on. When Miss Havisham had fixed her attention on me, she said, speaking as if there had been no lapse in our dialogue:

"What else?"

"Estella," said I, turning to her now, and trying to command my trembling voice, "you know I love you. You know that I have loved you long and dearly."

She raised her eyes to my face, on being thus addressed, and her fingers plied their work, and she looked at me with an unmoved countenance. I saw that Miss Havisham glanced from me to her, and from her to me.

"I should have said this sooner, but for my long mistake. It induced me to hope that Miss Havisham meant us for one another. While I thought you could not help yourself, as it were, I refrained from saying it. But I must say it now."

Preserving her unmoved countenance, and with her fingers still going, Estella shook her head.

"I know," said I, in answer to that action; "I know. I have no hope that I shall ever call you mine, Estella. I am ignorant what may become of me very soon, how poor I may be, or where I may go. Still, I love you. I have loved you ever since I first saw you in this house."

Looking at me perfectly unmoved and with her fingers busy, she shook her head again.

"It would have been cruel in Miss Havisham, horribly cruel, to practise on the susceptibility of a poor boy, and to torture me through all these years with a vain hope and an idle pursuit, if she had reflected on the gravity of what she did. But I think she did not. I think that in the endurance of her own trial, she forgot mine, Estella."

I saw Miss Havisham put her hand to her heart and hold it there, as she sat looking by turns at Estella and at me.

"It seems," said Estella, very calmly, "that there are sentiments, fancies — I don't know how to call them — which I am not able to comprehend. When you say you love me, I know what you mean, as a form of words; but nothing more. You address nothing in my breast, you touch nothing there. I don't care for what you say at all. I have tried to warn you of this; now, have I not?"

I said in a miserable manner, "Yes."

"Yes. But you would not be warned, for you thought I did not mean it. Now, did you not think so?"

"I thought and hoped you could not mean it. You, so young, untried, and beautiful, Estella! Surely it is not in Nature."

"It is in *my* nature," she returned. And then she added, with a stress upon the words, "It is in the nature formed within me. I make a great difference between you and all other people when I say so much. I can do no more."

"Is it not true," said I, "that Bentley Drummle is in town here, and pursuing you?"

"It is quite true," she replied, referring to him with the indifference of utter contempt.

"That you encourage him, and ride out with him, and that he dines with you this very day?"

She seemed a little surprised that I should know it, but again replied, "Quite true."

"You cannot love him, Estella!"

Her fingers stopped for the first time, as she retorted rather angrily, "What have I told you? Do you still think, in spite of it, that I do not mean what I say?"

"You would never marry him, Estella?"

She looked towards Miss Havisham, and considered for a moment with her work in her hands. Then she said, "Why not tell you the truth? I am going to be married to him."

I dropped my face into my hands, but was able to control myself better than I could have expected, considering what agony it gave me to hear her say those words. When I raised my face again, there was such a ghastly look upon Miss Havisham's, that it impressed me, even in my passionate hurry and grief.

"Estella, dearest dearest Estella, do not let Miss Havisham lead you into this fatal step. Put me aside for ever — you have done so, I well know — but bestow yourself on some worthier person than Drummle. Miss Havisham gives you to him, as the greatest slight and injury that could be done to the many far better men who admire you, and to the few who truly love you. Among those few, there may be one who loves you even as dearly, though he has not loved you as long, as I. Take him, and I can bear it better, for your sake!"

My earnestness awoke a wonder in her that seemed as if it would have been touched with compassion, if she could have rendered me at all intelligible to her own mind.

"I am going," she said again, in a gentler voice, "to be married to him. The preparations for my marriage are making, and I shall be married soon. Why do you injuriously introduce the name of my mother by adoption? It is my own act."

"Your own act, Estella, to fling yourself away upon a brute?"

"On whom should I fling myself away?" she retorted, with a smile. "Should I fling myself away upon the man who would the soonest feel (if people do feel such things) that I took nothing to him? There! It is done. I shall do well enough, and so will my husband. As to leading me into what you call this fatal step, Miss Havisham would have had me wait, and not marry yet; but I am tired of the life I have led, which has very few charms for me, and I am willing enough to change it. Say no more. We shall never understand each other."

"Such a mean brute, such a stupid brute!" I urged in despair.

"Don't be afraid of my being a blessing to him," said Estella; "I shall not be that. Come! Here is my hand. Do we part on this, you visionary boy — or man?"

"O Estella!" I answered, as my bitter tears fell fast on her hand, do what I would to restrain them; "even if I remained in England and could hold my head up with the rest, how could I see you Drummle's wife!"

"Nonsense," she returned, "nonsense. This will pass in no time."

"Never, Estella!"

"You will get me out of your thoughts in a week."

"Out of my thoughts! You are part of my existence, part of myself. You have been in every line I have ever read, since I first came here, the rough common boy whose poor heart you wounded even then. You have been in every prospect I have ever seen since — on the river, on the sails of the ships, on the marshes, in the clouds, in the light, in the darkness, in the wind, in the woods, in the sea, in the streets. You have been the embodiment of every graceful fancy that my mind has ever become acquainted with. The stones of which the strongest London buildings are made, are not more real, or more impossible to be displaced by your hands, than your presence and influence have been to me, there and everywhere, and will be. Estella, to the last hour of my life, you cannot choose but remain part of my character, part of the little good in me, part of the evil. But, in this separation I associate you only with the good, and I will faithfully hold you to that always, for you must have done me far more good than harm, let me feel now what sharp distress I may. O God bless you, God forgive you!"

In what ecstasy of unhappiness I got these broken words out of myself, I don't know. The rhapsody welled up within me, like blood from an inward wound, and gushed out. I held her hand to my lips some lingering moments, and so I left her. But ever afterwards, I remembered — and soon afterwards with stronger reason — that while Estella looked at me merely with incredulous wonder, the spectral figure of Miss Havisham, her hand still covering her heart, seemed all resolved into a ghastly stare of pity and remorse.

All done, all gone! So much was done and gone, that when I went out at the gate, the light of the day seemed of a darker colour than when I went in. For a while, I hid myself among some lanes and by-paths, and then struck off to walk all the way to London. For, I had by that time come to myself so far, as to consider that I could not go back to the inn and see Drummle there; that I could not bear to sit upon the coach and be spoken to; that I could do nothing half so good for myself as tire myself out.

It was past midnight when I crossed London Bridge. Pursuing the narrow intricacies of the streets which at that time tended westward near the Middlesex shore of the river, my readiest access to the Temple was close by the river-side, through Whitefriars. I was not expected till tomorrow, but I had my keys, and, if Herbert were gone to bed, could get to bed myself without disturbing him.

As it seldom happened that I came in at that Whitefriars gate after the Temple was closed, and as I was very muddy and weary, I did not take it ill that the night-porter examined me with much attention as he held the gate a little way open for me to pass in. To help his memory I mentioned my name.

"I was not quite sure, sir, but I thought so. Here's a note, sir. The messenger that brought it, said would you be so good as read it by my lantern?"

Much surprised by the request, I took the note. It was directed to Philip Pip, Esquire, and on the top of the superscription were the words, "PLEASE READ THIS, HERE." I opened it, the watchman holding up his light, and read inside, in Wemmick's writing:

"DON'T GO HOME."

CHAPTER VI

TURNING FROM the Temple gate as soon as I had read the warning, I made the best of my way to Fleet-street, and there got a late hackney chariot and drove to the Hummums in Covent Garden.[1] In those times a bed was always to be got there at any hour of the night, and the chamberlain, letting me in at his ready wicket, lighted the candle next in order on his shelf, and showed me straight into the bedroom next in order on his list. It was a sort of vault on the ground floor at the back, with a despotic

---

1. *the Hummums in Covent Garden:* large run-down hotel in the south-east corner of the market place, named for a Turkish bath which used to occupy the site, and scene of a ghost-story recounted in James Boswell's *Life of Samuel Johnson* (1791).

monster of a four-post bedstead in it, straddling over the whole place, putting one of his arbitrary legs into the fireplace and another into the doorway, and squeezing the wretched little washing-stand in quite a Divinely Righteous manner.[1]

As I had asked for a night-light, the chamberlain had brought me in, before he left me, the good old constitutional rushlight[2] of those virtuous days — an object like the ghost of a walking-cane, which instantly broke its back if it were touched, which nothing could ever be lighted at, and which was placed in solitary confinement at the bottom of a high tin tower, perforated with round holes that made a staringly wide-awake pattern on the walls. When I had got into bed, and lay there footsore, weary, and wretched, I found that I could no more close my own eyes than I could close the eyes of this foolish Argus.[3] And thus, in the gloom and death of the night, we stared at one another.

What a doleful night! How anxious, how dismal, how long! There was an inhospitable smell in the room, of cold soot and hot dust; and, as I looked up into the corners of the tester[4] over my head, I thought what a number of bluebottle flies from the butchers', and earwigs from the market, and grubs from the country, must be holding on up there, lying by for next summer. This led me to speculate whether any of them ever tumbled down, and then I fancied that I felt light falls on my face — a disagreeable turn of thought, suggesting other and more objectionable approaches up my back. When I had lain awake a little while, those extraordinary voices with which silence teems, began to make themselves audible. The closet whispered, the fireplace sighed, the little washing-stand ticked, and one guitar-string played occasionally in the chest of drawers. At about the same time, the eyes on the wall acquired a new expression, and in every one of those staring rounds I saw written, DON'T GO HOME.

---

1. *in quite a Divinely Righteous manner:* assuming arbitary and absolute power, by comic analogy with the "Divine Right" of kings, the idea that the sanction to rule comes from God rather than man.
2. *rushlight:* a cheap candle made from a reed dipped in grease and stood in a perforated cyclindrical container.
3. *Argus:* many-eyed monster of Greek mythology.
4. *tester:* the canopy of a four-poster bed.

Whatever night-fancies and night-noises crowded on me, they never warded off this DON'T GO HOME. It plaited itself into whatever I thought of, as a bodily pain would have done. Not long before, I had read in the newspapers, how a gentleman unknown had come to the Hummums in the night, and had gone to bed, and had destroyed himself, and had been found in the morning weltering in blood. It came into my head that he must have occupied this very vault of mine, and I got out of bed to assure myself that there were no red marks about; then opened the door to look out into the passages, and cheer myself with the companionship of a distant light, near which I knew the chamberlain to be dozing. But all this time, why I was not to go home, and what had happened at home, and when I should go home, and whether Provis was safe at home, were questions occupying my mind so busily, that one might have supposed there could be no more room in it for any other theme. Even when I thought of Estella, and how we had parted that day for ever, and when I recalled all the circumstances of our parting and all her looks and tones, and the action of her fingers while she knitted — even then I was pursuing, here and there and everywhere, the caution Don't go home. When at last I dozed, in sheer exhaustion of mind and body, it became a vast shadowy verb which I had to conjugate. Imperative mood, present tense: Do not thou go home, let him not go home, let us not go home, do not ye or you go home, let not them go home. Then, potentially: I may not and I cannot go home; and I might not, could not, would not, and should not go home; until I felt that I was going distracted, and rolled over on the pillow, and looked at the staring rounds upon the wall again.

I had left directions that I was to be called at seven; for it was plain that I must see Wemmick before seeing any one else, and equally plain that this was a case in which his Walworth sentiments, only, could be taken. It was a relief to get out of the room where the night had been so miserable, and I needed no second knocking at the door to startle me from my uneasy bed.

The Castle battlements arose upon my view at eight o'clock. The little servant happening to be entering the fortress with two hot rolls, I passed through the postern and crossed the drawbridge, in her company, and so came without announcement into the presence of Wemmick as he was making tea for himself and the Aged. An open door afforded a perspective view of the Aged in bed.

"Halloa, Mr. Pip!" said Wemmick. "You did come home, then?"

"Yes," I returned; "but I didn't go home."

"That's all right," said he, rubbing his hands. "I left a note for you at each of the Temple gates, on the chance. Which gate did you come to?"

I told him.

"I'll go round to the others in the course of the day and destroy the notes," said Wemmick; "it's a good rule never to leave documentary evidence if you can help it, because you don't know when it may be put in. I'm going to take a liberty with you. — *Would* you mind toasting this sausage for the Aged P.?"

I said I should be delighted to do it.

"Then you can go about your work, Mary Anne," said Wemmick to the little servant; "which leaves us to ourselves, don't you see, Mr. Pip?" he added, winking, as she disappeared.

I thanked him for his friendship and caution, and our discourse proceeded in a low tone, while I toasted the Aged's sausage and he buttered the crumb of the Aged's roll.

"Now, Mr. Pip, you know," said Wemmick, "you and I understand one another. We are in our private and personal capacities, and we have been engaged in a confidential transaction before to-day. Official sentiments are one thing. We are extra official."

I cordially assented. I was so very nervous, that I had already lighted the Aged's sausage like a torch, and been obliged to blow it out.

"I accidentally heard, yesterday morning," said Wemmick, "being in a certain place where I once took you — even between you and me, it's as well not to mention names when avoidable —"

"Much better not," said I. "I understand you."

"I heard there by chance, yesterday morning," said Wemmick, "that a certain person not altogether of uncolonial pursuits, and not unpossessed of portable property — I don't know who it may really be — we won't name this person —"

"Not necessary," said I.

"— had made some little stir in a certain part of the world where a good many people go, not always in gratification of their own inclinations, and not quite irrespective of the government expense —"

In watching his face, I made quite a firework of the Aged's sausage, and greatly discomposed both my own attention and Wemmick's; for which I apologised.

"— by disappearing from such place, and being no more heard of thereabouts. From which," said Wemmick, "conjectures had been raised and theories formed. I also heard that you at your chambers in Garden-court, Temple, had been watched, and might be watched again."

"By whom?" said I.

"I wouldn't go into that," said Wemmick, evasively, "it might clash with official responsibilities. I heard it, as I have in my time heard other curious things in the same place. I don't tell it you on information received. I heard it."

He took the toasting-fork and sausage from me as he spoke, and set forth the Aged's breakfast neatly on a little tray. Previous to placing it before him, he went into the Aged's room with a clean white cloth, and tied the same under the old gentleman's chin, and propped him up, and put his nightcap on one side, and gave him quite a rakish air. Then, he placed his breakfast before him with great care, and said, "All right, ain't you, Aged P.?" To which the cheerful Aged replied, "All right, John, my boy, all right!" As there seemed to be a tacit understanding that the Aged was not in a presentable state, and was therefore to be considered invisible, I made a pretence of being in complete ignorance of these proceedings.

"This watching of me at my chambers (which I have once had reason to suspect)," I said to Wemmick when he came back, "is inseparable from the person to whom you have adverted; is it?"

Wemmick looked very serious. "I couldn't undertake to say that, of my own knowledge. I mean, I couldn't undertake to say it was at first. But it either is, or it will be, or it's in great danger of being."

As I saw that he was restrained by fealty to Little Britain from saying as much as he could, and as I knew with thankfulness to him how far out of his way he went to say what he did, I could not press him. But I told him, after a little meditation over the fire, that I would like to ask him a question, subject to his answering or not answering, as he deemed right, and sure that his course would be right. He paused in his breakfast, and crossing his arms, and pinching his shirt-sleeves (his notion of in-door comfort was to sit without any coat), he nodded to me once, to put my question.

"You have heard of a man of bad character, whose true name is Compeyson?"

He answered with one other nod.

"Is he living?"

One other nod.

"Is he in London?"

He gave me one other nod, compressed the post-office exceedingly, gave me one last nod, and went on with his breakfast.

"Now" said Wemmick, "questioning being over;" which he emphasised and repeated for my guidance; "I come to what I did, after hearing what I heard. I went to Garden-court to find you; not finding you, I went to Clarriker's to find Mr. Herbert."

"And him you found?" said I, with great anxiety.

"And him I found. Without mentioning any names or going into any details, I gave him to understand that if he was aware of anybody — Tom, Jack, or Richard — being about the chambers, or about the immediate neighbourhood, he had better get Tom, Jack, or Richard, out of the way while you were out of the way."

"He would be greatly puzzled what to do?"

"He *was* puzzled what to do; not the less, because I gave him my opinion that it was not safe to try to get Tom, Jack, or Richard, too far out of the way at present. Mr. Pip, I'll tell you something. Under existing circumstances there is no place like a great city when you are once in it. Don't break cover too soon. Lie close. Wait till things slacken, before you try the open, even for foreign air."

I thanked him for his valuable advice, and asked him what Herbert had done?

"Mr. Herbert," said Wemmick, "after being all of a heap for half an hour, struck out a plan. He mentioned to me as a secret, that he is courting a young lady who has, as no doubt you are aware, a bedridden Pa. Which Pa, having been in the Purser line of life, lies a-bed in a bow-window where he can see the ships sail up and down the river. You are acquainted with the young lady, most probably?"

"Not personally," said I.

The truth was, that she had objected to me as an expensive companion who did Herbert no good, and that, when Herbert had first proposed to present me to her, she had received the proposal with such very moderate warmth, that Herbert had felt himself obliged to confide the state of the case to me, with a view to the lapse of a little time before I made her acquaintance. When I had begun to advance Herbert's prospects by stealth, I had been able to bear this with cheerful philosophy; he and his affianced, for their part, had naturally not been very anxious to introduce a third person into their interviews; and thus, although I was assured that I had risen in Clara's esteem, and although the young lady and I had long regularly interchanged messages and remembrances by Herbert, I had never seen her. However, I did not trouble Wemmick with these particulars.

"The house with the bow-window," said Wemmick, "being by the river-side, down the Pool there between Limehouse and Greenwich,* and being kept, it seems, by a very respectable widow who has a furnished upper floor to let, Mr. Herbert put it to me, what did I think of that as a temporary tenement for Tom, Jack, or Richard? Now, I thought very well of it, for three reasons I'll give you. That is to say. Firstly. It's altogether out of all your beats, and is well away from the usual heap of streets great and small. Secondly. Without going near it yourself, you could always hear of the safety of Tom, Jack, or Richard, through Mr. Herbert. Thirdly. After a while and when it might be prudent, if you should want to slip Tom, Jack, or Richard, on board a foreign packet-boat, there he is — ready."

Much comforted by these considerations, I thanked Wemmick again and again, and begged him to proceed.

"Well, sir! Mr. Herbert threw himself into the business with a will, and by nine o'clock last night he housed Tom, Jack, or Richard — whichever it may be — you and I don't want to know — quite successfully. At the old lodgings it was understood that he was summoned to Dover, and in fact he was taken down the Dover road and cornered out of it. Now, another great advantage of all this, is, that it was done without you, and when, if any one was concerning himself about your movements, you must be known to be ever so many miles off and quite otherwise engaged. This diverts suspicion and confuses it; and for the same reason I recommended that even if you came back last night, you should not go home. It brings in more confusion, and you want confusion."

Wemmick, having finished his breakfast, here looked at his watch, and began to get his coat on.

"And now, Mr. Pip," said he, with his hands still in the sleeves, "I have probably done the most I can do; but if I can ever do more — from a Walworth point of view, and in a strictly private and personal capacity — I shall be glad to do it. Here's the address. There can be no harm in your going here to-night and seeing for yourself that all is well with Tom, Jack, or Richard, before you go home — which is another reason for your not going home last night. But after you have gone home, don't go back here. You are very welcome, I am sure, Mr. Pip;" his hands were now out of his sleeves, and I was shaking them; "and let me finally impress one important point upon you." He laid his hands upon my shoulders, and added in a solemn whisper: "Avail yourself of this evening to lay hold of his portable property. You don't know what may happen to him. Don't let anything happen to the portable property."

Quite despairing of making my mind clear to Wemmick on this point, I forbore to try.

"Time's up," said Wemmick, "and I must be off. If you had nothing more pressing to do than to keep here till dark, that's what I should advise. You look very much worried, and it would do you good to have a perfectly quiet day with the Aged — he'll be up presently — and a little bit of — you remember the pig?"

"Of course," said I.

"Well; and a little bit of *him*. That sausage you toasted was his, and he was in all respects a first-rater. Do try him, if it is only for old acquaintance sake. Good-by, Aged Parent!" in a cheery shout.

"All right, John; all right, my boy!" piped the old man from within.

I soon fell asleep before Wemmick's fire, and the Aged and I enjoyed one another's society by falling asleep before it more or less all day. We had loin of pork for dinner, and greens grown on the estate, and I nodded at the Aged with a good intention whenever I failed to do it drowsily. When it was quite dark, I left the Aged preparing the fire for toast; and I inferred from the number of teacups, as well as from his glances at the two little doors in the wall, that Miss Skiffins was expected.

CHAPTER VII

EIGHT O'CLOCK had struck before I got into the air that was scented, not disagreeably, by the chips and shavings of the long-shore boat-builders, and mast oar and block makers. All that waterside region of the upper and lower Pool below Bridge,[1] was unknown ground to me, and when I struck down by the river, I found that the spot I wanted was not where I had supposed it to be, and was anything but easy to find. It was called Mill Pond Bank, Chinks's Basin; and I had no other guide to Chinks's Basin than the Old Green Copper Rope-Walk.[2]

It matters not what stranded ships repairing in dry docks I lost myself among, what old hulls of ships in course of being knocked to pieces, what ooze and slime and other dregs of tide, what yards of ship-builders and ship-breakers, what rusty anchors blindly biting into the ground though for years off duty, what mountainous country of accumulated casks and timber, how many rope-walks that were not the Old Green Copper. After several times falling short of my destination and as often over-shooting it, I came unexpectedly round a corner, upon Mill Pond Bank. It was a fresh kind of place, all circumstances considered, where the wind from the river had room to turn itself round; and there were two or three trees in it, and there was the stump of a ruined windmill, and there was the Old Green Copper Rope-Walk — whose long and narrow vista I could trace in the moonlight, along a series of wooden frames set in the ground, that looked like superannuated haymaking-rakes which had grown old and lost most of their teeth.

Selecting from the few queer houses upon Mill Pond Bank, a house with a wooden front and three stories of bow-window (not bay-window, which is another thing),* I looked at the plate upon the door, and read

---

1. *below Bridge:* i.e., below London Bridge.
2. *Mill Pond Bank, Chinks's Basin ... the Old Green Copper Rope-Walk:* the names Mill Pond Bank, Chinks's Basin, and the Old Green Copper Rope-Walk, entirely appropriate for this dockland area, are almost certainly of Dickens's invention; it is not even clear which bank of the river is intended, although the south seems more likely given that Pip walks from Walworth. A rope-walk is a long narrow strip of ground used for twisting rope.

there, Mrs. Whimple. That being the name I wanted, I knocked, and an elderly woman of a pleasant and thriving appearance responded. She was immediately deposed, however, by Herbert, who silently led me into the parlour and shut the door. It was an odd sensation to see his very familiar face established quite at home in that very unfamiliar room and region; and I found myself looking at him, much as I looked at the corner-cupboard with the glass and china, the shells upon the chimney-piece, and the coloured engravings on the wall, representing the death of Captain Cook,[1] a ship-launch, and his Majesty King George the Third in a state-coachman's wig, leather-breeches, and top-boots, on the terrace at Windsor.[2]

"All is well, Handel," said Herbert, "and he is quite satisfied, though eager to see you. My dear girl is with her father; and if you'll wait till she comes down, I'll make you known to her, and then we'll go up-stairs. — *That's* her father."

I had become aware of an alarming growling overhead, and had probably expressed the fact in my countenance.

"I am afraid he is a sad old rascal," said Herbert, smiling, "but I have never seen him. Don't you smell rum? He is always at it."

"At rum?" said I.

"Yes," returned Herbert, "and you may suppose how mild it makes his gout. He persists, too, in keeping all the provisions up-stairs in his room, and serving them out. He keeps them on shelves over his head, and *will* weigh them all. His room must be like a chandler's shop."

While he thus spoke, the growling noise became a prolonged roar, and then died away.

"What else can be the consequence," said Herbert, in explanation, "if he *will* cut the cheese? A man with the gout in his right hand — and everywhere else — can't expect to get through a Double Gloucester without hurting himself."

---

1. *the death of Captain Cook:* the British naval officer, who "discovered" Australia in 1770, was killed by the Hawaiians at Karakakoa Bay in 1779.
2. *his Majesty King George the Third in a state-coachman's wig, leather-breeches, and top-boots, on the terrace at Windsor:* George III was king from 1760 until his death at Windsor in 1820, though, due to his dementia, his son acted as Regent for the final decade of the reign.

He seemed to have hurt himself very much, for he gave another furious roar.

"To have Provis for an upper lodger is quite a godsend to Mrs. Whimple," said Herbert, "for of course people in general won't stand that noise. A curious place, Handel; isn't it?"

It was a curious place, indeed; but remarkably well kept and clean.

"Mrs. Whimple," said Herbert, when I told him so, "is the best of housewives, and I really do not know what my Clara would do without her motherly help. For, Clara has no mother of her own, Handel, and no relation in the world but old Gruffandgrim."

"Surely that's not his name, Herbert?"

"No, no," said Herbert, "that's my name for him. His name is Mr. Barley. But what a blessing it is for the son of my father and mother, to love a girl who has no relations, and who can never bother herself, or anybody else, about her family!"

Herbert had told me on former occasions, and now reminded me, that he first knew Miss Clara Barley when she was completing her education at an establishment at Hammersmith, and that on her being recalled home to nurse her father, he and she had confided their affection to the motherly Mrs. Whimple, by whom it had been fostered and regulated with equal kindness and discretion, ever since. It was understood that nothing of a tender nature could possibly be confided to old Barley, by reason of his being totally unequal to the consideration of any subject more psychological than Gout, Rum, and Purser's stores.

As we were thus conversing in a low tone while Old Barley's sustained growl vibrated in the beam that crossed the ceiling, the room door opened, and a very pretty slight dark-eyed girl of twenty or so, came in with a basket in her hand: whom Herbert tenderly relieved of the basket, and presented blushing, as "Clara." She really was a most charming girl, and might have passed for a captive fairy, whom that truculent Ogre, Old Barley, had pressed into his service.

"Look here," said Herbert, showing me the basket, with a compassionate and tender smile after we had talked a little; "here's poor Clara's supper, served out every night. Here's her allowance of bread, and here's her slice of cheese, and here's her rum — which I drink. This is Mr. Barley's breakfast for to-morrow, served out to be cooked. Two mutton chops, three potatoes, some split peas, a little flour, two ounces of butter, a pinch of salt, and all this black pepper. It's stewed up together, and taken hot, and it's a nice thing for the gout, I should think!"

There was something so natural and winning in Clara's resigned way of looking at these stores in detail, as Herbert pointed them out, — and something so confiding, loving, and innocent, in her modest manner of yielding herself to Herbert's embracing arm — and something so gentle in her, so much needing protection on Mill Pond Bank, by Chinks's Basin, and the Old Green Copper Rope-Walk, with Old Barley growling in the beam — that I would not have undone the engagement between her and Herbert, for all the money in the pocket-book I had never opened.

I was looking at her with pleasure and admiration, when suddenly the growl swelled into a roar again, and a frightful bumping noise was heard above, as if a giant with a wooden leg were trying to bore it through the ceiling to come at us. Upon this Clara said to Herbert, "Papa wants me, darling!" and ran away.

"There is an unconscionable old shark for you!" said Herbert. "What do you suppose he wants now, Handel?"

"I don't know," said I. "Something to drink?"

"That's it!" cried Herbert, as if I had made a guess of extraordinary merit. "He keeps his grog ready-mixed in a little tub on the table. Wait a moment, and you'll hear Clara lift him up to take some. — There he goes!" Another roar, with a prolonged shake at the end. "Now," said Herbert, as it was succeeded by silence, "he's drinking. Now," said Herbert, as the growl resounded in the beam once more, "he's down again on his back!"

Clara returned soon afterwards, and Herbert accompanied me up-stairs to see our charge. As we passed Mr. Barley's door, he was heard hoarsely muttering within, in a strain that rose and fell like wind, the following Refrain; in which I substitute good wishes for something quite the reverse.

"Ahoy! Bless your eyes, here's old Bill Barley. Here's old Bill Barley, bless your eyes. Here's old Bill Barley on the flat of his back, by the Lord. Lying on the flat of his back, like a drifting old dead flounder, here's your old Bill Barley, bless your eyes. Ahoy! Bless you."

In this strain of consolation, Herbert informed me the invisible Barley would commune with himself by the day and night together; often while it was light, having, at the same time, one eye at a telescope which was fitted on his bed for the convenience of sweeping the river.

In his two cabin rooms at the top of the house, which were fresh and airy, and in which Mr. Barley was less audible than below, I found Provis comfortably settled. He expressed no alarm, and seemed to feel none that was worth mentioning; but it struck me that he was softened — indefinably, for I could not have said how, and could never afterwards recal how when I tried; but certainly.

The opportunity that the day's rest had given me for reflection, had resulted in my fully determining to say nothing to him respecting Compeyson. For anything I knew, his animosity towards the man might otherwise lead to his seeking him out and rushing on his own destruction. Therefore, when Herbert and I sat down with him by his fire, I asked him first of all whether he relied on Wemmick's judgment and sources of information?

"Ay, ay, dear boy!" he answered, with a grave nod, "Jaggers's knows."

"Then, I have talked with Wemmick," said I, "and have come to tell you what caution he gave me and what advice."

This I did accurately, with the reservation just mentioned; and I told him how Wemmick had heard, in Newgate prison (whether from officers or prisoners I could not say), that he was under some suspicion, and that my chambers had been watched; how Wemmick had recommended his keeping close for a time, and my keeping away from him; and what Wemmick had said about getting him abroad. I added, that of course, when the time came, I should go with him, or should follow close upon him, as might be safest in Wemmick's judgment. What was to follow that, I did not touch upon; neither indeed was I at all clear or comfortable about it in my own mind, now that I saw him in that softer condition, and in declared peril for my sake. As to altering my way of living, by enlarging my expenses, I put it to him whether in our present unsettled and difficult circumstances, it would not be simply ridiculous, if it were no worse?

He could not deny this, and indeed was very reasonable throughout. His coming back was a venture, he said, and he had always known it to be a venture. He would do nothing to make it a desperate venture, and he had very little fear of his safety with such good help.

Herbert, who had been looking at the fire and pondering, here said that something had come into his thoughts arising out of Wemmick's suggestion, which it might be worth while to pursue. "We are both good watermen, Handel, and could take him down the river ourselves when the right time comes. No boat would then be hired for the purpose, and no boatmen; that would save at least a chance of suspicion, and any chance is worth saving. Never mind the season; don't you think it might be a good thing if you began at once to keep a boat at the Temple stairs, and were in the habit of rowing up and down the river? You fall into that habit, and then who notices or minds? Do it twenty or fifty times, and there is nothing special in your doing it the twenty-first or fifty-first."

I liked this scheme, and Provis was quite elated by it. We agreed that it should be carried into execution, and that Provis should never recognise us if we came below Bridge and rowed past Mill Pond Bank. But, we further agreed that he should pull down the blind in that part of his window which gave upon the east, whenever he saw us and all was right.

Our conference being now ended, and everything arranged, I rose to go; remarking to Herbert that he and I had better not go home together, and that I would take half an hour's start of him. "I don't like to leave you here," I said to Provis, "though I cannot doubt your being safer here than near me. Good-by!"

"Dear boy," he answered, clasping my hands, "I don't know when we may meet again, and I don't like Good-by. Say Good Night!"

"Good night! Herbert will go regularly between us, and when the time comes you may be certain I shall be ready. Good night, Good night!"

We thought it best that he should stay in his own rooms, and we left him on the landing outside his door, holding a light over the stair-rail to light us down-stairs. Looking back at him, I thought of the first night of his return when our positions were reversed, and when I little supposed my heart could ever be as heavy and anxious at parting from him as it was now.

Old Barley was growling and swearing when we repassed his door, with no appearance of having ceased or of meaning to cease. When we got to the foot of the stairs, I asked Herbert whether he had preserved the name of Provis. He replied, certainly not, and that the lodger was Mr. Campbell. He also explained that the utmost known of Mr. Campbell there, was, that he (Herbert) had Mr. Campbell consigned to him, and felt a strong personal interest in his being well cared for, and living a secluded life. So, when we went into the parlour where Mrs. Whimple and Clara were seated at work, I said nothing of my own interest in Mr. Campbell, but kept it to myself.

When I had taken leave of the pretty gentle dark-eyed girl, and of the motherly woman who had not outlived her honest sympathy with a little affair of true love, I felt as if the Old Green Copper Rope-Walk had grown quite a different place. Old Barley might be as old as the hills, and might swear like a whole field of troopers, but there were redeeming youth and trust and hope enough in Chinks's Basin to fill it to overflowing. And then I thought of Estella, and of our parting, and went home very sadly.

All things were as quiet in the Temple as ever I had seen them. The windows of the rooms on that side, lately occupied by Provis, were dark and still, and there was no lounger in Garden-court. I walked past the fountain twice or thrice before I descended the steps that were between me and my rooms, but I was quite alone. Herbert coming to my bedside when he came in — for I went straight to bed, dispirited and fatigued — made the same report. Opening one of the windows after that, he looked out into the moonlight, and told me that the pavement was as solemnly empty as the pavement of any Cathedral at that same hour.

Next day, I set myself to get the boat. It was soon done, and the boat was brought round to the Temple stairs, and lay where I could reach her within a minute or two. Then, I began to go out as for training and practice: sometimes alone, sometimes with Herbert. I was often out in cold, rain, and sleet, but nobody took much note of me after I had been out a few times. At first, I kept above Blackfriars Bridge; but as the hours of the tide changed, I took towards London Bridge. It was Old London Bridge in those days, and at certain states of the tide there was a race and a fall of water there which gave it a bad reputation. But I knew well enough how to "shoot" the bridge after seeing it done, and so began to row about among the shipping in the Pool, and down to Erith.[1] The first time I passed Mill Pond Bank, Herbert and I were pulling a pair of oars; and, both in going and returning, we saw the blind towards the east come down. Herbert was rarely there less frequently than three times in a week, and

---

1. *Erith:* small town on the Kent bank of the Thames. See Map A.

he never brought me a single word of intelligence that was at all alarming. Still, I knew that there was cause for alarm, and I could not get rid of the notion of being watched. Once received, it is a haunting idea; how many undesigning persons I suspected of watching me, it would be hard to calculate.

In short, I was always full of fears for the rash man who was in hiding. Herbert had sometimes said to me that he found it pleasant to stand at one of our windows after dark, when the tide was running down, and to think that it was flowing, with everything it bore, towards Clara. But I thought with dread that it was flowing towards Magwitch, and that any black mark on its surface might be his pursuers, going swiftly, silently, and surely, to take him.

CHAPTER VIII

SOME WEEKS passed without bringing any change. We waited for Wemmick, and he made no sign. If I had never known him out of Little Britain, and had never enjoyed the privilege of being on a familiar footing at the Castle, I might have doubted him; not so for a moment, knowing him as I did.

My worldly affairs began to wear a gloomy appearance, and I was pressed for money by more than one creditor. Even I myself began to know the want of money (I mean of ready money in my own pocket), and to relieve it by converting some easily spared articles of jewellery into cash. But I had quite determined that it would be a heartless fraud to take more money from my patron in the existing state of my uncertain thoughts and plans. Therefore, I had sent him the unopened pocket-book by Herbert, to hold in his own keeping and I felt a kind of satisfaction — whether it was a false kind or a true, I hardly know — in not having profited by his generosity since his revelation of himself.

As the time wore on, an impression settled heavily upon me that Estella was married. Fearful of having it confirmed, though it was all but a conviction, I avoided the newspapers, and begged Herbert (to whom I had confided the circumstances of our last interview) never to speak of her to me. Why I hoarded up this last wretched little rag of the robe of hope that was rent and given to the winds, how do I know! Why did you who read this, commit that not dissimilar inconsistency of your own, last year, last month, last week?

It was an unhappy life that I lived, and its one dominant anxiety, towering over all its other anxieties like a high mountain above a range of mountains, never disappeared from my view. Still, no new cause for fear arose. Let me start from my bed as I would, with the terror fresh upon me that he was discovered; let me sit listening as I would, with dread, for Herbert's returning step at night, lest it should be fleeter than ordinary, and winged with evil news; for all that, and much more to like purpose, the round of things went on. Condemned to inaction and a state of constant restlessness and suspense, I rowed about in my boat, and waited, waited, waited, as I best could.

There were states of the tide when, having been down the river, I could not get back through the eddy-chafed arches and starlings[1] of old London Bridge; then, I left my boat at a wharf near the Custom House,[2] to be brought up afterwards to the Temple stairs. I was not averse to doing this, as it served to make me and my boat a commoner incident among the waterside people there. From this slight occasion, sprang two meetings that I have now to tell of.

One afternoon, late in the month of February, I came ashore at the wharf at dusk. I had pulled down as far as Greenwich with the ebb tide, and had turned with the tide. It had been a fine bright day, but had become foggy as the sun dropped, and I had had to feel my way back among the shipping, pretty carefully. Both in going and returning, I had seen the signal in his window, All well.

As it was a raw evening and I was cold, I thought I would comfort myself with dinner at once; and as I had hours of dejection and solitude before me if I went home to the Temple, I thought I would afterwards go

---

1. *starlings:* outworks of piles, projecting beyond the lower part of the piers of a bridge, forming a protection for the piers themselves; Old London Bridge was a famous example of their use. See Illustration G.
2. *the Custom House:* then as today just east of London Bridge. See Map C.

to the play. The theatre where Mr. Wopsle had achieved his questionable triumph, was in that waterside neighbourhood (it is nowhere now),[1] and to that theatre I resolved to go. I was aware that Mr. Wopsle had not succeeded in reviving the Drama, but, on the contrary, had rather partaken of its decline. He had been ominously heard of, through the playbills, as a faithful Black, in connexion with a little girl of noble birth, and a monkey.[2] And Herbert had seen him as a predatory Tartar of comic propensities, with a face like a red brick, and an outrageous hat all over bells.[3]

I dined at what Herbert and I used to call a Geographical chop-house — where there were maps of the world in porter-pot rims on every half-yard of the tablecloths, and charts of gravy on every one of the knives — to this day there is scarcely a single chop-house within the Lord Mayor's dominions[4] which is not Geographical — and wore out the time in dozing over crumbs, staring at gas, and baking in a hot blast of dinners. By-and-by, I roused myself and went to the play.

There, I found a virtuous boatswain in his Majesty's service — a most excellent man, though I could have wished his trousers not quite so tight in some places and not quite so loose in others — who knocked all the little men's hats over their eyes, though he was very generous and brave, and who wouldn't hear of anybody's paying taxes, though he was very patriotic. He had a bag of money in his pocket, like a pudding in the cloth, and on that property married a young person in bed-furniture,[5] with great rejoicings; the whole population of Portsmouth (nine in number at the last Census) turning out on the beach, to rub their own hands and shake everybody else's, and sing "Fill, fill!"[6] A certain dark-

---

1. *The theatre where Mr. Wopsle had achieved his questionable triumph was in that waterside neighbourhood (it is nowhere now):* reference unknown.

2. *as a faithful Black, in connexion with a little girl of noble birth, and a monkey:* probably a reference to a popular drama, untraced.

3. *a predatory Tartar of comic propensities, with a face like a red brick, and an outrageous hat all over bells:* probably a reference to the story *Timour the Tartar* first popularized in an 1811 melodrama by M.G. ("Monk") Lewis.

4. *within the Lord Mayor's dominions:* i.e., within the City of London.

5. *in bed-furniture:* i.e., the costume was made from, or looked like, the hangings of a four-poster bed.

6. *"Fill, fill!":* probably James Hook's late eighteenth-century song for three voices, "Fill, fill my friend the flowing bowl."

complexioned Swab,[1] however, who wouldn't fill, or do anything else that was proposed to him, and whose heart was openly stated (by the boat-swain) to be as black as his figure-head,[2] proposed to two other Swabs to get all mankind into difficulties; which was so effectually done (the Swab family having considerable political influence) that it took half the evening to set things right, and then it was only brought about through an honest little grocer with a white hat, black gaiters, and red nose, getting into a clock, with a gridiron, and listening, and coming out, and knocking every-body down from behind with the gridiron whom he couldn't confute with what he had overheard. This led to Mr. Wopsle's (who had never been heard of before) coming in with a star and garter on, as a plenipo-tentiary of great power direct from the Admiralty, to say that the Swabs were all to go to prison on the spot, and that he had brought the boat-swain down the Union Jack, as a slight acknowledgment of his public services. The boatswain, unmanned for the first time, respectfully dried his eyes on the Jack, and then cheering up and addressing Mr. Wopsle as Your Honour, solicited permission to take him by the fin. Mr. Wopsle conceding his fin with a gracious dignity, was immediately shoved into a dusty corner while everybody danced a hornpipe; and from that corner, surveying the public with a discontented eye, became aware of me.

The second piece was the last new grand comic Christmas panto-mime, in the first scene of which, it pained me to suspect that I detected Mr. Wopsle with red worsted legs under a highly magnified phosphoric countenance and a shock of red curtain-fringe for his hair, engaged in the manufacture of thunderbolts in a mine, and displaying great coward-ice when his gigantic master came home (very hoarse) to dinner. But he presently presented himself under worthier circumstances; for, the Genius of Youthful Love being in want of assistance — on account of the paren-tal brutality of an ignorant farmer who opposed the choice of his daugh-ter's heart, by purposely falling upon the object, in a flour sack, out of the first-floor window — summoned a sententious Enchanter; and he, com-

---

1. *dark-complexioned Swab:* Negro sailor.
2. *figure-head:* face (nautical, from the ornamental carving of a human figure on the prow of a ship).

ing up from the antipodes rather unsteadily, after an apparently violent journey, proved to be Mr. Wopsle in a high-crowned hat, with a necromantic work in one volume under his arm. The business of this enchanter on earth, being principally to be talked at, sung at, butted at, danced at, and flashed at with fires of various colours, he had a good deal of time on his hands. And I observed with great surprise, that he devoted it to staring in my direction as if he were lost in amazement.

There was something so remarkable in the increasing glare of Mr. Wopsle's eye, and he seemed to be turning so many things over in his mind and to grow so confused, that I could not make it out. I sat thinking of it, long after he had ascended to the clouds in a large watch-case, and still I could not make it out. I was still thinking of it when I came out of the theatre an hour afterwards, and found him waiting for me near the door.

"How do you do?" said I, shaking hands with him as we turned down the street together. "I saw that you saw me."

"Saw you, Mr. Pip!" he returned. "Yes, of course I saw you. But who else was there?"

"Who else?"

"It is the strangest thing," said Mr. Wopsle, drifting into his lost look again; "and yet I could swear to him."

Becoming alarmed, I entreated Mr. Wopsle to explain his meaning.

"Whether I should have noticed him at first but for your being there," said Mr. Wopsle, going on in the same lost way, "I can't be positive; yet I think I should."

Involuntarily I looked round me, as I was accustomed to look round me when I went home; for, these mysterious words gave me a chill.

"Oh! He can't be in sight," said Mr. Wopsle. "He went out, before I went off, I saw him go."

Having the reason that I had, for being suspicious, I even suspected this poor actor. I mistrusted a design to entrap me into some admission. Therefore, I glanced at him as we walked on together, but said nothing.

"I had a ridiculous fancy that he must be with you, Mr. Pip, till I saw that you were quite unconscious of him, sitting behind you there, like a ghost."

My former chill crept over me again, but I was resolved not to speak yet, for it was quite consistent with his words that he might be set on to induce me to connect these references with Provis. Of course, I was perfectly sure and safe that Provis had not been there.

"I dare say you wonder at me, Mr. Pip; indeed I see you do. But it is so very strange! You'll hardly believe what I am going to tell you. I could hardly believe it myself, if you told me."

"Indeed?" said I.

"No, indeed. Mr. Pip, you remember in old times a certain Christmas Day, when you were quite a child, and I dined at Gargery's, and some soldiers came to the door to get a pair of handcuffs mended?"

"I remember it very well."

"And you remember that there was a chase after two convicts, and that we joined in it, and that Gargery took you on his back, and that I took the lead and you kept up with me as well as you could?"

"I remember it all very well." Better than he thought — except the last clause.

"And you remember that we came up with the two in a ditch, and that there was a scuffle between them, and that one of them had been severely handled and much mauled about the face, by the other?"

"I see it all before me."

"And that the soldiers lighted torches, and put the two in the centre, and that we went on to see the last of them, over the black marshes, with the torchlight shining on their faces — I am particular about that; with the torchlight shining on their faces, when there was an outer ring of dark night all about us?"

"Yes," said I. "I remember all that."

"Then, Mr. Pip, one of those two prisoners sat behind you to-night. I saw him over your shoulder."

"Steady!" I thought. I asked him then, "Which of the two do you suppose you saw?"

"The one who had been mauled," he answered readily, "and I'll swear I saw him! The more I think of him, the more certain I am of him."

"This is very curious!" said I, with the best assumption I could put on, of its being nothing more to me. "Very curious indeed!"

I cannot exaggerate the enhanced disquiet into which this conversation threw me, or the special and peculiar terror I felt at Compeyson's having been behind me "like a ghost." For, if he had ever been out of my thoughts for a few moments together since the hiding had begun, it was in those very moments when he was closest to me; and to think that I should be so unconscious and off my guard after all my care, was as if I had shut an avenue of a hundred doors to keep him out, and then had found him at my elbow. I could not doubt either that he was there, because I was there, and that however slight an appearance of danger there might be about us, danger was always near and active.

I put such questions to Mr. Wopsle as, When did the man come in? He could not tell me that; he saw me, and over my shoulder he saw the man. It was not until he had seen him for some time that he began to identify him; but he had from the first vaguely associated him with me, and known him as somehow belonging to me in the old village time. How was he dressed? Prosperously, but not noticeably otherwise; he thought, in black. Was his face at all disfigured? No, he believed not. I believed not, too, for, although in my brooding state I had taken no especial notice of the people behind me, I thought it likely that a face at all disfigured would have attracted my attention.

When Mr. Wopsle had imparted to me all that he could recal or I extract, and when I had treated him to a little appropriate refreshment after the fatigues of the evening, we parted. It was between twelve and one o'clock when I reached the Temple, and the gates were shut. No one was near me when I went in and went home.

Herbert had come in, and we held a very serious council by the fire. But there was nothing to be done, saving to communicate to Wemmick what I had that night found out, and to remind him that we waited for his hint. As I thought that I might compromise him if I went too often to the Castle, I made this communication by letter. I wrote it before I went to bed, and went out and posted it; and again no one was near me. Herbert and I agreed that we could do nothing else but be very cautious. And we were very cautious indeed — more cautious than before, if that were possible — and I for my part never went near Chinks's Basin, except when I rowed by, and then I only looked at Mill Pond Bank as I looked at anything else.

CHAPTER IX

THE SECOND of the two meetings referred to in the last chapter, occurred about a week after the first. I had again left my boat at the wharf below Bridge;[1] the time was an hour earlier in the afternoon; and, undecided where to dine, I had strolled up into Cheapside, and was strolling along it, surely the most unsettled person in all the busy concourse, when a large hand was laid upon my shoulder, by some one overtaking me. It was Mr. Jaggers's hand, and he passed it through my arm.

"As we are going in the same direction, Pip, we may walk together. Where are you bound for?"

"For the Temple, I think," said I.

"Don't you know?" said Mr. Jaggers.

"Well," I returned, glad for once to get the better of him in cross-examination, "I do *not* know, for I have not made up my mind."

"You are going to dine?" said Mr. Jaggers. "You don't mind admitting that, I suppose?"

"No," I returned, "I don't mind admitting that."

"And are not engaged?"

"I don't mind admitting also, that I am not engaged."

"Then," said Mr. Jaggers, "come and dine with me."

I was going to excuse myself, when he added, "Wemmick's coming." So, I changed my excuse into an acceptance — the few words I had uttered, serving for the beginning of either — and we went along Cheapside and slanted off to Little Britain, while the lights were springing up brilliantly in the shop windows, and the street lamp-lighters, scarcely finding ground enough to plant their ladders on in the midst of the afternoon's bustle, were skipping up and down and running in and out, opening more red eyes in the gathering fog than my rushlight tower at the Hummums had opened white eyes in the ghostly wall.

At the office in Little Britain there was the usual letter-writing, hand-washing, candle-snuffing, and safe-locking, that closed the business of the

---

1. *I had again left my boat at the wharf below Bridge:* i.e., the wharf near the Custom House below London Bridge (see note on p. 405).

day. As I stood idle by Mr. Jaggers's fire, its rising and falling flame made the two casts on the shelf look as if they were playing a diabolical game at bo-peep with me; while the pair of coarse fat office candles that dimly lighted Mr. Jaggers as he wrote in a corner, were decorated with dirty winding-sheets,[1] as if in remembrance of a host of hanged clients.

We went to Gerrard-street, all three together, in a hackney-coach: and as soon as we got there, dinner was served. Although I should not have thought of making, in that place, the most distant reference by so much as a look to Wemmick's Walworth sentiments, yet I should have had no objection to catching his eye now and then in a friendly way. But it was not to be done. He turned his eyes on Mr. Jaggers whenever he raised them from the table, and was as dry and distant to me as if there were twin Wemmicks and this was the wrong one.

"Did you send that note of Miss Havisham's to Mr. Pip, Wemmick?" Mr. Jaggers asked, soon after we began dinner.

"No, sir," returned Wemmick; "it was going by post, when you brought Mr. Pip into the office. Here it is." He handed it to his principal, instead of to me.

"It's a note of two lines, Pip," said Mr. Jaggers, handing it on, "sent up to me by Miss Havisham, on account of her not being sure of your address. She tells me that she wants to see you on a little matter of business you mentioned to her. You'll go down?"

"Yes," said I, casting my eyes over the note, which was exactly in those terms.

"When do you think of going down?"

"I have an impending engagement," said I, glancing at Wemmick, who was putting fish into the post-office, "that renders me rather uncertain of my time. At once, I think."

"If Mr. Pip has the intention of going at once," said Wemmick to Mr. Jaggers, "he needn't write an answer, you know."

Receiving this as an intimation that it was best not to delay I settled that I would go to-morrow, and said so. Wemmick drank a glass of wine and looked with a grimly satisfied air at Mr. Jaggers, but not at me.

---

1. *winding-sheets:* masses of solidified grease clinging to the side of a candle, resembling folded sheets, and thus compared to shrouds.

"So, Pip! Our friend the Spider," said Mr. Jaggers, "has played his cards. He has won the pool."

It was as much as I could do to assent.

"Hah! He is a promising fellow — in his way — but he may not have it all his own way. The stronger will win in the end, but the stronger has to be found out first. If he should turn to, and beat her —"

"Surely," I interrupted, with a burning face and heart, "you do not seriously think that he is scoundrel enough for that, Mr. Jaggers?"

"I didn't say so, Pip. I am putting a case. If he should turn to and beat her, he may possibly get the strength on his side; if it should be a question of intellect, he certainly will not. It would be chance work to give an opinion how a fellow of that sort will turn out in such circumstances, because it's a toss-up between two results."

"May I ask what they are?"

"A fellow like our friend the Spider," answered Mr. Jaggers, "either beats, or cringes. He may cringe and growl, or cringe and not growl; but he either beats or cringes. Ask Wemmick *his* opinion."

"Either beats or cringes," said Wemmick, not at all addressing himself to me.

"So, here's to Mrs. Bentley Drummle," said Mr. Jaggers, taking a decanter of choicer wine from his dumb-waiter, and filling for each of us and for himself, "and may the question of supremacy be settled to the lady's satisfaction! To the satisfaction of the lady *and* the gentleman, it never will be. Now, Molly, Molly, Molly, Molly, how slow you are to-day!"

She was at his elbow when he addressed her, putting a dish upon the table. As she withdrew her hands from it, she fell back a step or two, nervously muttering some excuse. And a certain action of her fingers as she spoke arrested my attention.

"What's the matter?" said Mr. Jaggers.

"Nothing. Only the subject we were speaking of," said I, "was rather painful to me."

The action of her fingers was like the action of knitting. She stood looking at her master, not understanding whether she was free to go, or whether he had more to say to her and would call her back if she did go. Her look was very intent. Surely, I had seen exactly such eyes and such hands, on a memorable occasion very lately!

He dismissed her, and she glided out of the room. But she remained before me, as plainly as if she were still there. I looked at those hands, I looked at those eyes, I looked at that flowing hair; and I compared them with other hands, other eyes, other hair, that I knew of, and with what those might be after twenty years of a brutal husband and a stormy life. I looked again at those hands and eyes of the housekeeper, and thought of the inexplicable feeling that had come over me when I last walked — not alone — in the ruined garden, and through the deserted brewery. I thought how the same feeling had come back when I saw a face looking at me, and a hand waving to me, from a stage-coach window; and how it had come back again and had flashed about me like Lightning, when I had passed in a carriage — not alone — through a sudden glare of light in a dark street. I thought how one link of association had helped that identification in the theatre, and how such a link, wanting before, had been riveted for me now, when I had passed by a chance, swift from Estella's name to the fingers with their knitting action, and the attentive eyes. And I felt absolutely certain that this woman was Estella's mother.

Mr. Jaggers had seen me with Estella, and was not likely to have missed the sentiments I had been at no pains to conceal. He nodded when I said the subject was painful to me, clapped me on the back, put round the wine again, and went on with his dinner.

Only twice more, did the housekeeper reappear, and then her stay in the room was very short, and Mr. Jaggers was sharp with her. But her hands were Estella's hands, and her eyes were Estella's eyes, and if she had reappeared a hundred times I could have been neither more sure nor less sure that my conviction was the truth.

It was a dull evening, for Wemmick drew his wine when it came round, quite as a matter of business — just as he might have drawn his salary when that came round — and with his eyes on his chief, sat in a state of perpetual readiness for cross-examination. As to the quantity of wine, his post-office was as indifferent and ready as any other post-office for its quantity of letters. From my point of view, he was the wrong twin all the time, and only externally like the Wemmick of Walworth.

We took our leave early, and left together. Even when we were groping among Mr. Jaggers's stock of boots for our hats, I felt that the right twin was on his way back; and we had not gone half a dozen yards down

Gerrard-street in the Walworth direction before I found that I was walking arm-in-arm with the right twin, and that the wrong twin had evaporated into the evening air.

"Well!" said Wemmick, "that's over! He's a wonderful man, without his living likeness; but I feel that I have to screw myself up when I dine with him — and I dine more comfortably unscrewed."

I felt that this was a good statement of the case, and told him so.

"Wouldn't say it to anybody but yourself," he answered. "I know that what is said between you and me, goes no further."

I asked him if he had ever seen Miss Havisham's adopted daughter, Mrs. Bentley Drummle? He said no. To avoid being too abrupt, I then spoke of the Aged, and of Miss Skiffins. He looked rather sly when I mentioned Miss Skiffins, and stopped in the street to blow his nose, with a roll of the head and a flourish not quite free from latent boastfulness.

"Wemmick," said I, "do you remember telling me before I first went to Mr. Jaggers's private house, to notice that housekeeper?"

"Did I?" he replied. "Ah, I dare say I did. Deuce take me," he added, suddenly, "I know I did. I find I am not quite unscrewed yet."

"A wild beast tamed, you called her."

"And what do *you* call her?"

"The same. How did Mr. Jaggers tame her, Wemmick?"

"That's his secret. She has been with him many a long year."

"I wish you would tell me her story. I feel a particular interest in being acquainted with it. You know that what is said between you and me goes no further."

"Well!" Wemmick replied, "I don't know her story — that is, I don't know all of it. But what I do know, I'll tell you. We are in our private and personal capacities, of course."

"Of course."

"A score or so of years ago, that woman was tried at the Old Bailey for murder, and was acquitted. She was a very handsome young woman, and I believe had some gipsy blood in her. Anyhow, it was hot enough when it was up, as you may suppose."

"But she was acquitted."

"Mr. Jaggers was for her," pursued Wemmick, with a look full of meaning, "and worked the case in a way quite astonishing. It was a desperate case, and it was comparatively early days with him then, and he worked it to general admiration; in fact, it may almost be said to have made him. He worked it himself at the police-office, day after day for many days, contending against even a committal; and at the trial where he couldn't work it himself, sat under Counsel, and — every one knew — put in all the salt and pepper. The murdered person was a woman; a woman, a good ten years older, very much larger, and very much stronger. It was a case of jealousy. They both led tramping lives, and this woman in Gerrard-street here had been married very young, over the broomstick[1] (as we say), to a tramping man, and was a perfect fury in point of jealousy. The murdered woman — more a match for the man, certainly, in point of years — was found dead in a barn near Hounslow Heath. There had been a violent struggle, perhaps a fight. She was bruised and scratched and torn, and had been held by the throat at last and choked. Now, there was no reasonable evidence to implicate any person but this woman, and, on the improbabilities of her having been able to do it, Mr. Jaggers principally rested his case. You may be sure," said Wemmick, touching me on the sleeve, "that he never dwelt upon the strength of her hands then, though he sometimes does now."

I had told Wemmick of his showing us her wrists, that day of the dinner party.

"Well, sir!" Wemmick went on; "it happened — happened, don't you see? — that this woman was so very artfully dressed from the time of her apprehension, that she looked much slighter than she really was; in particular, her sleeves are always remembered to have been so skilfully contrived that her arms had quite a delicate look. She had only a bruise or two about her — nothing for a tramp — but the backs of her hands were lacerated, and the question was, was it with finger-nails? Now, Mr. Jaggers showed that she had struggled through a great lot of brambles which were not as high as her face; but which she could not have got through and kept her hands out of; and bits of those brambles were actually found in her skin and put in evidence, as well as the fact that the brambles in question were found on examination to have been broken

---

1. *over the broomstick:* i.e., through an unofficial marriage ceremony.

through, and to have little shreds of her dress and little spots of blood upon them here and there. But the boldest point he made, was this. It was attempted to be set up in proof of her jealousy, that she was under strong suspicion of having, at about the time of the murder, frantically destroyed her child by this man — some three years old — to revenge herself upon him. Mr. Jaggers worked that, in this way. 'We say these are not marks of finger-nails, but marks of brambles, and we show you the brambles. You say they are marks of finger-nails, and you set up the hypothesis that she destroyed her child. You must accept all consequences of that hypothesis. For anything we know, she may have destroyed her child, and the child in clinging to her may have scratched her hands. What then? You are not trying her for the murder of her child; why don't you? As to this case, if you *will* have scratches, we say that, for any thing we know, you may have accounted for them, assuming for the sake of argument that you have not invented them?' To sum up, sir," said Wemmick, "Mr. Jaggers was altogether too many for the Jury, and they gave in."

"Has she been in his service ever since?"

"Yes; but not only that," said Wemmick. "She went into his service immediately after her acquittal, tamed as she is now. She has since been taught one thing and another in the way of her duties, but she was tamed from the beginning."

"Do you remember the sex of the child?"

"Said to have been a girl."

"You have nothing more to say to me to-night?"

"Nothing. I got your letter and destroyed it. Nothing."

We exchanged a cordial Good Night, and I went home, with new matter for my thoughts, though with no relief from the old.

CHAPTER X

PUTTING Miss Havisham's note in my pocket, that it might serve as my credentials for so soon reappearing at Satis House, in case her waywardness should lead her to express any surprise at seeing me, I went down again by the coach next day. But I alighted at the Half-way House, and breakfasted there, and walked the rest of the distance; for, I sought to get into the town quietly by the unfrequented ways, and to leave it in the same manner.

The best light of the day was gone when I passed along the quiet echoing courts behind the High-street. The nooks of ruin where the old monks had once had their refectories and gardens, and where the strong walls were now pressed into the service of humble sheds and stables, were almost as silent as the old monks in their graves. The cathedral chimes had at once a sadder and a more remote sound to me, as I hurried on avoiding observation, than they had ever had before; so, the swell of the old organ was borne to my ears like funeral music; and the rooks, as they hovered about the grey tower and swung in the bare high trees of the priory-garden, seemed to call to me that the place was changed, and that Estella was gone out of it for ever.[1]

An elderly woman whom I had seen before as one of the servants who lived in the supplementary house across the back court-yard, opened the gate. The lighted candle stood in the dark passage within, as of old, and I took it up and ascended the staircase alone. Miss Havisham was not in her own room, but was in the larger room across the landing. Looking in at the door, after knocking in vain, I saw her sitting on the hearth in a ragged chair, close before, and lost in the contemplation of, the ashy fire.

Doing as I had often done, I went in, and stood, touching the old chimney-piece, where she could see me when she raised her eyes. There was an air of utter loneliness upon her, that would have moved me to

---

1. *The best light of the day was gone when I passed along the quiet echoing courts ... Estella was gone out of it for ever:* Until the dissolution of the monasteries under Henry VIII, Rochester was the site of one of the richest abbeys in south-eastern England, the Benedictine Priory of St. Andrew, founded by Bishop Gundulf in the eleventh century. Only a few remnants now survive, including three fifteenth-century monastic gateways and fragments of the priory wall, although the cathedral itself, with its fine Chapter House doorway and Norman under-croft, still stands. Its tower and spire were constructed in the fourteenth century, though the latter was removed in 1823 and only replaced at the beginning of the present century. The pamphlet *Rochester's Heritage Trail* (1993), produced by the City of Rochester Society, offers useful plans, sketches, and descriptions of the area.

pity though she had wilfully done me a deeper injury than I could charge her with. As I stood compassionating her and thinking how in the progress of time I too had come to be a part of the wrecked fortunes of that house, her eyes rested on me. She stared, and said in a low voice, "Is it real?"

"It is I, Pip. Mr. Jaggers gave me your note yesterday, and I have lost no time."

"Thank you. Thank you."

As I brought another of the ragged chairs to the hearth and sat down, I remarked a new expression on her face, as if she were afraid of me.

"I want," she said, "to pursue that subject you mentioned to me when you were last here, and to show you that I am not all stone. But perhaps you can never believe, now, that there is anything human in my heart?"

When I said some reassuring words, she stretched out her tremulous right hand, as though she was going to touch me; but she recalled it again before I understood the action, or knew how to receive it.

"You said, speaking for your friend, that you could tell me how to do something useful and good. Something that you would like done, is it not?"

"Something that I would like done very much."

"What is it?"

I began explaining to her that secret history of the partnership. I had not got far into it, when I judged from her looks that she was thinking in a discursive way of me, rather than of what I said. It seemed to be so, for, when I stopped speaking, many moments passed before she showed that she was conscious of the fact.

"Do you break off," she asked then, with her former air of being afraid of me, "because you hate me too much to bear to speak to me?"

"No, no," I answered, "how can you think so, Miss Havisham! I stopped because I thought you were not following what I said."

"Perhaps I was not," she answered, putting a hand to her head. "Begin again, and let me look at something else. Stay! Now tell me."

She set her hand upon her stick, in the resolute way that sometimes was habitual to her, and looked at the fire with a strong expression of forcing herself to attend. I went on with my explanation, and told her how I had hoped to complete the transaction out of my means, but how in this I was disappointed. That part of the subject (I reminded her) involved matters which could form no part of my explanation, for they were the weighty secrets of another.

"So!" said she, assenting with her head, but not looking at me. "And how much money is wanting to complete the purchase?"

I was rather afraid of stating it, for it sounded a large sum. "Nine hundred pounds."

"If I give you the money for this purpose, will you keep my secret as you have kept your own?"

"Quite as faithfully."

"And your mind will be more at rest?"

"Much more at rest."

"Are you very unhappy now?"

She asked this question, still without looking at me, but in an unwonted tone of sympathy. I could not reply at the moment, for my voice failed me. She put her left arm across the head of her stick, and softly laid her forehead on it.

"I am far from happy, Miss Havisham; but I have other causes of disquiet than any you know of. They are the secrets I have mentioned."

After a little while, she raised her head and looked at the fire again.

"It is noble in you to tell me that you have other causes of unhappiness. Is it true?"

"Too true."

"Can I only serve you, Pip, by serving your friend? Regarding that as done, is there nothing I can do for you yourself?"

"Nothing. I thank you for the question. I thank you even more for the tone of the question. But, there is nothing."

She presently rose from her seat, and looked about the blighted room for the means of writing. There were none there, and she took from her pocket a yellow set of ivory tablets, mounted in tarnished gold, and wrote upon them with a pencil in a case of tarnished gold that hung from her neck.

"You are still on friendly terms with Mr. Jaggers?"

"Quite. I dined with him yesterday."

"This is an authority to him to pay you that money, to lay out at your irresponsible[1] discretion for your friend. I keep no money here; but if you

---

1. *irresponsible:* exempt from legal responsibility.

would rather Mr. Jaggers knew nothing of the matter, I will send it to you."

"Thank you, Miss Havisham; I have not the least objection to receiving it from him."

She read me what she had written, and it was direct and clear, and evidently intended to absolve me from any suspicion of profiting by the receipt of the money. I took the tablets from her hand, and it trembled again, and it trembled more as she took off the chain to which the pencil was attached, and put it in mine. All this she did, without looking at me.

"My name is on the first leaf. If you can ever write under my name, 'I forgive her,' though ever so long after my broken heart is dust — pray do it!"

"O Miss Havisham," said I, "I can do it now. There have been sore mistakes; and my life has been a blind and thankless one; and I want forgiveness and direction far too much, to be bitter with you."

She turned her face to me for the first time since she had averted it, and, to my amazement, I may even add to my terror, dropped on her knees at my feet; with her folded hands raised to me in the manner in which, when her poor heart was young and fresh and whole, they must often have been raised to heaven from her mother's side.

To see her with her white hair and her worn face kneeling at my feet, gave me a shock through all my frame. I entreated her to rise, and got my arms about her to help her up; but she only pressed that hand of mine which was nearest to her grasp, and hung her head over it and wept. I had never seen her shed a tear before, and, in the hope that the relief might do her good, I bent over her without speaking. She was not kneeling now, but was down upon the ground.

"O!" she cried, despairingly. "What have I done! What have I done!"

"If you mean, Miss Havisham, what have you done to injure me, let me answer. Very little. I should have loved her under any circumstances. — Is she married?"

"Yes."

It was a needless question, for a new desolation in the desolate house had told me so.

"What have I done! What have I done!" She wrung her hands, and crushed her white hair, and returned to this cry over and over again. "What have I done!"

I knew not how to answer, or how to comfort her. That she had done a grievous thing in taking an impressionable child to mould into the form that her wild resentment, spurned affection, and wounded pride, found vengeance in, I knew full well. But that, in shutting out the light of day, she had shut out infinitely more; that, in seclusion, she had secluded herself from a thousand natural and healing influences; that, her mind, brooding solitary, had grown diseased, as all minds do and must and will that reverse the appointed order of their Maker; I knew equally well. And could I look upon her without compassion, seeing her punishment in the ruin she was, in her profound unfitness for this earth on which she was placed, in the vanity of sorrow which had become a master mania, like the vanity of penitence, the vanity of remorse, the vanity of unworthiness, and other monstrous vanities that have been curses in this world?

"Until you spoke to her the other day, and until I saw in you a looking-glass that showed me what I once felt myself, I did not know what I had done. What have I done! What have I done!" And so again, twenty, fifty times over, What had she done!

"Miss Havisham," I said, when her cry had died away, "you may dismiss me from your mind and conscience. But Estella is a different case, and if you can ever undo any scrap of what you have done amiss in keeping a part of her right nature away from her, it will be better to do that, than to bemoan the past through a hundred years."

"Yes, yes, I know it. But, Pip — my Dear!" There was an earnest womanly compassion for me in her new affection. "My Dear! Believe this: when she first came to me, I meant to save her from misery like my own. At first I meant no more."

"Well, well!" said I. "I hope so."

"But as she grew, and promised to be very beautiful, I gradually did worse, and with my praises, and with my jewels, and with my teachings, and with this figure of myself always before her a warning to back and point my lessons, I stole her heart away and put ice in its place."

"Better," I could not help saying, "to have left her a natural heart, even to be bruised or broken."

With that, Miss Havisham looked distractedly at me for a while, and then burst out again, What had she done!

"If you knew all my story," she pleaded, "you would have some compassion for me and a better understanding of me."

"Miss Havisham," I answered, as delicately as I could, "I believe I may say that I do know your story, and have known it ever since I first left this neighbourhood. It has inspired me with great commiseration, and I hope I understand it and its influences. Does what has passed between us give me any excuse for asking you a question relative to Estella? Not as she is, but as she was when she first came here?"

She was seated on the ground, with her arms on the ragged chair, and her head leaning on them. She looked full at me when I said this, and replied, "Go on."

"Whose child was Estella?"

She shook her head.

"You don't know?"

She shook her head again.

"But Mr. Jaggers brought her here, or sent her here?"

"Brought her here."

"Will you tell me how that came about?"

She answered in a low whisper and with caution: "I had been shut up in these rooms a long time (I don't know how long; you know what time the clocks keep here), when I told him that I wanted a little girl to rear and love, and save from my fate. I had first seen him when I sent for him to lay this place waste for me; having read of him in the newspapers, before I and the world parted. He told me that he would look about him for such an orphan child. One night he brought her here asleep, and I called her Estella."

"Might I ask her age then?"

"Two or three. She herself knows nothing, but that she was left an orphan and I adopted her."

So convinced I was of that woman's being her mother, that I wanted no evidence to establish the fact in my own mind. But, to any mind, I thought, the connexion here was clear and straight.

What more could I hope to do by prolonging the interview? I had succeeded on behalf of Herbert, Miss Havisham had told me all she knew of Estella, I had said and done what I could to ease her mind. No matter with what other words we parted; we parted.

Twilight was closing in when I went down-stairs into the natural air.

I called to the woman who had opened the gate when I entered, that I would not trouble her just yet, but would walk round the place before leaving. For, I had a presentiment that I should never be there again, and I felt that the dying light was suited to my last view of it.

By the wilderness of casks that I had walked on long ago, and on which the rain of years had fallen since, rotting them in many places, and leaving miniature swamps and pools of water upon those that stood on end, I made my way to the ruined garden. I went all round it; round by the corner where Herbert and I had fought our battle; round by the paths where Estella and I had walked. So cold, so lonely, so dreary all!

Taking the brewery on my way back, I raised the rusty latch of a little door at the garden end of it, and walked through. I was going out at the opposite door — not easy to open now, for the damp wood had started and swelled, and the hinges were yielding, and the threshold was encumbered with a growth of fungus — when I turned my head to look back. A childish association revived with wonderful force in the moment of the slight action, and I fancied that I saw Miss Havisham hanging to the beam. So strong was the impression, that I stood under the beam shuddering from head to foot before I knew it was a fancy — though to be sure I was there in an instant.

The mournfulness of the place and time, and the great terror of this illusion, though it was but momentary, caused me to feel an indescribable awe as I came out between the open wooden gates where I had once wrung my hair after Estella had wrung my heart. Passing on into the front court-yard, I hesitated whether to call the woman to let me out at the locked gate of which she had the key, or first to go up-stairs and assure myself that Miss Havisham was as safe and well as I had left her. I took the latter course and went up.

I looked into the room where I had left her, and I saw her seated in the ragged chair upon the hearth close to the fire, with her back towards me. In the moment when I was withdrawing my head to go quietly away, I saw a great flaming light spring up. In the same moment, I saw her running at me, shrieking, with a whirl of fire blazing all about her, and soaring at least as many feet above her head as she was high.

I had a double-caped great-coat on, and over my arm another thick coat. That I got them off, closed with her, threw her down, and got them

over her; that I dragged the great cloth from the table for the same purpose, and with it dragged down the heap of rottenness in the midst, and
all the ugly things that sheltered there; that we were on the ground struggling like desperate enemies, and that the closer I covered her, the more
wildly she shrieked and tried to free herself; that this occurred I knew
through the result, but not through anything I felt, or thought, or knew I
did. I knew nothing until I knew that we were on the floor by the great
table, and that patches of tinder yet alight were floating in the smoky air,
which, a moment ago, had been her faded bridal dress.

Then, I looked round and saw the disturbed beetles and spiders running away over the floor, and the servants coming in with breathless cries
at the door. I still held her forcibly down with all my strength, like a prisoner who might escape; and I doubt if I even knew who she was, or why
we had struggled, or that she had been in flames, or that the flames were
out, until I saw the patches of tinder that had been her garments, no longer
alight but falling in a black shower around us.

She was insensible, and I was afraid to have her moved, or even touched.
Assistance was sent for and I held her until it came, as if I unreasonably
fancied (I think I did) that if I let her go, the fire would break out again
and consume her. When I got up, on the surgeon's coming to her with
other aid, I was astonished to see that both my hands were burnt; for, I
had no knowledge of it through the sense of feeling.

On examination it was pronounced that she had received serious hurts
but that they of themselves were far from hopeless; the danger lay mainly
in the nervous shock. By the surgeon's directions, her bed was carried
into that room and laid upon the great table: which happened to be well
suited to the dressing of her injuries. When I saw her again, an hour afterwards, she lay indeed where I had seen her strike her stick, and had
heard her say that she would lie one day.

Though every vestige of her dress was burnt, as they told me, she still
had something of her old ghastly bridal appearance; for, they had covered
her to the throat with white cotton-wool, and as she lay with a white
sheet loosely overlying that, the phantom air of something that had been
and was changed, was still upon her.

I found, on questioning the servants, that Estella was in Paris, and I
got a promise from the surgeon that he would write to her by the next

post. Miss Havisham's family I took upon myself; intending to communicate with Mr. Matthew Pocket only, and leave him to do as he liked about informing the rest. This I did next day, through Herbert, as soon as I returned to town.

There was a stage, that evening, when she spoke collectedly of what had happened, though with a certain terrible vivacity. Towards midnight she began to wander in her speech, and after that it gradually set in that she said innumerable times in a low solemn voice, "What have I done!" And then, "When she first came, I meant to save her from misery like mine." And then, — "Take the pencil and write under my name, 'I forgive her!'" She never changed the order of these three sentences, but she sometimes left out a word in one or other of them; never putting in another word, but always leaving a blank and going on to the next word.

As I could do no service there, and as I had, nearer home, that pressing reason for anxiety and fear which even her wanderings could not drive out of my mind, I decided in the course of the night that I would return by the early morning coach: walking on a mile or so, and being taken up clear of the town. At about six o'clock of the morning, therefore, I leaned over her and touched her lips with mine, just as they said, not stopping for being touched, "Take the pencil and write under my name, 'I forgive her.'"

CHAPTER XI

MY HANDS had been dressed twice or thrice in the night, and again in the morning. My left arm was a good deal burned to the elbow, and, less severely, as high as the shoulder; it was very painful, but the flames had set in that direction, and I felt thankful it was no worse. My right hand was not so badly burnt but that I could move the fingers. It was bandaged, of course, but much less inconveniently than my left hand and arm; those I carried in a sling; and I could only wear my coat like a cloak, loose over my shoulders and fastened at the neck. My hair had been caught by the fire, but not my head or face.

When Herbert had been down to Hammersmith and seen his father, he came back to me at our chambers, and devoted the day to attending on me. He was the kindest of nurses, and at stated times took off the bandages, and steeped them in the cooling liquid that was kept ready, and put them on again, with a patient tenderness that I was deeply grateful for.

At first, as I lay quiet on the sofa, I found it painfully difficult, I might say impossible, to get rid of the impression of the glare of the flames, their hurry and noise, and the fierce burning smell. If I dozed for a minute, I was awakened by Miss Havisham's cries, and by her running at me with all that height of fire above her head. This pain of the mind was much harder to strive against than any bodily pain I suffered; and Herbert, seeing that, did his utmost to hold my attention engaged.

Neither of us spoke of the boat, but we both thought of it. That was made apparent by our avoidance of the subject, and by our agreeing — without agreement — to make my recovery of the use of my hands, a question of so many hours, not of so many weeks.

My first question when I saw Herbert had been of course, whether all was well down the river? As he replied in the affirmative, with perfect confidence and cheerfulness, we did not resume the subject until the day was wearing away. But then, as Herbert changed the bandages, more by the light of the fire than by the outer light, he went back to it spontaneously.

"I sat with Provis last night, Handel, two good hours."

"Where was Clara?"

"Dear little thing!" said Herbert. "She was up and down with Gruffandgrim all the evening. He was perpetually pegging at the floor, the moment she left his sight. I doubt if he can hold out long though. What with rum and pepper — and pepper and rum — I should think his pegging must be nearly over."

"And then you will be married, Herbert?"

"How can I take care of the dear child otherwise? — Lay your arm out upon the back of the sofa, my dear boy, and I'll sit down here, and get the bandage off so gradually that you shall not know when it comes. I was speaking of Provis. Do you know, Handel, he improves?"

"I said to you I thought he was softened when I last saw him."

"So you did. And so he is. He was very communicative last night, and told me more of his life. You remember his breaking off here about some woman that he had had great trouble with. — Did I hurt you?"

I had started, but not under his touch. His words had given me a start.

"I had forgotten that, Herbert, but I remember it now you speak of it."

"Well! He went into that part of his life, and a dark wild part it is. Shall I tell you? Or would it worry you just now?"

"Tell me by all means. Every word."

Herbert bent forward to look at me more nearly, as if my reply had been rather more hurried or more eager than he could quite account for. "Your head is cool?" he said, touching it.

"Quite," said I. "Tell me what Provis said, my dear Herbert."

"It seems," said Herbert, "— there's a bandage off most charmingly, and now comes the cool one — makes you shrink at first, my poor dear fellow, don't it? but it will be comfortable presently — it seems that the woman was a young woman, and a jealous woman, and a revengeful woman; revengeful, Handel, to the last degree."

"To what last degree?"

"Murder. — Does it strike too cold on that sensitive place?"

"I don't feel it. How did she murder? Whom did she murder?"

"Why, the deed may not have merited quite so terrible a name," said Herbert, "but, she was tried for it, and Mr. Jaggers defended her, and the reputation of that defence first made his name known to Provis. It was another and a stronger woman who was the victim, and there had been a struggle — in a barn. Who began it, or how fair it was, or how unfair, may be doubtful; but how it ended, is certainly not doubtful, for the victim was found throttled."

"Was the woman brought in guilty?"

"No; she was acquitted. — My poor Handel, I hurt you!"

"It is impossible to be gentler, Herbert. Yes? What else?"

"This acquitted young woman and Provis," said Herbert, "had a little child: a little child of whom Provis was exceedingly fond. On the evening of the very night when the object of her jealousy was strangled as I tell you, the young woman presented herself before Provis for one moment, and swore that she would destroy the child (which was in her possession), and he should never see it again; then, she vanished. — There's the worst arm comfortably in the sling once more, and now there remains but the right hand, which is a far easier job. I can do it better by this light than by a stronger, for my hand is steadiest when I don't see the poor blistered patches too distinctly. — You don't think your breathing is affected, my dear boy? You seem to breathe quickly."

"Perhaps I do, Herbert. Did the woman keep her oath?"

"There comes the darkest part of Provis's life. She did."

"That is, he says she did."

"Why, of course, my dear boy," returned Herbert, in a tone of surprise, and again bending forward to get a nearer look at me. "He says it all. I have no other information."

"No, to be sure."

"Now, whether," pursued Herbert, "he had used the child's mother ill, or whether he had used the child's mother well, Provis doesn't say; but, she had shared some four or five years of the wretched life he described to us at this fireside, and he seems to have felt pity for her, and forbearance towards her. Therefore, fearing he should be called upon to depose about this destroyed child, and so be the cause of her death, he hid himself (much as he grieved for the child), kept himself dark, as he says, out of the way and out of the trial, and was only vaguely talked of as a certain man called Abel, out of whom the jealousy arose. After the acquittal she disappeared, and thus he lost the child and the child's mother."

"I want to ask —"

"A moment, my dear boy," said Herbert, " and I have done. That evil genius, Compeyson, the worst of scoundrels among many scoundrels, knowing of his keeping out of the way at that time, and of his reasons for doing so, of course afterwards held the knowledge over his head as a means of keeping him poorer, and working him harder. It was clear last night that this barbed the point of Provis's animosity."

"I want to know," said I, "and particularly, Herbert, whether he told you when this happened?"

"Particularly? Let me remember, then, what he said as to that. His expression was, 'a round score o' year ago, and a'most directly after I took up wi' Compeyson.' How old were you when you came upon him in the little churchyard?"

"I think in my seventh year."

"Ay. It had happened some three or four years then, he said, and you brought into his mind the little girl so tragically lost, who would have been about your age."

"Herbert," said I, after a short silence, in a hurried way, "can you see me best by the light of the window, or the light of the fire?"

"By the firelight," answered Herbert, coming close again.

"Look at me."

"I do look at you, my dear boy."

"Touch me."

"I do touch you, my dear boy."

"You are not afraid that I am in any fever, or that my head is much disordered by the accident of last night?"

"N-no, my dear boy," said Herbert, after taking time to examine me. "You are rather excited, but you are quite yourself."

"I know I am quite myself. And the man we have in hiding down the river, is Estella's Father."

CHAPTER XII

WHAT PURPOSE I had in view when I was hot on tracing out and proving Estella's parentage, I cannot say. It will presently be seen that the question was not before me in a distinct shape, until it was put before me by a wiser head than my own.

But, when Herbert and I had held our momentous conversation, I was seized with a feverish conviction that I ought to hunt the matter down — that I ought not to let it rest, but that I ought to see Mr. Jaggers, and come at the bare truth. I really do not know whether I felt that I did this for Estella's sake, or whether I was glad to transfer to the man in whose preservation I was so much concerned, some rays of the romantic interest that had so long surrounded her. Perhaps the latter possibility may be the nearer to the truth.

Any way, I could scarcely be withheld from going out to Gerrard-street that night. Herbert's representations that if I did, I should probably be laid up and stricken useless, when our fugitive's safety would depend upon me, alone restrained my impatience. On the understanding, again and again reiterated, that come what would, I was to go to Mr. Jaggers to-morrow, I at length submitted to keep quiet, and to have my hurts looked after, and to stay at home. Early next morning we went out together, and at the corner of Giltspur-street by Smithfield, I left Herbert to go his way into the City, and took my way to Little Britain.

There were periodical occasions when Mr. Jaggers and Wemmick went over the office accounts, and checked off the vouchers, and put all things straight. On those occasions Wemmick took his books and papers into Mr. Jaggers's room, and one of the up-stairs clerks came down into the outer office. Finding such clerk on Wemmick's post that morning, I knew what was going on; but, I was not sorry to have Mr. Jaggers and Wemmick together, as Wemmick would then hear for himself that I said nothing to compromise him.

My appearance with my arm bandaged and my coat loose over my shoulders, favoured my object. Although I had sent Mr. Jaggers a brief account of the accident as soon as I had arrived in town, yet I had to give him all the details now; and the speciality of the occasion caused our talk to be less dry and hard, and less strictly regulated by the rules of evidence, than it had been before. While I described the disaster, Mr. Jaggers stood, according to his wont, before the fire. Wemmick leaned back in his chair, staring at me, with his hands in the pockets of his trousers, and his pen put horizontally into the post. The two brutal casts, always inseparable in my mind from the official proceedings, seemed to be congestively considering whether they didn't smell fire at the present moment.

My narrative finished, and their questions exhausted, I then produced Miss Havisham's authority to receive the nine hundred pounds for Herbert. Mr. Jaggers's eyes retired a little deeper into his head when I handed him the tablets, but he presently handed them over to Wemmick, with instructions to draw the cheque for his signature. While that was in course of being done, I looked on at Wemmick as he wrote, and Mr. Jaggers, poising and swaying himself on his well-polished boots, looked on at me. "I am sorry, Pip," said he, as I put the cheque in my pocket, when he had signed it, "that we do nothing for *you*."

"Miss Havisham was good enough to ask me," I returned, "whether she could do nothing for me, and I told her No."

"Everybody should know his own business," said Mr. Jaggers. And I saw Wemmick's lips form the words "portable property."

"I should *not* have told her No, if I had been you," said Mr. Jaggers;

"but every man ought to know his own business best."

"Every man's business," said Wemmick, rather reproachfully towards me, "is portable property."

As I thought the time was now come for pursuing the theme I had at heart, I said, turning on Mr. Jaggers:

"I did ask something of Miss Havisham, however, sir. I asked her to give me some information relative to her adopted daughter, and she gave me all she possessed."

"Did she?" said Mr. Jaggers, bending forward to look at his boots and then straightening himself. "Hah! I don't think I should have done so, if I had been Miss Havisham. But *she* ought to know her own business best."

"I know more of the history of Miss Havisham's adopted child than Miss Havisham herself does, sir. I know her mother."

Mr. Jaggers looked at me inquiringly, and repeated "Mother?"

"I have seen her mother within these three days."

"Yes?" said Mr. Jaggers.

"And so have you, sir. And you have seen her still more recently."

"Yes?" said Mr. Jaggers.

"Perhaps I know more of Estella's history than even you do," said I. "I know her father too."

A certain stop that Mr. Jaggers came to in his manner — he was too self-possessed to change his manner, but he could not help its being brought to an indefinably attentive stop — assured me that he did not know who her father was. This I had strongly suspected from Provis's account (as Herbert had repeated it) of his having kept himself dark; which I pieced on to the fact that he himself was not Mr. Jaggers's client until some four years later, and when he could have no reason for claiming his identity. But, I could not be sure of this unconsciousness on Mr. Jaggers's part before, though I was quite sure of it now.

"So! You know the young lady's father, Pip?" said Mr. Jaggers.

"Yes," I replied, "and his name is Provis — from New South Wales."

Even Mr. Jaggers started when I said those words. It was the slightest start that could escape a man, the most carefully repressed and the soonest checked, but he did start, though he made it a part of the action of taking out his pocket-handkerchief. How Wemmick received the announcement I am unable to say, for I was afraid to look at him just then, lest Mr. Jaggers's sharpness should detect that there had been some communication unknown to him between us.

"And on what evidence, Pip," asked Mr. Jaggers, very coolly, as he paused with his handkerchief half way to his nose, "does Provis make this claim?"

"He does not make it," said I, "and has never made it, and has no knowledge or belief that his daughter is in existence."

For once, the powerful pocket-handkerchief failed. My reply was so unexpected that Mr. Jaggers put the handkerchief back into his pocket without completing the usual performance, folded his arms and looked with stern attention at me, though with an immovable face.

Then I told him all I knew, and how I knew it; with the one reservation that I left him to infer that I knew from Miss Havisham what I in fact knew from Wemmick. I was very careful indeed as to that. Nor, did I look towards Wemmick until I had finished all I had to tell, and had been for some time silently meeting Mr. Jaggers's look. When I did at last turn my eyes in Wemmick's direction, I found that he had unposted his pen, and was intent upon the table before him.

"Hah!" said Mr. Jaggers at last, as he moved towards the papers on the table. "—What item was it you were at, Wemmick, when Mr. Pip came in?"

But I could not submit to be thrown off in that way, and I made a passionate, almost an indignant, appeal to him to be more frank and manly with me. I reminded him of the false hopes into which I had lapsed, the length of time they had lasted, and the discovery I had made: and I hinted at the danger that weighed upon my spirits. I represented myself as being surely worthy of some little confidence from him, in return for the confidence I had just now imparted. I said that I did not blame him, or suspect him, or mistrust him, but I wanted assurance of the truth from him. And if he asked me why I wanted it and why I thought I had any right to it, I would tell him, little as he cared for such poor dreams, that I had loved Estella dearly and long, and that, although I had lost her and must live a bereaved life, whatever concerned her was still nearer and dearer to me than anything else in the world. And seeing that Mr. Jaggers stood quite still and silent, and apparently quite obdurate, under this appeal, I turned to Wemmick, and said, "Wemmick, I know you to be a man with a gentle heart. I have seen your pleasant home, and your old father, and all the innocent cheerful playful ways with which you refresh your business life. And I entreat you to say a word for me to Mr. Jaggers, and to represent to him that, all circumstances considered, he ought to be more open with me!"

I have never seen two men look more oddly at one another than Mr. Jaggers and Wemmick did after this apostrophe. At first, a misgiving crossed me that Wemmick would be instantly dismissed from his employment; but, it melted as I saw Mr. Jaggers relax into something like a smile, and Wemmick become bolder.

"What's all this?" said Mr. Jaggers. "You with an old father, and you with pleasant and playful ways?"

"Well!" returned Wemmick. "If I don't bring 'em here, what does it matter?"

"Pip," said Mr. Jaggers, laying his hand upon my arm, and smiling openly, "this man must be the most cunning impostor in all London."

"Not a bit of it," returned Wemmick, growing bolder and bolder. "I think you're another."

Again they exchanged their former odd looks, each apparently still distrustful that the other was taking him in.

"*You* with a pleasant home?" said Mr. Jaggers.

"Since it don't interfere with business," returned Wemmick, "let it be so. Now, I look at you, sir, I shouldn't wonder if *you* might be planning and contriving to have a pleasant home of your own, one of these days, when you're tired of all this work."

Mr. Jaggers nodded his head retrospectively two or three times, and actually drew a sigh. "Pip," said he, "we won't talk about 'poor dreams'; you know more about such things than I, having much fresher experience of that kind. But now, about this other matter. I'll put a case to you. Mind! I admit nothing."

He waited for me to declare that I quite understood that he expressly said that he admitted nothing.

"Now, Pip," said Mr. Jaggers, "put this case. Put the case that a woman, under such circumstances as you have mentioned, held her child concealed, and was obliged to communicate the fact to her legal adviser, on his representing to her that he must know, with an eye to the latitude of his defence, how the fact stood about that child. Put the case that at the same time he held a trust to find a child for an eccentric rich lady to adopt and bring up."

"I follow you, sir."

"Put the case that he lived in an atmosphere of evil, and that all he saw of children, was, their being generated in great numbers for certain destruction. Put the case that he often saw children solemnly tried at a criminal bar, where they were held up to be seen; put the case that he habitually knew of their being imprisoned, whipped, transported, neglected, cast out, qualified in all ways for the hangman, and growing up to be hanged. Put the case that pretty nigh all the children he saw in his daily business life, he had reason to look upon as so much spawn, to develop into the fish that were to come to his net — to be prosecuted, defended, forsworn, made orphans, be-devilled somehow."

"I follow you, sir."

"Put the case, Pip, that here was one pretty little child out of the heap, who could be saved; whom the father believed dead, and dared make no stir about; as to whom, over the mother, the legal adviser had this power: 'I know what you did, and how you did it. You came so and so, this was your manner of attack and this the manner of resistance, you went so and so, you did such and such things to divert suspicion. I have tracked you through it all, and I tell it you all. Part with the child, unless it should be necessary to produce it to clear you, and then it shall be produced. Give the child into my hands, and I will do my best to bring you off. If you are saved, your child is saved too; if you are lost, your child is still saved.' Put the case that this was done, and that the woman was cleared."

"I understand you perfectly."

"But that I make no admissions?"

"That you make no admissions." And Wemmick repeated, "No admissions."

"Put the case, Pip, that passion and the terror of death had a little shaken the woman's intellects, and that when she was set at liberty, she was scared out of the ways of the world and went to him to be sheltered. Put the case that he took her in, and that he kept down the old wild violent nature whenever he saw an inkling of its breaking out, by asserting his power over her in the old way. Do you comprehend the imaginary case?"

"Quite."

"Put the case that the child grew up, and was married for money. That the mother was still living. That the father was still living. That the mother and father unknown to one another, were dwelling within so many miles, furlongs, yards if you like, of one another. That the secret was still a secret, except that you had got wind of it. Put that last case to yourself very carefully."

"I do."

"I ask Wemmick to put it to *him*self very carefully."

And Wemmick said, "I do."

"For whose sake would you reveal the secret? For the father's? I think he would not be much the better for the mother. For the mother's? I think if she had done such a deed she would be safer where she was. For the daughter's? I think it would hardly serve her, to establish her parentage for the information of her husband, and to drag her back to disgrace, after an escape of twenty years, pretty secure to last for life. But, add the case that you had loved her, Pip, and had made her the subject of those 'poor dreams' which have, at one time or another, been in the heads of more men than you think likely, then I tell you that you had better — and would much sooner when you had thought well of it — chop off that bandaged left hand of yours with your bandaged right hand, and then pass the chopper on to Wemmick there, to cut *that* off, too."

I looked at Wemmick, whose face was very grave. He gravely touched his lips with his forefinger. I did the same. Mr. Jaggers did the same. "Now, Wemmick," said the latter then, resuming his usual manner, "what item was it you were at, when Mr. Pip came in?"

Standing by for a little, while they were at work, I observed that the odd looks they had cast at one another were repeated several times: with this difference now, that each of them seemed suspicious, not to say conscious, of having shown himself in a weak and unprofessional light to the other. For this reason, I suppose, they were now inflexible with one another; Mr. Jaggers being highly dictatorial, and Wemmick obstinately justifying himself whenever there was the smallest point in abeyance for a moment. I had never seen them on such ill terms; for generally they got on very well indeed together.

But, they were both happily relieved by the opportune appearance of

Mike, the client with the fur cap and the habit of wiping his nose on his sleeve, whom I had seen on the very first day of my appearance within those walls. This individual, who, either in his own person or in that of some member of his family, seemed to be always in trouble (which in that place meant Newgate), called to announce that his eldest daughter was taken up on suspicion of shoplifting. As he imparted this melancholy circumstance to Wemmick, Mr. Jaggers standing magisterially before the fire and taking no share in the proceedings, Mike's eye happened to twinkle with a tear.

"What are you about?" demanded Wemmick, with the utmost indignation. "What do you come snivelling here for?"

"I didn't* go to do it, Mr. Wemmick."

"You did," said Wemmick. "How dare you? You're not in a fit state to come here, if you can't come here without spluttering like a bad pen. What do you mean by it?"

"A man can't help his feelings, Mr. Wemmick," pleaded Mike.

"His what?" demanded Wemmick, quite savagely. "Say that again!"

"Now, look here my man," said Mr. Jaggers, advancing a step, and pointing to the door. "Get out of this office. I'll have no feelings here. Get out."

"It serves you right," said Wemmick. "Get out."

So the unfortunate Mike very humbly withdrew, and Mr. Jaggers and Wemmick appeared to have re-established their good understanding, and went to work again with an air of refreshment upon them as if they had just had lunch.

CHAPTER XIII

FROM LITTLE Britain, I went, with my cheque in my pocket, to Miss Skiffins's brother, the accountant; and Miss Skiffins's brother, the accountant, going straight to Clarriker's and bringing Clarriker to me, I had the great satisfaction of concluding that arrangement. It was the only good thing I had done, and the only completed thing I had done, since I was first apprised of my great expectations.

Clarriker informing me on that occasion that the affairs of the House were steadily progressing, that he would now be able to establish a small branch-house in the East which was much wanted for the extension of the business, and that Herbert in his new partnership capacity would go out and take charge of it, I found that I must have prepared for a separation from my friend, even though my own affairs had been more settled. And now indeed I felt as if my last anchor were loosening its hold, and I should soon be driving with the winds and waves.

But, there was recompense in the joy with which Herbert would come home of a night and tell me of these changes, little imagining that he told me no news, and would sketch airy pictures of himself conducting Clara Barley to the land of the Arabian Nights, and of me going out to join them (with a caravan of camels, I believe), and of our all going up the Nile and seeing wonders. Without being sanguine as to my own part in these bright plans, I felt that Herbert's way was clearing fast, and that old Bill Barley had but to stick to his pepper and rum, and his daughter would soon be happily provided for.

We had now got into the month of March. My left arm, though it presented no bad symptoms, took in the natural course so long to heal that I was still unable to get a coat on. My right arm was tolerably restored; — disfigured, but fairly serviceable.

On a Monday morning, when Herbert and I were at breakfast, I received the following letter from Wemmick by the post.

"Walworth. Burn this as soon as read. Early in the week, or say Wednesday, you might do what you know of, if you felt disposed to try it. Now burn."

When I had shown this to Herbert and had put it in the fire — but not before we had both got it by heart — we considered what to do. For, of course my being disabled could now be no longer kept out of view.

"I have thought it over, again and again," said Herbert, "and I think I know a better course than taking a Thames waterman. Take Startop. A good fellow, a skilled hand, fond of us, and enthusiastic and honourable."

I had thought of him, more than once.

"But how much would you tell him, Herbert?"

"It is necessary to tell him very little. Let him suppose it a mere freak, but a secret one, until the morning comes: then let him know that there is urgent reason for your getting Provis aboard and away. You go with him?"

"No doubt."

"Where?"

It had seemed to me, in the many anxious considerations I had given the point, almost indifferent what port we made for — Hamburg, Rotterdam, Antwerp — the place signified little, so that he was got out of England. Any foreign steamer that fell in our way and would take us up, would do. I had always proposed to myself to get him well down the river in the boat; certainly well beyond Gravesend,[1] which was a critical place for search or inquiry if suspicion were afoot. As foreign steamers would leave London at about the time of high-water, our plan would be to get down the river by a previous ebb-tide, and lie by in some quiet spot until we could pull off to one. The time when one would be due where we lay, wherever that might be, could be calculated pretty nearly, if we made inquiries beforehand.

Herbert assented to all this, and we went out immediately after breakfast to pursue our investigations. We found that a steamer for Hamburg was likely to suit our purpose best, and we directed our thoughts chiefly to that vessel. But we noted down what other foreign steamers would leave London with the same tide, and we satisfied ourselves that we knew the build and colour of each. We then separated for a few hours; I, to get at once such passports as were necessary; Herbert, to see Startop at his lodgings. We both did what we had to do without any hindrance, and when we met again at one o'clock reported it done. I, for my part, was prepared with passports; Herbert had seen Startop, and he was more than ready to join.

Those two should pull a pair of oars, we settled, and I would steer; our charge would be sitter,[2] and keep quiet; as speed was not our object, we should make way enough. We arranged that Herbert should not come home to dinner before going to Mill Pond Bank that evening; that he should not go there at all, to-morrow evening, Tuesday; that he should prepare Provis to come down to some Stairs hard by the house, on Wednes-

---

1. *Gravesend:* port on the Kent side of the Thames estuary. See Map A.
2. *sitter:* passenger in a small boat.

day, when he saw us approach, and not sooner; that all the arrangements with him should be concluded that Monday night; and that he should be communicated with no more in any way, until we took him on board.

These precautions well understood by both of us, I went home.

On opening the outer door of our chambers with my key, I found a letter in the box, directed to me; a very dirty letter, though not ill-written. It had been delivered by hand (of course since I left home), and its contents were these:

"If you are not afraid to come to the old marshes to-night or to-morrow night at Nine, and to come to the little sluice-house by the limekiln,[1] you had better come. If you want information regarding *your uncle Provis*, you had much better come and tell no one and lose no time. *You must come alone.* Bring this with you."

I had had load enough upon my mind before the receipt of this strange letter. What to do now, I could not tell. And the worst was, that I must decide quickly, or I should miss the afternoon coach, which would take me down in time for to-night. To-morrow night I could not think of going, for it would be too close upon the time of the flight. And again, for anything I knew, the proffered information might have some important bearing on the flight itself.

If I had had ample time for consideration, I believe I should still have gone. Having hardly any time for consideration — my watch showing me that the coach started within half an hour — I resolved to go. I should certainly not have gone, but for the reference to my Uncle Provis; that, coming on Wemmick's letter and the morning's busy preparation, turned the scale.

It is so difficult to become clearly possessed of the contents of almost any letter, in a violent hurry, that I had to read this mysterious epistle again, twice, before its injunction to me to be secret got mechanically into my mind. Yielding to it in the same mechanical kind of way, I left a note in pencil for Herbert, telling him that as I should be so soon going away, I knew not for how long, I had decided to hurry down and back, to ascertain for myself how Miss Havisham was faring. I had then barely time to get my great-coat, lock up the chambers, and make for the coach-

---

1. *limekiln:* for producing lime from limestone by roasting.

office by the short by-ways. If I had taken a hackney-chariot and gone by the streets, I should have missed my aim; going as I did, I caught the coach just as it came out of the yard. I was the only inside passenger, jolting away knee-deep in straw, when I came to myself.

For, I really had not been myself since the receipt of the letter; it had so bewildered me ensuing on the hurry of the morning. The morning hurry and flutter had been great, for, long and anxiously as I had waited for Wemmick, his hint had come like a surprise at last. And now, I began to wonder at myself for being in the coach, and to doubt whether I had sufficient reason for being there, and to consider whether I should get out presently and go back, and to argue against ever heeding an anonymous communication, and, in short, to pass through all those phases of contradiction and indecision to which I suppose very few hurried people are strangers. Still, the reference to Provis by name, mastered everything. I reasoned as I had reasoned already without knowing it — if that be reasoning — in case any harm should befal him through my not going, how could I ever forgive myself!

It was dark before we got down, and the journey seemed long and dreary to me who could see little of it inside, and who could not go outside in my disabled state. Avoiding the Blue Boar, I put up at an inn of minor reputation down the town, and ordered some dinner. While it was preparing, I went to Satis House and inquired for Miss Havisham; she was still very ill, though considered something better.

My inn had once been a part of an ancient ecclesiastical house, and I dined in a little octagonal common-room, like a font.[1] As I was not able to cut my dinner, the old landlord with a shining bald head did it for me. This bringing us into conversation, he was so good as to entertain me with my own story — of course with the popular feature that Pumblechook was my earliest benefactor and the founder of my fortunes.

"Do you know the young man?" said I.

"Know him!" repeated the landlord. "Ever since he was — no height at all."

"Does he ever come back to this neighbourhood?"

---

1. *My inn had once been a part of an ancient ecclesiastical house, and I dined in a little octagonal common-room, like a font:* see note on p. 418.

"Ay, he comes back," said the landlord, "to his great friends, now and again, and gives the cold shoulder to the man that made him."

"What man is that?"

"Him that I speak of," said the landlord. "Mr. Pumblechook."

"Is he ungrateful to no one else?"

"No doubt he would be, if he could," returned the landlord, "but he can't. And why? Because Pumblechook done everything for him."

"Does Pumblechook say so?"

"Say so!" replied the landlord. "He han't no call to say so."

"But does he say so?"

"It would turn a man's blood to white wine winegar to hear him tell of it, sir," said the landlord.

I thought, "Yet Joe, dear Joe, *you* never tell of it. Long-suffering and loving Joe, *you* never complain. Nor you, sweet-tempered Biddy!"

"Your appetite's been touched like, by your accident," said the landlord, glancing at the bandaged arm under my coat. "Try a tenderer bit."

"No thank you," I replied, turning from the table to brood over the fire. "I can eat no more. Please take it away."

I had never been struck at so keenly, for my thanklessness to Joe, as through the brazen impostor Pumblechook. The falser he, the truer Joe; the meaner he, the nobler Joe.

My heart was deeply and most deservedly humbled as I mused over the fire for an hour or more. The striking of the clock aroused me, but not from my dejection or remorse, and I got up and had my coat fastened round my neck, and went out. I had previously sought in my pockets for the letter, that I might refer to it again, but I could not find it, and was uneasy to think that it must have been dropped in the straw of the coach. I knew very well, however, that the appointed place was the little sluice-house by the limekiln on the marshes, and the hour nine. Towards the marshes I now went straight, having no time to spare.

CHAPTER XIV

IT WAS a dark night, though the full moon rose as I left the enclosed lands, and passed out upon the marshes. Beyond their dark line there was a ribbon of clear sky, hardly broad enough to hold the red large moon. In a few minutes she had ascended out of that clear field, in among the piled mountains of cloud.

There was a melancholy wind, and the marshes were very dismal. A stranger would have found them insupportable, and even to me they were so oppressive that I hesitated, half inclined to go back. But, I knew them well, and could have found my way on a far darker night, and had no excuse for returning, being there. So, having come there against my inclination, I went on against it.

The direction that I took, was not that in which my old home lay, nor that in which we had pursued the convicts. My back was turned towards the distant Hulks as I walked on, and, though I could see the old lights away on the spits of sand, I saw them over my shoulder. I knew the limekiln as well as I knew the old Battery, but they were miles apart; so that if a light had been burning at each point that night, there would have been a long strip of the blank horizon between the two bright specks.

At first, I had to shut some gates after me, and now and then to stand still while the cattle that were lying in the banked-up pathway, arose and blundered down among the grass and reeds. But after a little while, I seemed to have the whole flats to myself.

It was another half-hour before I drew near to the kiln. The lime was burning with a sluggish stifling smell, but the fires were made up and left, and no workmen were visible. Hard by, was a small stone-quarry. It lay directly in my way, and had been worked that day, as I saw by the tools and barrows that were lying about.

Coming up again to the marsh level out of this excavation — for the rude path lay through it — I saw a light in the old sluice-house. I quickened my pace, and knocked at the door with my hand. Waiting for some reply, I looked about me, noticing how the sluice was abandoned and broken, and how the house — of wood with a tiled roof — would not be proof against the weather much longer, if it were so even now, and how the mud and ooze were coated with lime, and how the choking vapour of the kiln crept in a ghostly way towards me. Still there was no answer, and I knocked again. No answer still, and I tried the latch.

It rose under my hand, and the door yielded. Looking in, I saw a lighted candle on a table, a bench, and a mattress on a truckle bedstead. As there was a loft above, I called, "Is there any one here?" but no voice answered. Then, I looked at my watch, and, finding that it was past nine, called again, "Is there any one here?" There being still no answer, I went out at the door, irresolute what to do.

It was beginning to rain fast. Seeing nothing save what I had seen already, I turned back into the house, and stood just within the shelter of the doorway, looking out into the night. While I was considering that some one must have been there lately and must soon be coming back, or the candle would not be burning, it came into my head to look if the wick were long. I turned round to do so, and had taken up the candle in my hand, when it was extinguished by some violent shock, and the next thing I comprehended, was, that I had been caught in a strong running noose, thrown over my head from behind.

"Now," said a suppressed voice with an oath, "I've got you!"

"What is this?" I cried, struggling. "Who is it? Help, help, help!"

Not only were my arms pulled close to my sides, but the pressure on my bad arm caused me exquisite pain. Sometimes, a strong man's hand, sometimes a strong man's breast, was set against my mouth to deaden my cries, and with a hot breath always close to me, I struggled ineffectually in the dark, while I was fastened tight to the wall. "And now," said the suppressed voice with another oath, "call out again, and I'll make short work of you!"

Faint and sick with the pain of my injured arm, bewildered by the surprise, and yet conscious how easily this threat could be put in execution, I desisted, and tried to ease my arm were it ever so little. But, it was bound too tight for that. I felt as if, having been burnt before, it were now being boiled.

The sudden exclusion of the night and the substitution of black darkness in its place, warned me that the man had closed a shutter. After groping about for a little, he found the flint and steel he wanted, and began to strike a light. I strained my sight upon the sparks that fell among the tinder, and upon which he breathed and breathed, match in hand, but I could only see his lips, and the blue point of the match; even those, but fitfully. The tinder was damp — no wonder there — and one after another the sparks died out.

The man was in no hurry, and struck again with the flint and steel. As the sparks fell thick and bright about him, I could see his hands, and touches of his face, and could make out that he was seated and bending over the table; but nothing more. Presently I saw his blue lips again, breathing on the tinder, and then a flare of light flashed up, and showed me Orlick.

Whom I had looked for, I don't know. I had not looked for him. Seeing him, I felt that I was in a dangerous strait indeed, and I kept my eyes upon him.

He lighted the candle from the flaring match with great deliberation, and dropped the match, and trod it out. Then, he put the candle away from him on the table, so that he could see me, and sat with his arms folded on the table and looked at me. I made out that I was fastened to a stout perpendicular ladder a few inches from the wall — a fixture there — the means of ascent to the loft above.

"Now," said he, when we had surveyed one another for some time, "I've got you."

"Unbind me. Let me go!"

"Ah!" he returned, "I'll let you go. I'll let you go to the moon, I'll let you go to the stars. All in good time."

"Why have you lured me here?"

"Don't you know?" said he, with a deadly look.

"Why have you set upon me in the dark?"

"Because I mean to do it all myself. One keeps a secret better than two. Oh you enemy, you enemy!"

His enjoyment of the spectacle I furnished, as he sat with his arms folded on the table, shaking his head at me and hugging himself, had a malignity in it that made me tremble. As I watched him in silence, he put his hand into the corner at his side, and took up a gun with a brass-bound stock.

"Do you know this?" said he, making as if he would take aim at me. "Do you know where you saw it afore? Speak, wolf!"

"Yes," I answered.

"You cost me that place. You did. Speak!"

"What else could I do?"

"You did that, and that would be enough, without more. How dared you to come betwixt me and a young woman I liked?"

"When did I?"

"When didn't you? It was you as always give Old Orlick a bad name to her."

"You gave it to yourself; you gained it for yourself. I could have done you no harm, if you had done yourself none."

"You're a liar. And you'll take any pains, and spend any money, to drive me out of this country, will you?" said he, repeating my words to Biddy in the last interview I had with her. "Now, I'll tell you a piece of information. It was never so well worth your while to get me out of this country as it is to-night. Ah! If it was all your money twenty times told, to the last brass farden!" As he shook his heavy hand at me, with his mouth snarling like a tiger's, I felt that it was true.

"What are you going to do to me?"

"I'm a going," said he, bringing his fist down upon the table with a heavy blow, and rising as the blow fell, to give it greater force, "I'm a going to have your life!"

He leaned forward staring at me, slowly unclenched his hand and drew it across his mouth as if his mouth watered for me, and sat down again.

"You wos always in Old Orlick's way since ever you wos a child. You goes out of his way, this present night. He'll have no more on you. You're dead."

I felt that I had come to the brink of my grave. For a moment I looked wildly round my trap for any chance of escape; but there was none.

"More than that," said he, folding his arms on the table again, "I won't have a rag of you, I won't have a bone of you, left on earth. I'll put your body in the kiln — I'd carry two such to it, on my shoulders — and, let people suppose what they may of you, they shall never know nothing."

My mind, with inconceivable rapidity, followed out all the consequences of such a death. Estella's father would believe I had deserted him, would be taken, would die accusing me; even Herbert would doubt me, when he compared the letter I had left for him, with the fact that I had called at Miss Havisham's gate for only a moment; Joe and Biddy would never know how sorry I had been that night; none would ever know what I had suffered, how true I had meant to be, what an agony I had passed through. The death close before me was terrible, but far more terrible than death was the dread of being misremembered after death. And so quick were my thoughts, that I saw myself despised by unborn generations — Estella's children, and their children — while the wretch's words were yet on his lips.

"Now, wolf," said he, "afore I kill you like any other beast — which is wot I mean to do and wot I have tied you up for — I'll have a good look at you and a good goad at you. Oh, you enemy!"

It had passed through my thoughts to cry out for help again; though few could know better than I, the solitary nature of the spot and the hopelessness of aid. But as he sat gloating over me, I was supported by a scornful detestation of him that sealed my lips. Above all things, I resolved that I would not entreat him, and that I would die making some last poor resistance to him. Softened as my thoughts of all the rest of men were in that dire extremity; humbly beseeching pardon, as I did, of Heaven; melted at heart, as I was, by the thought that I had taken no farewell, and never never now could take farewell, of those who were dear to me, or could explain myself to them, or ask for their compassion on my miserable errors; still, if I could have killed him, even in dying, I would have done it.

He had been drinking, and his eyes were red and bloodshot. Around his neck was slung a tin bottle, as I had often seen his meat and drink slung about him in other days. He brought the bottle to his lips, and took a fiery drink from it; and I smelt the strong spirits that I saw flash into his face.

"Wolf!" said he, folding his arms again, "Old Orlick's a going to tell you somethink. It was you as did for your shrew sister."

Again my mind, with its former inconceivable rapidity, had exhausted the whole subject of the attack upon my sister, her illness, and her death, before his slow and hesitating speech had formed these words.

"It was you, villain," said I.

"I tell you it was your doing — I tell you it was done through you," he retorted, catching up the gun, and making a blow with the stock at the vacant air between us. "I come upon her from behind, as I come upon you to-night. *I* giv' it her! I left her for dead, and if there had been a limekiln as nigh her as there is now nigh you, she shouldn't have come to life again. But it warn't Old Orlick as did it; it was you. You was favoured, and he was bullied and beat. Old Orlick bullied and beat, eh? Now you pays for it. You done it; now you pays for it."

He drank again, and became more ferocious. I saw by his tilting of the bottle that there was no great quantity left in it. I distinctly understood that he was working himself up with its contents, to make an end of me. I knew that every drop it held, was a drop of my life. I knew that when I was changed into a part of the vapour that had crept towards me but a little while before, like my own warning ghost he would do as he had done in my sister's case — make all haste to the town, and be seen slouching about there, drinking at the ale-houses. My rapid mind pursued him to the town, made a picture of the street with him in it, and contrasted its lights and life with the lonely marsh and the white vapour creeping over it, into which I should have dissolved.

It was not only that I could have summed up years and years and years while he said a dozen words, but that what he did say presented pictures to me, and not mere words. In the excited and exalted state of my brain, I could not think of a place without seeing it, or of persons without seeing them. It is impossible to over-state the vividness of these images, and yet I was so intent, all the time, upon him himself — who would not be intent on the tiger crouching to spring! — that I knew of the slightest action of his fingers.

When he had drunk this second time, he rose from the bench on which he sat, and pushed the table aside. Then, he took up the candle, and shading it with his murderous hand so as to throw its light on me, stood before me, looking at me and enjoying the sight.

"Wolf, I'll tell you something more. It was Old Orlick as you tumbled over on your stairs that night."

I saw the staircase with its extinguished lamps. I saw the shadows of the heavy stair-rails, thrown by the watchman's lantern on the wall. I saw the rooms that I was never to see again; here, a door half open; there, a door closed; all the articles of furniture around.

"And why was Old Orlick there? I'll tell you something more, wolf. You and her *have* pretty well hunted me out of this country, so far as getting a easy living in it goes, and I've took up with new companions, and new masters. Some of 'em writes my letters when I wants 'em wrote — do you mind? — writes my letters, wolf! They writes fifty hands; they're not like sneaking you, as writes but one. I've had a firm mind and a firm will to have your life, since you wos down here at your sister's burying. I han't seen a way to get you safe, and I've looked arter you to know your ins and outs. For, says Old Orlick to himself, 'Somehow or another I'll have him!' What! When I looks for you, I finds your uncle Provis, eh?"

Mill Pond Bank, and Chinks's Basin, and the Old Green Copper Rope-Walk, all so clear and plain! Provis in his rooms, the signal whose use was over, pretty Clara, the good motherly woman, old Bill Barley on his back, all drifting by, as on the swift stream of my life fast running out to sea!

"*You* with a uncle too! Why, I know'd you at Gargery's when you wos so small a wolf that I could have took your weazen[1] betwixt this finger and thumb and chucked you away dead (as I'd thoughts o' doing, odd times, when I see you loitering amongst the pollards on a Sunday), and you hadn't found no uncles then. No, not you! But when Old Orlick come for to hear that your uncle Provis had mostlike wore the leg-iron wot Old Orlick had picked up, filed asunder, on these meshes ever so many year ago, and wot he kep by him till he dropped your sister with it, like a bullock, as he means to drop you — hey? — when he come for to hear that — hey?" —

In his savage taunting, he flared the candle so close at me, that I turned my face aside, to save it from the flame.

"Ah!" he cried, laughing, after doing it again, "the burnt child dreads the fire! Old Orlick knowed you was burnt, Old Orlick knowed you was a smuggling your uncle Provis away, Old Orlick's a match for you and knowed you'd come to-night! Now I'll tell you something more, wolf, and this ends it. There's them that's as good a match for your uncle Provis as Old Orlick has been for you. Let him 'ware them, when he's lost his nevvy! Let him 'ware them, when no man can't find a rag of his dear relation's clothes, nor yet a bone of his body! There's them that can't and that won't have Magwitch — yes, *I* know the name! — alive in the same land with them, and that's had such sure information of him when he was alive in another land, as that he couldn't and shouldn't leave it un-

---

1. *weazen:* windpipe (dialect, more commonly transcribed "weasand").

beknown and put them in danger. P'raps it's them that writes fifty hands, and that's not like sneaking you as writes but one. 'Ware Compeyson, Magwitch, and the gallows!"

He flared the candle at me again, smoking my face and hair, and for an instant blinding me, and turned his powerful back as he replaced the light on the table. I had thought a prayer, and had been with Joe and Biddy and Herbert, before he turned towards me again.

There was a clear space of a few feet between the table and the opposite wall. Within this space, he now slouched backwards and forwards. His great strength seemed to sit stronger upon him than ever before, as he did this with his hands hanging loose and heavy at his sides, and with his eyes scowling at me. I had no grain of hope left. Wild as my inward hurry was, and wonderful the force of the pictures that rushed by me instead of thoughts, I could yet clearly understand that unless he had resolved that I was within a few moments of surely perishing out of all human knowledge, he would never have told me what he had told.

Of a sudden, he stopped, took the cork out of his bottle, and tossed it away. Light as it was, I heard it fall like a plummet. He swallowed slowly, tilting up the bottle by little and little, and now he looked at me no more. The last few drops of liquor he poured into the palm of his hand, and licked up. Then, with a sudden hurry of violence and swearing horribly, he threw the bottle from him, and stooped; and I saw in his hand a stone-hammer with a long heavy handle.

The resolution I had made did not desert me, for, without uttering one vain word of appeal to him, I shouted out with all my might, and struggled with all my might. It was only my head and my legs that I could move, but to that extent I struggled with all the force, until then unknown, that was within me. In the same instant I heard responsive shouts, saw figures and a gleam of light dash in at the door, heard voices and tumult, and saw Orlick emerge from a struggle of men, as if it were tumbling water, clear the table at a leap, and fly out into the night.

After a blank, I found that I was lying unbound, on the floor, in the same place, with my head on some one's knee. My eyes were fixed on the ladder against the wall, when I came to myself — had opened on it before my mind saw it — and thus as I recovered consciousness, I knew that I was in the place where I had lost it.

Too indifferent at first, even to look round and ascertain who supported me, I was lying looking at the ladder, when there came between me and it, a face. The face of Trabb's boy!

"I think he's all right!" said Trabb's boy, in a sober voice; "but ain't he just pale though!"

At these words, the face of him who supported me looked over into mine, and I saw my supporter to be —

"Herbert! Great Heaven!"

"Softly," said Herbert. "Gently, Handel. Don't be too eager."

"And our old comrade, Startop!" I cried, as he too bent over me.

"Remember what he is going to assist us in," said Herbert, "and be calm."

The allusion made me spring up; though I dropped again from the pain in my arm. "The time has not gone by, Herbert, has it? What night is to-night? How long have I been here?" For, I had a strange and strong misgiving that I had been lying there a long time — a day and a night — two days and nights — more.

"The time has not gone by. It is still Monday night."

"Thank God!"

"And you have all to-morrow, Tuesday, to rest in," said Herbert. "But you can't help groaning, my dear Handel. What hurt have you got? Can you stand?"

"Yes, yes," said I, "I can walk. I have no hurt but in this throbbing arm."

They laid it bare, and did what they could. It was violently swollen and inflamed, and I could scarcely endure to have it touched. But, they tore up their handkerchiefs to make fresh bandages, and carefully replaced it in the sling, until we could get to the town and obtain some cooling lotion to put upon it. In a little while we had shut the door of the dark and empty sluice-house, and were passing through the quarry on our way back. Trabb's boy — Trabb's overgrown young man now — went before us with a lantern, which was the light I had seen come in at the door. But, the moon was a good two hours higher than when I had last seen the sky, and the night though rainy was much lighter. The white vapour of the kiln was passing from us as we went by, and, as I had thought a prayer before, I thought a thanksgiving now.

Entreating Herbert to tell me how he had come to my rescue — which at first he had flatly refused to do, but had insisted on my remaining quiet — I learnt that I had in my hurry dropped the letter, open, in our chambers, where he, coming home to bring with him Startop whom he had met in the street on his way to me, found it, very soon after I was gone. Its tone made him uneasy, and the more so because of the inconsistency between it and the hasty letter I had left for him. His uneasiness increasing instead of subsiding after a quarter of an hour's consideration, he set off for the coach-office, with Startop, who volunteered his company, to make inquiry when the next coach went down. Finding that the afternoon coach was gone, and finding that his uneasiness grew into positive alarm, as obstacles came in his way, he resolved to follow in a post-chaise.[1] So, he and Startop arrived at the Blue Boar, fully expecting there to find me, or tidings of me; but, finding neither, went on to Miss Havisham's, where they lost me. Hereupon they went back to the hotel (doubtless at about the time when I was hearing the popular local version of my own story), to refresh themselves and to get some one to guide them out upon the marshes. Among the loungers under the Boar's archway, happened to be Trabb's boy — true to his ancient habit of happening to be everywhere where he had no business — and Trabb's boy had seen me passing from Miss Havisham's in the direction of my dining-place. Thus, Trabb's boy became their guide, and with him they went out to the sluice-house: though by the town way to the marshes, which I had avoided. Now, as they went along, Herbert reflected, that I might, after all, have been brought there on some genuine and serviceable errand tending to Provis's safety, and, bethinking himself that in that case interruption must be mischievous, left his guide and Startop on the edge of the quarry, and went on by himself, and stole round the house two or three times, endeavouring to ascertain whether all was right within. As he could hear nothing but indistinct sounds of one deep rough voice (this was while my mind was so busy), he even at last began to doubt whether I was there, when suddenly I cried out loudly, and he answered the cries, and rushed in, closely followed by the other two.

---

1. *post-chaise:* privately-hired travelling carriage.

When I told Herbert what had passed within the house, he was for our immediately going before a magistrate in the town, late at night as it was, and getting out a warrant. But, I had already considered that such a course, by detaining us there, or binding us to come back, might be fatal to Provis. There was no gainsaying this difficulty, and we relinquished all thoughts of pursuing Orlick at that time. For the present, under the circumstances, we deemed it prudent to make rather light of the matter to Trabb's boy; who I am convinced would have been much affected by disappointment, if he had known that his intervention saved me from the limekiln. Not that Trabb's boy was of a malignant nature, but that he had too much spare vivacity, and that it was in his constitution to want variety and excitement at anybody's expense. When we parted, I presented him with two guineas (which seemed to meet his views), and told him that I was sorry ever to have had an ill opinion of him (which made no impression on him at all).

Wednesday being so close upon us, we determined to go back to London that night, three in the post-chaise; the rather, as we should then be clear away, before the night's adventure began to be talked of. Herbert got a large bottle of stuff for my arm, and by dint of having this stuff dropped over it all the night through, I was just able to bear its pain on the journey. It was daylight when we reached the Temple, and I went at once to bed, and lay in bed all day.

My terror, as I lay there, of falling ill and being unfitted for to-morrow, was so besetting, that I wonder it did not disable me of itself. It would have done so, pretty surely, in conjunction with the mental wear and tear I had suffered, but for the unnatural strain upon me that to-morrow was. So anxiously looked forward to, charged with such consequences, its results so impenetrably hidden though so near.

No precaution could have been more obvious than our refraining from communication with him that day; yet this again increased my restlessness. I started at every footstep and every sound, believing that he was discovered and taken, and this was the messenger to tell me so. I persuaded myself that I knew he was taken; that there was something more upon my mind than a fear or a presentiment; that the fact had occurred, and I had a mysterious knowledge of it. As the day wore on and no ill news came, as the day closed in and darkness fell, my overshadowing dread of being disabled by illness before to-morrow morning, altogether mastered me. My burning arm throbbed, and my burning head throbbed, and I fancied I was beginning to wander. I counted up to high numbers, to make sure of myself, and repeated passages that I knew in prose and verse. It happened sometimes that in the mere escape of a fatigued mind, I dozed for some moments or forgot; then I would say to myself with a start, "Now it has come, and I am turning delirious!"

They kept me very quiet all day, and kept my arm constantly dressed and gave me cooling drinks. Whenever I fell asleep, I awoke with the notion I had had in the sluice-house, that a long time had elapsed and the opportunity to save him was gone. About midnight I got out of bed and went to Herbert, with the conviction that I had been asleep for four-and-twenty hours, and that Wednesday was past. It was the last self-exhausting effort of my fretfulness, for, after that, I slept soundly.

Wednesday morning was dawning when I looked out of window. The winking lights upon the bridges were already pale, the coming sun was like a marsh of fire on the horizon. The river, still dark and mysterious, was spanned by bridges that were turning coldly grey, with here and there at top a warm touch from the burning in the sky. As I looked along the clustered roofs, with Church towers and spires shooting into the unusually clear air, the sun rose up, and a veil seemed to be drawn from the river, and millions of sparkles burst out upon its waters. From me too, a veil seemed to be drawn, and I felt strong and well.

Herbert lay asleep in his bed, and our old fellow-student lay asleep on the sofa. I could not dress myself without help, but I made up the fire, which was still burning, and got some coffee ready for them. In good time they too started up strong and well, and we admitted the sharp morning air at the windows, and looked at the tide that was still flowing towards us.

"When it turns at nine o'clock," said Herbert, cheerfully, "look out for us, and stand ready, you over there at Mill Pond Bank!"

CHAPTER XV

IT WAS one of those March days when the sun shines hot and the wind blows cold: when it is summer in the light, and winter in the shade. We had our pea-coats with us, and I took a bag. Of all my worldly possessions I took no more than the few necessaries that filled the bag. Where I might go, what I might do, or when I might return, were questions utterly unknown to me; nor did I vex my mind with them, for it was wholly set on Provis's safety. I only wondered for the passing moment, as I stopped at the door and looked back, under what altered circumstances I should next see those rooms, if ever.

We loitered down to the Temple stairs, and stood loitering there, as if we were not quite decided to go upon the water at all. Of course I had taken care that the boat should be ready and everything in order. After a little show of indecision, which there were none to see but the two or three amphibious creatures belonging to our Temple stairs, we went on board and cast off; Herbert in the bow, I steering. It was then about high-water — half-past eight.

Our plan was this. The tide, beginning to run down at nine and being with us until three, we intended still to creep on after it had turned, and row against it until dark. We should then be well in those long reaches below Gravesend, between Kent and Essex, where the river is broad and solitary, where the waterside inhabitants are very few, and where lone public-houses are scattered here and there, of which we could choose one for a resting-place. There we meant to lie by, all night. The steamer for Hamburg, and the steamer for Rotterdam, would start from London at about nine on Thursday morning. We should know at what time to expect them, according to where we were, and would hail the first; so that if by any accident we were not taken aboard, we should have another chance. We knew the distinguishing marks of each vessel.

The relief of being at last engaged in the execution of the purpose, was so great to me that I felt it difficult to realise the condition in which I had been a few hours before. The crisp air, the sunlight, the movement on the river, and the moving river itself — the road that ran with us, seeming to sympathise with us, animate us, and encourage us on — freshened me with new hope. I felt mortified to be of so little use in the boat;

but, there were few better oarsmen than my two friends, and they rowed with a steady stroke that was to last all day.

At that time, the steam-traffic on the Thames was far below its present extent, and watermen's boats were far more numerous. Of barges, sailing colliers, and coasting-traders, there were perhaps as many as now; but, of steam-ships, great and small, not a tithe or a twentieth part so many. Early as it was, there were plenty of scullers going here and there that morning, and plenty of barges dropping down with the tide; the navigation of the river between bridges, in an open boat, was a much easier and commoner matter in those days than it is in these; and we went ahead among many skiffs and wherries, briskly.

Old London Bridge was soon passed, and old Billingsgate market with its oyster-boats and Dutchmen, and the White Tower and Traitor's Gate,[1] and we were in among the tiers of shipping. Here, were the Leith, Aberdeen, and Glasgow steamers, loading and unloading goods, and looking immensely high out of the water as we passed alongside; here, were colliers by the score and score, with the coal-whippers[2] plunging off stages on deck, as counterweights to measures of coal swinging up, which were then rattled over the side into barges; here, at her moorings was to-morrow's steamer for Rotterdam, of which we took good notice; and here to-morrow's for Hamburg, under whose bowsprit we crossed. And now I, sitting in the stern, could see with a faster beating heart, Mill Pond Bank and Mill Pond stairs.

"Is he there?" said Herbert.

"Not yet."

"Right! He was not to come down till he saw us. Can you see his signal?"

"Not well from here; but I think I see it. — Now, I see him! Pull both. Easy, Herbert. Oars!"

We touched the stairs lightly for a single moment, and he was on board

---

1. *old Billingsgate market with its oyster-boats and Dutchmen, and the White Tower and Traitor's Gate:* the old Billingsgate fish market stood next to and east of the Custom House, with the Tower of London to the west. See Map C and Illustration H.
2. *coal-whippers:* dock labourers who raise coal out of a ship's hold by using a pulley with their own bodies acting as counter-balances.

and we were off again. He had a boat-cloak with him, and a black canvas bag, and he looked as like a river-pilot as my heart could have wished. "Dear boy!" he said, putting his arm on my shoulder as he took his seat. "Faithful dear boy, well done. Thankye, thankye!"

Again among the tiers of shipping, in and out, avoiding rusty chain-cables frayed hempen hawsers and bobbing buoys, sinking for the moment floating broken baskets, scattering floating chips of wood and shaving, cleaving floating scum of coal, in and out, under the figure-head of the John of Sunderland making a speech to the winds (as is done by many Johns),[1] and the Betsy of Yarmouth with a firm formality of bosom and her nobby eyes starting two inches out of her head,[2] in and out, hammers going in ship-builders' yards, saws going at timber, clashing engines going at things unknown, pumps going in leaky ships, capstans going, ships going out to sea, and unintelligible sea-creatures roaring curses over the bulwarks at respondent lightermen, in and out — out at last upon the clearer river, where the ships' boys might take their fenders[3] in, no longer fishing in troubled waters with them over the side, and where the festooned sails might fly out to the wind.

At the Stairs where we had taken him aboard, and ever since, I had looked warily for any token of our being suspected. I had seen none. We certainly had not been, and at that time as certainly we were not, either attended or followed by any boat. If we had been waited on by any boat, I should have run in to shore, and have obliged her to go on, or to make her purpose evident. But, we held our own, without any appearance of molestation.

He had his boat-cloak on him, and looked, as I have said, a natural part of the scene. It was remarkable (but perhaps the wretched life he had led, accounted for it), that he was the least anxious of any of us. He was not indifferent, for he told me that he hoped to live to see his gentleman

---

1. *(as is done by many Johns):* "John," here, is probably used as a generic name, with no specific reference intended.

2. *her nobby eyes starting two inches out of her head:* referring to the eyes carved on the figure-head.

3. *fenders:* lengths of old cable etc., hung over a ship's side, protecting it in harbour from collision with the wharf or other vessels.

one of the best of gentlemen in a foreign country; he was not disposed to be passive or resigned, as I understood it; but he had no notion of meeting danger half way. When it came upon him, he confronted it, but it must come before he troubled himself.

"If you knowed, dear boy," he said to me, "wot it is to sit here alonger my dear boy and have my smoke, arter having been day by day betwixt four walls, you'd envy me. But you don't know wot it is."

"I think I know the delights of freedom," I answered.

"Ah," said he, shaking his head gravely. "But you don't know it equal to me. You must have been under lock and key, dear boy, to know it equal to me — but I ain't a going to be low."

It occurred to me as inconsistent, that for any mastering idea, he should have endangered his freedom and even his life. But I reflected that perhaps freedom without danger was too much apart from all the habit of his existence to be to him what it would be to another man. I was not far out, since he said, after smoking a little:

"You see dear boy, when I was over yonder, t'other side the world, I was always a looking to this side; and it come flat to be there, for all I wos a growing rich. Everybody knowed Magwitch, and Magwitch could come, and Magwitch could go, and nobody's head would be troubled about him. They ain't so easy concerning me here, dear boy — wouldn't be, leastwise, if they knowed where I was."

"If all goes well," said I, "you will be perfectly free and safe again, within a few hours."

"Well," he returned, drawing a long breath, "I hope so."

"And think so?"

He dipped his hand in the water over the boat's gunwale, and said, smiling with that softened air upon him which was not new to me:

"Ay, I s'pose I think so, dear boy. We'd be puzzled to be more quiet and easy-going than we are at present. But — it's a flowing so soft and pleasant through the water, p'raps, as makes me think it — I was a thinking through my smoke just then, that we can no more see to the bottom of the next few hours, than we can see to the bottom of this river what I catches hold of. Nor yet we can't no more hold their tide than I can hold this. And it's run through my fingers and gone, you see!" holding up his dripping hand.

"But for your face, I should think you were a little despondent," said I. "Not a bit on it, dear boy! It comes of flowing on so quiet, and of that there rippling at the boat's head making a sort of a Sunday tune. Maybe I'm a growing a trifle old besides."

He put his pipe back in his mouth with an undisturbed expression of face, and sat as composed and contented as if we were already out of England. Yet he was as submissive to a word of advice as if he had been in constant terror, for, when we ran ashore to get some bottles of beer into the boat, and he was stepping out, I hinted that I thought he would be safest where he was, and he said, "Do you, dear boy?" and quietly sat down again.

The air felt cold upon the river, but it was a bright day, and the sunshine was very cheering. The tide ran strong, I took care to lose none of it, and our steady stroke carried us on thoroughly well. By imperceptible degrees, as the tide ran out, we lost more and more of the nearer woods and hills, and dropped lower and lower between the muddy banks, but the tide was yet with us when we were off Gravesend. As our charge was wrapped in his cloak, I purposely passed within a boat or two's length of the floating Custom House, and so out to catch the stream, alongside of two emigrant ships, and under the bows of a large transport with troops on the forecastle looking down at us. And soon the tide began to slacken, and the craft lying at anchor to swing, and presently they had all swung round, and the ships that were taking advantage of the new tide to get up to the Pool, began to crowd upon us in a fleet, and we kept under the shore, as much out of the strength of the tide now as we could, standing carefully off from low shallows and mud-banks.

Our oarsmen were so fresh, by dint of having occasionally let her drive with the tide for a minute or two, that a quarter of an hour's rest proved full as much as they wanted. We got ashore among some slippery stones while we ate and drank what we had with us, and looked about. It was like my own marsh country, flat and monotonous, and with a dim horizon; while the winding river turned and turned, and the great floating buoys upon it turned and turned, and everything else seemed stranded and still. For, now, the last of the fleet of ships was round the last low point we had headed; and the last green barge, straw-laden, with a brown sail, had followed; and some ballast-lighters,[1] shaped like a child's first rude imitation of a boat, lay low in the mud; and a little squat shoal-lighthouse on open piles, stood crippled in the mud on stilts and crutches; and slimy stakes stuck out of the mud, and slimy stones stuck out of the mud, and red landmarks and tidemarks stuck out of the mud, and an old landing-stage and an old roofless building slipped into the mud, and all about us was stagnation and mud.

We pushed off again, and made what way we could. It was much harder work now, but Herbert and Startop persevered, and rowed, and rowed, and rowed, until the sun went down. By that time the river had lifted us a little, so that we could see above the bank. There was the red sun, on the low level of the shore, in a purple haze, fast deepening into black; and there was the solitary flat marsh; and far away there were the rising grounds, between which and us there seemed to be no life, save here and there in the foreground a melancholy gull.

As the night was fast falling, and as the moon, being past the full, would not rise early, we held a little council: a short one, for clearly our course was to lie by at the first lonely tavern we could find. So, they plied their oars once more, and I looked out for anything like a house. Thus we held on, speaking little, for four or five dull miles. It was very cold, and, a collier coming by us, with her galley-fire smoking and flaring, looked like a comfortable home. The night was as dark by this time as it would be until morning; and what light we had, seemed to come more from the river than the sky, as the oars in their dipping struck at a few reflected stars.

At this dismal time we were evidently all possessed by the idea that we were followed. As the tide made, it flapped heavily at irregular intervals against the shore; and whenever such a sound came, one or other of us was sure to start and look in that direction. Here and there, the set of the current had worn down the bank into a little creek, and we were all suspicious of such places, and eyed them narrowly. Sometimes, "What was that ripple?" one of us would say in a low voice. Or another, "Is that a

---

1. *ballast-lighters:* boats carrying heavy material such as gravel or sand for use as ballast in unladen sea-going vessels, to prevent them riding too high in the water and capsizing.

boat yonder?" And afterwards, we would fall into a dead silence, and I would sit impatiently thinking with what an unusual amount of noise the oars worked in the thowels.[1]

At length we descried a light and a roof, and presently afterwards ran alongside a little causeway made of stones that had been picked up hard-by. Leaving the rest in the boat, I stepped ashore, and found the light to be in a window of a public-house. It was a dirty place enough, and I dare say not unknown to smuggling adventurers; but there was a good fire in the kitchen, and there were eggs and bacon to eat, and various liquors to drink. Also, there were two double-bedded rooms — "such as they were," the landlord said. No other company was in the house than the landlord, his wife, and a grizzled male creature, the "Jack"[2] of the little causeway, who was as slimy and smeary as if he had been low-water mark too.

With this assistant, I went down to the boat again, and we all came ashore, and brought out the oars, and rudder, and boat-hook, and all else, and hauled her up for the night. We made a very good meal by the kitchen fire, and then apportioned the bedrooms: Herbert and Startop were to occupy one; I and our charge the other. We found the air as carefully excluded from both, as if air were fatal to life; and there were more dirty clothes and bandboxes under the beds than I should have thought the family possessed. But, we considered ourselves well off, notwithstanding, for a more solitary place we could not have found.

While we were comforting ourselves by the fire after our meal, the Jack — who was sitting in a corner, and who had a bloated pair of shoes on, which he had exhibited while we were eating our eggs and bacon, as interesting relics that he had taken a few days ago from the feet of a drowned seaman washed ashore — asked me if we had seen a four-oared galley going up with the tide? When I told him No, he said she must have gone down then, and yet she "took up too," when she left there.

"They must ha' thought better on't for some reason or another," said the Jack, "and gone down."

---

1. *thowels:* wooden rowlocks (pegs to secure the oars on a rowing-boat).
2. *"Jack":* odd-job man; the following reference to "low-water mark" probably relies on a pun with "jack" meaning the small flag flown at the bow of a ship.

"A four-oared galley, did you say?" said I.

"A four," said the Jack, "and two sitters."

"Did they come ashore here?"

"They put in with a stone two-gallon jar, for some beer. I'd ha' been glad to pison the beer myself," said the Jack, "or put some rattling physic[1] in it."

"Why?"

"*I* know why," said the Jack. He spoke in a slushy voice, as if much mud had washed into his throat.

"He thinks," said the landlord: a weakly meditative man with a pale eye, who seemed to rely greatly on his Jack: "he thinks they was, what they wasn't."

"*I* knows what I thinks," observed the Jack.

"*You* thinks Custum 'Us,[2] Jack?" said the landlord.

"I do," said the Jack.

"Then you're wrong, Jack."

"Aм I!"

In the infinite meaning of his reply and his boundless confidence in his views, the Jack took one of his bloated shoes off, looked into it, knocked a few stones out of it on the kitchen floor, and put it on again. He did this with the air of a Jack who was so right that he could afford to do anything.

"Why, what do you make out that they done with their buttons then, Jack?" asked the landlord, vacillating weakly.

"Done with their buttons?" returned the Jack. "Chucked 'em overboard. Swallered 'em. Sowed 'em, to come up small salad.[3] Done with their buttons!"

"Don't be cheeky, Jack," remonstrated the landlord, in a melancholy and pathetic way.

"A Custum 'Us officer knows what to do with his Buttons," said the Jack, repeating the obnoxious word with the greatest contempt, "when

---

1. *rattling physic:* strong laxative.
2. *Custum 'Us:* i.e., excise men from the Custom House.
3. *small salad:* shoots of mustard and cress.

they comes betwixt him and his own light. A Four and two sitters don't go hanging and hovering, up with one tide and down with another, and both with and against another, without there being Custum 'Us at the bottom of it." Saying which he went out in disdain; and the landlord, having no one to rely upon, found it impracticable to pursue the subject.

This dialogue made us all uneasy, and me very uneasy. The dismal wind was muttering round the house, the tide was flapping at the shore, and I had a feeling that we were caged and threatened. A four-oared galley hovering about in so unusual a way as to attract this notice, was an ugly circumstance that I could not get rid of. When I had induced Provis to go up to bed, I went outside with my two companions (Startop by this time knew the state of the case), and held another council. Whether we should remain at the house until near the steamer's time, which would be about one in the afternoon; or whether we should put off early in the morning; was the question we discussed. On the whole we deemed it the better course to lie where we were, until within an hour or so of the steamer's time, and then to get out in her track, and drift easily with the tide. Having settled to do this, we returned into the house and went to bed.

I lay down with the greater part of my clothes on, and slept well for a few hours. When I awoke, the wind had risen, and the sign of the house (the Ship) was creaking and banging about, with noises that startled me. Rising softly, for my charge lay fast asleep, I looked out of the window. It commanded the causeway where we had hauled up our boat, and, as my eyes adapted themselves to the light of the clouded moon, I saw two men looking into her. They passed by under the window, looking at nothing else, and they did not go down to the landing-place which I could discern to be empty, but struck across the marsh in the direction of the Nore.[1]

My first impulse was to call up Herbert, and show him the two men going away. But, reflecting before I got into his room, which was at the back of the house and adjoined mine, that he and Startop had had a harder day than I, and were fatigued, I forbore. Going back to my window, I could see the two men moving over the marsh. In that light, however, I soon lost them, and feeling very cold, lay down to think of the matter, and fell asleep again.

---

1. *the Nore:* large sandbank off the eastern extremity of the Hoo peninsula. See Map A.

We were up early. As we walked to and fro, all four together, before breakfast, I deemed it right to recount what I had seen. Again our charge was the least anxious of the party. It was very likely that the men belonged to the Custom House, he said quietly, and that they had no thought of us. I tried to persuade myself that it was so — as, indeed, it might easily be. However, I proposed that he and I should walk away together to a distant point we could see, and that the boat should take us aboard there, or as near there as might prove feasible, at about noon. This being considered a good precaution, soon after breakfast he and I set forth, without saying anything at the tavern.

He smoked his pipe as we went along, and sometimes stopped to clap me on the shoulder. One would have supposed that it was I who was in danger, not he, and that he was reassuring me. We spoke very little. As we approached the point, I begged him to remain in a sheltered place, while I went on to reconnoitre; for, it was towards it that the men had passed in the night. He complied, and I went on alone. There was no boat off the point, nor any boat drawn up anywhere near it, nor were there any signs of the men having embarked there. But, to be sure the tide was high, and there might have been some footprints under water.

When he looked out from his shelter in the distance, and saw that I waved my hat to him to come up, he rejoined me, and there we waited; sometimes lying on the bank wrapped in our coats, and sometimes moving about to warm ourselves: until we saw our boat coming round. We got aboard easily, and rowed out into the track of the steamer. By that time it wanted but ten minutes of one o'clock, and we began to look out for her smoke.

But, it was half-past one before we saw her smoke, and soon afterwards we saw behind it the smoke of another steamer. As they were coming on at full speed, we got the two bags ready, and took that opportunity of saying good-by to Herbert and Startop. We had all shaken hands cordially, and neither Herbert's eyes nor mine were quite dry, when I saw a four-oared galley shoot out from under the bank but a little way ahead of us, and row out into the same track.

A stretch of shore had been as yet between us and the steamer's smoke, by reason of the bend and wind of the river; but now she was visible, coming head on. I called to Herbert and Startop to keep before the tide, that she might see us lying by for her, and I adjured Provis to sit quite still, wrapped in his cloak. He answered cheerily, "Trust to me, dear boy," and sat like a statue. Meantime the galley, which was very skilfully handled, had crossed us, let us come up with her, and fallen alongside. Leaving just room enough for the play of the oars, she kept alongside, drifting when we drifted, and pulling a stroke or two when we pulled. Of the two sitters, one held the rudder lines, and looked at us attentively — as did all the rowers; the other sitter was wrapped up, much as Provis was, and seemed to shrink, and whisper some instruction to the steerer as he looked at us. Not a word was spoken in either boat.

Startop could make out, after a few minutes, which steamer was first, and gave me the word "Hamburg," in a low voice as we sat face to face. She was nearing us very fast, and the beating of her paddles grew louder and louder. I felt as if her shadow were absolutely upon us, when the galley hailed us. I answered.

"You have a returned Transport there," said the man who held the lines. "That's the man, wrapped in the cloak. His name is Abel Magwitch, otherwise Provis. I apprehend that man, and call upon him to surrender, and you to assist."

At the same moment, without giving any audible direction to his crew, he ran the galley aboard of us. They had pulled one sudden stroke ahead, had got their oars in, had run athwart us, and were holding on to our gunwale, before we knew what they were doing. This caused great confusion on board the steamer, and I heard them calling to us, and heard the order given to stop the paddles, and heard them stop, but felt her driving down upon us irresistibly. In the same moment, I saw the steersman of the galley lay his hand on his prisoner's shoulder, and saw that both boats were swinging round with the force of the tide, and saw that all hands on board the steamer were running forward quite frantically. Still in the same moment I saw the prisoner start up, lean across his captor, and pull the cloak from the neck of the shrinking sitter in the galley. Still in the same moment, I saw that the face disclosed, was the face of the other convict of long ago. Still in the same moment, I saw the face tilt backward with a white terror on it that I shall never forget, and heard a great cry on board the steamer and a loud splash in the water, and felt the boat sink from under me.

It was but for an instant that I seemed to struggle with a thousand mill-weirs and a thousand flashes of light; that instant past, I was taken on board the galley. Herbert was there, and Startop was there; but our boat was gone, and the two convicts were gone.

What with the cries aboard the steamer, and the furious blowing-off of her steam, and her driving on, and our driving on, I could not at first distinguish sky from water or shore from shore; but, the crew of the galley righted her with great speed, and, pulling certain swift strong strokes ahead, lay upon their oars, every man looking silently and eagerly at the water astern. Presently a dark object was seen in it, bearing towards us on the tide. No man spoke, but the steersman held up his hand, and all softly backed water, and kept the boat straight and true before it. As it came nearer, I saw it to be Magwitch, swimming, but not swimming freely. He was taken on board, and instantly manacled at the wrists and ankles.

The galley was kept steady, and the silent eager look-out at the water was resumed. But, the Rotterdam steamer now came up and apparently not understanding what had happened, came on at speed. By the time she had been hailed and stopped, both steamers were drifting away from us, and we were rising and falling in a troubled wake of water. The look-out was kept, long after all was still again and the two steamers were gone; but, everybody knew that it was hopeless now.

At length we gave it up, and pulled under the shore towards the tavern we had lately left, where we were received with no little surprise. Here, I was able to get some comforts for Magwitch — Provis no longer — who had received some very severe injury in the chest and a deep cut in the head.

He told me that he believed himself to have gone under the keel of the steamer, and to have been struck on the head in rising. The injury to his chest (which rendered his breathing extremely painful) he thought he had received against the side of the galley. He added that he did not pretend to say what he might or might not have done to Compeyson, but, that in the moment of his laying his hand on his cloak to identify him, that villain had staggered up and staggered back, and they had both gone overboard together; when the sudden wrenching of him (Magwitch) out of our boat, and the endeavour of his captor to keep him in it, had capsized us. He told me in a whisper that they had gone down, fiercely locked in each other's arms, and that there had been a struggle under water, and that he had disengaged himself, struck out, and swum away.

I never had any reason to doubt the exact truth of what he thus told me. The officer who steered the galley gave the same account of their going overboard.

When I asked this officer's permission to change the prisoner's wet clothes by purchasing any spare garments I could get at the public-house, he gave it readily: merely observing that he must take charge of everything his prisoner had about him. So the pocket-book which had once been in my hands, passed into the officer's. He further gave me leave to accompany the prisoner to London; but, declined to accord that grace to my two friends.

The Jack at the Ship was instructed where the drowned man had gone down, and undertook to search for the body in the places where it was likeliest to come ashore. His interest in its recovery seemed to me to be much heightened when he heard that it had stockings on. Probably, it took about a dozen drowned men to fit him out completely; and that may have been the reason why the different articles of his dress were in various stages of decay.

We remained at the public-house until the tide turned, and then Magwitch was carried down to the galley and put on board. Herbert and Startop were to get to London by land, as soon as they could. We had a doleful parting, and when I took my place by Magwitch's side, I felt that that was my place henceforth while he lived.

For now, my repugnance to him had all melted away, and in the hunted wounded shackled creature who held my hand in his, I only saw a man who had meant to be my benefactor, and who had felt affectionately, gratefully, and generously, towards me with great constancy through a series of years. I only saw in him a much better man than I had been to Joe.

His breathing became more difficult and painful as the night drew on, and often he could not repress a groan. I tried to rest him on the arm I could use, in any easy position; but, it was dreadful to think that I could not be sorry at heart for his being badly hurt, since it was unquestionably best that he should die. That there were, still living, people enough who were able and willing to identify him, I could not doubt. That he would be leniently treated, I could not hope. He who had been presented in the worst light at his trial, who had since broken prison and had been tried again, who had returned from transportation under a life sentence, and who had occasioned the death of the man who was the cause of his arrest.

As we returned towards the setting sun we had yesterday left behind us, and as the stream of our hopes seemed all running back, I told him how grieved I was to think that he had come home for my sake.

"Dear boy," he answered, "I'm quite content to take my chance. I've seen my boy, and he can be a gentleman without me."

No. Apart from any inclinations of my own, I had thought about that, while we had been there side by side. I understood Wemmick's hint now. I foresaw that, being convicted, his possessions would be forfeited to the Crown.

"Lookee here, dear boy," said he. "It's best as a gentleman should not be knowed to belong to me now. Only come to see me as if you come by chance alonger Wemmick. Sit where I can see you when I am swore to, for the last o' many times, and I don't ask no more."

"I will never stir from your side," said I, "when I am suffered to be near you. Please God, I will be as true to you, as you have been to me!"

I felt his hand tremble as it held mine, and he turned his face away as he lay in the bottom of the boat, and I heard that old sound in his throat — softened now, like all the rest of him. It was a good thing that he had touched this point, for it put into my mind what I might not otherwise have thought of until too late: That he need never know how his hopes of enriching me had perished.

CHAPTER XVI

HE WAS taken to the Police Court[1] next day, and would have been immediately committed for trial, but that it was necessary to send down for an old officer of the prison-ship from which he had once escaped,

---

1. *Police Court:* since Magwitch is arrested on the river, this would presumably be the Marine Police Office at Wapping New Stairs (see Map C), established in 1798.

to speak to his identity. Nobody doubted it; but, Compeyson, who had meant to depose to it, was tumbling on the tides, dead, and it happened that there was not at that time any prison officer in London who could give the required evidence. I had gone direct to Mr. Jaggers at his private house, on my arrival over-night, to retain his assistance, and Mr. Jaggers on the prisoner's behalf would admit nothing. It was the sole resource, for he told me that the case must be over in five minutes when the witness was there, and that no power on earth could prevent its going against us.

I imparted to Mr. Jaggers my design of keeping him in ignorance of the fate of his wealth. Mr. Jaggers was querulous and angry with me for having "let it slip through my fingers," and said we must memorialise by-and-by, and try at all events for some of it. But, he did not conceal from me that although there might be many cases in which the forfeiture would not be exacted, there were no circumstances in this case to make it one of them. I understood that, very well. I was not related to the outlaw, or connected with him by any recognisable tie; he had put his hand to no writing or settlement in my favour before his apprehension, and to do so now would be idle. I had no claim, and I finally resolved, and ever afterwards abided by the resolution, that my heart should never be sickened with the hopeless task of attempting to establish one.

There appeared to be reason for supposing that the drowned informer had hoped for a reward out of this forfeiture, and had obtained some accurate knowledge of Magwitch's affairs. When his body was found, many miles from the scene of his death, and so horribly disfigured that he was only recognisable by the contents of his pockets, notes were still legible, folded in a case he carried. Among these, were the name of a banking-house in New South Wales where a sum of money was, and the designation of certain lands of considerable value. Both these heads of information were in a list that Magwitch, while in prison, gave to Mr. Jaggers, of the possessions he supposed I should inherit. His ignorance, poor fellow, at last served him; he never mistrusted but that my inheritance was quite safe, with Mr. Jaggers's aid.

After three days' delay, during which the crown prosecution stood over for the production of the witness from the prison-ship, the witness came, and completed the easy case. He was committed to take his trial at the next Sessions,[1] which would come on in a month.

It was at this dark time of my life that Herbert returned home one evening, a good deal cast down, and said:

"My dear Handel, I fear I shall soon have to leave you."

His partner having prepared me for that, I was less surprised than he thought.

"We shall lose a fine opportunity if I put off going to Cairo, and I am very much afraid I must go, Handel, when you most need me."

"Herbert, I shall always need you, because I shall always love you; but my need is no greater now, than at another time."

"You will be so lonely."

"I have not leisure to think of that," said I. "You know that I am always with him to the full extent of the time allowed, and that I should be with him all day long, if I could. And when I come away from him, you know that my thoughts are with him."

The dreadful condition to which he was brought, was so appalling to both of us, that we could not refer to it in plainer words.

"My dear fellow," said Herbert, "let the near prospect of our separation — for, it is very near — be my justification for troubling you about yourself. Have you thought of your future?"

"No, for I have been afraid to think of any future."

"But yours cannot be dismissed; indeed, my dear dear Handel, it must not be dismissed. I wish you would enter on it now, as far as a few friendly words go, with me."

"I will," said I.

"In this branch house of ours, Handel, we must have a —"

I saw that his delicacy was avoiding the right word, so I said, "A clerk."

"A clerk. And I hope it is not at all unlikely that he may expand (as a clerk of your acquaintance has expanded) into a partner. Now, Handel — in short, my dear boy, will you come to me?"

There was something charmingly cordial and engaging in the manner in which after saying "Now, Handel," as if it were the grave begin-

---

1. *Sessions:* Quarter Sessions, the lower criminal and civil court then held four times a year by the justices of the peace, here at the Session House next to Newgate Prison along the Old Bailey (see Map B).

ning of a portentous business exordium, he had suddenly given up that tone, stretched out his honest hand, and spoken like a schoolboy.

"Clara and I have talked about it again and again," Herbert pursued, "and the dear little thing begged me only this evening, with tears in her eyes, to say to you that if you will live with us when we come together, she will do her best to make you happy, and to convince her husband's friend that he is her friend too. We should get on so well, Handel!"

I thanked her heartily, and I thanked him heartily, but said I could not yet make sure of joining him as he so kindly offered. Firstly, my mind was too preoccupied to be able to take in the subject clearly. Secondly — Yes! Secondly, there was a vague something lingering in my thoughts that will come out very near the end of this slight narrative.

"But if you thought, Herbert, that you could, without doing any injury to your business, leave the question open for a little while —"

"For any while," cried Herbert. "Six months, a year!"

"Not so long as that," said I. "Two or three months at most."

Herbert was highly delighted when we shook hands on this arrangement, and said he could now take courage to tell me that he believed he must go away at the end of the week.

"And Clara?" said I.

"The dear little thing," returned Herbert, "holds dutifully to her father as long as he lasts; but he won't last long. Mrs. Whimple confides to me that he is certainly going."

"Not to say an unfeeling thing," said I, "he cannot do better than go."

"I am afraid that must be admitted," said Herbert: "and then I shall come back for the dear little thing, and the dear little thing and I will walk quietly into the nearest church. Remember! The blessed darling comes of no family, my dear Handel, and never looked into the red book,[1] and hasn't a notion about her grandpapa. What a fortune for the son of my mother!"

On the Saturday in that same week, I took my leave of Herbert — full of bright hope, but sad and sorry to leave me — as he sat on one of

---

1. *red book:* published guide to the members of the Court and Aristocracy, conventionally bound in red and gold, such as *Debrett's Peerage* (from 1784) or Webster's *Royal Red Book* (from 1797).

the seaport mail coaches. I went into a coffee-house to write a little note to Clara, telling her he had gone off, sending his love to her over and over again, and then went to my lonely home — if it deserved the name, for it was now no home to me, and I had no home anywhere.

On the stairs I encountered Wemmick, who was coming down, after an unsuccessful application of his knuckles to my door. I had not seen him alone, since the disastrous issue of the attempted flight; and he had come, in his private and personal capacity, to say a few words of explanation in reference to that failure.

"The late Compeyson," said Wemmick, "had by little and little got at the bottom of half of the regular business now transacted, and it was from the talk of some of his people in trouble (some of his people being always in trouble) that I heard what I did. I kept my ears open, seeming to have them shut, until I heard that he was absent, and I thought that would be the best time for making the attempt. I can only suppose now, that it was a part of his policy, as a very clever man, habitually to deceive his own instruments. You don't blame me, I hope, Mr. Pip? I am sure I tried to serve you, with all my heart."

"I am as sure of that, Wemmick, as you can be, and I thank you most earnestly for all your interest and friendship."

"Thank you, thank you very much. It's a bad job," said Wemmick, scratching his head, "and I assure you I haven't been so cut up for a long time. What I look at, is the sacrifice of so much portable property. Dear me!"

"What I think of, Wemmick, is the poor owner of the property."

"Yes, to be sure," said Wemmick. "Of course there can be no objection to your being sorry for him, and I'd put down a five-pound note myself to get him out of it. But what I look at, is this. The late Compeyson having been beforehand with him in intelligence of his return, and being so determined to bring him to book, I do not think he could have been saved. Whereas, the portable property certainly could have been saved. That's the difference between the property and the owner, don't you see?"

I invited Wemmick to come up-stairs, and refresh himself with a glass of grog before walking to Walworth. He accepted the invitation. While he was drinking his moderate allowance, he said, with nothing to lead up to it, and after having appeared rather fidgety:

"What do you think of my meaning to take a holiday on Monday, Mr. Pip?"

"Why, I suppose you have not done such a thing these twelve months."

"These twelve years, more likely," said Wemmick. "Yes. I'm going to take a holiday. More than that; I'm going to take a walk. More than that; I'm going to ask you to take a walk with me."

I was about to excuse myself, as being but a bad companion just then, when Wemmick anticipated me.

"I know your engagements," said he, "and I know you are out of sorts, Mr. Pip. But if you *could* oblige me, I should take it as a kindness. It ain't a long walk, and it's an early one. Say it might occupy you (including breakfast on the walk) from eight to twelve. Couldn't you stretch a point and manage it?"

He had done so much for me at various times, that this was very little to do for him. I said I could manage it — would manage it — and he was so very much pleased by my acquiescence, that I was pleased too. At his particular request, I appointed to call for him at the Castle at half-past eight on Monday morning, and so we parted for the time.

Punctual to my appointment, I rang at the Castle gate on the Monday morning, and was received by Wemmick himself: who struck me as looking tighter than usual, and having a sleeker hat on. Within, there were two glasses of rum-and-milk prepared, and two biscuits. The Aged must have been stirring with the lark, for, glancing into the perspective of his bedroom, I observed that his bed was empty.

When we had fortified ourselves with the rum-and-milk and biscuits, and were going out for the walk with that training preparation on us, I was considerably surprised to see Wemmick take up a fishing-rod, and put it over his shoulder. "Why, we are not going fishing!" said I. "No," returned Wemmick, "but I like to walk with one."

I thought this odd; however, I said nothing, and we set off. We went towards Camberwell Green,[1] and when we were thereabouts, Wemmick said suddenly:

---

1. *Camberwell Green:* large common at the centre of the village not far south of Walworth. See Map C.

"Halloa! Here's a church!"

There was nothing very surprising in that; but again, I was rather surprised, when he said, as if he were animated by a brilliant idea:

"Let's go in!"

We went in, Wemmick leaving his fishing-rod in the porch, and looked all round. In the mean time, Wemmick was diving into his coat-pockets, and getting something out of paper there.

"Halloa!" said he. "Here's a couple of pair of gloves! Let's put 'em on!"

As the gloves were white kid gloves, and as the post-office was widened to its utmost extent, I now began to have my strong suspicions. They were strengthened into certainty when I beheld the Aged enter at a side door, escorting a lady.

"Halloa!" said Wemmick. "Here's Miss Skiffins! Let's have a wedding."

That discreet damsel was attired as usual, except that she was now engaged in substituting for her green kid gloves, a pair of white. The Aged was likewise occupied in preparing a similar sacrifice for the altar of Hymen.[1] The old gentleman, however, experienced so much difficulty in getting his gloves on, that Wemmick found it necessary to put him with his back against a pillar, and then to get behind the pillar himself and pull away at them, while I for my part held the old gentleman round the waist, that he might present an equal and safe resistance. By dint of this ingenious scheme, his gloves were got on to perfection.

The clerk and clergyman then appearing, we were ranged in order at those fatal rails. True to his notion of seeming to do it all without preparation, I heard Wemmick say to himself as he took something out of his waistcoat-pocket before the service began, "Halloa! Here's a ring!"

I acted in the capacity of backer, or best-man, to the bridegroom; while a little limp pew opener in a soft bonnet like a baby's, made a feint of being the bosom friend of Miss Skiffins. The responsibility of giving the lady away, devolved upon the Aged, which led to the clergyman's being unintentionally scandalised, and it happened thus. When he said, "Who giveth this woman to be married to this man?" the old gentlemen, not in the least knowing what point of the ceremony we had arrived at, stood

---

1. *Hymen:* God of marriage in Greek myth.

most amiably beaming at the ten commandments. Upon which, the clergyman said again, "WHO giveth this woman to be married to this man?" The old gentleman being still in a state of most estimable unconsciousness, the bridegroom cried out in his accustomed voice, "Now Aged P. you know; who giveth?" To which the Aged replied with great briskness, before saying that *he* gave, "All right, John, all right, my boy!" And the clergyman came to so gloomy a pause upon it, that I had doubts for the moment whether we should get completely married that day.

It was completely done, however, and when we were going out of church, Wemmick took the cover off the font, and put his white gloves in it, and put the cover on again. Mrs. Wemmick, more heedful of the future, put her white gloves in her pocket and assumed her green. "*Now*, Mr. Pip," said Wemmick, triumphantly shouldering the fishing-rod as we came out, "let me ask you whether anybody would suppose this to be a wedding party!"

Breakfast had been ordered at a pleasant little tavern, a mile or so away upon the rising-ground beyond the Green; and there was a bagatelle board in the room, in case we should desire to unbend our minds after the solemnity. It was pleasant to observe that Mrs. Wemmick no longer unwound Wemmick's arm when it adapted itself to her figure, but sat in a high-backed chair against the wall, like a violoncello in its case, and submitted to be embraced as that melodious instrument might have done.

We had an excellent breakfast, and when any one declined anything on table, Wemmick said, "Provided by contract, you know; don't be afraid of it!" I drank to the new couple, drank to the Aged, drank to the Castle, saluted the bride at parting, and made myself as agreeable as I could.

Wemmick came down to the door with me, and I again shook hands with him, and wished him joy.

"Thankee!" said Wemmick, rubbing his hands. "She's such a manager of fowls you have no idea. You shall have some eggs, and judge for yourself. I say, Mr. Pip!" calling me back, and speaking low. "This is altogether a Walworth sentiment, please."

"I understand. Not to be mentioned in Little Britain," said I.

Wemmick nodded. "After what you let out the other day, Mr. Jaggers may as well not know of it. He might think my brain was softening, or something of the kind."

CHAPTER XVII

HE LAY in prison very ill, during the whole interval between his committal for trial, and the coming round of the Sessions. He had broken two ribs, they had wounded one of his lungs, and he breathed with great pain and difficulty, which increased daily. It was a consequence of his hurt, that he spoke so low as to be scarcely audible; therefore, he spoke very little. But, he was ever ready to listen to me, and it became the first duty of my life to say to him, and read to him, what I knew he ought to hear.

Being far too ill to remain in the common prison, he was removed, after the first day or so, into the infirmary. This gave me opportunities of being with him that I could not otherwise have had. And but for his illness he would have been put in irons, for he was regarded as a determined prison-breaker, and I know not what else.

Although I saw him every day, it was for only a short time; hence, the regularly recurring spaces of our separation were long enough to record on his face any slight changes that occurred in his physical state. I do not recollect that I once saw any change in it for the better; he wasted, and became slowly weaker and worse, day by day, from the day when the prison door closed upon him.

The kind of submission or resignation that he showed, was that of a man who was tired out. I sometimes derived an impression, from his manner or from a whispered word or two which escaped him, that he pondered over the question whether he might have been a better man under better circumstances. But, he never justified himself by a hint tending that way, or tried to bend the past out of its eternal shape.

It happened on two or three occasions in my presence, that his desperate reputation was alluded to by one or other of the people in attendance on him. A smile crossed his face then, and he turned his eyes on me with a trustful look, as if he were confident that I had seen some small redeeming touch in him, even so long ago as when I was a little child. As to all the rest, he was humble and contrite, and I never knew him complain.

When the Sessions came round, Mr. Jaggers caused an application to be made for the postponement of his trial until the following Sessions. It was obviously made with the assurance that he could not live so long, and was refused. The trial came on at once, and, when he was put to the bar, he was seated in a chair. No objection was made to my getting close to the dock, on the outside of it, and holding the hand that he stretched forth to me.

The trial was very short and very clear. Such things as could be said for him, were said — how he had taken to industrious habits, and had thriven lawfully and reputably. But, nothing could unsay the fact that he had returned, and was there in presence of the Judge and Jury. It was impossible to try him for that, and do otherwise than find him Guilty.

At that time, it was the custom (as I learnt from my terrible experience of that Sessions) to devote a concluding day to the passing of Sentences, and to make a finishing effect with the Sentence of Death. But for the indelible picture that my remembrance now holds before me, I could scarcely believe, even as I write these words, that I saw two-and-thirty men and women put before the Judge to receive that sentence together.* Foremost among the two-and-thirty, was he; seated, that he might get breath enough to keep life in him.

The whole scene starts out again in the vivid colours of the moment, down to the drops of April rain on the windows of the court, glittering in the rays of April sun. Penned in the dock, as I again stood outside it at the corner with his hand in mine, were the two-and-thirty men and women; some defiant, some stricken with terror, some sobbing and weeping, some covering their faces, some staring gloomily about. There had been shrieks from among the women convicts, but they had been stilled, and a hush had succeeded. The sheriffs with their great chains and nosegays, other civic gewgaws and monsters, criers, ushers, a great gallery full of people — a large theatrical audience — looked on, as the two-and-thirty and the Judge were solemnly confronted. Then, the Judge addressed them. Among the wretched creatures before him whom he must single out for special address, was one who almost from his infancy had been an offender against the laws; who, after repeated imprisonments and punishments, had been at length sentenced to exile for a term of years; and who, under circumstances of great violence and daring had made his escape and been re-sentenced to exile for life. That miserable man would seem for a time to have become convinced of his errors, when far removed from the scenes of his old offences, and to have lived a peaceable and honest life. But in a fatal moment, yielding to those propensities and passions, the indulgence of which had so long rendered him a scourge to society, he had quitted his haven of rest and repentance, and had come back to the country where he was proscribed. Being here presently denounced, he had for a time succeeded in evading the officers of Justice, but being at length seized while in the act of flight, he had resisted them, and had — he best knew whether by express design, or in the blindness of his hardihood — caused the death of his denouncer, to whom his whole career was known. The appointed punishment for his return to the land that had cast him out, being Death, and his case being this aggravated case, he must prepare himself to Die.

The sun was striking in at the great windows of the court, through the glittering drops of rain upon the glass, and it made a broad shaft of light between the two-and-thirty and the Judge, linking both together, and perhaps reminding some among the audience, how both were passing on, with absolute equality, to the greater Judgment that knoweth all things and cannot err. Rising for a moment, a distinct speck of face in this way of light, the prisoner said, "My Lord, I have received my sentence of Death from the Almighty, but I bow to yours," and sat down again. There was some hushing, and the Judge went on with what he had to say to the rest. Then, they were all formally doomed, and some of them were supported out, and some of them sauntered out with a haggard look of bravery, and a few nodded to the gallery, and two or three shook hands, and others went out chewing the fragments of herb they had taken from the sweet herbs lying about. He went last of all, because of having to be helped from his chair and to go very slowly; and he held my hand while all the others were removed, and while the audience got up (putting their dresses right, as they might at church or elsewhere) and pointed down at this criminal or at that, and most of all at him and me.

I earnestly hoped and prayed that he might die before the Recorder's Report was made,[1] but, in the dread of his lingering on, I began that night to write out a petition to the Home Secretary of State, setting forth my knowledge of him, and how it was that he had come back for my sake. I wrote it as fervently and pathetically as I could, and when I had

---

1. *before the Recorder's Report was made:* see note on p. 290.

finished it and sent it in, I wrote out other petitions to such men in authority as I hoped were the most merciful, and drew up one to the Crown itself.* For several days and nights after he was sentenced I took no rest except when I fell asleep in my chair, but was wholly absorbed in these appeals. And after I had sent them in, I could not keep away from the places where they were, but felt as if they were more hopeful and less desperate when I was near them. In this unreasonable restlessness and pain of mind, I would roam the streets of an evening, wandering by those offices and houses where I had left the petitions. To the present hour, the weary western streets of London on a cold dusty spring night, with their ranges of stern shut-up mansions and their long rows of lamps, are melancholy to me from this association.

The daily visits I could make him were shortened now, and he was more strictly kept. Seeing, or fancying, that I was suspected of an intention of carrying poison to him, I asked to be searched before I sat down at his bedside, and told the officer who was always there, that I was willing to do anything that would assure him of the singleness of my designs. Nobody was hard with him, or with me. There was duty to be done, and it was done, but not harshly. The officer always gave me the assurance that he was worse, and some other sick prisoners in the room, and some other prisoners who attended on them as sick nurses (malefactors, but not incapable of kindness, GOD be thanked!), always joined in the same report.

As the days went on, I noticed more and more that he would lie placidly looking at the white ceiling, with an absence of light in his face, until some word of mine brightened it for an instant, and then it would subside again. Sometimes he was almost, or quite, unable to speak; then, he would answer me with slight pressures on my hand, and I grew to understand his meaning very well.

The number of the days had risen to ten, when I saw a greater change in him than I had seen yet. His eyes were turned towards the door, and lighted up as I entered.

"Dear boy," he said, as I sat down by his bed: "I thought you was late. But I knowed you couldn't be that."

"It is just the time," said I. "I waited for it at the gate."

"You always waits at the gate; don't you, dear boy?"

"Yes. Not to lose a moment of the time."

"Thankee dear boy, thankee. God bless you! You've never deserted me, dear boy."

I pressed his hand in silence, for I could not forget that I had once meant to desert him.

"And what's the best of all," he said, "you've been more comfortable alonger me, since I was under a dark cloud, than when the sun shone. That's best of all."

He lay on his back, breathing with great difficulty. Do what he would, and love me though he did, the light left his face ever and again, and a film came over the placid look at the white ceiling.

"Are you in much pain to-day?"

"I don't complain of none, dear boy."

"You never do complain."

He had spoken his last words. He smiled, and I understood his touch to mean that he wished to lift my hand, and lay it on his breast. I laid it there, and he smiled again, and put both his hands upon it.

The allotted time ran out, while we were thus; but, looking round, I found the governor of the prison standing near me, and he whispered, "You needn't go yet." I thanked him gratefully, and asked, "Might I speak to him, if he can hear me?"

The governor stepped aside, and beckoned the officer away. The change, though it was made without noise, drew back the film from the placid look at the white ceiling, and he looked most affectionately at me.

"Dear Magwitch, I must tell you, now at last. You understand what I say?"

A gentle pressure on my hand.

"You had a child once, whom you loved and lost."

A stronger pressure on my hand.

"She lived and found powerful friends. She is living now. She is a lady and very beautiful. And I love her!"

With a last faint effort, which would have been powerless but for my yielding to it and assisting it, he raised my hand to his lips. Then, he gently let it sink upon his breast again, with his own hands lying on it. The placid look at the white ceiling came back, and passed away, and his head dropped quietly on his breast.

Mindful, then, of what we had read together, I thought of the two men who went up into the Temple to pray, and I knew there were no better words that I could say beside his bed, than "O Lord, be merciful to him, a sinner!"[1]

CHAPTER XVIII

NOW THAT I was left wholly to myself, I gave notice of my intention to quit the chambers in the Temple as soon as my tenancy could legally determine, and in the meanwhile to underlet them. At once I put bills up in the windows; for, I was in debt, and had scarcely any money, and began to be seriously alarmed by the state of my affairs. I ought rather to write that I should have been alarmed if I had had energy and concentration enough to help me to the clear perception of any truth beyond the fact that I was falling very ill. The late stress upon me had enabled me to put off illness, but not to put it away; I knew that it was coming on me now, and I knew very little else, and was even careless as to that.

For a day or two, I lay on the sofa, or on the floor — anywhere, according as I happened to sink down — with a heavy head and aching limbs, and no purpose, and no power. Then there came one night which appeared of great duration, and which teemed with anxiety and horror; and when in the morning I tried to sit up in my bed and think of it, I found I could not do so.

Whether I really had been down in Garden-court in the dead of the night, groping about for the boat that I supposed to be there; whether I had two or three times come to myself on the staircase with great terror, not knowing how I had got out of bed; whether I had found myself lighting the lamp, possessed by the idea that he was coming up the stairs, and that the lights were blown out; whether I had been inexpressibly harassed by the distracted talking, laughing, and groaning, of some one, and had

---

1. *Mindful, then, of what we had read together … merciful to him, a sinner!":* See Jesus's parable of the Pharisee and the Publican in Luke 18:9–14, especially verse 13: "And the publican, standing afar off, would not lift up so much as his eyes unto heaven, but smote upon his breast, saying, God be merciful to me a sinner."

half suspected those sounds to be of my own making; whether there had been a closed iron furnace in a dark corner of the room, and a voice had called out over and over again that Miss Havisham was consuming within it; these were things that I tried to settle with myself and get into some order, as I lay that morning on my bed. But, the vapour of a limekiln would come between me and them, disordering them all, and it was through the vapour at last that I saw two men looking at me.

"What do you want?" I asked, starting; "I don't know you."

"Well, sir," returned one of them, bending down and touching me on the shoulder, "this is a matter that you'll soon arrange, I dare say, but you're arrested."

"What is the debt?"

"Hundred and twenty-three pound, fifteen, six. Jeweller's account, I think."

"What is to be done?"

"You had better come to my house," said the man. "I keep a very nice house."[1]

I made some attempt to get up and dress myself. When I next attended to them, they were standing a little off from the bed, looking at me. I still lay there.

"You see my state," said I. "I would come with you if I could; but indeed I am quite unable. If you take me from here, I think I shall die by the way."

Perhaps they replied, or argued the point, or tried to encourage me to believe that I was better than I thought. Forasmuch as they hang in my memory by only this one slender thread, I don't know what they did, except that they forbore to remove me.

That I had a fever and was avoided, that I suffered greatly, that I often lost my reason, that the time seemed interminable, that I confounded impossible existences with my own identity; that I was a brick in the house wall, and yet entreating to be released from the giddy place where the

---

1. *"You had better come to my house," said the man. "I keep a very nice house.":* a sponging-house, a place for the preliminary confinement of debtors run by a bailiff or Sheriff's officer.

builders had set me; that I was a steel beam of a vast engine, clashing and whirling over a gulf, and yet that I implored in my own person to have the engine stopped, and my part in it hammered off; that I passed through these phases of disease, I know of my own remembrance, and did in some sort know at the time. That I sometimes struggled with real people, in the belief that they were murderers, and that I would all at once comprehend that they meant to do me good, and would then sink exhausted in their arms, and suffer them to lay me down, I also knew at the time. But, above all, I knew that there was a constant tendency in all these people — who, when I was very ill, would present all kinds of extraordinary transformations of the human face, and would be much dilated in size — above all, I say, I knew that there was an extraordinary tendency in all these people, sooner or later to settle down into the likeness of Joe.

After I had turned the worst point of my illness, I began to notice that while all its other features changed, this one consistent feature did not change. Whoever came about me, still settled down into Joe. I opened my eyes in the night, and I saw in the great chair at the bedside, Joe. I opened my eyes in the day, and, sitting on the window-seat, smoking his pipe in the shaded open window, still I saw Joe. I asked for cooling drink, and the dear hand that gave it me was Joe's. I sank back on my pillow after drinking, and the face that looked so hopefully and tenderly upon me was the face of Joe.

At last, one day, I took courage, and said, "*Is* it Joe?"

And the dear old home-voice answered, "Which it air, old chap."

"O Joe, you break my heart! Look angry at me, Joe. Strike me, Joe. Tell me of my ingratitude. Don't be so good to me!"

For, Joe had actually laid his head down on the pillow at my side and put his arm round my neck, in his joy that I knew him.

"Which dear old Pip, old chap," said Joe, "you and me was ever friends. And when you're well enough to go out for a ride — what larks!"

After which, Joe withdrew to the window, and stood with his back towards me, wiping his eyes. And as my extreme weakness prevented me from getting up and going to him, I lay there, penitently whispering, "O God bless him! O God bless this gentle Christian man!"

Joe's eyes were red when I next found him beside me; but, I was holding his hand, and we both felt happy.

"How long, dear Joe?"

"Which you meantersay, Pip, how long have your illness lasted, dear old chap?"

"Yes, Joe."

"It's the end of May, Pip. To-morrow is the first of June."

"And have you been here all the time, dear Joe?"

"Pretty nigh, old chap. For, as I says to Biddy when the news of your being ill were brought by letter, which it were brought by the post and being formerly single he is now married though underpaid for a deal of walking and shoe-leather, but wealth were not a object on his part, and marriage were the great wish of his hart —"

"It is so delightful to hear you, Joe! But I interrupt you in what you said to Biddy."

"Which it were," said Joe, "that how you might be amongst strangers, and that how you and me having been ever friends, a wisit at such a moment might not prove unacceptabobble. And Biddy, her word were, 'Go to him, without loss of time.' That," said Joe, summing up with his judicial air, "were the word of Biddy. 'Go to him,' Biddy say, 'without loss of time.' In short, I shouldn't greatly deceive you," Joe added, after a little grave reflection, "if I represented to you that the word of that young woman were, 'without a minute's loss of time.'"

There Joe cut himself short, and informed me that I was to be talked to in great moderation, and that I was to take a little nourishment at stated frequent times, whether I felt inclined for it or not, and that I was to submit myself to all his orders. So, I kissed his hand, and lay quiet, while he proceeded to indite a note to Biddy, with my love in it.

Evidently, Biddy had taught Joe to write. As I lay in bed looking at him, it made me, in my weak state, cry again with pleasure to see the pride with which he set about his letter. My bedstead, divested of its curtains, had been removed, with me upon it, into the sitting-room, as the airiest and largest, and the carpet had been taken away, and the room kept always fresh and wholesome night and day. At my own writing-table, pushed into a corner and cumbered with little bottles, Joe now sat down to his great work, first choosing a pen from the pen-tray as if it were a chest of large tools, and tucking up his sleeves as if he were going to wield a crowbar or sledge-hammer. It was necessary for Joe to hold on heavily to the table with his left elbow, and to get his right leg well out behind him, before he could begin, and when he did begin, he made every down-stroke so slowly that it might have been six feet long, while at every up-stroke I could hear his pen spluttering extensively. He had a curious idea that the inkstand was on the side of him where it was not, and constantly dipped his pen into space, and seemed quite satisfied with the result. Occasionally, he was tripped up by some orthographical stumbling-block, but on the whole he got on very well indeed, and when he had signed his name, and had removed a finishing blot from the paper to the crown of his head with his two forefingers, he got up and hovered about the table, trying the effect of his performance from various points of view as it lay there, with unbounded satisfaction.

Not to make Joe uneasy by talking too much, even if I had been able to talk much, I deferred asking him about Miss Havisham until next day. He shook his head when I then asked him if she had recovered.

"Is she dead, Joe?"

"Why you see, old chap," said Joe, in tone of remonstrance, and by way of getting at it by degrees, "I wouldn't go so far as to say that, for that's a deal to say; but she ain't —"

"Living, Joe?"

"That's nigher where it is," said Joe; "she ain't living."

"Did she linger long, Joe?"

"Arter you was took ill, pretty much about what you might call (if you was put to it) a week," said Joe; still determined, on my account, to come at everything by degrees.

"Dear Joe, have you heard what becomes of her property?"

"Well, old chap," said Joe, "it do appear that she had settled the most of it, which I meantersay tied it up, on Miss Estella. But she had wrote out a little coddleshell[1] in her own hand a day or two afore the accident, leaving a cool four thousand to Mr. Matthew Pocket. And why, do you suppose, above all things, Pip, she left that cool four thousand unto him? 'Because of Pip's account of him the said Matthew.' I am told by Biddy, that air the writing," said Joe, repeating the legal turn as if it did him

---

1. *coddleshell:* Joe's idiosyncratic rendering of "codicil."

infinite good, "'account of him the said Matthew.' And a cool four thousand, Pip!"

I never discovered from whom Joe derived the conventional temperature of the four thousand pounds, but it appeared to make the sum of money more to him, and he had a manifest relish in insisting on its being cool.

This account gave me great joy, as it perfected the only good thing I had done. I asked Joe whether he had heard if any of the other relations had any legacies?

"Miss Sarah," said Joe, "she have twenty-five pound perannium fur to buy pills, on account of being bilious. Miss Georgiana, she have twenty pound down. Mrs. — what's the name of them wild beasts with humps, old chap?"

"Camels?" said I, wondering why he could possibly want to know.

Joe nodded. "Mrs. Camels," by which I presently understood he meant Camilla, "she have five pound fur to buy rushlights to put her in spirits when she wake up in the night."

The accuracy of these recitals was sufficiently obvious to me, to give me great confidence in Joe's information. "And now," said Joe, "you ain't that strong yet, old chap, that you can take in more nor one additional shovel-full to-day. Old Orlick he's been a bustin' open a dwelling-ouse."

"Whose?" said I.

"Not, I grant, you, but what his manners is given to blusterous," said Joe, apologetically; "still, a Englishman's ouse is his Castle, and castles must not be busted 'cept when done in war time. And wotsume'er the failings on his part, he were a corn and seedsman in his hart."

"Is it Pumblechook's house that has been broken into, then?"

"That's it, Pip," said Joe; "and they took his till, and they took his cash-box, and they drinked his wine, and they partook of his wittles, and they slapped his face, and they pulled his nose, and they tied him up to his bedpust, and they giv' him a dozen, and they stuffed his mouth full of flowering annuals to prewent his crying out. But he knowed Orlick, and Orlick's in the county jail."

By these approaches we arrived at unrestricted conversation. I was slow to gain strength, but I did slowly and surely become less weak, and Joe stayed with me, and I fancied I was little Pip again.

For, the tenderness of Joe was so beautifully proportioned to my need, that I was like a child in his hands. He would sit and talk to me in the old confidence, and with the old simplicity, and in the old unassertive protecting way, so that I would half believe that all my life since the days of the old kitchen was one of the mental troubles of the fever that was gone. He did everything for me except the household work, for which he had engaged a very decent woman, after paying off the laundress on his first arrival. "Which I do assure you, Pip," he would often say, in explanation of that liberty; "I found her a tapping the spare bed, like a cask of beer, and drawing off the feathers in a bucket, for sale. Which she would have tapped yourn next, and draw'd it off with you a laying on it, and was then a carrying away the coals gradiwally in the soup-tureen and wegetable-dishes, and the wine and spirits in your Wellington boots."

We looked forward to the day when I should go out for a ride, as we had once looked forward to the day of my apprenticeship. And when the day came, and an open carriage was got into the Lane, Joe wrapped me up, took me in his arms, carried me down to it, and put me in, as if I were still the small helpless creature to whom he had so abundantly given of the wealth of his great nature.

And Joe got in beside me, and we drove away together into the country, where the rich summer growth was already on the trees and on the grass, and sweet summer scents filled all the air. The day happened to be Sunday, and when I looked on the loveliness around me, and thought how it had grown and changed, and how the little wild flowers had been forming, and the voices of the birds had been strengthening, by day and by night, under the sun and under the stars, while poor I lay burning and tossing on my bed, the mere remembrance of having burned and tossed there, came like a check upon my peace. But, when I heard the Sunday bells, and looked around a little more upon the outspread beauty, I felt that I was not nearly thankful enough — that I was too weak yet, to be even that — and I laid my head on Joe's shoulder, as I had laid it long ago when he had taken me to the Fair or where not, and it was too much for my young senses.

More composure came to me after a while, and we talked as we used to talk, lying on the grass at the old Battery. There was no change whatever in Joe. Exactly what he had been in my eyes then, he was in my eyes still; just as simply faithful, and as simply right.

When we got back again and he lifted me out, and carried me — so easily — across the court and up the stairs, I thought of that eventful Christmas Day when he had carried me over the marshes. We had not yet made any allusion to my change of fortune, nor did I know how much of my late history he was acquainted with. I was so doubtful of myself now, and put so much trust in him, that I could not satisfy myself whether I ought to refer to it when he did not.

"Have you heard, Joe," I asked him that evening, upon further consideration, as he smoked his pipe at the window, "who my patron was?"

"I heerd," returned Joe, "as it were not Miss Havisham, old chap."

"Did you hear who it was, Joe?"

"Well! I heerd as it were a person what sent the person what giv' you the bank-notes at the Jolly Bargemen, Pip."

"So it was."

"Astonishing!" said Joe, in the placidest way.

"Did you hear that he was dead, Joe?" I presently asked, with increasing diffidence.

"Which? Him as sent the bank-notes, Pip?"

"Yes."

"I think," said Joe, after meditating a long time, and looking rather evasively at the window-seat, "as I *did* hear tell that how he were something or another in a general way in that direction."

"Did you hear anything of his circumstances, Joe?"

"Not partickler, Pip."

"If you would like to hear, Joe —" I was beginning, when Joe got up and came to my sofa.

"Lookee here, old chap," said Joe, bending over me. "Ever the best of friends; ain't us, Pip?"

I was ashamed to answer him.

"Wery good, then," said Joe, as if I *had* answered; "that's all right, that's agreed upon. Then why go into subjects, old chap, which as betwixt two sech must be for ever onnecessary? There's subjects enough as betwixt two sech, without onnecessary ones. Lord! To think of your poor sister and her Rampages! And don't you remember Tickler?"

"I do indeed, Joe."

"Lookee here, old chap," said Joe. "I done what I could to keep you and Tickler in sunders, but my power were not always fully equal to my inclinations. For when your poor sister had a mind to drop into you, it were notsermuch," said Joe, in his favourite argumentative way, "that she dropped into me too, if I put myself in opposition to her but that she dropped into you always heavier for it. I noticed that. It ain't a grab at a man's whisker, nor yet a shake or two of a man (to which your sister was quite welcome), that 'ud put a man off from getting a little child out of punishment. But when that little child is dropped into, heavier, for that grab of whisker or shaking, then that man naterally up and says to himself, 'Where is the good as you are a doing? I grant you I see the 'arm,' says the man, 'but I don't see the good. I call upon you, sir, theerfore, to pint out the good.'"

"The man says?" I observed, as Joe waited for me to speak.

"The man says," Joe assented. "Is he right, that man?"

"Dear Joe, he is always right."

"Well, old chap," said Joe, "then abide by your words. If he's always right (which in general he's more likely wrong), he's right when he says this: — Supposing ever you kep any little matter to yourself, when you was a little child, you kep it mostly because you know'd as J. Gargery's power to part you and Tickler in sunders, were not fully equal to his inclinations. Theerfore, think no more of it as betwixt two sech, and do not let us pass remarks upon onnecessary subjects. Biddy giv' herself a deal o' trouble with me afore I left (for I am almost awful dull), as I should view it in this light, and, viewing it in this light, as I shouldser put it. Both of which," said Joe, quite charmed with his logical arrangement, "being done, now this to you a true friend, say. Namely. You mustn't go a over-doing on it, but you must have your supper and your wine-and-water, and you must be put betwixt the sheets."

The delicacy with which Joe dismissed this theme, and the sweet tact and kindness with which Biddy — who with her woman's wit had found me out so soon — had prepared him for it, made a deep impression on my mind. But whether Joe knew how poor I was, and how my great expectations had all dissolved, like our own marsh mists before the sun, I could not understand.

Another thing in Joe that I could not understand when it first began to develop itself, but which I soon arrived at a sorrowful comprehension of, was this: As I became stronger and better, Joe became a little less easy with me. In my weakness and entire dependence on him, the dear fellow had fallen into the old tone, and called me by the old names, the dear "old Pip, old chap," that now were music in my ears. I too had fallen into the old ways, only happy and thankful that he let me. But, imperceptibly, though I held by them fast, Joe's hold upon them began to slacken; and whereas I wondered at this, at first, I soon began to understand that the cause of it was in me, and that the fault of it was all mine.

Ah! Had I given Joe no reason to doubt my constancy, and to think that in prosperity I should grow cold to him and cast him off? Had I given Joe's innocent heart no cause to feel instinctively that as I got stronger, his hold upon me would be weaker, and that he had better loosen it in time and let me go, before I plucked myself away?

It was on the third or fourth occasion of my going out walking in the Temple Gardens leaning on Joe's arm, that I saw this change in him very plainly. We had been sitting in the bright warm sunlight, looking at the river, and I chanced to say as we got up:

"See, Joe! I can walk quite strongly. Now, you shall see me walk back by myself."

"Which do not over-do it, Pip," said Joe; "but I shall be happy fur to see you able, sir."

The last word grated on me; but how could I remonstrate! I walked no further than the gate of the gardens, and then pretended to be weaker than I was, and asked Joe for his arm. Joe gave it me, but was thoughtful.

I, for my part, was thoughtful too; for, how best to check this growing change in Joe, was a great perplexity to my remorseful thoughts. That I was ashamed to tell him exactly how I was placed, and what I had come down to, I do not seek to conceal; but, I hope my reluctance was not quite an unworthy one. He would want to help me out of his little savings, I knew, and I knew that he ought not to help me, and that I must not suffer him to do it.

It was a thoughtful evening with both of us. But, before we went to bed, I had resolved that I would wait over to-morrow, to-morrow being Sunday, and would begin my new course with the new week. On Monday morning I would speak to Joe about this change, I would lay aside this last vestige of reserve, I would tell him what I had in my thoughts (that Secondly, not yet arrived at),[1] and why I had not decided to go out to Herbert, and then the change would be conquered for ever. As I cleared, Joe cleared, and it seemed as though he had sympathetically arrived at a resolution too.

We had a quiet day on the Sunday, and we rode out into the country, and then walked in the fields.

"I feel thankful that I have been ill, Joe," I said.

"Dear old Pip, old chap, you're a'most come round, sir."

"It has been a memorable time for me, Joe."

"Likeways for myself, sir," Joe returned.

"We have had a time together, Joe, that I can never forget. There were days once, I know, that I did for a while forget; but I never shall forget these."

"Pip," said Joe, appearing a little hurried and troubled, "there has been larks. And, dear sir, what have been betwixt us — have been."

At night, when I had gone to bed, Joe came into my room, as he had done all through my recovery. He asked me if I felt sure that I was as well as in the morning?

"Yes, dear Joe, quite."

"And are always a getting stronger, old chap?"

"Yes, dear Joe, steadily."

Joe patted the coverlet on my shoulder with his great good hand, and said, in what I thought a husky voice, "Good night!"

When I got up in the morning, refreshed and stronger yet, I was full of my resolution to tell Joe all, without delay. I would tell him before breakfast. I would dress at once and go to his room and surprise him; for, it was the first day I had been up early. I went to his room, and he was not there. Not only was he not there, but his box was gone.

I hurried then to the breakfast-table, and on it found a letter. These were its brief contents.

"Not wishful to intrude I have departured fur you are well again dear Pip and will do better without   "Jo.

"P.S. Ever the best of friends."

---

1. *(that Secondly, not yet arrived at):* first mentioned in Vol. III Ch. 16 p. 471, and finally revealed on p. 492.

Enclosed in the letter, was a receipt for the debt and costs on which I had been arrested. Down to that moment I had vainly supposed that my creditor had withdrawn or suspended proceedings until I should be quite recovered. I had never dreamed of Joe's having paid the money; but, Joe had paid it, and the receipt was in his name.

What remained for me now, but to follow him to the dear old forge, and there to have out my disclosure to him, and my penitent remonstrance with him, and there to relieve my mind and heart of that reserved Secondly, which had begun as a vague something lingering in my thoughts, and had formed into a settled purpose?

The purpose was, that I would go to Biddy, that I would show her how humbled and repentant I came back, that I would tell her how I had lost all I once hoped for, that I would remind her of our old confidences in my first unhappy time. Then, I would say to her, "Biddy, I think you once liked me very well, when my errant heart, even while it strayed away from you, was quieter and better with you than it ever has been since. If you can like me only half as well once more, if you can take me with all my faults and disappointments on my head, if you can receive me like a forgiven child (and indeed I am as sorry, Biddy, and have as much need of a hushing voice and a soothing hand), I hope I am a little worthier of you than I was — not much, but a little. And, Biddy, it shall rest with you to say whether I shall work at the forge with Joe, or whether I shall try for any different occupation down in this country, or whether we shall go away to a distant place where an opportunity awaits me, which I set aside when it was offered, until I knew your answer. And now, dear Biddy, if you can tell me that you will go through the world with me, you will surely make it a better world for me, and me a better man for it, and I will try hard to make it a better world for you."

Such was my purpose. After three days more of recovery, I went down to the old place, to put it in execution; and how I sped in it, is all I have left to tell.

CHAPTER XIX

THE TIDINGS of my high fortunes having had a heavy fall, had got down to my native place and its neighbourhood, before I got there. I found the Blue Boar in possession of the intelligence, and I found that it made a great change in the Boar's demeanour. Whereas the Boar had cultivated my good opinion with warm assiduity when I was coming into property, the Boar was exceedingly cool on the subject now that I was going out of property.

It was evening when I arrived, much fatigued by the journey I had so often made so easily. The Boar could not put me into my usual bedroom, which was engaged (probably by some one who had expectations), and could only assign me a very indifferent chamber among the pigeons and post-chaises up the yard. But, I had as sound a sleep in that lodging as in the most superior accommodation the Boar could have given me, and the quality of my dreams was about the same as in the best bedroom.

Early in the morning while my breakfast was getting ready, I strolled round by Satis House. There were printed bills on the gate, and on bits of carpet hanging out of the windows, announcing a sale by auction of the Household Furniture and Effects, next week. The House itself was to be sold as old building materials and pulled down. LOT 1 was marked in whitewashed knock-knee letters on the brewhouse; LOT 2 on that part of the main building which had been so long shut up. Other lots were marked off on other parts of the structure, and the ivy had been torn down to make room for the inscriptions, and much of it trailed low in the dust and was withered already. Stepping in for a moment at the open gate and looking around me with the uncomfortable air of a stranger who had no business there, I saw the auctioneer's clerk walking on the casks and telling them off for the information of a catalogue-compiler, pen in hand, who made a temporary desk of the wheeled chair I had so often pushed along to the tune of Old Clem.

When I got back to my breakfast in the Boar's coffee-room, I found Mr. Pumblechook conversing with the landlord. Mr. Pumblechook (not improved in appearance by his late nocturnal adventure) was waiting for me, and addressed me in the following terms.

"Young man, I am sorry to see you brought low. But what else could be expected! What else could be expected!"

As he extended his hand with a magnificently forgiving air, and as I was broken by illness and unfit to quarrel, I took it.

"William," said Mr. Pumblechook to the waiter, "put a muffin on table. And has it come to this! Has it come to this!"

I frowningly sat down to my breakfast. Mr. Pumblechook stood over me and poured out my tea — before I could touch the teapot — with the air of a benefactor who was resolved to be true to the last.

"William," said Mr. Pumblechook, mournfully, "put the salt on. In happier times," addressing me, "I think you took sugar? And did you take milk? You did. Sugar and milk. William, bring a watercress."

"Thank you," said I, shortly, "but I don't eat watercresses."

"You don't eat 'em," returned Mr. Pumblechook, sighing and nodding his head several times, as if he might have expected that, and as if abstinence from watercresses were consistent with my downfall. "True. The simple fruits of the earth. No. You needn't bring any, William."

I went on with my breakfast, and Mr. Pumblechook continued to stand over me, staring fishily and breathing noisily, as he always did.

"Little more than skin and bone!" mused Mr. Pumblechook, aloud. "And yet when he went away from here (I may say with my blessing), and I spread afore him my humble store, like the Bee, he was as plump as a Peach!"

This reminded me of the wonderful difference between the servile manner in which he had offered his hand in my new prosperity, saying, "May I?" and the ostentatious clemency with which he had just now exhibited the same fat five fingers.

"Hah!" he went on, handing me the bread-and-butter. "And air you a going to Joseph?"

"In Heaven's name," said I, firing in spite of myself, "what does it matter to you where I am going? Leave that teapot alone."

It was the worst course I could have taken, because it gave Pumblechook the opportunity he wanted.

"Yes, young man," said he, releasing the handle of the article in question, retiring a step or two from my table, and speaking for the behoof of the landlord and waiter at the door, "I *will* leave that teapot alone. You are right, young man. For once, you are right. I forgit myself when I take such an interest in your breakfast, as to wish your frame, exhausted by the

debilitating effects of prodigygality, to be stimilated by the 'olesome nourishment of your forefathers. And yet," said Pumblechook, turning to the
landlord and waiter, and pointing me out at arm's length, "this is him as I
ever sported with in his days of happy infancy! Tell me not it cannot be; I
tell you this is him!"

A low murmur from the two replied. The waiter appeared to be particularly affected.

"This is him," said Pumblechook, "as I have rode in my shay-cart. This
is him as I have seen brought up by hand. This is him untoe the sister of
which I was uncle by marriage, as her name was Georgiana M'ria from
her own mother, let him deny it if he can!"

The waiter seemed convinced that I could not deny it, and that it
gave the case a black look.

"Young man," said Pumblechook, screwing his head at me in the old
fashion, "you air a going to Joseph. What does it matter to me, you ask
me, where you air a going? I say to you, Sir, you air a going to Joseph."

The waiter coughed, as if he modestly invited me to get over that.

"Now," said Pumblechook, and all this with a most exasperating air
of saying in the cause of virtue what was perfectly convincing and conclusive, "I will tell you what to say to Joseph. Here is Squires of the Boar
present, known and respected in this town, and here is William, which his
father's name was Potkins if I do not deceive myself."

"You do not, sir," said William.

"In their presence," pursued Pumblechook, "I will tell you, young man,
what to say to Joseph. Says you, 'Joseph, I have this day seen my earliest
benefactor and the founder of my fortun's. I will name no names, Joseph,
but so they are pleased to call him up-town, and I have seen that man.'"

"I swear I don't see him here," said I.

"Say that likewise," retorted Pumblechook. "Say you said that, and even
Joseph will probably betray surprise."

"There you quite mistake him," said I. "I know better."

"Says you," Pumblechook went on, "'Joseph, I have seen that man,
and that man bears you no malice and bears me no malice. He knows
your character, Joseph, and is well acquainted with your pig-headedness
and ignorance; and he knows my character, Joseph, and he knows my want
of gratitoode. Yes, Joseph,' says you," here Pumblechook shook his head

and hand at me, "'he knows my total deficiency of common human gratitoode. *He* knows it, Joseph, as none can. *You* do not know it, Joseph, having no call to know it, but that man do.'"

Windy donkey as he was, it really amazed me that he could have the face to talk thus to mine.

"Says you, 'Joseph, he gave me a little message, which I will now repeat. It was, that in my being brought low, he saw the finger of Providence. He knowed that finger when he saw it, Joseph, and he saw it plain. It pinted out this writing, Joseph. *Reward of ingratitoode to earliest benefactor, and founder of fortun's.* But that man said that he did not repent of what he had done, Joseph. Not at all. It was right to do it, it was kind to do it, it was benevolent to do it, and he would do it again.'"

"It's a pity," said I, scornfully, as I finished my interrupted breakfast, "that the man did not say what he had done and would do again."

"Squires of the Boar!" Pumblechook was now addressing the landlord, "and William! I have no objections to your mentioning, either uptown or down-town, if such should be your wishes, that it was right to do it, kind to do it, benevolent to do it, and that I would do it again."

With those words the Impostor shook them both by the hand, with an air, and left the house; leaving me much more astonished than delighted by the virtues of that same indefinite "it." I was not long after him in leaving the house too, and when I went down the High-street I saw him holding forth (no doubt to the same effect) at his shop door to a select group, who honoured me with very unfavourable glances as I passed on the opposite side of the way.

But, it was only the pleasanter to turn to Biddy and to Joe, whose great forbearance shone more brightly than before, if that could be, contrasted with this brazen pretender. I went towards them slowly, for my limbs were weak, but with a sense of increasing relief as I drew nearer to them, and a sense of leaving arrogance and untruthfulness further and further behind.

The June weather was delicious. The sky was blue, the larks were soaring high over the green corn, I thought all that country-side more beautiful and peaceful by far than I had ever known it to be yet. Many pleasant pictures of the life that I would lead there, and of the change for the better that would come over my character when I had a guiding spirit at my side whose simple faith and clear home-wisdom I had proved, beguiled my way. They awakened a tender emotion in me; for, my heart was softened by my return, and such a change had come to pass, that I felt like one who was toiling home barefoot from distant travel, and whose wanderings had lasted many years.

The schoolhouse where Biddy was mistress, I had never seen; but, the little roundabout lane by which I entered the village for quietness' sake, took me past it. I was disappointed to find that the day was a holiday; no children were there, and Biddy's house was closed. Some hopeful notion of seeing her busily engaged in her daily duties, before she saw me, had been in my mind and was defeated.

But, the forge was a very short distance off, and I went towards it under the sweet green limes, listening for the clink of Joe's hammer. Long after I ought to have heard it, and long after I had fancied I heard it and found it but a fancy, all was still. The limes were there, and the white thorns were there, and the chestnut-trees were there, and their leaves rustled harmoniously when I stopped to listen; but, the clink of Joe's hammer was not in the midsummer wind.

Almost fearing, without knowing why, to come in view of the forge, I saw it at last, and saw that it was closed. No gleam of fire, no glittering shower of sparks, no roar of bellows; all shut up, and still.

But, the house was not deserted, and the best parlour seemed to be in use, for there were white curtains fluttering in its window, and the window was open and gay with flowers. I went softly towards it, meaning to peep over the flowers, when Joe and Biddy stood before me, arm in arm.

At first Biddy gave a cry, as if she thought it was my apparition, but in another moment she was in my embrace. I wept to see her, and she wept to see me; I, because she looked so fresh and pleasant; she, because I looked so worn and white.

"But dear Biddy, how smart you are!"

"Yes, dear Pip."

"And Joe, how smart *you* are!"

"Yes, dear old Pip, old chap."

I looked at both of them, from one to the other, and then —

"It's my wedding-day," cried Biddy, in a burst of happiness, "and I am married to Joe!"

* * * * *

They had taken me into the kitchen, and I had laid my head down on the old deal table. Biddy held one of my hands to her lips, and Joe's restoring touch was on my shoulder. "Which he warn't strong enough, my dear, fur to be surprised," said Joe. And Biddy said, "I ought to have thought of it, dear Joe, but I was too happy." They were both so overjoyed to see me, so proud to see me, so touched by my coming to them, so delighted that I should have come by accident to make their day complete!

My first thought was one of great thankfulness that I had never breathed this last baffled hope to Joe. How often, while he was with me in my illness, had it risen to my lips. How irrevocable would have been his knowledge of it, if he had remained with me but another hour!

"Dear Biddy," said I, "you have the best husband in the whole world, and if you could have seen him by my bed you would have — But no, you couldn't love him better than you do."

"No, I couldn't indeed," said Biddy.

"And, dear Joe, you have the best wife in the whole world, and she will make you as happy as even you deserve to be, you dear, good, noble Joe!"

Joe looked at me with a quivering lip, and fairly put his sleeve before his eyes.

"And Joe and Biddy both, as you have been to church to-day, and are in charity and love with all mankind, receive my humble thanks for all you have done for me and all I have so ill repaid! And when I say that I am going away within the hour, for I am soon going abroad, and that I shall never rest until I have worked for the money with which you have kept me out of prison, and have sent it to you, don't think, dear Joe and Biddy, that if I could repay it a thousand times over, I suppose I could cancel a farthing of the debt I owe you, or that I would do so if I could!"

They were both melted by these words, and both entreated me to say no more.

"But I must say more. Dear Joe, I hope you will have children to love, and that some little fellow will sit in this chimney corner of a winter night, who may remind you of another little fellow gone out of it for ever. Don't tell him, Joe, that I was thankless; don't tell him, Biddy, that I was ungenerous and unjust; only tell him that I honoured you both, because you were both so good and true, and that, as your child, I said it would be natural to him to grow up a much better man than I did."

"I ain't a going," said Joe, from behind his sleeve, "to tell him nothink o' that natur, Pip. Nor Biddy ain't. Nor yet no one ain't."

"And now, though I know you have already done it in your own kind hearts, pray tell me, both, that you forgive me! Pray let me hear you say the words, that I may carry the sound of them away with me, and then I shall be able to believe that you can trust me, and think better of me, in the time to come!"

"O dear old Pip, old chap," said Joe. "God knows as I forgive you, if I have anythink to forgive!"

"Amen! And God knows I do!" echoed Biddy.

"Now let me go up and look at my old little room, and rest there a few minutes by myself, and then when I have eaten and drunk with you, go with me as far as the finger-post, dear Joe and Biddy, before we say good-by!"

I sold all I had, and put aside as much as I could, for a composition with my creditors — who gave me ample time to pay them in full — and I went out and joined Herbert. Within a month, I had quitted England, and within two months I was clerk to Clarriker and Co., and within four months I assumed my first undivided responsibility. For, the beam across the parlour ceiling at Mill Pond Bank, had then ceased to tremble under old Bill Barley's growls and was at peace, and Herbert had gone away to marry Clara, and I was left in sole charge of the Eastern Branch until he brought her back.

Many a year went round, before I was a partner in the House; but, I lived happily with Herbert and his wife, and lived frugally, and paid my debts, and maintained a constant correspondence with Biddy and Joe. It was not until I became third in the Firm, that Clarriker betrayed me to Herbert; but, he then declared that the secret of Herbert's partnership had been long enough upon his conscience, and he must tell it. So, he told it, and Herbert was as much moved as amazed, and the dear fellow and I were not the worse friends for the long concealment. I must not leave it to be supposed that we were ever a great House, or that we made mints of money. We were not in a grand way of business, but we had a good name, and worked for our profits, and did very well. We owed so much to Herbert's ever cheerful industry and readiness, that I often wondered how I had conceived that old idea of his inaptitude, until I was one day enlightened by the reflection, that perhaps the inaptitude had never been in him at all, but had been in me.

CHAPTER XX

FOR ELEVEN years, I had not seen Joe nor Biddy with my bodily eyes — though they had both been often before my fancy in the East — when, upon an evening in December, an hour or two after dark, I laid my hand softly on the latch of the old kitchen door. I touched it so softly that I was not heard, and looked in unseen. There, smoking his pipe in the old place by the kitchen firelight, as hale and as strong as ever though a little grey, sat Joe; and there, fenced into the corner with Joe's leg, and sitting on my own little stool looking at the fire, was — I again!

"We giv' him the name of Pip for your sake, dear old chap," said Joe, delighted when I took another stool by the child's side (but I did *not* rumple his hair), "and we hoped he might grow a little bit like you, and we think he do."

I thought so too, and I took him out for a walk next morning, and we talked immensely, understanding one another to perfection. And I took him down to the churchyard, and set him on a certain tombstone there, and he showed me from that elevation which stone was sacred to the memory of Philip Pirrip, late of this Parish, and Also Georgiana, Wife of the Above.

"Biddy," said I, when I talked with her after dinner, as her little girl lay sleeping in her lap, "you must give Pip to me, one of these days; or lend him, at all events."

"No, no," said Biddy, gently. "You must marry."

"So Herbert and Clara say, but I don't think I shall, Biddy. I have so settled down in their home, that it's not at all likely. I am already quite an old bachelor."

Biddy looked down at her child, and put its little hand to her lips, and then put the good matronly hand with which she had touched it, into mine. There was something in the action and in the light pressure of Biddy's wedding-ring, that had a very pretty eloquence in it.

"Dear Pip," said Biddy, "you are sure you don't fret for her?"

"O no — I think not, Biddy."

"Tell me as an old, old friend. Have you quite forgotten her?"

"My dear Biddy, I have forgotten nothing in my life that ever had a foremost place there, and little that ever had any place there. But that poor dream, as I once used to call it, has all gone by, Biddy, all gone by!"*

Nevertheless, I knew while I said those words, that I secretly intended to revisit the site of the old house that evening, alone, for her sake. Yes even so. For Estella's sake.

I had heard of her as leading a most unhappy life, and as being separated from her husband, who had used her with great cruelty, and who had become quite renowned as a compound of pride, avarice, brutality, and meanness. And I had heard of the death of her husband, from an accident consequent on his ill-treatment of a horse. This release had befallen her some two years before; for anything I knew, she was married again.

The early dinner-hour at Joe's, left me abundance of time, without hurrying my talk with Biddy, to walk over to the old spot before dark. But, what with loitering on the way, to look at old objects and to think of old times, the day had quite declined when I came to the place.

There was no house now, no brewery, no building whatever left, but the wall of the old garden. The cleared space had been enclosed with a rough fence, and, looking over it, I saw that some of the old ivy had struck root anew, and was growing green on low quiet mounds of ruin. A gate in the fence standing ajar, I pushed it open, and went in.

A cold silvery mist had veiled the afternoon, and the moon was not yet up to scatter it. But, the stars were shining beyond the mist, and the moon was coming, and the evening was not dark. I could trace out where every part of the old house had been, and where the brewery had been, and where the gates, and where the casks. I had done so, and was looking along the desolate garden-walk, when I beheld a solitary figure in it.

The figure showed itself aware of me, as I advanced. It had been moving towards me, but it stood still. As I drew nearer, I saw it to be the figure of a woman. As I drew nearer yet, it was about to turn away, when it stopped, and let me come up with it. Then, it faltered as if much surprised, and uttered my name, and I cried out:

"Estella!"

"I am greatly changed. I wonder you know me."

The freshness of her beauty was indeed gone, but its indescribable majesty and its indescribable charm remained. Those attractions in it, I had seen before; what I had never seen before, was the saddened softened light of the once proud eyes; what I had never felt before, was the friendly touch of the once insensible hand.

We sat down on a bench that was near, and I said, "After so many years, it is strange that we should thus meet again, Estella, here where our first meeting was! Do you often come back?"

"I have never been here since."

"Nor I."

The moon began to rise, and I thought of the placid look at the white ceiling, which had passed away. The moon began to rise, and I thought of the pressure on my hand when I had spoken the last words he had heard on earth.

Estella was the next to break the silence that ensued between us.

"I have very often hoped and intended to come back, but have been prevented by many circumstances. Poor, poor old place!"

The silvery mist was touched with the first rays of the moonlight, and the same rays touched the tears that dropped from her eyes. Not knowing that I saw them, and setting herself to get the better of them, she said quietly:

"Were you wondering, as you walked along, how it came to be left in this condition?"

"Yes, Estella."

"The ground belongs to me. It is the only possession I have not relinquished. Everything else has gone from me, little by little, but I have kept this. It was the subject of the only determined resistance I made in all the wretched years."

"Is it to be built on?"

"At last it is. I came here to take leave of it before its change. And you," she said, in a voice of touching interest to a wanderer, "you live abroad still?"

"Still."

"And do well, I am sure?"

"I work pretty hard for a sufficient living, and therefore — Yes, I do well."

"I have often thought of you," said Estella.

"Have you?"

"Of late, very often. There was a long hard time when I kept far from me, the remembrance of what I had thrown away when I was quite ignorant of its worth. But, since my duty has not been incompatible with the admission of that remembrance, I have given it a place in my heart."

"You have always held your place in my heart," I answered. And we were silent again, until she spoke.

"I little thought," said Estella, "that I should take leave of you in taking leave of this spot. I am very glad to do so."

"Glad to part again, Estella? To me, parting is a painful thing. To me, the remembrance of our last parting has been ever mournful and painful."

"But you said to me," returned Estella, very earnestly, "'God bless you, God forgive you!' And if you could say that to me then, you will not hesitate to say that to me now — now, when suffering has been stronger than all other teaching, and has taught me to understand what your heart used to be. I have been bent and broken, but — I hope — into a better shape. Be as considerate and good to me as you were, and tell me we are friends."

"We are friends," said I, rising and bending over her, as she rose from the bench.

"And will continue friends apart," said Estella.

I took her hand in mine, and we went out of the ruined place; and, as the morning mists had risen long ago when I first left the forge, so, the evening mists were rising now, and in all the broad expanse of tranquil light they showed to me, I saw the shadow of no parting from her.*

THE END

Explanatory Notes

Dedication

38   *Chauncy Hare Townshend*

Dickens and Townshend (1798–1868) met in 1840, and remained friends, having a common interest in mesmerism. Educated at Eton and Cambridge, Townshend took holy orders but was only briefly a beneficed clergyman; his private means enabled him to indulge in an amateurish fashion in painting, music, writing, and collecting, while also travelling widely. He appointed Dickens his literary executor, which, on his death, left Dickens the unexpected and uncongenial task of editing his chaotic collection of papers, which duly appeared in 1869 as *Religious Opinions of the Late Reverend Chauncy Hare Townshend*. In addition to this dedication, Townshend was presented with the manuscript of the novel.

VOLUME I

Chapter 1

39   *that universal struggle*

Probably referring to Darwin's theories of evolution by natural section, recently summarized in *On the Origin of Species by Means of Natural Selection, or the Preservation of Favoured Races in the Struggle for Life* (1859), and discussed three times around this period in Dickens's family journal *All the Year Round* (June 2 & July 7 1860, & March 29 1861).

40   *the marsh country ... twenty miles of the sea*

Clearly the northern part of the Hoo peninsula, the tongue of low-lying land between the mouths of the Thames and the Medway in Kent — see Map A. In childhood Dickens lived for some time nearby in Sheerness and later Chatham. He returned to the area frequently after 1856 when he bought Gad's Hill Place, a house on the Gravesend road above the village of Higham outside Rochester, where he went to live permanently shortly before the writing of *Great Expectations*. A number of details in the following pages reinforce this specific setting: convict Hulks (p. 50) were moored in the Medway at Upnor, Chatham; there is a churchyard with a series of distinctive children's graves (p. 39) at Cooling, an old Battery (p. 42) at the mouth of Cliffe Creek, and blacksmith's forges (p. 44) in the villages of Cliffe, Chalk, and High Halstow. The prevalence of pollarded trees (p. 40), clapboard houses (p. 44), chalk pits (p. 109) and limekilns (p. 440), and the pronunciation of "marshes" (p. 51) are all consistent with life on the Kent estuaries. From references to the Cathedral and the ruined priory (p. 418), the "nearest town" (p. 60) clearly derives from the city of Rochester, on the River Medway, and on Watling Street, the old Roman road from London to Canterbury.

40   *"Hold your noise! ... cut your throat!"*

On the representation of non-standard speech in the novel, see Brook Ch. 3.

Chapter 3

56   *Didn't you hear the cannon last night?*
      A slip by Dickens, confusing the real second convict with Magwitch's imaginary companion the "young man," since in Vol. I Ch. 1 Pip had been led to believe that the latter escaped at the same time as Magwitch.

Chapter 4

65   *like a Medium of the present day*
      In London in the late 1850s and early 1860s, there was something of a "Spirit-moving mania," in the words of *Punch*, a mania that was roundly mocked not only in that comic weekly but also in the family weeklies conducted by Dickens. See, for example, "Well-Authenticated Rappings" *Household Words* 20 February 1858 or "Modern Magic" *All the Year Round* 28 July 1860.

Chapter 7

79   *Mr. Wopsle's great-aunt ... seeing her do it.*
      Mr. Wopsle's great-aunt's establishment is merely an exaggerated example of the notorious Dame Schools of the first half of the nineteenth century. See Collins 1963 pp. 94–7 and Appendix C 12/1.

Chapter 10

113   *One-Pound notes*
      Such notes were only generally issued between 1797 and 1821. Dickens's familiarity with this fact is suggested by "Two Chapters on Bank Note Forgeries" published in his first family journal *Household Words* (7 & 21 Sept. 1850).

Chapter 13

137   *five-and-twenty pound*
      Presumably a slip by Dickens, as the sum mentioned by Miss Havisham is in guineas, not pounds (p. 135). A pound was worth twenty shillings, a guinea twenty-one. The last guinea coins were minted in 1813.

Chapter 16

154   *the Bow-street men ... extinct red-waistcoated police*
      The Bow Street Runners (detectives) and the Bow Street Patrols (who in fact wore the distinctive red waistcoats) were founded in the mid-eighteenth century by John and Henry Fielding. They were replaced by the professional police force set up by Sir Robert Peel in the metropolis in 1829 and in the rest of the country from 1839. Dickens had criticized the older establishment on several previous occasions. See Collins 1962 Ch. IX.

VOLUME II

Chapter 1

193   *The journey from our town ... Cheapside, London.*

The Cross-Keys coaching-inn in the City of London was the destination of the stage-coach from Rochester (see Maps A & B). Dickens nostalgically describes his childhood journey over the same route on the "Timpson's Blue-Eyed Maid," when his family moved from Chatham to Camden in 1822, in "Dullborough Town," one of the sketches in *The Uncommercial Traveller*.

Chapter 3

210   *I don't know why ... genteel as never was and brew.*

Baking and brewing are of course linked by their common use of yeast for fermentation; the social difference is clearly between retail and wholesale trade, between being a shopkeeper and a manufacturer, as is made clear by the following comment on the incompatibily of running a public-house and being a gentleman. On the complex compatibilities and incompatibilities of trade and gentility in Victorian England, see Phillips 93–101.

214   *A capitalist — an Insurer of Ships*

"A merchant" in the manuscript. All subsequent references to shipping insurance were added at a later stage. The references to trading, now slightly incongruous, were already present in the manuscript, with the addition of a reference to trading to China for tea, cut in all printed versions.

217   *with an appearance of amiable dignity*

In the manuscript, "with an appearance of amiable enthusiasm, and I thought she was the sweetest woman I had ever seen." The repeated emphasis on Mrs. Pocket's obsession with aristocracy in printed versions replaces an equally emphatic concern with her cloying amiability in the manuscript.

Chapter 4

220   *by name Drummle and Startop*

In the manuscript, "Jumble and Startop."

221   *a toady neighbour ... This lady's name was Mrs. Coiler*

In the manuscript, the character is Mrs. Pocket's mother, who bears a particular animus against Mr. Pocket, instead of Mrs. Coiler's universal amiability.

Chapter 5

233   *police-court*

The court of initial investigation of charges preferred by the police, known at the time the story is set as "public-offices" or "police-offices," as Dickens was aware — see "The Prisoners' Van" *Sketches by Boz*. Beside the central office in Bow Street, after 1792 there were seven public-offices in other London parishes, including one at Hatton Garden (see Map B), presumably that referred to here.

Chapter 8

247 *MY DEAR MR. PIP ... BIDDY*
Dickens made three small but significant changes to Biddy's letter to Pip at the beginning of Vol. II Ch. 8 for the 1868 Charles Dickens edition, all of which tend to suggest a Biddy already slightly more formal and educated that in the version preferred here, which is that of the edition of 1861. The changes were:
1) in company of Mr. Wopsle → in company with Mr. Wopsle
2) Tuesday morning 9 o'clock → Tuesday morning at nine o'clock
3) Your ever obliged and affectionate
> Servant,
>> Biddy.

→

Your ever obliged and affectionate servant,
> Biddy.

252 *Blacking Ware'us*
Presumably "Warren's Blacking" on the Thames at Hungerford Stairs, off the Strand (see Map C). It was then a famous landmark, according to Dickens, who was forced to work in a rival establishment during the period of his father's insolvency (see Appendix C 1).

Chapter 9

257 *that curious flavour ... the convict presence*
Convict fare relied heavily on stale bread soaked in warm water (a compound also often applied to the skin as a medicament); convict uniforms were often made of the coarse green cotton cloth known as baize; and convict labour typically consisted of picking oakum (untwisting old rope) and breaking stones ("hearthstone" was made from powdered stone mixed with clay and was used for whitening and polishing stone).

Chapter 13

288 *At that time, jails ... improving the flavour of their soup.*
Topical reference to the riots in Chatham Convict Prison in February 1861, brought on principally by a sudden reduction in the prisoners' diet. On Dickens's criticism elsewhere of "soft" conditions in new model and reformed prisons, see Collins 1962 Ch. I, Introduction p. 21, and Appendix D 10.

Chapter 16

310 *the new school nearly finished here*
Presumably one of the new schools founded from the second decade of the century by the Church of England National Society, which, along with those run by the Nonconformist Royal Lancasterian Society, employed more systematic methods and gradually began to put the often chaotic old Dame Schools (see Explanatory Note to p. 79) out of business. See Collins 1963 Ch IV and Appendix C 12.

Chapter 17

318 *the names of the various bridges ... Vauxhall, six.*
See Map C. This information helps to date the action with some precision. South-wark Bridge was the last completed in 1819; Old London Bridge (referred to here, as Vol. III Ch. 7 p. 403 makes clear) was not pulled down until 1831, although construction of the new bridge had begun in 1824. Tower Bridge was not constructed until towards the end of the century.

Chapter 20

349 *I should of a certainty be hanged if took*
Dickens clearly exaggerated the danger. Although theoretically the offence remained a capital one until 1835, no returned transports were in fact hanged after 1810. See Collins 1962 p. 281.

VOLUME III

Chapter 2

367 *raving off*
The collocation is unrecorded in the Oxford English Dictionary, but in context presumably means "avoiding by behaving wildly." The first American edition had "staving off."

Chapter 4

379 *your Shropshire*
Presumably a slip by Dickens, since Drummle is described as coming "of rich people down in Somersetshire" in Vol. II Ch. 6 p. 233.

Chapter 6

395 *down the Pool there between Limehouse and Greenwich*
An uncharacteristic slip by Dickens concerning the topography of London. The Pool, divided into upper and lower, is the broad stretch of the river below the Tower of London (see Map C); the stretch beyond Limehouse going south around the Isle of Dogs is known as Limehouse Reach.

Chapter 7

397 *bow-window (not bay-window, which is another thing)*
Dickens's point is presumably that a bay-window must form a recess (bay) in a room, whereas a bow-window may be merely a curved projection from the wall; however, according to the Oxford English Dictionary the two terms were and are often used synonymously.

Chapter 12

437 *didn't*
The British 1861 edition reads "did't," and some editors have argued that Dickens

was consciously reflecting Mike's "constitutional cold" first mentioned in Vol. II Ch. 1 p. 199, and again referred to here. But in such a case consistency would demand that "can't" a few lines below be written "ca't." So we have preferred the alternative, less problematic, reading found in the manuscript, serialized versions, and first American editions.

Chapter 17

477 *At that time, it was the custom ... receive that sentence together.*
See Dickens's description of the proceedings of the court of quarter session in "Criminal Courts" in *Sketches by Boz* and reproduced in Appendix D 2.

479 *I began that night to write ... one to the Crown itself.*
On the frequency of petitions for clemency and subsequent reprieves under the "Bloody Code," see Collins (1962) Ch. II.

Chapter 20

501 *"My dear Biddy ... all gone by!"*
From here on the manuscript originally carried a different and much briefer ending, in which Pip and Estella meet again but are not united, and which Dickens abandoned on the advice of Sir Edward Bulwer Lytton, the founding father of Victorian fiction. The original ending is preserved in three forms: 1) the first four lines are still legible under erasure on the original manuscript, though the remainder is lost; 2) the whole is preserved legibly in proofs of the novel now held at the Pierpoint Morgan Library, after being recovered from beneath the revised ending which had been pasted over; and 3) the whole is reprinted, presumably from a proof, in Forster Vol. III p. 336n. Variations in the versions are recorded in the Clarendon edition of the novel, while the Pierpoint Morgan version is reproduced below:

> It was four years more, before I saw herself. I had heard of her as leading a most unhappy life, and as being separated from her husband who had used her with great cruelty, and who had become quite renowned as a compound of pride, brutality, and meanness. I had heard of the death of her husband (from an accident consequent on ill-treating a horse), and of her being married again to a Shropshire doctor, who, against his interest, had once very manfully interposed, on an occasion when he was in professional attendance on Mr. Drummle, and had witnessed some outrageous treatment of her. I had heard that the Shropshire doctor was not rich, and that they lived on her own personal fortune.
>
> I was in England again — in London, and walking along Piccadilly with little Pip — when a servant came running after me to ask would I step back to a lady in a carriage who wished to speak to me. It was a little pony carriage, which the lady was driving; and the lady and I looked sadly enough on one another.
>
> "I am greatly changed, I know; but I thought you would like to

shake hands with Estella too, Pip. Lift up that pretty child and let me kiss it!" (She supposed the child, I think, to be my child.)

I was very glad afterwards to have had the interview; for, in her face and in her voice, and in her touch, she gave me the assurance, that suffering had been stronger than Miss Havisham's teaching, and had given her a heart to understand what my heart used to be.

503   *the shadow of no parting from her*
The revised manuscript and one extant proof have "the shadow of no parting from her but one" (clearly the final parting of death), while the final words were altered to "no shadow of another parting from her" in all volumes supervised by Dickens from the single-volume edition of 1862.

Appendices: Contemporary Documents

APPENDIX A. THE COMPOSITION OF THE NOVEL

A1. Dickens's Working Memoranda

[Now held in the Wisbech and Fenland Museum Library, along with the manuscript of the novel. Facsimiles of the Memoranda appear in Stone. The following transcription attempts to follow Dickens's arrangement on the page as closely as possible.]

<u>Dates</u>

Herbert Pocket speaks of Miss Havisham's
matter having happened "five and twenty years
ago." at that time, Pip is — say 18 or 19.
Consequently it happened 6 or 7 years before
Pip, ~~xx~~ and Estella — who is about his age —
were born.

But say that the matter was a year or so in
hand — which it would be — that would reduce
it to ~~4 or 5 years~~ 5 or 6 years before
they were born.

Magwitch tells his story in the Temple, when
Pip is 23.   Magwitch is then about 60.
Say Pip was about 7 at the opening of the story. Magwitch's
                              about
escape would then be ∧ 16 years ago. If Magwitch
says he first knew Compey about 20 years ago, that
would leave about 4 years for his knowledge of
Compey and whole association with him up to the
time of the escape.   That would also make him
about 40 when he knew Compey, and Compey was
younger than he.

When Magwitch ~~knew Comp~~ became known to Compey

the end of Miss Havisham's matter would thus have
taken place about 7 or 8 years before.

Estella, as Magwitch's child, must have been born

(Dates) 2
about 3 years before he knew Compey.

The Ages in the last stage of Pip's Expectations — stand thus:

Pip	about	23
Estella	"	23
Herbert	"	23
Magwitch	"	60
Compey	"	52 or 53
Miss Havisham	"	56 (I judge her to have been the elder in the love time.)
Biddy	"	24 or 25
Joe	"	45

Jaggers 55, Wemmick near 50, and so forth.

General Mems: 1

Miss Havisham and Pip, and the Money for Herbert. So
Herbert made a partner in clarriker's

Compeyson. How brought in?

Estella, Magwitch's daughter

Orlick — and Pip's entrapment — and escape

— To the flight

Start

Pursuit

xx Both overboard
Struggle — xxxx the upturned
together — Compeyson drowned —
Magwitch rescued by Pip. And
taken.

Then:

Magwitch tried, found guilty, & left for

<u>Death</u>

Dies presently in Newgate

Property confiscated to the Crown.

Herbert goes abroad:

Pip perhaps to follow.

Pip arrested when i too ill to be moved — lies in the

chambers in Fever. Ministering Angel <u>Joe</u>.

Recovered again, Pip goes humbly down to the

old marsh Village, to propose to Biddy.

Finds Biddy married to Joe

<u>General Mems: 2.</u>

So goes abroad to Herbert (happily married to Clara
Barley), and becomes his clerk.

The one good thing he did in his prosperity,
the only thing that endures and bears good fruit

<u>Tide</u>

Down at	up
9 AM	3 PM
till	till
3 PM	9 P. M
Down 9 PM	
till 3 morg	

Down at 9 ⅄ A.M.	till 3 P.M Wednesday
Up at 3 PM —	till 9. P.M. Wednesday
Down at 9 PM.	till 3 A M Thursday morg
Up at 3 AM.	till 9. A M Thursday morg
	<u>when the boat starts</u>

A2. Extracts from Dickens's Letters relating to the composition and publication of the novel

[Reprinted with the permission of the Clarendon Press from the *Letters of Charles Dickens* Vol. IX, 1859-61 (1997), ed. Graham Storey.]

1. From letter to The Earl of Carlisle, 8 August 1860, Gad's Hill Place.

This is Falstaff's own Gad's Hill, and I live on the top of it. All goes well with me, thank God. I should be thoroughly delighted to see you again, and to show you where the robbery was done. My eldest daughter keeps my house, and it is one I was extraordinarily fond of when a child.... I am prowling about, meditating a new book.

2. From letter to Frederic Chapman, 24 August 1860, Gad's Hill Place.

You will probably hear from me concerning a new Serial Story before long. You won't object to one, I dare say.

3. From letter to John Forster, [? Mid–September 1860], [?].

For a little piece I have been writing—or am writing; for I hope to finish it to-day—such a very fine, new, and grotesque idea has opened upon me, that I begin to doubt whether I had not better cancel the little paper, and reserve the notion for a new book. You shall judge as soon as I get it printed. But it so opens out before *me* that I can see the whole of a serial revolving on it, in a most singular and comic manner.

4. From letter to John Forster, 4 October, 1860, Gad's Hill Place.

Last week I got to work on the new story. I had previously very carefully considered the state and prospects of *All the Year Round*, and, the more I considered them, the less hope I saw of being able to get back, *now*, to the profit of a separate publication in the old 20 numbers. However I worked on, knowing that what I was doing would run into another groove; and I called a council of war at the office on Tuesday. It was perfectly clear that the one thing to be done was, for me to strike in. I have therefore decided to begin the story as of the length of the *Tale of Two Cities* on the first of December — begin publishing, that is. I must make the most I can out of the book. You shall have the first two or three weekly parts to-morrow. The name is GREAT EXPECTATIONS. I think a good name?

5. From letter to John Forster, [6 October 1860], [?].

The sacrifice of *Great Expectations* is really and truly made for myself. The property of *All the Year Round* is far too valuable, in every way, to be much endangered. Our fall is not large, but we have a considerable advance in hand of the story we are now publishing, and there is no vitality in it, and no chance whatever of stopping the fall; which on the contrary would be certain to increase. Now, if I went into a twenty-number serial, I should cut off my power of doing anything serial here for two good years — and that would be a most perilous thing. On the other hand, by dashing in now, I come in when most wanted; and if Reade and Wilkie follow me our course will be shaped out handsomely and hopefully for between two and three years. A thousand pounds are to be paid for early proofs of the story to America.

6. From letter to Charles Lever, 6 October 1860, Office of All the Year Round.

We drop, rapidly and continuously, with the Day's Ride. Whether it is too detached and discursive in its interest for the audience and the form of publication, I can not say positively; but it does not *take hold*. The consequence is, that the circulation becomes affected, and that the subscribers complain. I have waited week after week, for these three or four weeks, watching for any sign of encouragement. The least sign would have been enough. But all the tokens that appear, are in the other direction; and therefore I have been driven upon the necessity of considering how to act, and of writing to you.

There is but one thing to be done. I had begun a book which I intended for one of my long twenty-number Serials. I must abandon that design and forego its profit (a very serious consideration, you may believe), and shape the story for these pages. I must get into these pages, as soon as possible, and must consequently begin my story in the No. for the 1st. of December. For as long a time as you continue afterwards, we must go on together.

This is the whole case. If the publication were to go steadily down, too long, it would be very, very, very, difficult to raise again. I do not fear the difficulty at all, by taking this early and vigorous action. But without it there is not a doubt that the position would be serious.

7. From letter to John Forster, [Early October 1860], [?].

The book will be written in the first person throughout, and during these first three weekly numbers you will find the hero to be a boy-child, like David. Then he will be an apprentice. You will not have to complain of the want of humour as in *The Tale of Two Cities*. I have made the opening, I hope, in its general effect exceedingly droll. I have put a child and a good-natured foolish man, in relations that seem to me very funny. Of course I have got in the pivot on which the story will turn too — and which indeed, as you remember, was the grotesque tragic-comic conception that first encouraged me. To be quite sure I had fallen into no unconscious repetitions, I read *David Copperfield* again the other day, and was affected by it to a degree you would hardly believe.

8. From letter to Wilkie Collins, 24 October 1860, Office of All the Year Round.

What a pity I am not there [Paris], at Meurice's, to sleep the sleep of infancy through the long plays where the gentlemen stand with their backs to mantel-pieces. What a pity I am not with you to make a Third at the Trois frères, and drink no end of bottles of Bordeaux without ever getting a touch of redness in my (poet's phrase again) "innocent nose"! But I must go down to Gad's tonight, and get to work again. Four weekly numbers have been ground off the wheel, and at least another must be turned, afore we meet. They shall be yours in the slumberous Railway carriage.

9. From letter to Baron Bernhard Tauchnitz, [? Mid-November 1860], Gad's Hill Place.

The *Uncommercial Traveller* is finished *for the present*, but I may very probably write another series under the same title, but bye and bye. I bring it to a close now, because I am about to produce in All the Year Round a new serial story of my own writing, which will be continued every week for nine months. It will be rather longer than *A Tale of Two Cities*. Its title will be *Great Expectations*....

10. From letter to Austen Henry Layard M.P., 4 December 1860, Gad's Hill Place.

I know you will readily believe that I would come if I could, and that I am heartily sorry I cannot.

A new story of my writing, nine months long, is just begun in All the Year Round. I have been taken off it for a month by other Christmas work, and for a few days have not been well. I am pledged to the active chairmanship of a certain public committee, and thus my time is so closely portioned out that I dare not interfere with my hours of retreat and occupation here. Tomorrow I MUST write. A certain allotment of my time when I have that story-demand upon me, has, all through my Author life, been an essential condition of my health and success. I have just returned here to work so many hours every day for so many days. It is really impossible for me to break my bond.

11. From letter to Sir Edward Bulwer Lytton, 4 December 1860, Gad's Hill Place.

As I have just begun a story of my own in All the Year Round we could not begin advantageously to publish yours before the 1st. of August — which would bring the publication of the book to the very best time of the year. But all the agreements could be immediately made, and the All the Year Round money is ready to be paid down.

12. From letter to Baron Bernhard Tauchnitz, 22 December 1860, Gad's Hill Place.

I cannot consent to name the sum you shall pay for Great Expectations. I have too great a regard for you, and too high a sense of your honorable dealing, to wish to depart from the custom we have always observed. Whatever price you put upon it will satisfy me. You have already proposed the terms yourself, on former occasions, and I entreat you to do so now.

13. From letter to Miss Mary Boyle, 28 December 1860, Office of All the Year Round.

I have no news, except that I am not quite well, and am being doctored. Pray read Great Expectations. I think it is very droll. It is a very great success, and seems universally liked — I suppose because it opens funnily and with an interest too.

14. From letter to Miss Georgina Hogarth, 17 January 1861, Office of All the Year Round.

When I was calculating yesterday about coming down, I was under an unaccountable impression that there was a day less in the week than there is. It seems to me that I cannot do better than come down at once, and get my Number [the next serial installment of *Great Expectations*] done at Gad's. Will you meet me, therefore, at Gravesend tomorrow (Friday), and I will come by the 2.20 Train. I think the best thing I can do, will be to take possession of the best Spare Room, if you will have its fire lighted and will put my odds and ends there.

15. From letter to Mrs Cowden Clarke, 25 January 1861, Office of All the Year Round.

I am glad to find you so faithfully following Great Expectations, which story is an immense success.

16. From letter to W.W.F. de Cerjat, 1 February 1861, Office of All the Year Round.

This journal is doing gloriously, and Great Expectations is a great success. Lever's story has been a dead-weight, and obliged me to rush in to the rescue. But it will soon be finished now, and we shall be all the better yet for that desirable consummation.

17. From letter to Edmund Yates, 24 February 1861, 3 Hanover Terrace, Regents Park.

Before Christmas, my story and what I had to do for Christmas kept me in actual bondage for weeks together. After Christmas (that is from the 26th. of December to past the middle of January) I was unwell, at the office to be near my Doctor, and did not once get to Gad's Hill where all the household were. Chronically, when I have a book to write I give myself up to it.

18. From letter to Sir Edward Bulwer Lytton, 4 April 1861, 3 Hanover Terrace, Regents Park.

My story will finish in the first week in August. Yours ought to begin in the last week of July, or the last week but one. Wilkie Collins will be at work to follow you. The publication has made a very great success with "Great Expectations", and could not present a finer time for you.

19. From letter to John Forster, [? Mid-April 1861], [?].

It is a pity that the third portion [i.e., the last stage of Pip's Expectations] cannot be read all at once, because its purpose would be much more apparent; and the pity is the greater, because the general turn and tone of the working out and winding up, will be away from all such things as they conventionally go. But what must be, must be. As to the planning out from week to week, nobody can imagine what the difficulty is, without trying. But, as in all such cases, when it is overcome the pleasure is proportionate. Two months more will see me through it, I trust. All the iron is in the fire, and I have "only" to beat it out.

20. From letter to Sir Edward Bulwer Lytton, 28 April 1861, 3 Hanover Terrace, Regents Park.

You cannot think how happy you make me by what you write of Great Expectations. There is nothing like the pride of making such an effect on such a writer as you.

21. From letter to Wilkie Collins, 24 May 1861, Lord Ward Hotel, Dover.

I hope — begin to hope — that somewhere about the 12th. of June will see me out of the book. I am anxious for some days at Gad's Hill, and settlement of Christmas No. with you. The idea I have, will certainly do (I think), and save us a quantity of beating about.

22. From letter to W.C. Macready, 11 June 1861, Office of All the Year Round.

I have just finished my book of Great Expectations, and am the worse for wear. Neuralgic pains in the face have troubled me a good deal, and the work has been pretty close. But I hope that the book is a good book, and I have no doubt of very soon throwing off the little damage it has done me.

23. From letter to [Frederic Chapman], 15 June 1861, 3 Hanover Terrace, Regents Park.

Pray keep Whiting's people well up to the mark, and fix a day for publishing Great Expectations, and let them and Eeles know that it *must* be out on the day appointed.

24. From letter to Wilkie Collins, 23 June 1861, Gad's Hill Place.

As yet, I have hardly got into the enjoyment of thorough laziness. Bulwer was so very anxious that I should alter the end of Great Expectations — the extreme end, I mean, after Biddy and Joe are done with — and stated his reasons so well, that I have resumed the wheel, and taken another turn at it. Upon the whole I think it is for the better. You shall see the change when we meet.

25. From letter to Sir Edward Bulwer Lytton, 24 June 1861, Gad's Hill Place.

I send you enclosed, the whole of the concluding weekly No. of Great Expectations, in order that you may the more readily understand where I have made the change.

My difficulty was, to avoid doing too much. My tendency — when I began to unwind the thread that I thought I had wound for ever — was to labour it, and get out of proportion.

So I have done it in as few words as possible; and I hope you will like the alteration that is entirely due to you.

26.　From letter to John Forster, 1 July 1861, Gad's Hill Place.

You will be surprised to hear that I have changed the end of *Great Expectations* from and after Pip's return to Joe's, and finding his little likeness there. Bulwer, who has been, as I think you know, extraordinarily taken by the book, so strongly urged it upon me, after reading the proofs, and supported his views with such good reasons, that I resolved to make the change. You shall have it when you come back to town. I have put in as pretty a little piece of writing as I could, and I have no doubt the story will be more acceptable through the alteration.

I have not seen Bulwer's changed story. I brought back the first month with me, and I know the nature of his changes throughout; but I have not yet had the revised proofs.

27.　From letter to T.R. Eeles, 6 July 1861, Gad's Hill Place.

Be so good as bind a Dedication copy of Great Expectations in Russia Leather and Gold, and to do it as soon as you can. Mr. Townshend, to whom the book is dedicated, will soon be leaving town. This note will be a sufficient authority to Chapman and Hall to supply you with a copy on my account.

28.　From letter to the Hon. Mrs. Richard Watson, 8 July, 1861, Gad's Hill Place.

I have owed you a letter for so long a time, that I fear you may sometimes have misconstrued my silence. But I hope that the sight of the handwriting of your old friend will undeceive you if you have, and will put that right.

During the progress of my last story, I have been working so hard that very, very little correspondence — except enforced correspondence on business — has passed this pen. And now that I am free again, I devote a few of my first leisure moments to this note.

29.　From letter to Baron Bernhard Tauchnitz, 15 July 1861, Office of All the Year Round.

The book has been a very great success indeed, here. I hope it will prove to answer your purpose also.

30.　From letter to W.C. Macready, 31 July 1861, Gad's Hill Place.

Though it is always inexpressibly interesting and delightful to me to hear from you, I felt an unwonted kind of reproach in your last, because I had not sent you Great Expectations. But you will not think I forgot it. The book is an immense success; and a compound of bungling on the part of the publisher and of the printer, has caused it to be out of print for a fortnight! Imagine that, with a Second Edition all sold to the trade, a third Edition already being ordered away, and not a copy of either producible until next Saturday! In this disordered state of things every stray copy has been swept into Piccadilly, and I have had not one to bless my self and family with.

So I shall bring your copy to Cheltenham when I come to read there.

31. From letter to Sir Edward Bulwer Lytton, 28 August 1861, Office of All the Year Round.

We are doing extremely well here, as to circulation. We certainly have not in the least lost ground since Great Expectations finished; and to the best of our belief, we have risen a thousand. I use this qualified phrase, simply because it requires some weeks to assure us what the circulation is — to a nicety, I mean. Under any other circumstances, we should unquestionably have dropped. That we most decidedly have not done so, is a fact as solid as the Monument. More, when I know more. In the meanwhile be sure that all is as right as you could possibly desire.

32. From letter to John Forster, [Late August 1861], [?].

The fourth edition of *Great Expectations* is now going to press; the third being nearly out. Bulwer's story keeps us up bravely. As well as we can make out, we have even risen fifteen hundred.

33. From letter to W.H. Wills, 31 August 1861, Gad's Hill Place.

From Frederick Chapman concerning Great Expectations, I have a note this very morning. There are only 90 copies left of the Third Edition, and we are now going to Press with the Fourth.

34. From letter to W.C. Macready, 13 October 1861, Gad's Hill Place.

Fourth Edition of Great Expectations, almost gone!

Appendix B. Contemporary Responses to the Novel

B1. Unsigned [H.F. Chorley] *Athenaeum* (13 July 1861) No. 1759 pp. 43–5.

[Prestigious literary weekly (1828–1921) then edited by W. Hepworth Dixon. *Athenaeum* reviews normally appeared almost immediately on a book's publication.]

Whether the library of English fiction contains a romance comparable with "Great Expectations" is a matter which admits of doubt — because with the breathless interest of a tale of mystery and adventure, with descriptions in which familiar and tame scenery is wrought up so as to exceed in picturesqueness the Apennine landscapes of a Radcliffe, or the deep-sea storms of a Fenimore Cooper, are combined such variety of humour, such deep and tender knowledge of the secrets of a yearning human heart, as belong to a novel of the highest order. Grant the two leading inventions of the tale as romantic, but not impossible; grant a certain exaggeration, so artfully distributed over the whole work as to amount to nothing more than a high tone of colour, and "Great Expectations" can be charged with only one fault; — that of being too short. It stands the test of collection, too, as few tales published in its fragmentary fashion can. Every week almost, as it came out, we were artfully stopped at some juncture which made Suspense count the days till the next number appeared, — again to be baulked, and anew to count. — Yet, on reading through the romance as a whole, there is no feeling of shock or spasm, still less any impression of "dropped stitches," but a sense that we have to do with a work of Art arranged from the first moment of conception with power, progress, and a minuteness consistent with the widest apparent freedom. Trying Mr. Dickens by himself, we find in this his last tale as much force as in the most forcible portions of "Oliver Twist," — as much delicacy as in the most delicate passages of "David Copperfield," — as much quaint humour as in "Pickwick." In short, that this is the creation of a great artist in his prime we have felt from the very first moment of its appearance, and can deliberately sign and seal the conviction, even though the catastrophe is before us, and though we have been just devouring the solution of "Great Expectations."

It is not lost time, neither a case of "painting the lily," to insist on certain details and characteristics of a tale already in thousands of hands. — No scenery could be imagined less romantic than the marshes in which the romance begins and ends; the soaking flat country, with its pollards, — with its "broads," in the furthest of which lie moored the convict-hulks, the old churchyard on the verge of this district, the sluices, and the limekiln. — But out of such common materials a Cuyp, or a Ruysdael, or a Hobbema makes a poetical landscape; and so with his pen does Mr. Dickens. The scene holds the reader from the first; the boy, born to be tormented by his "great expectations," is as much a dreamer, in right of his natural surroundings, as if he had been born at the feet of the Jungfrau, or bred in that Paradise of heaven, earth and sea, "the Golden Shell" of Palermo. — That Nature has influences apart from her sublimities, and that these speak to all who have ears to hear, is told with the decision of a key-note clearly touched, in the very first lines of this strong story. The return to the key, from time to time, is masterly, in the fullest sense of the word, because never monotonous.

The hero of the tale, — a dreaming, ambitious boy, with a grain of genius in him, and flung out by Fate into a narrow and cramping existence, which in no respect contents his yearnings, — may interest few people; and yet he is true to a life with which many have struggled, to dreams which have put right, or put wrong, many a better man than himself. His shrewish guardian sister, with her perpetual apron (a household ephod of self-defence and assertion), and her sycophants, may be, we trust, more shrewish than are the sisters of many child-dreamers; but how admirably is her bitterness and vulgarity (fed by parasites) balanced by the sweet, truthful nature of Joe, with his dull wits and his meandering speech, and his huge hands like two forge hammers, and his tender, loving heart. If we take the following scene of his farewell appearance in the story, it is not because it is the best in which he figures, — but because his discourse on the inexpediency of offering a present of blacksmith work to Miss Havisham — his visit to the thankless boy in London in the hour of his prosperity — above all, the scene of his wife's burial (which is like one of Hogarth's best pictures put into writing), have already been got by heart by thousands on thousands of readers. What is offered will enlighten some by a few days in advance. Pip's "great expectations" have landed him in a violent fever — and the faithful, neglected friend tends him as under: —

[Long quotation from Vol. 3 Ch. 18 pp. 483–486 omitted]

Most admirable is the manner in which the plot of the tale winds round the wretched hunted jail-bird. Those who from the first understand the delusion of the boy's great expectations, — who felt or saw that they had nothing to do with the ghastly recluse in the deserted house, and her brooding revengeful sense of the wicked wrong which had laid her woman's life waste — were, therefore, all the more terribly held in thrall by the knowledge that the convict would return some day, and the air-castle be blown into fragments as by a whirlwind. — It is much to say, that the suspense so strongly excited is followed by a catastrophe as fearfully and forcibly outdoing expectation as if it had not been foreseen. There is nothing in English fiction, not even "the print of the man's foot in the sand" in "Robinson Crusoe," fuller of engrossing and legitimate terror than the night scene of the convict's return, dogged from its first moment by Death. — From this point to its close, the interest of the romance increases with a resistless and steady power never before attained by Mr. Dickens. Nor has he ever used his own language with such poignant muscular force as here. Not an epithet is lost; not a touch is laid on carelessly; not a sentence is mannered. Adventure follows adventure — each one more riveting than the last — each one, too, adding some softening and redeeming light to the character of the poor hunted "warmint," without making the close of his sad story maudlin or sentimental. Everything is as it should be, great and small; — from the tremendous murder-scene in the limekiln down to Wemmick's lamentation over "the portable property."

There are those who will say that Miss Havisham's strange mad life is over-drawn; but such have not been conversant with the freaks and eccentricities which a haughty spirit in agony can assume: nor the manner in which a resolution once taken becomes a law never to be broken. We have no doubt, that, even now, in remote places of England, rich old mansions might be found as strangely peopled as the deserted brewery — with its spectre in white. Satis House, with its dank and weed-grown garden and the moldering bridal feast, is as real, to us, as the lonely church on the marshes — or as the wonderful estate in Walworth, with its works of art and ingenuity — the original of which, by the way, we have heard claimed for half-a-dozen different localities.

One word more. In no late fiction has Mr. Dickens been so happy in his group of what may be called accessory characters. Mr. Jaggers, with his handker-chief; Mr. Wopsle, with his dramatic instincts, — the greedy, sycophantic seedsman, — that wonderful thorn in everyone's side, Trabb's boy — are all capital. We fancy that at the outset he may have meant to make more of Mr. and Mrs. Matthew Pocket, — but they are not missed — Herbert is as fresh and genial an *Horatio* as a hero could desire; and most particularly are we grateful for the uncertainty in which the tale closes, as we interpret it. We do not believe that Pip *did* marry Estella, though there are two opinions on the subject.

We part from this tale with as much reluctance as if we had never before known the dear delight of reading a romance. So strong a sensation of pleasure is too rarely received in this wilderness of dubious literature of ours. "Great Expectations," we are satisfied, will add to Mr. Dickens's reputation, and is the imaginative book of the year.

B2. Unsigned [John Forster] *Examiner* (20 July 1861) pp. 452–3.

[Radical then liberal weekly review of politics and literature (1808–81), edited from 1847 by Dickens's friend and biographer John Forster.]

All who have read this story from week to week, as it appeared in the vigorous and entertaining pages of Mr. Dickens's popular journal, should join those who now read it for the first time as a finished work. It is a finished work in the best sense. There are, we believe, some readers whose taste goes no further than enjoyment of the wit and animal spirits of Pickwick, and who prefer the amply joyous humour of that book to the maturest and best work of the mind that produced it. Such readers may and do cling as they will to their own pleasures of the past. Let it not be forgotten that to the sober middle-aged man who believes only in Pickwick and Nicholas Nickleby, those books were among the choicest delights of twenty years ago, when he read only for enjoyment, delighted openly and heartily in all that he enjoyed, and had a mind that he could deliver alive into the hands of his entertainer. Such power of enjoyment may be blunted, but very sure we are that in the author of Pickwick the power of giving a true and high pleasure has been sharpened and refined. Mr. Dickens is at this day not only a writer of rare and original genius — when at his best, we say it most deliberately, the greatest master of the whimsical and the pathetic yet to be found in any age among the prose writers of Europe — but he has wrought himself into a novelist who is a master in his art. In place of the old sketch books of adventure lengthened at will, and the pathetic or humorous personifications of life that were the spontaneous outpouring of an earnest mind and a swift fancy, we have now the same wit that has so vividly represented detached scenes concentrated with its whole strength upon the construction of a plot that shall knit every fragment of its detail into one round and perfect whole. We dwelt upon the singular success with which this result had been achieved in the *Tale of Two Cities*. In the story of *Great Expectations* the same thing is equally remarkable. And the new story has this advantage over its predecessor, that its scene is in England, and that its contrivance allows scope for a fuller display of the author's comic power. There is not a character that does not fit into the plot as a stone into an arch. Every dialogue is necessary to the outline or the proper colour of the one thing told. The opening pages could not have been written until the contents of the last pages were known. Chance phrases in the very first chapter bear so directly — though at the time imperceptibly — upon events to come, that after they have served their first purpose in giving the sense of a perfect continuity and harmony to the whole work, it is worth any man's while, and the better the man the more it is worth his while, to read the tale twice — for the second time critically, in order to observe the exquisite art of passages that at the first reading influence, at the author's will with unsuspected subtlety, alike the cunning and the simple.

Everything in art, good or bad, should have, and usually has, a central thought to which its parts bear some harmonious relation. In *Great Expectations* the thought is one often enforced by Mr. Dickens: that far greater than great expectations from without is the worth of an honest man's own wholesome labour. Joe Gargery lies at the core of the tale, an illiterate blacksmith living by his own large arm and loving with his own large heart, strong as a man, simple as a child, but like a good woman gentle and true, and unconsciously self-denying. About him revolves Pip, the orphan child he has reared and loved; good fellow enough and bright fellow enough, but not greater than the vanity of youth, he is unwilling to be seen with his simple friend of the forge when a mysterious provision of money as to the source of which he has made a wrong guess, and the assurance of great expecta-tions from the same unknown source, transform him suddenly into a gentleman. His great expectations are the fairy gold that turns to dead leaves in the morning. There is gold enough, but his benefactor is only a convict who has amassed for-tune in Australia, and whose craze it has been to make a gentleman of the boy who fed him upon one occasion of his greatest misery and need. He escapes from Australia to see and rejoice in the gentleman of his own making, and thus be-comes a sort of upside down and altogether human Frankenstein monster to the youth, who is threatened with a life-long companionship, not of the monster that he made, but of the poor monster that made him. The monster, a born "warmint" and jail-bird, is sketched with a generous and wise humour. That he is a humiliat-ing patron from whom great expectations cannot rationally be allowed to flow, Pip sees and feels. But the wealth he would not take from such hands becomes forfeit when the man is condemned as an escaped convict to the gallows; and from the deathbed that only anticipates the sentence of the law, Pip turns to his neglected foster-father, Joe Gargery, the blacksmith; Joe, who had in these late years found the fallen Pip in his distress, tenderly nursed him in sickness, quietly bought out the execution for an extravagant jeweller's bill with the coin earned with his own daily sweat, and vanished when his work of patient love was done. Pip turns to the true-souled labourer at his forge with the old childish love again before he goes abroad to begin life anew dependent on his own day-labour.

One with this story is that of Miss Havisham and *her* foster child, Estella, who becomes the object of Pip's love, and by a network of incidents in no point vio-lating probability is shown to be his convict benefactor's daughter. Wealthy Miss

Havisham, courted in fraud by a villain and by the deceit, made manifest upon her wedding morning, turned so far mad that she shuts out the light of day, stops the clock at the hour fatal to her great expectations, and cherishes the wedding garments yellow with time and the mouldy marriage feast, is only unnatural inasmuch as she is insane. Yet the unwholesome cherishing and the perversion of her passion are so true in art that, as it has usually happened with the most singular creations of the novelist, living types have already been pointed out that claim resemblance to them. Upon Miss Havisham, who is rich, a knot of greedy relatives found their great expectations, while her own expectations now are of the revenge she will take by training up the beautiful Estella to win and wring the hearts of men. She lives to see a piteous end to her sick hopes.

[Series of lengthy extracts with brief commentary omitted.]

The connexion of Pip's great expectations with the great old Bailey lawyer, and the ingenious blending of Newgate associations with Pip's fortunes, before many readers will have discovered any relation between Newgate and the source of his prosperity, we may note as another instance of the skill with which the unity of the story is preserved throughout. We may expect nothing from the fact that there was in the village by the marsh a stage-struck parish clerk with a theatrical delivery; but he comes to London as an actor, Pip looks in upon him once or twice at a minor theatre, and on one occasion his early history applied to the recognition of a second person who is among the audience, is of great value in the conduct of the tale to its catastrophe. When Pip becomes a pupil of Mr. Matthew Pocket, whose wife, with a grandfather who ought to have been in the Peerage, was in her way a woman of great expectations and is not a blessing to her house, there are two fellow pupils, Startop and Bentley Drummle. They are not produced as detached sketches; each of these also becomes in his turn essential to the story. Even the audacious tailor's boy in the village, who mocks Pip in the street when he appears in his best clothes, has his own time and place for an important action necessary to the plot. But Mr. Pumblechook does nothing. It is his part to be nothing while claiming to be everything; a servile flatterer of wealth for its own sake, the pompous and coarse pretender is there to represent the baser chorus of the world that will sing hymns even to a boy whom it has bullied in his poverty when he becomes, by no act of his own merit, a lad of great expectations in the way of cash.

We are tempted to quote largely from the wit and wisdom of this book, but it is in every reader's hand. Rich as it is in scenes vivid with life and truth, and in those phrases and sentences which occur only in what is written for more than one generation of readers, it is better that it should be read, as it is being read, in its entirety. No other writer can construct a story with more skill than is shown in the construction of *Great Expectations*; and most certainly no other writer can unite with a natural presentment of life and character an equal force of original genius.

B3. Unsigned *Saturday Review* (20 July 1861) pp. 69–70.

[Influential review (1855–1938), with a social rather than literary emphasis in its earlier years, when J.F. Stephen (see Appendix C 4) was a frequent contributor.]

Mr. Dickens may be reasonably proud of these volumes. After the long series of his varied works — after passing under the cloud of *Little Dorrit* and *Bleak House* — he has written a story that is new, original, powerful, and very entertaining. It has its weaknesses, as most compositions have, but it is astonishing that a writer who has written so much should still have so much novelty to offer us. He does not serve up the hashes of his old entertainments, and live on repeated resuscitations of his defunct creation. He does not bring in David Copperfield at every stage of his life, and David Copperfield's sons and granddaughters. He thinks of new characters, makes new jokes, contrives new incidents. He ought to have the thanks of the wearied public, and the admiration of those who know how hard it is to observe when the first zest of observation is passed away, and how much courage and resolution it demands to note the comic in life and manners amid the tragedy and farce of declining years. *Great Expectations* restores Mr. Dickens and his readers to the old level. It is in his best vein, and although unfortunately it is too slight, and bears many traces of hasty writing, it is quite worthy to stand beside *Martin Chuzzlewit* and *David Copperfield*. It has characters in it that will become part of common talk, and live even in the mouths of those who do not read novels. Wemmick strikes us as the great creation of the book, and his marriage as the funniest incident. How often will future jokers observe, "Halloa, here's a church; let's have a wedding." It is impossible not to regret that a book so good should not have been better. Probably the form in which it was first published may have had something to do with its faults. The plot ends before it ought to do. The heroine is married, reclaimed from harshness to gentleness, widowed, made love to, and remarried, in a page or two. This is too stiff a pace for the emotions of readers to live up to. We do not like to go beyond a canter through the moral restoration of a young lady. Characters, too, are entirely altered, in order to make the story end rapidly. Herbert, one of the most pleasing characters Mr. Dickens ever drew, starts as an amiable dreamy creature, incapable of business, and living on the vaguest hopes. But at the close of the tale it becomes necessary to provide for the hero. So Herbert comes out all at once as a shrewd, successful Levant merchant, and takes the hero into partnership. Villains, again, are sketched in and then smeared out again. Old Orlick, the gigantic lout of a blacksmith, commits every kind of atrocity, from breaking the skull of his mistress to purposing to burn the hero in a limekiln, and yet all we hear of him at the end is, that he is taken up for a burglary which forms no part of the story. These are little things, but they might have been avoided. There appears to be no reason why *Great Expectations* should fall below any of Mr. Dickens' works, and yet it undoubtedly does. It is rather a story with excellent things in it than an excellent story.

Mr. Dickens has always had one great fault, and it was not to be supposed that he would suddenly shake this fault off. *Great Expectations* is strongly marked with it. This fault is that of exaggerating one particular set of facts, a comic side in a character, or a comic turn of expression, until all reality fades away, and the person who is the centre of the extravagance becomes a mere peg or clothes-horse on which the rags of comedy hang loosely and flutter backwards and forwards. Miss Havisham is one of Mr. Dickens' regular pieces of melodramatic exaggeration. She is represented as having lived for a quarter of a century in a room never dusted or cleaned, and always lighted with candles. During all this time she has worn her bridal dress, and everything on her and in the room has remained exactly the same and exactly in the same position for this enormous length of time. Human life cannot go on in this way. [...]

But if this new tale is marked with the faults of its predecessors, it appears to us to surpass them in one point. There are passages and conceptions in it which indicate a more profound study of the general nature of human character than Mr. Dickens usually betrays. The hero writes an autobiography of his own life, tells the story of his childhood, of his struggles with poverty, and of his gradual rise in the world until he attains what, in Mr. Dickens' novels, is the very vague position of a gentleman. Every one is a gentleman there who is not a comic servant or labourer or tradesman on the one hand; or a bloated aristocrat on the other. The adventures of Pip, therefore, threaten to trespass very closely on the adventures of David Copperfield, and the power of novel creation which Mr. Dickens possesses is shown in nothing more than that he should have succeeded in keeping two stories of a boy's childhood so wholly distinct. The method he has adopted to create the distinction lies not only in the contrivance of an entirely different set of incidents, but also in making Pip a much more thorough study of character than David Copperfield was. [...]

B4. Unsigned [Edwin P. Whipple] *Atlantic Monthly* (September 1861) Vol. VIII No. 47 pp. 380–2.

[Leading American literary and political magazine, founded in Boston, Massachusetts, in 1857; J.R. Lowell was its editor until 1861.]

The very title of this book indicates the confidence of conscious genius. In a new aspirant for public favor, such a title might have been a good device to attract attention; but the most famous novelist of the day, watched by jealous rivals and critics, could hardly have selected it, had he inwardly felt the capacity to meet all the expectations he raised. We have read it, as we have read all Mr. Dickens's previous works, as it appeared in instalments, and can testify to the felicity with which expectation was excited and prolonged, and to the series of surprises which accompanied the unfolding of the plot of the story. In no other of his romances has the author succeeded so perfectly in at once stimulating and baffling the curiosity of his readers. He stirred the dullest minds to guess the secret of his mystery; but, so far as we have learned, the guesses of his most intelligent readers have been almost as wide of the mark as those of the least apprehensive. It has been all the more provoking to the former class, that each surprise was the result of art, and not of trick; for a rapid review of previous chapters has shown that the materials of a strictly logical development of the story were freely given. Even after the first, second, third, and even fourth of these surprises gave their pleasing electric shocks to Intelligent curiosity, the *dénouement* was still hidden, though confidentially foretold. The plot of the romance is therefore universally admitted to be the best that Dickens has ever invented. Its leading events are, as we read the story consecutively, artistically necessary, yet, at the same time, the processes are artistically concealed. We follow the movement of a logic of passion and character, the real premises of which we detect only when we are startled by the conclusions.

The plot of "Great Expectations" is also noticeable as indicating, better than any of his previous stories, the individuality of Dickens's genius. Everybody must have discerned in the action of his mind two diverging tendencies, which, in this novel, are harmonized. He possesses a singularly wide, clear, and minute power of accurate observation, both of things and of persons; but that observation, keen and true to actualities as it independently is, is not a dominant faculty, and is opposed or controlled by the strong tendency of his disposition to pathetic or humorous idealization. Perhaps in "The Old Curiosity Shop" those qualities are best seen in their struggle and divergence, and the result is a magnificent juxtaposition of romantic tenderness, melodramatic improbabilities, and broad farce. The humorous characterization is joyously exaggerated into caricature, — the serious characterization into romantic unreality. Richard Swiveller and Little Nell refuse to combine. There is abundant evidence of genius both in the humorous and the pathetic parts, but the artistic impression is one of anarchy rather than unity.

In "Great Expectations," on the contrary, Dickens seems to have attained the mastery of powers which formerly more or less mastered him. He has fairly discovered that he cannot, like Thackeray, narrate a story as if he were a mere looker-on, a mere "knowing" observer of what he describes and represents; and he has therefore taken observation simply as the basis of his plot and his characterization. As we read "Vanity Fair" and "The Newcomes," we are impressed with the actuality of the persons and incidents. There is an absence both of directing ideas and disturbing idealizations. Everything drifts to its end, as in real life. In "Great Expectations" there is shown a power of external observation finer and deeper even than Thackeray's; and yet, owing to the presence of other qualities, the general impression is not one of objective reality. The author palpably uses his observations as materials for his creative faculties to work upon; he does not record, but invents; and he produces something which is natural only under conditions prescribed by his own mind. He shapes, disposes, penetrates, colors, and contrives everything, and the whole action is a series of events which could have occurred only in his own brain, and which it is difficult to conceive of as actually "happening." And yet in none of his other works does he evince a shrewder insight into real life, and a clearer perception and knowledge of what is called "the world." The book is, indeed, an artistic creation, and not a mere succession of humorous and pathetic scenes, and demonstrates that Dickens is now in the prime, and not in the decline of his great powers.

The characters of the novel also show how deeply it has been meditated; for, though none of them may excite the personal interest which clings to Sam Weller or little Dombey, they are better fitted to each other and to the story in which they appear than is usual with Dickens. They all combine to produce that unity of impression which the work leaves on the mind. Individually they will rank among the most original of the author's creations. Magwitch and Joe Gargery, Jaggers and Wemmick, Pip and Herbert, Wopsle, Pumblechook, and "the Aged," Miss Havisham, Estella, and Biddy, are personages which the most assiduous readers of Dickens must pronounce positive additions to the characters his rich and various genius had already created.

Pip, the hero, from whose mind the whole representation takes its form and color, is admirably delineated throughout. Weak, dreamy, amiable, apprehensive, aspiring, inefficient, the subject and the victim of "Great Expectations," his individuality is, as it were, diffused through the whole narrative. Joe is a noble character, with a heart too great for his powers of expression to utter in words, but whose patience, fortitude, tenderness, and beneficence shine lucidly through his confused and mangled English. Magwitch, the "warmint" who "grew up took up," whose memory extended only to that period of his childhood when he was "a-thieving turnips for his living" down in Essex, but in whom a life of crime had only intensified the feeling of gratitude for the one kind action of which he was the object, is hardly equalled in grotesque grandeur by anything which Dickens has previously done. The character is not only powerful in itself, but it furnishes pregnant and original hints to all philosophical investigators into the phenomena of crime. In this wonderful creation Dickens follows the maxim of the great master of characterization, and seeks "the soul of goodness in things evil."

The style of the romance is rigorously close to things. The author is so engrossed with the objects before his mind, is so thoroughly in earnest, that he has fewer of those humorous caprices of expression in which formerly he was wont to wanton. Some of the old hilarity and play of fancy is gone, but we hardly miss it in our admiration of the effects produced by his almost stern devotion to the main idea of his work. There are passages of description and narrative in which we are hardly conscious of the words, in our clear apprehension of the objects and incidents they convey. The quotable epithets and phrases are less numerous than in "Dombey & Son" and "David Copperfield"; but the scenes and events impressed on the imagination are perhaps greater in number and more vivid in representation. The poetical element of the writer's genius, his modification of the forms, hues, and sounds of Nature by viewing them through the medium of an imagined mind, is especially prominent throughout the descriptions with which the work abounds. Nature is not only described, but individualized and humanized.

Altogether we take great joy in recording our conviction that "Great Expectations" is a masterpiece. We have never sympathized in the mean delight which some critics seem to experience in detecting the signs which subtly indicate the decay of power in creative intellects. We sympathize still less in the stupid and ungenerous judgments of those who find a still meaner delight in wilfully asserting that the last book of a popular writer is unworthy of the genius which produced his first. In our opinion, "Great Expectations" is a work which proves that we may expect from Dickens a series of romances far exceeding in power and artistic skill the productions which have already given him such a preëminence among the novelists of the age.

B5. Unsigned [E.S. Dallas] *The Times* (17 October 1861) p. 6.

[Prestigious daily newspaper linked to establishment views and running continuously from the 1780s. This notice emphasizes the influence of weekly serialization on the novel's form.]

Mr. Dickens has good-naturedly granted to his hosts of readers the desire of their hearts. They have been complaining that in his later works he has adopted a new style, to the neglect of that old manner which first won our admiration. Give us back the old *Pickwick* style, they cried, with its contempt of art, its loose story, its jumbled characters, and all its jesting that made us laugh so lustily; give us back Sam Weller and Mrs. Gamp and Bob Sawyer, and Mrs. Nickleby, Pecksniff, Bumble, and the rest, and we are willing to sacrifice serious purpose, consistent plot, finished writing, and all else. Without calling upon his readers for any alarming sacrifices, Mr. Dickens has in the present work given us more of his earlier fancies than we have had for years. *Great Expectations* is not, indeed, his best work, but it is to be ranked among his happiest. There is that flowing humour in it which disarms criticism, and which is all the more enjoyable because it defies criticism. Faults there are in abundance, but who is going to find fault when the very essence of the fun is to commit faults? Does the reader who, after feasting on the *Pickwick Papers* for the fifth time, begins to get fastidious suppose that Mr. Dickens is not fully alive to all the absurdities which he has committed in that work? In foregoing, to some extent, the correct and highly proper style of his more recent productions, and in falling back upon the jovial extravagances of his younger days, is it to be supposed that so masterly a writer is not quite aware of what he has done, and has not deliberately chosen his path? A wild story, odd characters, absurd situations, whimsical descriptions — it is easy to make a long catalogue of such crimes. To do so, however, were merely to give the body without the soul, — to hang, draw, and quarter the body, and to present its dead fragments as specimens of the living man. Lord Chesterfield advised his son not to laugh, because laughter disfigures the countenance. All comedy is liable to the same objection. If the comical element predominates in a story, it is impossible to avoid some distortion of feature, and for the sake of a good laugh most readers are prepared to tolerate a good many violations of symmetry in plot, passion, and character.

The method of publishing an important work of fiction in monthly instalments was considered a hazardous experiment, which could not fail to set its mark upon the novel as a whole. Mr. Dickens led the way in making the experiment, and his enterprise was crowned with such success that most of the good novels now find their way to the public in the form of a monthly dole. We cannot say that we have ever met with a man who would confess to having read a tale regularly month by month, and who, if asked how he liked Dickens's or Thackeray's last number, did not instantly insist upon the impossibility of his getting through a story piecemeal. Nevertheless, the monthly publication succeeds, and thousands of a novel are sold in minute doses, where only hundreds would have been disposed of in the lump. Charles Lamb somewhere speaks of books which are not books, and there is a reading which men accustomed to study will not permit themselves to regard as reading. There are little half-hours and quarters throughout the day which we sometimes know not how to fill up, and in which our idle humour would not allow of our taking up any important work, unless it came before us in the fragments of a monthly issue. Rolling in the railway train or waiting for dinner at the club we get through a chapter or two. We are amused, but we cannot call it reading, and our chief pleasure in turning over the pages is to ascertain whether the novel will be worthy of perusal when it comes out complete. On the whole, perhaps, the periodical publication of the novel has been of use to it, and has forced English writers to develop a plot and work up the incidents. Lingering over the delineation of character and of manners, our novelists began to lose sight of the story and to avoid action. Periodical publication compelled them to a different course. They could not afford, like Scheherazade, to let the devourers of their tales go to sleep at the end of a chapter. As modern stories are intended not to set people to sleep, but to keep them awake, instead of the narrative breaking down into a soporific dulness, it was necessary that it should rise at the close into startling incident. Hence a disposition to wind up every month with a melodramatic surprise that awakens curiosity in the succeeding number. Even the least melodramatic novelist of the day, Mr. Thackeray, who, so far from feasting us with surprises, goes to the other extreme, and is at particular pains to assure us that the conduct and the character of his personages are not in the least surprising, falls into the way of finishing off his monthly work with a flourish of some sort to sustain the interest.

But what are we to say to the new experiment which is now being tried of publishing good novels week by week? Hitherto the weekly issue of fiction has been connected with publication of the lowest class — small penny and half-penny serials that found in the multitude some compensation for the degradation of their readers. The sale of these journals extended to hundreds of thousands, and so largely did this circulation depend on the weekly tale, that on the conclusion of a good story it has been known to suffer a fall of 40,000 or 50,000. The favourite authors were Mr. J. F. Smith, Mr. Pierce Egan, and Mr. G. W. Reynolds, and the favourite subjects were stories from high life, in which the vices of an aristocracy were portrayed, now with withering sarcasm, and now with fascinating allurements. Lust was the alpha and murder the omega of these tales. When the attempt was made to introduce the readers of the penny journals to better authors and to a more wholesome species of fiction, it was an ignominious failure. And the question was naturally raised — is this failure due to the taste of the readers or to the form of the publication? One of the penny journals reproduced Sir Walter Scott's novels in its columns, and it was found that the fictions of Sir Walter were quite unsuited to the tastes of its weekly readers. Was this, however, entirely the fault of the readers? we ask. Was it not in a great measure due to the form of publication? Not one of Sir Walter's novels was intended to be read in weekly instalments, and it is not wonderful that appearing chapter by chapter in a penny journal they should suffer. Mr. Dickens has tried another experiment. The periodical which he conducts is addressed to a much higher class of readers than any which the penny journals would reach, and he has spread before them novel after novel specially adapted to their tastes. The first of these fictions which achieved a decided success was that of Mr. Wilkie Collins — *The Woman in White*. It was read with avidity by hosts of weekly readers, and the momentum which it acquired when published in fragments carried it through several large editions when published as a whole. The novel was most successful, but if we are from it to form a judgement of the sort of story which succeeds in a weekly issue our estimate will not be very high. Everything is sacrificed to the plot — character, dialogue, passion, description; and the plot, when we come to examine it, is not merely improbable — it is impossible. We are fascinated with a first reading of the tale, but, having once had our curiosity appeased, we never wish to take it up again. After Mr. Wilkie Collins's tale, the next great hit was this story of Mr. Dickens's to which we invite the attention of our readers. It is quite equal to *The Woman in White* in the management of the plot, but, perhaps, this is not saying much when we have to add that the story, though not impossible like Mr. Wilkie Collins's, is very improbable. If Mr. Dickens, however, chose to keep the common herd of readers together by the marvels of an improbable story, he attracted the better class of readers by his fancy, his fun, and his sentiment. Altogether, his success was so great as to warrant the conclusion, which four goodly editions already justify, that the weekly form of publication is not incompatible with a very high order of fiction. And now there is being published, in the same periodical another novel, which promises still more. It is by one who of all our novelists is the greatest master of construction, and who knows how to keep an exciting story within the bounds of probability. The *Strange Story* which Sir Edward Lytton is now relating week by week, is not only interesting as an experiment in hebdomadal publication, it is doubly interesting as a scientific novel. Scientific novels are generally

dull, dead things. Sir Edward Lytton undertakes the most difficult of all tasks —
to write a scientific novel in weekly parts. It appears to be the greatest of all the
successes achieved by *All the Year Round*. Hundreds of thousands of readers rush to
read "the fairy tales of science and the long results of time" as recorded by Sir E.
B. Lytton.

Great Expectations is republished as a three-volume novel. Mr. Dickens, we
believe, only once before published a three-volume tale — *Oliver Twist*. We mention the fact because the resemblance between the two tales is not merely the
superficial one that they are both in the same number of volumes, but is also one
of subject very much and of treatment. The hero of the present tale, Pip, is a sort
of Oliver. He is low-born, fatherless and motherless, and he rises out of the cheerless
degradation of his childhood into quite another sphere. The thieves got a hold of
Oliver, tried to make him a pickpocket, and were succeeded in their friendly intentions by Mr. Brownlow, who thought that he could manage better for the lad.
Pip's life is not less mixed up with the ways of convicts. He befriends a convict in
his need, and henceforth his destiny is involved in that of the prisoner. The convict in the new story takes the place of Mr. Brownlow in the old, and supplies
Master Pip with every luxury. In either tale, through some unaccountable caprice
of fortune, the puny son of poverty suddenly finds himself the child of affluence.
If we are asked which of the tales we like best, the reply must be that the earlier
one is the more fresh in style, and rich in detail, but that the later one is the more
free in handling, and the more powerful in effect. It is so, even though we have to
acknowledge in the work some of Mr. Dickens's worst mannerisms. For example,
it is a mere mannerism that in all his tales there should be introduced some one
— generally a woman — who has been confined indoors for years, and who,
either from compulsion or from settled purpose, should live in dirt and gloom,
never breathing the fresh air and enjoying the sunshine. A lady who has a whim
of this sort is here, as in most of Mr. Dickens's tales, the blind of the story. Making
every allowance, however, for repetitions, the tale is really worthy of its author's
reputation, and is well worth reading.

[...]

B6. Unsigned *British Quarterly Review* (January 1862) Vol. XXXV No. 69 pp. 154–5.

[Nonconformist evangelical quarterly (1845–86), with a wide cov-
erage including theology, literature, politics and science. The issue
contained a lengthy review of *The Collected Works of Charles Dickens*

published in 1861, though only the paragraphs referring to *Great Expectations* are reproduced here.]

The last tale, read by so many thousands during its appearance in *All the Year Round*, and still so eagerly sought for that a fifth edition is even now advertised — *Great Expectations* — may fairly rank among Dickens' most powerful works. We should have been well pleased had the story been less sombre in character, and some of the incidents less unnatural; but to its great merit in delineation of character, and its careful construction, we willingly bear testimony. The hero, to whom we wish a better name than Pip had been given, is most naturally drawn, and the story of his boyhood may well stand beside David Copperfield's. The convict, with whose fortunes he becomes so mysteriously linked, will rank high in Mr. Dickens' gallery of portraits. There is nothing melodramatic about him; he is the fierce, ignorant outcast, accustomed to find every man's hand against him, and for that very reason more likely to remember with gratitude the little boy who came out over the marshes that cold, misty Christmas morning, to bring the food for which he was starving, and the file without which he could not escape. Even the great fortune which he makes, and which he lavishes with such reckless generosity on his young benefactor, is not an unnatural incident, when we remember the well-authenticated tales told of convicts some forty or fifty years ago. And then, when the returned convict makes his startling appearance at Pip's elegant chambers, and slowly finds out that there can be little real sympathy between them, we almost pity the poor lifer who has incurred so terrible a risk, only to find that in making his boy "a gentleman" he has placed an insurmountable bar between them. The progress of the story here is very admirable. Pip, gradually awakening to the sense of what he owes the poor outcast — although until then believing his good fortune to have arisen from a very different source; and then, while determinately refusing to receive his gifts, striving so devotedly to effect his escape; and all the incidents of that escape too — the delays, the obstacles, the unforeseen disappointments, how admirably are they drawn — and the last scenes, where the convict sinks into death, with Pip keeping gentle watch by his side; invest the poor hunted outcast with a lasting interest.

Far less natural is the character of disappointed, half-crazed Miss Havisham. That under the shock of a sudden disappointment, the room where the bridal-feast was laid should have been shut up, is a fact that has really occurred; but a woman never seeing the light of day for twenty years is too extravagant for any one but a complete lunatic; while her constant wearing, through the same long period, the white satin dress, and the bridal veil, is an obvious impossibility; two or three years constant wear would reduce both lace and satin to the veriest rags.

We wish the story could have been managed without the intervention of either Miss Havisham or Estella, or that their characters had been softened. Both are most unpleasing; the latter especially, cold and cruel through mere waywardness. Indeed, the child of convicts, and the adopted daughter of so implacable a woman, we greatly doubt if the mere discipline of a brutal husband for some five or six years could have availed to tame Estella sufficiently to make her a suitable wife for Pip. After his disappointments and strivings, we think he deserves a better fate. But then what an admirable character is Joe Gargery, the blacksmith — one of the finest Dickens has ever drawn, although one of the most amusing — making such extravagant blunders in words, but never in deeds; so simple, truthful, up-right; the very husband for poor Biddy, simple, upright, kind-hearted as he. Jaggers, the Old Bailey lawyer, looks like a portrait, but a very repulsive one. Wemmick, his clerk, is scarcely natural, — ruralising at his "castle" at Walworth, and tending his aged father with such affectionate care, and yet the adviser of thieves and murderers during all his working hours; the contrast is too great. On the whole, *Great Expectations* is a most powerful story; and though we could have wished for a little more sunshine, still the marvellous force with which the darker scenes are painted place it very high among Dickens' works.

B7. Unsigned [J.M. Capes with J.E.E.D. Acton] *Rambler* (January 1862) Vol. VI Pt. 17 pp. 274–6.

[Catholic monthly review founded in 1848 by Capes. The then editor Richard Simpson sent Capes's notice of *Great Expectations* to the historian Lord Acton for his comments, which he then incorporated into the review.]

If we were asked to name the walk in which English literature has in late years most distinguished itself by the side of the literatures of other European countries, we should be disposed to give the palm to our novelists. Not that their works form the most important body of books in positive value; but, in comparison with what is done in other countries, they have carried their peculiar matter to a pitch of excellence unknown elsewhere. In this excellence we must give a very high place to the moral respectability that characterises all our great novelists since Bulwer's reformation, with only so few exceptions — perhaps Currer Bell, and perhaps Kingsley — that they serve rather as a foil to the rest. But this respect-ability was not in fashion when "Boz" began to write; then, the corrupt Bulwer was in the ascendent, and the author of *Pickwick*, to his immense credit, resisted and overcame the evil influence, and won the foremost place in popularity, without pandering for a moment to the prevailing taste for indecency. The thorough youthfulness, fun, and animal spirits of *Pickwick* will always make it the characteristic work of the author; but it is not so decidedly his best book as to deserve to be always referred to as such. Nancy refusing to be delivered from Sikes, when her love for the child had brought her a chance of redemption, and Charley Bates turning against the murderer, are in a higher style than any thing in *Pickwick*.

But both the fun of *Pickwick* and the genuine pathos of *Oliver Twist* soon degenerated into a tedious reiteration of some superficial absurdity that does duty for humour, and into the pathos of a melodrama at a minor theatre. We trace this fall partly to Mr. Dickens's views about religion; he reminds us of certain Germans of the last century, of whom we may take Herder as the type: they saw no divine element in Christianity, but they made humanity their God, and so made their religion simply human, and taught that man was perfectible, but childhood perfect. So they used to die full of benevolence for all men, and of admiration for the sun, the moon, their children, their dog, and their home. They hated intolerance, exclusiveness, and any positive religion. With a comprehensive charity they embraced all mankind, and branded with the same condemnation both the mutual excommunication of different faiths and the distinction of ranks, as treason against the broad human nature that was common to all alike. They professed a kind of natural religion, adorned with poetry and enthusiasm, quite superior to the narrowness and lowness of Christianity.

Mr. Dickens is very like these men. Nothing can be more indefinite or more human than his religion. He loves his neighbour for his neighbour's sake, and knows nothing of sin when it is not crime. Thus one whole lobe of the human soul is dark to him; he cannot see a whole character, or perhaps has disabled himself from seeing it by his persevering purpose to write up his own particular views. This partly explains his defects of humour — his giving us so few characters and so many caricatures. And these caricatures have been the winding-sheet and the leaden coffin of his humour. For what fun can any one person find in describing a man by an ever-recurring absurdity, by his ever sucking his thumb, by his having a mouth like a letter-box, or by his firing a gun at sundown? It is the mere poverty of an imagination self-restrained to one narrow field of human nature, that makes him search curiously for such follies, and ransack newspapers for incidents to put into his books. A novelist of a more creative genius describes not a particular individual, but a general character, summed up in one, but fitting many, like Major Pendennis.

It is the determination to make every thing subservient to this fetishism of sentimental civilisation that spoils not only the humour of Mr. Dickens, but the temper of his intelligent readers. They do not choose to be insulted with the negative sermons of those pathetic death-beds which are made so much happier by the want of all spiritual assistance, and where the "babbling of green fields" is the all-sufficient substitute for the sterner truths of which dying Christians naturally think.

Yet, with all his faults, we should be puzzled to name Mr. Dickens's equal in the perception of the purely farcical, ludicrous, and preposterously funny, though not so much now, perhaps, as in the days when he had not adopted the stage-trick of putting some queer saying into his characters' mouths, and making them utter it on every possible occasion. It is by a partial flickering up of this bright gift that *Great Expectations* has proved an agreeable surprise to so many of his readers. The story is as exaggerated and impossible as any he ever perpetrated; it is uncomfortable, too, and abounds with those tedious repetitions to which he has become so grievously addicted. Mr. Jaggers is always biting his forefinger; Provis begins his speeches with a stereotyped phrase. But there is some very good fun in the story, nevertheless; not jovial, not hearty, not Pickwickian indeed, but really comic, and sufficient to excite a pleasant quiet laugh on a dull winter-day. Wemmick, the lawyer's clerk, who lives in a cockney castle at Walworth, and fires off his gun at sundown every night, is a conception, barring the last characteristic, worthy of Dickens's happiest days. The walk to the wedding is delicious. And, on the whole, then, we may rejoice that even in Mr. Dickens's ashes still live his wonted fires. Perhaps, if he would but lie fallow for a year or two, and let his thoughts range at will, and eschew every thing that is tragic, sentimental, or improving, especially in his particular line of improvement, we need not despair of seeing a still more lively reproduction of the delightful absurdities with which he charmed his readers a quarter of a century ago.

B8. Unsigned [Margaret Oliphant] "Sensation Novels" *Blackwood's Magazine* (May 1862) No. 91 pp. 574–80.

[Scottish conservative monthly miscellany (1817–1980). "Sensation Novels" is a lengthy essay by novelist and journalist Margaret Oliphant, a regular reviewer for *Blackwood's* with little sympathy for Dickens's genius. Here, Oliphant contrasts Dickens's novel unfavourably with Wilkie Collins's *The Woman in White*, which finished its run in *All the Year Round* in August 1860. Only the comments on *Great Expectations* are reproduced.]

There can scarcely be a greater contrast between two works which aim in their different individualities at something of a similar effect, than there exists between Mr Wilkie Collins's powerful story and the last work of his Master in Art. Mr Dickens's successes in sensation are great. Even in "Great Expectations," which is far from being one of his best works, he manages to impress distinct images of horror, surprise, and pain upon the mind of his reader with vivid power and distinctness; but his performances go on an entirely different principle, and use other agencies than those which, in the hands of his disciple, heighten the effect by the evident simplicity of the means. Mr Dickens was one of the first popular writers who brought pictures of what is called common life into fashion. It is he who has been mainly instrumental in leading the present generation of authors to disregard to a great extent the pictorial advantages of life on the upper levels of society, and to find a counter-picturesqueness in the experiences of the poor. But while this is the case, it is equally certain that Mr Dickens, for his own part, has never ventured to depend for his special effects upon the common incidents of life. He has shifted the fashionable ground, and sought his heroes among penniless clerks and adventurers, as little beholden to their ancestors as to fortune. He has made washerwomen as interesting as duchesses, and found domestic angels among the vagabonds of a circus, on the very edge between lawlessness and crime; but whenever he has aimed at a scene, he has hurried aside to regions of exaggeration, and shown distrust of the common and usual by fantastic eccentricities, and accumulations of every description of high-strained oddity. The characters upon which he depends are not individual only, with a due recognisable difference to distinguish them from their fellows, but always peculiar, and set forth with a quaintly exaggerated distortion, by which we identify in a moment, not the character described, but the author who has made it, and of whom these oddities are characteristic. If it were possible to quicken these curious originals into life, what an odd crowd of ragamuffins and monsters would that be which should pursue this Frankenstein through the world! In the flush of fresh life and invention, when Sam Wellers and Mark Tapleys led the throng, we all awaited with impatience and received with delight the new oddities with which the great novelist filled his pages; but it is impossible to deny that nowadays that fertile fulness has failed, and that the persistent devotion to the eccentric which has distinguished Mr Dickens through all his literary life, does now no longer produce fruits such as earn him our forgiveness for all the daring steps he takes beyond the modesty of nature. In his last work, symptoms of a dangerous adherence to, and departure from, his old habitudes, will strike most of his faithful readers. The oddity remains, but much of the character has evaporated. The personages in "Great Expectations" are less out of the way, and the circumstances more so. Strange situations and fantastic predicaments have very much taken the place of those quaint and overstrained but still lifelike phases of humanity in which the author used to delight. He now carves his furniture grotesquely, and makes quaint masks upon his friezes; but he has no longer patience to keep up the strain so long as is necessary for the perfection of a character. After an indication of what he means this and that figure to be, he goes on with his story, too indifferent about it, one could suppose, to enter into the old elaboration. The book reminds us of a painter's rapid memoranda of some picture, in which he uses his pencil to help his memory. After he has dashed in the outline and composition, he scribbles a hasty "carmine" or "ultramarine" where those colours come. So the reds and blues of Mr Dickens's picture are only written in. He means us to fill in the glow of the natural hue from the feeble symbol of the word which represents it, or perhaps to go back in our own memory to those forcible and abundant days when he wrought out his own odd conceptions minutely as if he loved them. Perhaps it was not at any time the wholesomest kind of art, but it was certainly much more satisfactory and piquant than now.

So far as "Great Expectations" is a sensation novel, it occupies itself with incidents all but impossible, and in themselves strange, dangerous, and exciting; but so far as it is one of the series of Mr Dickens's works, it is feeble, fatigued, and colourless. One feels that he must have got tired of it as the work went on, and that the creatures he had called into being, but who are no longer the lively men and women they used to be, must have bored him unspeakably before it was time to cut short their career, and throw a hasty and impatient hint of their future to stop the tiresome public appetite. Joe Gargery the blacksmith alone represents the ancient mood of the author. He is as good, as true, patient, and affectionate, as ungrammatical and confused in his faculty of speech, as could be desired; and shields the poor little Pip when he is a child on his hands, and forgives him when he is a man too grand for the blacksmith, with all that affecting tenderness and refinement of affection with which Mr Dickens has the faculty of making his poor blacksmiths and fishermen much more interesting than anything he has ever produced in the condition of gentlemen. Near Joe's abode, however, dwells a lady who is intended to have much more influence upon the fortunes of the hero than his humble protector. Here is the first sight of Miss Havisham and her surroundings, as they are disclosed to little Pip and to the reader: —

[Long extracts from Vol. I Ch. 8 pp. 92–94 omitted]

This is fancy run mad. As the story progresses, we learn that this poor lady, who is perfectly sane, much as appearances are against her, has lived in this miraculous condition for five-and-twenty years. Not very long ago we heard an eminent Scotch divine pause in the middle of his exposition to assure his hearers that it was not necessary to believe that the garments of the children of Israel were literally preserved from the wear and tear of the forty years in the wilderness, but simply that God provided them with clothing as well as food. We should like to know what the reverend gentleman would say to that wedding-dress of Miss Havisham's, which, in five-and-twenty years, had only grown yellow and faded, but was still, it appears, extant in all its integrity, no tatters being so much as inferred, except on the shoeless foot, the silk stocking on which "had been trodden ragged." In this ghastly company lived a pretty young girl called Estella, whom Miss Havisham had reared with the avowed intention of avenging her own wrongs against men in general by breaking as many hearts as possible. The unlucky little Pip is the first victim selected. He is brought there to be operated upon in the special hope he may learn to love Estella, and by her means have his heart broken — though the unfortunate little individual in question has no connection whatever with the breaking of Miss Havisham's heart, nor any other title to be considered as a representative of male humanity. If startling effects were to be produced by any combination of circumstances or arrangement of still life, here, surely, was the very scene for a sensation. But somehow the sensation does not come. The wretched old heroine of this masquerade is, after all, notwithstanding her dire intentions of revenge upon the world, a very harmless and rather amiable old woman, totally incapable of any such determined folly. Estella grows up everything she ought not to grow up, but breaks nobody's heart but his, so far as there is any evidence, and instead of carrying out the benevolent intentions of her benefactress, only fulfils a vulgar fate by marrying a man without any heart to be broken, and being miserable herself instead. Here there is the most perfect contrast to the subtle successes of the "Woman in White." Mr Dickens's indifference or languor has left the field open to his disciple. With the most fantastic exaggeration of means, here is no result at all achieved, and no sensation produced upon the composed intelligence of the reader. The shut-up house does not deceive that wary and experienced observer: he waits to see what comes of the bridal dress of twenty-five years' standing, and its poor old occupant; and as nothing in the least startling comes of either the one or the other, declines to be excited on the subject. The whole of this scene, and of the other scenes which follow in this house, and the entire connection between Miss Havisham, Pip, and Estella, is a failure. It is a mere piece of masquerading which deceives nobody, and carries to the utmost bounds of uninteresting extravagance that love of the odd and eccentric which has already brought Mr Dickens to occasional misfortune in his long and well-deserved round of success.

Very different, however, is the darker side of the story. The appearance of the escaped convict in the squalid and dismal solitude of the marsh — the melancholy landscape with that one wretched figure embodying the forlorn and desolate sentiment of the scene — is perhaps as vivid and effective a sketch as Mr Dickens ever drew. It is made in fewer words than usual, done at a breath, as if the author felt what he was saying this time, and saw the scene too vividly himself to think a full development of every detail necessary to enable his reader to see it also. Here is the apparition and the scene: —

[Long extracts from Vol. I Ch. 1 pp. 40–43 omitted]

After another very vivid picture of the same marshes under the wild torch-light of a convict-hunt, this horrible figure disappears out of the book, and only comes to life again at the end of the second volume, when, as Pip's unknown benefactor, the mysterious secret friend who has made the young blacksmith a gentleman, he re-emerges, humanised and horribly affectionate, out of the darkness. The young fellow's utter despair when he finds himself held fast in the clutches of this man's gratitude and bounty — compelled to be grateful in his turn while loathing the very thought of the obligation which he has been unwittingly incurring — is very powerfully drawn, and the predicament perhaps as strange and frightful as could be conceived. The terrible benefactor appears without the slightest warning in the young man's chambers, startling his harmless youthful life into the rudest, yet most intense tragedy; for his convict patron is a "Lifer," and the penalty of his return, if found out, is death. The sudden change which thus clouds over a hitherto harmless and aimless existence; the precautions necessary to keep the stranger safe; the gradual concentration of all interests into this one; the way in which, when hunted and in danger, the unfortunate young hero grows first tolerant, then anxious, and at last affectionate, to his strange and uncongenial friend — is carefully done, and contains all that there is of interest and excitement in the book. It is a struggle against an unseen enemy — always an exciting spectacle; and the fact that it is not the imperilled criminal himself for whom we are principally concerned, but the generous young men who have devoted themselves to save him, refines the contest, and gives it an interest less coarsely tragical. Through the whole, he, the man specially in danger, is acquiescent, passive; while the unlucky object of his bounty contrives and plots for him, accepting the bond between them with hearty youthful generosity as soon as his dreadful patron is in trouble. The narrative is close and rapid, and told without much unnecessary detail; but notwithstanding its undeniable effectiveness as a whole, it must be admitted that neither its successive incidents nor even its crisis strikes sharp upon the course of the story, or stands out with any distinctness from its general level. We watch the second boat stealing out upon the river without any sudden thrill of interest. We see the two convicts go down together into the water churned by the agitating passage of the great steamer which lowers over them like a castle in the water, but we draw our breath as calm as before. The means, in short, are superabundant, and full of all the natural elements of wonder, pity, and terror, but the effect is *not* produced. Perhaps most readers will make sure of what is going to happen to Abel Magwitch before they retire to their peaceful pillows, but once there, the returned convict will not haunt them. He will neither interfere with their sleep, nor startle their leisure with any uncomfortable consciousness of his own lurking, clandestine figure. At first, when he was out on the marsh, there seemed some likelihood that he might — but he has died, so far as his faculty of exciting a sensation goes, for long before he dies in prison. By means almost as exciting as those which, in the case of Bill Sykes, made the reading world hold its breath, and invested with all the dark grandeur of tragedy the vulgar fate of a brutal wretch, too debased for sympathy, Mr Dickens has this time made nothing but a narrative, powerful, indeed, but not pictorial, and from which we cannot quote any one incident sufficiently vivid and distinct to concentrate the attention of the reader. The following deathbed sketch, however, is full of a subdued pathos and tenderness, without exaggeration or overdoing, dismissing in pity and charity, but without any attempt to make him a wonder either of remorse or reforma- tion, the lawless soul who has been the overshadowing terror of the book: —

[Long extracts from Vol. III Ch. 17 pp. 476–480 omitted]

This picture is affecting in its simplicity and composure. The man has been a criminal, but he is not remorseful, or even affected by the solemn agitation and thrill of expectancy which we naturally associate with the approach of death. He is only weary and worn out, as most people are when they come to that inevita- ble hour, unsusceptible of impression. A wonderful mystery among all the mys- teries of this life is the quietness with which most people die. Guilty as they may happen to be, going to sleep like innocent creatures, with subdued demonstra- tions of childlike simple emotion, tearful pleasure, grateful affection — a wonder as great as anything in life, and only coming to be acknowledged as experience of what *is*, takes the place, in all true representations of our various and strange ex- istence, of theories and imaginations of what ought to be. The convict dies with a certain subdued halo of patience and gentleness about him; yet he has been a troublesome ruffian enough as long as he had any opportunities that way, and very shortly before the end of his life has exhibited towards his persecutor senti- ments which were anything but Christian. But notwithstanding these drawbacks, Abel Magwitch makes, on the whole, an edifying end; and Mr Dickens senses the opportunity to note with delicate skill that pathetic gratification in the affection shown them, which is common to the old and weak of all classes. The tender pride with which the dying man dwells on the fact that his "dear boy" always waits at the gate for the hour of entrance is a touch as true to nature as it is affecting in itself.

The secondary persons of this book, however — almost entirely separated as they are from the main action, which is connected only in the very slightest way with the rest of the story — are, so far as they possess any individual character at all, specimens of oddity run mad. The incredible ghost, in the wedding-dress which has lasted for five-and-twenty years, is scarcely more *outré* than the ridiculous Mrs Pocket, whom the hero finds seated in her garden, oblivious of everything that is going on around her, absorbed in a book which it is natural to suppose must be a novel — for popular superstition still believes in the existence of individuals capable of abandoning all the duties of life for the superior charms of fiction. But it is not a novel, but a Red book, which wraps the lady in an ideal world. Of the same description is the ingenious Mr Wemmick, the lawyer's clerk, who lives in a little castle at Walworth, and calls his old father the Aged, and exclaims, "Hulloa! here's a church — let's go in!" when he is going to be married. Is this fun? Mr Dickens ought to be an authority in that respect, seeing he has made more honest laughter in his day than any man living, and called forth as many honest tears; but we confess it looks exceedingly dull pleasantry to us, and that we are slow to accept Mr Wemmick's carpentry as a substitute for all the homely wit and wisdom in which Mr Dickens's privileged humorists used to abound. Besides all this heavy sport, there is a sensation episode of a still heavier description, for the introduction of which we are totally unable to discover any motive, except that of filling a few additional pages — unless, perhaps, it might be a desperate expedient on the part of the author to rouse his own languid interest in the conduct of the piece. Otherwise, why Pip should be seduced into the clutches of the senseless brute Orlick, and made to endure all the agonies of death for nothing, is a mystery quite beyond our powers of guessing. And again Mr Dickens misses fire — he rouses himself up, indeed, and bethinks himself of his old arts of word and composition, and does his best to galvanise his figures into momentary life. But it is plain to see all along that he means nothing by it; we are as sure that help will come at the right moment, as if we saw it approaching all the time; and the whole affair is the most arbitrary and causeless stoppage in the story — perhaps acceptable to weekly readers, as a prick of meretricious excitement on the languid road, perhaps a little stimulant to the mind of the writer, who was bored with his own production — but as a part of a narrative totally uncalled for, an interruption and encumbrance, interfering with the legitimate interest of the story, which is never so strong as to bear much trifling with. In every way, Mr Dickens's performance must yield precedence to the companion work of his disciple and assistant. The elder writer, rich in genius and natural power, has, from indolence or caprice, or the confidence of established popularity, produced, with all his unquestionable advantages, and with a subject admirably qualified to afford the most striking and picturesque effects, a very ineffective and colourless work; the younger, with no such gifts, has employed the common action of life so as to call forth the most original and startling impressions upon the mind of the reader. The lesson to be read therefrom is one so profoundly improving that it might form the moral of any Good-child story. Mr Dickens is the careless, clever boy who could do it twice as well, but won't take pains. Mr Wilkie Collins is the steady fellow, who pegs at his lesson like a hero, and wins the rise over the other's head. Let the big children and the little prepend and profit by the lesson. The most popular of writers would do well to pause before he yawns and flings his careless essay at the public, and to consider that the reputation which makes everything he produces externally successful is itself mortal, and requires a substance more substantial than a languid owner can be expected to give.

B9. Unsigned "My Convict Experiences" *Temple Bar* (September 1861) Vol. III pp. 193–4.

[This is not a review of *Great Expectations*, but an essay on penal reform which invokes the humanitarian spirit of the recently-published novel. Appearing in one of the new metropolitan literary monthlies, operated by Richard Bentley, it is a spirited reply to an accusation that the coercive penal system in force in Ireland was more effective than the liberal regime replacing mass transportation in England. Here, "license-holders" refers to those remitted for good behaviour, under the system instituted by the Penal Servitude Act of 1853, on an "order of licence," know colloquially as a "ticket-of-leave." "Sir Joshua" is Sir Joshua Jebb, Surveyor-General of Convict Prisons and designer of those at Pentonville and Portland.]

[...]

It is within the memory of the oldest inhabitants that only last April the whole land was thrown into a panic by the announcement, on undoubted authority, that 90 per cent of the released convicts were returned into prison after committing the most frightful ravages on society, and that the remaining 10 per cent were no better than they should be. This was "too bad" for even Sir Joshua; and we had an indignant denial of the fact and protest against the systematic manner in which attempts to disparage the convict system in this country had for years been carried on. In regard to the 90 per cent, it was all found to be a mistake, and that from 20 to 25 per cent was about the mark. It appears that out of 9180 license-holders discharged between 1853 and March 1861, only 30 forfeited their licenses in the year 1860, and only 54 were again sentenced to penal servitude. In the seven years and six months between October 1853 and December 1860, 9 per cent only of the whole number have forfeited their licenses, and 11.3 per cent have been again sentenced to penal servitude; of these, two-thirds of the number have been convicted of the lighter crimes. It also appears that of 764 females licensed during the same period, only 4 had their licenses revoked in 1860, and 8 were subjected to fresh convictions, — the percentage during the whole period of seven and a half years being only 8½ in each case.

Another remarkable feature is, that whereas a few years ago we annually got rid of some 3000 to 4000 of our worst criminals by deportation to a distant colony, yet now that we release the great majority at home, and have to submit to the relapse into crime of say 25 per cent of them, the number sentenced to penal servitude and transportation has been reduced from an average of 3698 males, in the five years from 1840 to 1844, to an average of about 2300 in the years from 1856 to 1860; and this when crime all over the country has diminished, and the population has increased.

To any one who recollects the fearful anticipations which prevailed when the abolition of transportation, as the highest of our secondary punishments, was first talked of, these results will appear almost fabulous; indeed, it would be difficult to assign causes for so favourable a result under the great difficulties which have been experienced.

Giving due weight to the great difference in the conditions, and the far greater difficulties which have been encountered in working the system in England, we may confidently affirm that the results have been fully equal to any that have been secured in Ireland.

This is the system of discipline which has replaced the hulks, of which it is stated, in a report for 1852, that, "speaking humanly, the demoralisation of every individual sentenced to transportation was certain. No matter what might have been his previous character, what the amount of his contrition, or what the sincerity of his efforts and resolutions to retrace his steps, he was placed within the influence of a moral pestilence, from which, like death itself, there was no escape." This is the state of moral and mental training which has replaced the crime-breeding and soul-staining contamination so feelingly described by the convict Magwitch in Mr. Dickens's latest and most perfect work, *Great Expectations*. Looking at our English system and its results, I think we have reason to be proud of it, and that we may fairly say, "They do *not* manage these things better in — Ireland!"

Appendix C. On Class and Language

C1. Charles Dickens "Hard Experiences in Boyhood" Autobiographical Fragment recorded in John Forster *The Life of Charles Dickens* (1872–4) Bk. I Ch. 2.

[The following passages, extracted from Forster's biography, record Dickens's intense feelings of shame and abandonment as a boy during and immediately following the period of his father's imprisonment for debt in 1824, when Dickens was sent to work in a blacking-warehouse owned by a family relative. The three extracts belong to three distinct periods: first, when Dickens was living with his mother and the other children; second, when the rest of the family went to stay with the father at the Marshalsea Prison and Dickens was put in lodgings alone; and finally, after his father's discharge, when he was united with his family but remained in employment at the warehouse.]

This speculation was a rivalry of "Warren's Blacking, 30, Strand," — at that time very famous. One Jonathan Warren (the famous one was Robert), living at 30, Hungerford Stairs, or Market, Strand (for I forget which it was called then), claimed to have been the original inventor or proprietor of the blacking recipe, and to have been deposed and ill-used by his renowned relation. At last he put himself in the way of selling his recipe, and his name, and his 30, Hungerford Stairs, Strand (30, Strand, very large, and the intermediate direction very small), for an annuity; and he set forth by his agents that a little capital would make a great business of it. The man of some property was found in George Lamert, the cousin and brother-in-law of James. He bought this right and title, and went into the blacking business and the blacking premises.

    — In an evil hour for me, as I often bitterly thought. Its chief manager, James Lamert, the relative who had lived with us in Bayham Street, seeing how I was employed from day to day, and knowing what our domestic circumstances then were, proposed that I should go into the blacking warehouse, to be as useful as I could at a salary, I think, of six shillings a week. I am not clear whether it was six or seven. I am inclined to believe, from my uncertainty on this head, that it was six at first, and seven afterwards. At any rate, the offer was accepted very willingly by my father and mother, and on a Monday morning I went down to the blacking warehouse to begin my business life.

It is wonderful to me how I could have been so easily cast away at such an age. It is wonderful to me that, even after my descent into the poor little drudge I had been since we came to London, no one had compassion enough on me — a child of singular abilities: quick, eager, delicate, and soon hurt, bodily or mentally — to suggest that something might have been spared, as certainly it might have been, to place me at any common school. Our friends, I take it, were tired out. No one made any sign. My father and mother were quite satisfied. They could hardly have been more so, if I had been twenty years of age, distinguished at a grammar-school, and going to Cambridge.

The blacking warehouse was the last house on the left-hand side of the way, at old Hungerford Stairs. It was a crazy, tumble-down old house, abutting of course on the river, and literally overrun with rats. Its wainscoted rooms and its rotten floors and staircase, and the old grey rats swarming down in the cellars, and the sound of their squeaking and scuffling coming up the stairs at all times, and the dirt and decay of the place, rise up visibly before me, as if I were there again. The counting-house was on the first floor, looking over the coal-barges and the river. There was a recess in it, in which I was to sit and work. My work was to cover the pots of paste-blacking: first with a piece of oil-paper, and then with a piece of blue paper; to tie them round with a string; and then to clip the paper close and neat all round, until it looked as smart as a pot of ointment from an apothecary's shop. When a certain number of grosses of pots had attained this pitch of perfection, I was to paste on each a printed label; and then go on again with more pots. Two or three other boys were kept at similar duty downstairs on similar wages. One of them came up, in a ragged apron and a paper cap, on the first Monday morning, to show me the trick of using the string and tying the knot. His name was Bob Fagin; and I took the liberty of using his name, long afterwards, in *Oliver Twist*.

Our relative had kindly arranged to teach me something in the dinner-hour; from twelve to one, I think it was; every day. But an arrangement so incompatible with counting-house business soon died away, from no fault of his or mine; and for the same reason, my small work-table, and my grosses of pots, my papers, string, scissors, paste-pot and labels, by little and little, vanished out of the recess in the counting-house, and kept company with the other small work-tables, grosses of pots, papers, string, scissors and paste-pots downstairs. It was not long before Bob Fagin and I, and another boy whose name was Paul Green, but who was currently believed to have been christened Poll (a belief which I transferred, long afterwards, again, to Mr. Sweedlepipe, in *Martin Chuzzlewit*), worked generally, side by side. Bob Fagin was an orphan, and lived with his brother-in-law, a waterman. Poll Green's father had the additional distinction of being a fireman, and was employed at Drury Lane theatre; where another relation of Poll's, I think his little sister, did imps in the pantomimes.

No words can express the secret agony of my soul as I sunk into this companionship; compared these everyday associates with those of my happier childhood; and felt my early hopes of growing up to be a learned and distinguished man crushed in my breast. The deep remembrance of the sense I had of being utterly neglected and hopeless; of the shame I felt in my position; of the misery it was to my young heart to believe that, day by day, what I had learned, and thought, and delighted in, and raised my fancy and my emulation up by, was passing away from me, never to be brought back any more; cannot be written. My whole nature was so penetrated with the grief and humiliation of such considerations, that even now, famous and caressed and happy, I often forget in my dreams that I have a dear wife and children; even that I am a man; and wander desolately back to that time of my life.

[...]

The key of the house was sent back to the landlord, who was very glad to get it; and I (small Cain that I was, except that I had never done harm to anyone) was handed over as a lodger to a reduced old lady, long known to our family, in Little College Street, Camden Town, who took children in to board, and had once done so at Brighton; and who, with a few alterations and embellishments, unconsciously began to sit for Mrs. Pipchin in *Dombey*, when she took in me.

She had a little brother and sister under her care then; somebody's natural children, who were very irregularly paid for; and a widow's little son. The two boys and I slept in the same room. My own exclusive breakfast, of a penny cottage loaf and a pennyworth of milk, I provided for myself. I kept another small loaf, and a quarter of a pound of cheese, on a particular shelf of a particular cupboard: to make my supper on when I came back at night. They made a hole in the six or seven shillings, I know well; and I was out at the blacking warehouse all day, and had to support myself upon that money all the week. I suppose my lodging was paid for, by my father. I certainly did not pay it myself; and I certainly had no other assistance whatever (the making of my clothes, I think, excepted), from Monday morning until Saturday night. No advice, no counsel, no encouragement, no consolation, no support, from anyone that I can call to mind, so help me God....

I was so young and childish, and so little qualified — how could I be otherwise? — to undertake the whole charge of my own existence that, in going to Hungerford Stairs of a morning, I could not resist the stale pastry put out at half-price on trays at the confectioners' doors in Tottenham Court Road; and I often spent in that the money I should have kept for my dinner. Then I went without my dinner, or bought a roll, or a slice of pudding. There were two pudding shops between which I was divided, according to my finances. One was in a court close to St. Martin's Church (at the back of the church), which is now removed altogether. The pudding at that shop was made with currants, and was rather a special pudding, but was dear: two penn'orth not being larger than a penn'orth of more ordinary pudding. A good shop for the latter was in the Strand, somewhere near where the Lowther Arcade is now. It was a stout, hale pudding, heavy and flabby; with great raisins in it, stuck in whole, at great distances apart. It came up hot, at about noon every day: and many and many a day did I dine off it.

We had half an hour, I think, for tea. When I had money enough, I used to go to a coffee-shop, and have half a pint of coffee, and a slice of bread and butter. When I had no money, I took a turn in Covent Garden Market, and stared at the pineapples. The coffee-shops to which I most resorted were, one in Maiden Lane; one in a court (non-existent now) close to Hungerford Market; and one in St. Martin's Lane, of which I only recollect that it stood near the church, and that in the door there was an oval glass plate, with COFFEE-ROOM painted on it, addressed towards the street. If I ever find myself in a very different kind of coffee-room now, but where there is such an inscription on glass, and read it backward on the wrong side MOOR-EEFFOC (as I often used to do then, in a dismal reverie) a shock goes through my blood.

I know I do not exaggerate, unconsciously and unintentionally, the scantiness of my resources and the difficulties of my life. I know that if a shilling or so were given me by anyone, I spent it in a dinner or a tea. I know that I worked, from morning to night, with common men and boys, a shabby child. I know that I tried, but ineffectually, not to anticipate my money, and to make it last the week through by putting it away in a drawer I had in the counting-house, wrapped into six little parcels, each parcel containing the same amount, and labelled with a different day. I know that I have lounged about the streets, insufficiently and unsatisfactorily fed. I know that, but for the mercy of God, I might easily have been, for any care that was taken of me, a little robber or a little vagabond.

But I held some station at the blacking warehouse too. Besides that my relative at the counting-house did what a man so occupied, and dealing with a thing so anomalous, could, to treat me as one upon a different footing from the rest, I never said, to man or boy, how it was that I came to be there, or gave the least indication of being sorry that I was there. That I suffered in secret, and that I suffered exquisitely, no one ever knew but I. How much I suffered, it is, as I have said already, utterly beyond my power to tell. No man's imagination can overstep the reality. But I kept my own counsel, and I did my work. I knew from the first that, if I could not do my work as well as any of the rest, I could not hold myself above a slight and contempt. I soon became at least as expeditious and as skilful with my hands as either of the other boys. Though perfectly familiar with them, my conduct and manners were different enough from theirs to place a space between us. They, and the men, always spoke of me as "the young gentleman." A certain man (a soldier once) named Thomas, who was the foreman, and another named Harry, who was the carman and wore a red jacket, used to call me "Charles" sometimes, in speaking to me; but I think it was mostly when we were very confidential, and when I had made some efforts to entertain them over our work with the results of some of the old readings, which were fast perishing out of my mind. Poll Green uprose once, and rebelled against the "young-gentleman" usage; but Bob Fagin settled him speedily.

[...]

I am not sure that it was before this time, or after it, that the blacking warehouse was removed to Chandos Street, Covent Garden. It is no matter. Next to the shop at the corner of Bedford Street, in Chandos Street, are two rather old-fashioned houses and shops adjoining one another. They were one then, or thrown into one, for the blacking business; and had been a butter shop. Opposite to them was, and is, a public-house, where I got my ale, under these new circumstances. The stones in the street may be smoothed by my small feet going across to it at dinner-time, and back again. The establishment was larger now, and we had one or two new boys. Bob Fagin and I had attained to great dexterity in tying up the pots. I forget how many we could do in five minutes. We worked, for the light's sake, near the second window as you come from Bedford Street and we were so brisk at it, that the people used to stop and look in. Sometimes there would be quite a little crowd there. I saw my father coming in at the door one day when we were very busy, and I wondered how he could bear it.

Now, I generally had my dinner in the warehouse. Sometimes I brought it from home, so I was better off. I see myself coming across Russell Square from Somers Town, one morning, with some cold hotch-potch in a small basin tied up in a handkerchief. I had the same wanderings about the streets as I used to have, and was just as solitary and self-dependent as before; but I had not the same difficulty in merely living. I never, however, heard a word of being taken away, or of being otherwise than quite provided for.

At last, one day, my father and the relative so often mentioned quarrelled; quarrelled by letter, for I took the letter from my father to him which caused the explosion, but quarrelled very fiercely. It was about me. It may have had some backward reference, in part, for anything I know, to my employment at the window. All I am certain of is that, soon after I had given him the letter, my cousin (he was a sort of cousin, by marriage) told me he was very much insulted about me; and that it was impossible to keep me, after that. I cried very much partly because it was so sudden, and partly because in his anger he was violent about my father, though gentle to me. Thomas, the old soldier, comforted me, and said he was sure it was for the best. With a relief so strange that it was like oppression, I went home.

My mother set herself to accommodate the quarrel, and did so next day. She brought home a request for me to return next morning, and a high character of me, which I am very sure I deserved. My father said I should go back no more, and should go to school. I do not write resentfully or angrily: for I know how all these things have worked together to make me what I am: but I never afterwards forgot, I never shall forget, I never can forget, that my mother was warm for my being sent back.

From that hour until this at which I write, no word of that part of my childhood which I have now gladly brought to a close, has passed my lips to any human being. I have no idea how long it lasted; whether for a year, or much more, or less. From that hour, until this, my father and my mother have been stricken dumb upon it. I have never heard the least allusion to it, however far off and remote, from either of them. I have never, until I now impart it to this paper, in any burst of confidence with anyone, my own wife not excepted, raised the curtain I then dropped, thank God.

Until old Hungerford Market was pulled down, until old Hungerford Stairs were destroyed, and the very nature of the ground changed, I never had the courage to go back to the place where my servitude began. I never saw it. I could not endure to go near it. For many years, when I came near to Robert Warrens' in the Strand, I crossed over to the opposite side of the way, to avoid a certain smell of the cement they put upon the blacking-corks, which reminded me of what I was once. It was a very long time before I liked to go up Chandos Street. My old way home by the Borough made me cry, after my eldest child could speak.

In my walks at night I have walked there often, since then, and by degrees I have come to write this. It does not seem a tithe of what I might have written, or of what I meant to write.

C2. Charles Dickens "Travelling Abroad" *The Uncommercial Traveller* First Edition (1861) VII.

[First appearing in *All the Year Round* on 7 April 1860, "Travelling Abroad" is a fantastic narrative, which in its final paragraphs is revealed to be composed of the jumbled memories of travel which pass through Dickens's mind as he tries out a carriage in a London emporium on behalf of a friend. In this first scene, he encounters himself as child of nine on the road between Gravesend and Rochester (see Map A).]

I got into the travelling chariot — it was of German make, roomy, heavy, and unvarnished — I got into the traveling chariot, pulled up the steps after me, shut myself in with a smart bang of the door, and gave the word "Go on!"

Immediately, all that W. and S.W. division of London began to slide away at a pace so lively, that I was over the river, and past the Old Kent-road, and out on Blackheath, and even ascending Shooter's Hill, before I had had time to look about me in the carriage, like a collected traveller.

I had two ample Imperials on the roof, other fitted storage for luggage in front, and other up behind; I had a net for books overhead, great pockets to all the windows, a leathern pouch or two hung up for odds and ends, and a reading-lamp fixed in the back of the chariot, in case I should be benighted. I was amply provided in all respects, and had no idea where I was going (which was delightful), except that I was going abroad.

So smooth was the old high-road, and so fresh were the horses, and so fast went I, that it was midway between Gravesend and Rochester, and the widening river was bearing the ships, white sailed or black smoked, out to sea, when I noticed by the wayside a very queer small boy.

"Halloa!" said I to the very queer small boy, "where do you live?"

"At Chatham," says he.

"What do you do there?" says I.

"I go to school," says he.

I took him up in a moment, and we went on. Presently, the very queer small boy said, "This is Gadshill we are coming to, where Falstaff went out to rob those travellers, and ran away."

"You know something about Falstaff, eh?" said I.

"All about him," said the very queer small boy. "I am old (I am nine), and I read all sorts of books. But *do* let us stop at the top of the hill, and look at the house there, if you please!"

"You admire that house?" said I.

"Bless you, sir," said the very queer small boy, "when I was not more than half as old as nine, it used to be a treat for me to be brought to look at it. And ever since I can recollect, my father, seeing me so fond of it, has often said to me, 'If you were to be very persevering and were to work hard, you might some day come to live in it.' Though that's impossible!" said the very queer small boy, drawing a low breath, and now staring at the house out of window with all his might.

I was rather amazed to be told this by the very queer small boy; for that house happens to be *my* house, and I have reason to believe that what he said was true.

C3. Alexis de Tocqueville *The Old Regime and the French Revolution* (1856; trans. John Bonner 1856) Pt. II Ch. 9.

[Tocqueville (1805–59), French statesman and political scientist, whose major writings are on American democracy and the French Revolution. Here, Tocqueville comments on the modernity of the English social system and its use of the term "gentleman," in contrast with their French equivalents.]

It seems extremely probable that, at the time of the first establishment of the feudal system in Europe, the class which was subsequently called the nobility did not at once form a *caste,* but was originally composed of the chief men of the nation, and was therefore, in the beginning, merely an aristocracy. This, however, is a question which I have no intention of discussing here; it will be sufficient to remark that, during the Middle Ages, the nobility had become a caste, that is to say, that its distinctive mark was birth.

It retained, indeed, one of the proper characteristics of an aristocracy, that of being a governing body of citizens; but birth alone decided who should be at the head of this body. Whoever was not born noble was excluded from this close and particular class, and could only fill a position more or less exalted but still subordinate in the State.

Wherever on the continent of Europe the feudal system had been established it ended in caste; in England alone it returned to aristocracy.

It has always excited my surprise that a fact which distinguishes England from all other modern nations, and which alone can throw light upon the peculiarities of its laws, its spirit, and its history, has not attracted to a still greater degree the attention of philosophers and statesmen, and that habit has rendered it, as it were, imperceptible to the English themselves. It has frequently been seen by glimpses, and imperfectly described, but no complete and distinct view has, I believe, ever been taken of it. Montesquieu, it is true, on visiting Great Britain in 1739, wrote, "I am now in a country which has little resemblance to the rest of Europe:" but that is all.

It was indeed, not so much its parliament, its liberty, its publicity, or its jury, which at that time rendered England so unlike the rest of Europe; it was something far more peculiar and far more powerful. England was the only country in which the system of caste had been not only modified, but effectually destroyed. The nobility and the middle classes in England followed the same business, embraced the same professions, and, what is far more significant, intermarried with each other. The daughter of the greatest nobleman could already without disgrace marry a man of yesterday.

In order to ascertain whether caste, with the ideas, habits, and barriers it creates amongst a nation, is definitely destroyed, look at its marriages. They alone give the decisive feature which we seek. At this very day, in France, after sixty years of democracy, we shall generally seek it in vain. The old and the new families, between which no distinction any longer appears to exist, avoid as much as possible to intermingle with each other by marriage.

It has often been remarked that the English nobility has been more prudent, more able, and less exclusive than any other. It would have been much nearer the truth to say, that in England, for a very long time past, no nobility, properly so called, has existed, if we take the word in the ancient and limited sense it has everywhere else retained.

This singular revolution is lost in the night of ages, but a living witness of it yet survives in the idiom of language. For several centuries the word *gentleman* has altogether changed its meaning in England, and the word *roturier* has ceased to exist. It would have been impossible to translate literally into English the well-known line from the "Tartuffe," even when Molière wrote it in 1664: —

Et tel qu'on le voit, il est bon gentilhomme.

If we make a further application of the science of languages to the science of history, and pursue the fate of the word *gentleman* through time and through space, — the offspring of the French word *gentilhomme*, — we shall find its application extending in England in the same proportion in which classes draw near one another and amalgamate. In each succeeding century it is applied to persons placed somewhat lower in the social scale. At length it travelled with the English to America, where it is used to designate every citizen indiscriminately. Its history is that of democracy itself.

In France the word *gentilhomme* has always been strictly limited to its original meaning; since the Revolution it has been almost disused, but its application has never changed. The word which was used to designate the members of the caste was kept intact, because the caste itself was maintained as separate from all the rest as it had ever been.

I go even further, and assert that this caste had become far more exclusive than it was when the word was first invented, and that in France a change had taken place in the direction opposed to that which had occurred in England.

C4. Unsigned [Sir James Fitzjames Stephen] "Gentlemen" *Cornhill Magazine* (March 1862) Vol. V pp. 330–2.

[Stephen (1829–94) was a lawyer who wrote widely on contemporary social issues. Here he argues that the moral and aesthetic implications of the term "gentleman" are now more important than its original social meaning. The comments reproducd here form part of a response to a provocative lecture at Salisbury in January of the same year by John Arthur Roebuck, maverick Liberal M.P. for Sheffield. In the lecture Roebuck had attacked the debasement of the rural and urban proletariat, and recommended the increased provision of popular education as a remedy.]

The characteristic moral distinctions by which society is as it were divided into two halves, are summed up in the one word "Gentleman." The division between those who are, and those who are not, entitled to this appellation, is as real and important as it is indefinite. It may, therefore, be worth while, in the first place, to examine the proper meaning of the word. The original meaning of the word gentleman, which it has never entirely lost, was nearly, if not quite, the same as that of its French equivalent *gentilhomme*. It denoted the fact that the person to whom it was applied was a member of one of a certain set of families, or the holder of a certain definite official or professional rank. As these families and officials were supposed to be distinguished from the rest of the world by the degree in which they possessed particular qualities, physical, moral, and intellectual, the word came by degrees to denote the combination of the two sets of distinctions; and as people came to perceive that the moral and intellectual qualities were far the most important and distinctive, they learned to attribute to the word a moral rather than a personal meaning. Hence, in the present day, the word implies the combination of a certain degree of social rank with a certain amount of the qualities which the possession of such rank ought to imply; but there is a constantly increasing disposition to insist more upon the moral and less upon the social element of the word, and it is not impossible that in course of time its use may come to be altogether dissociated from any merely conventional distinction. Leaving, then, on one side that part of the meaning of the word which relates to external social rank, these questions suggest themselves: — What are the personal qualities denoted or connoted by the word? How far, in point of fact, are the poor deficient in the possession of those qualities? To what is that deficiency to be ascribed? And how far can it be remedied?

A fashion has prevailed of describing every sort of sin or vice as being ungentlemanlike, and as deserving, on that ground, to be avoided. It is said, for example, that it is ungentlemanlike to swear; that no man deserves to be called a gentleman who would be guilty of the selfishness and treachery of seduction; and some popular writers have delighted in contrasting the claims of such a man (for example) as George IV to be considered the first gentleman of Europe, with the innumerable acts of perfidy, debauchery, falsehood, and meanness which stained his whole career, personal and political. No doubt the result of this fashion has been to enable lay preachers, who had a natural reluctance to enter upon the deeper foundations on which morality rests, to preach very effective sermons. But to use words usefully is one thing; to use them correctly is quite another; and many reasons make the latter a hardly less important habit than the former.

Like many other words, the word gentleman, considered merely in its personal sense, is used upon a tacit assumption which must become express if its full meaning is to be understood. This tacit assumption is that the persons to whom the word applies form a body associated together for the sake of the pleasure which is to be derived from each other's society, and not for those more serious purposes which great associations of men, such as states, churches, armies, legislative and political bodies, and the like, are intended to promote. A man whose personal qualities fit him to take his place in such a society may properly, or at least intelligibly, be described as a gentleman, whatever else he may either have or want. It would be difficult, if not impossible, to give a complete list of the qualities which such a position implies, but they may be ranged under three great heads: some of them are artistic, some moral, and some intellectual: and of these the artistic qualities are the most definite, the most easily ascertained, and the most universally required. Thus it is equally inconsistent with the character of a gentleman to blow one's nose with one's fingers, to tell gross lies, or to be unable to read; but of the three offences the first is most obviously and most fundamentally irreconcilable with the character in question. Indeed the two others are ungentlemanlike principally, if not entirely, because of their inartistic nature. The reason why a lie is ungentlemanlike is because lying is not merely a vice, but an ugly and displeasing vice. Lies which are not ugly and displeasing, exaggerations for example, or inaccuracies, are not ungentlemanlike. Breaches of morality quite as decided and to the full as injurious to society, are not in the least inconsistent with the character of a gentleman. A man, for example, might be a perfect gentleman who was utterly dead to all sense of religious duty, or entirely devoid of charity towards his neighbour. Indeed the graver kinds of crime are not of necessity ungentlemanlike. Perhaps picking pockets, or obtaining money by false pretences, might be so described; but if a man from jealousy committed murder or arson it would be an abuse of language to give such a name to his conduct. No doubt the moral quality of an action is one of the elements which contribute to its beauty, or at least to our opinion of its beauty, for admiration is to a great extent the creature of association, so that we learn to admire and consider as beautiful those acts which we associate with beneficial result. Still it is by reason of their beauty, whether derived from their moral excellence or not, that we call certain dispositions gentlemanlike, and others not; nor is it to every kind of beauty that we ascribe that name, but only to those descriptions of beauty which are sufficiently striking and obvious to command the attention and sympathy of persons who associate together for the purpose of enjoying each other's society, whilst they are engaged in that enjoyment. Hence it follows that when we speak of a gentleman we do not mean either a good man, or a wise man, but a man socially pleasant, and we consider his goodness and wisdom, his moral and intellectual qualities as relevant to his claims to be considered a gentleman only in so far as they contribute to his social pleasantness.

This may appear to some persons to give a lower notion of what is meant by a gentleman than is conveyed by that vague mode of speaking upon the subject, which aims at denouncing all faults and vices whatever as being offences against good manners. In fact, however, it is always important to use language correctly; and the exaggerations referred to have a strong tendency to conceal the fact that the object of preserving the beauty, dignity, and pleasantness of life has a value of its own altogether independent of the general utility of the qualities by which those objects are brought about. It may seem at first sight a small thing to consider moral virtues with reference to the amount of social pleasure which they confer, but, in reality, it is by no means a small thing.

C5. William Sewell "Gentlemanly Manners" *Sermons to Boys at Radley School* (1854–69) Vol. II pp. 453–4.

[William Sewell (1804–74), High Church clergyman, Oxford don, and afterwards headmaster of St. Peter's College, Radley, the Oxfordshire public school which he helped to found in 1847. In this and other sermons delivered to the boys of the school, Sewell takes the simple line that prevailing English class divisions are ordained by God. In 1854 Sewell sent Dickens a copy of the first volume, which the latter returned with a comment on how far apart their views were (*Letters of Charles Dickens* Vol. VII p. 307).]

We have, I think, in England, owing to the freedom of our constitution, and the happy providential blessings which God has heaped upon us, followed the division of mankind which God himself has made, and struck the line between those who are gentlemen, that is, of a higher and superior class, and those who are not, where He himself has struck it. Some men He has made to rule and govern; some to be ruled and governed. And in England, the term gentleman is generally given to all those who are in those positions of society, in which they are trusted with power and authority, and are required to exercise the higher faculties of nature, in influencing, guiding, and benefiting others. And now you can see that in this sense, the term gentleman is applicable to every one of you. You are all the sons of gentlemen, of persons who, at least, are in liberal, respected professions and occupations. This place is not intended for any others.

C6. John Ruskin "Of Vulgarity" *Modern Painters* Vol. V (1860) Pt. IX Ch. VII.

[John Ruskin (1819–1900), English art historian and social critic, who rejected the growth of competition and economic self-interest under capitalism, and struggled for the restoration of the Mediaeval Christian ideals of feudal responsibility and chivalry. Here, Ruskin argues that gentlemanliness has nothing to do with social class, but derives from a genetic inheritance ("race"), which can be elevated or degraded from generation to generation. Sensitiveness is the hallmark which distinguishes gentlemanliness from vulgarity. Significantly, Ruskin's examples of the former derive largely from Biblical and Classical sources; those of the latter tend to be found among Dickens's characters. Authorial footnotes are omitted.]

§ 1. Two great errors, colouring, or rather discolouring, severally, the minds of the higher and lower class, have sown wide dissension, and wider misfortune, through the society of modern days. These errors are in our modes of interpreting the word "gentleman."

Its primal, literal, and perpetual meaning is "a man of pure race;" well bred, in the sense that a horse or dog is well bred.

The so-called higher classes, being generally of purer race than the lower, have retained the true idea, and the convictions associated with it; but are afraid to speak it out, and equivocate about it in public; this equivocation mainly proceeding from their desire to connect another meaning with it, and a false one; — that of "a man living in idleness on other people's labour;" — with which idea the term has nothing whatever to do.

The lower classes, denying vigorously, and with reason, the notion that a gentleman means an idler, and rightly feeling that the more any one works, the more of a gentleman he becomes, and is likely to become, — have nevertheless got little of the good they otherwise might, from the truth, because, with it, they wanted to hold a falsehood, — namely, that race was of no consequence. It being precisely of as much consequence in man as it is in any other animal.

§ 2. The nation cannot truly prosper till both these errors are finally got quit of. Gentlemen have to learn that it is no part of their duty or privilege to live on other people's toil. They have to learn that there is no degradation in the hardest manual, or the humblest servile, labour, when it is honest. But that there *is* degradation, and that deep, in extravagance, in bribery, in indolence, in pride, in taking places they are not fit for, or in coining places for which there is no need. It does not disgrace a gentleman to become an errand boy, or a day labourer; but it disgraces him much to become a knave, or a thief. And knavery is not the less knavery because it involves large interests, nor theft the less theft because it is countenanced by usage, or accompanied by failure in undertaken duty. It is an incomparably less guilty form of robbery to cut a purse out of a man's pocket, than to take it out of his hand on the understanding that you are to steer his ship up channel, when you do not know the soundings.

§ 3. On the other hand, the lower orders, and all orders, have to learn that every vicious habit and chronic disease communicates itself by descent; and that by purity of birth the entire system of the human body and soul may be gradually elevated, or, by recklessness of birth, degraded; until there shall be as much difference between the well-bred and ill-bred human creature (whatever pains be taken with their education) as between a wolf-hound and the vilest mongrel cur. And the knowledge of this great fact ought to regulate the education of our youth, and the entire conduct of the nation.

§ 4. Gentlemanliness, however, in ordinary parlance, must be taken to signify those qualities which are usually the evidence of high breeding, and which, so far as they can be acquired, it should be every man's effort to acquire; or, if he has them by nature, to preserve and exalt. Vulgarity, on the other hand, will signify qualities usually characteristic of ill-breeding, which, according to his power, it becomes every person's duty to subdue. We have briefly to note what these are.

§ 5. A gentleman's first characteristic is that fineness of structure in the body, which renders it capable of the most delicate sensation; and of structure in the mind which renders it capable of the most delicate sympathies — one may say, simply, "fineness of nature." This is, of course, compatible with heroic bodily strength and mental firmness; in fact, heroic strength is not conceivable without such delicacy. Elephantine strength may drive its way through a forest and feel no touch of the boughs; but the white skin of Homer's Atrides would have felt a bent rose leaf, yet subdue its feeling in glow of battle, and behave itself like iron. I do not mean to call an elephant a vulgar animal; but if you think about him carefully, you will find that his non-vulgarity consists in such gentleness as is possible to elephantine nature; not in his insensitive hide nor in his clumsy foot; but in the way he will lift his foot if a child lies in his way; and in his sensitive trunk, and still more sensitive mind, and capability of pique on points of honour.

§ 6. And, though rightness of moral conduct is ultimately the great purifier of race, the sign of nobleness is not in this rightness of moral conduct, but in sensitiveness. When the make of the creature is fine, its temptations are strong, as well as its perceptions; it is liable to all kinds of impressions from without in their most violent form; liable therefore to be abused and hurt by all kinds of rough things which would do a coarser creature little harm, and thus to fall into frightful wrong if its fate will have it so. Thus David, coming of gentlest as well as royalest race, of Ruth as well as of Judah, is sensitiveness through all flesh and spirit; not that his compassion will restrain him from murder when his terror urges him to it; nay, he is driven to the murder all the more by his sensitiveness to the shame which otherwise threatens him. But when his own story is told him under a disguise, though only a lamb is now concerned, his passion about it leaves him no time for thought. "The man shall die" — note the reason — "because he had no pity." He is so eager and indignant that it never occurs to him as strange that Nathan hides the name. This is true gentleman. A vulgar man would assuredly have been cautious, and asked "who it was?"

§ 7. Hence it will follow that one of the probable signs of high-breeding in men generally, will be their kindness and mercifulness; these always indicating more or less fineness of make in the mind; and miserliness and cruelty the contrary; hence that of Isaiah: "The vile person shall no more be called liberal, nor the churl said to be bountiful." But a thousand things may prevent this kindness from displaying or continuing itself; the mind of the man may be warped so as to bear mainly on his own interests, and then all his sensibilities will take the form of pride, or fastidiousness, or revengefulness; and other wicked, but not ungentlemanly tempers; or, farther, they may run into utter sensuality and covetousness, if he is bent on pleasure, accompanied with quite infinite cruelty when the pride is wounded or the passions thwarted; — until your gentleman becomes Ezzelin, and your lady, the deadly Lucrece; yet, still gentleman and lady, quite incapable of making anything else of themselves, being so born.

§ 8. A truer sign of breeding than mere kindness is therefore sympathy; — a vulgar man may often be kind in a hard way, on principle, and because he thinks he ought to be; whereas, a highly-bred man, even when cruel, will be cruel in a softer way, understanding and feeling what he inflicts, and pitying his victim. Only we must carefully remember that the quantity of sympathy a gentleman feels can never be judged of by its outward expression, for another of his chief characteristics is apparent reserve. I say "apparent" reserve; for the sympathy is real, but the reserve not: a perfect gentleman is never reserved, but sweetly and entirely open, so far as it is good for others, or possible, that he should be. In a great many respects it is impossible that he should be open except to men of his own kind. To them, he can open himself, by a word, or syllable, or a glance; but to men not of his kind he cannot open himself, though he tried it through an eternity of clear grammatical speech. By the very acuteness of his sympathy he knows how much of himself he can give to anybody; and he gives that much frankly; — would always be glad to give more if he could, but is obliged, nevertheless, in his general intercourse with the world, to be a somewhat silent person; silence is to most people, he finds, less reserve than speech. Whatever he said, a vulgar man would misinterpret: no words that he could use would bear the same sense to the vulgar man that they do to him; if he used any, the vulgar man would go away saying, "He had said so and so, and meant so and so" (something assuredly he never meant); but he keeps silence, and the vulgar man goes away saying, "He didn't know what to make of him." Which is precisely the fact, and the only fact which he is anywise able to announce to the vulgar man concerning himself.

§ 9. There is yet another quite as efficient cause of the apparent reserve of a gentleman. His sensibility being constant and intelligent, it will be seldom that a feeling touches him, however acutely, but it has touched him in the same way often before, and in some sort is touching him always. It is not that he feels little, but that he feels habitually; a vulgar man having some heart at the bottom of him, if you can by talk or by sight fairly force the pathos of anything down to his heart, will be excited about it and demonstrative; the sensation of pity being strange to him, and wonderful. But your gentleman has walked in pity all day long; the tears have never been out of his eyes; you thought the eyes were bright only; but they were wet. You tell him a sorrowful story, and his countenance does not change; the eyes can but be wet still; he does not speak neither, there being, in fact, nothing to be said, only something to be done; some vulgar person, beside you both, goes away saying, "How hard he is!" Next day he hears that the hard person has put good end to the sorrow he said nothing about; — and then he changes his wonder, and exclaims, "How reserved he is!"

§ 10. Self-command is often thought a characteristic of high-breeding: and to a certain extent it is so, at least it is one of the means of forming and strengthening character; but it is rather a way of imitating a gentleman than a characteristic of him; a true gentleman has no need of self-command; he simply feels rightly on all occasions; and desiring to express only so much of his feeling as it is right to express, does not need to command himself. Hence perfect ease is indeed characteristic of him; but perfect ease is inconsistent with self-restraint. Nevertheless gentlemen, so far as they fail of their own ideal, need to command themselves, and do so; while, on the contrary, to feel unwisely, and to be unable to restrain the expression of the unwise feeling, is vulgarity, and yet even then, the vulgarity, at its root, is not in the mistimed expression, but in the unseemly feeling; and when we find fault with a vulgar person for "exposing himself," it is not his openness, but clumsiness; and yet more the want of sensibility to his own failure, which we blame; so that still the vulgarity resolves itself into want of sensibility. Also, it is to be noted that great powers of self-restraint may be attained by very vulgar persons, when it suits their purposes.

§ 11. Closely, but strangely, connected with this openness is that form of truthfulness which is opposed to cunning yet not opposed to falsity absolute. And herein is a distinction of great importance.

Cunning signifies especially a habit or gift of overreaching, accompanied with enjoyment and a sense of superiority. It is associated with small and dull conceit, and with an absolute want of sympathy or affection. Its essential connection with vulgarity may be at once exemplified by the expression of the butcher's dog in Landseer's "Low Life." Cruikshank's "Noah Claypole," in the illustrations to Oliver Twist, in the interview with the Jew, is, however, still more characteristic. It is the intensest rendering of vulgarity absolute and utter with which I am acquainted.

The truthfulness which is opposed to cunning ought, perhaps, rather to be called the desire of truthfulness; it consists more in unwillingness to deceive than in not deceiving, — an unwillingness implying sympathy with and respect for the person deceived; and a fond observance of truth up to the possible point, as in a good soldier's mode of retaining his honour through a *ruse-de-guerre*. A cunning person seeks for opportunities to deceive; a gentleman shuns them. A cunning person triumphs in deceiving; a gentleman is humiliated by his success, or at least by so much of the success as is dependent merely on the falsehood, and not on his intellectual superiority.

§ 12. The absolute disdain of all lying belongs rather to Christian chivalry than to mere high breeding; as connected merely with this latter, and with general refinement and courage, the exact relations of truthfulness may be best studied in the well-trained Greek mind. The Greeks believed that mercy and truth were co-relative virtues — cruelty and falsehood, co-relative vices. But they did not call necessary severity, cruelty; nor necessary deception, falsehood. It was needful sometimes to slay men, and sometimes to deceive them. When this had to be done, it should be done well and thoroughly; so that to direct a spear well to its mark, or a lie well to its end, was equally the accomplishment of a perfect gentleman. Hence, in the pretty diamond-cut-diamond scene between Pallas and Ulysses, when she receives him on the coast of Ithaca, the goddess laughs delightedly at her hero's good lying, and gives him her hand upon it; — showing herself then in her woman's form, as just a little more than his match. "Subtle would he be, and stealthy, who should go beyond thee in deceit, even were he a god, thou many-witted! What! here in thine own land, too, wilt thou not cease from cheating? Knowest thou not me, Pallas Athena, maid of Jove, who am with thee in all thy labours, and gave thee favour with the Phaeacians, and keep thee, and have come now to weave cunning with thee?" But how completely this kind of cunning was looked upon as a part of a man's power, and not as a diminution of faithfulness, is perhaps best shown by the single line of praise in which the high qualities of his servant are summed up by Chremulus in the Plutus — "Of all my house servants, I hold you to be the faithfullest, and the greatest cheat (or thief)."

§ 13. Thus, the primal difference between honourable and base lying in the Greek mind lay in honourable purpose. A man who used his strength wantonly to hurt others was a monster; so, also, a man who used his cunning wantonly to hurt others. Strength and cunning were to be used only in self-defence, or to save the weak, and then were alike admirable. This was their first idea. Then the second, and perhaps the more essential, difference between noble and ignoble lying in the Greek mind, was that the honourable lie — or, if we may use the strange, yet just, expression, the true lie — knew and confessed itself for such — was ready to take the full responsibility of what it did. As the sword answered for its blow, so the lie for its snare. But what the Greeks hated with all their heart was the false lie; — the lie that did not know itself, feared to confess itself, which slunk to its aim under a cloak of truth, and sought to do liars' work, and yet not take liars' pay, excusing itself to the conscience by quibble and quirk. Hence the great expression of Jesuit principle by Euripides, "The tongue has sworn, but not the heart," was a subject of execration throughout Greece, and the satirists exhausted their arrows on it — no audience was ever tired hearing … "that Euripidean thing" brought to shame.

§ 14. And this is especially to be insisted on in the early education of young people. It should be pointed out to them with continual earnestness that the essence of lying is in deception, not in words; a lie may be told by silence, by equivocation, by the accent on a syllable, by a glance of the eye attaching a peculiar significance to a sentence; and all these kinds of lies are worse and baser by many degrees than a lie plainly worded; so that no form of blinded conscience is so far sunk as that which comforts itself for having deceived, because the deception was by gesture or silence, instead of utterance; and, finally, according to Tennyson's deep and trenchant line, "A lie which is half a truth is ever the worst of lies."

§ 15. Although, however, ungenerous cunning is usually so distinct an outward manifestation of vulgarity, that I name it separately from insensibility, it is in truth only an effect of insensibility, producing want of affection to others, and blindness to the beauty of truth. The degree in which political subtlety in men such as Richelieu, Machiavel, or Metternich, will efface the gentleman, depends on the selfishness of political purpose to which the cunning is directed, and on the base delight taken in its use. The command, "Be ye wise as serpents, harmless as doves," is the ultimate expression of this principle, misunderstood usually because the word "wise," is referred to the intellectual power instead of the subtlety of the serpent. The serpent has very little intellectual power, but according to that which it has, it is yet, as of old, the subtlest of the beasts of the field.

§ 16. Another great sign of vulgarity is also, when traced to its root, another phase of insensibility, namely, the undue regard to appearances and manners, as in the households of vulgar persons, of all stations, and the assumption of behaviour, language, or dress unsuited to them, by persons in inferior stations of life. I say "undue" regard to appearances, because in the undueness consists, of course, the vulgarity. It is due and wise in some sort to care for appearances, in another sort undue and unwise. Wherein lies the difference?

At first one is apt to answer quickly: the vulgarity is simply in pretending to be what you are not. But that answer will not stand. A queen may dress like a waiting-maid, — perhaps succeed, if she chooses, in passing for one; but she will not, therefore, be vulgar; nay, a waiting-maid may dress like a queen, and pretend to be one, and yet need not be vulgar, unless there is inherent vulgarity in her. In Scribe's very absurd but very amusing *Reine d'un jour,* a milliner's girl sustains the part of a queen for a day. She several times amazes and disgusts her courtiers by her straightforwardness; and once or twice very nearly betrays herself to her maids of honour by an unqueenly knowledge of sewing; but she is not in the least vulgar, for she is sensitive, simple, and generous, and a queen could be no more.

§ 17. Is the vulgarity, then, only in trying to play a part you cannot play, so as to be continually detected? No; a bad amateur actor may be continually detected in his part, but yet continually detected to be a gentleman: a vulgar regard to appearances has nothing in it necessarily of hypocrisy. You shall know a man not to be a gentleman by the perfect and neat pronunciation of his words: but he does not pretend to pronounce accurately; he *does* pronounce accurately, and the vulgarity is in the real (not assumed) scrupulousness.

§ 18. It will be found on farther thought, that a vulgar regard for appearances is, primarily, a selfish one, resulting, not out of a wish to give pleasure (as a wife's wish to make herself beautiful for her husband), but out of an endeavour to mortify others, or attract for pride's sake; — the common "keeping up appearances" of society, being a mere selfish struggle of the vain with the vain. But the deepest stain of the vulgarity depends on this being done, not selfishly only, but stupidly, without understanding the impression which is really produced, nor the relations of importance between oneself and others, so as to suppose that their attention is fixed upon us, when we are in reality ciphers in their eyes — all which comes of insensibility. Hence pride simple is not vulgar (the looking down on others because of their true inferiority to us), nor vanity simple (the desire of praise), but conceit simple (the attribution to ourselves of qualities we have not), is always so. In cases of overstudied pronunciation, etc., there is insensibility, first, in the person's thinking more of himself than of what he is saying; and, secondly, in his not having musical fineness of ear enough to feel that his talking is uneasy and strained.

§ 19. Finally, vulgarity is indicated by coarseness of language or manners, only so far as this coarseness has been contracted under circumstances not necessarily producing it. The illiterateness of a Spanish or Calabrian peasant is not vulgar, because they had never an opportunity of acquiring letters; but the illiterateness of an English school-boy is. So again, provincial dialect is not vulgar; but cockney dialect, the corruption, by blunted sense, of a finer language continually heard, is so in a deep degree; and again, of this corrupted dialect, that is the worst which consists, not in the direct or expressive alteration of the form of a word, but in an unmusical destruction of it by dead utterance and bad or swollen formation of lip. There is no vulgarity in —

> "Blythe, blythe, blythe was she,
> Blythe was she, but and ben,
> And weel she liked a Hawick gill,
> And leugh to see a tappit hen;"

but much in Mrs. Gamp's inarticulate "bottle on the chumley-piece, and let me put my lips to it when I am so dispoged."

§ 20. So also of personal defects, those only are vulgar which imply insensibility or dissipation.

There is no vulgarity in the emaciation of Don Quixote, the deformity of the Black Dwarf, or the corpulence of Falstaff; but much in the same personal characters, as they are seen in Uriah Heep, Quilp, and Chadband.

C7. J.H. Newman "Liberal Knowledge Viewed in Relation to Religion" *The Scope and Nature of University Education* (1859) Discourse VIII Sections 8–10.

[John Henry Newman (1801–90), leading figure in the High Church Oxford Movement of the 1830s, who moved to the Church of Rome in 1845. He served as rector of the new Catholic University in Dublin from 1854. Originally addressed in 1852 to interested Catholics in Dublin, Newman's discourses on university education were later incorporated into *The Idea of a University* (1873). Here, he argues for the final separateness of liberal knowledge and religious truth, and thus of English gentlemanliness and Christian virtue. The former Newman associates with the formulations of the 3rd Earl of Shaftesbury in *Characteristics of Men* (1711), which he cites extensively in the preceding section. It is significant that his concept of the gentleman derives almost entirely from eighteenth-century models rather than reflecting contemporary Victorian redefinitions.]

§ 8. Taking these passages as specimens of what I call the Religion of Philosophy, it is obvious to observe that there is no doctrine contained in them which is not in a certain sense true; yet, on the other hand, that almost every statement is perverted and made false, because it is not the whole truth. They are exhibitions of truth under one aspect, and therefore insufficient; conscience is most certainly a moral sense, but it is more; vice again, is a deformity, but it is worse. Lord Shaftesbury may insist, if he will, that simple and solitary fear cannot effect a moral conversion, and we are not concerned to answer him; but he will have a difficulty in proving that any real conversion follows from a doctrine which makes virtue a mere point of good taste, and vice vulgar and ungentlemanlike.

Such a doctrine is essentially superficial, and such will be its effects. It has no better measure of right and wrong than that of visible beauty and tangible fitness. Conscience indeed inflicts an acute pang, but that pang, forsooth, is irrational, and to reverence it is an illiberal superstition. But, if we will make light of what is deepest within us, nothing is left but to pay homage to what is more upon the surface. To *seem* becomes to *be*; what looks fair will be good, what causes offence will be evil; virtue will be what pleases, vice what pains. As well may we measure virtue by utility as by such a rule. Nor is this an imaginary apprehension; we all must recollect the celebrated sentiment into which a great and wise man was betrayed, in the glowing eloquence of his valediction to the spirit of chivalry. "It is gone," cries Mr. Burke; "that sensibility of principle, that chastity of honour, which felt a stain like a wound; which inspired courage, while it mitigated ferocity; which ennobled whatever it touched, and under which *vice lost half its evil by losing all its grossness.*" In the last clause of this beautiful sentence we have too apt an illustration of the ethical temperament of a civilized age. It is detection, not the sin, which is the crime; private life is sacred, and inquiry into it is intolerable; and decency is virtue. Scandals, vulgarities, whatever shocks, whatever disgusts, are offences of the first order. Drinking and swearing, squalid poverty, improvidence, laziness, slovenly disorder, make up the idea of profligacy: poets may say any thing, however wicked, with impunity; works of genius may be read without danger or shame, whatever their principles; fashion, celebrity, the beautiful, the heroic, will suffice to force any evil upon the community. The splendours of a court, and the charms of good society, wit, imagination, taste, and high breeding, the *prestige* of rank, and the resources of wealth, are a screen, an instrument, and an apology for vice and irreligion. And thus at length we find, surprising as the change may be, that that very refinement of Intellectualism, which began by repelling sensuality, ends by excusing it. Under the shadow indeed of the Church, and in its due development, Philosophy does service to the cause of morality; but, when it is strong enough to have a will of its own, and is lifted up with an idea of its own importance, and attempts to form a theory, and to lay down a principle, and to carry out a system of ethics, and undertakes the moral education of the man, then it does but abet evils to which at first it seemed instinctively opposed. True Religion is slow in growth, and, when once planted, is difficult of dislodgement; but its intellectual counterfeit has no root in itself: it springs up suddenly, it suddenly withers. It appeals to what is in nature, and it falls under the dominion of the old Adam. Then, like dethroned princes, it keeps up a state and majesty, when it has lost the real power. Deformity is its abhorrence; accordingly, since it cannot dissuade men from vice, therefore in order to escape the sight of its deformity, it embellishes it. It "skins and films the ulcerous place," which it cannot probe or heal,

> "While rank corruption, mining all within,
> Infects unseen."

And from this shallowness of philosophical Religion it comes to pass that it seems able to fulfil certain precepts of Christianity more readily and exactly than Christians themselves. St. Paul, as I have said, gives us a pattern of evangelical perfection; he draws the Christian character in its most graceful form, and its most beautiful hues. He discourses of that charity which is patient and meek, humble and single-minded, disinterested, contented, and persevering. He tells us to prefer each other before ourselves, to give way to each other, to abstain from rude words and evil speech, to avoid self-conceit, to be calm and grave, to be cheerful and happy, to observe peace with all men, truth and justice, courtesy and gentleness, all that is modest, amiable, virtuous, and of good repute. Such is St. Paul's exemplar of the Christian in his external relations; and, I repeat, the school of the world seems to send out living copies of this typical excellence with greater success than the Church. At this day the "gentleman" is the creation, not of Christianity, but of civilization. But the reason is obvious. The world is content with setting right the surface of things; the Church aims at regenerating the very depths of the heart. She ever begins with the beginning; and, as regards the multitude of her children, is never able to get beyond the beginning, but is continually employed in laying the foundation. She is engaged with what is essential, as previous and as introductory to the ornamental and the attractive. She is curing men and keeping them clear of mortal sin; she is "treating of justice and chastity, and the judgment to come": she is insisting on faith and hope, and devotion, and honesty, and the elements of charity; and has so much to do with precept, that she almost leaves it to inspirations from Heaven to suggest what is of counsel and perfection. She aims at what is necessary rather than at what is desirable. She is for the many as well as for the few. She is putting souls in the way of salvation, that they may then be in a condition, if they shall be called upon, to aspire to the heroic, and to attain the substance, as well as the semblance, of the beautiful.

§ 9. Such is the method, or the policy (so to call it), of the Church; but Philosophy looks at the matter from a very different point of view: what have Philosophers to do with the terror of judgment or the saving of the soul? Lord Shaftesbury calls the former a sort of "panic fear." Of the latter he scoffingly complains that "the saving of souls is now the heroic passion of exalted spirits." Of course he is at liberty, on his principles, to pick and choose out of Christianity what he will; he discards the theological, the mysterious, the spiritual; he makes selection of the morally or esthetically beautiful. To him it matters not at all that he begins his teaching where he should end it; it matters not that, instead of planting the tree, he merely crops its flowers for his banquet; he only aims at the present life, his philosophy dies with him; if his flowers do but last to the end of his revel, he has nothing more to seek. When night comes, the withered leaves may be mingled with his own ashes; he and they will have done their work, he and they will be no more. Certainly, it costs little to make men virtuous on conditions such as these; it is like teaching them a language or an accomplishment, to write Latin or to play on an instrument, — the profession of an artist, not the commission of an Apostle.

This embellishment of the exterior is almost the beginning and the end of philosophical morality. This is why it aims at being modest rather than humble; this is how it can be proud at the very time that it is unassuming. To humility indeed it does not even aspire; humility is one of the most difficult of virtues both to attain and to ascertain. It lies close upon the heart itself, and its tests are exceedingly delicate and subtle. Its counterfeits abound; however, we are little concerned with them here, for, I repeat, it is hardly professed even by name in the code of ethics which we are reviewing. As has been often observed, ancient civilization had not the idea, and had no word to express it: or rather, it had the idea, and considered it a defect of mind, not a virtue, so that the word which denoted it conveyed a reproach. As to the modern world, you may gather its ignorance of it by its perversion of the somewhat parallel term "condescension." Humility or condescension, viewed as a virtue of conduct, may be said to consist, as in other things, so in our placing ourselves in our thoughts on a level with our inferiors; it is not only a voluntary relinquishment of the privileges of our own station, but an actual participation or assumption of the condition of those to whom we stoop. This is true humility, to feel and to behave as if we were low; not, to cherish a notion of our importance, while we affect a low position. Such was St. Paul's humility, when he called himself "the least of the saints"; such the humility of those many holy men who have considered themselves the greatest of sinners. It is an abdication, as far as their own thoughts are concerned, of those prerogatives or privileges to which others deem them entitled. Now it is not a little instructive to contrast with this idea, Gentlemen, — with this theological meaning of the word "condescension," — its proper English sense; put them in juxta-position and you will at once see the difference between the world's humility and the humility of the Gospel. As the world uses the word, "condescension" is a stooping indeed of the person, but a bending forward, unattended with any the slightest effort to leave by a single inch the seat in which it is so firmly established. It is the act of a superior, who protests to himself, while he commits it, that he is superior still, and that he is doing nothing else but an act of grace towards those on whose level, in theory, he is placing himself. And this is the nearest idea which the philosopher can form of the virtue of self-abasement; to do more than this is to his mind a meanness or an hypocrisy, and at once excites his suspicion and disgust. What the world is, such it has ever been; we know the contempt which the educated pagans had for the martyrs and confessors of the Church; and it is shared by the anti-Catholic bodies of this day.

Such are the ethics of Philosophy, when faithfully represented; but an age like this, not pagan, but professedly Christian, cannot venture to reprobate humility in set terms, or to make a boast of pride. Accordingly, it looks out for some expedient by which it may blind itself to the real state of the case. Humility, with its grave and self-denying attributes, it cannot love; but what is more beautiful, what more winning, than modesty? what virtue, at first sight, simulates humility so well? though what in fact is more radically distinct from it? In truth, great as is its charm, modesty is not the deepest or the most religious of virtues. Rather it is the advanced guard or sentinel of the soul militant, and watches continually over its nascent intercourse with the world about it. It goes the round of the senses; it mounts up into the countenance; it protects the eye and ear; it reigns in the voice and gesture. Its province is the outward deportment, as other virtues have relation to matters theological, others to society, and others to the mind itself. And being more superficial than other virtues, it is more easily disjoined from their company; it admits of being associated with principles or qualities naturally foreign to it, and is often made the cloak of feelings or ends for which it was never given to us. So little is it the necessary index of humility, that it is even compatible with pride. The better for the purpose of Philosophy; humble it cannot be, so forthwith modesty becomes its humility.

Pride, under such training, instead of running to waste in the education of the mind, is turned to account; it gets a new name; it is called self-respect; and ceases to be the disagreeable, uncompanionable quality which it is in itself. Though it be the motive principle of the soul, it seldom comes to view; and when it shows itself, then delicacy and gentleness are its attire, and good sense and sense of honour direct its motions. It is no longer a restless agent, without definite aim; it has a large field of exertion assigned to it, and it subserves those social interests which it would naturally trouble. It is directed into the channel of industry, frugality, honesty, and obedience; and it becomes the very staple of the religion and morality held in honour in a day like our own. It becomes the safeguard of chastity, the guarantee of veracity, in high and low; it is the very household god of society, as at present constituted, inspiring neatness and decency in the servant girl, propriety of carriage and refined manners in her mistress, uprightness, manliness, and generosity in the head of the family. It diffuses a light over town and country; it covers the soil with handsome edifices and smiling gardens; it tills the field, it stocks and embellishes the shop. It is the stimulating principle of providence on the one hand, and of free expenditure on the other; of an honourable ambition, and of elegant enjoyment. It breathes upon the face of the community, and the hollow sepulchre is forthwith beautiful to look upon.

Refined by the civilization which has brought it into activity, this self-respect infuses into the mind an intense horror of exposure, and a keen sensitiveness of notoriety and ridicule. It becomes the enemy of extravagances of any kind; it shrinks from what are called scenes; it has no mercy on the mock-heroic, on pretence or egotism, on verbosity in language, or what is called prosiness in conversation. It detests gross adulation; not that it tends at all to the eradication of the appetite to which the flatterer ministers, but it sees the absurdity of indulging it, it understands the annoyance thereby given to others, and if a tribute must be paid to the wealthy or the powerful, it demands greater subtlety and art in the preparation. Thus vanity is changed into a more dangerous self-conceit, as being checked in its natural eruption. It teaches men to suppress their feelings, and to control their tempers, and to mitigate both the severity and the tone of their judgments. As Lord Shaftesbury would desire, it prefers playful wit and satire in putting down what is objectionable, as a more refined and good-natured, as well as a more effectual method, than the expedient which is natural to uneducated minds. It is from this impatience of the tragic and the bombastic that it is now quietly but energetically opposing itself to the unchristian practice of duelling, which it brands as simply out of taste, and as the remnant of a barbarous age; and certainly it seems likely to effect what Religion has aimed at abolishing in vain.

§ 10. Hence it is that it is almost a definition of a gentleman to say he is one who never inflicts pain. This description is both refined and, as far as it goes, accurate. He is mainly occupied in merely removing the obstacles which hinder the free and unembarrassed action of those about him; and he concurs with their movements rather than takes the initiative himself. His benefits may be considered as parallel to what are called comforts or conveniences in arrangements of a personal nature: like an easy chair or a good fire, which do their part in dispelling cold and fatigue, though nature provides both means of rest and animal heat without them. The true gentleman in like manner carefully avoids whatever may cause a jar or a jolt in the minds of those with whom he is cast; — all clashing of opinion, or collision of feeling, all restraint, or suspicion, or gloom, or resentment; his great concern being to make every one at their ease and at home. He has his eyes on all his company; he is tender towards the bashful, gentle towards the distant, and merciful towards the absurd; he can recollect to whom he is speaking; he guards against unseasonable allusions, or topics which may irritate; he is seldom prominent in conversation, and never wearisome. He makes light of favours while he does them, and seems to be receiving when he is conferring. He never speaks of himself except when compelled, never defends himself by a mere retort, he has no ears for slander or gossip, is scrupulous in imputing motives to those who interfere with him, and interprets every thing for the best. He is never mean or little in his disputes, never takes unfair advantage, never mistakes personalities or sharp sayings for arguments, or insinuates evil which he dare not say out. From a long-sighted prudence, he observes the maxim of the ancient sage, that we should ever conduct ourselves towards our enemy as if he were one day to be our friend. He has too much good sense to be affronted at insults, he is too well employed to remember injuries, and too indolent to bear malice. He is patient, forbearing, and resigned, on philosophical principles; he submits to pain, because it is inevitable, to bereavement, because it is irreparable, and to death, because it is his destiny. If he engages in controversy of any kind, his disciplined intellect preserves him from the blundering discourtesy of better, though less educated minds; who, like blunt weapons, tear and hack instead of cutting clean, who mistake the point in argument, waste their strength on trifles, misconceive their adversary, and leave the question more involved than they find it. He may be right or wrong in his opinion, but he is too clear-headed to be unjust; he is as simple as he is forcible, and as brief as he is decisive. Nowhere shall we find greater candour, consideration, indulgence: he throws himself into the minds of his opponents, he accounts for their mistakes. He knows the weakness of human reason as well as its strength, its province and its limits. If he be an unbeliever, he will be too profound and large-minded to ridicule religion or to act against it; he is too wise to be a dogmatist or fanatic in his infidelity. He respects piety and devotion; he even supports institutions as venerable, beautiful, or useful, to which he does not assent; he honours the ministers of religion, and he is contented with declining its mysteries without assailing or denouncing them. He is a friend of religious toleration, and that, not only because his philosophy has taught him to look on all forms of faith with an impartial eye, but also from the gentleness and effeminacy of feeling, which is the attendant on civilization.

Not that he may not hold a religion too, in his own way, even when he is not a Christian. In that case his religion is one of imagination and sentiment; it is the embodiment of those ideas of the sublime, majestic, and beautiful, without which there can be no large philosophy. Sometimes he acknowledges the being of God, sometimes he invests an unknown principle or quality with the attributes of perfection. And this deduction of his reason, or creation of his fancy, he makes the occasion of such excellent thoughts, and the starting-point of so varied and systematic a teaching, that he even seems like a disciple of Christianity itself. From the very accuracy and steadiness of his logical powers, he is able to see what sentiments are consistent in those who hold any religious doctrine at all, and he appears to others to feel and to hold a whole circle of theological truths, which exist in his mind no otherwise than as a number of deductions.

Such are some of the lineaments of the ethical character, which the culti-vated intellect will form, apart from religious principle. They are seen within the pale of the Church and without it, in holy men, and in profligate; they form the *beau-ideal* of the world; they partly assist and partly distort the development of the Catholic. They may subserve the education of a St. Francis de Sales or a Cardinal Pole; they may be the limits of the virtue of a Shaftesbury or a Gibbon. Basil and Julian were fellow-students at the schools of Athens; and one became the Saint and Doctor of the Church, the other her scoffing and relentless foe.

C8. Thomas Carlyle "Labour" *Past and Present* (1843) Bk. III Ch. 11

[Thomas Carlyle (1795–1881), Scottish social historian and politi-cal philosopher. *Past and Present* compares social and spiritual con-ditions in contemporary industrial England unfavourably with those in a twelfth-century abbey. In this chapter, Carlyle preaches the "gos-pel of labour," condemning the idleness and dilettantism of the modern aristocracy.]

For there is a perennial nobleness, and even sacredness, in Work. Were he never so benighted, forgetful of his high calling, there is always hope in a man that actually and earnestly works: in Idleness alone is there perpetual despair. Work, never so Mammonish, mean, *is* in communication with Nature; the real desire to get Work done will itself lead one more and more to truth, to Nature's appointments and regulations, which are truth.

The latest Gospel in this world is, Know thy work and do it. "Know thyself": long enough has that poor "self" of thine tormented thee; thou wilt never get to "know" it, I believe! Think it not thy business, this of knowing thyself; thou art an unknowable individual: know what thou canst work at; and work at it, like a Hercules! That will be thy better plan.

It has been written, "an endless significance lies in Work"; a man perfects him-self by working. Foul jungles are cleared away, fair seedfields rise instead, and stately cities; and withal the man himself first ceases to be a jungle and foul unwhole-some desert thereby. Consider how, even in the meanest sorts of Labour, the whole soul of a man is composed into a kind of real harmony, the instant he sets himself to work! Doubt, Desire, Sorrow, Remorse, Indignation, Despair itself, all these like helldogs lie beleaguering the soul of the poor dayworker, as of every man: but he bends himself with free valour against his task, and all these are stilled, all these shrink murmuring far off into their caves. The man is now a man. The blessed glow of Labour in him, is it not as purifying fire, wherein all poison is burnt up, and of sour smoke itself there is made bright blessed flame!

Destiny, on the whole, has no other way of cultivating us. A formless Chaos, once set it *revolving*, grows round and ever rounder; ranges itself, by mere force of gravity, into strata, spherical courses; is no longer a Chaos, but a round compacted World. What would become of the Earth, did she cease to revolve? In the poor old Earth, so long as she revolves, all inequalities, irregularities disperse themselves; all irregularities are incessantly becoming regular. Hast thou looked on the Potter's wheel, — one of the venerablest objects; old as the Prophet Ezechiel and far older? Rude lumps of clay, how they spin themselves up, by mere quick whirling, into beautiful circular dishes. And fancy the most assiduous Potter, but without his wheel; reduced to make dishes, or rather amorphous botches, by mere kneading and baking! Even such a Potter were Destiny, with a human soul that would rest and lie at ease, that would not work and spin! Of an idle unrevolving man the kindest Destiny, like the most assiduous Potter without wheel, can bake and knead nothing other than a botch; let her spend on him what expensive colouring, what gilding and enamelling she will, he is but a botch. Not a dish; no, a bulging, kneaded, crooked, shambling, squint-cornered, amorphous botch, — a mere enamelled vessel of dishonour! Let the idle think of this.

Blessed is he who has found his work; let him ask no other blessedness. He has a work, a life-purpose; he has found it, and will follow it! How, as a free-flowing channel, dug, and torn by noble force through the sour mud-swamp of one's existence, like an ever-deepening river there, it runs and flows; — draining-off the sour festering water, gradually from the root of the remotest grass-blade; making, instead of pestilential swamp, a green fruitful meadow with its clear-flowing stream. How blessed for the meadow itself, let the stream and *its* value be great or small! Labour is Life: from the inmost heart of the Worker rises his god-given Force, the sacred celestial Life-essence breathed into him by Almighty God; from his inmost heart awakens him to all nobleness, — to all knowledge, "self-knowledge" and much else, so soon as Work fitly begins. Knowledge? The knowledge that will hold good in working, cleave thou to that; for Nature herself accredits that, says Yea to that. Properly thou hast no other knowledge but what thou hast got by working: the rest is yet all a hypothesis of knowledge; a thing to be argued of in schools, a thing floating in the clouds, in endless logic-vortices, till we try it and fix it. "Doubt, of whatever kind, can be ended by Action alone."

C9. Samuel Smiles "Character: The True Gentleman" *Self-Help* (1859) Ch. XIII

[Samuel Smiles (1812–1904), Scottish advocate of political and social reform and biographer of a number of industrial leaders. *Self-Help*, a sequence of biographical anecdotes in praise of thrift, industry, and self-improvement, is his best-known work. Here, he attempts, not entirely successfully, to define gentlemanliness as a moral quality independent of social status.]

The inbred politeness which springs from right-heartedness and kindly feelings is of no exclusive rank or station. The mechanic who works at the bench may possess it, as well as the clergyman or the peer. It is by no means a necessary condition of labour that it should, in any respect, be either rough or coarse. The politeness and refinement which distinguish all classes of the people in many continental countries show that those qualities might become ours too — as doubtless they will become with increased culture and more general social intercourse — without sacrificing any of our more genuine qualities as men. From the highest to the lowest, the richest to the poorest, to no rank or condition in life has nature denied her highest boon — the great heart. There never yet existed a gentleman but was lord of a great heart. And this may exhibit itself under the hodden grey of the peasant as well as under the laced coat of the noble. Robert Burns was once taken to task by a young Edinburgh blood, with whom he was walking, for recognizing an honest farmer in the open street. "Why you fantastic gomeral," exclaimed Burns, "it was not the great-coat, the scone bonnet, and the saunders-boot hose that I spoke to, but *the man* that was in them; and the man, sir, for true worth, would weigh down you and me, and ten more such, any day."

William and Charles Grant were the sons of a farmer in Inverness-shire, whom a sudden flood stripped of everything, even to the very soil which he tilled. The farmer and his sons, with the world before them where to choose, made their way southward in search of employment until they arrived in the neighbourhood of Bury, in Lancashire. From the crown of the hill near Walmersley they surveyed the wide extent of country which lay before them, the river Irwell making its circuitous course through the valley. They were utter strangers in the neighbourhood, and knew not which way to turn. To decide their course they put up a stick and agreed to pursue the direction in which it fell. Thus their decision was made, and they journeyed on accordingly until they reached the village of Ramsbotham, not far distant. They found employment in a print-work, in which William served his apprenticeship; and they commended themselves to their employers by their diligence, sobriety, and strict integrity. They plodded on, rising from one station to another, until at length the two men themselves became employers, and after many long years of industry, enterprise, and benevolence, they became rich, honoured, and respected by all who knew them. Their cotton-mills and print-works gave employment to a large population. Their well directed diligence made the valley teem with activity, joy, health, and opulence. Out of their abundant wealth they gave liberally to all worthy objects, erecting churches, founding schools, and in all ways promoting the well-being of the class of workingmen from which they had sprung. They afterwards erected, on the top of the hill above Walmersley, a lofty tower in commemoration of the early event in their history which had determined the place of their settlement. The brothers Grant became widely celebrated for their benevolence and their various goodness, and it is said that Mr. Dickens had them in his mind's eye when delineating the character of the brothers Cheeryble.

One amongst many anecdotes of a similar kind may be cited to show that the character was by no means exaggerated. A Manchester warehouseman published an exceedingly scurrilous pamphlet against the firm of Grant Brothers, holding up the elder partner to ridicule as "Billy Button". William was informed by some one of the nature of the pamphlet, and his observation was that the man would live to repent of it. "Oh!" said the libeller, when informed of the remark, "he thinks that some time or other I shall be in his debt; but I will take good care of that." It happens, however, that men in business do not always foresee who shall be their creditor, and it so turned out that the Grants' libeller became a bankrupt, and could not complete his certificate and begin business again without obtaining their signature. It seemed to him a hopeless case to call upon that firm for any favour, but the pressing claims of his family forced him to make the application. He appeared before the man whom he had ridiculed as "Billy Button" accordingly. He told his tale and produced his certificate. "You wrote a pamphlet against us once?" said Mr. Grant. The supplicant expected to see his document thrown into the fire; instead of which Grant signed the name of the firm, and thus completed the necessary certificate. "We make it a rule", said he, handing it back, "never to refuse signing the certificate of an honest tradesman, and we have never heard that you were anything else." The tears started into the man's eyes. "Ah," continued Mr. Grant, "you see my saying was true that you would live to repent writing that pamphlet. I did not mean it as a threat — I only meant that one day you would know us better, and repent having tried to injure us." "I do, I do, indeed, repent it." "Well, well, you know us now. But how do you get on — what are you going to do?" The poor man stated that he had friends who would assist him when his certificate was obtained. "But how are you off in the meantime?" The answer was, that, having given up every farthing to his creditors, he had been compelled to stint his family in even the common necessaries of life, that he might be enabled to pay for his certificate. "My good fellow, this will never do; your wife and family must not suffer in this way; be kind enough to take this ten-pound note to your wife from me: there, there, now — don't cry, it will be all well with you yet; keep up your spirits, set to work like a man, and you will raise your head among the best of us yet." The overpowered man endeavoured with choking utterance to express his gratitude, but in vain; and putting his hand to his face, he went out of the room sobbing like a child.

The True Gentleman is one whose nature has been fashioned after the highest models. It is a grand old name, that of Gentleman, and has been recognized as a rank and power in all stages of society. "The Gentleman is always the Gentleman,' said the old French General to his regiment of Scottish gentry at Rousillon, "and invariably proves himself such in need and in danger." To possess this character is a dignity of itself, commanding the instinctive homage of every generous mind, and those who will not bow to titular rank will yet do homage to the gentleman. His qualities depend not upon fashion or manners, but upon moral worth — not on personal possessions, but on personal qualities. The Psalmist briefly describes him as one "that walketh uprightly, and worketh righteously, and speaketh the truth in his heart".

[…]

Riches and rank have no necessary connexion with genuine gentlemanly qualities. The poor man may be a true gentleman — in spirit and in daily life. He may be honest, truthful, upright, polite, temperate, courageous, self-respecting, and self-helping — that is, be a true gentleman. The poor man with a rich spirit is in all ways superior to the rich man with a poor spirit. To borrow St. Paul's words, the former is as "having nothing, yet possessing all things", while the other, though possessing all things, has nothing. The former hopes everything, and fears nothing; the latter hopes nothing, and fears everything. Only the poor in spirit are really poor.

C10. Dinah Maria Mulock [Mrs. Craik] *John Halifax, Gentleman* (1856) Ch. 16.

[Dinah Maria Mulock (1826–87), known as Mrs. Craik after her marriage in 1864, a prolific writer of stories for both adults and children. *John Halifax, Gentleman*, her best-known work, is the story of a foundling with "a mind and breeding above his outward condition," who, through industry and integrity, plus an inner conviction that he was born the son of a gentleman, gradually rises to become an industrial magnate. His first step is to be befriended by the narrator, Phineas Fletcher, the weakling son of the owner of a tannery in the town of Norton Bury; his second is to fall in love with and eventually marry the aristocratic Miss Ursula March. The following scene occurs when difference of social class seems to make John Halifax's desire hopeless.]

It was winter-time. All the summer-days at Enderley were gone, "like a dream when one awaketh." Of her who had been the beautiful centre of the dream we had never heard nor spoken since.

John and I were walking together along the road towards the Mythe; we could just see the frosty sunset reflected on the windows of the Mythe House, now closed for months, the family being away. The meadows alongside, where the Avon had overflowed and frozen, were a popular skating-ground: and the road was alive with lookers-on of every class. All Norton Bury seemed abroad and half Norton Bury exchanged salutations with my companion, till I was amused to notice how large John's acquaintance had grown.

Among the rest there overtook us a little elderly lady, as prim and neat as an old maid, and as bright-looking as a happy matron. I saw at once who it was — Mrs. Jessop, our good doctor's new wife, and old love; whom he had lately brought home, to the great amazement and curiosity of Norton Bury.

"She seems to like you very much," I said; as, after a cordial greeting, which John returned rather formally, she trotted on.

"They were both very kind to me in London, last month, as I think I told you."

"Ay!" It was one of the few things he had mentioned about that same London journey, for he had grown into a painful habit of silence now. Yet I dreaded to break it, lest any wounds rankling beneath might thereby be caused to smart once more. And our love to one another was too faithful for a little reserve to have power to influence it in any way.

We came once more upon the old lady, watching the skaters. She again spoke to John, and looked at me with her keen, kind, blue eyes.

"I think I know who your friend is, though you do not introduce him." (John hastily performed that ceremony.) "Tom, and I" (how funny to hear her call our old bachelor doctor, 'Tom!') "were wondering what had become, of you, Mr. Halifax. Are you stronger than you were in London?"

"Was he ill in London, madam?"

"No, indeed, Phineas! Or only enough to win for me Dr. and Mrs. Jessop's great kindness."

"Which you have never come to thank us for. Never crossed our door-sill since we returned home! Does not your conscience sting you for your ingratitude?"

He coloured deeply.

"Indeed, Mrs. Jessop, it was not ingratitude."

"I know it; I believe it," she answered, with much kindness. "Tell me what it was."

He hesitated.

"You ought to believe the warm interest we both take in you. Tell me the plain truth."

"I will. It is that your kindness to me in London was no reason for my intruding on you at Norton Bury. It might not be agreeable for you and Dr. Jessop to have my acquaintance here. I am a tradesman."

The little old lady's eyes brightened into something beyond mere kindness as she looked at him.

"Mr. Halifax, I thank you for that 'plain truth.' Truth is always best. Now for mine. I had heard you were a tradesman; I found out for myself that you were a gentleman. I do not think the two facts incompatible, nor does my husband. We shall be happy to see you at our house at all times and under all circumstances."

She offered him her hand. John bowed over it in silence, but it was long since I had seen him look more pleased.

"Well, then, suppose you come this evening, both of you?"

We assented; and on her further invitation John and I and the little old lady walked on together.

I could not help watching Mrs. Jessop with some amusement. Norton Bury said she had been a poor governess all her days; but that hard life had left no shadow on the cheerful sunset of her existence now. It was a frank, bright, happy face, in spite of its wrinkles, and its somewhat hard Welsh features. And it was pleasant to hear her talk, even though she talked a good deal, and in a decidedly Welsh accent. Sometimes a tone or two reminded me slightly of—— Ay, it was easy to guess why John evidently liked the old lady.

"I know this road well, Mr. Halifax. Once I spent a summer here, with an old pupil, now grown up. I am going to-day to inquire about her at the Mythe House. The Brithwoods came home yesterday."

I was afraid to look at John. Even to me the news was startling. How I blessed Mrs. Jessop's innocent garrulousness.

"I hope they will remain here some time. I have a special interest in their stay. Not on Lady Caroline's account, though. She patronizes me very kindly; but I doubt if she ever forgets — what Tom says I am rather too proud of remembering — that I was the poor governess, Jane Cardigan."

"Jane Cardigan!" I exclaimed.

"What, Mr. Fletcher, you know my name! And really, now I think of it, I believe I have heard yours. Not from Tom, either. It couldn't possibly be — Yes! it certainly was — How strange! Did you ever hear tell of a Miss Ursula March?"

The live crimson rushed madly over John's face. Mrs. Jessop saw it; she could not but see. At first she looked astounded, then exceedingly grave.

I replied, "that we had had the honour of meeting Miss March last summer at Enderley."

"Yes," the old lady continued, somewhat formally. "Now I recollect, Miss March told me of the circumstance; of two gentlemen there, who were very kind to her when her father died; a Mr. Fletcher and his friend — was that Mr. Halifax?"

"It was," I answered: for John was speechless. Alas! I saw at once that all my hopes for him, all the design of my long silence on this subject, had been in vain. No, he had not forgotten her. It was not in his nature to forget.

Mrs. Jessop went on, still addressing herself to me.

"I am sure I ought, on behalf of my dear pupil, to offer you both my warmest thanks. Hers was a most trying position. She never told me of it till afterwards, poor child! I am thankful her trouble was softened to her by finding that *strangers*" (was it only my fancy that detected a slight stress on the word?) — "mere strangers could be at once so thoughtful and so kind."

"No one could be otherwise to Miss March. Is she well? Has she recovered from her trial?"

"I hope so. Happily, few sorrows, few feelings of any kind, take lasting hold at eighteen. She is a noble girl. She did her duty, and it was no light one, to him who is gone; now her life begins anew. It is sure to be prosperous — I trust it may be very happy. — Now I must bid you both good-bye."

She stopped at the gates of the Mythe House; great iron gates, a barrier as proud and impassable as that which in these times the rich shut against the poor, the aristocrat against the plebeian. John, glancing once up at them, hurriedly moved on.

"Stay; you will come and see us, Mr. Halifax? Promise!"

"If you wish it."

"And promise, too, that under all circumstances you will tell me, as you did this morning, the 'plain truth'? Yes, I see you will. Good-bye."

The iron gates closed upon her, and against us. We took our silent way up to the Mythe to our favourite stile. There we leaned — still in silence, for many minutes.

"The wind is keen, Phineas; you must be cold."

Now I could speak to him — could ask him to tell me of his pain.

"It is so long since you have told me anything. It might do you good."

"Nothing can do me good. Nothing but bearing it. My God! what have I not borne! Five whole months to be dying of thirst, and not a drop of water to cool my tongue."

He bared his head and throat to the cutting wind — his chest heaved, his eyes seemed in a flame.

"God forgive me! — but I sometimes think I would give myself body and soul to the devil for one glimpse of her face, one touch of her little hand."

I made no answer. What answer could be made to such words as these? I waited — all I could do — till the paroxysm had gone by. Then I hinted — as indeed seemed not unlikely — that he might see her soon.

"Yes, a great way off, like that cloud up there. But I want her near — close — in my home — at my heart; — Phineas," he gasped, "talk to me — about something else — anything. Don't let me think, or I shall go clean mad."

And indeed he looked so. I was terrified. So quiet as I had always seen him when we met, so steadily as he had pursued his daily duties; and with all this underneath — this torment, conflict, despair, of a young man's love. It must come out — better it should.

"And you have gone on working all this while?"

"I was obliged. Nothing but work kept me in my senses. Besides" — and he laughed hoarsely — "I was safest in the tan-yard. The thought of her could not come there. I was glad of it. I tried to be solely and altogether what I am — a 'prentice lad — a mere clown."

"Nay, that was wrong."

"Was it? Well, at last it struck me so. I thought I would be a gentleman again — just for a pretence, you know — a dream — a bit of the old dream back again. So I went to London."

"And met the Jessops there?"

"Yes; though I did not know she was Jane Cardigan. But I liked her — I liked my life with them. It was like breathing a higher air, the same air that—— Oh, Phineas, it was horrible to come back to my life here — to that accursed tan-yard!"

I said nothing.

"You see, now" — and that hard laugh smote me to the heart again — "you see, Phineas, how wicked I am growing. You will have to cut my acquaintance presently."

"Tell me the rest — I mean, the rest of your life in London," I said, after a pause. "Did you ever hear of her?"

"Of course not; though I knew she was there. I saw it in the 'Court Circular.' Fancy a lady, whose name was in the 'Court Circular,' being inquired after by a tanner's lad! But I wanted to look at her — any beggar might do that, you know — so I watched in streets and parks, by theatre-doors at night, and by church-doors on Sunday mornings; yet I never saw her once. Only think, not once for five whole months."

"John, how could you tell me you were happy?"

"I don't know. Perhaps because of my pride; perhaps because — Ah, don't look so wretched! Why did you let me say all this? You are too good for such as I."

Of course I took no heed of idle words like these. I let him stand there, leaning against the stile, now and then grasping it with his nervous, muscular hands, as if he would tear it down; then I said quietly —

"What do you intend to do?"

"Do? Nothing! What can I do? Though sometimes a score of wild plans rush into my mind such as to run away to the Indies, like that young Warren Hastings we were talking of, come back twenty years hence a nabob, and — marry her."

"Marry her," I repeated, mournfully.

"Ay, I could. That is what maddens me. If now she and I were to meet and stand together, equal man and woman, I could make her love me; I feel I could. Instead of crawling after her thus I would go boldly in at those very gates — do you think she is there?"

He trembled, actually trembled, at the mere thought of her being so near.

"Oh, it's hard, hard! I could despise myself. Why cannot I trust my manhood, my honest manhood that I was born with, go straight to her and tell her that I love her; that God meant her for me and me for her — true husband and true wife? Phineas, mark my words" — and, wild as his manner was, it had a certain force which sounded almost like prophecy — "if ever Ursula March marries she will be my wife — *my* wife!"

I could only murmur — "Heaven grant it!"

"But we shall never marry, neither one nor the other of us; we shall go on apart and alone till the next world. Perhaps she will come to me then: I may have her in my heart there."

John looked upward: there was in the west a broad, red frosty cloud, and just beyond it, nay, all but resting on it, the new moon — a little, wintry, soft new moon. A sight that might well have hushed the maddest storm of passion: it hushed his. He stood, still looking up, for many minutes, then his eyes closed, the lashes all wet.

"We'll never speak of this again, Phineas; I'll not grieve thee any more; I'll try and be a better brother to thee for the future. Come along!"

He drew my arm in his, and we went home.

[...]

C11. "An Old Boy" [Thomas Hughes]
Tom Brown's Schooldays (1857) Pt. II Ch. 6
"Fever in the School"

[Thomas Hughes (1822–96), barrister and Liberal M.P., much influenced by the Christian Socialism of F.D. Maurice. *Tom Brown's Schooldays* is an evocation of the Rugby School of his youth, and the spirit of its reformist headmaster Dr. Thomas Arnold. In this scene, from near the end of the novel, the muscular and sporty Tom is talking to Arthur, the physically weak but academically superior boy who he shares a study with, while the latter recovers from the fever which nearly killed him.]

The locking-up bell began to toll, and the two boys were silent, and listened to it. The sound soon carried Tom off to the river and the woods, and he began to go over in his mind the many occasions on which he had heard that toll coming faintly down the breeze, and had to pack his rod in a hurry and make a run for it, to get in before the gates were shut. He was roused with a start from his memories by Arthur's voice, gentle and weak from his late illness.

"Tom, will you be angry if I talk to you very seriously?"

"No, dear old boy, not I. But ain't you faint, Arthur, or ill? What can I get you? Don't say anything to hurt yourself now — you are very weak; let me come up again."

"No, no, I shan't hurt myself. I'd sooner speak to you now, if you don't mind. I've asked Mary to tell the Doctor that you are with me, so you needn't go down to calling-over; and I mayn't have another chance, for I shall most likely have to go home for change of air to get well, and mayn't come back this half."

"Oh, do you think you must go away before the end of the half? I'm so sorry. It's more than five weeks yet to the holidays, and all the fifth-form examination and half the cricket-matches to come yet. And what shall I do all that time alone in our study? Why, Arthur, it will be more than twelve weeks before I see you again. Oh, hang it, I can't stand that! Besides, who's to keep me up to working at the examination books? I shall come out bottom of the form, as sure as eggs is eggs."

Tom was rattling on, half in joke, half in earnest, for he wanted to get Arthur out of his serious vein, thinking it would do him harm; but Arthur broke in —

"Oh, please, Tom, stop, or you'll drive all I had to say out of my head. And I'm already horribly afraid I'm going to make you angry."

"Don't gammon, young 'un," rejoined Tom (the use of the old name, dear to him from old recollections, made Arthur start and smile, and feel quite happy); "you know you ain't afraid, and you've never made me angry since the first month we chummed together. Now I'm going to be quite sober for a quarter of an hour, which is more than I am once in a year; so make the most of it; heave ahead, and pitch into me right and left."

"Dear Tom, I ain't going to pitch into you," said Arthur, piteously; "and it seems so cocky in me to be advising you, who've been my backbone ever since I've been at Rugby, and have made the school a paradise to me. Ah, I see I shall never do it, unless I go head-over-heels at once, as you said when you taught me to swim. Tom, I want you to give up using vulgus-books and cribs."

Arthur sank back on to his pillow with a sigh, as if the effort had been great; but the worst was now over, and he looked straight at Tom, who was evidently taken aback. He leant his elbows on his knees, and stuck his hands into his hair, whistled a verse of "Billy Taylor," and then was quite silent for another minute. Not a shade crossed his face, but he was clearly puzzled. At last he looked up, and caught Arthur's anxious look, took his hand, and said simply —

"Why, young 'un?"

"Because you're the honestest boy in Rugby, and that ain't honest."

"I don't see that."

"What were you sent to Rugby for?"

"Well, I don't know exactly — nobody ever told me. I suppose because all boys are sent to a public school in England."

"But what do you think yourself? What do you want to do here, and to carry away?"

Tom thought a minute. "I want to be A 1 at cricket and football, and all the other games, and to make my hands keep my head against any fellow, lout or gentleman. I want to get into the sixth before I leave, and to please the Doctor; and I want to carry away just as much Latin and Greek as will take me through Oxford respectably. There now, young 'un, I never thought of it before, but that's pretty much about my figure. Ain't it all on the square? What have you got to say to that?"

"Why, that you are pretty sure to do all that you want, then."

"Well, I hope so. But you've forgot one thing, what I want to leave behind me. I want to leave behind me," said Tom, speaking slow, and looking much moved, "the name of a fellow who never bullied a little boy, or turned his back on a big one."

Arthur pressed his hand, and after a moment's silence went on: "You say, Tom, you want to please the Doctor. Now, do you want to please him by what he thinks you do, or by what you really do?"

"By what I really do, of course."

"Does he think you use cribs and vulgus-books?"

Tom felt at once that his flank was turned, but he couldn't give in. "He was at Winchester himself," said he; "he knows all about it."

"Yes, but does he think *you* use them? Do you think he approves of it?"

"You young villain!" said Tom, shaking his fist at Arthur, half vexed and half pleased, "I never think about it. Hang it — there, perhaps he don't. Well, I suppose he don't."

Arthur saw that he had got his point; he knew his friend well, and was wise in silence as in speech. He only said, "I would sooner have the doctor's good opinion of me as I really am, than any man's in the world."

After another minute, Tom began again: "Look here, young 'un, how on earth am I to get time to play the matches this half, if I give up cribs? We're in the middle of that long crabbed chorus in the Agamemnon; I can only just make head or tail of it with the crib. Then there's Pericles's speech coming on in Thucydides, and 'The Birds' to get up for the examination, besides the Tacitus." Tom groaned at the thought of his accumulated labours. "I say, young 'un, there's only five weeks or so left to holidays; mayn't I go on as usual for this half? I'll tell the Doctor about it some day, or you may."

Arthur looked out of the window; the twilight had come on, and all was silent. He repeated in a low voice, "In this thing the Lord pardon thy servant, that when my master goeth into the house of Rimmon to worship there, and he leaneth on my hand, and I bow down myself in the house of Rimmon, when I bow down myself in the house of Rimmon, the Lord pardon thy servant in this thing."

Not a word more was said on the subject, and the boys were again silent — one of those blessed, short silences in which the resolves which colour a life are so often taken.

D12. *Reports of the Assistant Commissioners Appointed to Inquire into the State of Popular Education in England* (1861).

[The following short extracts are from three volumes of regional reports into popular education throughout England, presented to Parliament by the Education Commission. They offer an insight into contemporary official attitudes towards spoken and written language, class, and education.]

12/1. From the Report of Mr. Cumin — The West of England (Vol. II pp. 83–4)

But the superiority of the inspected school-room over the private school-room is most apparent when the infant school is compared with the dames' school. I have already explained the vital importance of good schools for the infant poor, and the evidence in the Appendix will show that I have not been guilty of any exaggeration. It is quite true that there are some excellent dames' or women's schools. I have myself visited some of them. I have been told by dames themselves that although they were in the neighbourhood of good public infant schools, their numbers had in no respect diminished; and I readily understand why parents prefer to send their children to the best sort of dames' school rather than to the public infant school. But these are the exception. In every case the dame carries on her school in the same house in which she lives, — in Plymouth and Devonport the school-room is the same as that in which she "and her family live, and do their household work by day, as well as sleep by night." One witness says, and my own observation confirms the truth of the picture: "The dames most commonly have only one room for every purpose, and their scholars may often be seen sitting round the sides of a four-post bed, on low forms, the sides of the bed forming a back to the seat; sometimes on the sides of the bed. When the children are present the atmosphere is always oppressive to me, and often, if I stay in it for ten minutes without opening the window, it makes me sick." Another witness says: "They (the dames) obtain numbers of young children, whose health, as well as that of the teachers, suffers from the confinement in crowded and ill-ventilated rooms. A female teacher lately came before me whose health had been much impaired, if not ruined, from this cause, and who was obliged to relinquish her occupation." Moreover, the room is often so small that the children cannot stand in a semicircle round the teacher. Indeed, I have seen the children as closely packed as birds in a nest, and tumbling over each other like puppies in a kennel. In some cases cooking of various sorts goes on, so that the atmosphere, besides being polluted by a crowd, is further contaminated by fried bacon or potatoes. Again, only in a few cases are the children provided with books, and those they do have contain only the alphabet. But in the public infant schools the picture is very different. The rooms are generally large and well ventilated; the young children are furnished with every convenience, and books, pictures, and even games are supplied in abundance.

12/2. From Mr. Foster's Report — Cumberland and Durham (Vol. III pp. 338–40)

I met with very few day schools indeed in which it seemed that the words read or repeated from a book, even with apparent ease, conveyed any idea to the mind of the pupil. For instance, a smart little boy read the first verse of the ninth chapter of St. Matthew's Gospel, "And he entered into a ship, and passed over, and came into his own city." I asked, "What did he enter into?" "Don't know, thank you, Sir," replied the boy politely. "Read it again. Now what did he come into?" "Don't know, thank you, Sir." In another school, a girl of about 13 years of age was directed to "say her geography" to me, and after she had repeated the boundaries of several countries, I asked, "What is a boundary?' "It's a year's wages." My question had suggested to her mind the terms on which the pitmen are in some collieries *bound* for a year to their employment. Doubtless she did not dream of its connexion with the lesson she had just repeated. These are fair specimens of the usual results of any effort to elicit the children's apprehension of what they were learning — either total silence or an answer perfectly irrelevant. The truth which has been forced upon me in a way it never was before is, that the language of books is an unknown tongue to the children of the illiterate, especially in remote situations. It is utterly unlike their vernacular dialect, both in its vocabulary and construction, and, perhaps, not less unintelligible than Latin generally was to the vulgar in the middle ages. The gulf between is the more impassable wherever, as in the collier villages, there is little or no intercourse with persons of the middle class. Only a very small proportion of the children seem to attain any adequate understanding of the language of books during their school life, and whether they do afterwards or not depends much upon the circumstances of their lot. A maidservant told me she could read and write, adding, complacently, that she had been at a *natural* school for six years, "at least," she added, apprehending she had made some mistake, "it was a kind of sort of natural school." That which schoolmasters proudly call intellectual training is nothing else than an attempt to familiarize the pupils with the use of literary language, and thus to supply them with a key to all the stores of knowledge contained in books. The other type of education would be realized if knowledge, secular and religious, were conveyed to the mind in such language as the children already understand. I cannot say that I have seen either of these systems carried out with any distinctness; that is, I have seen no systematic effort to put children in possession of the language of books apart from the immediate design of conveying the knowledge embodied in that language. The teaching is at best as though one put a Latin geography into a boy's hand and made him understand it, so that he was acquiring Latin and geography at the same time, but each, of course, less perfectly than if it had been the sole object of study for the time being. Still less have I observed any considerable effort to convey knowledge directly in terms well understood, and apart from the literary language of a text book. The choice lies for the most part between knowledge embodied in formularies which are in an unknown tongue, and are committed to memory without an idea attached to them on the one hand; and, on the other, similar formularies interpreted with a view to effecting for the knowledge an entrance into the understanding. In other words, I have seen little of what is called intellectual training apart from the immediate object of imparting information; and still less of information really communicated to the mind except through the process which is called intellectual training. But I believe the latter prevails to a great extent in the Nonconformist Sunday schools, and probably the chief secret of their superior popularity and success lies in the fact that they thus attend to one thing at a time. In one of the best Sunday schools I visited, where, besides the perfection of good order, there was an amount of Biblical knowledge truly surprising, the teachers conducted their earnest catechising, and the pupils their eager and intelligent answering, in one of the most uncouth dialects it was ever my lot to hear. These teachers are plain earnest members of the congregation, very little, if at all above the children in social position, and using their own dialect for the inculcation of sacred truth. I know not whether it is from any deliberate recognition of this principle, but the fact is so, that whereas the Church Sunday schools are very generally supplied with volunteers from the families of the clergyman or the squire, it is a thing very unusual among the Dissenters for the wealthy and educated, where there are such, to engage in this work; they leave it to the humbler members. To a similar cause may probably be attributed, at least in part, the superior success which has always been deemed to attend Scotch education. The better classes in Scotland all understand the lingua of the people, and use it in their intercourse with them. A Scotch parish schoolmaster employs an English text book just as, fifty years ago, "Ruddiman's Latin Grammar" was committed and repeated in Latin; but if he attempts familiar explanation or extempore teaching of any kind, he speaks as broad Scotch as is necessary for being understood. It well accords with this to mention that, with a single exception, the most successful teachers I found in the north were Scotchmen by birth, or trained in Glasgow; and for this I could assign no reason so probable as the fact, that there they must have learned the dialect of the people, and acquired more or less the habit of using it when necessary. By this they can gain an access to the minds of children in the north of England which is impossible to a teacher of mere metropolitan education. I could myself have held no free or satisfactory intercourse with the labouring classes in my district, had I not been familiar with Lowland Scotch.

12/3. From the Report of J.S. Winder — Rochdale and Bradford, as examples of the manufacturing districts of Lancashire and Yorkshire (Vol II p. 175).

Up to a short time ago hardly any means of public instruction existed except Sunday schools, and the habits of the people were in the highest degree uncivilized and rude. Even now, language and manners, particularly in the remoter corners, are strikingly blunt and abrupt, and many primitive customs, amongst others, that of dispensing with surnames, still linger in parts of the district. Milnrow, the recognized metropolis and classic centre of the Lancashire dialect, where the true idiom is said to be still preserved in great purity, is within two miles of the town [Rochdale], and a stranger finds no little difficulty in following a dialogue in the broad unadulterated provincialism which still holds its ground [...]

12/4. From the Report of Mr. Wilkinson — London (Vol. II p. 399).

Had a stranger accompanied me on my Sunday morning walks through some of the worst haunts of St. George-in-the-East, he would indeed have found it difficult to imagine that a ray of educational improvement had penetrated into those black regions of vice and brutality; not so the policeman who accompanied me; he had known the classical district of Bluegate Fields for 30 years; his proof of the great practical improvement resulting from education was the fact that we were both walking there in safety and without insult. In the most wretched of these foul alleys, from a group of drunken men and vicious women, would start out the little forms of bright-eyed and smartly dressed girls on their way to the Sunday schools; and even the foul-mouthed and brutalized ruffians looked at them with a kindly eye, and an apparent consciousness that they belonged to a different race, and that the generation of savages was passing away.

So, in conversation with the more intelligent among the old inmates of workhouses in all my three parishes, I have received such descriptions of the old times, contrasted with the present, as have left no doubt in my mind of the beneficial influence which education, imperfect as it yet is, has exerted.

Appendix D. On Crime & Punishment

D1. Mrs. Trimmer *The Charity School Spelling Book* (1818) Pt. II pp. 17–18.

[Typical of early nineteenth-century spelling primers, this spelling book progressed from the alphabet, through graded spelling lessons, to short anecdotes. Like the one cited below, No. 24 in the section "Lessons Consisting of Words not Exceeding Two Syllables," these were generally of an improving nature.]

Philip Howlet was a sharp lad, very quick at his learning. Ralph Howard was as sharp as he, but he made nothing out at his book, because he would not apply himself as he ought to do. Philip would learn a whole page of spelling, while Ralph got a dozen words. Philip took delight in reading, Ralph hated the sight of a book; all his delight was play. Philip minded what his parents and teachers said to him: Ralph scorned all good advice. Philip and Ralph were both put out 'prentice about the same time; one to a joiner, the other to a turner. Philip was a good 'prentice; and when his time was out, worked for the master he served his time with, who gave him good wages. Ralph was a very bad 'prentice, and ran away before his time was half out, but his master had him taken up, and he was sent to Bridewell; after that he went back to his master, but he grew worse and worse so his master gave him the rest of the time he had to serve, rather than be troubled with such a bad 'prentice. Then Ralph got among sots and drunkards; and at last became a thief, and was taken up and hanged.

D2. Charles Dickens "Criminal Courts" *Sketches by Boz* (1839; revised 1850) XXIV.

[Originally appeared as "The Old Bailey" in the *Morning Chronicle* of 23 October 1834, one of five "Street Sketches." (On the process of revision, see Butt Ch. 2) The sketch is composed of four parts, each in turn exhibiting a remarkably different, but nevertheless characteristic, tone and attitude towards crime and punishment: the fearsome childhood memories of Newgate, the sentimentality of the story of the wayward son, the melodramatic account of the guilty verdict in the Old Court, and the ironic description of incorrigible juvenile depravity in the New Court.]

We shall never forget the mingled feelings of awe and respect with which we used to gaze on the exterior of Newgate in our school-boy days. How dreadful its rough heavy walls, and low massive doors, appeared to us — the latter looking as if they were made for the express purpose of letting people in, and never letting them out again. Then the fetters over the debtors' door, which we used to think were a *bona fide* set of irons, just hung up there for convenience' sake, ready to be taken down at a moment's notice, and riveted on the limbs of some refractory felon! We were never tired of wondering how the hackney coachmen on the opposite stand could cut jokes in the presence of such horrors, and drink pots of half-and-half so near the last drop.

Often have we strayed here, in session-time, to catch a glimpse of the whipping-place, and that dark building on one side of the yard, in which is kept the gibbet with all its dreadful apparatus, and on the door of which we half expected to see a brass plate, with the inscription "Mr. Ketch;" for we never imagined that the distinguished functionary could by possibility live anywhere else! The days of these childish dreams have passed away, and with them many other boyish ideas of a gayer nature. But we still retain so much of our original feeling, that to this hour we never pass the building without something like a shudder.

What London pedestrian is there who has not, at some time or other, cast a hurried glance through the wicket at which prisoners are admitted into this gloomy mansion, and surveyed the few objects he could discern with an indescribable feeling of curiosity? The thick door, plated with iron and mounted with spikes, just low enough to enable you to see, leaning over them, an ill-looking fellow, in a broad-brimmed hat, Belcher handkerchief, and top-boots: with a brown coat, something between a great-coat and a "sporting" jacket, on his back, and an immense key in his left hand. Perhaps you are lucky enough to pass just as the gate is being opened; then you see, on the other side of the lodge, another gate, the image of its predecessor, and two or three more turnkeys, who look like multiplications of the first one, seated round a fire which just lights up the whitewashed apartment sufficiently to enable you to catch a hasty glimpse of these different objects. We have a great respect for Mrs. Fry, but she certainly ought to have written more romances than Mrs. Radcliffe.

We were walking leisurely down the Old Bailey, some time ago, when, as we passed this identical gate, it was opened by the officiating turnkey. We turned quickly round, as a matter of course, and saw two persons descending the steps. We could not help stopping and observing them.

They were an elderly woman of decent appearance, though evidently poor, and a boy of about fourteen or fifteen. The woman was crying bitterly; she carried a small bundle in her hand, and the boy followed at a short distance behind her. Their little history was obvious. The boy was her son, to whose early comfort she had, perhaps, sacrificed her own — for whose sake she had borne misery without repining, and poverty without a murmur — looking steadily forward to the time when he, who had so long witnessed her struggles for himself, might be enabled to make some exertions for their joint support. He had formed dissolute connections; idleness had led to crime; and he had been committed to take his trial for some petty theft. He had been long in prison, and, after receiving some trifling additional punishment, had been ordered to be discharged that morning. It was his first offence, and his poor old mother, still hoping to reclaim him, had been waiting at the gate to implore him to return home.

We cannot forget the boy; he descended the steps with a dogged look, shaking his head with an air of bravado and obstinate determination. They walked a few paces, and paused. The woman put her hand upon his shoulder in an agony of entreaty, and the boy sullenly raised his head as if in refusal. It was a brilliant morning, and every object looked fresh and happy in the broad, gay sun-light; he gazed round him for a few moments, bewildered with the brightness of the scene, for it was long since he had beheld anything save the gloomy walls of a prison. Perhaps the wretchedness of his mother made some impression on the boy's heart; perhaps some undefined recollection of the time when he was a happy child, and she his only friend and best companion, crowded on him — he burst into tears; and covering his face with one hand, and hurriedly placing the other in his mother's, walked away with her.

Curiosity has occasionally led us into both Courts at the Old Bailey. Nothing is so likely to strike the person who enters them for the first time as the calm indifference with which the proceedings are conducted; every trial seems a mere matter of business. There is a great deal of form, but no compassion; considerable interest, but no sympathy. Take the Old Court, for example. There sit the Judges, with whose great dignity everybody is acquainted, and of whom, therefore, we need say no more. Then, there is the Lord Mayor in the centre, looking as cool as a Lord Mayor *can* look, with an immense *bouquet* before him, and habited in all the splendour of his office. Then, there are the Sheriffs, who are almost as dignified as the Lord Mayor himself; and the Barristers, who are quite dignified enough in their own opinion; and the spectators, who, having paid for their admission, look upon the whole scene as if it were got up especially for their amusement. Look upon the whole group in the body of the Court — some wholly engrossed in the morning papers, others carelessly conversing in low whispers, and others, again, quietly dozing away an hour — and you can scarcely believe that the result of the trial is a matter of life or death to one wretched being present. But turn your eyes to the dock; watch the prisoner attentively for a few moments; and the fact is before you, in all its painful reality. Mark how restlessly he has been engaged, for the last ten minutes, in forming all sorts of fantastic figures with the herbs which are strewed upon the ledge before him; observe the ashy paleness of his face when a particular witness appears, and how he changes his position, and wipes his clammy forehead and feverish hands, when the case for the prosecution is closed, as if it were a relief to him to feel that the jury knew the worst.

The defence is concluded; the judge proceeds to sum up the evidence; and the prisoner watches the countenances of the jury, as a dying man, clinging to life to the very last, vainly looks in the face of his physician for a slight ray of hope. They turn round to consult; you can almost hear the man's heart beat, as he bites the stalk of rosemary, with a desperate effort to appear composed. They resume their places — a dead silence prevails as the foreman delivers in the verdict — "Guilty!" A shriek bursts from a female in the gallery; the prisoner casts one look at the quarter from whence the noise proceeded; and is immediately hurried from the dock by the gaoler. The clerk directs one of the officers of the Court to "take the woman out," and fresh business is proceeded with, as if nothing had occurred.

No imaginary contrast to a case like this could be as complete as that which is constantly presented in the New Court, the gravity of which is frequently disturbed, in no small degree, by the cunning and pertinacity of juvenile offenders. A boy of thirteen is tried, say, for picking the pocket of some subject of her Majesty, and the offence is about as clearly proved as an offence can be. He is called upon for his defence, and contents himself with a little declamation about the jurymen and his country — asserts that all the witnesses have committed perjury, and hints that the police force generally have entered into a conspiracy "again" him. However probable this statement may be, it fails to convince the Court, and some such scene as the following then takes place:

> *Court:* Have you any witnesses to speak to your character, boy?
> *Boy:* Yes, my Lord; fifteen gen'l'm'n is a vaten outside, and vos a vaten all day yesterday, vich they told me the night afore my trial vos a-comin' on.
> *Court:* Inquire for these witnesses.

Here a stout beadle runs out, and vociferates for the witnesses at the very top of his voice; for you hear his cry grow fainter and fainter as he descends the steps into the courtyard below. After an absence of five minutes, he returns, very warm and hoarse, and informs the Court of what it knew perfectly well before — namely, that there are no such witnesses in attendance. Hereupon the boy sets up a most awful howling; screws the lower part of the palms of his hands into the corners of his eyes; and endeavours to look the picture of injured innocence. The jury at once find him "guilty," and his endeavours to squeeze out a tear or two are redoubled. The governor of the gaol then states, in reply to an inquiry from the bench, that the prisoner has been under his care twice before. This the urchin resolutely denies in some such terms as — "S'elp me, gen'l'm'n, I never vos in trouble afore — indeed, my Lord, I never vos. It's all a howen to my having a twin brother, vich has wrongfully got into trouble, and vich is so exactly like me, that, no vun ever knows the difference atween us."

This representation, like the defence, fails in producing the desired effect, and the boy is sentenced, perhaps, to seven years' transportation. Finding it impossible to excite compassion, he gives vent to his feelings in an imprecation bearing reference to the eyes of "old big vig!" and, as he declines to take the trouble of walking from the dock, is forthwith carried out, congratulating himself on having succeeded in giving everybody as much trouble as possible.

D3. Charles Dickens "A Visit to Newgate" *Sketches by Boz* (1839; revised 1850) XXV.

[Dickens first visited Newgate Prison in November 1835, to collect material for this sketch, written especially for the First Series of *Sketches by Boz*, issued in early 1836. (On the process of revision, again see Butt Ch. 2) The central section, describing the apartments devoted to women, boys, and "respectable" prisoners, plus the prison chapel and press yard, is omitted. It is interesting to compare this description of the condemned cell with the more heightened account of Fagin's last night alive in the penultimate chapter of *Oliver Twist* (1838).]

"The force of habit" is a trite phrase in everybody's mouth; and it is not a little remarkable that those who use it most, as applied to others, unconsciously afford in their own persons singular examples of the power which habit and custom exercise over the minds of men, and of the little reflection they are apt to bestow on subjects with which every day's experience has rendered them familiar. If Bedlam could be suddenly removed like another Aladdin's palace, and set down on the space now occupied by Newgate, scarcely one man out of a hundred, whose road to business every morning lies through Newgate Street or the Old Bailey, would pass the building without bestowing a hasty glance on its small, grated windows, and a transient thought upon the condition of the unhappy beings immured in its dismal cells; and yet these same men, day by day, and hour by hour, pass and repass this gloomy depository of the guilt and misery of London, in one perpetual stream of life and bustle, utterly unmindful of the throng of wretched creatures pent up within it — nay, not even knowing, or, if they do, not heeding, the fact that, as they pass one particular angle of the massive wall with a light laugh or a merry whistle, they stand within one yard of a fellow-creature, bound and helpless, whose hours are numbered, from whom the last feeble ray of hope has fled for ever, and whose miserable career will shortly terminate in a violent and shameful death. Contact with death, even in its least terrible shape, is solemn and appalling. How much more awful is it to reflect on this near vicinity to the dying — to men in full health and vigour, in the flower of youth or the prime of life, with all their faculties and perceptions as acute and perfect as your own; but dying, nevertheless — dying as surely — with the hand of death imprinted upon them as indelibly — as if mortal disease had wasted their frames to shadows, and corruption had already begun!

It was with some such thoughts as these that we determined, not many weeks since, to visit the interior of Newgate — in an amateur capacity, of course; and, having carried our intention into effect, we proceed to lay its results before our readers, in the hope — founded more upon the nature of the subject than on any presumptuous confidence in our own descriptive powers — that this paper may not be found wholly devoid of interest. We have only to premise, that we do not intend to fatigue the reader with any statistical accounts of the prison; they will be found at length in numerous reports of numerous committees, and a variety of authorities of equal weight. We took no notes, made no memoranda, measured none of the yards, ascertained the exact number of inches in no particular room: are unable even to report of how many apartments the gaol is composed.

We saw the prison, and saw the prisoners; and what we did see, and what we thought, we will tell at once in our own way.

Having delivered our credentials to the servant who answered our knock at the door of the governor's house, we were ushered into the "office;" a little room, on the right-hand side as you enter, with two windows looking into the Old Bailey: fitted up like an ordinary attorney's office, or merchant's counting-house, with the usual fixtures — a wainscoted partition, a shelf or two, a desk, a couple of stools, a pair of clerks, an almanac, a clock, and a few maps. After a little delay, occasioned by sending into the interior of the prison for the officer whose duty it was to conduct us, that functionary arrived; a respectable-looking man of about two or three and fifty, in a broad-brimmed hat and full suit of black, who, but for his keys, would have looked quite as much like a clergyman as a turnkey. We were disappointed; he had not even top-boots on. Following our conductor by a door opposite to that at which we had entered, we arrived at a small room, without any other furniture than a little desk, with a book for visitors' autographs, and a shelf, on which were a few boxes for papers, and casts of the heads and faces of the two notorious murderers, Bishop and Williams; the former, in particular, exhibiting a style of head and set of features which might have afforded sufficient moral grounds for his instant execution at any time, even had there been no other evidence against him. Leaving this room also by an opposite door, we found ourself in the lodge which opens on the Old Bailey; one side of which is plentifully garnished with a choice collection of heavy sets of irons, including those worn by the redoubtable Jack Sheppard — genuine; and those *said* to have been graced by the sturdy limbs of the no less celebrated Dick Turpin — doubtful. From this lodge, a heavy oaken gate, bound with iron, studded with nails of the same material, and guarded by another turnkey, opens on a few steps, if we remember right, which terminate in a narrow and dismal stone passage, running parallel with the Old Bailey, and leading to the different yards, through a number of tortuous and intricate windings, guarded in their turn by huge gates and gratings, whose appearance is sufficient to dispel at once the slightest hope of escape that any newcomer may have entertained; and the very recollection of which, on eventually traversing the place again, involves one in a maze of confusion.

[...]

A few paces up the yard, and forming a continuation of the building, in which are the two rooms we have just quitted, lie the condemned cells. The entrance is by a narrow and obscure staircase leading to a dark passage, in which a charcoal stove casts a lurid tint over the objects in its immediate vicinity, and diffuses something like warmth around. From the left-hand side of this passage, the massive door of every cell on the story opens; and from it alone can they be approached. There are three of these passages, and three of these ranges of cells, one above the other; but in size, furniture, and appearance they are all precisely alike. Prior to the recorder's report being made, all the prisoners under sentence of death are removed from the day-room at five o'clock in the afternoon, and locked up in these cells, where they are allowed a candle until ten o'clock; and here they remain until seven next morning. When the warrant for a prisoner's execution arrives, he is removed to the cells, and confined in one of them until he leaves it for the scaffold. He is at liberty to walk in the yard; but, both in his walks and in his cell, he is constantly attended by a turnkey, who never leaves him on any pretence.

We entered the first cell. It was a stone dungeon, eight feet long by six wide, with a bench at the upper end, under which were a common rug, a Bible, and Prayer-book. An iron candlestick was fixed into the wall at the side; and a small high window in the back admitted as much air and light as could struggle in between a double row of heavy, crossed iron bars. It contained no other furniture of any description.

Conceive the situation of a man spending his last night on earth in this cell.

Buoyed up with some vague and undefined hope of reprieve, he knew not why — indulging in some wild and visionary idea of escaping, he knew not how — hour after hour of the three preceding days allowed him for preparation has fled with a speed which no man living would deem possible, for none but this dying man can know. He has wearied his friends with entreaties, exhausted the attendants with importunities, neglected in his feverish restlessness the timely warnings of his spiritual consoler; and, now that the illusion is at last dispelled, now that eternity is before him and guilt behind, now that his fears of death amount almost to madness, and an overwhelming sense of his helpless, hopeless state rushes upon him, he is lost and stupefied, and has neither thoughts to turn to, nor power to call upon, the Almighty Being from whom alone he can seek mercy and forgiveness, and before whom his repentance can alone avail. Hours have glided by, and still he sits upon the same stone bench with folded arms, heedless alike of the fast decreasing time before him, and the urgent entreaties of the good man at his side. The feeble light is wasting gradually, and the death-like stillness of the street without, broken only by the rumbling of some passing vehicle which echoes mournfully through the empty yards, warns him that the night is waning fast away. The deep bell of St. Paul's strikes — one! He heard it; it has roused him. Seven hours left! He paces the narrow limits of his cell with rapid strides, cold drops of terror starting on his forehead, and every muscle of his frame quivering with agony. Seven hours! He suffers himself to be led to his seat, mechanically takes the Bible which is placed in his hand, and tries to read and listen. No: his thoughts will wander. The book is torn and soiled by use — and like the book he read his lesson in, at school, just forty years ago! He has never bestowed a thought upon it, perhaps, since he left it as a child: and yet the place, the time, the room — nay, the very boys he played with, crowd as vividly before him as if they were scenes of yesterday; and some forgotten phrase, some childish word, rings in his ears like the echo of one uttered but a minute since. The voice of the clergyman recalls him to himself. He is reading from its sacred book its solemn promises of pardon for repentance, and its awful denunciation of obdurate men. He falls upon his knees and clasps his hands to pray. Hush! what sound was that? He starts upon his feet. It cannot be two yet. Hark! Two quarters have struck; — the third — the fourth. It is! Six hours left. Tell him not of repentance! Six hours' repentance for eight times six years of guilt and sin. He buries his face in his hands, and throws himself on the bench.

Worn with watching and excitement, he sleeps, and the same unsettled state of mind pursues him in his dreams. An insupportable load is taken from his breast; he is walking with his wife in a pleasant field, with the bright sky above them, and a fresh and boundless prospect on every side — how different from the stone walls of Newgate! She is looking — not as she did when he saw her for the last time in that dreadful place, but as she used when he loved her — long, long ago, before misery and ill-treatment had altered her looks, and vice had changed his nature, and she is leaning upon his arm, and looking up into his face with tenderness and affection — and he does *not* strike her now, nor rudely shake her from him. And oh! how glad he is to tell her all he had forgotten in that last hurried interview, and to fall on his knees before her, and fervently beseech her pardon for all the unkindness and cruelty that wasted her form and broke her heart! The scene suddenly changes. He is on his trial again: there are the judge and jury, and prosecutors, and witnesses, just as they were before. How full the Court is — what a sea of heads — with a gallows, too, and a scaffold — and how all those people stare at *him*! Verdict, "Guilty." No matter; he will escape.

The night is dark and cold, the gates have been left open, and in an instant he is in the street, flying from the scene of his imprisonment like the wind. The streets are cleared, the open fields are gained, and the broad wide country lies before him. Onward he dashes in the midst of darkness, over hedge and ditch, through mud and pool, bounding from spot to spot with a speed and lightness astonishing even to himself. At length he pauses; he must be safe from pursuit now; he will stretch himself on that bank, and sleep till sunrise.

A period of unconsciousness succeeds. He wakes, cold and wretched. The dull grey light of morning is stealing into the cell, and falls upon the form of the attendant turnkey. Confused by his dreams, he starts from his uneasy bed in momentary uncertainty. It is but momentary. Every object in the narrow cell is too frightfully real to admit of doubt or mistake. He is the condemned felon again, guilty and despairing; and in two hours more will be dead.

D4. *Report from the Select Committee on Transportation (1838) pp. 2–10 & 17–8.*

[A parliamentary committee set up by the Whig administration under the chairmanship of the young Sir William Molesworth, with Lord John Russell, the Home Secretary, and Lord Grey the Colonial Under-Secretary, as prominent members. Its remit was "to inquire into the System of Transportation, its Efficacy as a punishment, its Influence on the Moral State of Society in the Penal Colonies, and how far it is susceptible of Improvement." Its conclusions were resoundingly negative and heralded a major shift from a penal policy based on transportation to distant colonies to one based on model penitentiaries on British soil. Only the early sections of the Report focusing on the Australian colonies are reproduced here. (References omitted.)]

[...]

The present condition of a transported felon is mainly determined by the 5th Geo. 4, c. 84, the Transportation Act, which authorizes Her Majesty in Council "to appoint any place or places beyond the seas, either within or without Her Majesty's dominions," to which offenders so sentenced shall be conveyed; the order for their removal must be given by one of the principal Secretaries of State. The places so appointed are, the two Australian colonies of New South Wales and Van Diemen's Land, the small volcanic island, called Norfolk Island, situated about 1,000 miles from the eastern shores of Australia, and Bermuda. Seventy-five thousand two hundred convicts have been transported to New South Wales since its settlement in 1787; on the average of the last five years 3,544 offenders have been annually sent there; and the whole convict population of the colony in 1836, amounted to 25,254 men, and 2,577 women; in all, 27,831. 27,759 convicts have been sent to Van Diemen's Land since the year 1817; the number annually transported there on the average of the last five years is 2,078; and the convict population in 1835 was 14,914 men and 2,054 women; in all, 16,968. At Norfolk Island the number of convicts, most of whom had been re-transported for offences committed in New South Wales, was, in 1837, above 1,200, and at Bermuda the number of convicts does not exceed 900.

The 5 Geo. 4, c. 84, likewise gives to the governor of a penal colony a property in the services of a transported offender for the period of his sentence, and authorizes the governor to assign over such offender to any other person. The only other imperial statutes with regard to transportation, which ought to be mentioned are, the 30 Geo. 3, c. 47, which enables Her Majesty to authorize the governor of a penal colony to remit, absolutely or conditionally, a part or the whole of the sentences of convicts; the 9 Geo. 4, c. 83, which empowers the governor to grant a temporary or partial remission of sentence; and the 2 & 3 Will. 4, c. 62, which limits the power of the governor in this respect. No reference need be made to other statutes, which merely determine for what crimes Transportation is the punishment. In New South Wales and Van Diemen's Land convicts are subjected to a variety of colonial laws, framed by the local Legislatures, established under the New South Wales Act, 9 Geo. 4, c. 83.

After sentence of transportation has been passed, convicts are sent to the hulks or gaols, where they remain till the period of their departure arrives. On board convict vessels the convicts are under the sole control of the surgeon-superintendent, who is furnished with instructions, as to his conduct, from the Admiralty.

The precautions, which have been taken against disease, and the better discipline now preserved in these ships, have applied an effectual remedy to the physical evils of the long voyage to Australia, and prevented the mortality amongst the prisoners, which prevailed to a fearful extent during the earlier periods of trans-portation. Little diminution, however, has taken place in those moral evils, which seem to be the necessary consequences of the close contact and communication between so many criminals, both during the period of confinement previous to embarkation, and during the weariness of a long voyage.

As soon as a convict vessel reaches its place of destination, a report is made by the surgeon-superintendent to the governor. A day is then appointed for the co-lonial secretary, or for his deputy, to go on board, to muster the convicts, and to hear their complaints if they have any to make. The male convicts are, subsequently, removed to the convict barracks; the females to the penitentiaries. In New South Wales, however, regulations have lately been established, by which, in most cases, female convicts are enabled to proceed at once from the ship to private service. It is the duty of an officer, called the principal superintendent of convicts, to classify the newly-arrived convicts; the greater portion of whom are distributed amongst the settlers as assigned servants; the remainder are either retained in the employ-ment of the government, or some few of them are sent to the penal settlements.

In 1836 the number of assigned convicts in Van Diemen's Land was 6,475; in New South Wales in 1835 the number was 20,207. In the earlier periods of the colony of New South Wales the supply of convicts so much exceeded the de-mand for their services by the settlers, that the Government used to grant certain indulgences to those settlers, who were willing to maintain convicts. More re-cently, the demand has exceeded the supply; the obtaining convict labourers has become, therefore, to a certain degree a matter of favour, which has given rise to complaints of abuse in the distribution, especially of the more valuable convicts. All applications for convicts are now made to an officer, called the commissioner for the assignment of convict servants, who is guided in his distribution of them by certain Government regulations. Settlers, to whom convicts are assigned, are bound to send for them within a certain period of time and to pay the sum of 1*l.* a head for the clothing and bedding of each assigned convict. An assigned convict is entitled to a fixed amount of food and clothing, consisting, in New South Wales, of 12 lbs. of wheat, or of an equivalent in flour and maize meal, 7 lbs. of mutton or beef, or 4½ lbs. of salt pork, 2 oz. of salt, and 2 oz. of soap weekly; two frocks or jackets, three shirts, two pair of trousers, three pair of shoes, and a hat or a cap, annually. Each man is likewise supplied with one good blanket, and a palliasse or wool mattress, which are considered the property of the master. Any articles, which the master may supply beyond these, are voluntary indulgences. The allowance in

Van Diemen's Land differs in some particulars, and on the whole is more liberal.

Male assigned convicts may be classed under the various heads of field labourers, domestic servants, and mechanics: the services of the last class being of more value than those of the two former, are estimated in assignment as equal to those of two or more field labourers. In the assignment of convicts scarcely any distinction is made either on account of the period of the sentence, or on account of the age, the character, or the nature of the offence of the convict. The previous occupation of a convict in this country mainly determines his condition in the penal colonies. For instance, domestic servants, transported for any offence, are assigned as domestic servants in Australia: for the greater portion of such servants in those colonies, even in the establishments of the wealthiest classes, have hitherto been transported felons. They are well fed, well clothed, and receive wages from 10l. to 15l. a year, and are as well treated in respectable families, as similar descriptions of servants are in this country. In many instances, masters have even carried to an illegal extent their indulgences to their convict servants.

Convicts, who are mechanics, are as well, if not better, treated, than those, who are domestic servants; for as every kind of skilled labour is very scarce in New South Wales, a convict, who has been a blacksmith, carpenter, mason, cooper, wheelwright, or gardener, is a most valuable servant, worth three or four ordinary convicts; he is eagerly sought after, and great interest is made to obtain him. As a mechanic can scarcely be compelled by punishment to exert his skill, it is for the interest of the master to conciliate his convict mechanic in order to induce him to work well; in too many cases this is effected by granting to the skilled convict various indulgences; by paying him wages; by allotting to him task-work, and by permitting him, after the performance of the task, to work on his own account; and, lastly, by conniving at, or overlooking disorderly conduct; for the most skilful mechanics are generally the worst behaved, and most drunken.

The condition, however, of by far the most numerous class of convicts, those, who are employed, as shepherds or neatherds, (of whom in 1837 there were above 8,000 in New South Wales), and in agriculture generally, is undoubtedly inferior to that of a convict, who is either a domestic servant or a mechanic; they are, however, according to most of the witnesses better fed, than the generality of agricultural labourers in this country; most masters either pay them wages in money, or give them, instead of money, tea, sugar, tobacco, spirits, and other trifling indulgences.

On the whole, therefore, Your Committee may assert that, in the families of well-conducted and respectable settlers, the condition of assigned convicts is much the same, as the condition of similar descriptions of servants in this country; but this is by no means the case in the establishments of all settlers. As the lot of a slave depends upon the character of his master, so the condition of a convict depends upon the temper and disposition of the settler, to whom he is assigned. On this account Sir George Arthur, late Governor of Van Diemen's Land, likened the convict to a slave, and described him "as deprived of liberty, exposed to all the caprice of the family to whose service he may happen to be assigned, and subject to the most summary laws;" "his condition (said Sir George) in no respect differs from that of the slave, except that his master cannot apply corporal punishment by his own hands, or those of his overseer, and has a property in him for a limited period. Idleness and insolence of expression, or of looks, anything betraying the insurgent spirit, subject him to the chain-gang or the triangle, or hard labour on the roads." Sir R. Bourke, the late Governor of New South Wales, has designated as a slave code, the law which, in that colony, enables a magistrate, generally himself a master of convicts, to inflict 50 lashes on a convict for "drunkenness, disobedience of orders, neglect of work, absconding, abusive language to his master or overseer, or any other disorderly or dishonest conduct." For these offences the convict may likewise be punished by imprisonment, solitary confinement, and labour in irons on the roads. That this law is by no means inoperative, is proved by the fact that, in 1835, the number of summary convictions in New South Wales amounted to 22,000, though the number of convicts in the colony did not exceed 28,000; that in one month in 1833, 247 convicts were flogged in that colony, and 9,784 lashes inflicted, which would give for the year, 2,964 floggings, and above 108,000 lashes inflicted chiefly for insolence, insubordination, and neglect of work. In Van Diemen's Land the law, which determines the condition of a convict servant, is severer, and the number of summary convictions proportionately more numerous, than in New South Wales. In 1834 the number of convicts in Van Diemen's Land was about 15,000; the summary convictions amounted to about 15,000; and the number of lashes inflicted was about 50,000. On the other hand, a convict, if ill-treated, may complain of his master; and if he substantiate his charge, the master is deprived of his services; but for this purpose the convict must go before a bench, sometimes 100 miles distant, composed of magistrates, most of whom are owners of convict labour. Legal redress is therefore rarely sought for, and still more rarely obtained by the injured convict.

With regard to the general conduct of assigned convicts, Your Committee would observe, that the misconduct and licentiousness of convict mechanics, and of convict domestic servants in the towns were complained of by every witness connected with either penal colony. Mr. Burton, judge of the Supreme Court in New South Wales, in a charge delivered in 1835, attributed to convict domestic servants the number of burglaries and robberies, which were committed in Sydney; and it was the opinion of most of the witnesses from New South Wales, that the assignment of convicts in towns should be immediately discontinued.

With regard to the general conduct of assigned agricultural labourers, there was a considerable diversity of opinion amongst the witnesses examined by Your Committee; convict labourers were said to behave ill or well, according as they were treated by their masters. The evidence, however, of Sir G. Arthur, appears to Your Committee to be conclusive on this point, with regard to which he wrote to the Secretary of State for the Colonies in the following terms:

> You cannot, my Lord, have an idea of the vexations, which accompany the employment of convicts, or of the vicissitudes attendant upon their assignment. Their crimes and misconduct involve the settlers in daily trouble, expense, and disappointment. The discipline and control of the convicts in Van Diemen's Land is carried, perhaps, to a higher degree, than could ever have been contemplated. Many of the convicts have been greatly reformed, when in the service of considerate and judicious masters; but, with all this abatement, there is so much peculation, so much insubordination, insolence, disobedience of lawful orders, and so much drunkenness, that reference to the magisterial authority is constant, and always attended with loss of time and expense to the settlers. There can be no doubt, things appear better in the colony than they really are; for, in numberless instances, masters are known to submit to peculation rather than incur the additional expense of prosecuting their servants. Two hundred felons, after having been for a long time under confinement in the gaols or hulks of England, and subsequently pent up on board a transport, are placed in charge of the masters or their agents, to whom they have been assigned. The master has then to take the convict to his home (either to the other extremity of the island, a distance of 140 miles, or nearer, as the case may be); and well would it be, if he could get him quietly there, but the contrary is of too frequent occurrence. Either with some money the convict has secreted, or from the bounty of some old acquaintance, the assigned servant, now relieved for the first time for some months from personal restraint, eludes the vigilance of his new master, finds his way into a public-house, and the first notice the settler of his servant, for whom he has travelled to Hobart Town, for whose clothing he has paid the Government, for whose comfort he has, perhaps, made other little advances, is, that he is lodged

in the watch-house with the loss of half his clothing, or committed to gaol for felony.

This is not in the slightest degree, an overdrawn picture, but a plain matter of every day occurrence. A settler, newly arrived, thinks it a vexation not to be endured; but he soon falls into compliance with difficulties, which are visited alike upon all; and, finding there is no escape from them, he is forced to participate in the common mischief, which he cannot avert.

From the preceding description of the condition of assigned convicts, the great inequality of that punishment must have been apparent; but on this subject Your Committee would now wish to direct the attention of The House to the written opinions of some of the highest authorities in the penal colonies. Amongst others to that of the late Governor of New South Wales, Sir R. Bourke, who stated that;

> It is one of the most apparent and necessary results of the system of assignment to render the condition of convicts, so placed, extremely unequal, depending, as it must, on a variety of circumstances, over which the Government cannot possibly exercise any control. It would be quite impracticable to lay down regulations, sufficient to remedy this inequality. The temper, character, station in society of the master, the occupation in which it might be found convenient to employ their servant, and the degree of connexion or variance, that might happen to subsist between this and his previous habits, have an unmeasurable influence over his condition, both physical and mental, which no regulations whatever can anticipate or control.

The only other authority, with regard to the effects of the assignment system, which Your Committee deem it necessary to quote, is Captain Maconochie, secretary to Sir John Franklin, the present Governor of Van Diemen's Land. In a report to the Government on the state of convict discipline in Van Diemen's Land, Captain Maconochie has stated that:

> The practice of assigning convicts to masters is cruel, uncertain, prodigal, ineffectual either for reform or example; can only be maintained in some degree of vigour by extreme severity; some of its most important enactments are systematically broken by the Government itself, which issues them; they are, of course, disregarded by the community. Others, when enforced, are deemed Acts of individual oppression; and the state of society

thus brought about, becomes the most annoying, perplexing, unruly, complicated, and unnatural that can be conceived. The severe coercive discipline, which is its principal element, is carried so far as to be at issue with every natural, and in many cases even every laudable, impulse of the human mind. It defeats, in consequence, its own most important objects; instead of reforming, it degrades humanity, vitiates all under its influence, multiplies petty business, postpones that, which is of higher interest, retards improvement, and is, in many instances, even the direct occasion of vice and crime.

Now, when it is considered that these are the deliberate opinions in writing of the late governor of the two penal colonies, and of the secretary of the present governor of Van Diemen's Land; and that in the year 1835, out of 27,000 convicts in New South Wales 20,000 were assigned servants, that one half, at least, of the convicts in Van Diemen's Land were similarly situated; it will hardly be necessary for Your Committee to produce further proof, as could easily be done, to show, that the condition of a transported convict is a mere lottery; that it may and does range between the extremes of comfort and misery; that no single case can be looked upon as a type of the whole system, or as one, from which any general conclusion can be drawn as to the condition of the assigned convict; that the most contradictory statements on the subject may be made with perfect truth, according as the person. who makes the statement, has seen one or other class, the convicts who are miserable or in a state of comfort; that, in short, to use the words of the late chief justice of Australia, "It frequently happens, that lesser offenders against the law come to be punished with disproportionate severity, while greater criminals escape with comparative impunity."

Assignment is the punishment for female, as well as for male convicts; the proportion of the former to the latter is about one to ten. In respectable families the condition of convict women, as respects their food, clothing, and indulgences, is much the same as that of women servants in this country. Their general conduct, according to the testimony of every witness examined before Your Committee, is (to use the words of Sir E. Parry) "as bad as anything could well be;" he could "hardly conceive anything worse." At times they are excessively ferocious, and the tendency of assignment is to render them still more profligate; they are all of them, with scarcely an exception, drunken and abandoned prostitutes; and even were any of them inclined to be well-conducted, the disproportion of sexes in the penal colonies is so great, that they are exposed to irresistible temptations; for instance, in a private family, in the interior of either colony, a convict woman, frequently the only one in the service, perhaps in the neighbourhood, is surrounded by a number of depraved characters, to whom she becomes an object of constant pursuit and solicitation; she is generally obliged to select one man, as a paramour, to defend her from the importunities of the rest; she seldom remains long in the same place; she either commits some offence, for which she is returned to the Government; or she becomes pregnant, in which case she is sent to the factory, to be there confined at the expense of the Government; at the expiration of the period of confinement or punishment, she is reassigned, and again goes through the same course; such is too generally the career of convict women, even in respectable families. It can be easily imagined, what a pernicious effect must be produced upon the character of the rising generation of the Australian colonies, in consequence of the children of settlers living, too frequently, in their tenderest years, under the charge of such persons. Many respectable settlers are, however, unwilling to receive convict women as assigned servants, when they can possibly dispense with the services of females; and in many instances convict men-servants are preferred for those domestic occupations, which are performed in this country by women only. A considerable portion, therefore, of the female convicts are retained in the service of the lower description of settlers, by whom, it is notorious, that they are not uncommonly employed as public prostitutes.

Female convicts are allowed to marry free men, but they remain under the surveillance of the police, and are liable to be sent back to the factory in case of misconduct; marriages between female convicts and persons who have been convicts are encouraged; and the Government even permits the marriage of convicts in assigned service, provided that the permission of the master is obtained, and a security given by the master to the Government, that the offspring will not become chargeable to the state. From the female factory at Paramatta, most of the convicts, who are permitted to marry, obtain their wives. Such marriages among convicts rarely however turn out well; for the woman not infrequently becomes the common property of the convict servants on the establishment; and gives rise to innumerable quarrels among the men, who purchase her favours generally by petty larcenies upon their master.

In delineating the characteristic features and effects of the assignment system, Your Committee have abstained from dwelling upon the enormous and complicated abuses, which at times have existed, and which perhaps even now, in spite of the utmost efforts of the colonial authorities, exist in various parts of that system; those abuses may chiefly be summed up under the following heads. First, the assignment of convicts to their wives or other relations, that have followed them to the colony, with the proceeds of the offences, for which they were transported, and upon which they have set up a profitable business, have become wealthy, and thus have held out to their acquaintances in this country strong temptations to pursue a similar career of crime; second the employment of convicts as clerks in the various departments of Government, where they have had means of acquiring knowledge, of which the most corrupt and dangerous use has been made; third, the employment of convicts, as clerks to attornies, with free access to the gaols, which has given rise in the colony to an unparalleled system of bribery and connivance at crime; at one time even the clerk of the Attorney-general was a convict, and performed all the legal business of his master; and lastly, the entrusting to convicts of the education of youth in the various public seminaries; the connexion of convicts with the press; these and other abuses, of which mention is to be found in every page of the evidence, appear, to a greater or less degree, to be inherent in the system of assignment.

[…]

Your Committee will now turn to the condition, in the penal colonies, of those offenders against the laws of this country, who have either become free by the expiration of their sentence, or have obtained conditional pardons, or what is termed a ticket of leave. A convict, transported for seven years, obtains, at the end of four years; for 14 years, at the end of six years; and for life, at the end of eight years, as a matter of course, unless his conduct has been very bad, a ticket of leave, which enables him, according to certain regulations, to work on his own account. This indulgence on the whole has a very useful effect, as it holds out hope to a convict if he behave well, and is liable to be reassumed in case of misconduct. Ticket-of-leave men find no difficulty in obtaining work at high wages; and having acquired experience in the colony, they are frequently preferred to lately arrived emigrants. They fill many situations of trust in both colonies; such, for instance, as constables in the police, overseers of road-parties and chain-gangs; the better educated have been employed as superintendents of estates, as clerks to bankers, to lawyers and to shopkeepers, and even as tutors in private families; some have married free women, are in prosperous circumstances, and have even become wealthy; and the real editor of one of the leading journals in the colony of New South Wales was a ticket-of-leave convict.

Great abuses, undoubtedly, have existed in the granting of tickets of leave; nevertheless, on the whole, as has been already observed, the institution of tickets of leave has a useful and beneficial effect. Your Committee, however, cannot help remarking that there is a strange legal absurdity connected with the system of granting tickets of leave, which ought to be removed. A convict was, by common law, as convict, subject to attaint, and unable to acquire property, or to maintain a suit in a court of justice; this law was nearly inoperative, because it is all but impossible, according to the strict rules of evidence, to prove convict attaint, as it was necessary to produce in court the record of conviction, and proof of identity of the person, said to be a convict. In New South Wales a Colonial Act was therefore passed, which rendered the fact of coming to the colony as a transport *prima facie* evidence of the person being a convict; at the same time, however, it extended the protection of the law to convicts under partial remission of sentence; this law is now repealed, or rather, is at variance with the express terms of an Act of the 2 & 3 Will. 4; and the consequence is, that though a ticket-of-leave man is permitted to work on his own account, yet, being a convict, he cannot recover wages for work so done, or call in his debts, and is consequently liable to be defrauded; and cases of frauds of this description have not been uncommon.

In order to complete the description of the various conditions, in which persons who have been transported, are to be found in the penal colonies, Your Committee must mention those who have obtained a conditional or absolute pardon, or have become free by the expiration of their sentences: they are termed emancipists or expirees. In this class are to be found some individuals who are very wealthy, and have accumulated immense fortunes; one is said to have possessed as much as 40,000*l*. a year. Every witness examined gave the same account of the mode in which these fortunes have been made. The emancipist who acquires wealth, in most cases commences his career by keeping a public-house, then lending money on mortgage; he then obtains landed property and large flocks, the latter frequently consisting of stolen cattle which he has purchased. As a case in point, Dr. Lang and Mr. Mudie mentioned that of the individual whom they stated to be in possession of 40,000*l*. a year. This individual was transported, about the end of the last century, for stealing geese on the commons of Yorkshire. He began his career as a prisoner in the employment of Government, in building the gaol at Parramatta; at that time rum was occasionally allowed to convicts; he was, however, a very temperate man, and sold his rations of spirits; he thus accumulated some money, and was enabled, when he became free, to set up a public-house, and keep a gig and horse for hire. On one occasion he was hired to drive to Parramatta, a female emancipist, who was likewise in possession of some property. This led to an acquaintance between them; he subsequently married her, and was enabled to increase his business considerably. At the period referred to, there was no regular market at Sydney. The farmers brought their loads of wheat and other produce to the town, and made exchanges with persons who paid them partly in money, partly in the commodities which they required. The farmers were chiefly emancipists, who, at the expiration of their sentence, had obtained grants of land near Windsor: an ignorant and dissolute set of people, totally unreformed by their punishment, and unable to resist any temptation. They mostly frequented the house of the emancipist above mentioned; there they would remain drunk for days, unconscious of what they had consumed or what they had given away. When recovered from the stupor of intoxication, they were frequently charged by their host for a sum far exceeding their means of payment. Credit was always given, on condition of signing warrants of attorney, which were at hand ready filled up. The instruments were drawn up by convicts, for in those days amongst that class only could persons be found qualified to perform the duties of the legal profession. When the farmers were once under the control of the individual, whose career Your Committee are describing, they were obliged to return to his house, till the amount of debt was such, that he feared lest it might surpass the value of their property. He then dispossessed them of their estates, and by this system of measures he had at one time obtained possession of a great proportion of the cultivated land in the colony of New South Wales. Such were the means, according to Dr. Lang, by which both the emancipist in question, and many others, have acquired great wealth. The greater portion, however, of this class are labourers and small shopkeepers; and if industrious, they have every facility for making an honest livelihood, but as, on the expiration of their sentence, they are exposed to every description of temptation, the greater portion of them retain the habits of profligacy which first led them into crime, and become still more worthless and dissipated. Of the numerous crimes committed in the colony, the greater portion are perpetrated by this class. Among the emancipists and ticket-of-leave men are to be found the cattle-stealers, receivers of stolen goods, keepers of illicit spirit-shops, and squatters, of the number and extent of whose offences every witness spoke in the strongest terms. In Van Diemen's Land the number of expirees or emancipists probably does not exceed 3,000. Sir George Arthur described them as the worst class in the colony.

D5. Anon. [Henry Savery] *Quintus Servinton* (1831) Bk. III Ch. 3

[*Quintus Servinton*, first published in Hobart, Tasmania, in 1831, is a semi-autobiographical novel by Henry Savery, who was convicted of forgery and transported to the Australian penal colonies. It was the first novel published in Australia, and one of the first to deal with the theme of Australian transportation. In this chapter is described Quintus's arrival at Woolwich on the Thames, where he is to be held in the hulks and assigned to forced labour, pending the departure of his transport ship. Here he quickly discovers that his lot is made much easier by his claims to be a gentleman.]

A short while sufficed to bring Quintus to the termination of his journey, and to open to him new and unexpected scenes.

Like many others, he had read unmoved in the hour of his prosperity, the tales of suffering, endured by criminals at their various places of punishment; he had glanced slightly over occasional paragraphs in the newspapers, connected with those floating prisons, the hulks, but intelligence of this sort had passed him unheeded, and he had never thought of acquainting himself with any other than general information, respecting their internal management and condition. Little dreaming that it might ever fall to his own lot to acquire such knowledge by personal experience, he had merely felt, as is commonly the case, that bad as they might be, they were quite good enough for their inhabitants, and had troubled himself no farther about them. Hitherto he had endured few of the pangs of imprisonment beyond the loss of liberty. He had been allowed an unrestrained intercourse with his friends, had been kept separate and apart from other unfortunates, had been free from all distinguishing emblems of his condition, all which circumstances had greatly tended to mitigate the severity of his fate. But, as the carriage that was rapidly conveying him to Woolwich, approached the Arsenal, and he saw crowds of men in irons, all dressed alike, some dragging carts filled with rubbish, some up to their middle in water, labouring by the river side at excavations, some carrying timber or other burthens, others in saw-pits, or employed upon different sorts of artificers' work, but observed that every gang or set was closely attended by soldiers, with muskets and fixed bayonets, and that here and there a task-master was watching a party, apparently under his immediate charge, an apprehension crept over his mind, that all distinction between himself and others, was now at an end. He derived some little consolation however from reflecting, that a few days would accomplish his departure from England, and he willingly associated brighter prospects with a foreign land.

Leaving the Warren, and turning a sharp angle of the road, the stupendous, black, dismal looking hulk, which was to be his temporary abode, met his eye, as it floated on the still water, its towering sides rising an immense height, and its crowded decks presenting a mixture of busy activity with idle curiosity, many being the lookers on at the "swell," who was coming to add to the number of its inhabitants. No sooner had he ascended the wooden stairs, fixed to the side of the vessel, than he was conducted to the superintendent, or captain as he was usually styled, who scarcely however deigned to look at his new charge, but turning to a writing-desk and signing his name to a paper, laconically said to the person who accompanied Quintus, "Here, sir, take your receipt, and now we change situations as to this notable gentleman. I would rather have twenty of the common sort, than one of these swells, but they must all herd in the same mess at my shop."

Quintus caught part of this uncourteous speech, and met the glance that was turned to survey him by a certain look, which induced the man to relax somewhat of his asperity. The fact was, this Captain had been elevated to his present rank, such as it was, as a reward for long and faithful services in subordinate situations, and he thought perhaps to strike awe upon the minds of strangers, by assuming a monstrous pomposity of deportment, calculated, as he conceived, to give a wonderful idea of his own importance. In this he sometimes failed, although at the same time, he was successful in concealing qualities, of which he might well have been proud; as under the assumed garb of official severity, he really possessed a good and feeling heart. His appearance was in keeping with his manners — smart, but vulgar in his dress — unpolished in his style of speaking, and evidently illiterate — prone to obsequiousness towards his superiors — fond of being flattered — haughty to his equals and inferiors, but kind at the bottom towards the wretches, over whom he held nearly uncontrolled sway. Quintus had mixed too much in good society, to be easily abashed by such a person as he now encountered, and assuming perhaps a rather more than usual elevation of mien upon the occasion, feeling too, his pride a little hurt by the levelling system now adopted, and for which he had been little prepared, soon saw the character of the man, and in a few minutes so contrived to impress his new master in his favor, that he received civility from him, to say the least, in the remainder of their interview, and the pains and penalties attached to his situation, were softened in point of rigour, compared with many of the others who were around him.

Yet, although mitigated, he thought them sufficiently severe; for no sooner had he withdrawn from the superior's presence, than a veteran, grown grey in the service, approached him and said, "Come along with me, my smart chum; we'll see how the grey uniform suits your complexion;" then leading the way, conducted him to a small apartment, filled with stores of all sorts, where, looking at a paper he held in his hand, he read aloud, "Let's see — five feet eight — fair complexion — brown hair — hazel eyes — ah! let's see, a suit No. 2 will do — No. 2 shoes too, I think. We'll make the best we can of him." Presently he handed him a bundle, in which were a grey cloth jacket, waistcoat and breeches; worsted stockings, and thick heavy shoes; two check shirts, and a broad brimmed, low crowned hat. "Here, my master," said he, "doff them there handsome traps, and put on these — we don't make fish of one, and flesh of another, here. Give all your gew-gaws, and what else is in your pockets to the clerk there in the office, who'll give you a receipt for them — we don't allow no money here, but 'twill all be returned safe to you when you goes away — I supposes we shan't have you no great while."

"I hope not," replied Quintus, in a good humoured tone, determined to conciliate those around him as much as lay in his power, well knowing that, bad as any thing is, it is capable of being made either worse or better by our manner of treating it. "I hope not, but so long as I remain here, I hope to meet with no worse friends than yourself, for I see you do not seek to add to my troubles more than can be helped, and I am obliged to you."

"Lord love your heart," said the man, "I always tells a real gentleman by the very cut of his jib, and I know how to behave to him. We be all born to trouble, rich and poor, as the saying is, and there's many a swell, I dare say, as ought to be here now worse than you, and yet holds up his head as high as the highest. I loves to take down the conceit of some of them there flash gentry as comes under my hands, cutting such capers as if King George was their uncle; but you won't find nobody behave bad to you here — any body can see you are of another kidney; but I say — I am afraid he'll have to clap the darbies on you."

"I trust not," said Quintus. "I'm sure he needn't be apprehensive of my trying to escape — that's the farthest thing in the world from my thoughts."

"'Tisn't for that," answered the man, "but you see as how there's near a thousand chaps here, and many of 'em are real hell-fire devils — thorough out and outers — and 'twont do to draw no distinctions like, with new chums — howsomever don't say nothing, whatever happens — there be more ways of killing dogs than hanging 'em, as the saying is, so cheer up my fine cock, and now, as you be ready, come along with me to the captain."

This dialogue had taken place during the time Quintus was changing his dress; and being now apparelled in his new livery, he ascended the steps of one of the gangways and was again ushered upon the quarter deck, in the presence of the captain of the hulk.

Approaching him with a bow, the man of authority slightly returned it, calling aloud, "Let Quintus Servinton be placed in the second class, and have a single basil," waving with his hand at the same moment for him to withdraw. He immediately retired therefore, with his veteran friend, and underwent the ceremony of having a small iron ring, fixed by a rivet, upon his right ancle, and which completed the equipments for his new habitation. — Whilst this was going on, the old man said to him, with a look of satisfaction, "I told you to cheer up — see how much better you be off than the rest of 'em," directing Quintus's notice to the crowds of men heavily ironed, by whom he was surrounded — "and besides," added he, "he has given you the best berth in the place — and where you'll have the best company as is going — there's a soldier officer as was lagged three years back, and he's a proper cock-of-the-walk there — and a fine fellow he is too. Him and you will suit one another exactly — come along, and I'll take you to him."

Thus encouraged, he descended the steps leading to his quarters, with tolerable cheerfulness; and was speedily introduced to the unfortunate soldier officer

— as he had been called, and who was now to be his companion. It was certainly a relief to him, to find upon entering the apartment, which was one of several, formed by divisions of the lower decks of an old seventy-four, that by the style of its principal inmates, manner and address, he was a gentleman; and Quintus, adapting himself to his circumstances with the best grace he could assume, they were soon engaged in general conversation, with as much life and energy, particularly on the part of the *ci devant* officer, as if they had known one another for years, and had now re-met in a state of mutual prosperity.

It may perhaps appear strange to those, who have never experienced a reverse of fortune — who have always basked in its sun-shine, free from the storms and troubles of adversity, that such a situation as two gentlemen now found themselves in, the one Quintus, as he has been described to the reader, and the other, the once gallant, gay, fashionable captain Spendall, formerly of His Majesty's —— regiment of infantry, they should have been able so to forget their calamities, so to lose sight of their falls, or so to unbend their oppressed minds, as to enter upon any light, or trifling subjects of conversation; but the fact is, that through all "the changes and chances of this mortal life," man is, more or less, the creature of circumstances; nor is it among the least of the merciful dispensations we receive at the hands of a Divine Providence, that the back is ever suited to the burthen, and that even the worst of our afflictions, are invariably attended by some extenuations. [...]

D6. Marcus Clarke *His Natural Life* (1870–2)
Bk. II Ch. 5 "How Society Made its Criminals Forty Years Ago"

[Marcus Clarke (1846–81) was born and educated in London, but, on his father's sudden death, emigrated to the Colony of Victoria in 1863, where he worked principally as a journalist. Published first as a serial in the *Australian Journal*, *His Natural Life* is an epic of colonial Australia. Based on research into records of the transportation system in Melbourne Public Library, it describes the fortunes of Richard Dawes, transported convict. Here, we have a vivid description of convict conditions aboard the transportation vessel.]

In the prison of the 'tween decks reigned a darkness pregnant with murmurs. The sentry at the entrance to the hatchway was supposed to "prevent the prisoners from making a noise," but he put a very liberal interpretation upon the clause, and as long as the prisoners refrained from shouting, yelling and fighting — eccentricities in which they sometimes indulged — he did not disturb them. This course of conduct was dictated by prudence, no less than by convenience, for one sentry was but little over so many; and the convicts, if pressed too hard, would raise a sort of bestial boo-hoo, in which all voices were confounded, and which, while it made noise enough and to spare, utterly precluded all notion of individual punishment. One could not flog a hundred and eighty men, and it was impossible to distinguish any particular offender. So, in virtue of this last appeal, convictism had established a tacit right to converse in whispers, and to move about inside its oaken cage.

To one coming in from the upper air, the place would have seemed in pitchy darkness; but the convict eye, accustomed to the sinister twilight, was enabled to discern surrounding objects with tolerable distinctness. The prison was about fifty feet long and fifty feet wide, and ran the full height of the 'tween decks, viz., about five feet ten inches high. The barricade was loop-holed here and there, and the planks were in some places wide enough to admit a musket barrel. On the aft side, next the soldiers' berths, was a trap door, like the stoke hole of a furnace. At first sight, this appeared to be contrived for the humane purpose of ventilation, but a second glance dispelled this weak conclusion. The opening was just large enough to admit the muzzle of a small howitzer, secured on the deck below. In case of a mutiny, the soldiers could sweep the prison from end to end with grape shot. Such fresh air as there was, filtered through those loop-holes, and came in somewhat larger quantity through a wind-sail passed into the prison from the hatchway. But the wind-sail, being necessarily but at one end of the place, the air it brought was pretty well absorbed by the twenty or thirty lucky fellows near it, and the other hundred and fifty did not come so well off. The scuttles were open certainly, but as the row of bunks had been built against them, the air *they* brought was the peculiar property of such men as occupied the berths into which they penetrated. These berths were twenty-eight in number, each containing six men. They ran in a double tier round three sides of the prison, twenty at each side, and eight affixed to that portion of the forward barricade opposite the door. Each berth was presumed to be five feet six inches square, but the necessities of stowage had deprived them of six inches, and even under that pressure twelve men were compelled to sleep on the deck. Pine did not exaggerate when he spoke of the custom of overcrowding convict ships; and as he was entitled to half a guinea for every man he delivered safely in Hobart Town, he had some reason to complain.

When Frere had come down, an hour before, the prisoners were all snugly between their blankets. They were not so now; though, at the first clink of the bolts, they would be back again in their old positions, to all appearances sound asleep. As the eye became accustomed to the fœtid duskiness of the prison, a strange picture presented itself. Groups of men, in all imaginable attitudes, were lying, standing, sitting, or pacing up and down. It was the scene on the poop deck over again, only, here being no fear of restraining keepers, the wild beasts were a little more free in their movements. It is impossible to convey, in words, any idea of the hideous phantasmagoria of shifting limbs and faces which moved through the evil smelling twilight of this terrible prison-house. Callot might have drawn it, Dante might have suggested it, but a minute attempt to describe its horrors would but disgust. There are depths in humanity which one cannot explore, as there are mephitic caverns into which one dare not penetrate.

Old men, young men, and boys, stalwart burglars and highway robbers, side by side with wizened pickpockets or cunning-featured area-sneaks. The forger occupied the same berth with the body-snatcher. The man of education learned strange secrets of house-breakers' craft, and the vulgar ruffian of St Giles took lessons in self-control from the keener intellect of the professional swindler. The fraudulent clerk and the flash "cracksman" interchanged experiences. The smuggler's stories of lucky ventures and successful runs were capped by the footpad's reminiscences of foggy nights and stolen watches. The poacher, grimly thinking of his sick wife and orphaned children, would start as the night-house ruffian clapped him on the shoulder and bade him, with a curse, to take good heart, and "be a man." The fast shop-boy, whose love of fine company and high living had brought him to this pass, had shaken off the first shame that was on him, and listened eagerly to the narratives of successful vice that fell so glibly from the lips of his older companions. To be transported seemed no such uncommon fate. The old fellows laughed, and wagged their grey heads with all the glee of past experience, and listening youth longed for the time when it might do likewise. Society was the common foe, and magistrates, jailers, and parsons, the natural prey of all noteworthy mankind. Only fools were honest, only cowards kissed the rod, and refused to meditate revenge on that world of respectability which had wronged them. Each new comer was one more recruit to the ranks of Ruffianism, and not a man penned in that reeking den of infamy but became a sworn hater of law, order and "free men." What he might have been before mattered not. He was now a prisoner, and — thrust into a suffocating barracoon, herded with the foulest of mankind; with all imaginable depths of blasphemy and indecency sounded hourly in his sight and hearing — he lost his self-respect, and became what his jailers took him to be — a wild beast to be locked under bolts and bars, lest he should break out and tear them.

D7. Anon. "The Autobiography of a Convict" *The Voice of our Exiles: Stray Leaves from a Prison Ship* (1854) ed. Daniel Ritchie pp. 159–64.

[This is the brief life of a transported convict, written by himself on board the "Pestonjee Bomanjee," the boat carrying him to exile in New South Wales. Ritchie, the Scottish chaplain of the vessel, organized the writing of a journal during the voyage, and afterwards published extracts from it on his return to Britain. The account reproduced here is in the form of a Christian confession or testimony.]

I was born in London, of decent parents, who bestowed on my youth every care and attention that the most tender affection could suggest. By economising their limited means, they were enabled to keep me at school until I had acquired a fair knowledge of reading, writing, and arithmetic. At thirteen years of age I was apprenticed, according to my own desire, to a tailor, who carried on a flourishing business in the *West End*. I was then fond of play and idleness, and although the conversation of some of my associates had familiarised me with crime, my boyhood innocence was still unsoiled.

I must confess, however unwilling I am to throw reflections on that loving mother who so patiently bore my caprices, and on that indulgent father who so studiously provided for my wants, that they did view my errors with too much lenity, and too seldom, by private admonition and personal example, tried to train and correct my unguarded impulses, or restrain my earliest aberrations from the line of rectitude. On this account I was placed in a slippery position, without any fixed support — neither a lowly dependence on the arm of God nor a proud self esteem; — and thus tottering, I was liable to be impelled in a virtuous or vicious direction, according to the nature of the slightest external force or circumstance. This condition, without fixed principles, although often very temporary, with me endured for several years — the happiest of my life — during which I was gradually losing the innocence of youth, without feeling the tortures of remorse.

My apprenticeship being now finished, and having become a skilful workman, I was employed by my old master at high wages. This is the precarious point in the lives of most men, and, according to their conduct at this time, their future welfare or woe is determined. Unless when actually employed, earning the means of gratification — rather let me say ruin — my only object was the enjoyment of the passing hour. This I madly endeavoured to find among the degraded frequenters of taverns, or places more abandoned. There, in the company of persons equally or more reckless than myself, I squandered my wages, my time, and my character. Their insane dissipation had a kind of fascination for me, and I began to regard some of them with feelings of admiration and friendship.

It was not long, however, before these feelings were concentrated upon one individual. That man, while profusely scattering his money, maintained a degree of reserve and personal respect that stimulated my curiosity. The indifference with which he at first met my advances was conquered by repeated civilities, and a submissive attention to his opinions. I succeeded slowly in gaining his esteem, and ultimately his confidence.

He had forsaken the trade of an engineer for the more lucrative one — which he pursued — of a burglar. His ability as a mechanic gave him peculiar advantages in his career, and had enabled him to follow it successfully for about three years. He described himself as a redresser of the wrongs of the poor, by taking from the rich their superfluous wealth; thus leading me to look upon him as a champion of the oppressed. In this view, theft — no longer a crime — is converted into an act of justice.

By these and similar sophisms my conscience was deadened, and I began to believe — oh fatal error! — that there was little or no difference between virtue and vice, between moral purity and impurity. This besotted folly was also partly the result of the habits I had acquired. The curse of intemperance had crippled my physical ability; my mind was blunted and depraved by listening to the recitals of crime; and at last every barrier was broken down, by permitting the desire to be fully formed of committing an act which my judgment pronounced wrong, although my necessities pointed the other way.

In this frame of mind I became the ready accomplice of the tempter, who plunged me into an abyss, from which I have only emerged stained with crime, and after suffering the most excruciating mental anguish. That man, who had become my *beau ideal* of a hero, proposed that I should assist him in perpetrating a burglary he meditated. No feeling of guilt, no sentiment of remorse influenced for a moment his character, hardened by crime — his conscience dead or benumbed by vicious gratifications. His callousness made itself contagious; my scruples were overcome by his reasoning; my vacillation was changed into a settled purpose, and I acceded to his request.

The object contemplated was the robbery of a house in Bedford Square. We gained admission while the family were at dinner, by means of a key previously made for the purpose. In felt shoes we succeeded in creeping softly up stairs to the bedrooms, without attracting attention. My duty was to remain on the stair and give notice of danger, while my more practised companion, with a dark lantern, sought for plunder. Our object was accomplished without interruption, and we had descended for the purpose of effecting our egress, when we found an unexpected barrier. Some one in the interim had placed a chain on the door, which was secured by a patent lock we had not the means of opening. The delay this occasioned led to our discovery, when, to avoid capture, we ran up stairs and gained the roof of the house, intending to descend through one of those adjoining. The police having been promptly called in, pursued us before we could succeed in doing so. In the hurry and darkness my foot slipped and I tumbled into a water-cistern, which saved me from being dashed on the pavement below. While in this situation I was made prisoner, and at once conveyed to the police office, where I had scarcely arrived when my companion was also brought in.

I could not help admiring the unflinching obstinacy of that man during the personal search which was immediately instituted. On me nothing was found, but from his pockets some money and articles of jewellery were removed. To this he offered no opposition, but he steadily refused to open one of his hands, which he kept firmly clenched in spite of every attempt that was made to relax it. It was struck with a baton, trodden on the ground by an iron heel until the blood was streaming, yet not for a moment did he loosen his grip. With a determination of tone there was no mistaking, he declared they might cut his hand off, but that nothing would force him to open it, as he had already sworn that he concealed nothing — an atrocious lie, for at that moment he held a ring which he then believed was a valuable diamond one, and which the family subsequently valued at more than L.100. He succeeded in keeping it, but his disappointment was extreme when he discovered afterwards from his knowledge of *stones*, that his firmness had been exerted in preserving a paltry counterfeit.

How bitterly I cursed fortune, how madly I condemned my wicked folly, when I found myself in the grasp of justice, are remembrances which haunt me still. But after having been restored to the right use of my reason by probationary discipline — to the just guidance of an awakened conscience by solitude and reflection, I beheld with thankfulness the merciful hand of God visibly stretched forth to pluck me out of the gulf into which I had recklessly leaped. The sins of my past life felt like burning cinders heaped upon my heart; but now, in the consciousness of being actuated by just and virtuous motives, I feel a new and comparatively happy man. With a resolution to act with integrity and according to the laws of my merciful God, I shall, trusting in him, begin a new life in the land of my exile, hoping to acquire by diligence and industry, contentment and repose.

D8. John Binny "Thieves and Swindlers" in Henry Mayhew's *London Labour and the London Poor* Vol. IV (1861–2) pp. 273–6 & 376–7.

[Henry Mayhew (1812–87) was, with Dickens, the greatest Victorian observer of the lower reaches of London society. *London Labour and the London Poor* began as a series of sketches in the *Morning Chronicle* around 1850. In the supplementary fourth volume of the 1861–2 edition, devoted to criminals and beggars and the agencies set up to police them, and largely written by other hands such as Binny's, the emphasis is on the social causes of crime. Only the introduction to the catalogue of thieves and swindlers, plus a short and remarkably detached autobiographical account of a returned convict, are reproduced here.]

8/1. Introduction

In tracing the geography of a river it is interesting to go to its source, possibly a tiny spring in the cleft of a rock in some mountain glen. You follow its windings, observing each tributary which flows into its gathering flood until it discharges its waters into the sea. We proceed in a similar manner to treat of the thieves and swindlers of the metropolis.

Thousands of our felons are trained from their infancy in the bosom of crime; a large proportion of them are born in the homes of habitual thieves and other persons of bad character, and are familiarized with vice from their earliest years; frequently the first words they lisp are oaths and curses. Many of them are often carried to the beershop or gin palace on the breast of worthless drunken mothers, while others, clothed in rags, run at their heels or hang by the skirts of their petticoats. In their wretched abodes they soon learn to be deceitful and artful and are in many cases very precocious. The greater number are never sent to school; some run idle about the streets in low neighbourhoods; others are sent out to beg throughout the city; others go out with their mothers and sit beside their stalls; while others sell a handful of matches or small wares in our public thoroughfares.

One day, in going down a dark alley in the Borough, near Horsemonger Lane Gaol, we saw a little boy — an Irish cockney, who had been tempted to steal by other boys he was in the habit of associating with. He was stripped entirely naked, and was looking over a window on the first floor with a curious grin on his countenance. His mother had kept his clothes from him that day as a punishment for stealing, and to prevent him getting out of the house while she went out to her street-stall.

In our brief sketch of the criminals of the metropolis, we have in the outset directed our attention to the sneaks or common thieves — by far the larger number of our criminal population — from whose ranks the expert pickpockets and the ingenious and daring burglars in most cases emerge. We have treated of the incipient stage of thieving, when the child of five or six years of age steals an apple, or an orange, or a handful of nuts from a stall, or an old pair of boots from a shop door, and then traced the after-stages of more daring crime.

There are thousands of neglected children loitering about the low neighbourhoods of the metropolis, and prowling about the streets, begging and stealing for their daily bread. They are to be found in Westminster, Whitechapel, Shoreditch, St. Giles's, New Cut, Lambeth, the Borough, and other localities. Hundreds of them may be seen leaving their parents' homes and low lodging-houses every morning sallying forth in search of food and plunder. They are fluttering in rags and in the most motley attire. Some are orphans and have no one to care for them; others have left their homes and live in lodging-houses in the most improvident manner, never thinking of to-morrow; others are sent out by their unprincipled parents to beg and steal for a livelihood; others are the children of poor but honest and industrious people, who have been led to steal through the bad companionship of juvenile thieves. Many of them have never been at a day-school nor attended a Sunday or ragged-school, and have had no moral or religious instruction. On the contrary, they have been surrounded by the most baneful and degrading influences, and have been set a bad example by their parents and others with whom they came in contact, and are shunned by the honest and industrious classes of society. The chief agencies which have tended to ameliorate their condition are the ragged-schools, where they receive sound secular and religious instruction; the shoeblacks' brigades, where they are trained in habits of honest industry; and the juvenile reformatories, which have been instituted for their moral and social elevation.

Many of them are hungry, and have no food to eat nor money to purchase it, and readily steal when they find a suitable opportunity. Not having received the benefit of a sound moral training, they have not the conscientious scruples possessed by the children of honest parents; their only care is to avoid being detected in their felonies. When they successfully steal some article from a stall or shop-door, or rifle a till by entering the shop, they are congratulated on their expertness by their companions and enjoy a larger share of plunder.

The public streets of the metropolis are regarded by these ragged little felons and the children of honest industrious parents in a very different aspect. The latter walk the streets with their eyes sparkling with wonder and delight at the beautiful and grand sights of the metropolis. They are struck with the splendour of the shops and the elegance and stateliness of the public buildings, and with the dense crowds of people of various orders, and trains of vehicles thronging the streets. These little ragged thieves walk along the streets with very different emotions. They, too, in their own way, enjoy the sights and sounds of London. Amid the busy crowds many of them are to be seen sitting in groups on the pavement or loitering about in good-humour and merriment; yet ever and anon their keen roguish eyes sparkle as they look into the windows of the confectioners', bakers', and greengrocers' shops, at the same time keeping a sharp eye on the policeman as he passes on his beat.

These juvenile thieves find an ample field for plunder at the stalls and shop-doors in Whitechapel, Shoreditch, Edgeware Road, and similar localities, where many articles are exposed for sale, which can be easily disposed of to some of the low fences. In this manner thousands of our felons are trained to be expert and daring in crime, and are frequently tried and convicted before the Police Courts.

This is the main source of the habitual felons of the metropolis. As these boys and girls grow up they commence a system of sneaking thefts over the metropolis, some purloining in shops, others gliding into areas and lobbies on various pretences, stealing articles from the kitchen, and when opportunity occurs carrying off the plate.

As these young felons advance in years they branch off into three different classes, determined partly by their natural disposition and personal qualities, and partly by the circumstances in which they are placed. Many of them continue through life to sneak as common thieves; others become expert pickpockets, and some ultimately figure as burglars.

A vast number of juvenile thieves as they grow up continue to carry on a system of petty felonies over the metropolis, and reside in the lowest neighbourhoods. Some pretend to sell laces and small wares to get a pretext to call at the houses of labouring people and tradesmen, and to go down the areas and enter the lobbies in fashionable streets. In addition to the paltry profits arising from these sales they get a livelihood by begging, and as a matter of course do not scruple to steal when they can find an opportunity.

These common thieves are of both sexes, and of various ages, and are often characterized by mental imbecility and low cunning. Many of them are lazy in disposition and lack energy both of body and mind. They go out daily in vast shoals over the metropolis picking up a miserable and precarious livelihood, sometimes committing felonies in the houses they visit of considerable value.

The pickpockets are of various ages and of different degrees of proficiency, from the little ragged urchin in St. Giles's stealing a handkerchief at the tail of a gentleman's coat, to the elegantly dressed and expert pickpocket promenading in the West-end and attending fashionable assemblies. Some are dressed as mechanics, others as clerks, some as smart business men, and others in fashionable attire. They are to be found on all public occasions, some of them clumsy and timid, others daring and most expert. Many of them continue to pursue this class of felonies in preference to any other. They receive a considerable accession to their numbers by young women, frequently servants who have been seduced, and cohabit with burglars, pick-pockets, and others, and who are trained to this infamous profession, and in many cases are shoplifters.

Many are trained to commit house-breaking and burglaries from fourteen to fifteen years of age. Boys are occasionally employed to enter through fanlights and windows, and to assist otherwise in plundering dwellings and shops. Some of them commit burglaries of small value in working neighbourhoods, where comparatively little ingenuity and skill are required, others plunder shops and warehouses and fashionable dwellings, which is generally done with greater care and ingenuity, and where the booty is often of higher value.

In addition to the three classes we have named, the common thief, the pickpocket, and the burglar, there is another class of low ruffians who frequently cohabit with low women and prostitutes, and commit highway robberies. They often follow these degraded females on the streets, and attack persons who accost them, believing them to be prostitutes. At other times they garotte men on the street at midnight, or in the by-streets in the evening, and plunder them with violence. This class of persons are generally hardened in crime, and many of them are returned convicts.

The habitual crime of the female portion of the community is in most cases associated with prostitution. We learn from statistics collected by the metropolitan constabulary for 1860, that there are nearly 7000 open prostitutes or street-walkers in London, three fourths of whom we have reason to believe are addicted to stealing. While many of these belong to our native-born felon population, a large proportion have been seduced from the ranks of honest and industrious people in London, or have come up from the provinces, while a few of them are from the Continent.

We believe that the most effective means of checking the crime of the metropolis is to have an efficient machinery of ragged schools in those low neighbourhoods, where neglected children are to be found, similar to the ragged school in George's Yard, and to train them in honest employment, as in the shoeblack brigades or industrial schools.

We learn from the statistics of the constabulary of the metropolis that juvenile crime has been considerably reduced within the past ten years. Several of our police inspectors have laboured with untiring industry to reform the lodging-houses and to introduce cleanliness and decency, where immorality and filth formerly prevailed. And noble exertions have been made by Christian societies to illumine these dark localities with the light of Christian truth.

Yet much still remains to be done. And it is a problem worthy of our highest and wisest statesmen to consider whether adequate means to elevate this abandoned class are to be provided by voluntary effort, or by the paternal care of our Government from the public treasury.

It is far easier to train the young in virtuous and industrious habits, than to reform the grown-up felon who has become callous in crime, and it is besides far more profitable to the State. To neglect them or inadequately to attend to their welfare gives encouragement to the growth of this dangerous class. On the other hand how noble the aim, to adopt wise and vigorous measures to provide for these children of adversity and misfortune, and to transform them into useful members of society!

Our national reformatories are very useful in reclaiming those juveniles who have fallen into crime; but ragged schools efficiently conducted would be of still higher value — as prevention is better than cure. In providing those noble machineries by voluntary effort, or by the State, we would wisely act as the minister of Divine Providence, and would thereby promote the best interests and prosperity of our country.

We have also endeavoured to give a cursory sketch of the swindlers of the metropolis, who are generally of a different class from our felon population. They consist of persons embezzling the property of their employers; of sharpers plundering their dupes by tricks at card-playing, skittles, or otherwise; and of rogues abstracting the property of the public by false pretences. Many of these formerly belonged to the ranks of the honest and industrious working and middle-classes, and not a few of them are well connected, and have lived in fashionable society. By improvidence, extravagance, or dissipation, they have squandered their means, and have now basely adopted a course of systematic dishonesty rather than lead an industrious life. Some of them have led a fast life in the metropolis, and are persons of ruined fortune. Others are indolent in disposition, and carry on a subtle system of public robbery rather than pursue some honest occupation or calling. [...]

8/2. Narrative of a Returned Convict

We give the following brief autobiography of a person who has recently returned from one of our penal settlements, having been transported for life. In character he is very different from the generality of our London thieves, having hot African blood in his veins and being a man of passionate, unbridled character. He was formerly a daring highway robber. He was introduced to us accidentally in Drury-lane, by a Bow-street police officer, who occasionally acts as a detective. On this occasion the latter displayed very little tact and discretion, which made it exceedingly difficult for us to get from him even the following brief tale: —

"I was born in a tent at Southampton, on the skirts of a forest, among the gipsies, my father and mother being of that stock of people. We had generally about seven or eight tents in our encampment, and were frequently in the forest between Surrey and Southampton. The chief of our gang, termed the gipsey king, had great influence among us. He was then a very old, silver-headed man, and had a great number of children. I learned when a boy to play the violin, and was tolerably expert at it. I went to the public-houses and other dwellings in the neighbourhood, with three or four other gipsey boys, who played the triangle and drum, as some of the Italian minstrels do. We went during the day and often in the evening. At other times we had amusement beside the tents, jumping, running, and single-stick, and begged from the people passing by in the vehicles or on foot.

"During the day some of the men of our tribe went about the district, and looked out over the fields for horses which would suit them, and came during the night and stole them away. They never carried away horses from the stables. They generally got their booty along the by-roads, and took them to the fairs in the neighbourhood and sold them, usually for about 10*l.* or 12*l.* The horses they stole were generally light and nimble, such as might be useful to themselves. They disfigured them by putting a false mark on them, and by clipping their mane and tail. When a horse is in good order they keep it for a time till it becomes more thin and lank, to make it look older. They let the horse generally go loose on the side of a road at a distance from their encampment, till they have an opportunity to sell it; and it is generally placed alongside one or two other horses, so that it is not so much observed. The same person who steals it frequently takes it to the fair to be sold.

"The gipsies are not so much addicted to stealing from farms as is generally supposed. They are assisted in gaining a livelihoood by their wives and other women going over the district telling fortunes. Some of them take to hawking for a livelihood. This is done by boys and girls, as well as old men and women. They sell baskets, brushes, brooms, and other articles.

"I spent my early years wandering among the gipsies till I was thirteen years of age, and was generally employed going about the country with my violin along with some of my brothers.

"My father died when I was about six years of age. A lady in Southampton, of the Methodist connexion, took an interest in my brothers and me, and we settled there with our mother, and afterwards learned coach-making. I lived with my mother in Southampton for five or six years. My brothers were well-behaved, industrious boys, but I was wild and disobedient.

"The first depredation I committed was when thirteen years old. I robbed my mother of a box of old-fashioned coins and other articles, and went to Canterbury, where I got into company with prostitutes and thieves. The little money I had was soon spent.

"After this I broke the window of a pawnbroker's shop as a cart was passing, put my hand through the broken pane of glass, and carried off a bowl of gold and silver coins, and ran off with them and made my way to Chatham.

"Some time after this I was, one day at noon, in the highway between Chatham and Woolwich, when I saw a carriage come up. The postillion was driving the horses smartly along. A gentleman and lady were inside, and the butler and a female servant were on the seat behind. I leaped on the back of the conveyance as it was driving past, and took away the portmanteau with the butler's clothes, and carried it off to the adjoining woods. I sold them to a Jew at Southampton for 3*l*. or 4*l*.

"Shortly after I came up to London, and became acquainted with a gang of young thieves in Ratcliffe Highway. I lived in a coffee-house there for about eighteen months. The boys gained their livelihood picking gentlemen's pockets, at which I soon became expert. After this I joined a gang of men, and picked ladies' pockets, and resided for some time at Whitechapel.

"Several years after I engaged with some other men in highway robbery. I recollect on one occasion we learned that a person was in the habit of going to one of the City banks once a week for a large sum of money — possibly to pay his workmen. He was generally in the habit of calling at other places in town on business, and carried the money with him in a blue serge bag. We followed him from the bank to several places where he made calls, until he came to a quiet by-street, near London bridge. It was a dark wintry night, and very stormy. I rushed upon him and garotted him, while one of my companions plundered him of his bag. He was a stout old man, dressed like a farmer. I was then about twenty-two years of age.

"At this time I went to music and dancing saloons, and played on my violin.

"Soon after I went to a fair at Maldstone with several thieves, all young men like myself. One of us saw a farmer in the market, a robust middle-aged man, take out his purse with a large sum of money. We followed him from the market. I went a little in advance of my companions for a distance of sixteen miles, till we came to a lonely cross turning surrounded with woods. The night happened to be dark. I went up to him and seized him by the leg, pulled him violently off his horse, and my companions came up to assist me. While he lay on the ground we rifled his pockets of a purse containing about 500*l*. and some silver money. He did not make very much resistance and we did not injure him. We came back to London and shared the booty among us.

"About the time of the great gathering of the Chartists on Kennington Common, in 1848, I broke into a pawnbroker's shop in the metropolis, and stole jewellery to the amount of 2,000*l.*, consisting of watches, rings, &c., and also carried off some money. I sold the jewels to a Jewish receiver for about 500*l.* I was arrested some time after, and tried for this offence, and sentenced to transportation for life.

"I returned from one of the penal settlements about a year ago, and have since led an honest life."

D9. Thomas Carlyle *Model Prisons* (Latter-Day Pamphlets 2) (March 1850).

[The *Latter-Day Pamphlets* are a series of virulent attacks on contemporary public practices and institutions, written when Carlyle's disillusion with social and democratic reform was at its most desperate. Here, following a visit to one of the new prisons — probably Coldbath Fields in Clerkenwell, which employed the "Silent System," under Captain George Laval Chesterton, its governor from 1829–1854 — Carlyle lambasts philanthropic reforms in the treatment of convicts.]

Several months ago, some friends took me with them to see one of the London Prisons; a Prison of the exemplary or model kind. An immense circuit of buildings; cut-out, girt with a high ring-wall, from the lanes and streets of the quarter, which is a dim and crowded one. Gateway as to a fortified place; then a spacious court, like the square of a city; broad staircases, passages to interior courts; fronts of stately architecture all round. It lodges some Thousand or Twelve-hundred prisoners, besides the officers of the establishment. Surely one of the most perfect buildings, within the compass of London. We looked at the apartments, sleeping-cells, dining-rooms, working-rooms, general courts or special and private: excellent all, the ne-plus-ultra of human care and ingenuity; in my life I never saw so clean a building; probably no Duke in England lives in a mansion of such perfect and thorough cleanness.

The bread, the cocoa, soup, meat, all the various sorts of food, in their respective cooking-places, we tasted: found them of excellence superlative. The prisoners sat at work, light work, picking oakum, and the like, in airy apartments with glass roofs, of agreeable temperature and perfect ventilation; silent, or at least conversing only by secret signs: others were out, taking their hour of promenade in clean flagged courts: methodic composure, cleanliness, peace, substantial whole-some comfort reigned everywhere supreme. The women in other apartments, some notable murderesses among them, all in the like state of methodic composure and substantial wholesome comfort, sat sewing: in long ranges of wash-houses, dry-ing-houses and whatever pertains to the getting-up of clean linen, were certain others, with all conceivable mechanical furtherances, not too arduously working. The notable murderesses were, though with great precautions of privacy, pointed out to us; and we were requested not to look openly at them, or seem to notice them at all, as it was found to "cherish their vanity" when visitors looked at them. Schools too were there; intelligent teachers of both sexes, studiously instructing the still ignorant of these thieves.

[…]

The Captain of the place, a gentleman of ancient Military or Royal-Navy habits, was one of the most perfect governors; professionally and by nature zeal-ous for cleanliness, punctuality, good order of every kind; a humane heart and yet a strong one; soft of speech and manner, yet with an inflexible rigour of com-mand, so far as his limits went: "iron hand in a velvet glove," as Napoleon defined it. A man of real worth, challenging at once love and respect: the light of those mild bright eyes seemed to permeate the place as with an all-pervading vigilance, and kindly yet victorious illumination; in the soft definite voice it was as if Na-ture herself were promulgating her orders, gentlest mildest orders, which how-ever, in the end, there would be no disobeying, which in the end there would be no living without fulfilment of. A true "*aristos*," and commander of men. A man worthy to have commanded and guided forward, in good ways, Twelve-hundred of the best commonpeople in London or the world: he was here, for many years past, giving all his care and faculty to command, and guide forward in such ways as there were, Twelve-hundred of the worst. I looked with considerable admira-tion on this gentleman; and with considerable astonishment, the reverse of admi-ration, on the work he had here been set upon.

This excellent Captain was too old a Commander to complain of anything; indeed he struggled visibly the other way, to find in his own mind that all here was best; but I could sufficiently discern that, in his natural instincts, if not mounting up to the region of his thoughts, there was a continual protest going on against much of it; that nature and all his inarticulate persuasion (however much forbid-den to articulate itself) taught him the futility and unfeasibility of the system fol-lowed here. The Visiting Magistrates, he gently regretted rather than complained, had lately taken his treadwheel from him, men were just now pulling it down; and how he was henceforth to enforce discipline on these bad subjects, was much a difficulty with him. "They cared for nothing but the treadwheel, and for having their rations cut short": of the two sole penalties, hard work and occasional hunger, there remained now only one, and that by no means the better one, as he thought. The "sympathy" of visitors, too, their "pity" for his interesting scoundrel-subjects, though he tried to like it, was evidently no joy to this practical mind. Pity, yes: — but pity for the scoundrel-species? For those who will not have pity on themselves, and will force the Universe and the Laws of Nature to have no "pity" on them? Meseems I could discover fitter objects of pity!

In fact it too was clear, this excellent man had got a field for his faculties which, in several respects, was by no means the suitable one. To drill Twelve-hundred scoundrels by "the method of kindness," and of abolishing your very treadwheel, — how could any commander rejoice to have such a work cut-out for him? You had but to look in the faces of these Twelve-hundred, and despair, for most part, of ever "commanding" them at all. Miserable distorted blockheads, the generality; ape-faces, imp-faces, angry dog-faces, heavy sullen ox-faces; degraded underfoot perverse creatures, sons of *in*-docility, greedy mutinous darkness, and in one word, of STUPIDITY, which is the general mother of such. Stupidity intellectual and stupidity moral (for the one always means the other, as you will, with surprise or not, discover if you look) had born this progeny: base-natured beings, on whom in the course of a maleficent subterranean life of London Scoundrelism, the Genius of Darkness (called Satan, Devil, and other names) had now visibly impressed his seal, and had marked them out as soldiers of Chaos and of him, — appointed to serve in *his* Regiments, First of the line, Second ditto, and so on in their order. Him, you could perceive, they would serve; but not easily another than him. These were the subjects whom our brave Captain and Prison-Governor was appointed to command, and reclaim to *other* service, by "the method of love," with a treadwheel abolished.

Hopeless forevermore such a project. These abject, ape, wolf, ox, imp and other diabolic-animal specimens of humanity, who of the very gods could ever have commanded them by love? A collar round the neck, and a cartwhip flourished over the back; these, in a just and steady human hand, were what the gods would have appointed them; and now when, by long misconduct and neglect, they had sworn themselves into the Devil's regiments of the line, and got the seal of Chaos impressed on their visage, it was very doubtful whether even these would be of avail for the unfortunate commander of Twelve-hundred men! By "love," without hope except of peaceably teasing oakum, or fear except of a temporary loss of dinner, he was to guide these men, and wisely constrain them, — whitherward? No-whither: that was his goal, if you will think well of it; that was a second fundamental falsity in his problem. False in the warp and false in the woof, thought one of us; about as false a problem as any I have seen a good man set upon lately!

To guide scoundrels by "love"; that is a false woof, I take it, a method that will not hold together; hardly for the flower of men will love alone do; and for the sediment and scoundrelism of men it has not even a chance to do. And then to guide any class of men, scoundrel or other, *No-whither,* which was this poor Captain's problem, in this Prison with oakum for its one element of hope or outlook, how can that prosper by "love" or by any conceivable method? That is a warp wholly false. Out of which false warp, or originally false condition to start from, combined and daily woven into by your false woof, or methods of "love" and suchlike, there arises for our poor Captain the falsest of problems, and for a man of his faculty the unfairest of situations. His problem was, not to command good men to do something, but bad men to do (with superficial disguises) nothing.

D10. Unsigned [Thomas Beard] "A Dialogue Concerning Convicts" *All the Year Round* (11 May 1861) pp. 155–6.

[Thomas Beard (1807–91), journalist, and lifelong friend of Dickens. Dickens commissioned Beard to write the dialogue according to his own specifications, provided him with the pamphlet of which it forms a summary (C.P. Measor's *The Convict Service* of 1861), and altered the piece substantially before publication. See Dickens's letters to Beard of 25 March and 18 April 1861 (*Letters of Charles Dickens* IX pp. 395 & 404.) In particular, the article attacks the expense and ineffectiveness of the newer model penitentiaries.]

Not a word. I hate the subject. Convict service! Convict discipline! Bah! a worn-out, dull, dreary hopeless tale.

But if I can show you, at the hazard of being dull only for a few minutes — say, five or six at the outside — that the system as it at present exists is open to the gravest objections, and fails of accomplishing any of the aims for which it was principally designed, surely you will listen to me?

Will you swear to be short?

I promise. I abstain, therefore, from entering into any of the statistics which lie ready to my hand, and by which it is distinctly and incontrovertibly shown that whilst, during the last ten years, the class of minor offences punished in the ordinary jails of the country have diminished by very nearly a full third, the heavier offences, punishable in the penal prisons to which the system of convict discipline is applied, have remained almost stationary in amount, or, if they have diminished at all, have diminished only in so slight a degree as to be scarcely appreciable.

Well, what do you infer from that?

Naturally, that the penal prisons, notwithstanding their supposed terrors, are in truth less formidable to the vicious than the common county and borough gaols.

An instance. Come, give me an instance.

I suppose you will not dispute the testimony of such a man as the Deputy-Governor of the convict prison at Chatham. In a pamphlet he has recently published, MR. MEASOR says, "I found last year a man in Kirkdale jail, who, having been discharged from Portsmouth convict prison, had again fallen into crime, and being sentenced to two years' imprisonment, candidly expressed to me his regret that he had not been sent back to a convict prison, saying that he would willingly have done at least three full years in lieu of the two, had he been allowed to choose the better living and comparative liberty of Portsmouth."

Upon my word I had no notion that these fellows were so fastidious. I should have thought that a jail was a jail; and pretty much the same all over England.

By no means. England in that respect boasts of variety, and for popularity with the customary tenant the convict prisons now undoubtedly hold the first rank. How little they are held in abhorrence, and how little the discipline enforced in them operates as a deterrent to crime, may be further judged of by the number of offenders that are constantly returning to them. During the last year, out of fourteen hundred prisoners who passed through Millbank prison, not fewer than three hundred were identified as having been there under previous sentences of transportation or penal servitude. Observe! *There* — in that one prison and within the memory of the present warders.

I wonder if three hundred out of fourteen hundred of life's ordinary travellers would ever dream of returning to the same hotel! These penal places must surely be pleasant places.

Money enough has been spent upon them to make them so; and when I tell you that the cost of keeping some six thousand two hundred prisoners in these convict prisons, ten years ago, was nearly two hundred thousand pounds, and that in the last year the cost of maintaining some eight thousand two hundred was upwards of three hundred and twenty-three thousand, you will easily comprehend that the conveniences and comforts of the inmates are undergoing no diminution as the establishments grow older.

Three hundred and twenty thousand pounds odd, for eight thousand men! Why, that's nearly forty pounds a head — or just double what a Dorsetshire labourer gets, by the sweat of his honest brow, for the maintenance of himself, his wife, and maybe half a score of children. And the Dorsetshire labourer has not the advantage of buying the necessaries of life, wholesale, and by contract, either.

Right! But we won't insist on that part of the question, lest you should by-and-by tell me, as some of our philosophers do, that, as a bird in the cage, a horse in the stable, and a pig in the pound, is in many respects better off than the creatures of the same race who run wild, so it would be a scandal to humanity if a man deprived of his liberty, no matter for what cause, should eat, drink, or sleep worse than the man who is free.

Worse! But he eats, drinks, and sleeps, much better!

Let us go on. We have seen that as matters at present stand, the convictions for the graver class of offences remain undiminished, while those of a lighter nature are reduced by a third. That the proportion of reconvictions to penal prisons is something enormous. And that the expenses of penal servitude have largely increased. That being so, the next question that presents itself is — how far does the present convict system accomplish the great object at which it professes to aim: that object being the *reclaiming of the criminal?*

And the punishing of him too.

Yes, the punishing of him too, as far as the humanity of the age will admit of anything in the shape of physical restraint as a corrective of evil or deterrent of crime; but the prime object of the system, no doubt, is to send the criminal out of the prison a better man than he comes in. Now, what I complain of is, that that object has not been attained in anything like the degree that might be secured.

[...]

D11. Charles Dickens "The Ruffian"
The Uncommercial Traveller Expanded Edition (1868) XXXVI.

[First appearing in *All the Year Round* on 10 October 1868, "The Ruffian" is a one of Dickens's last, and least liberal, responses to the problems of crime in London.]

I entertain so strong an objection to the euphonious softening of Ruffian into Rough, which has lately become popular, that I restore the right word to the heading of this paper; the rather as my object is to dwell upon the fact that the Ruffian is tolerated among us to an extent that goes beyond all unruffianly endurance. I take the liberty to believe that if the Ruffian besets my life, a professional Ruffian at large in the open streets of a great city, notoriously having no other calling than that of Ruffian, and of disquieting and despoiling me as I go peacefully about my lawful business, interfering with no one, then the Government under which I have the great constitutional privilege, supreme honour and happiness, and all the rest of it, to exist, breaks down in the discharge of any Government's most simple elementary duty.

What did I read in the London daily papers in the early days of this last September? That the Police had "AT LENGTH SUCCEEDED IN CAPTURING TWO OF THE NOTORIOUS GANG THAT HAVE SO LONG INFESTED THE WATERLOO ROAD." Is it possible? What a wonderful Police! Here is a straight, broad, public thoroughfare of immense resort; half a mile long; gas-lighted by night; with a great gas-lighted railway station in it, extra the street lamps; full of shops; traversed by two popular cross-thoroughfares of considerable traffic; itself the main road to the South of London; and the admirable Police have, after long infestment of this dark and lonely spot by a gang of Ruffians, actually got hold of two of them. Why, can it be doubted that any man of fair London knowledge and common resolution, armed with the powers of the Law, could have captured the whole confederacy in a week?

It is to the saving up of the Ruffian class by the Magistracy and Police — to the conventional preserving of them, as if they were Partridges — that their number and audacity must be in great part referred. Why is a notorious Thief and Ruffian ever left at large? He never turns his liberty to any account but violence and plunder, he never did a day's work out of gaol, he never will do a day's work out of gaol. As a proved notorious Thief, he is always consignable to prison for three months. When he comes out, he is surely as notorious a Thief as he was when he went in. Then send him back again. "Just Heaven!" cries the Society for the protection of remonstrant Ruffians. "This is equivalent to a sentence of perpetual imprisonment!" Precisely for that reason it has my advocacy. I demand to have the Ruffian kept out of my way, and out of the way of all decent people. I demand to have the Ruffian employed, perforce, in hewing wood and drawing water somewhere for the general service, instead of hewing at her Majesty's subjects, and drawing their watches out of their pockets. If this be termed an unreasonable demand, then the tax-gatherer's demand on me must be far more unreasonable, and cannot be otherwise than extortionate and unjust.

It will be seen that I treat of the Thief and Ruffian as one. I do so, because I know the two characters to be one, in the vast majority of cases, just as well as the Police know it. (As to the Magistracy, with a few exceptions, they know nothing about it but what the Police choose to tell them.) There are disorderly classes of men who are not thieves; as railway navigators, brickmakers, wood-sawyers, costermongers. These classes are often disorderly and troublesome; but it is mostly among themselves, and at any rate they have their industrious avocations, they work early and late, and work hard. The generic Ruffian — honourable member for what is tenderly called the Rough Element — is either a Thief, or the companion of Thieves. When he infamously molests women coming out of chapel on Sunday evenings (for which I would have his back scarified often and deep), it is not only for the gratification of his pleasant instincts, but that there may be a confusion raised by which either he or his friends may profit, in the commission of highway robberies or in picking pockets. When he gets a police-constable down and kicks him helpless for life, it is because that constable once did his duty in bringing him to justice. When he rushes into the bar of a public house, and scoops an eye out of one of the company there, or bites his ear off, it is because the man he maims gave evidence against him. When he and a line of comrades extending across the footway — say of that solitary mountain-spur of the Abruzzi, the Waterloo Road — advance towards me "skylarking" among themselves, my purse or shirt-pin is in predestined peril from his playfulness. Always a Ruffian, always a Thief. Always a Thief, always a Ruffian.

Now, when I, who am not paid to know these things, know them daily on the evidence of my senses and experience; when I know that the Ruffian never jostles a lady in the street, or knocks a hat off, but in order that the Thief may profit, is it surprising that I should require, from those who *are* paid to know these things, prevention of them?

Look at this group at a street corner. Number One is a shirking fellow of five-and-twenty, in an ill-favoured and ill-savoured suit, his trousers of corduroy, his coat of some indiscernible groundwork for the deposition of grease, his neckerchief like an eel, his complexion like dirty dough, his mangy fur cap pulled low upon his beetle brows to hide the prison cut of his hair. His hands are in his pockets. He puts them there when they are idle, as naturally as in other people's pockets when they are busy, for he knows that they are not roughened by work, and that they tell a tale. Hence, whenever he takes one out to draw a sleeve across his nose — which is often, for he has weak eyes and a constitutional cold in his head — he restores it to its pocket immediately afterwards. Number Two is a burly brute of five-and-thirty, in a tall stiff hat; is a composite, as to his clothes, of betting-man and fighting-man; is whiskered; has a staring pin in his breast, along with his right hand; has insolent and cruel eyes; large shoulders; strong legs, booted and tipped for kicking. Number Three is forty years of age; is short, thick-set, strong, and bow-legged; wears knee cords and white stockings, a very long-sleeved waistcoat, a very large neckerchief doubled or trebled round his throat, and a crumpled white hat crowns his ghastly parchment face. This fellow looks like an executed postboy of other days, cut down from the gallows too soon, and restored and preserved by express diabolical agency. Numbers Five, Six, and Seven are hulking, idle, slouching young men, patched and shabby, too short in the sleeves and too tight in the legs, slimly clothed, foul-spoken, repulsive wretches inside and out. In all the party there obtains a certain twitching character of mouth and furtiveness of eye, that hint how the coward is lurking under the bully. The hint is quite correct, for they are a slinking, sneaking set, far more prone to lie down on their backs and kick out, when in difficulty, than to make a stand for it. (This may account for the street mud on the backs of Numbers Five, Six, and Seven being much fresher than the stale splashes on their legs.)

These engaging gentry a Police-constable stands contemplating. His station, with a Reserve of assistance, is very near at hand. They cannot pretend to any trade, not even to be porters or messengers. It would be idle if they did, for he knows them, and they know that he knows them, to be nothing but professed Thieves and Ruffians. He knows where they resort, knows by what slang names they call one another, knows how often they have been in prison, and how long, and for what. All this is known at his Station, too, and is (or ought to be) known at Scotland Yard, too. But does he know or does his Station know, or does Scotland Yard know or does anybody know, why these fellows should be here at liberty, when, as reputed Thieves to whom a whole Division of Police could swear, they might all be under lock and key at hard labour? Not he; truly he would be a wise man if he did! He only knows that these are members of the "notorious gang," which, according to the newspaper Police-Office reports of this last past September, "have so long infested" the awful solitudes of the Waterloo Road, and out of which almost impregnable fastnesses the Police have at length dragged Two, to the unspeakable admiration of all good civilians.

[…]

Maps and Illustrations Showing Settings

1. Maps

Based on maps from around the period 1800-20

Map A: Estuaries of the Thames and Medway
Map B: City of London
Map C: Pip's London

2. Illustrations

London scenes of around 1800-20 reproduced from engravings in Walter Thornbury and Edward Walford's *Old and New London* in six volumes (London: Cassell, Petter, & Galpin, 1897).

A. Smithfield Market
B. Barnard's Inn
C. The River Front at Hammersmith
D. Covent Garden Market
E. The Royal Exchange
F. The Temple Stairs
G. London Bridge
H. Billingsgate Market

MAP A. ESTUARIES OF THE THAMES AND MEDWAY

MAP B. CITY OF LONDON

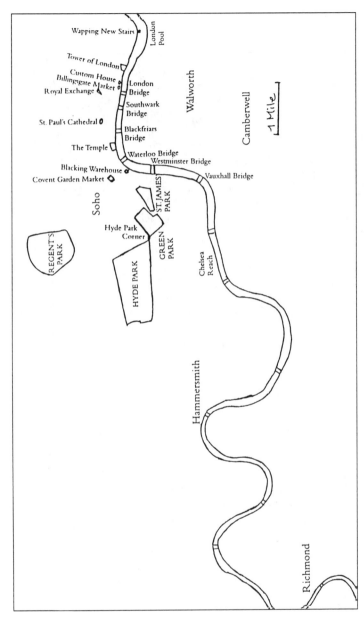

Wapping New Stairs

London Pool

Tower of London

Custom House
Billingsgate Market
Royal Exchange

London Bridge

Southwark Bridge

St. Paul's Cathedral

Blackfriars Bridge

The Temple

Waterloo Bridge

Westminster Bridge

Blacking Warehouse

Vauxhall Bridge

Covent Garden Market

Soho

ST. JAMES PARK

Hyde Park Corner

GREEN PARK

Chelsea Reach

REGENT'S PARK

HYDE PARK

Walworth

Camberwell

1 Mile

Hammersmith

Richmond

Map C. Pip's London

ILLUSTRATION A. SMITHFIELD MARKET

ILLUSTRATION B. BARNARD'S INN

ILLUSTRATION C. THE RIVER FRONT AT HAMMERSMITH

ILLUSTRATION D. COVENT GARDEN MARKET